DANGEROUS LITTLE DARES

Charlie Lennon

To shop books and merch directly from Charlie's bookstore visit:
www.CharlieLennonBooks.com

Author Photo © Charlie Lennon
Cover Design: A.R. Tarter
Cover Formatting: Ashley Santoro
Crest Design: A. Smiian
eBook ISBN: 979-8-9990849-4-1
Paperback ISBN: 979-8-9990849-2-7
First Published September 2025

The Society
of Secrets

Book 1

"Fiercely romantic, and hilariously clever!"
@CharlieLennonAuthor

"Sweet and spicy, because we love a man who yearns, and we definitely love a man who *CRAWLS*." @CharlieLennonAuthor

"Reads like a decadent vanilla cupcake with morally gray confetti sprinkles."
@CharlieLennonAuthor

"Hilariously sexy, thrillingly dangerous, and terribly heartfelt."
@CharlieLennonAuthor

"A brilliant smash-up between a romantic comedy and a romantic suspense! Great for readers of romantasy and contemporary alike." @CharlieLennonAuthor

"A delightfully sweet take on a contemporary, morally gray hero."
@CharlieLennonAuthor

"Heartwarming, intense, funny, this is the book will have you tearing through every thrilling page!" @CharlieLennonAuthor

Hey, Gorgeous, it's me, Charlie!
Want to make me do a little happy dance?
You can shop books and exclusive merch, directly from my author bookstore!

www.CharlieLennonBooks.com

Dedication

This is for the girls who swooned over Westley from Princess Bride.

If Westley was a billionaire instead of a farm-boy-pirate, and you love a Golden Retriever hero who lives by the words:
Touch her and die...
Meet Carter Kensington.

And to younger me. We did it. No more hiding.

Dangerous Little Dares is a thrilling romantic comedy, romantic suspense smash-up. These characters are filthy rich, morally gray, and will use whatever means necessary to get what they want. Throughout every thrilling and heartfelt page of this book, you might laugh and you might cry, and I promise, you'll most definitely clench your thighs.

Now be a good girl, grab some tissues, your emotional support water bottle, maybe even a little snack, and settle in, because you're about to enter the luxurious and treacherous world of Briar Rose for the very first time...

♥

This book contains subject matter that may be sensitive to some

I hope that I have thoughtfully handled the sensitive themes in this book with the care and attention they deserve. I've chosen to omit the full list of sensitive subject matter from this book, as it contains spoilers. The complete list can be found on my website. www.CharlieLennonBooks.com/contentwarnings

Contents

Prologue

I Hate Gambling
Carter

I was dealt a damn good hand in this life. Some might even consider it an unbeatable hand. But there are three things I wish I could put back in the toothpaste tube.

One, being orphaned at the tender age of fifteen.

Two, subsequently inheriting the responsibility for the family estate, all its related assets, and the mess my father left behind the moment I turned eighteen.

Three, *I sure as hell never asked to fall madly, deeply, in love with my best friend's little sister.*

But here's the thing with cards, you get what you get. And with toothpaste, you can't put it back in the tube, no matter how hard you try.

Now, obviously, there's nothing I can do about the first two problems. The third, however, isn't so much a problem as a waking nightmare. Just so we're clear, I've tried to ignore my feelings, but that's basically like pretending to be a non-sentient sea slug. No eyes. No feelings. No problems.

Right?

Abso-fucking-lutely wrong.

To put it lightly, she is the gravity my world revolves around.

It's like playing a constant game of tug-of-war that I'm never going to win. Like Atlas carrying the world on his shoulders—only I'm not an all-powerful Titan, and the force I'm fighting is way more powerful than gravity. It's a mischievous ball of sunshine with a smile that pierces right through your very soul, and trying to stay out of her orbit is futile.

Some might say I have it all, *power, status, wealth,* but when it comes down to it, I can't afford the most important thing of all. Because she's not for sale.

So, it doesn't matter that I was dealt a damn good hand because here's the thing about playing cards, no matter how good your hand is—*somebody's always sitting on an ace.*

CHAPTER 1

Cupcake or Bride

CARTER

I scrubbed a hand down my face and paced, knowing I was running out of time. Sara was already on the auction stage looking like a frosted cupcake—or a bride. I couldn't decide which. Either way, it was only a matter of minutes before some schmuck was going to bid on her, and there wasn't a damn thing I could do about it. Not officially, anyway.

It'd been months since she'd been home in Briar Rose, and I hadn't had an actual conversation with her in even longer. Tonight, she looked devastatingly beautiful, dark curly hair, elegantly piled on top of her head, cheeks flushed, eyes wide—she always stole my breath, but tonight was different. Tonight was my last chance, and I was quickly losing my window.

Across the ballroom, every rich old bastard was busy eye-fucking her like a frosted dessert they wanted to take a bite out of. So I paced, reminding myself why it was an incredibly bad idea to go on a neck-breaking spree, and why it was an even worse idea to place a bid on her.

"Carter Kensington." A reporter shoved a tape recorder in my face. "It seems like you have your eyes on a special someone." Shit. I wasn't even supposed to be here tonight, and I definitely did *not* need this hitting the news cycle and causing yet *another* frenzy.

"Tell us, who will the city's most eligible bachelor be taking home tonight?" She touched my arm, her sultry expression speaking volumes.

I smiled thinly. "Excuse me, I'm not taking press interviews tonight." I slipped out of her grip and quickly headed through the crowd towards the bar for a desperately needed drink, but I didn't make it that far because I spotted one of my late father's associates heading my way. *Perfect.*

Everywhere I looked, *someone* was blocking my path, and it resulted in me cutting through the crowd like a bat out of hell.

I felt my skin prickle, and I did a double take—still on stage, Sara was making her best attempt to stifle a laugh and regain composure, watching my predicament down in the shark pit.

Of course, she would find this funny.

Feeling far too brazen, I shot her a wink, watching her cheeks turn a satisfying shade of red before she quickly looked away.

I nearly crashed into Liam when he appeared out of seemingly nowhere. "You bid on a date yet?" My best friend asked.

"What?" I startled, ripping my gaze away from his very off-limits little sister. "Uh, no." I recovered quickly. "I wasn't planning on bidding tonight."

"Come on, you know it's for a good cause." Liam prodded with a smirk. "You're not feeling *charitable*?"

"Please." I rolled my eyes, looking around the room. "Don't give me that shit. I know these things get you two, hot and heavy."

"I don't have the faintest idea what you're talking about." Liam chuckled, sending a smirk to his long-time girlfriend up on the stage. "I'm just donating to a good cause."

Over my shoulder, I noticed Richard fucking Sinclair strolling into the ballroom. "Listen." I groaned, the seconds ticking down. "Unlike you and Gina, I don't have a kink for spending an exorbitant amount of money on something that's already mine." I relaxed, as Richard headed across the room and ambushed Taggart and Eric instead. I smirked, knowing he'd probably talk their ears off long enough to keep them from bidding on Sara. *Good.*

Liam raised a brow. "Do you know anything about foreplay?"

"If I wanted to make a donation to a shitty charity, I'd just cut a check." Yet another reason I couldn't stand most of the people in this room, the vast majority of these charity events were complete fraud. Shell companies, owned by the people standing all around us. I lowered my voice. "Besides, you know I don't find it particularly appealing to buy a date with a woman when she's only drooling over my inheritance and not me."

"Can't it be both?" Liam asked, not taking his eyes off the stage.

I huffed out a breath. "Sure, but it never is."

"Suit yourself." He shrugged, lifting his paddle as the auctioneer opened the bidding for Gina. "If you don't have game, just say so."

Across the room, the other half of our crew was busy stirring up shit as usual. Cade and Theo snickered, taking turns counter-bidding Liam, and I rolled my eyes. "You know they're just going to push you to your ceiling."

"Eh, she's worth it." Liam raised his paddle again. "Besides, this isn't completely selfless."

"Like I said, I don't want to know." I raised my hands in surrender and backed away with a chuckle. "I'm going to get some fresh air. It's a bit hot in here." Sara was up next and I knew it was an incredibly bad idea for me to stand here, *in front of her brother*, while someone else bid on the girl that I'd burn my entire inheritance for, let alone the chance to take on a real date.

It also occurred to me that if I timed it right, maybe I could catch her backstage and steal her away without anyone seeing.

"Kensington, where are you going?" Cade called a head above the crowd as I headed for the hallway. "The fun is just getting started." He threw his long arms out with a grin, while Theo avoided my gaze altogether.

"I'll be back in a bit." I waved my hand at Cade, still heading for the door.

"Sure you will." Cade rolled his blue eyes at me. "You're coming tonight, right? You know, I'm not taking no for an answer." He joked, but I could see the worry in his expression, and I quickly shoved the guilt down.

"Yeah, I'll be there." I chuckled as the auctioneer prattled on in the background and Cade and Theo both threw their paddles up in unison.

"*I will hurt you.*" Liam mouthed silently to them across the ballroom.

I made it about three steps outside the ballroom before a man with graying hair, a red velvet tux, and a cigar hanging out of his mouth ambushed me. "Richard." I greeted him thinly, sliding my hands into my pockets to hide the tension in my curling fingers.

"You should be in there, bidding on your future wife." He scolded me, and it was a struggle to keep from rolling my eyes. "When I was your age..." I tuned him out as he launched into an aspirational lecture that made me grit my teeth.

Eyeing the door just beyond the curved staircase, I wondered if I could slip backstage and steal Sara away before her date did. Eric was no longer occupied and would probably bid on her tonight, *he usually did.* The two of them had the most unexciting, on-again-off-again situation-ship I'd ever seen. Sara could do so much better than him, and it was almost comical seeing the two of them together, because he was just so incredibly dull compared to Sara. Why she continued to entertain him, I honestly had no idea; her father seemed to like him a lot more than she did.

I blew out a slow breath, trying to find some sort of Zen while Richard badgered me for an investment. That's all I was to the people in this room, a walking money bag, ripe for the picking. Not only was it exhausting, but it made me suspicious of every-one's intentions, and left me feeling even more isolated than I already was.

As grateful as I was for the life I had, sometimes I couldn't help feeling like it wasn't even mine. Like I'd been backed into a corner that I'd never walked into in the first place.

Right now, I desperately wanted to steal a quiet moment away from everything and clear my head, because in a matter of hours, everything was about to change and I wasn't entirely sure I was ready.

"Come on, what will it take for you to open your pocket-book?" Richard nudged me as if we had that sort of friendliness. "Your father, rest his soul, was a huge advocate of the arts and very generous. What do you think he would do?" So fucking conde-scending, as if I wasn't running the art curation and asset manage-ment business my father left behind day in and day out.

I grimaced. "I can assure you, the estate backs many amazing charities as it is." *Just not the ones that funnel into your pocket.* Greedy bastard.

Richard was like a bug-eyed lizard who couldn't generate any of his own warmth. He had to find some little rock to leech from so he could survive, and I'd be damned if I let him perch on my back. I was so sick of playing this game that my temper was about to boil over and scald his little lizard feet.

"Have you considered my offer?" Richard asked.

"As I've said before, I can appreciate that my father did busi-ness with you, but I'm just not in a place to continue that at this time." Joining the *elite* secret Society that was possibly involved in my parents' untimely deaths wasn't exactly at the top of my bucket list.

Richard reached up to squeeze my shoulder. "I just worry about you, son. It pities me to think of you navigating your career without your father's guidance." *And here it comes.* "Let me take you under my wing, show you the benefits of being part of the organization."

What exactly he wanted from me, I was never quite sure, but I knew it was about more than just joining the *organization*.

"To be blunt, you're not qualified to advise me on the matters of *my* estate." I bit out, knowing Sara had to be up any minute now. I checked the time on my vintage Patek, desperately wishing it was a time machine out of this wretched conversation.

Richard chuckled. "And you are?" The minutes were ticking down, making me even more agitated than I already was.

"Frankly, Richard, it's really none of your business how I handle the estate. I can assure you, everything is being properly managed, and I will not be redirecting assets, regardless of my father's history with you." What I really wanted to say was *hey asshole, let me paint a picture for you. The art portfolio is thriving, and I've more than doubled the estate since taking it over. P.S. you're not getting a dime. Not just because I hate your guts, but because you're suspicious as fuck and you have a creepy obsession with my parents' mortality.* "But thank you for the offer." I bit out sharply.

He kept a smile painted on, but I could see the facade cracking, exposing the ugliness underneath. "I know you're a sensible man." He squeezed my shoulder too hard, the way people with too little power do. "There was a reason your father was in business with me." He lifted a finger, shaking it in my face. "You may have your mother's fire, but you'll come around eventually." His smile was so incredibly slimy, it made my skin crawl.

"If you'll excuse me." I stepped away, not waiting for his response.

The more I resisted, the harder they all seemed to push, and it wasn't just Richard. All my late father's associates aggressively badgered me about joining the organization. It was like they desperately needed something from me, but what that was, I had no idea, because no one would come right out and say it.

I'd nearly made it backstage when a shaky old voice, akin to a dying bird, called after me. "Carter Kensington."

My shoulders sagged as I turned, recognizing the voice. *Escape effectively sabotaged.*

"Come here, young man."

"Mrs. Bishop." It was an effort not to sigh.

Decadently dressed as usual, she reached out a wrinkled hand clad in outrageous jewels, and I grimaced, bracing for the conversation she *always* wanted to have. "Have you found yourself a wife yet?" She could hardly crane her neck up to meet my gaze.

I gently guided her over to a set of deep-seated armchairs against the wall, taking the one next to her. "No. Not yet."

She laid her ornate walking cane across her lap, and a ruby the size of an egg sparkled, catching the flickering candlelight above us. "You must be so lonely in that big house without your parents."

I forced a smile. "I'm doing just fine, but thank you for asking." Except that I wasn't. I found it harder and harder to control the anger that was always bubbling up because I was sick of talking about this. Sick of being alone. Sick of wanting what I couldn't have. Sick of dealing with the bullshit my father left behind. Sick of playing the game that was living in this world. I blew out a long, slow breath, feeling more and more unhinged, but chewing out a little old lady wasn't high on my priority list right now.

"If I had a granddaughter, I'd set you up." She offered brightly, as if the idea had just popped into her head, except that she offered her nonexistent granddaughter to me *every time we spoke*. "You're too handsome to be alone, surely there must be someone?" But she didn't wait for my response as she started listing her friends and *their* granddaughters while I smiled politely, slowly dying inside.

By the time I escaped, it was at least ten minutes later, and I was on the verge of panic as I raced backstage. This was my only chance to talk to Sara tonight, and I *had* to talk to her.

I burst into the dressing room, and a chorus of voices and whistles immediately greeted me as I scanned the room.

"Hey Carter—hi handsome—wanna buy out my contract, Kensington? Old man Campbell bought my date."

Sara wasn't here.

I hurried back down the hallway towards the stage.

"You missed her." Sloane, Sara's best friend, chimed as I rushed past her. "She's already gone."

I whirled around, lowering my voice. "Eric?" I asked breath-lessly, knowing I shouldn't even act like I cared.

"It's always Eric," Jules, Sara's other best friend, offered, shooting me a sympathetic look over her shoulder, and then her eyes slid past me, flashing with something as her boyfriend Douglass called after her.

Filled with defeat, I sagged against the wall in the dimly lit hallway and shuttered my eyes. A moment later, my tie was hissing against my suit as I yanked it off, and then my pearl cuff-links were jingling as I angrily stuffed them into my pocket.

Damn it, this was not a conversation to have via text message or even over the phone. I'd blown it, and Sara was going to be so hurt that I didn't tell her myself.

"There you are," Liam said, coming around the corner with his hard-earned prize slung over his shoulder. Gina giggled while her thick blonde hair bounced with his every step. "After party?" He asked, jaw flexing with apprehension.

"Of course." I pushed off the wall, even though going to some debauched party with people I mostly hated was the last thing I wanted to do. Especially when I had an early morning tomorrow.

Heading towards the valet, we descended the crushed-velvet stairs of the grand ballroom, our dress shoes glinting in the fading light as we stepped into the cool night air.

When the valet pulled up with Liam's cherry red Bugatti, Liam, so very gently, *reverently,* pulled Gina down and helped her into the passenger seat. When he stooped down to gather the long ends of her delicate gown into the car, her eyes heated, and I suddenly realized why—Liam's hand was hiding somewhere under all that fabric and I suddenly found the vining flowers on the stone archway above me wildly interesting.

A moment later, I slid behind the wheel of my black McLaren, asking, "I'll see you over there?"

Liam nodded in response, his expression wary and sad all at once, and I felt my chest tighten with guilt that I didn't know exactly where to put.

"Drive safe." I called knowing I was definitely going to beat them over there. *Fucking rabbits.*

Part of me envied their relationship, while the other part of me knew I wasn't cut out for it, because even if I craved that sort of intimacy, there was always something holding me back.

I sighed as I hit the narrow road that led out to the country-side estates. There weren't street lamps out here, and the stars speckled the dark night sky like an eerie, beautiful painting, casting a pale glow on the tall grass that flanked either side of the road.

I wondered if leaving Briar Rose was a mistake, but what other choice did I have? I'd tried to follow in my father's footsteps for years now, and it was eating me alive. I hated it—making big numbers even bigger. What was even the point? *Especially* when I didn't have anyone to share it with.

Everyone around me seemed to find it so easy to carve out their spot in life, and I was tired of being miserable and alone. I needed to move on, try something new.

Liam was off in the city starting his new restaurant, and Sara was busy painting, pursuing her art degree. Theo would hardly talk to me, things had been strained ever since I bailed him out of prison. And Cade, as much as I loved the guy—whatever it was he was working on these days was most defi-nitely illegal. He didn't say, and I didn't ask, but he was probably the next person I was going to have to bail out of prison.

Our tight-knit group was slowly drifting apart, and there was nothing left for me here. I was falling apart from the inside out, and the one thing that might put me back together was always just out of my grasp.

White-knuckling the steering wheel, I tried to hold on to something, anything that felt tangible, real.

Suddenly, as I came flying around the next bend, a blur of white flashed against the headlights, snapping me out of my rumination.

A split second before I ran it over, I registered the red-bottomed high heel in the middle of the road.

What the hell?

My attention snapped back to the ditch as the massive blob of white moved, and then pure shock washed over me as I suddenly realized what it was.

A woman.

I slammed on the brakes as the dark brown hair came into view—and then a hand.

Covered in blood.

CHAPTER 2
Yellow Gatorade
CARTER

The car came skidding to a stop, and I threw my door open, rounding the car in the next instant.

Heart pounding, I rushed to the edge of the embankment and peered over. My shadow blocked the light, but I heard a whimper and without a second thought I slid into the muddy ditch expecting the worst, and that's exactly what I got.

"Sara?" I froze, fear slicing through me as I registered the horrifying red smears painted across her dress.

A split second later, I was moving, and my brogues squelched through the thick mud as I closed the space between us in several long strides.

"C-Carter?" She stumbled back, voice paper thin.

"I'm here now. Everything's going to be okay." I forced the panic down, but I could hear the unsteady pitch of my voice as I spoke. "Where are you bleeding?" I deftly unclasped my belt, yanking it off in one fluid motion, ready to make a tourniquet, but she just stared at me, a wild look in her eyes, and I realized she must be in shock. When I reached for her, she backed away, mumbling utter nonsense.

"Sara, it's Carter." I lifted my hands, palms open. "I'm not going to hurt you."

She had her high heel in her hand and was just staring at it. "I can't find my other shoe. I lost it." She murmured, and then mumbled something about losing her buttons, and I wondered if she meant marbles.

She was definitely going into shock.

"We'll find your other shoe." I promised, and very carefully, I reached for her.

She stood there stiffly, as if she hardly registered me in front of her at all, while I frantically combed over her exposed skin, hunting for the source of the bleeding.

Swearing under my breath, I realized she had a pretty sizable gash on her arm—clean cut. It was fairly dirty, but it was already clotting. Other than that, she was just covered in small nicks and scratches, none of them even remotely large enough to be the source of *so* much blood. Which meant she was bleeding somewhere I couldn't see. I swallowed hard.

"You shouldn't be here." Sara murmured, still staring at the shoe in her hands. "You should leave."

Shit. Head wound. *Had to be.* I was frantic as I started pulling pins out of her soft hair.

"W-What are you doing?" She choked out in surprise.

"I'm checking to see if you smacked your pretty little head because, you know, I'd never leave you out here." I breathed, finding only a small gash on her temple. "Sara." I started slowly, the lump in my throat hardening as I steadied myself. "Where exactly are you bleeding?"

She stared at me blankly, looked me dead in the eye for the longest minute of my life and then, as if she finally realized that I had her, that she was safe—a broken little sound like I'd never heard before, cracked out of her and I pulled her into my arms as she began to sob.

"You're safe now. I've got you." I murmured, feeling more panicked by the second. "Everything is going to be okay. Whatever happened, you're safe now."

It was a surreal feeling. Not knowing what the hell was going on. Simultaneously realizing how perfectly she fit into my arms. I'd never held her like this before. *Ever.* The fact that it was tonight, like this, was devastating. *I was devastated.*

My throat was slowly closing up, but I asked as gently as I could muster. "Sara, I'm really worried about how much blood you've lost, and I don't know where exactly you're injured. Do you know if you're still bleeding?"

She only cried harder.

"You think we could take a look?" I asked gently, my mind swirling with a thousand terrible possibilities.

She shook her head, shoulders shaking violently.

I swallowed hard. "Can you tell me what happened? Or who you were with at least?" She couldn't form a full word between her sobs, let alone get a full breath in. "Sara, I need you to try and take some deep breaths for me." I gently cupped her face with both my hands, forcing her eyes to meet mine. "Can you do that for me, sweet girl? Take some deep breaths with me?"

Shoulder-shaking sobs were her only response as she crumpled against me. Oh God, I needed to get her to a hospital. *Now.*

"He—he and I—I—was supposed to—but I couldn't." She was nearly inaudible between her sobs.

My ears started to ring, fingers started to go numb. "Did Eric hurt you? Did something happen between the two of you?" I asked so, *so* gently, even while I battled the protective fury that was steadily unraveling inside of me.

"I wasn't with Eric." She sobbed as I cradled the back of her head.

"*Who were you with?*" I felt dizzy as each breath came faster and faster.

"N-no." she cried, "It's fine, I'm fine." She chanted to herself over and over again, and I knew it was more for *her* sake than mine.

All around us, the tall grass rasped eerily in the wind, and as I surveyed our surroundings, realization slowly washed over me. Maybe this wasn't her blood at all...

Oh fuck. Was I going to bury a body tonight?

I would. *For her, I would.*

"Whatever this is, everything's going to be okay." I murmured, knowing I'd move heaven and earth to protect her.

Suddenly, the car headlights clicked off, plunging us into the night, and my skin prickled, knowing that whatever had happened out here, we needed to leave. Right now. We could sort out the details at the hospital, but right now we were exposed, and literally anything or anyone could be out there.

My feet slipped as I tried to find purchase on the slippery embankment, and if it hadn't been for my height, I wasn't sure if I would have been able to climb out at all.

At the top, I pulled Sara up onto the road in one swift movement. "Come on." I ushered her towards the car, taking another cautious glance over my shoulder.

Her voice pitched up. "I can't."

My chest was so tight, I could hardly pull in a full breath as I begged, "Please, get in the car, Sara."

"No." She stumbled back, and my eyes blew wide as I lunged for her, grabbing her before she fell into the ditch again.

"I'm not asking, we need to get you out of the cold, probably to a hospital."

"I just can't, okay?" Tears rolled down her cheeks, shimmering in the hardly there moonlight as she shoved me back.

"Sara, get in the car." I demanded more sternly. "I'm serious."

She whimpered, "I can't."

I gripped the back of my neck in disbelief because now she was just being plain stubborn. "Why the hell not?" I pleaded, my pulse spiking as I eyed the blood on her dress, total confusion washing over me. "Because you're hurt?"

"Because I'm covered in mud, and the blood will stain your seats." She cried.

"You think I care about my *car*? You are out of your Goddamn mind if you think I'm leaving you out here." I snapped incredulously.

She took another step away, and panic threatened to swallow me whole.

"Okay. Okay." I rasped more to myself. "Ambulance. Yeah, we'll call an ambulance." I nodded, immediately dialing.

"No, don't do that." She lunged for the phone.

I stood tall, keeping the phone out of her reach. "Sweetheart, you're in shock, but everything is going to be okay." I promised. "Whatever this is, I'll protect you, but we need to get you to a doctor."

"Don't!" she shouted, just as emergency services answered.

"Hi, we need an ambulan—"

"No," she screamed, knocking my phone out of my hand, and it slid across the pavement before it disappeared over the edge of the embankment.

I turned to her, utterly stunned, wondering what the hell was going on. "If you don't get in my car right now," I threatened, "I swear to God, I'll haul you over my shoulder and *hike* to the nearest hospital."

Her lower lip wobbled. "I can't."

"You can."

"Please, Carter."

"Get in the car." I begged, pleaded, desperately. "I'm trying to help you. Why won't you let me? You won't tell me where you're bleeding, and I'm seriously worried about how much blood you've lost."

"It's period blood. Okay!" Sara screamed. "I don't need an ambulance."

"What?" I stood there, pure surprise washing over me before I quickly recovered. "And what about the cut on your arm? Why were you in the ditch?" I demanded gently enough.

"No. You don't get to ask me those questions." She looked me dead in the eye, and I knew she was hiding something. "And just so we're clear, I'm *not* going to a hospital." She gritted out with more determination than I think I'd ever seen.

"Fine." I gripped the back of my neck, realizing I needed to change tactics. "No ambulance, no questions, no hospital." I opened the passenger door like I was luring a lamb to the slaughter. Nice and easy. No sudden movements. "Will you please just get into the car so I can take you home?"

She nodded, albeit reluctantly, and I blew out a breath I didn't realize I'd been holding.

～

After a few silent miles, I took the next exit. The heat was blasting, but Sara pulled my suit jacket tighter around herself like she couldn't get warm.

"Where are we going?" She asked nervously, probably wondering if I was in-fact taking her to the hospital. Part of me wondered if I should.

"I'm getting you something to eat." I said, already heading towards a drive-through. "Did you eat today?"

After a long moment, she confessed quietly, "I may have forgotten."

"Sara." I groaned, not totally surprised because she always forgot to eat when she was stressed out.

"I don't need a lecture, Kensington."

I swallowed hard. "I'm not trying to lecture you, I just hate knowing you've been running on fumes all day."

A moment later she full out panicked when I pulled up to a drugstore. "Carter, I can't go in like this."

"I know." I smiled softly as I unbuckled. "I'm just going to pop in and get you some supplies. I'll be right back."

"You're going to buy me tampons?" She asked, entirely horrified.

"Is that what you'd prefer? Tampons?"

She turned beet red, and the only response I got was a groan from behind her hands. "This is not information I want *you* knowing."

"Well, tough luck, Rookie." I slid out of the car with a wink.

"You need supplies, and I'm the only one with two shoes." I *had* looked for her other shoe, but it was nowhere to be found by the time I'd finally gotten her into the car.

Inside the drugstore though, it was *me* who was the rookie. I gripped the back of my neck, staring at the wall of period products feeling totally lost. I wasn't particularly shy about buying this stuff, but I'd never had sisters, or any long-term girlfriends for that matter, so I didn't really know the lingo all that well.

I reached for a box that said heavy flow, deciding this situation definitely called for proper reinforcements. Except Sara was relatively short, and as I compared the pictures on the box between the light and heavy options, it left me wondering, what if the big ones were *too* big to fit? Was that a thing? And if they *were* too big —nope. Never mind. I shook my head, wondering what the hell was wrong with me.

Just to be safe, I grabbed one of everything. That left me balancing a precarious stack of *supplies* in one hand, wet wipes and hand sanitizer in the other, while I grabbed our drinks out of the cooler. There was an entire wall of cold yellow Gatorade *my favorite*, but I didn't hesitate as I grabbed one yellow and one blue.

It wasn't until I reached the register, adding a bag of Sara's favorite Sour Patch candy to the top of the pile, that I finally realized what a mess I was. The woman ringing me up eyed me warily, and I took inventory of myself, realizing I probably looked like a serial killer taking a midnight snack break. *Fan-freaking-tastic.*

Sara rifled through the bag as I dropped the blue Gatorade into my cupholder and the yellow one into hers. "This is *a lot* of stuff." She finally commented.

"I wasn't sure what to get." I admitted. "Do you need anything else? I can go back in if I missed something."

"No, this definitely, *definitely* covers it."

I reparked the car in a dark corner of the lot and slipped into the cool night air, so she could sort herself out. As I leaned against the trunk of my McLaren, the cold didn't bother me at all because

I was fuming. My blood was practically boiling as I considered five different ways to beat someone to a pulp, and the second I figured out who she was with, I was going to use them all. Over the years, I'd always tried to keep an eye out for her, and this was so beyond unacceptable, I couldn't even wrap my brain around it.

"Better?" I asked quietly as I settled back into the car with the smell of hand sanitizer in the air.

"It's as good as it's gonna get until I get home." She murmured, staring too hard at her hands in her lap.

"It's not a big deal." I pulled back out onto the road.

"It's embarrassing." She had a strange quality in her voice that made my stomach knot. "*I'm* disgusting."

"You don't think that." I said gently, not sure if I was asking her or telling her, but she was quiet, far too quiet. "Is that what your date said?" I finally asked, pulling into the Burrito Bell drive-through and rolling my window down.

"Welcome to Burrito Bell, home of the Bell..." A tired voice crackled through the static speakerphone with the specials as I looked at Sara, waiting for an answer.

"No questions, remember?" She huffed, shooting me a glare.

I gave her a pointed look, to the effect of *we're coming back to this* and turned to order our usual. "Four deluxe soft tacos, that'll be all." I said, already pulling forward towards the drive-through window. Two for her, two for me, except they were huge and she almost never finished the second one.

"What if I don't want a soft taco?" Sara crossed her arms over her chest and threw me a defiant look as one brow shot up.

Yes. A sparkling ray of her glorious mischief was singing, *let's play.* Whether she realized it or not, that was everything I needed to know—that she was going to be okay, despite whatever shit-storm she'd just been through. *And tonight*, I desperately needed to know that she'd be okay.

"Would you like something else?" I asked skeptically, the corner of my mouth quirking up as I suppressed a full-on grin.

"Maybe I do, but I didn't get the chance to look at the menu."

She complained, her long lashes fluttering in a way that had me white-knuckling my steering wheel again.

"Well, we can't have that, can we?" My eyes darted down to her seatbelt, checking that she was still buckled in—*she was.*

My grin broke free, and her eyes went wide with realization. "Carter, no." She barely got the words out as I punched the pedal.

We accelerated past the first window, then the second, in a blur. Her scream was a delight to my ears as I drifted around the parking lot in a tight circle and came to a screeching stop in front of the ordering menu again.

"Carter!" she reprimanded me, but her scowl broke into a small grin that she immediately tried to cover, but I caught it anyway and threw my head back, barking a satisfied, throaty laugh. "I hate it when you do that." She complained.

"No, you don't." I teased. "So let's hear it, what *would* you like, pretty girl?"

She glared at me and unbuckled, but when she leaned across me, my laughter was cut off at the knees—I froze as the scent of strawberry, amber, and something warmly sweet, like honey, invaded my adrenaline-spiked senses while she shouted through my window, "Could I have one soft taco, please?"

I stifled a laugh and added with a smug gleam. "Deluxe."

"Yes, deluxe." She emphasized tartly, giving me a roll of her eyes before sliding back down into her seat. Stubborn as ever.

I slowly rolled towards the first window, passing my credit card to the annoyed-looking worker, who was not amused with my apology.

"Don't forget, I always know what you want." I reminded Sara and leaned back against the headrest, just watching her.

"Not always." She muttered, giving me a look I couldn't quite decipher. "For your information, I don't *always* get a soft taco."

"*Yes*, you do." I chuckled, passing her the warm paper bag.

Sara casually sorted the tacos between the two of us while I parked the car facing an empty field.

"Nice try." I chuckled, moving the extra one she'd ordered back over to her side.

"You're going to make me eat all this?!" she demanded with mock offense, even as she devoured her first one, already completely ensconced in the task.

I shrugged. "Clean plate club, don't let me down, Devereux."

"No promises." She rolled her eyes, mumbling through an adorable mouthful, and I watched intently as she took another massive bite.

I couldn't help but admire the way the streetlamp illuminated the rogue curl that was hanging over her face, like a baroque painting. The image was certainly more beautiful than any of the priceless paintings I had hanging on my walls or hidden away in my portfolio.

I desperately wished I could take a picture of her, something to take with me, but I knew it'd spoil the moment. Not to mention, my phone was back in the ditch. So I just watched her with quiet admiration instead, trying to burn the image of her into my mind—every little perfect, bewitching detail.

Earlier tonight she'd been flawlessly elegant, just like she'd planned, no doubt. She'd descended those stairs with her shoulders back, smile wide, not a hair out of place, looking enchantingly beautiful and *now*—her natural curls were fighting their way out of her polished hair style with a vengeance and it wasn't even a question in my mind. I preferred her like *this*, hair a bit frizzy— partly my doing, I supposed—a little undone, comfortable, guard down. It was so *us*.

These moments with her, there was something vastly intimate about it, and I knew I'd miss it. *Miss her.*

I smiled to myself as she inhaled her food like a cute little gremlin, heavy breathing intermixed with small sounds of satisfaction. It made my mind wander, despite my best efforts.

She suddenly looked up at me with a sheepish grin, wiping the corner of her mouth with the back of her hand. "What?"

I smiled softly. "Nothing." *Everything.*

"You'd better hurry up, Kensington, or I'm going to beat you." She threatened, always so competitive.

I chuckled, knowing exactly how this would go as I reached for a taco. "It's not a race, you know."

"You're just saying that because you're behind." She said through another adorably determined mouthful, while I proceeded to shove the entire thing into my mouth in what was essentially two big bites. *Not behind anymore.*

She tried to match my pace, but it left her with furious eyes and chipmunk cheeks.

"Rookie move." I teased, already crumpling the wrapper and dusting off my hands.

She mumbled something I couldn't interpret through her mouthful, but I was pretty sure it was a colorful string of curses. I smiled to myself, knowing everyone always thought she was such a goody two-shoes, but I knew better. She was comfortable enough to let her guard down with me, and show that unfiltered side, *and I loved it.*

I opened her yellow Gatorade with a grin. "Almost there, don't fold yet."

She rolled her eyes but grunted in thanks, taking the drink. A moment later, after several slow, laborious bites, she finally *with great defeat* passed her leftovers over the console, which I happily polished off, *like I always did.*

We just sat like that for a long while, staring out into the dark field, neither of us saying anything. Comfortable silence. Easy. Familiar.

Until the question burning in my mind finally had to be acknowledged. "So, who were you with?" Her gaze dropped, and I nudged her with my elbow. "Come on, you can tell me anything."

"I'm tired, Carter. Will you please just take me home?" She looked out her window, refusing to look back at me.

"Well, that's too bad." I argued gently enough as I crossed my arms over my chest and settled in. "I guess it's going to be a long night for the both of us, because I'm not moving until I have a name. So you think it over, and when you're ready, you can tell me which scum bag abandoned you on the side of the road covered in blood."

She was staring at her hands again. "Please don't be mad, I just can't."

"I'm already mad." The understatement of the century.

"Just promise me you won't do anything."

I grabbed her chin between my fingers, and her breath hitched when I turned her head towards me, looking her square in the eye. "The only thing I can promise you is that when I'm done with whoever he is, he's a dead man."

Pure fear flashed through her eyes, and in that moment, all the terrible scenarios that had been running through my mind won, and I snapped.

CHAPTER 3
My Traitorous Car
CARTER

"Goddamn it." I muttered under my breath, eyes shuttering as I reached across Sara's seat and buckled her in.

I put the car in reverse and whipped back out onto the road.

"Carter." She gripped my arm in panic. "What are you doing? Where are we going?"

"If you won't tell me who you were with, then we'll go to the party and I'll find him myself." I bit out, seeing nothing but red. I wasn't going to let this go, wasn't going to sweep it under the rug. *I couldn't.*

"No, don't!" She lunged for the steering wheel, begging me to stop.

"Sweetheart, I don't know what the hell happened out there, and honestly it doesn't matter. *Somebody hurt you*—left you on the side of the goddamn road, covered in blood." I clenched and unclenched my jaw. "Whoever he is, *I'm gonna kill him.*"

"Please," she begged. "If I tell you, will you turn around?"

"Not a chance in hell," I muttered, already heading back out towards the Bishop Estate, feeling myself press deeper into my seat as the needle on the speedometer struggled to match my growing rage.

"Please, Carter, don't do this to *me*. You're just going to make this worse than it already is. Please turn around, I'm begging you. I don't want to go there." Sara started sobbing, and I realized she was *terrified*. Of what exactly, I didn't know. "I *can't* go there."

My shoulders sagged as I blew out a defeated breath, because no matter how angry I was, no matter how determined I was, I couldn't bear to hear her beg me like that, and definitely couldn't bear to make her cry.

"Fine." I murmured, quickly realizing I was only making things worse.

Despite what I *should* do, I rerouted, knowing she had me completely wrapped around her finger—I doubt she realized it.

"Thank you." She collapsed against her seat.

"Don't thank me, Sara. You *will* tell me who it was."

She was quiet.

"*Right now.*" I demanded far harsher than I should have.

In the smallest voice I'd ever heard her speak in, she whispered meekly, "Someday I'll tell you. Just not tonight."

I ground my teeth, wondering if my jaw could shatter from clenching it so hard, but I didn't know where to put the fierce protectiveness that was washing over me. I was going to tear someone limb from limb before severing them from their favorite one.

We drove the rest of the way home in tense silence, while I suppressed every awful scenario that flipped through my mind, knowing if she was so worked up about this, it was for a damn good reason.

When we were back in Briar Rose, I pulled down the long Devereux Estate driveway, past the circular fountain and parked under the flowering porte-cochere before I killed the headlights.

"Sara, just answer me this, is there a dead body back in that field? Because if there is, I need to deal with it." I sighed, dragging my hands down my face. "Preferably tonight."

She turned to me, mouth agape. "You think I murdered someone?"

"I honestly don't know what to think. I know you're lying

about something, I just don't know what. The girls said Eric won the bid for your date, you're saying you weren't with Eric. Either way, there's no explanation for why the hell you were in the ditch. Even if you are telling the truth about your period, you're covered in scrapes, which tells me there's a high likelihood that you either jumped out of a moving car or you were pushed." I watched her closely, and she swallowed nervously. "I can only protect you if you tell me what happened. So who the hell were you with, Sara?"

"I don't need protection." She swallowed thickly. "Please just let this go."

"You are not getting out of this car until you give me something. Anything." I demanded firmly before adding more softly. "You can trust me. I know, you know that. So cut the bullshit and stop trying to do this on your own."

"Fine. You want the truth?" She snapped. "I've been basically alienated on campus! Wanting a normal college experience was nothing but a pipe dream. I've somehow finished my first year of college, and I've never been lonelier. The photos they got—" She cut herself off, lower lip quivering. "Everything is so fucked."

She looked me dead in the eye for the longest minute of my life, and then I saw it—the moment she broke.

"Carter, please." Her voice was a trembling push of air. "I don't want to talk about this anymore."

Shit.

She buried her face in her hands, and her shoulders shook with each silent sob.

"It's okay." I tried to reassure her, tried to force breath into my own lungs as she cried for reasons that weren't entirely clear. "We won't talk about it anymore. We'll talk about something else." Except I had no idea what to say.

I swallowed hard, hesitating as I reached for her, not even sure if I should touch her now. Seeing her like this left me feeling panicked in a way that I was completely unfamiliar with. "Sara?" I reached over and tentatively rubbed her back. "Is this okay?"

"Yeah." A small strangled noise escaped from her.

"Can I hold you?"

"Yeah," she sobbed, but didn't move.

I carefully slid an arm under and around her as I pulled her over the console and into my lap, and she immediately buried her face in my chest, hiding it.

Her voice was muffled. "I'll ruin your suit."

"It's already ruined, and I don't care." Settling her small frame against my body, I wrapped my arms around her, all while my ears were ringing. "I'm sorry, Sara. I wasn't mad at *you*. You have to know that. Just know—I'm here whenever you're ready to talk."

She cried harder, and I wished so badly I could just make everything better tonight, whatever was happening on campus, everything—but all I could do was hold her. So that's exactly what I did, all the while hating how right it felt. *Having her in my arms.*

We sat like that for a long while until her sobs eventually quieted, and when she finally pulled back and looked up at me through those thick dark lashes, her eyes were on my mouth.

I tensed as the heat of her breath brushed across my skin like a tempting invitation.

A glimmer of nervous but mischievous sparkle crept across her expression. "Carter?"

"Yeah?" I asked, utterly frozen.

She didn't quite form a word as she slowly, carefully sat up. *Not like this. Not like this. Not like this.*

Her hands settled against my chest, delicate and warm. "Can I ask you something?"

I knew right then and there, no matter what I did, no matter what I said, I was going to be so utterly fucked. I wasn't prepared for this, and I was pretty damn sure she was about to cross that line we'd always flirted with but never stepped over, and I couldn't possibly bear to cross that line. *Not tonight.* Not when I knew it'd crush her. *Crush me.*

"Sara." I swallowed hard, her name on my tongue was a mere push of air coming out of me, even as her admission made my skin light up with want, even as the temptation of claiming her mouth sang to me like the deadly call of a siren.

She was right, everything was *so* fucked.

"I trust you." She breathed, referencing my damned speech from earlier. "I know you wouldn't hurt me, right?"

"Sara." I rasped.

"You want to play our game?" She murmured.

I swallowed hard, knowing exactly where this was going. "Sar, this isn't a good idea."

"Didn't you miss me while I was gone?" She asked softly, her expression shifting to something more sensuous.

"Yes." I swallowed hard. *So damn bad.*

"Truth or dare." She started slowly, but didn't wait for me to answer at all. "I dare you to tell me what you're thinking right now."

It wasn't hard to guess. "Sara." I pleaded, not exactly sure what I was pleading for.

"Fine." Her eyes dropped to my mouth again. "I'll go first." She swallowed thickly. "Truth. I'm thinking your lips look... so incredibly soft." Her wide brown eyes searched mine. "Dare." The word lingered between us like a bomb ready to go off.

"Carter?" She breathed, and time probably stopped as she hesitated, searching my eyes, trepidation and longing there as she inched forward.

Even with heartbreak already pulsing through my veins, I gently stopped her, detonating an entirely different kind of bomb. "Sara, I have to tell you something."

She tensed in my arms, and while she didn't physically move a muscle, everything in her body recoiled. The hurt that instantly bloomed across her expression made my stomach twist as I watched it all play out on her face, like my own personal horror film. Watched her discover that I would in-fact hurt her, and that I just did.

"Sara, you know why we can't. We'd never—you're so amazing but," I was grasping at straws, trying to find the right words, but everything was coming out so wrong. Why did I always get so tongue-tied around her? Every word seemed to etch the hurt and rejection deeper and deeper into her expression, when all I was trying to do was protect her. Or maybe I was trying to protect myself. Fuck, this was all happening, all wrong.

Just then the car announced, text message from Blonde Reporter, before it auto-played.

Where are you, Carter? I can't wait to get you out of that suit, so I can taste every inch of your body tonight.

I scrambled for the dashboard, but it was too late. My traitorous car continued reading the text message that was going to seal my damnation.

I'll even let you do that thing you did to me last time.

I could have curled up and died as it ended the message, listing a long string of sexual emojis, one after the other.

Sara was already reaching for the door when I grabbed her.

"I'm so sorry." What could I even say? It had only been a one-time thing, but it didn't matter.

"Don't worry about it." Sara said flatly. "I got it. You're not interested."

I grabbed her hand. "Please don't be like that."

She lunged for the door handle with her other hand, and I grabbed that one too. "I'm not being like anything." She snapped, her eyes already filling with tears.

I held on tight enough not to hurt her, but tight enough that she couldn't go anywhere because I just couldn't bear to let her go. "Please don't get out of this car right now." I begged.

"Carter, I'm tired." Her gaze dropped, and she refused to look at me. "Please just let me go."

Could I do it? Let her go?

"You've had a shit night and your judgment is clouded. I can't let you out of the car. Not until I know you're not mad at me." It was selfish, but I didn't care, because in a matter of hours all this was going away. *Forever.*

"We'll be sitting here for a long time." She muttered.

"Please don't be upset, Sara. I can't *leave* knowing you're upset with me."

Her eyes snapped up to mine, and I swallowed hard, knowing I should have told her sooner. Why the hell didn't I tell her sooner?

"Leave?" She narrowed her eyes.

My mouth opened, but nothing came out because all the anger dissolved out of her expression in an instant, and it was quickly replaced with a look of betrayal.

"Tell me you're lying." She gripped my shirt and shoved against my chest in weak protest. "Carter, tell me you didn't do it."

I let her beat against me, let my hands slide down her arms to rest on the swaths of white fabric gathered around her waist, in surrender.

"I ship out first thing tomorrow." I admitted softly.

She collapsed against me, her voice a strangled sob of devastation. "Why?"

"Because I can't keep living someone else's life." I stroked her hair, committing the sweet, sun-warmed strawberry smell to memory.

"Please don't go." She sobbed into my shirt. "Please, Carter, I'm *begging* you."

"I'll think about you every day." I promised, hating that I was leaving just weeks before her birthday.

She could hardly get the words out. "You're going to get yourself killed."

I smiled sadly. "Have a little faith in me."

"I do." She argued, and I realized that's exactly why I had to leave. But I couldn't help wondering if I was making the biggest mistake of my life as I made the only girl I'd ever really cared about, cry harder than I'd ever seen her cry.

I didn't have a choice.

It was terrifying to stay and terrifying to leave, but if I didn't get out now, this life would smother me and there would be nothing to stop me from doing something horribly, terribly, stupid—something that would blow up my life even more than leaving would.

Maybe I'd made an assumption about what she was going to do, but it was too late now.

Letting her go was for the best, *at least that's what I tried to tell myself.*

CHAPTER 4
Boola Boola

CARTER

Two years later...

"Casanova, check your six, you've got a bandit coming up behind you." Tatum's voice crackled through the comms in warning.

The sensors in my jet were blaring as I pulled on the throttle. "Copy, I see him." I began a steep climb until the nose of my jet was pointed towards the endless blue skies. Bracing against the G-force, I maneuvered into a flip and dropped behind my target.

The sensors beeped in confirmation a moment later—target hit—which meant the skies were clear.

"Always going for the yank and bank." Mike muttered over the comms.

I flipped my jet upside down, mirroring my wingman's cockpit from above. "Aww, is Jinx upset because he can't keep up?" I teased.

He flipped me the bird. "Show off." I flashed him a toothy grin he couldn't see from inside my helmet.

"Formation, fall in." I called through the comms and proceeded to barrel roll off Jinx as our squad shifted into a tight V formation.

"Nothing but beautiful blue skies." Ezra sighed contentedly

from beside me in his own jet. "In fact, it's the perfect day to join the Martin Baker Fan Club, don't you think, Jinx?"

"Shut up." Mike groaned.

"You make it too easy." Tatum chimed, and I could hear the smug grin on his face from his own cockpit.

"Yeah, he'll be the first one to yank that oh-shit-stick." I agreed, knowing if one of us ever ejected, it'd be Jinx and we'd never let him live it down.

"Some of us aren't fangs out twenty-four seven." Mike complained.

I shrugged. "If you can't keep up, just say so."

"Seriously, you fly like a senior citizen." Tatum added. "Hey Casanova, you think we should change Jinx's call sign to Snail?"

"Sounds good to me." I doubled down. "Or Grandma."

"Actually, I amend my earlier statement—you go *so* slow, I doubt you'd even be able to *pull* the oh-shit-stick in time."

"Oh, fuck off." Mike complained, but I could hear the amusement in his voice. He *was* slow as hell and definitely deserved the rib, but he was always a good sport about it.

"Look alive. We've got a cluster incoming." I warned, that focused calm settling over me as my fingers moved over switches and dials with pure muscle memory. The plane sensors blared, and all I could do was grin. "Boys, I believe it's time to party." *Cue thematic fight song because I fucking loved this shit.*

We split off, falling into a coordinated set of movements, and it was the most beautiful thing I'd ever seen. Sure, every flight started and ended the same way, but everything in-between was pure instinct. I lived for those long minutes when I was slicing through the air at mock speeds. It was a high you couldn't get from anything else—it's where I finally found my *calm*. Nothing else pacified my nerves, quieted my mind, quite like the drag of my jet through the sky. It was a heady cocktail, adrenaline, focus, muscle memory—something I craved, day and night.

The moment I'd taken my baby up for the first time, I'd found myself. I realized being a pilot defined me as a person. I loved it, and it didn't hurt that I was damn good at it too. I didn't know if I'd personally use the word prodigy, but I'd certainly heard it thrown around when my superiors thought I wasn't listening.

Honestly, the only thing I cared about was being the best. *And I was.* I'd always loved going fast, and in the sky, it was even better. *It was pure freedom.*

"Jinx, you've got one incoming on your six." I murmured into the comms, barrel rolling away from my bogey.

"Yeah, I got it padlocked." Mike replied.

Alarms blared in the cockpit as I danced through the sky like my life depended on it—because it did.

Focused breaths in-and-out, G-force increasing every second, anchoring into my seat, letting go of everything else, flow, instinct, foresight, and then my crosshairs locked onto my target.

The sensors blared in confirmation a moment later.

"Smasher, you got a couple bandits coming up on your three and six," Tatum warned his wingman Ezra before he shifted into a set of complex maneuvers, repositioning around his own bogey.

"Headed your way, Smasher." I dropped in and lured one of the bandits off Ezra and moved the dogfight away.

Maneuvering a series of tight rolls and climbs, I attempted to get the target into my sights, but every single time, just when I thought I had him, he'd slip out of the crosshairs again. "Shit." I hissed, blood thrumming, frustration pumping through my veins as the target kept up with me, move for move. As rare as it was, I quickly realized my target was just as good as me, which meant it was down to whoever fucked up first. If I didn't do something fast, the end of this flight was going to look very different from all the rest. "See how you like this." I muttered, the ground blurring beneath me as I dropped low to cut through the mountainous terrain.

"You're below the hard deck," Tatum warned.

"Copy." I continued my flight path.

"Casanova, get the hell out of there. I can't get to you down there."

"Almost there." I murmured as the ground came closer with each alarming second—I snapped up in a quick maneuver, and the sensors beeped in confirmation a moment later. Target hit, but Jinx, my wingman, was still in trouble.

I sliced back up through the sky and dropped in, taking out the last bandit that was hot on his tail a mere moment later. Cheers sounded through the comms, and I grinned, heart pounding, high on adrenaline, knowing I was born for this.

As I brought my jet down, that familiar swell of disappointment settled in my chest. This was the worst part of flying— kissing the sky goodbye, at least until my next flight.

I climbed out of my jet and pulled off my helmet, raking a hand through my damp, sweaty hair, realizing my captain was headed my way, and he looked *pissed*.

"I should suspend you for pulling that bullshit." He growled, and I straightened, for whatever reprimand was about to follow. "But unfortunately for me, your impulsive stunts caught the attention of the suits. Long before today, it seems." There was genuine pity in his eyes as he motioned me towards the hangar.

Oh shit.

~

A woman wearing a tight bun stared me down from across the table. "I'm curious why someone who could sit on a yacht drinking gin and tonics all day, decided to enlist."

"Actually, I'm more of an old-fashioned kind of guy." I countered, but she did *not* find that amusing. So I shrugged, "I wanted to serve my country." *And fly fucking fast.*

Her eyes narrowed. "Bullshit."

The corner of my mouth hooked up, knowing she was absolutely right. People usually ate the whole *I wanted to serve my country* shit up, but truthfully, my reasons were my own, and they were none of her damn business.

"Despite running away from your old life, you still own your family estate." Her eyes twinkled, albeit coldly, like she was sitting on one of those proverbial aces, and I couldn't freaking wait. "Not to mention you still maintain a foothold in the art world."

I shrugged. "I have no heir to handle my affairs."

"One might assume you intended to return to your old life."

I pressed my lips into a thin line. "I don't." Part of me wished I'd left Briar Rose even sooner. *With caveats.*

"Don't you? You've continued to acquire land." She tapped the folder on the table. "Half of Briar Rose, to be exact."

My lips twitched. "Well, I would own the other half, but someone beat me to it."

"Yes, we know all about Cade Blackthorn." She hummed even more unamused. "But we're not talking about *him*—we're talking about *you*."

"Well, you seem to know everything there is to know, so I'm not exactly sure what it is you need from me." I gave her a lazy smile.

Her face remained impassive. "Some things you can't know until you look a man in the eye." I shifted, an odd feeling washing over me. "At present you live quite modestly and here on base, you've successfully maintained secrecy about who you are—I'm curious what exactly your motivations are, for your career, for your old life."

"I'm just here to protect and serve." I gave her a flat smile.

She scoffed, thumbing through a folder on the table. "You have no surviving family, you indulge in the occasional one-night stand here and there but never with the same person twice. *No girlfriend?*" She raised a brow, looking at me again.

I smirked. "Who's asking?"

"That's above your pay grade, *Lieutenant.*" She bit out sharply, putting me in my place as she tapped the folder in front of her. "You're unattached." It was a statement this time. "You're driven to be the best. Just impulsive enough to take the necessary risks that are required, and even worse—your risks usually pay off. Today was just another one of those calculated risks, wasn't it?"

I sat forward, folding my hands on the table. "Risks required for what?"

"We're recruiting you." She said simply, and I raised a skeptical brow, waiting as she continued. "To a black ops task force."

I chuckled and tapped the wings on my flight suit a bit obtusely. "I don't know if you know this, but this is the Air Force, not the Marines." She smiled thinly as I continued. "I'm a *pilot*, not a tactical officer." And that's precisely the way I wanted to keep it.

She gave me a smile that didn't meet her eyes. "*Exactly.* You're not *just* impulsive, you're smart, you think strategically—you're always several moves ahead of your opponents, and your aerial skills are rare, *unmatched,* actually. This covert task force targets remote locations that are *only* accessible aerially. For obvious reasons, these *high-profile* assassinations can't lead back to us, and we need someone with enough guts to get in, and enough brains to get back out."

"And you think I'm your guy?" I scoffed, wondering if this was actually a joke. Tatum was going to get a kick out of this.

"I know you are. You're an excellent pilot, so you should have no problem getting through the airspace unnoticed, and the rest can be trained easily enough."

I mean, I *was* good, but I hadn't been doing this all that long —why they wanted *me* was honestly a bit bizarre. I had career plans, and creeping through the night to assassinate God knows who was not part of those very important plans. *To say the least.* In the air, I did what I had to—there was an agreement though, when you went up into the sky, you knew what you were getting into—any pilot did. On the ground, sneaking up and offing people in their sleep, well, it wasn't exactly my flavor of justice to say the least, not that this had ever been about that for me anyway. Like I said, all I wanted was to fly fast. *That was it.*

"Don't you want someone with more experience?" I shifted uneasily, hating how out of control I felt here on the ground.

"No. I want the best, and lucky for us, that now includes

you." She hummed, all too authoritatively, reminding me I didn't really have a say when it came down to it. "This team includes some of the cockiest, riskiest pilots we have. Don't worry, Lieutenant, I'm sure you'll fit right in."

"I'm not tactically trained." I reminded her.

"Oh, but you have excellent instincts, don't you?" She placed a knife on the table and snapped her wrist, sending the blade slicing towards me as she murmured, "Let's see how fast you are on your feet, Lieutenant." Her eyes shifted behind me, and I lunged.

Knife in hand, I went flying backwards, realizing with horror that I couldn't breathe as something tight cinched around my throat. My chair hit the ground hard, and then I was up and moving, shoving the shock and panic down.

The next several seconds were pure instinct and survival, and there wasn't a second to hesitate as I slid the knife around the back of my neck and cut the thin wire around my throat.

I was gasping for air, but avoiding suffocation cost me. My eyes blew wide as a tree trunk of a man rammed into me, tackling me to the ground, and I grunted as we hit the concrete floor, me underneath taking all the impact, because he was a damn tank.

We were a pile of limbs and blades, rolling around, each of us desperately fighting for the upper hand, as I tried to get my head on straight and calculate his next move.

I was already bleeding from somewhere when the woman said, "He's been instructed to kill you, so I suggest you do it first."

"What the fuck is this?" I demanded, just as his knife slashed over my face. I cursed, realizing I'd been struck. *Again.*

"Your interview."

I could hardly see out of one eye as blood trickled down my face and I was sloppy and confused as I struggled to get the upper hand, using the only thing I could, *speed*, by some miracle, I managed to gain the advantage, but I wasn't stupid enough to believe I would have it for long.

"Yield." I demanded, knife to his throat as I spat a mouthful of blood on the ground.

My assailant bellowed and lunged, slashing at me again as I went tumbling back, and as his blade found its mark, I realized that unlike the way Liam or Cade and I would fight, this guy wasn't about to tap out. It was me or him. Scrambling up, I growled a curse, finally understanding he *was* going to kill me if I didn't kill him first. Only, I wasn't really in the mood to kill someone with my bare hands before I'd even eaten lunch.

When he came charging at me, I defaulted to a move I'd used on Theo before and used his body weight against him, flipping him over the top of me with his own momentum. I locked him into a chokehold for what seemed like hours but was probably only a minute or two—relief coursing through me when he finally went limp.

"Don't worry, we'll train that mercy right out of you." The woman amended, now standing above me.

Gasping for breath, I shoved him off me and collapsed onto the floor, feeling warmth trickle down my face, down my arm. Adrenaline was in charge, and nothing hurt yet, but it would. Later, it most definitely would.

The suit narrowed her eyes. "The next time I hand you a knife, I suggest you use it." She dropped the file onto my chest as I panted, tasting metal in my mouth. "Welcome to the team. You start on Monday."

"I didn't ask for this." I groaned, hating how powerless I felt.

"I think the expression you're looking for, Lieutenant, is *Yes, Ma'am.*"

Shit-motherfucker.

I closed my eyes and submitted to the cold concrete floor, heart sinking as I slowly accepted that the dream career I'd been working towards had just gotten flushed down the toilet. That was what I got for signing my life away, so much for all that freedom I'd been feeling a mere twenty minutes ago. Fucking suits.

A gunshot suddenly echoed across the hangar, and I jolted up, watching in disbelief as they dragged away the man I'd just been fighting without a word of explanation or apology.

Ohhh fuck.

I stared down at my arm, at the flap of skin there, and wondered if I was going to be sick. Flopping back down onto the floor, I couldn't help but feel nauseas as I stared up at the rafters feeling sorry for myself. Just when I felt like I had a grip on my life, everything was shifting *again*.

I'd been so damn close to everything I wanted—well, except for one thing. That one tiny little empty place inside me that was always nagging at me—no matter how hard I tried to seal it off, because there was only one person the right size to fill it.

But she had probably moved on, and I would probably be dead in a few years anyway, because now, I was officially disposable.

CHAPTER 5

Ghosts Always Return

SARAFINA

One year later, present day...

I gasped, slamming on the brakes as the car chasing me finally ran me off the road—my front tires slid up over the sidewalk as I screeched to a stop. Cranking the wheel, I punched the petal to gun it around the car, but I was thrown forward against my seatbelt as I hit the brakes, because just then another van screeched to a stop right next to me, and then another, right behind me—*boxing me in.*

Hands trembling, I whipped my head from window to window, frantically looking for a way out, jolting when a man started banging on my car, his camera bulb flashing as he violently yanked on the door handle, which was locked, thank God.

I quickly realized the only way out was *backwards.* Throwing the car in reverse, I braced a hand on the passenger headrest, eyes sweeping oncoming traffic before I gunned it up over the sidewalk —bumper scraping when I squeezed around the van, and then twisted the wheel *hard*—flipping back around as I threw my car in drive.

My tires squealed as I peeled out, feeling myself press against my seat while I accelerated towards oncoming traffic. Cars honked at me as I carefully cut between them, veering for the first side street, and then I braced, teeth gritting as I hand-over-hand cranked the wheel, and pulled a hard left, drifting around the corner in a controlled swing.

I shot onto the side street and floored it, catching air as I zipped through one green after another, grateful the traffic lights were on my side today. I took turn after turn, eyes flicking up to the rearview mirror, while my body shook with adrenaline.

A few miles out, when I was finally sure no one was following me, I slowed down and headed back to my university. My heart was still pounding, and I realized I'd sweat through my shirt as I cruised through the rolling green hills towards the center of campus.

The paparazzi weren't allowed on the private property, and even though they sometimes snuck onto campus anyway, this was better than leading them back to my house. I'd finally settled into a new apartment, and I was not about to start packing *again*.

The sun was already low in the sky as I parked, and I knew I really needed to get back to Briar Rose before it got too late, but right now, what I really needed to do was calm the fuck down, because I was so freaking tired of this shit.

I walked the long way around the old brick buildings covered in ivy, avoiding the dorms, because even here on campus, I had to be careful. Now that I was pursuing my master's, most of the people who'd been out to get me those early years had already graduated, but that didn't stop my hyper vigilance and it didn't stop my anxiety about walking past the campus dorms.

Inside the Cobalt building, I was hit by the comforting smell of paint and art supplies, and then everything finally loosened as I stepped into my art studio and released a heavy breath.

Ditching my sweaty shirt, I pulled my painting overalls on over my bra and threw my hair up into a messy ball on top of my head before I *cranked* the music. The playlist was gritty, with a pulsing base, and feminine rage lyrics, and I let it thunder through me like a war cry while I bounced around, shaking off the anxiety.

As I plopped down on my rolling stool and shoved myself

towards my almost finished art piece, I knocked over a cup that apparently still had paint thinner in it, and proceeded to coat myself, *and* a corner of my almost finished canvas. *Shit!*

I grumbled to myself and quickly cleaned everything up before I stared at the corner and rolled my eyes. So much for finishing my piece tonight. *Great freaking work, Sara.*

As I grabbed my brushes and palette and stood there, head tilted, staring at the piece, deciding on the final finishing touches, I suddenly felt overstimulated by the music and opted for a light-hearted musical instead.

Humming along, I eventually zoned out, falling into a deep flow state as I painted, letting all my worries disappear into the paint. Each line, each stroke, was a little part of my heart and soul, a little piece of everything I was, until it all blended together into something entirely new. Something beautiful and meaningful.

Dip, dab, stroke. Over and over again. The scrape and drag of the brush over the canvas, the specifically weird smell of the blue paint I was using—so incredibly familiar, yet something I'd almost grown to like even though it stunk a bit.

Until I suddenly realized what time it was. As I pushed back to stare at my painting, I forced myself to get up, knowing I needed to hit the road before I got too tired to make it home at all.

I reluctantly locked my studio up, really wishing I'd finished the piece first, but it was already dark outside. Halfway back to my car, a grunt in the darkness caught my attention, and I tensed, heart instantly pounding as I paused under the leafless trees.

Tightly clutching my bag over my shoulder, I blinked, frantically trying to get my eyes to adjust as I squinted across the parking lot. There was an echoing thud and another grunt, and then I realized with great relief that it was just Carmen. One of the few people who hadn't gone out of their way to make my life a living hell these past few years.

She was struggling to load a large object into the back of a moving truck. "Carmen," I called, hurrying across the parking lot. "Do you need some help?"

"You're a lifesaver." Carmen panted from above me. "I don't know why I thought I could move this by myself."

I lifted a corner and my eyes blew wide, realizing her cargo wasn't just massive, it was freaking *heavy*. "Good God, how did you even get this outside by yourself?" I shoved hard, relieved when the object finally started to slide with me pushing and her pulling in unison.

"Determination?" She huffed, with a quizzical look, and extended me a hand, pulling me up into the bed of the truck.

We dragged the canvas-wrapped object towards the front before she secured it, explaining, "It's mixed media, and I assembled it in pieces, not realizing how heavy it was getting."

I laughed, dusting off my hands. "Yeah, I've definitely made that mistake before."

"It's my first commission." She beamed and then rolled her eyes, adding, "Well, sort of. It's for my aunt's friend, but whatever."

"Hey that totally counts." I hopped out of the truck and grabbed my bag off the ground.

She grinned from above. "Long drive ahead of you, Devereux?"

"Eh, it's just a few hours." I shrugged with a laugh that was still a bit breathy from exertion. "Can't complain."

"Well, you better get to it, it's getting late." She pulled the rolling door closed and rounded the truck with a wave. "Happy Thanksgiving, Sara. Drive safe."

Three hours into the drive home, I was definitely complaining.

I desperately needed to pee, but I didn't want to stop at some sketchy gas station in the middle of the night, especially being deliriously tired and all. So, I did what any good driver would do to stay awake. I turned to the reliable power of Disney musicals, frigid air, and floored it.

By the time I was finally cruising through the towering topiaries lining the entrance to Briar Rose Estates, my fingers were nearly frozen, and I was on my umpteenth loop of *let's get down to business.*

As I entered the massive roundabout, about halfway around the floral-landscaped turn, an imposing figure jogging on the other side of the stone fountain made me do a double take. My pulse spiked, but I shook my head, knowing it was late and I was probably just imagining things.

But when I drove past the sprawling estate just across the street from my parent's manor, I couldn't help but squint a little harder, just to see if there *was* a car in the courtyard. There wasn't, because of course there wasn't. That obscenely large manor had been vacant for years now, its occupant just another ghost from my past.

My tires crunched over the pebbled stone as I headed down the long driveway and into the courtyard, before I rounded the winterized fountain, and drove beneath the porte-cochere back towards the garage. After parking my discreet school SUV next to the long row of Liam's extra cars, I headed inside, wincing when my heavy bag slipped off my shoulder and whacked one of his Maseratis. *Oopsie.*

It was late as I quietly crept into my parents' house, but the moment I stepped inside, I grinned, realizing half the neighborhood was in the kitchen. Dropping my bag in the grand marble entry, I made a much needed pit stop and then headed towards the warm sound of laughter.

"Da Vinci." Cade, one of my older brother's best friends, crooned, immediately draping an arm around my shoulders. "Welcome home, Gorgeous. Did you miss me?"

"Hey Sar-Bear." Liam grinned at me from across the kitchen and then his gaze shifted to Cade's arm, his dark eyes turning to ice. "Blackthorn, you have three seconds flat to get your filthy paws off my sister."

Towering over me, Cade pulled me closer into his muscled

side with a grin. "Wow, I get an extra second this time?!" His jet black hair flopped over his tanned forehead as he tilted his head counting, "Two. Three. Ahh." Liam had already picked up a butter knife, and was rounding the kitchen island when Cade finally lifted his hands in surrender. "Alright, alright. Take it easy." Liam shot him a lethal look while Cade coughed behind his hand. "Hell's kitchen over here. Am I right?" Cade winked at me, blue eyes twinkling, as he shoved his ear-length hair back, and I just rolled my eyes. *Typical Cade.*

"I heard that." Liam grumbled, not bothering to look up from the massive dessert he was piping perfect little shapes onto with his steady hands.

"Hey lady." Gina, my brother's longtime girlfriend, pressed a long-stemmed wineglass into my hand, and her shelf of thick blonde hair fell over me as she pulled me in for a warm hug. "We missed you."

I shook my head with a laugh. "What's everybody doing up so late?"

"Waiting for you, of course." My best friend Sloane answered, her baby blue eyes twinkling as she scrunched her nose and patted the kitchen stool between her and Ariana.

Meanwhile, Gina hopped up onto the counter next to Liam, and stuck her finger out in request. He smirked and paused working on the dessert to pipe a little heart onto her finger.

After she'd sucked her finger clean, Liam murmured, "You going to give me a taste?"

"Only if you come and get it." Gina giggled, sinking her fingers into his dark wavy hair.

Liam parted her legs and stepped between them, grinning as he hauled her to the edge of the counter and against his broad frame. He gripped her chin and bent to murmur something against her ear that had her squirming before he chuckled low and deep, and gave her a long, slow kiss. The second they started making out, I rolled my eyes, because if there was one thing you needed to know about Liam and Gina—it didn't matter the place or time, they were always all over each other, *no matter who was watching.*

"How was the drive?" Ariana asked, tucking a strand of her bouncy, strawberry blonde hair behind her ear.

"Long but uneventful." I sighed, settling into the chair between the blonde duo of my best friends. "Glad to be home." *An understatement.*

"Sar, it's way too late for you to be driving by yourself." Liam bristled, going all protective. "You should have just let the driver pick you up."

"Thanks, Mom." I rolled my eyes sarcastically. "But I'm fine, really. I'm here safe and sound, aren't I?"

Liam returned to his dessert and started placing edible flowers all over it with a pair of culinary tweezers, not looking very convinced, but he knew *I'd* never give up driving for the same reason *he* wouldn't. Besides, driving myself meant I could blend in on campus a little easier, and *try* to enjoy a more normal college experience. Driving was the last thing I had left, because everything else had basically gone to shit. It was pathetic, but it was mine, and I wasn't giving it up. Liam, of course, had no idea what had happened during my freshman year. *Nobody* in this room knew because *if they did*—I'd be stuck with some stuffy bodyguard glued to my hip, and that was *not* normal. I found Liam watching me, and I gave him a big smile and then gulped down a heavy sip of wine, avoiding his discerning gaze.

"How is your women's charity going?" I asked Ariana, "I heard that you opened up another shelter last week? That's so great!"

"We're doing really amazing." Ariana grinned, "We were actually able to get another investor on board a couple of months ago, and we'll be opening up several more shelters next year." Ariana was one of the Vandenbergh Hotel heiresses, and her latest passion was helping women find housing while they were getting back on their feet. She was incredibly business savvy and driven, and she'd very successfully managed to step out of the role of socialite and into the role of an activist—something her father wasn't incredibly thrilled with, unfortunately.

"Ariana, that's so great." Sloane exclaimed.

"I know, I'm really excited. I feel like we're finally starting to get some momentum." Ariana beamed proudly. "And once we—"

"*There you are.*" Theo, another one of Liam's friends, strolled into the kitchen looking grumpy as shit as his dark eyes locked in on Ariana. "I've been calling you for an hour, why the hell didn't you answer?"

"My phone is *dead.*" Ariana's eyes instantly narrowed. "And don't you have anything better to do than continually ruin my social life?"

"Your father is looking for you." Theo muttered, "Let's go."

"Now?" she complained.

"Yes, now. You're not walking home alone in the dark, and I've got shit to do, so let's go."

"I think it's past somebody's bedtime." Ariana muttered under her breath to me and Sloane, curling her lip with a face that Theo definitely saw, but pretended to ignore. "Sorry, I'll see you guys tomorrow." Ariana sighed, and her shoulders sagged as she threw her arms around me, giving me a hug. "I'm glad you're home, Sara. We've all missed you."

Bye, everyone chimed, and Ariana's high heels clicked in defiance as she stalked past Theo, not even bothering to acknowledge him.

Theo's hands curled and uncurled at his sides as he lumbered behind her, and Cade just rolled his eyes at Liam, who shook his head with a knowing look.

"So." I grinned, kicking my feet up into Sloane's lap. "How was Paris?! I saw the photos, and you looked *amazing.*"

Sloane tossed her silky blonde hair to the other side and shook her head with a crazed look in her eye. "*It was insane, you would not believe what happened.*"

An hour later, several more people had shown up, and everyone was still going strong, but I was delirious and in desperate need of some shut-eye, so I dragged myself upstairs and headed down mine and Liam's wing of the house.

The housekeeper had left my bag in the hallway, and as I pushed into my room and flicked the lights on, I realized why. Jules was already fast asleep in my king-sized bed, her deep auburn-brown hair fanned across the pillow her face was currently smashed into.

"Sorry, Jules!" I whispered, quickly turning off the main light.

She only grunted in response and groggily patted the bed as I shuffled across the room in the dark. As quietly as I could, I rifled through my armoire looking for pajamas and grabbed the first thing I could find, yanking it on.

"Sorry, I smell like paint thinner." I whispered, crawling between the sheets, too tired to do anything about it.

Jules responded with another sleepy grunt, but threaded her arm through mine, and I smiled because God, it was good to be home, back with my best friends, *back with safe people.*

I wasn't sure what time it was when I finally woke up, but the sun was blasting through a crack in the brocaded curtains spanning my bedroom, and the crystal chandelier hanging from the ceiling was an explosion of rainbows painted across my wallpapered room.

Finding my tongue practically glued to the roof of my mouth, I reached for my emotional support water bottle and groaned when I realized I'd never brought it inside. The bed was empty, and the sitting room was quiet, which meant the girls were probably already downstairs.

With the faint smell of maple syrup in the air, I headed towards the kitchen for liquids and sustenance. My eyes were still half closed as I wandered down the dimly lit corridor, padding over cold marble floors until I reached the silk rugs leading to the main living areas.

Overhead, Christmas music tinkled through the surround sound speakers, and even though *Thanksgiving* was tomorrow, I knew my mother had probably been playing Christmas tunes since October. She loved the holidays and, maybe even more; she loved hosting parties.

I, on the other hand, loved eating all the delicious food she and my brother Liam whipped up, and this week I was going to do nothing but eat and sleep and be gloriously lazy. *A respite I so desperately needed, and I couldn't wait.*

As I rounded the corner into the kitchen, the morning light was a full-out assault to my eyes, blasting through the giant windows that spanned the entire length of one wall.

"Good morning, sleepyhead." My mother chimed from the stovetop as I stumbled into the kitchen on pure muscle memory. "You got in late last night."

I grunted and groggily poured myself a glass of freshly squeezed orange juice from the ceramic pitcher we always used at Thanksgiving. It was one of my elementary school art projects that had unfortunately found permanent residence among our holiday dishes. Despite being slightly misshapen, with one droopy eye and lopsided feathers, Mr. Turkey had survived, year after year. *He was sturdy, I'd give him that.*

I took a heavy sip of orange juice, and that's when I finally looked over the rim of my glass and saw who had been sitting at the breakfast table, *watching me,* this entire time.

Carter freaking Kensington.

Naturally, I immediately choked.

CHAPTER 6

Cave Lady Instincts

SARAFINA

Nothing about it was dainty, little, or cute as I stared straight into the eyes of my brother's best friend—the biggest crush I'd ever had in my life, and proceeded to inhale a full three ounces of orange juice down the wrong windpipe.

The glass nearly shattered as I slammed it onto the counter, wheezing wet pulp out of my airway. Sweat beaded the back of my neck as I hacked up my left lung, desperately trying to stay alive, because today was not the day I was going to die by citrus. Humiliation? Yeah, maybe. But not citrus, for Christ's sake!

"Annnd now she's awake." Liam grinned, clearly enjoying my suffering as I smoothed my hair and tried to find some semblance of composure, suppressing another cough.

My mother gave me a curious look but didn't say anything, and my father was completely unbothered. He was still reading his newspaper with a cup of piping hot black coffee, probably his second cup this morning.

"You okay?" Carter asked with an amused smile, fork in hand, eyes bright and expectant. *Oh God.* His gaze flicked over me just once before he quickly shoved a forkful of eggs into his mouth, suddenly focusing far too intently on his plate.

When I looked down, I immediately realized why. *Oh, mother-*

fucker. My tits were hard, on display for all to see and—what the hell was I even wearing?!

My cheeks heated as I slowly processed the horrifying little number I'd pulled on in the dark. A princess t-shirt that I'd had since I was twelve, that was so yellow, dingy and full of little holes that I wasn't even sure it was clean. *Far too small* sleeping shorts that I'd honestly never seen before in my life. I most definitely had make-up smudged around my eyes, given the fact that I hadn't bothered to wash my face last night, and just when I thought it couldn't get any worse, my gaze dropped and I realized with complete horror—I'd forgotten to shave one of my legs, several times in a row, apparently. I could have disintegrated into the tiled floor. Halo of frizzy hair and all.

Carter, on the other hand, looked like a freaking male model because, of course, he did. His toffee-brown hair was perfectly mussed, the only sign he'd recently woken up. Or maybe he'd styled it that way? I couldn't decide. And he was wearing some sort of tight athletic shirt that was honestly *criminal.* It was practically screaming, *hey look! Man muscles!* And not only was he huge, he had a new scar slashing across one of his eyebrows and a split lip that made me realize those new muscles weren't just hard-earned, they were a necessity to surviving his new life. I swallowed hard, trying to ignore the way that made me feel. He was all *man* now, and his figure was utterly imposing—not his burnt sienna-colored eyes though, they still had that same boyish warmth, still sparkled with those golden flecks of amber and crinkled at the corners—it was at that moment I became acutely aware of every part of my body because I realized I was *staring,* and worse, everybody was watching *me* stare at *him. Shit.*

Carter's lips quirked across his stubbled jaw, and I quickly pivoted and then realized that gave him a perfect view of my half-covered ass.

Crap. Nowhere to go!

I was in full-out panic as I quickly grabbed a plate, knocking over the napkin holder in my attempt to reach for a piece of French toast with my bare hands.

Liam chuckled, still chowing down. "Somebody's hungover."

Asshole.

I cleared my throat trying to steady my voice. "No, I only had a glass and a half." I bit out, focusing on the pattern circling the edge of my plate. "I'm just a little tired since I was cramming before winter break."

I was screaming internally. Did I look halfway composed on the outside? I had no idea. Where the hell were the girls?! Why hadn't anybody warned me he was coming?

"Sure." Liam scoffed, and I shot him a dirty look, but he only grinned.

I moved behind the shelter of the kitchen island and started pouring syrup on my French toast. When I finally dared another look in Carter's direction, I was horrified to find he was *already* looking at me. I suddenly turned into a wild animal, posturing, refusing to be the weaker one and break eye contact first. Carter's gaze shifted lower, and I internally fist-pumped at being the winning primate, until I realized he was watching me make a maple syrup moat on my plate. *For fuck's sake.*

"I didn't know you were coming." I said as casually as I could muster while I smashed another piece of French toast onto my plate, hoping it'd mop up all the extra syrup, but I was freaking the fuck out, and my voice was high and pitchy, despite my best efforts.

"Neither did I." He was watching me *so intently*. "It was a last-second thing."

"You look good." This time, my voice sounded oddly flat. Crap. Too far the other way.

Carter opened his mouth as if to return the compliment and then refrained, his Adam's apple bobbing as he swallowed, the tension tightening between us by the second.

I crossed my arms over my boobs in an attempt to shield my embarrassingly hard nipples and rocked back on my bare heels, feeling alarmingly unhinged. "You know, I haven't heard from you in years. I didn't even know if you were still alive." My voice held far too much emotion, and I winced, knowing I sounded erratic. So much for playing it cool. I sounded like I was in theater class doing different line takes, with my tone swinging from way too interested, to panicked, to outright rude.

"Sara." My mother scolded me, pulling fruit out of the extra sub-zero refrigerator. "That's not something to joke about, you know Carter puts his life in danger every day." She arranged the fruit on a pretty platter and pushed it towards me before she turned to Carter, scolding, "You are taking care of yourself, being safe, aren't you?"

He chuckled. "Yes, of course." Was he? How'd he get the split lip, the scar? Was this a regular thing for him to look this banged up? Then he added, "As much as I can be, anyway."

I shoved a handful of blueberries into my mouth, chomping nervously.

"I talk to him every week." Liam shrugged indifferently. "You could have joined one of our many, many video chats." I shot Liam a death glare.

"You want to sit down?" Carter asked, motioning to the empty chair next to him in the breakfast nook.

No, I did *not* want to sit down. Not in this outfit and not next to him, but before I could protest, he pulled out the chair for me.

I gritted my teeth. Of course, he was ever the gentleman, always polite and cool as a cucumber. "Sure," I said tightly, trying not to draw any further attention to myself as I set my plate down next to his and slid into the velvet tufted, high-backed chair, feeling like it had suddenly turned into an interrogation seat.

I cut into my French toast far too aggressively. "Just would have been nice to hear something from you. You said—" I stopped myself, feeling the heavy rise and fall of my chest. Why was I so worked up? I thought I was over him. I *was* over him.

"You should have reached out." Carter offered softly, still staring at me with those beautiful brown eyes.

"Or *you* could have." I bit out before shoving a bite of French toast into my mouth.

"Sara, what has gotten into you?" My mother scolded, looking absolutely bewildered as she flipped another piece of French toast. "You two used to be thick as thieves. I thought you'd be happy Carter's finally home for the holidays again."

"She's hungover." Liam didn't bother looking up from his phone to torture me.

"It's fine, Charlotte." Carter looked totally unbothered. "She's right. I could have reached out. *Should* have reached out." He corrected.

"See." I said with a raise of my brows, but my sweet mother just gave me a look like, *what the hell is your problem?*

"I just wasn't sure if you wanted to hear from me after..." Carter's voice trailed off as my eyes went wide, silently begging him to shut his goddamn trap. He pivoted, thank God. At least I wasn't totally dead to him. "Well, you just seemed pretty upset when I told you I was leaving back then." Annnd never mind. Thanks for outing me to the whole table.

Carter looked down, cutting his already cut French toast into an even smaller piece, and I ignored Liam's suspicious gaze darting between the two of us.

I hadn't seen Carter since the charity auction. That awful, horrible night. We hadn't spoken since he'd rejected my almost kiss, which in hindsight might not have been my smoothest move —trying to kiss him on a dare. But still. He'd broken my heart in more ways than one that night, and then he'd left, and I'd never heard from him. Not once. He'd wanted to leave his old life behind, and I guess that included me.

I was devastated. He was more than a crush. He was my best friend, and now I had no idea what we were. If there even was a *we*. It was embarrassing, thinking our friendship had ever been more than that. He'd always been Liam's friend first—a fact I was continually reminded of.

Despite my current behavior, I *was* genuinely relieved he was safe. Maybe a little too relieved for my liking.

I suddenly realized everyone at the table was staring at me, waiting for me to respond to whatever Carter had just said. "I'm just glad you're home safe and sound." My smile was forced, and I couldn't quite meet his gaze.

~

I ate quickly, refusing to look Carter in the eye again before I excused myself upstairs to get ready for the festivities. After I'd showered, I threw on a *cute* oversized t-shirt from my duffle bag and vowed to burn the princess shirt along with my dignity the moment I got the chance.

My dripping wet hair soaked the back of my shirt as I dumped out my Hermès cosmetics bag onto the glass surface of my makeup vanity, neatly organizing everything into the drawers for the week. There was no way in hell I would be caught looking that haggard *ever again*.

I zoned out, staring at nothing, and thinking about everything. My pulse fluttered as I closed my eyes, *he was home*. It was bound to happen eventually, I just hadn't expected to have such a visceral reaction.

It was like my cave lady instincts were kicking in, *yoo-hoo* here's a man that could whack dinner over the head with a big stick, and drag it back to the cave for you. I would reprimand myself for noticing, but honestly, you'd have to be blind to miss it. Even then, he had smelled too good, minty and familiar, but more manly and musky. Just entirely too sexy. I was just a mere mortal, and he was like a tempting—

A sharp knock startled me at the door, and I yelped, banging my knee into the vanity. "It's me." Carter's deep, velvety voice called from the other side, and my stomach flipped.

CHAPTER 7
Stolen Pink Thing
SARAFINA

Hearing Carter at the bedroom door, Jules poked her head out of the sitting room with wide eyes, and I frantically waved her away.

She grinned at me before quietly disappearing around the corner.

"What do you want?" I asked, wincing as my voice came out irritated once again. What was wrong with me? I was glad to see him. More than glad, but I also felt off, weird, unsure of how to act. Jumpy. Neurotic. *Need I go on?* Because I *definitely* could.

"Can I come in—are you decent?" Carter asked.

I forced myself to take a slow breath before responding, "Yeah, come on in." I turned on my tufted stool with arms crossed as the door cracked open.

"Yes?" he confirmed again.

"What do you need?" I asked, and his head finally popped through the door *slowly,* making sure the coast was definitely clear.

He stepped into the threshold, filling the doorway as he gripped the frame just above him, and I watched as the sleeves of that obscene athletic shirt were victimized by the biceps he'd mercilessly shoved into them. He'd always been outrageously tall and athletic, but now he was *thick*, covered in lean muscle that rippled with his every fidgety movement.

"Can I talk to you for a minute?" He looked nervous. Carter never looked nervous, and there was something oddly cute about it. Giant hulking man afraid of tiny little woman. *Ugh. Stop.*

I nodded, any response getting stuck in my throat when he slipped into my room and softly closed the door behind him, before he leaned his massive frame against it—*effectively trapping me in!*

Just the proximity of him and all sorts of things were shifting inside me with sinful delight. Traitor. Traitor. Traitor! What the hell was wrong with me?

Carter rubbed the palm of his hand with his thumb, his eyes a mixture of emotions as he searched my face, and I broke eye contact first. So much for being the winning primate.

"Are we okay?" He asked softly.

I spun around on my stool to face the mirror and tried to act casual as I started applying makeup, or rather attempting to, because I couldn't think straight—let alone remember the makeup routine I'd done every day for the past, however many years. "Of course we're okay. Why wouldn't we be okay?" My voice sounded high and pitchy, and even I didn't believe myself. *Oy.*

I dared a peek at him through the gilded mirror, and he gripped the back of his neck, mouth parting as he searched for the right words. "I uh—I figured Liam and your mom would update you—about what was going on with me." He winced.

"They did." I said flatly and dug around in the mother-of-pearl inlaid drawers for absolutely nothing at all, because I couldn't think, couldn't breathe, couldn't process anything with him so close. He was sucking all the oxygen out of the room, and suffocation would be *oh so sweet* right about now.

He was quiet for a long while, and when I finally looked at him in the mirror again, he was just watching me. I dropped my gaze, feeling my cheeks heat, though I couldn't explain exactly why.

He pushed his massive frame off the back of my door, and every cell in my being buzzed with awareness as he padded across the plush floral rugs *towards me*.

Slowly, *carefully*, he leaned against the edge of my vanity—my bare knee brushed against his leg, and I quickly readjusted, but he didn't move at all. No, he was exceptionally still. Except for the quick rise and fall of his broad chest.

We both stayed like that, frozen, until he finally grabbed the hair tie off my vanity and played with it for what seemed like an eternity. Just spinning that little pink band, round and round, while I watched, like I was being hypnotized, because maybe I was. His corded arms flexed with the motion, muscles rippling under the floral tattoo inked up one of his arms. He'd never been a mere mortal man. Ever. But me, I was as average as they came. Which is exactly why I needed to remember, why I'd tried *so freaking hard* to move on back then.

"I'm really sorry if I hurt your feelings—and uh, how I handled that night—there are some things I would have done differently." He murmured, finally looking at me, and this time I held his gaze even though I felt like I might disintegrate. "You were just so upset with me..." He trailed off, eyes searching mine. "I just—I didn't know if you'd want to hear from me after I left— after everything that had happened, and uh, I thought maybe I should give you some space." His Adam's apple worked as he swallowed thickly and then quickly added. "Maybe that wasn't the right choice on my part. I just... um." He was *never* at a loss for words. "I didn't know what you needed, and I—I guess I was just scared that if I reached out too soon, I'd push you away and..." He searched my eyes, lips parted, desperately struggling to decide exactly what to say.

My shoulders sagged, realizing he was incredibly nervous while I was busy trying to play tough. "I know." I murmured quietly, hating that I'd let him leave, thinking we weren't on good terms. "I'm really sorry too, for letting you leave like that."

If anything had happened to him, I would have been completely devastated. I was being *so* petty for acting like this. Letting him put his life on the line with old grievances at home. I was being the worst, and I decided right then and there I would do better. Carter deserved way better than I was treating him, and even if my feelings were hurt—it wasn't his fault, it was mine. Me wanting something that was never going to happen. The sooner I got over it, the sooner we could get back to normal. Get back to being friends. Easier said than done.

Carter twisted the hair tie around either finger, again and again, and I found myself laser-focused on his hands. God, why did he have to have such nice hands? Big, wide, covered in rough calluses, *long fingers*. I swallowed hard.

"I missed you a lot, you know." He confessed it so quietly I wondered if I'd misheard him, but I hadn't.

I chewed on my lip, trying to suppress the smile that was threatening to consume my entire face. "You did?" I said nonchalantly as I could manage, but years of deciding I didn't care, that convincing myself what was between us was actually nothing—it all went straight out the window. Perfect.

"Of course." He said, his golden brown eyes lighting ever so softly. "I thought about you ev—" He cleared his throat and shrugged. "Of course I missed you. You're yellow and I'm blue."

My smile broke free, I just couldn't help it. "I'm really glad you're home. I thought you might have forgotten about me." I admitted and then internally rolled my eyes at myself. *Why? Just why in the hell would I admit that out loud?*

"You? Never." He grinned, focusing back on the hair tie he was playing with.

How could someone I knew so well feel so damn unfamiliar? Even back then, when I'd had a huge crush, there had always been a comfort between us, an easiness—because out of all my brother's friends, Carter had always been the kindest to me.

Now, I felt uncertain, like I didn't want to say or do the wrong thing.

"Are things going well for you?" I asked slowly, knowing that was the stupidest question in the world.

"Yeah," he said with a soft smile. "Really well. I'm up for a promotion soon."

"Yeah?" I waited for him to continue, but he didn't. "That's good." I nodded, unsure where to go from here. Truth was, there were a million and one things I wanted to ask him, a million and one things I wanted to *tell* him—I just didn't know how.

We looked at each other dead in the eye, and for a mere moment, everything was right—just for a millisecond, it was like no time had passed at all.

He looked at me expectantly, and I wondered if I should stand and hug him. Realized a part of me was aching to touch him, to remember what it felt like to be wrapped in those rare, strong-armed hugs that seemed to make the world disappear.

I could almost read the same thought in his eyes, but just then my bedroom door burst open, and a tall blonde blur of other-worldly beauty exploded into the room.

"Carter!?" Sloane squealed, with her silky blonde hair and effortlessly perfect makeup—she was always picture perfect, because she was quite literally a runway model. Meanwhile, I sat like a wet rat on my vanity stool, suddenly so unsure of what to do with my hands.

"Hey!" Carter said, his voice immediately full of his usual pep, dissolving all the tension in the room. "Good to see you, Sloane."

"Carters home." Sloane grinned at me before turning back to Carter. "Damn, you got ripped, Kensington." She didn't apologize as she checked him out unabashedly, and while his attention was focused on her, I used the opportunity to greedily do the same.

He chuckled. "That tends to happen when you work out for a living."

Sloane, not one for subtly, yanked him up off the vanity and spun him in a circle like a debutante. She was tall, but he still had to duck under her arm to oblige her, and I chuckled because he was always such a good sport—putting up with our antics over the years.

"Not bad." Sloane critiqued and gave him a slow, dramatic clap of approval. I couldn't help but smile. She was right. His transformation was *real good*.

Carter shook his head, a blush spreading across his tanned cheeks, and I wondered where he'd gotten so much sun. "Alright, I guess I'll leave you girls to it." He cast a long look at me before closing the door behind him, but not before—I caught a flash of pink around his wrist.

My heart tripped realizing what it was.

My freaking hair tie.

Sloane hooked a thumb over her shoulder as the door clicked shut. "Carters home." She whisper-screamed, her eyes wide with knowing.

I rolled my lips over my teeth and quickly spun back to the mirror, as Jules reappeared, shaking her head with a grin.

"What'd he say? No, what'd you say?" Sloane begged, eyes gleaming as she hugged the bedpost, comically sashed by the drapes hanging over my bed. "You two were awfully cozy up here."

"He just wanted to make sure we were okay." I started casually applying my mascara even while my heart continued racing.

"And are you?"

"Of course." I shrugged. "It's Carter we're talking about here, you know he doesn't have beef with anyone."

"I'm pretty sure he'd give his beef to *you*." Sloane grinned, coming closer while Jules groaned.

"Sloane!" I threw a lipstick at her.

"What?! I'm just saying." She caught the tube straight out of the air and proceeded to apply a swipe. "You're both older and wiser. Who knows?"

"*I know.*" I groaned. "We're just friends. That's all." I emphasized, trying to convince myself just as much as her.

"Okay, suuure." Sloane nudged me knowingly before climbing all the way into my bed, under the pillowy covers and all. She tucked one of my childhood stuffed animals under her arm before pulling her phone out and adding smugly, "Today should be fun, I've always loved a little holiday romance."

"Me too." Jules chimed, heading to the ensuite to finish drying her hair.

"There's no romance!" I groaned, but my heart fluttered at the thought of what the rest of the day might bring.

Carter was home. *And he'd just stolen my only hair tie.*

I smiled to myself. *Aww crap.*

CHAPTER 8
Don't Break The Egg
CARTER

Next to me, Liam and Sara argued fervently on the lawn. "You did not get the Turkey Ball into the Cornucopia before the timer went off," Liam shouted, his breath curling in the cold air.

I blew into my mitten-clad hands, knowing she definitely didn't. "Uh, yes, we did!" Sara parried right back, eyes sparkling with mischief as she accused, "*You're* the one who's cheating."

"You would know, you little cheater." Liam grabbed at Sara, but she ducked behind me with a grin just before he could grab her.

"Alright, you two, break it up, break it up." I finally wiggled my arms between them, pushing them apart.

Jules tapped in, and I rested my arm on Sara's shoulder, and rolled my eyes watching. "You guys are going down," Jules threatened, shoving Liam's chest. It was all play, of course, but it was comical how she postured big and tough, at more than a full foot shorter than Liam.

"Ladies, this has been child's play." Liam bowed out, giving the girls a wink. "Doesn't matter if you cheated, because we're still gonna win anyway."

"We did *not* cheat." Jules rolled her eyes at him.

Sloane came up with a hot drink in hand and linked arms

with Sara, pulling her out from under my arm with an astute look on her face. "You're going down, Kensington."

"Yeah, we'll see about that." I rolled my eyes and lifted my chin to greet Remi Devereux, one of Liam's cousins, several paces away.

Similar competitive squabbles erupted across the Devereux's perfectly manicured lawn—most of Briar Rose was out here, and everyone was bundled in colorful scarves identifying which team they were on.

On the other side of me, Cade crooned, "Come on, don't deny it."

"Literally, I'm not discussing this with you." Ariana rolled her eyes.

"Because you know it's true." Cade smirked, but his eyes blew wide, and he quickly headed the other way when he saw Theo closing in—Ariana followed suit, diligently avoiding Theo like she always did.

"Settle down everyone, settle down." Charlotte Devereux called from the deck with her bullhorn. "We'll tally up the scores and then move to our last and final competition, the Egg Master Race." Behind her, the smaller kids and the older adults sat bundled up in a row of chairs with steaming mugs, watching the annual Devereux Turkey Games. *I didn't realize how much I'd missed this.*

"Are you ready to race, Kensington?" Sara cocked her head at me smugly.

"You ready to lose your title, Rookie?" I teased, albeit a bit nervously. "Because this year, I'm going to smoke your ass."

"Oh, Kensington." She smiled patronizingly, sweetly, and I knew I was back in. "You'll never be faster than me, but that's so cute."

I grinned. "We'll see about that." Thanks to soccer and track, Sara *was* faster than most everyone, even me and Cade on occasion, but not today. Just on the *possibility* that I might come home this year, I'd been running sprints. *For over a month.*

From the raised deck, Liam and Sara's mom, Charlotte, used the bullhorn to detail out the instructions for the Egg Master Race.

"Here you go." River's tiny voice chirped as she strained to lift her basket up to me.

I chuckled, tousling her already windblown hair. "Did you help paint these?" I asked, and she smiled proudly, nodding that she did. I dug through the sparkly, puff-painted eggs and selected a gold one. "Thanks, River."

"You're welcome." She grinned shyly and then skipped over to the girls, who *oohed and awed* over her. I chuckled, watching River eat the attention right up.

Sara shot me a mischievous look before squatting down and whispering something into River's ear from behind a mitten'd hand. River laughed gleefully before sprinting away, and I chuckled watching her lose half her eggs in the process.

"What was that all about?" I closed the distance between us and nudged Sara's shoulder.

"Just a little surprise for later." Sara shrugged, her expression giving way to a genuine grin.

"Great, I can't wait." I rolled my eyes, secretly eating it up. I'd always loved Sara's mischievous streak, and being on the receiving end of whatever little prank she was planning, brought me immense relief.

Actually, after our little chat this morning, she'd been all smiles, acting like nothing had ever been wrong. It made me feel like an idiot for staying so distant these last few years. It was Sara. *Of course, we were fine.* I was such a moron for letting years slip by, thinking she hated my guts. Regret didn't even begin to cover it.

"So who's going first?" I asked, already formulating a plan. "Ladies first?"

"Absolutely not." Sara raised a brow suspiciously. "*You* can go first."

"As you wish." I shrugged, concealing a smile because she'd

taken the bait all too easily. She was going to attempt to wear me out by making me run first. Too bad it wouldn't work.

"Alright, the first Egg Master can line up." Charlotte's voice crackled through the bullhorn. "And as a reminder, the Egg Masters will get a four-second head start, *and no cheating.*" She emphasized. "I'm looking at you, Damon Kingsley."

"I would never." Theo's older cousin clutched his chest and shouted back with a devious grin, several paces away from us.

The long row of people next to us rolled their eyes in unison. A competitive streak ran through nearly everyone here. The unspoken rule was to *win,* no matter what. We all took that extremely seriously, because the Egg Master Crown was the highest honor you could earn at the Turkey Games.

"Ready?" I asked, carefully holding my sparkly hard-boiled egg.

"Are you?" Sara postured, with a little smirk.

I crossed my arms to hide the slight tremor in my hands. "Oh, I was born ready," I smirked, stealing a second glance the second she wasn't looking. Seeing her today—it was difficult not to stare.

River's tiny voice crackled through the bullhorn. "On your mark, get set, go!"

I snapped back to reality, and heart already pounding, I took off, running towards the other side of the still-green lawn. Several seconds later, I heard River's tiny voice again. "Chasers go!"

When I was almost to the podium, lined with colorful bowls —one for each team—I felt Sara's fingertips graze my back. "Gotcha!" She shouted, slightly out of breath.

I chuckled with a shrug. "Damn, girl, I guess you're still faster."

She raised her eyebrows, panting hard. "Told ya."

"Double or nothing?" I extended my hand, adding my gold egg to her red one.

"Double." She agreed, taking the egg with a determined glimmer in her eye, and I realized we were making up our own rules now.

While the teams lined up to switch, River used her opportunity with the bullhorn to tell everyone what she wanted for Christmas, *though she forgot to push the button for half of it.*

Sara was already in a runner's stance, stretching, when I leaned over the top of her, catching a familiar whiff of something sweet that made me swallow hard.

I whispered into her ear with a chuckle, "Hey Rookie."

"Hmm?"

"You'd better give it all you've got, because I *let* you catch me." I admitted with a smirk.

Sara's eyes snapped up to mine with wide-eyed understanding, right as River shouted. "Go!"

"Shit." Sara took off, a full footstep behind everyone else.

I counted down the seconds, heart pounding, ready to chase her—*ready to catch her.*

Sara *was* fast, always had been—*and she was competitive.* Even with the late start, she was already ahead of most of the group, and for a split second, I genuinely wondered if I'd overestimated myself.

When the moment came, I was focused on one thing, and one thing alone. Her. The cold air stung my cheeks as I passed the bulk of the group in long, hard strides, quickly closing the gap between us. *Naw, I totally had her. Knew it.*

"Going somewhere?" I sprinted alongside Sara, a mere pace away that I could easily close if I wanted to.

"Agh!" She dodged away from me, but I cut her off, and we did a lunge back and forth as she tried to get around me to get her egg into the pink bowl on the podium.

"Fine, I guess I'll just take the scenic route." Sara shouted with a wild grin before sprinting off the platform; she darted through an archway that led into the elaborate gardens her mother kept.

Game on.

Finding people who didn't want to be found was my expertise. Finding the girl I couldn't keep my eyes off of—well, that was just too damn easy.

Inside the maze of evergreen shrubs, I lost the sound of her footsteps, and I listened with a grin, knowing she couldn't have gotten very far. "You can run, but you can't hide." I taunted, every cell in my body awake and electrified.

Pebbled stone exploded from the next row over, and I grinned, not quite close enough to grab her before she ducked through another archway and out into the damp woods behind the estate.

The soft ground absorbed the sound of her sprinting steps, but now she had nowhere to hide. Her pink knit hat was like a beacon amidst all the dead winter foliage, and it wasn't long before I was pacing right behind her.

Sara looked over her shoulder, giving me the most beautiful grin, and then she tripped on a tree branch and promptly ate it.

Right behind, with no time to slow down, I slammed into her and we both went down in a tangle of limbs.

She yelped as I twisted, hitting the ground first, and we tumbled a few times before landing in a hard heap of grunts and groans with her every supple curve draped over the top of me.

Her eyes blew wide as she gazed down at me for a split second before she frantically scrambled across me—or tried to, at least.

I grabbed her foot with a grin of my own. "Nah uh—not so fast, Rookie."

She shrieked with laughter as I dragged her towards me. "You're going to break it." She accused when I yanked her zippered pocket shut before she could stuff one of the eggs into it.

"*You're* going to break it." I argued, dirt and leaves sticking in both our hair as I wrestled her mercilessly for that egg, effectively destroying it as sparkles crumbled everywhere.

"Cheater!" she shouted, her voice gloriously joyful.

"Just give. Me. The egg." I gritted, but suddenly she paused, looking at me with a devious grin. I stopped and gave her a goofy smile back—only to be hit in the face with a handful of leaves.

With a dirt-covered leaf stuck to my mouth, I narrowed my eyes. "Oh, you're in for it now, you little troublemaker." I was bigger and stronger, and I'd be damned if this wasn't the year I finally stole her smug little Egg Master Crown. No more Mr. Nice Guy.

I rolled on top of her and secured her hips between my knees while she laughed hysterically, going for another handful of leaves. "You already used that little trick." I grinned, pinning her hands above her head before she could throw another pile of dirt at me.

"Hah! I got it!" I cried triumphantly as I wrenched the egg out of her hand, holding the broken thing up in the air, like the victor I was.

Beneath me, Sara had finally gone still, and when I finally looked down, time stopped moving in an instant.

I froze as the air suddenly charged with something wild and forbidden. Her every panting breath curled into the cool air, each warm wisp an inviting caress across my face as it danced past.

All the feelings I'd had this morning—that I'd so carefully tucked away when she'd walked downstairs half-naked—came rushing back with a vengeance. Only now, Sara was lying underneath me, looking like she'd let me do one of the many things I'd shoved out of my mind this morning.

The pink hat was long gone, and her curly chocolate brown hair was fanned out underneath her, framing her rosy, wind-burned cheeks. Her dark lashes fluttered as she laid beneath me, giving me a doe-eyed look that was completely submissive.

I slowly slid my free hand into her other jacket pocket and retrieved the second egg. "I win." I rasped, watching her gaze drop to my mouth, finding her eyes dilated to the size of quarters.

"I know you broke the eggs, because there's glitter all over the ground!" Sloane and Jules burst through the trees.

I immediately let go of Sara's hands, the trance broken.

"So who was—" Sloane immediately clocked us, or rather me, on top of Sara. "You know what? I'm starving." Sloane grabbed Jules, whose mouth dropped open with a grin before they both abruptly spun around.

Underneath me, Sara still hadn't moved, she was still just

staring at me, and I swallowed hard as I rocked back and hauled her up off the ground in one quick motion.

"Told you I'd catch you." I said, the blood still roaring in my ears as I quickly let go, but when she swayed, my hand shot right back out to steady her, realizing she hadn't found her footing. As I gripped her, Sara just stared up at me with a look I couldn't quite make sense of. "We should probably head back." I offered, heart hammering so wildly against my chest, I wondered if she could hear it.

Her mouth opened and closed before she nodded just once and then finally stepped back.

As we headed back towards the house, she walked slightly ahead of me, giving me a perfect view of her leaf-covered backside.

I tried not to look, but it didn't matter—I didn't know if I'd ever get the feeling of her lying underneath me out of my mind. *Didn't know if I wanted to.*

CHAPTER 9
Over My Dead Body
CARTER

"Carter, I'd like a word with you." Brad Devereux, Sara's father, called from the doorway.

"Of course." I reluctantly followed Brad into his office and took a seat in the leather chair across from his desk, realizing it was an ambush. Richard Sinclair and Samuel Mortarulo were seated on the leather couch off to the side, smoking cigars and sipping amber drinks.

I'd sat in here many times before, and while I was wildly grateful to the Devereux family for keeping an eye on me after my parents had died, I wasn't that uncertain teenager anymore, hadn't been for a long while now.

I knew Brad meant well, but I didn't come back for these pressure-filled conversations. If anything, I'd come back for personal reasons, and the smell of Sara's spiced apple cobbler wafting through the house was certainly one of them.

Brad lit up a cigar before motioning to the box, offering me one, but I shook my head and settled into the plush leather chair with my old-fashioned still in hand.

"Have you considered The Society's offer?" He asked, and I realized we were getting straight to it today.

Of course, I had seen the stack of letters that had somehow mysteriously appeared on my kitchen counter when I'd come home. How or who had left them there, I wasn't entirely sure because the security cameras didn't log anyone entering or exiting. Violating didn't even begin to cover it.

"I'm still thinking it over." I lied, watching him and the other men carefully. Even now, I could sense Brad was in deep, just like my father had been, and it made me uneasy. At this point, he was just another voice badgering me to come back to Briar Rose, and it wasn't much better than any of my father's friends, haranguing me to do the same.

He nodded. "I understand you're going through a phase right now, Carter, but I can assure you, your father would have wanted you to follow in his footsteps, especially in joining the organization."

I cringed at the comparison. I loved my father, I truly did, but I wasn't all that confident I was anything like him. In fact, I really hoped I wasn't. "Well, he's not here anymore, so unfortunately he doesn't get a say." I said, cramming all my emotions back down as politely as I could.

Brad sat forward, and the tension in the room increased as something frustrated, or maybe even panicked, flashed across his expression. "Carter, I've hesitated to say this until now, but there are agreements that were made long before you took over the estate. Do you understand?" That was a new piece of information.

"What agreements?" I asked warily.

Brad's gaze shifted to Samuel, almost as if he were looking for permission. "Your father was right in the middle of some very important work with the organization, and we've all been very patient over the years, waiting for you to continue what he started."

"Brad, I have a career." I countered skeptically, "Aside from maintaining the estate itself, I'm not interested in settling down in Briar Rose. I'm sorry, it's just not in the cards for me anymore."

"I've already spoken with The Society Director and they've agreed to make an exception. They will allow you to join, even if you're only here part time." Desperation saturated his request under the unyielding timber of his tone.

"You're not hearing me."

Brad put his hand up. "If you're going to refuse, then I would implore you to turn the estate over to *me,* so that I can uphold the agreements your father made." Was he serious? There was no way in hell that was happening. "There are requirements that must be met to uphold your family name. Your membership is long over-due, and The Society is growing restless. They've been *very* patient over the years, letting you run rampant, and I fear that patience is running thin."

I was stunned, actually couldn't believe the words coming out of his mouth. "You know I'm not going to do that." I scoffed as he indifferently puffed his cigar again. "Brad, why don't we just cut the bullshit because I'm honestly pretty sick of this cloak and dagger nonsense with the three of you. Maybe if you tell me about these *agreements* you're referring to, we can figure something out, but frankly, I've had just about enough of this. "

"Son, the details are completely irrelevant, and whether you like it or not, you're a cornerstone of the Briar Rose community, so you *will* uphold this longstanding tradition."

I shook my head, growing more frustrated by the minute. One of the few people who'd stood by my side in all this was suddenly turning on me, and in that moment, I realized he'd never been on my side to begin with.

"If you were to join, I would consider giving you my bless-ing." Brad stared at me for a long time until realization slowly washed over me. "I only want the very best for my little girl, and I already have several offers." He added, shooting a glance in Richard's direction. "After she completes her master's degree, of course."

"Offers?" I puzzled, desperately hoping he didn't mean what I thought he did.

"For her hand."

I laughed humorlessly. "Brad, you can't possibly be serious." Another indifferent puff of his cigar. "You can't force her into an arranged marriage—that's—that's absurd." I honestly wasn't entirely sure if Richard was offering himself or negotiating for someone else. Someone younger, hopefully. What was I even thinking? *Fuck no*, none of this was happening at all. Over my dead body.

"Like I said, it's a longstanding tradition." Brad murmured as I gaped at him. "I could be persuaded to shift my approval in another direction. If you were to concede, that is."

"What the hell does Sara think of this?" I demanded.

"She'll do as she's told."

"And what about Charlotte? What does she think?" Surely Sara's mother was against this.

"How do you think Charlotte and I met?"

What? I shook my head in disbelief. This had to be some sort of strange fever dream. "She won't do it." I practically growled, knowing Sarafina was incredibly stubborn, not to mention she absolutely hated being told what to do.

Brad sighed, leaning back in his chair. "I know my daughter, and despite what you may think, I do know what's important to her."

"Oh, and what's that?" I scoffed incredulously.

"Stability." He murmured, and I hated knowing he was right, at least about that. "She'll never have that with you. Not unless you return to Briar Rose and uphold the commitments you've so ignorantly left fraying." He snapped, practically trembling with frustration.

Stunned would have been an understatement.

Just then, Sara's mother came into the office, gaze sweeping over Richard and Samuel before she gave her husband a pointed look. "Come on, you three, this is a day for fun." Charlotte looked at me warily. "Carter, can you help me with something in the kitchen?"

I was being rescued, thank God. "Of course." I nodded to Brad, not bothering to acknowledge the other two. "Thanks for the *chat*."

What the actual hell was I supposed to do with all this information? There was no way in hell I was going to stand by while Sara was bartered off like a mail-order bride.

What. The. Actual. Fuck.

"It looked like you needed saving." Charlotte said, looping her arm through mine as we headed down the long corridor, our footsteps echoing as we headed away from Brad's office towards the main living areas.

"It's alright, I know he means well." I assured her, even though I was quickly coming to the realization that wasn't even remotely true.

Charlotte stopped and faced me, reaching up to cup my face while her voice lowered. "I know he likes to talk about all that Society nonsense with you, but I want you to know your parents would be proud of you, no matter what." She smiled, emphasizing, "*I'm* proud of you, Carter."

She patted my chest in a motherly way that made me *ache* for my own mother, even if I was a grown man who flew fucking fast planes and beat people to a bloody pulp, professionally—*if they were lucky.* "I admire you, actually, for knowing what you want, and being able to go after it. It's an honorable quality." She smiled while I blinked rapidly and cleared my throat, any response getting stuck there.

We continued down the corridor, her voice turning pragmatic. "As a reminder, Liam and Sara aren't aware of The Society and I'd appreciate it if we could keep it that way."

I hesitated. "Charlotte, what exactly do you know about the organization?"

She hummed, "You know, Carter, that is an excellent question, and I wish your father were around to tell you more, but if he were, you probably wouldn't even be dealing with all this." She was quiet for a moment. "If you really want to know, you ought to respond to their requests to meet with you—it might be worth finally sorting all this out for yourself."

"Are *you* in The Society?" I quietly asked, knowing if there was anyone in Briar Rose I could trust. It was her.

She chuckled softly. "Membership is strictly confidential."

"Oh." Maybe she didn't trust *me*.

"But no, Carter, from what I gather from Brad, they only extend invitations to the head of each household."

"So the men." I swallowed hard, unease washing over me as I strung everything together.

"You're quick." She chuckled with a glint in her eye as she shook her head at the truth of my realization.

"Charlotte," I treaded *very* carefully. "He mentioned some arrangements after Sara's college graduation."

"He said that?" She immediately stopped walking and studied me for a moment, her eyes swirling with alarm.

I cleared my throat, uncertain if I should even bring it up. "He also mentioned that's how the two of you met."

She looked surprised, if not a little anxious. "About that." It was almost a plea. "The kids don't know."

"I won't say anything." I quickly promised, feeling my heart split in half—after everything she'd done for me, and all this time, I'd had no idea. "It's not my place, but, Charlotte, if any of you ever need *anything*."

She huffed a laugh. "You're a sweet boy, Carter, you always have been, but I try to keep the things that aren't in my control out of my worries." She smiled up at me, taking on a motherly tone that told me we were done discussing it. "But that's enough of all that. With regard to Sara, don't worry. I'll talk to Brad and set things straight."

Then she muttered more to herself. "He'd never get her down the aisle anyway. What was he thinking, negotiating her future like that? Just ridiculous." I grimaced in agreement as her tone shifted. "I'm just glad you're doing well and that you can finally join us for the holidays again. We *all* are." Her tone turned curious. "Especially Liam, *and Sara,* of course." She looked up at me, searching my eyes, and I did my best to keep my expression blank.

"It's good to be home." I agreed quickly, looking away after an inconspicuous amount of time had passed.

She chuckled and patted my arm affectionately. "Just remember, all good things take time. Be patient, and most of all, Carter, *be persistent."* She stopped before we hit the dining room and looked me dead in the eyes. "If you haven't figured it out already, you have more leeway than you realize, and I think now might be the perfect time to start using it. Time is a fickle thing, don't let too much of it pass or you might regret it."

I opened my mouth to ask what exactly she meant by that because if she meant what I thought she did—but River started crying, a tiny little howl amidst the clatter of small, arguing voices at the end of the wide hallway.

"Oh dear, I wonder what that's all about." Charlotte quickly headed towards the sound of tiny, upset voices chiming like the mother hen she was. "Now, now, who did what?"

I stepped into an alcove and, for a long moment, I just stood in the dimly lit hallway and let the silent tears fall. Charlotte wasn't my mother, but she was certainly the next best thing, and she was proud of me. Who I was. Who I'd become. I know she didn't know all the dirty little details of my life and my violent career, but part of me knew even if she did, she still wouldn't judge me. I liked to think my own mother would feel the same.

But it didn't take long before Brad's words were replaying in my head like a broken record. *She'll do as she's told.* Like hell she would.

I thumbed the damp from under my eyes and threw one long gaze over my shoulder towards Brad's office, realizing in that moment that he wasn't any different from any of my father's associates. He was ignorant, and selfish, and possibly incredibly dangerous.

He wanted something from me, needed it so desperately he was willing to use his own daughter as a bargaining chip, and the realization chilled me to the bone.

Sara wasn't a bargaining chip though, she was the dealer, controlling the entire game, and maybe—it was time I dealt myself in.

CHAPTER 10

Netflix and So Not Chill

SARAFINA

I plopped the last scoop of fresh whipped cream onto the still-warm apple cobbler when I felt a presence suddenly looming behind me. I didn't need to turn to know exactly who it was.

"If you need a volunteer to lick the bowl, I'd be happy to oblige." Carter crooned, already reaching around me, but I moved quicker, pulling the bowl away with a smirk.

Wide hands hit the counter on either side of me, and I turned, intending to say something snappy, but the closeness of him, *the look in his expression*, stole the breath right out from under me.

Nerves hit me like a freight train as I shyly dropped my gaze, realizing he wasn't about to budge. "Maybe I was going to eat that." It came out a meager whisper.

"Yeah?" He murmured with a lazy grin, while the scent of him invaded all my senses. All manly, musky, and damningly intoxicating. Like sexy fresh laundry, if that was even a thing.

"Yeah." I slowly ran my finger around the rim of the bowl, collecting the last bits of whipped cream for myself.

He chuckled low and deep. "Oh, you shouldn't have done that, pretty girl. I'm faster, remember?"

It *was* a fast glance Carter made behind him, confirming we were alone in the kitchen, and then it happened all at once—he gripped my wrist, and before I could put my finger into my own mouth, *his* plush lips slid over *my* finger instead.

I gasped as his tongue swirled over the pad of my finger and he sucked the whipped cream clean off it. I nearly dropped the mixing bowl, but Carter was already there, steadying it in my hands.

I might have been gaping as he gave me a lopsided grin and slowly backed away without offering another word.

When he finally disappeared around the corner, towards the sound of laughter, I collapsed against the counter, still hardly able to catch my breath. What in the ever-living fuck was that? Maybe it was nothing. We were just friends... because friends totally sucked things off each other's fingers. Right? It was certainly a first for me.

In a complete daze, I carried the spiced cobbler to the buffet table, completely forgetting to dust it with cinnamon.

Sloane grabbed me the moment the cobbler hit the table. "Wow, that smells amazing." She lowered her voice, eyes glimmering as I murmured thanks. "But why do you look like you just got a lobotomy?"

"What?" I asked, shaking myself out of my stupor as Jules closed in.

"We just saw you-know-who sneaking out of the kitchen, like he didn't want to be seen." Jules explained with a raised brow.

Sloane was desperate for answers. "Did he make a move?"

"Of course he didn't." Jules answered for me, handing me a plate of cobbler as the corner of her mouth pulled into a smirk. "But did he?"

Jules served Sloane the next scoop as I struggled to explain. "We just uh—he uh—well I—"

"What?" they begged.

Right on cue, one of my mom's friends appeared and affectionately rubbed my back. "This smells delicious, Sara."

"Help yourself." I smiled, shooting the girls a warning look. "The apples are from the Bishop's orchard."

"Oh, how lovely." She chimed, serving herself a plate.

The sound of River's voice startled me from above. "Cookie." She demanded, from Carter's shoulders. He was wearing a red reindeer nose, and she was clearly already on a sugar high, but he lifted a cookie anyway. River promptly stuffed it into her mouth so she could slap her ribbon reins. "Mush! Dasher. Mush!" she chanted, and a puff of crumbs flew out of her mouth, straight into Carter's hair, making him groan.

A strange feeling washed over me as he gripped her little feet and galloped away, making the sound effects and all.

"I think someone has a little crush." Jules commented while I stared at the last place Carter had just been. "River." She clarified quietly. "He's good with her—with all the kids."

"Yeah, he is." I agreed quietly. During the lawn games, the kids had figured out he was a real-life G.I. Joe no thanks to Liam and Cade—the two of them had gotten a real good laugh when Carter was mobbed by about a dozen very small, very demanding tyrants begging for an airplane ride. At one point Carter had five different kids hanging off him, hounding him for another turn— he'd put on a good show, letting them tackle him to the ground, which made them all cheer with delight. And then, he of course gave them all another ride, because Jules was right, he was a total natural. I tried not to dwell on it as I shook my head. "Today has been so weird."

"Good weird, or bad weird?" Jules brows crunched with concern.

"To be determined?" I sighed, and she looped her arm through mine, pulling me towards the living room. "How's Doug?" I asked, changing the subject.

"I don't know, long distance sucks." She rolled her eyes. "I do not recommend."

Liam walked by, and Jules plucked a cookie off his plate, and he grumbled, but let me do the same. "Thanks, Lee." Jules called sweetly. "Just helping you keep your figure."

Liam practically grunted at us as he headed past us to grab a seat for the Tricky Turkey gift exchange.

~

"Wow, this is exactly what I wanted." Carter chuckled, pulling the t-shirt out of the gift bag. "Who intercepted my Christmas list from Santa?" He held the shirt up against his chest, and I grinned as the room erupted into cheers and chants, begging him *to put it on.*

"Take your top off!" Cade called across the room with a smirk.

Carter shook his head with a disbelieving grin. It was clear the shirt was going to be far too small to fit his massive frame, but he tried anyway. A moment later, his arms were tangled above his head because he couldn't get the damn thing over his massive shoulders.

"Sorry, guys." His voice was muffled as he struggled to get the shirt off, and I breathily dropped my gaze when his undershirt rode up, revealing row upon row of muscled stomach. "It's too small." He huffed, finally freeing himself.

"Shall we make some alterations?" Theo grinned and flicked out a pocket knife, looking at Cade.

"Guys." Carter's hair was mussed as he put his hands up, backing away with a smirk. "Don't make me hurt you."

"Yeah, sorry, there's no way in hell you're getting out of this one." Liam grinned and whipped off his sweater, leaving him in a fitted white t-shirt.

Across the room, chairs were already being shifted out of the way.

"Don't you want to play dress-up?" Cade rammed into Carter, tackling him to the floor in front of the Christmas tree before my brother and Theo piled on.

The room was filled with laughter and clapping as the heaping pile of flailing muscles shifted across the floor. And because he was being a good sport, I could tell Carter was only halfheartedly fighting back by the time they finally pinned him.

"Hmmm," Jules muttered with a roll of her eyes. "Dinner and a show."

Sloane hummed in agreement.

"Come on, guys." Carter complained with an amused chuckle as the sound of fabric ripped. "Really?"

They hauled him up a moment later, and Cade was already howling with laughter as I clapped a hand over my mouth. Stretched over Carter's broad frame was a way too tight *bikini t-shirt*. One of those vacation shirts with a slender woman's torso, big boobs, clad in a hot pink triangle bikini.

"That's one ugly broad!" One of my father's friends, Richard, shouted.

Carter shook his head with an amused laugh, the tips of his ears burning an adorable shade of pink. When his eyes met mine across the room, there was something soft and almost pleading in them. I bit my lip, concealing a grin, and circled my finger in the air. His chest shook with silent laughter as he appeased me, lifting his arms out. He did a slow spin for the room, and the peanut gallery erupted in approval, clapping, whistling, and just generally making Carter blush.

As I looked around the room, everything felt right. Everyone who was supposed to be here was. The sounds of my friends and family's laughter, the smells of spiced desserts, and reheated leftovers filled the air, and I didn't know if anything could be more perfect or more comforting.

I honestly couldn't remember the last time I'd felt this way. I'd had all these huge dreams and aspirations for college, and it hadn't been long before I'd realized it was all just a big pipe dream. Not only was I beginning to doubt myself more and more, and overthink things, but part of me wondered if I was even cut out to be an artist. None of my work was all that groundbreaking, anyway.

Not to mention, the dream of a normal college experience was long gone. Part of me wasn't even entirely sure why I was pursuing my master's degree, not when I just desperately wanted to get the hell out of there. My grandiose plans of living in the college dorms, of making new friends—it couldn't have been further from my reality.

Apparently, it was never in the cards for me, because I was a socialite from Briar Rose, and all people saw was a chance to make a quick buck off of me. I was the girl the paparazzi would pay an arm and a leg for a photo of, *especially a nude.* A harsh reality I'd learned the very first week I'd showered in the communal dorm bathrooms.

The last several years had been incredibly lonely, but nobody in this room knew. It didn't matter though; after graduation, I'd come back to Briar Rose and forget all about college. This was my home, and these were the people who loved me, and I couldn't wait to come home for good.

I blinked, realizing the game had long been over, and I'd gotten stuck with an oversized dog calendar that featured a different dog pooping every month. I chuckled, I'd probably give it to River, she'd get a kick out of it, *though I doubted her mom would.*

Snacking on some of Liam's leftover smoked turkey, I looked out over the sea of heads crammed into the theater room, realizing I was going to have to sit on the floor.

Before I could make it to the front, River's tiny voice chirped at me. "Sara, I saved you a seat."

My gaze swung across the dark room as the projector flickered with previews, and I was simultaneously filled with dread and anticipation when I found her. She was sitting with her new best friend, Carter, and I realized I couldn't very well turn down a five-year-old, so I reluctantly headed their way.

"Here." River patted the crack between the two cushions on the loveseat.

"Why don't you sit in the middle since you're smaller?" I suggested, feeling Carter's gaze on me.

She didn't bother looking up at me as she continued sorting her collection of candy. "Then I'd have to move all my stuff." She said simply.

Great, the kid had airtight logic, not to mention, it looked like she'd pillaged every candy dish across the house like she was trick-or-treating.

I avoided the unwrapped chocolates—each with a single bite taken out of them—and reluctantly squeezed in *next to Carter.*

As I sank into the cushion, I panicked, realizing there were way too many points of contact with his muscled arm, and I quickly attempted to lean forward, but Carter's calloused fingers slipped around the nape of my neck, halting me. "Stay." He murmured, "I'll get it."

I nodded wordlessly, instantly unable to get my voice to work as he reached out a long arm and grabbed a fuzzy blanket from the basket in front of us.

When he settled back in and tossed the blanket over the two of us—making sure I had enough of it—I could have sworn he shifted even closer.

Either way, there was no avoiding it. There were about a million points of contact between our bodies, and every single one of them made me feel like I was about to combust.

No matter how hard I tried, I couldn't focus on the movie. Couldn't even tell you what was on if my life depended on it.

I was finally pulled out of my strange trance when Carter threw his head back and barked a rich, throaty laugh. I smiled to myself as River looked at Carter for a beat too long and then burst into her own fit of laughter. She definitely hadn't caught the adult innuendo her new friend was laughing at, but it was cute all the same.

He kind of felt like my new friend, too. Or at least, we were finding a brand new rhythm today. I dared a glance out of the corner of my eye and nearly jumped out of my skin when Liam suddenly appeared.

The movie flickered against his tanned skin in the darkness. "Sorry, kiddo, you're gonna have to sit in my lap. All the seats are gone." River made a pouty face but collected her candy into her pockets before Liam lifted her and settled in next to me—shoving me *even further* onto Carter.

So I sat there, squished like the cream filling between the broad-shouldered sandwich of my brother and his best friend, while my heart threatened to beat straight through my chest. Carter didn't seem rattled at all. Nope, perfectly at ease. He slipped an arm over the back of the couch—to give his shoulders more room because we were so crammed. Right?

Why was I so wound up? I needed to get a grip.

"Stop fidgeting." Liam elbowed me. "Can't you get situated?"

I narrowed my eyes and whispered, "River, do you remember what we talked about earlier?"

Her eyes lit up, and she nodded, already scurrying towards the kitchen.

"You'd think she's never eaten candy before in her life." Liam brushed the cookie crumbs off his pants with a shake of his head. "What was that all about?"

"Oh, you'll see." I hummed, "River's just making you a little treat."

Just as I was about to go check on her, River came back, carefully carrying two mugs filled to the brim with mostly marshmallows. Undoubtedly, to hide our little secret. I was impressed, she was a master prankster already.

"Here." She grunted, giving one mug to Liam and the other to Carter, who only smirked knowingly.

"Thanks, River." Liam said, still watching the screen, completely oblivious to her standing there, waiting for his reaction. I winked at her while we all waited for an unsuspecting Liam to take the first sip.

Finally, he took a heavy swig and then immediately coughed, nearly spitting it out.

I chuckled as the smaller kids aggressively shushed him. "What's in this?" Liam raised an amused brow.

Hardly able to contain herself, River twisted back and forth, a naughty grin on her face. "Lots of hot sauce."

"Oh, that's very creative." Liam chuckled, setting his drink down. "I think I need a palate cleanser, though." Liam loved spicy food, so I knew she must have poured *a ton* into his mug.

"It's just a joke. I can make you a real one if you want." River sprinted off to the kitchen, not waiting for Liam.

I leaned in to whisper to Carter, "Liam has chocolate on his ass." I breathed, realizing he was *right there* when I turned my head a moment later.

Carter's eyes flicked up to look, but he didn't shift away from me as he chuckled low and deep, the sound vibrating against me. "Sure does." His face was a mere breath away from mine, and I swallowed hard before shyly dropping my gaze. "I'll just stick with my old-fashioned, I think." Carter drummed his fingers on the back of the couch, wisely leaving his hot chocolate untouched. "Let me guess, that was your sneaky little idea from earlier?"

I shrugged, keeping my voice low. "You did break both of the eggs. Had to pay you back somehow." I met his gaze again. It was *so* intense, eyes so warm and focused only on me. I wondered what exactly he was thinking.

"You got me there." Carter licked his lips, and I studied his split lip before he finally brought his glass to his mouth after what felt like a lifetime. His Adam's apple worked as he swallowed and then he passed me the glass. "I'll remind you, you started your little prank *before* the eggs broke."

"Maybe." I shrugged, taking the glass from him. "Whiskey?"

He nodded. "Whiskey, bitters, turkey cheer. You know, the essentials."

I rolled my eyes and took a small sip, testing it out. "I don't know what I expected, I hate whiskey." I grimaced as it burned all the way down.

Carter chuckled and sat forward. "Come on, I'll make you something sweet." His fingers wiggled behind him, reaching for me as we weaved through the packed crowd towards the door. His finger wiggling became more and more aggressive until I finally swatted him, and my stomach flipped when he grabbed on with a rough, calloused hand and didn't let go. Not until we hit the hallway.

Liam and River passed by, heading back to the movie. "You've got chocolate on your ass," Liam chimed from behind me.

I looked down, my mouth falling open in surprise, and River shot me a guilty look, flashing me a theatrical clenched smile.

"So do you!" I called back to Liam.

"Shit. These are new." He muttered, twisting to look at the back of his pants. "Hey, bring me a drink when you come back." He called over his shoulder, and then I could hear him explaining to River the importance of candy-eating zones using the theory of mise en place as they disappeared back into the theater.

Carter gave me a soft smile and tilted his head, motioning for me to follow him, and as we walked down the quiet hallway towards the bar, I suddenly felt incredibly nervous.

CHAPTER 11

Drinking Games

SARAFINA

In the bar, the lights were dim, and a few battery votives flickered amidst the fragrant holiday garland draped across the bar top. I pulled up a leather barstool, realizing literally everyone else was in the theater, leaving Carter and me utterly *alone,* and that realization sucked all the air out of the room.

Carter slipped behind the bar. "What'll it be, pretty girl?" He flipped a cocktail shaker with a flourish and I laughed, realizing he was still wearing that ridiculous bikini shirt.

"Lime jello shots?" I shrugged innocently.

He laughed, loud and throaty. "I can see you're taking your college drinking very seriously."

"What can I say? I'm a pro at jello shots." I mimed it out for him—the sticking my finger in, giving it a swirl, and knocking it back. It earned me a genuine laugh that warmed me all the way down to my toes.

Carter disappeared as he dropped down and rooted around in the liquor cabinet, reemerging a moment later. "I'm sorry to say, it looks like we're all out of the clear stuff." He gripped the back of his neck. "We do, however, have enough whiskey left for the apocalypse, though."

"Just my luck." I muttered.

"How about a seven-and-seven?" He asked.

"Sure." I shrugged, knowing I'd take literally anything he gave me.

Carter made my drink, looking far too good doing it, and then he topped it off with one of the edible flowers my mother kept the bar stocked with.

I tucked the flower behind my ear. "How do I look?" I playfully rested my chin on the bare skin that my sweater had slid down to expose on my shoulder.

Carter just stared at me for a long while, fingers gripping the countertop. "You look good." He nodded, but didn't add anything else, or apologize as he watched me so incredibly intently.

A long moment stretched between us before I smiled shyly and dropped my gaze.

"Well, how is it?" He asked as I finally took a sip of the drink.

"It's great." I grimaced, throwing it back in several eye-twitching gulps.

"Damn, should I just leave you the bottle?" Carter joked, sliding the whiskey my way.

My heart tripped noticing my pink hair tie was *still* on his wrist.

Heart pounding, I leaned over the bar and grabbed two shot glasses, sloppily pouring a shot in each. "Let's play truth or dare." He gave me a look I couldn't quite decipher, and I wondered if I was about to lose my gumption. "You haven't forgotten how to play, have you?" I teased, albeit a bit nervously.

"I don't forget anything when it comes to you." He crossed his arms, leaning forward onto the counter, which made his buff arms look even bigger. "Tell me what you want to know, pretty girl." His eyes glimmered suspiciously.

I ran my finger around the rim of the shot glass slowly. So many things I could ask. So many things I was *dying* to ask, but I chickened out. "Why did you leave?" I asked quietly.

He shrugged before giving me his canned answer. "I wanted to serve my country."

"If you lie, you drink." I warned, and he lifted his glass to drink. "Come on." I groaned, wondering if we didn't have that familiar cadence between us anymore. "Seriously, why did you leave?"

He set the shot glass down with a lazy smirk. "I don't know. Just wanted to change things up. Needed to get out of here."

I swallowed hard. "Was it really so bad here? Was there nothing worth staying for?" Shit, did I really just say that part out loud? I blew out a slow breath, feeling my cheeks heat.

"I needed to figure out who I was without all this." His mouth twitched in an almost smile that didn't meet his eyes. "Things were complicated back then. They still are." He was unapologetic as he stared at me for a moment too long *again,* and I shifted nervously.

"What happened to your lip?" I finally asked.

He shrugged. "Bar fight."

"You? Never." I knew he was lying, and my heart sank a bit, realizing he didn't trust me as much as he used to.

He chuckled, ignoring my question altogether. "It's your turn, and you don't get to pick truth or dare because you picked for me. So tell me something, pretty girl."

There was a long pause. "Tell you what?" I puzzled.

"Everything." He said simply, his caramel brown eyes twinkling with something achingly beautiful—something that I was never going to have.

"Ah, well, that would be a lot." I traced the rim of my shot glass and swallowed thickly. "Where to even begin?"

"Start at the beginning and we'll go from there." He shifted his head, trying to catch my gaze. "I want to know the things nobody else knows, the things I know you're shouldering all on your own."

"I mean, there's not much to tell." I shrugged.

"Liar." He teased, though there was genuine concern swirling in his expression.

I rolled my eyes. "Fine. What do you want to know?"

"Boyfriend?"

I scoffed. "Really? That's your burning question?"

His jaw fanned. "Someone from Briar Rose?"

I blushed and suppressed a small smile. "No boyfriend." *Because only douchebags and assholes seemed to be interested in a romantic relationship with me.*

"Hmmm." He murmured in approval. "How's your painting coming along?"

"Fine, I guess." I shrugged. *It was a heaping pile of crap.*

"You have any pictures of your work? I'd love to see it."

"My phone's in the theater." It was in my back pocket, but I'd never shown my family or friends my work, and I was not about to start with Carter. The bona fide art investor. Hell to the naw.

"Fine." He drawled mischievously. "Then tell me a secret, something nobody else knows."

I stared at him, wondering how so much time had passed so quickly. "Carter... you already know something no one else knows." I admitted quietly.

He inhaled a sharp breath. "You never talked to Sloane or Jules?"

"No." I fiddled with a berry on the decorative garland.

"Your mom?"

I shook my head, and when I finally glanced at him, his expression was so incredibly concerned. I forced a smile, hating that Carter had been the one to find me that night. The one who knew even a sliver of my dirty little secret. I rolled my eyes, with a small smile. "I still can't believe you thought I murdered Tag."

Carter chuckled lowly to himself and nodded, something sharp flashing through his expression. *"So that's who you were with."* My pulse spiked, but Carter didn't miss a beat. "I could have killed him for even looking your way, let alone whatever happened between the two of you that night." He didn't press, but I knew he was asking me to finally explain. I didn't. The fact that I'd just admitted I was with Tag was damning enough. Taggart Caldwell had a reputation, and Carter certainly knew about it. It was complicated, but I was ashamed all the same. Carter's jaw fanned as something lethal flashed through his expression, and he dropped his gaze, practically drilling through the countertop with his quiet simmering rage. "Still could kill him." He considered.

I realized in that moment that I believed him. "*Have you ever killed someone?*" The question was out before I could think better.

"No." He responded all too quickly and then, after a moment, he looked dead into my eyes and took the shot. I swallowed hard as he quietly poured himself another, immediately downing that one too.

I felt like I couldn't breathe. "Carter, I have no idea why I asked you that." Hot, I felt so incredibly hot. "I shouldn't have asked you that. I'm so, so sorry."

"Don't be sorry." He murmured. "You're always allowed to ask me anything."

I nodded, at a complete loss for words.

When I looked up, he was watching me carefully, and I couldn't stand the pity in his eyes. Not for himself. *For me.*

The only thing worse than having his pity for my shit luck in the relationship department was the fact that I'd do anything to meet someone exactly like Carter. Someone kind, funny, driven, passionate, someone who understood me, but unfortunately, that had never been in the cards for me.

"Your turn." I forced a deep breath in, breaking the tension. "Truth or dare."

"Dare." He tilted his head, cocky as ever.

Why I did what I did next, I couldn't tell you. Something possessed me. "I dare you to go kiss Sloane."

"What?" He pushed up off the counter abruptly.

"Kiss Sloane or drink." I said tightly.

"Why would you dare me to kiss *Sloane*?" His tone was clipped.

"I don't know?" Except that I did. Blondes had always been his type, and Sloane wasn't just blonde, she was beautiful, and funny, and exactly Carter's type. My stomach churned just waiting for him to go do it. "Is there a reason you don't want to?" I asked innocently, while my heart pounded a mile a minute.

"Uh yeah, there's a lot of reasons." He downed the shot with a heavy roll of his eyes. "Your turn, a dare for you." He refilled his shot glass.

"I don't get to pick?"

"Nope." The firm tenor of his voice demanded submission.

I scoffed, shoving the fluttering feeling down. "Alright, let's have it."

With a totally straight face, he said, "Kiss *me*."

I almost fell off my stool. "What?" I breathed nervously. "You don't seriously mean that."

"Oh, I'm very serious, Sarafina." He repeated slowly. "I dare you to kiss me, or drink."

"Carter, that would be totally weird." As if I hadn't spent all day replaying the feeling of him on top of me in the woods, wondering exactly what it'd be like to be swept up in those corded arms and then devoured by that perfect mouth of his. Would he be gentle and soft? Or would he be demanding and passionate? Honestly, I could see either with him.

"Kiss me or drink." Carter hummed, his voice lower and more gravelly this time.

How long had I been staring at his lips? "That would be too weird." I stuttered out.

"Would it?" He rounded the counter, making my breath catch. "Give me one good reason it would be weird."

"Because you're—you're you." I stuttered out ineloquently, breath pulsing, as he neared.

"And you're you." He hovered in front of me, oozing sex and

promise, and I suddenly worried it was a joke I wasn't in on. "Do you want a minute to consider?" He asked.

"No." I could hardly get the word out. *I was a filthy, fucking liar.*

Carter cocked his head, looking neither relieved nor disappointed. "Then drink."

My throat closed up as I quickly downed the shot, and everything burned, just like I deserved. He refilled my glass, his gaze drilling through me with such intensity I wished he'd just do it anyway, but he didn't.

He finally sat on the barstool next to me, and didn't look away, didn't do anything but wait.

"Why didn't you call?" I focused on my shot glass too hard, still feeling confused.

"I was busy."

"Liar." I muttered, and he drank, confirming it.

"Why didn't *you* call?" he asked.

"I was busy." I shrugged, parroting him.

"Liar." he parroted right back, and I simultaneously drank.

The tension between us was a band ready to snap as I filled both our glasses again. "Why did you do that thing in the kitchen?" I could hardly hold his gaze.

He broke first and fiddled with the pink hair tie stretched tight across his wrist. *My* freaking hair tie. "What thing?"

"You know *exactly* what thing."

"Why do you think?" I could have sworn his gaze dropped to my lips for a millisecond.

I swallowed hard, had he been serious about the kiss? I honestly couldn't tell. "Dare—I dare you to model for my art class next week."

"I leave town in two days." He said, his eyes darting between mine, regret possibly dancing somewhere in between.

Confusion washed over me, and I felt like a humiliated idiot. "Then drink." I lifted my shot glass and tapped it to his before I knocked it back.

"You didn't lose." He said tightly.

"Yes, I did." I could feel tears welling up in my traitorous eyes as I slid off the barstool, but he moved faster, bracketing me in at the countertop before I could escape.

"*Sara*." He murmured, and I couldn't possibly think straight with him standing that close. There was nowhere to go as one tear and then another slipped down my cheeks. Nowhere to hide as I desperately tried not to crumble in front of him, failing miserably with every second that passed.

I could feel his body heat radiating off him as he lifted a trembling hand. "Don't cry, pretty girl." He pleaded quietly before a callused thumb brushed across my cheek, carefully wiping away the tear. "Tell me what to do, and I'll do it." He tipped my gaze to his and split me in half with just a look.

"I lied." I admitted against my better judgment. "And I hate that I don't know if you were serious or not."

His words were a deluge. "I know—I was—I'm sorry—I just can't go another three years without talking to you."

"Then don't." I might have pleaded.

"If you don't tell me to stop," he murmured, eyes wild. "Then I'm going to kiss you." I froze, feeling the heat of him brush against my face as he pleaded. "Just tell me to stop. Remind me why this is a terrible idea."

I knew I should pull away, but I wasn't even remotely strong enough to exercise that much willpower, as everything I'd ever wanted dangled in front of me like bait—tempting and dangerously deadly all at once. And maybe that's all this was to him, a catch and release—another one of our silly games that would leave me gutted once he got what he wanted and threw me back—*just like everyone else had.*

My fingers tangled in the fabric of his shirt as he pressed closer, eyes fluttered as the heat of his breath rushed across my mouth, right there, just waiting for me to cave and close that last tiny little bit of terrifying distance.

"What the fuck is going on in here?" Liam growled from the doorway, and we both froze.

Suddenly, Carter wasn't in front of me anymore, he was flying backwards. They went crashing to the ground in a stupid heap of testosterone while I bolted for the door, biting back a sob.

"Sara," Carter begged, but I didn't stop.

Outside, I laid across the porch swing on the side of the house and cried. Ugly cried, snot and all. I didn't even know exactly why I was crying, but I couldn't hold it in anymore. Relief, nerves, anxiety. He knew my secret. He'd tried to kiss me. Liam had found us. It was all too much and simultaneously not enough.

Carter's quiet, calm voice appeared behind me a little while later. "Truth."

I sat up and wiped my nose. "Oh, my God." I gasped, realizing one of his eyes was nearly swollen shut. "Carter."

"It's fine." He said, "I'm sorry. I shouldn't have done that. We were drinking, and I wasn't thinking clearly." My chest collapsed like a sinkhole with no bottom.

Oh, that was the story we were going with.

"Truth," Carter murmured from behind me again. "Yellow Gatorade is my favorite. Always was, always will be."

I chewed on that for a minute, confusion washing over me, but when I turned to argue, a lump formed in my throat, realizing he was already gone. When I would see him again, I had no idea.

I wasn't sure how long I sat there by the time the screen door finally opened again. "You doing okay, sweetie?" My mother sat next to me, rubbing my back. "You seemed a little surprised that Carter was back today."

"I think I'm just tired." I lied. "And maybe a little drunk." That part was true. All those whiskey shots had finally caught up with me, and I felt disgusting.

My mother shook her head with a chuckle. "Let's get you to bed, you wild girl."

The rest of the house was already quiet as we walked arm in arm up to my room. She deposited me in my bed, clothes and all, before she pulled the covers up and pushed my hair out of my face. "I'm so proud of you, Sarafina." My lower lip quivered, and my mother's brows crunched sympathetically. "Oh, sweetie, it will all work itself out." She promised. "It always does. Timing is everything."

I nodded, another tear streaking down my face as I rolled onto my back and stared at the ceiling. "There's chocolate melted on the loveseat." I didn't bother explaining which one.

She rubbed her temple, probably even more exhausted than I was, since she'd been up since dawn preparing for the party. "I'll let the house staff know." She leaned down and planted a kiss on my temple. "Sweet dreams, honey. It's good to have you home."

If only that were true. I felt like I was losing something I never had in the first place.

CHAPTER 12
Swirly Girly
CARTER

"What building are you looking for, hon?" The woman behind the information desk was barely visible over the counter as she chomped away on her gum.

"The Cobalt building? I'm looking for Sarafina Devereux's class at noon."

She motioned over her shoulder. "Head down this hallway and exit through the back. It's the last building at the end of the sidewalk. If you hit a parking lot, you went too far."

"Thanks." I tapped the desk as I stepped away.

"You active?" She nodded to my Air Force hoodie and then asked with a tilt of her head, "Career guy?"

"That's the plan."

She looked me up and down. "Must be hard on your girl-friend, unless you're single?"

I opened my mouth to correct her, but changed my mind. "We make it work."

"Good for you." She turned back to her computer indifferently.

I wandered through the maze of hallways, hoping it wasn't an epic mistake to show up unannounced. After the clusterfuck that had been Thanksgiving, I wasn't sure how Sara would feel about seeing me, especially on her turf. But I was scheduled to be over-seas for Christmas, which meant this was my last chance to try and fix things. Otherwise, another three years was going to slip by, and there was no telling where that would leave us.

Inside the Cobalt building, the smell of art supplies filled the air. Paint, canvas, and something acrid—in an open classroom, someone was working on a massive piece, wearing long gloves and a respirator. As I hurried down the hallway, trying to get the smell out of my lungs, I seriously hoped Sara wasn't dealing with these kinds of noxious chemicals on a daily basis.

Feeling incredibly nervous, I slid my phone into my back pocket and slowly approached her classroom. The door was open, and when I peered inside *there she was.*

My heart skipped a beat. I felt like I couldn't move, couldn't walk inside, couldn't take my eyes off her at all. She was thankfully too preoccupied to notice me lurking.

She looked incredible for *so* many reasons. One being that I'd never seen her so in her element before, and the other being her *outfit.*

God, that innocent little outfit was anything but. She was wearing the kind of thing you'd expect to see on your high school art teacher, but the hot as hell version. A strappy little tank top, tucked into wide-leg pants that were covered in paint smears, conveniently hugging all the right places. That gloriously thick hair of hers was unsurprisingly piled on top of her head, curls escaping left and right, the whole of it a bit frizzy and entirely sexy.

I crossed my arms and anchored against the doorframe, not quite ready to make my presence known as I unabashedly feasted on her with my eyes. *Surely, just looking couldn't hurt.* She'd always been exceptionally beautiful, of course, but seeing her at Thanksgiving after all those years—how three years had slipped by in the blink of an eye, I had no idea. What had started out as giving each other space had turned into something else entirely. I'd convinced myself that's what she needed after everything that had happened that awful night I'd found her in the ditch, but I wasn't entirely sure that had been the right choice at all. In fact, I was positive it wasn't. I'd been a complete idiot, and now she was—I didn't bother finishing the thought. *She was off limits, is what she was, and I had a fading bruise to prove it.*

I'd been impulsive on Thanksgiving, and Sara deserved so much better than that, *she deserved to know she wasn't just a game to me.* It wasn't a mistake I was going to make again. Not when it came to her.

I knew I should make my presence known, but I couldn't peel myself off the doorframe, never wanting the little movie in front of me to end. Sara had a concentrated look on her face as she dragged the easels across the room, one after another. She'd stand, head tilted for a moment, before moving it another imperceptible inch and then another, until she had it just right. I chuckled to myself, knowing that was Sara in a nutshell. An overthinking perfectionist, through and through.

She'd always been too hard on herself, always run a little anxious, and sometimes I wished she could see what I saw. Those moments when her guard slipped down, when she was wild and free, and so much freaking fun. I was positive she was going to be an incredibly successful artist. One, because she was clearly good enough to oversee classes by herself, and two, because everything about her was fucking magic. Always had been.

As if sensing my gaze, Sara looked up, her blank expression turning confused. "Carter?" She headed my way. "What are you doing here?" Her hands landed on her hips as if I were in trouble, and I wondered if I was about to be.

"I couldn't make it home for the Christmas party, so I thought I'd visit you before you went back on break." I loomed in the doorway, waiting to see if she was going to kick me out.

"Why?" she puzzled, like it wasn't completely obvious.

I raked a hand through my hair, a nervous tic. It did nothing, however, to steady the heady buzz that seemed to emanate from inside my very bones. "I wanted to see you." I said simply, *was dying to see you*, I didn't add.

"I do not get you, Kensington." She cocked her head, and a smile pulled at the corner of her mouth. "Well, come in, you're blocking the door." She grabbed my arm and pulled me out of the way while several students filed in around us.

God, I wanted to pull her into a hug, but I didn't. "I heard you needed a model."

"Oh!" She thought for a moment and then frowned. "I didn't know you were coming. We already have a model and besides—"

"*I'm* actually your model." I grinned, all too proud of myself. "I called ahead and made the arrangements."

"*You're* the model?" She clapped a hand over her mouth, concealing a laugh.

I shifted uneasily. "What's so funny?"

She chuckled with pure amusement. "Carter, this is a *nude* composition class."

Oh fuuuuuck.

"Nude?" I puffed out my cheeks before blowing out a heavy breath. "No shit."

She shook her head, already composing a text as she chuckled like an adorable little gremlin. "It's alright, I've got a few models on standby, you'd be surprised how often they back out. Even when they *know* it's nude."

I dragged a hand over my face. *Shit-mother-fucker.* This was my moment. Buck up or walk away.

"Hey now," I grabbed her phone before she could send the message. "If you need me to strip, then I'll strip."

She crossed her arms and skeptically nodded towards the podium. "You're going to stand up there, butt naked, for an hour?"

"I was not aware that's what this class was, but yes." I started pulling my hoodie over my head before I could change my mind.

"Woah there, flyboy, slow your roll. The models definitely don't strip down in the middle of the room." She practically dragged me towards the small ensuite bathroom. "You can dress down in here. There's a locker for all your stuff, and you'll use the robe until it's go-time."

"So proper." I chuckled. "But dressing room or not, it doesn't change the fact that you're about to see me in my birthday suit." Her gaze dropped to my crotch and then snapped to my eyes in realization, like she hadn't fully processed what was about to happen.

Which made it all the more satisfying as her neck went redder by the minute, visible to me by the compliments of her skimpy little tank top. I stifled a groan, realizing her black bra was visible through the too-thin fabric. Instead of staring, I offered her a lazy grin while she desperately tried to regain her composure.

"Carter, I appreciate the gesture, but you really don't have to do this." She was nervous, wringing her hands. "I'll call for a backup, yeah, that's probably for the best."

"I said I would do it, and I will." I was not about to let her down because of my poor planning.

"Oh God. Oooookay." She laughed maniacally and clapped her hands together, rambling nervously as she slowly backed away. "Okay. Yup. This. Is. Happening."

I followed her like a magnet who had no other choice, because I didn't.

"I think you're forgetting, *I'm* the one who's gotta get naked." It was too much fun watching her unravel.

Her voice went up an octave. "I have to finish prepping for the class." She motioned over her shoulder. "Yes, I'll be over here." She walked away and then abruptly turned back to me, trying to get back into professional mode. "But please let me know if you need anything."

"I like you, swirly." I said with a chuckle.

"I am *not* swirly." She argued as she proceeded to actually twirl a loose curl around her finger—her expression went glazed before she abruptly turned on her heel, leaving me with just my nerves and my quickly dwindling gumption.

~

I had never been particularly prude or shy about my body, and frankly, I was pretty happy with how I looked these days, but as I stood there on that platform—I realized I had a big problem on my hands. How the hell was I going to look at her for an entire hour without getting hard? I shouldn't have watched her, looking so goddamn sexy, for so goddamn long before I'd come in. Total. Rookie. Move.

"Hey." Sara crossed through the circle of easels, voice low. "Are you totally and completely sure about this?"

"I've never been so sure of anything in my life." I winked, and she rolled her eyes at me, but honestly, she looked even more nervous than I felt.

"So I'll give everyone instructions and then, when you're ready, you can give me your robe. Just try to find a position that's comfortable, since you'll be standing in the same pose for a while." She was trying *so* hard to be all business. "For this particular class, we'll do four poses, so you won't be stuck in the same position for the entire hour." She nodded, assuring herself more than me.

"You good?" I asked.

"Great." She swallowed thickly. "You?"

I grinned, "You know, I actually woke up this morning and thought, I'm in the mood to flash someone." I bobbed my head back and forth. "I wasn't, however, in the mood to get arrested, so you're really solving a problem for me."

She grinned at that. "I'm not one to kink shame, Carter. To each their own."

I nearly groaned, trying not to let my mind wander from *that* comment.

Her face got stern. "Seriously, though, you don't have to do this. I really appreciate you showing up, but honestly, you don't have to prove anything." Her gaze dropped for a long moment, before she finally peeked up at me through her lashes, voice lowered. "I'm so sorry about how things ended the other night."

"Me too." I offered her a smile before I raised a brow teasing, "And I know you're not calling me a quitter, Devereux, because I'm *so* doing this."

"Oh, I would never call you a quitter." She smirked and patted my arm. "Good luck, Kensington."

She whirled back nervously, rubbing her neck. "Oh, sorry, I almost forgot—if you uh, you know, *go up.*" She motioned a rising erection with her pointer finger. "Don't worry, it happens all the time. *Totally normal.*" I nearly choked as Sara practically sprinted away, leaving me with that zipper-tenting little nugget.

As she left, I didn't dare peek at the back of her. Instead, I focused on every disgusting thing I could think of, because having my best friend's little sister talk about my erection right before I had to stay flaccid for an hour—was a recipe for disaster.

CHAPTER 13

Greek Statue Weens

CARTER

Slowly but surely, the seats filled up, and I couldn't help but admire watching Sarafina in her element. When it was finally time to strip, Sara focused *comically* hard on my eyes as she took the robe from me and hung it on a nearby hook.

To her credit, she didn't look once. Not even a little peek.

For the entire hour, she had her hand glued to her neck, breathily looking at each student's work, while she made quiet comments, pointing things out. Her gaze flicked up to me *very professionally* and I could sense she still hadn't looked where she really wanted to.

Sara nodded at me, and I shifted into a new pose before attempting to stay perfectly still again, which was a hell of a lot harder than it looked.

"He looks like a Greek statue. Like he's *actually* carved out of a piece of marble." One student commented under her breath.

That's when Sara looked, like *really* looked, and this time, she avoided my eyes altogether. Her neck immediately turned a shade of red that resembled a very cute, very ripe tomato, and I smirked as her eyes shuttered for a beat too long, and then she moved to the next student without comment.

Fuck yeah, I looked like a Greek statue. I'd worked my ass off for this body.

When I finally moved into the last position, I could feel my foot starting to cramp up, probably because I was straining too hard to stay flaccid.

Sara seemed to notice and passed me the robe a little early, a sparkly little grin on her face that she shared only with me. *Mine.* "You can go change now." Her voice was a push of air as she dared a look up at me through her lashes.

As soon as I slipped the robe on, it was game over. Instant boner. And that fucker would not go down. I was so damn hard I had to wait it out in the bathroom. I realized everyone probably thought I was rubbing one out in here, and looking at the walls, I was sure I wouldn't have been the first.

When I finally emerged, Sara was busy on the computer again, and the classroom was empty. *Perfect.*

As I neared, she stood abruptly and nearly knocked over her chair, but I was already there, steadying her by the elbow. "Careful." I hummed, and she was jittery as I stepped towards her—I couldn't help it.

She stumbled back, eyes flared as I closed the space again. I wasn't thinking, I was just compelled to be closer to her.

We repeated this slowly, like it was essential, until she startled, finally bumping into the wall behind her.

I caged her in, one arm resting next to her head, while I boldly twirled a loose strand of her hair around my finger, unable to resist. "Do I make you nervous, pretty girl?"

"What?" she rasped.

"You hardly looked at me once." I murmured.

"I—" She breathily searched my face. "I looked at you—I just didn't want to make you uncomfortable."

"Oh, I was perfectly comfortable." I said lowly and stepped a bit closer, wanting to add, *you can stare at me naked anytime you want,* but I didn't.

"Good." She swallowed hard, chest brushing mine on her next inhale. "I'm glad."

God, I wanted to kiss her so bad. Nothing was more torturous than the almost kiss we'd nearly shared the other night. This past month I'd been driving myself crazy, because I couldn't decide if she'd actually leaned in right at the last second or if I'd just imagined it. I'd never know for sure, and I wouldn't risk fucking things up again. I needed to go slow, test the waters.

"Well, you survived." She said with a nervous laugh, filling the silence.

I licked my lips. "We both did."

She fidgeted. "Let me buy you lunch, you earned it." But she didn't move. Neither of us moved for a *long* moment.

What the hell was I doing? Liam would castrate me if I tried to kiss his sister again. Maybe he'd be right to, *and maybe it'd be worth it.*

"You bet your ass I earned it." I pushed off the wall, breaking the tension. "Was I the best nudie you've ever had?"

"Oh, I never kiss and tell." She gave me a devious look as she reached for her bag.

"Fair enough." I nudged her with my arm as we headed toward the door, and she nudged me back, lingering for a moment, making my boner come right back. *Sigh.*

In the hallway, Sara pivoted suddenly, and she was chewing on her lip like she was trying to make a meal out of it. "Can I show you something?"

"What did you have in mind?" I gave her a devilish grin, and hooked a finger through her belt loop, tugging her closer, before I'd even realized what I'd done. She sucked in a breath as I quickly let go, appalled at myself. What the hell was wrong with me.

"Um, do you want to see my work?" She asked breathily.

Knowing Sara, this invitation might have been even more intimate than what I'd had in mind. "Hell yeah, I do." I smiled wide. "Lead the way."

Sara looked at me over her shoulder and hesitated for a

moment before she unlocked the door at the end of the hallway and slowly pushed it open.

Inside the dark room, row after row of massive canvases were lined up, and I grinned, knowing how much this must mean to her. She'd always been extremely secretive about her art.

"Which one's yours?"

"All of them." She fidgeted nervously. "This is my private studio."

I reached for the light switch, and my mouth dropped open. "Holy shit, Sara, these are really fucking good."

She was still furiously chewing her lip.

"I'm serious, you're an *incredible* artist." I scratched my head. "I mean, I always knew you would be, but seeing what you've been working on..." I honestly felt a little guilty in that moment. I'd always believed in her, but seeing her work with my own two eyes, I realized even *I'd* underestimated her skill.

"I'm obviously still learning."

"You could sell these *right now*." I said, already heading across the room to have a closer look. "Have you sold anything yet?" I asked, knowing they were better than some of the paintings I'd recently bought, which was insane.

"No, not yet. I'm not quite ready to put my stuff out there yet. I just feel like it would be humiliating if they didn't sell. Maybe after I complete my master's." Sara brushed a strand of hair out of her face. "I don't know, maybe I'm not cut out for this, maybe—"

I turned, looking her square in the eye. "I wanna buy your first painting."

"Carter." She rolled her eyes. "You don't have—"

"I want. To buy. Your first. Painting." I practically demanded, because not only did I want to support her, I wanted bragging rights.

She searched my face. "You're serious?" She clearly had no idea how good she was.

I headed for a medium-sized canvas on the far wall. "How much?"

"Uh, a hundred bucks?" She shrugged, bewildered. "I don't know."

I pulled all the cash I had out of my wallet—a stack of hundred-dollar bills—and handed it to her, still staring at the painting. "Consider this a down payment."

"Don't be silly." She scoffed. "I'd just give it to you. Besides, this doesn't even look like your style at all."

"Exactly." I murmured. "It's all you." All the complexity and depth and *joy* of Sara was written all over the canvas, in every single brushstroke. It'd be like having a piece of her in my house— *I was ecstatic.*

"This is going to be worth a fortune someday, and you're going to regret letting it go for so little." I teased, hearing a small sniffle behind me. I whirled around, finding Sara fanning her eyes frantically. "What's wrong?" I pulled her into the hug I'd been dying to give her all day.

"I don't even know if I can do this." She sniffled against my chest.

"I've got news for ya, sweetheart, you're already doing it." I closed my eyes and inhaled deeply. Strawberry and amber. Sweet and sexy. *She smelled like home.* "You're gonna be a star." I said, in an old-timey accent, trying to lighten the mood, all while feeling like there was a tight band constricting around my chest. Why the hell did this feel so damn right? *Her in my arms.*

She laughed, and I pulled back, taking her face in my hands as I looked her in the eyes a little breathlessly. "You're incredible, Sara, you know that? I've never met anyone like you."

She immediately looked down. *Nervous.*

Good.

"Same to you." She playfully punched my arm, breaking the tension. "I guess I have to figure out how to ship this thing to you, huh?"

I chuckled, "Damn right you do, and by the way, there is no way in hell I'm letting you pay for lunch."

She wiped her nose and shook her head, trying to shake the emotions off. "I can live with that, I guess."

"Yeah, that's my girl." *I wished she really were.*

~

At lunch, I couldn't stop grinning at her.

"*What?*" She giggled, giving me a crazed look.

I shrugged. "You look good in my sweatshirt, that's all." It was one of my old Air Force hoodies, and damn, she *did* look good in my clothes, never mind that my arms were freezing.

"What can I say? I look good in everything." She winked. "Even this ratty ol' thing."

"Can't argue there." I stuck my tongue in my cheek with a smirk, not bothering to add it must not be *too ratty* if she kept burying her nose in it—every time she thought I wasn't looking.

Sara reached across the table, serving herself more lamb kofta, and I was always impressed at how much she could put down for such a tiny little thing. She'd always had such a hunger for life, food, friends. It was infectious. Her *joy* was infectious. Felt essential, somehow.

She caught me staring, and her very full cheeks turned pink. I just grinned, knowing I'd already placed a to-go order, so she'd have enough leftovers for the week. She *loved* leftovers.

Sara dragged a piece of pita bread through the hummus contemplatively. "So, flyboy, what's your call sign?" She finally asked, a heated look painting her expression.

I smiled to myself. "You really wanna know?"

"Obviously." She swatted my hand when I tried to steal the piece of meat she was already going for, and I grinned.

"The boys gave it to me, I don't know, it's kind of embarrassing." I admitted.

Her eyes sparkled. "Now you definitely have to tell me."

I leaned back and gripped my neck. "Casanova." I said it so quietly that she made me repeat myself, but I think she might have heard me the first time.

Sara's nose scrunched as she grinned with pure amusement. "Casanova?" I nodded, more than a little embarrassed. "I think they hit the nail on the head." She shoved the pita bread into her mouth with a wildly amused smirk, and I groaned. "Well, Casanova, maybe you'll take me flying sometime."

"You trust me that much?" I teased.

She chewed slowly and then swallowed. "I've always trusted you, Carter. I can't help it."

I stopped mid bite, I couldn't help it either. My stomach bottomed out, knowing that in an hour, I had to head back and there was always the chance that this would be my last visit home. I needed more time. *We* needed more time.

Christmas and New Year's came and went, and I spent the holidays flying into remote areas, covered in mud and other less savory substances. This last few months had been especially brutal, and because I wasn't sleeping well, I was running on fumes.

While I couldn't get Sara out of my mind, or out of my dreams for that matter, I'd been so busy juggling *so many things*, it hadn't occurred to me, that I hadn't heard from Liam or Sara in weeks—despite our agreement that we would try to text more regularly.

Finally back home from an exhausting black ops mission, I grabbed the mail and jogged up the stairs to my modest one-bedroom apartment, and headed inside. It was just off base, and of course I could afford something more luxurious, but when I'd enlisted, nobody knew who I was. It was a fresh start, and I wasn't about to out myself by renting an extravagant apartment or driving a flashy car. I was hardly ever at home anyway.

I quickly went through my mail, finding a thick black enve-lope in the stack. Thinking it was another society letter, I almost threw it away, but the return address in the corner caught my eye.

It was from the Devereuxs—a Christmas card, probably. I smiled and slid my finger through the seal, pulling the card out. My face dropped, realizing it was a funeral invitation.

The date had already passed—I folded over and puked right onto the kitchen floor, as a wave of guilt punched through me like a freight train. After everything she'd done for me, I'd missed the fucking funeral.

CHAPTER 14

Death Can Go Fuck Itself

SARAFINA

It was nearly a month before I even bothered to turn my cell phone back on. And when I finally did, text-after-text and voice-mail-after-voicemail pushed through until the battery just gave up and died.

After I'd charged my phone, I'd deleted it all. Every. Single. Message. Didn't bother reading a single one. There was nothing anybody could say. Nothing that would bring her back, nothing that would soothe the gaping hole I knew I'd never be able to fill.

I stood in front of the refrigerator, not caring that I was letting all the cold air out. It was basically empty anyway. Just like my heart.

Liam was back in the city working, and my father, who was hardly ever home anymore, had grown reliant on microwave dinners since he'd fired the housekeeping staff. So I was here, mostly alone, surviving off of cheese sticks and prepackaged cookies. It was the only thing I could get down since I'd completely lost my appetite, and I couldn't find it in me to care that I was slowly wasting away. Nothing mattered anymore. Especially not me.

The house was deathly quiet, which was in stark contrast to how it looked. Festive, filled to the brim with echoes of our ignorant happiness in every corner. Filled to the brim with *Christmas decorations*. In March.

Christmas was the one thing she had loved most, and none of us had been able to stomach putting all the decorations away. I knew it would never be the same.

Christmas. The holidays. My life.

I knew we could never recreate the fun, the gatherings, *the comfort* that only she could create. The worst part was that it wasn't just the holidays, either. It was quickly becoming evident that she was the glue that had held *everything* together. *Everyone* together.

I'd lost my mother, but it felt like I'd lost my dad and brother, too. We were all scattered to the wind, processing our grief in different ways.

I'd never known I was taking it all for granted, because I'd actually been one of those lucky girls, one who'd genuinely gotten along with her mother. Of course, we'd had the occasional spat here and there, but she'd always supported me, given me the room I needed to figure out who I was, room to become my own person, without judgment or expectation.

In all these months that had passed, I just kept wondering why the people that seemed to burn the brightest were always the ones that were taken from us first.

Her death had been sudden.

A total shock.

Brain aneurism.

Shortly after New Years.

The doctor's report had been both comforting and infuriating. The knowing there was nothing anyone could have done, so at least we didn't have to live with the guilt that we could have changed the outcome.

On the other hand. Fuck death. She wasn't supposed to go like that. We were supposed to have more time. She was supposed to be with me when I had *my* babies. Supposed to show me how to grow up, how to *be* a mother.

I needed her. For *everything*. I wasn't ready to live in a world without a mother.

Now, I didn't even know if I wanted to *be* a mother anymore. In an instant, everything in my life had changed. Everything felt so foreign and wrong and unfamiliar, and I wondered if I would ever stop feeling this terrible. If the ache would ever ease. It'd been three whole months, and it felt like three days. It'd been three whole months, and I still felt like I couldn't breathe. I honestly didn't know how anyone ever recovered from grief like this, because it was *all-consuming*. People kept telling me *it comes in waves,* but it didn't. Waves would have been a relief. No, it was a rip current, drowning me, every hour of every day. It was all-consuming, all the time, with no reprieve. Just grief and anger, and more of that layered right on top, and it was all just far, far too much to handle.

I'd taken some time off school because I literally couldn't function, but staying home hadn't really been all that comforting, because what had made home so comforting was *her*, but she wasn't here. Not anymore. So now the house felt like a living graveyard, and there was nowhere I could go to escape the grief, nowhere to hide from it.

"Knock knock." Sloane's voice echoed in the distance, and I let go of the refrigerator door, realizing it'd been chiming at me for some time.

I forced myself to sit at the breakfast table in an attempt to look somewhat normal, rather than the hollow shell that had been reflected back to me in the refrigerator glass.

"We brought soup." Jules announced, carrying several grocery bags into the kitchen. Someone turned the lights on, and I winced as my eyes protested to the adjustment.

"Where do you want these?" Douglass, Jules boyfriend, asked, holding up a paper grocery bag.

I just stared at him. Couldn't formulate an answer. What was even in the bag? How could I possibly answer that question? Everything felt hard. Including speaking.

"The fridge, obviously the fridge." Jules steered him towards it and then proceeded to dig through the produce they'd left the last time they were here—it was probably rotten now.

Sloane dumped an ungodly amount of cheese sticks into the deli drawer and then started arranging far too many types of cookies on the kitchen island.

A moment later, Sloane was pulling down a bowl from the cupboard and microwaving some sort of soup that I knew I wouldn't be able to eat even if I wanted to.

Nothing else existed as my eyes locked onto something shimmering near the sink, and I wasn't sure when I'd gotten up, but I was already floating towards it. It was sort of horrifying the way it was just sitting in the soap dish, *waiting*, like she was coming back for it at any moment. *Her wedding ring.*

These tiny little habits and memories of my mother were all over the house, and you'd stumble across them when you least expected it. Every time it happened, it was always bittersweet.

I slipped my mother's ring on, finding it loose, but I knew, three months ago it probably would have fit. God, my hands looked so much like hers. I didn't know if I hated or loved that— the never being able to look at my hands and not think of my mother.

Sloane placed the bowl of soup on the table. "I got my grandma's chicken noodle soup recipe. Do you think you can try to get something down today?" She asked gently.

The smell of it was already making me nauseas, and I shook my head *no* and wandered down the hall.

Collapsing onto the nearest couch, I closed my eyes, twisting the ring with my thumb as if it were a magic genie lamp that could somehow bring my mother back. Maybe if I rubbed it long enough, wished hard enough.

Even from down the hall, I could hear them all whispering about *what to do,* and I couldn't find it in me to care. I was just too exhausted.

I felt someone sink into the couch cushion next to me, and

Jules gentle voice spoke, "Sloane called Liam. He's going to come pick you up tomorrow and take you over to his place."

I hummed in response as I let myself drift off into a tormented sleep. I hoped I wouldn't dream. Peaceful darkness would be nice for once.

It was the middle of the night when I finally woke up on the couch, groggy, with a pounding headache. Slowly trudging upstairs, I noticed my father's car still wasn't in the driveway.

He hardly came home anymore. Where he went, I had no idea, but when he *was* home, he didn't even sleep in his bedroom, he opted for the couch in his office. We hadn't spoken more than a few passing words in weeks, and I knew he was in pain, *but so was I.*

As I collapsed into my bed, I suddenly wondered if I'd ever really had a relationship with my father at all. My mother was never coming back, I knew that, but for some reason it felt like I'd lost my father too.

"Sorry for your loss." A tall, ominous presence continued to hover in front of me.

I started to respond before I realized who it was. "Thank you." I tensed the moment I looked up at that sneering face.

"I am *truly sorry*." Taggart Caldwell said, looking vaguely sympathetic and then, "You should have tried harder to save her."

Anger and grief slammed into me, but I didn't say anything. I couldn't for some reason.

Sloane was on one side of me, Jules and Ariana on the other. "You've done enough." They seethed at him, their voices sounding like snakes.

"He's right, you know." My brother turned to me. "Why

didn't you trade places with her? You're the one who deserves to be in that casket."

I tried to speak, but I couldn't, and as I looked down into my mother's casket, I realized she was gone. I tried to scream, to tell someone she was missing, but I couldn't. Not a sound would come out of my mouth.

I was suffocating. Silken fabric pressed against my face.

I was in the casket. *I* was my mother, and we were dead.

I woke up screaming, gasping for breath, and nobody was there to hear me.

I was lost in my own thoughts, just waiting, when the front door pushed open. "Hey Sar-Bear." Liam said, a sad, lopsided smile on his face. "Damn, you look terrible." I knew it was meant to be a joke, but it came out far too sincere.

My lower lip quivered, and his eyes were shiny as he pulled me against his broad frame—as the first sob cracked out of me, I was already being crushed into my brother's warm, solid embrace.

"I know." His voice wavered. "I miss her too."

We stood in the entryway, neither of us saying much more, until I finally let go first.

Liam cleared his throat, thumbing away the damp beneath his eyes, and asked, "Is Dad home?" I shook my head, and Liam grimaced, dragging a hand over his stubbled jaw. "I thought you were on campus."

"I was." I said, wiping my own cheeks. "And then I came home."

"Why didn't you tell me?"

I shrugged. "Didn't want to bug you."

"Sarafina." He groaned, "If I'd have known you were here." His eyes flitted around the entry, horror slowly setting in. "The decorations are still up."

"I didn't have the energy to take them down." I admitted.

"Dad should have hired someone to pack all this up." Liam groaned, his voice subtly lit with frustration.

I chewed my lip, zoning out a bit. "When he is home, he just throws stuff away."

"What do you mean?" Liam puzzled, alarm lacing his voice. "*What* exactly has he been throwing away?"

I shrugged. "I don't know. Last week, the bedroom curtains were in the can."

Liam grumbled under his breath and headed upstairs to our parent's wing of the house. I sighed and reluctantly followed after him, but when I got upstairs he was just standing in the doorway, mouth parted in shock.

My pulse thundered in my ears. "What is it?" I peered around him, discovering their room was *empty*. "Oh my God, where is *everything*?"

Both of us just stood there, utterly dumbfounded, before Liam finally made a beeline for the closet, and I raced after him, hand flying to my throat when I realized it too was completely emptied out.

All of my mother's clothes were gone.

No. My body was moving for me as I sprinted down the stairs, tearing into the garage. I heaved the trashcan onto its side and got onto my hands and knees, ripping apart bags of garbage, hoping I wasn't too late.

Please, please, please. I desperately searched, hoping something of hers would appear, but it didn't.

Liam hovered nearby, his voice calm but pleading. "Sara." His footsteps were soft, cautious even, as he approached, but I didn't scream or cry, or hardly react at all, because what was even the point anymore?

If there had been any room left for me to feel emotion, it was gone now. All of this was entirely too much, and I felt myself shutting down, letting everything go numb. *No more pain.*

"Why would he do that?" I asked, my voice hollow as I sat

between the ripped garbage bags of Christmas garland and broken ornaments.

"I don't know, but we need to get your stuff together and go, you can't stay here."

"I need a minute." I sighed, my voice muffled in my hands.

"Alright." Liam reluctantly propped the door open and allowed me a few minutes to collect myself.

When I finally got up, I didn't bother cleaning up the garbage bags. I'd let my father deal with the consequences of what he'd done whenever he finally decided to come home.

Inside, I found Liam in my father's office, going through the desk drawers. "When was the last time you saw him?" Liam asked, flipping through the stacks of paperwork.

"I'm not actually sure." I admitted. "It's been several weeks, at least."

"Sara." Liam groaned, and his eyes shuttered for a long moment. "You've been here all by yourself for weeks?"

"What are you looking for?" I asked, ignoring him.

"Anything worth finding." Liam replied, slumping back into my father's leatherback chair, blowing out a defeated breath.

"Are those Mom's journals?" I asked, floating towards the box on the desk.

Liam rested his chin on his fist. "Mhmm."

I pulled one out and thumbed through it, cherishing the pages and pages of my mother's handwriting. "Where did these come from?" I wondered, finding it odd that these were the only things my father hadn't gotten rid of. On the other hand, what better thing to keep.

"I don't know, but we're certainly not leaving them here, that's for damn sure." Liam huffed, and I nodded in agreement.

Liam and I gathered some of my belongings, and then he loaded my bags into the trunk of his Bentley along with my mother's journals.

I watched our house as we drove away and wondered when my father would come back. If he would even notice I was gone.

For all I knew, we were dead to him too. The realization was sobering.

Suddenly, my favorite musical was blasting through the speakers, and Liam was belting along to the lyrics while he wiggled his brows at me. "Come on, you love this song."

I only groaned at him and rolled my eyes.

Liam grinned and turned the song down quiet enough to talk over. "My supplier brought me some truffles this morning—we could do grilled cheese for dinner? *Your favorite.*"

"Sounds great." I slipped on his sunglasses because I could feel him watching me out of the corner of his eye while he drove, and I could hardly bear it.

This is exactly why I hadn't called him, because he was going to try to fix me, and I couldn't burden him with that, not when I couldn't *be* fixed. Not when he'd already sacrificed so much for me already.

Inside Liam's city penthouse, I stood in the guest room and suddenly realized the cozy room wasn't a *guest room* at all. It was *my* room, and it was already filled with so many of my favorite things. One of the cashmere throw blankets I was obsessed with was neatly folded over an armchair, the room smelled amazing because several of my favorite Loewe candles were scattered around, and a brand new pair of my favorite fuzzy slippers were sitting in the closet. As I wandered into the bathroom, I discovered the drawers were filled with all the skincare products I liked. And when I sank onto the edge of the upholstered bed, I realized it was already made up with a set of beautiful flower-printed sheets—to match the soft, feminine decor of the rest of the room.

Liam came through the doorway a moment later, hauling in another one of my bags, as he huffed, "I'm going to get dinner started, but you could take a little nap if you want—I'll wake you up when it's ready."

I swallowed thickly. "All my favorite stuff is in here."

He rolled my bag into the walk-in closet, his deep voice calling from inside. "Yeah. And?" He braced an arm on top of the closet door, filling it as his eyes crinkled with amusement.

I just stared at him for a long moment, while he patiently waited. "When did you set this room up for me?"

Liam huffed a soft laugh. "Right after I moved in—I told you that." He shoved a hand through his dark wavy hair, heading for the hallway again. "Which is why you should have called me sooner, kiddo."

"I didn't know I had my own room here."

He only chuckled, shaking his head. "Sar, I think you seriously need to get your ears cleaned out—you and Gina both." He muttered.

"Dinner's ready." Liam called gently, leaning in the doorway, waiting, while I dragged myself out of bed.

As we walked towards the kitchen, I was hit by the sickening smell of food. I stared at the *stack* of perfectly toasted grilled cheese sandwiches, tomato soup, and green salad, knowing nothing had ever looked so overwhelming—and I was right. Even though Liam's cooking was incredible, I could hardly get more than a few bites down.

Nausea swirled in my stomach as I tried to force yet another bite down, because I could feel Liam's quiet gaze on me, and it was that extra bite that did me in.

My stomach surged, and I bolted out of the chair, knocking it to the ground as I raced to the kitchen sink with my mouth covered, knowing there was no way I was going to make it to the bathroom—and I was right because I barely made it to the sink in time.

Liam was instantly at my side, holding my hair back as I shakily held myself up while I lost my dinner. "Do you have the flu?" He asked, pressing a hand to my forehead when I'd finally finished retching.

"I haven't really been able to eat." I admitted spitting into the sink.

"What do you mean?" He asked, alarm lacing his voice as I ran the water and turned on the garbage disposal.

I stuck my head under the faucet and rinsed out my mouth before I shakily slid against the cabinets to sit on the floor.

Liam squatted down in front of me, handing me an open bottle of water and a hand towel. "Maybe that was too rich." He murmured more to himself, "I'll make you some clear broth."

"Liam." I grabbed his arm before he could stand. "*Later*—I can't possibly eat right now."

He nodded with a heavy sigh, and settled in against the kitchen cabinets next to me, arms propped on his knees.

We sat there, a heavy silence hanging between us before I finally asked, "How are you even functioning?"

He huffed a sad, quiet laugh, head sagging between his shoulders as he shook it. "I'm not even remotely functional right now, Sarafina."

"I have awful nightmares." I murmured, staring at the cabinets in front of us.

"I can hardly sleep at all." He countered, suddenly grabbing my hand.

When I finally looked over at him, I realized his face was tear-streaked, and I squeezed his hand, *hard*, as silent tears streaked down my own cheeks.

I didn't see an end in sight, but knowing we at least had each other, suddenly made everything feel the tiniest bit more bearable.

CHAPTER 15
Birthday Cake and Chocolate Shakes

CARTER

"Open sesame." I knocked again, but nobody answered, leaving me standing in the hallway outside Liam's penthouse, juggling a duffle bag full of sand in one hand and a *massive* bag of Sour Patch candy in the other. As I reached for my phone, my bag slipped off my shoulder, hitting the floor with a solid thud, and just then, the door inched open.

When I finally looked up, the breath whooshed out of me as I stared into the deep brown eyes of the girl I'd been dying to see for months now. Only her eyes weren't alive and sparkling with mischief like the last time I'd seen her—they were hollow and gaunt, and I realized with utter devastation that she was *way* too thin.

"Happy birthday." I chimed, my heart beating a mile a minute while I processed her far too emaciated appearance. "Alas, Sour Patch." I murmured, the words nearly dying on my tongue as I held out the candy, trying to school my features.

"Hi?" Sara said, a little perplexed, though a small *almost* smile tugged at the corner of her wan lips, and then she shot a look over her shoulder. "Please tell me you didn't plan anything for my birthday." She complained to Liam, who had a sneaky grin plastered across his face.

"Okay, I didn't plan anything for your birthday." Liam put his hands up in fake surrender.

"Liar." I coughed under my breath, throwing Sara a wink.

"Yeah, okay, maybe I planned a *little* something," Liam confessed, pinching his fingers in the air for emphasis.

"Liam, I seriously do not have the energy." Sara complained, and looking at her—I believed her.

"Don't worry, we won't make you do a damn thing unless it involves fun." I promised cheekily, realizing she still hadn't smiled, not really. I pulled her into a hug, being careful not to crush her small frame. "Good to see you too, by the way. Absolutely incredible hospitality." I said with dry sarcasm.

Liam waved me inside with a shake of his head and closed the door behind me as I shuffled forward, still embracing Sara. It was her birthday, so I supposed I could get away with an extra-long hug, but I decided not to push it, and let go a moment later.

"You two are unbelievable." Sara rolled her eyes, and I caught the tiniest glimmer of something alive in there.

Liam took my duffel bag off my shoulders, brows shooting up in surprise. "Geez, Kensington, what did you even pack? You might have Gina beat for the heaviest overnight bag." He didn't wait for an answer as he continued in a medieval accent. "Come on, good sir, I'll show you to your quarters."

"Giddy up, squire." Sara swung her arm half-heartedly, motioning for me to get a move on, and I swallowed hard, wondering how much weight she'd lost since the last time I'd seen her. Whatever the number was, it was far too much.

I followed Liam down the hallway as he asked, "How was the drive?"

"Long." Did he even notice? Or was he too preoccupied with his own grief, dealing with his own demons?

"Yeah, I bet. Well, I'm glad you could make this work with your schedule." He walked into one of the guest bedrooms ahead of me. "I know Sara really appreciates it, even if she doesn't look like it."

I peered down the hall, making sure the coast was clear, and then quickly shut the door behind us as he dropped my duffel on the guest bed. Eyes wild, I silently, frantically, motioned to Sara through the door, but Liam spoke first.

He put his hand up, voice low. "I know."

"She's fucking skin and bones." I whisper-shouted.

"I know." Liam hissed back, the happy smile he'd just had plastered across his face, long gone. "Why the fuck do you think I tried to plan something fun this weekend?"

"Is she even eating?"

"A bit." He grimaced.

"A bit?" I dragged both hands down my face. "Has she been to a doctor?" I demanded quietly.

Liam aggressively motioned for me to lower my voice as he whispered, "I'm finally making some progress with her this week."

"What the hell does that even mean?" I threw my arms out.

Liam's eyes shuttered. "She ate a piece of fruit yesterday." He gripped the back of his neck, and I knew he was aware of the utter absurdity of that statement.

"Fruit?!" I whisper-shouted. "She needs more than fucking fruit, Liam."

"You think I don't know that? You think I'm not doing enough?" Liam snapped. "I'm doing everything I can possibly think of! I make her all her favorite foods every fucking day." He started counting on his fingers. "Lasagna, truffle grilled cheese, Chicken Piccata, stir-fry, Lebanese. I've baked her every type of goddamn cookie I can think of, and she hardly touches any of it." He threw his hands up. "Last week, I sourced the most insane ingredients from one of my contacts and made her a fucking omakase." He wiped his hand through the air. "Nothing." Sheer panic filled his eyes. "She used to beg me for that kind of shit all the time and now—all she eats are those shitty little cheese sticks." He laughed wildly. "Cheese sticks, Carter."

I motioned for him to lower his voice.

"I could make her any dish she wanted, but she won't eat." He hissed, the exhaustion taking over. "I can't force the food down her fucking throat—though trust me, I've debated it. Honestly, I don't know what the fuck to do anymore." He was on the verge of hyperventilating.

"Liam, breathe." I gripped his shoulder supportively. "I'm sorry, I didn't mean *you* aren't doing enough." I lowered my voice, continuing carefully. "But I think she needs actual medical attent—"

Liam pinched the bridge of his nose and cut me off. "Just," he blew out a breath, begging, "*Please*, just for this weekend, don't make a big deal about it, okay?" His shoulders slumped in defeat. "She *needs* this weekend to go well. *I* need for her to enjoy her birthday." He conceded authoritatively, "I promise I'll take her in. After the weekend is over."

There was a knock at the door, and Liam ripped it open and leaned against it, looking only mildly guilty.

Sara looked between the two of us. "You two making out in here or something?"

"Yup." I forced a smile. "Bromance for the win."

"Right." Her tired eyes darted between us, trying to figure out the weird energy. "Well, I need some long arms. I don't care which ones."

"At your service, milady." I followed her back into the hallway, shooting Liam a stern look over my shoulder. "First thing Monday." I mouthed a silent shout.

"I know." He mouthed back.

Sara had a small journal tucked under her arm, and at the end of the hallway, she opened a set of built-in cabinets and pointed to a dark green felt box on the top shelf.

I pulled the box down, realizing it was far heavier than it looked.

"Thanks," Sara said, her long hair falling limply over her shoulder as she opened the box and carefully tucked the journal inside, next to several rows of identical journals.

"What is all this?" I asked curiously, if not hopefully, because projects were good, staying busy was good.

She put the lid back on the box and smiled sadly. "My mother's journals. I don't want them out, you know, if people are coming over."

I nodded, waiting to see if she would say anything else, but she didn't as I slid the box back up on the shelf.

"Thanks." She tucked her hair behind her ear and left me standing there, trying to figure out how to make the next two days as happy as humanly possible for her.

While we grazed on appetizers at the kitchen island, I kept my gaze casual as I kept track of what Sara ate—which was all of nothing, so far. The wine, however, was a different story.

"Can I do anything to help?" Gina asked, sliding her arms around Liam's neck.

"No, baby." Liam threaded an arm around her waist and hauled her against him, while he whisked something on the stove with his free hand. "You've been working so hard, and I want you to go sit down and rest." He paused, giving her a long, slow kiss with enough tongue that I awkwardly fidgeted with my watch, pretending not to notice. "Think you can do that for me?" He asked.

"Are you sure?" She hummed, a sound that was definitely a moan, and I was glad he had her to help him cope with all this, but I certainly didn't need to hear *that*.

Liam smirked and leaned into Gina's ear, whispering something that had her biting her lip, and moment later, when he dragged his finger through some sort of sauce and slid his finger into her mouth—Sara and I both picked up our phones, getting awkwardly busy.

Liam eventually carried Gina around the kitchen island and

planted her on a barstool next to me and Sara, before he returned to the stove. As Liam milled around the kitchen, sleeves rolled up his tatted arms, towel tucked neatly into his waist apron, he was totally in the zone. Liam moved through the kitchen the way I maneuvered my jet through the skies—with utter precision and focus.

One minute he was skewering a spoon in and out of a shiny sauce so fast you'd wondered if he'd even tasted it, and the next he was plating something with such intensity, you didn't dare breathe while you watched.

Where Sara was an artist with paint and brushes, Liam was an artist with ingredients and flavors. He created tiny little pieces of architecture, each plate so beautiful you wondered if it was even edible. He was a master at his craft.

In between Liam moving through his kitchen with such fluidity that you could almost consider it a form of dance, he had a small staff working on a variety of dishes—and I knew, there was no way the four of us were going to make a dent in all this food.

I wasn't sure if the full-scale production was just for Sara's birthday weekend, or if Liam had been keeping this whole thing up for weeks now, but it was clear he was trying, really fucking hard to take care of her, and I hoped he was taking care of himself too. I shook my head, knowing at least Gina was.

Next to me, Sara finished her second glass of wine, and Gina wasted no time refilling it. I groaned internally, but all I could do was head to the fridge to get her a bottle of water and try to keep her hydrated.

Staying out of the staff's way, I opened the fridge, and that's when it *really* hit me. The scale at which Liam had been trying to coax Sara into eating, as if this dinner hadn't been evidence enough.

The fridge was stocked with every kind of food I imagined Sara had ever eaten. All of it was staged beautifully to Liam's credit, ready to grab and go, just waiting for her to partake. Colorful little ceramic bowls of different kinds of berries were perched at the front of the shelves. Gourmet snack-packs filled with the best quality ingredients money could buy. Stacks and stacks of individual servings of food were labeled neatly, ready to be reheated on demand—small servings of pasta, soup, little meat dishes. And heartbreakingly, filling the entire middle rack of his commercial refrigerator was bin after bin, *filled with every type of cheese stick imaginable.* Panic pricked through me, taking it all in. We had to do something, and soon.

Next to a rainbow of bottled juices, I spotted the glass water bottles and reached for several, knowing it was no doubt some specialty spring water from some obscure mountain.

I returned to the kitchen island knowing I'd need to tread carefully or Sara would dehydrate herself—just because she was actually that stubborn.

"Staying hydrated, ladies?" I asked, passing each of the girls a bottle.

"Oh thanks, Carter." Gina slid off her stool, texting furiously before she answered a work call. "Tell him to take the plea deal, it's his best option." She demanded, stepping outside.

I stood there, holding Sara's gaze while I guzzled down my own water.

"Can I help you?" She saw straight through me, and I knew she was about to shut me down.

Glancing over, I confirmed Liam was distracted in the kitchen. "I don't know, can you?" I flirted, trying something.

I offered her my already open bottle, and her eyes flickered between me and Liam before she took it, smirking while she obnoxiously wiped the rim off with a napkin.

"What's the matter, don't wanna touch something my lips have touched?" I crooned quietly, chest thundering, hoping she'd play along, hoping that spark was somewhere in there. I'd hardly seen a glimmer of it since I'd arrived.

"Oh, I never said that." She parried right back. "I'm sure your lips are perfectly touchable, *Casanova*, but I wouldn't know, since I've never actually touched them." She smirked, adding. "You feel like playing another game—risking another black eye?"

Oh, fuck me.

She took a tiny sip and gave me a coy smile, teasing melodically. "What's the matter, Kensington? Cat got your tongue?"

I rolled my eyes. "Just drink your damn water."

"Or what, flyboy? What are you gonna do—pin me down again and make me?"

"*Careful.*" I warned, dragging my fingers over hers as I took the bottle back—her eyes flared with nerves. *There it was, she was always all talk.*

But she quirked a brow, and to my complete surprise, she kept going. "Do you lay in bed at night and think about what it felt like—*me underneath of you?* You tell me your truth, and maybe I'll tell you mine."

"Don't play with fire if you don't want to get burned." I warned, my skin heating from the inside out as she gave me a heavy-lidded look. *God, she had no idea what she could do to me with a simple look.*

She didn't miss a beat as she responded with a murmur, "Would you do it? Would you light me up if I asked you to?"

Mother of God, this woman.

I'd never seen her flirt so shamelessly before.

Game on.

"If you asked me nicely, I'd do a hell of a lot more than that, sweetheart." I rasped completely recklessly, lowering my voice to a mere push of air. "But the question is, would you be a good girl for me and do what you're told?" I knew I'd gone too far the moment it was out of my mouth—except she sucked in a small breath, and nodded, *yes,* almost imperceptibly.

Ohhh, fuck me. Was she serious?

A quick glance into the kitchen confirmed nobody was paying attention to us, and I was practically panting at the realization.

I knew I shouldn't, but I reached for the leg of her chair anyway, dragging her towards me—watching her eyes flare as I pulled her legs between my spread knees. "*Prove it.*" I murmured, waiting in pulse-thrumming anticipation as I pushed her water across the countertop. "Show me you can be a good girl and drink every last drop." I challenged whisper soft.

She searched my eyes, lips parted on a retort that never made it past her lips.

"*I dare you.*" I hummed low and egged her on, knowing I had her. "Unless you don't know how, *Rookie.*" I smirked as something electric hummed in the air between us.

Oh so slowly, nervously, Sara picked up the bottle, and my eyes dropped to her lips as she tipped the bottle against that temptingly smart mouth of hers in compliance—watching as that slender throat worked while she swallowed.

"Atta girl." I murmured breathlessly. "But I know you can take a little more, can't you?" Sara's eyes went wide as I rasped. "Unless you need me to teach you how."

"Sorry about that." Gina tossed her blonde hair over her shoulder as she slid back onto the barstool on the other side of Sara.

Sara jumped so hard that she nearly fell off the stool, and I only grinned, steadying her back into her seat as she sputtered water everywhere. *Checkmate.*

Sarah was coughing as Gina spread some caviar on a chive blini and popped it into her mouth. "What I'd miss?"

"Nothing at all." I said casually, sliding Sara a wink that made her narrow her eyes.

Sara rested an elbow on the counter and leaned on her hand, scratching her face with her middle finger—*subtly flipping me off.*

There she is. I dropped my gaze and suppressed a smile.

"Dinner's ready." Liam announced and tipped his head, motioning for us to follow him into the dining room as he headed that way with several plates in hand.

I followed behind Sara and purred into her ear, "Don't think this is over, pretty girl. I want you to drink every last drop, and *swallow,* like the good girl I know you are." I smirked as she nearly tripped, but I was right there to catch her, and I always would be.

~

The most beautiful plates of food were spread across the flower-dressed table, soft music played in the background, and candles flickered all around us.

"Birthday girl first." Gina beamed, inviting Sara to start us off.

Liam and I exchanged a look while we waited with bated breath to see what Sara would serve herself. She gingerly took a very small amount from the dishes directly in front of her and then quickly passed the plates to Gina.

Liam wasted no time. "Here, have some of this too." He plopped a comically large pile of shredded meat onto Sara's plate before she could object, and I passed a few more plates towards Liam to aid in the effort.

Gina, to my frustration, uncorked yet *another* bottle of wine, topping everyone off, and I realized Liam and Gina were definitely not on the same page regarding Sara. Had they even discussed this at all? They were usually so in sync.

After the girls had served themselves, I loaded up my plate, and Liam did the same, keeping a bright smile on his face as we worked overtime to keep the conversation light and easy.

"This is so cute," Gina commented halfway through the meal. "It's like a little double date."

My chest tightened as Liam scoffed. "Hardly. Carter isn't Sara's type." He shot a look at me. "And she's definitely not yours."

I felt Sara's gaze flick up to me for a millisecond, but I didn't dare look back. I was still on thin ice from Thanksgiving.

Throughout dinner, Sara made a good effort of *looking* like she was eating, but by the end, I knew she'd just pushed most of the food around on her plate.

The only thing she *had* finished was her wine, because Gina kept refilling everyone's damn glasses the moment they'd emptied.

After dinner, we all crammed onto the deep-seated sofa with Liam and me on the ends, and the girls in the middle, but about ten minutes into the movie—Gina leaned over to Liam and whispered something before they disappeared down the hallway and didn't return.

Sara brushed against me as she quickly reached for the remote and cranked the volume up, muttering, "When Gina's in town, they're like this *every freaking night.*"

I chuckled and laid my arm over the back of the couch. "I guess that means it's just you and me now, birthday girl."

"Guess so." Sara's eyes darted to mine and then quickly away, not full of so much tease now that we were actually alone.

There was a heavy thump from down the hallway and then a muffled squeal from Gina, and a deep laugh from Liam.

"Let it begin." Sara groaned and turned the TV up a little more.

A few minutes later, Sara started stuffing pillows around herself, and when she finally settled, I smiled to myself, knowing she was the tiniest bit closer. Her head was *almost* resting in the crook of my arm, where it draped over the back of the couch, and I didn't mind one bit.

Throughout the entire movie, we awkwardly tried to ignore the moans that carried down the hallway, some louder than others —until a muffled scream from Gina cut through the chorus of thumping.

"Oh my God! I'm about to stab a Q-tip into my ear, so I never have to hear them again." Sara groaned, "She's gotta be faking that, right—I've never heard someone sound like that in my life."

I opened my mouth, and then immediately shut it—*nope, not even remotely appropriate.* "Probably." I muttered, trying to ignore what she'd just unknowingly admitted to me. *Motherfucker.*

Eventually, the banging down the hallway quieted, and as I watched Sara out of the corner of my eye—she got sleepier and sleepier, until her head finally did tip onto my shoulder, making me hyper-aware of every point of contact. I sighed contentedly, relishing in the feeling, and while I didn't dare move, I was watching the hallway like a hawk, *just in case.*

When the credits started rolling and Sara still hadn't moved, my heart thundered in my chest, wondering what to do. Should I wake her up? Carry her to bed? Sleep right here, sitting up, so I didn't disturb her, while she got the rest it looked like she so desperately needed? I was not about to ruin possibly the best moment of my life.

Her wine glass made the decision for me—it was still in her hand and barely upright, threatening to make a mess at any second, as it tipped little by little, getting alarmingly close to spilling.

As I reached for it, she made a tiny noise, and her fingers tightened around the glass just before I could grab it.

Her eyes fluttered open. "What time is it?"

"Late." I murmured.

She pushed up to stand, but when she stumbled, I shot up—hands instinctively going to her waist as she swayed. "You good?" I swallowed hard because she felt *so impossibly frail beneath my grip.*

"Mhmm," she clutched the wineglass, and my heart sank.

I swallowed hard, trying my best to sound casual. "You want me to finish that for you?"

"Helps me sleep." She said, tucking the glass into her shoulder before heading towards her bedroom. Her hand trailed along the wall for stability. "Night." She called.

"Sweet dreams." I sighed, and let my head drop back onto the couch.

I had to do *something.*

∾

It was party day, and I was standing at the stovetop making eggs, panicking about the fact that Sara hadn't even bothered to open the candy I'd brought her when she strolled into the kitchen.

She offered me a small smile as she turned the electric teakettle on.

"Can I make you some eggs?"

"No thanks." She didn't look at me as she started digging through the loose-leaf tea drawer, and my chest tightened.

Frick. I stared into the pan, treading very carefully. "I make a mean blueberry oatmeal, what about that?"

She shook her head, and my shoulders sagged as I stared at my eggs, suddenly not feeling very hungry myself.

"What about a walk after breakfast?"

"A walk?"

"Yeah, just a short one." I shrugged. "Might be nice to get some fresh air."

"I don't think so." She immediately shot me down.

"Come on." I stared into the pan, frantically trying to salvage my idea. "We could go look at the puppies. It's only a couple blocks away." I snuck a glance as her mouth twisted, getting ready to say no. "I'll even carry you if you get tired." I offered.

"I don't know." She clutched an empty mug, deciding.

"Please?" I stuck out my lower lip, switching tactics—making it about me. "I *really* wanted to see the puppies."

"Alright." She folded almost instantly, and I grinned, grateful my new strategy worked, but heartbroken all the same. She'd do it for me, apparently, but not for herself. My sweet, sweet girl. She needed to find some strength to take care of herself, otherwise, she wouldn't be able to do it for anyone else. I wondered if she knew that.

When we started our walk, I was so proud of myself for luring her out of Liam's penthouse. I genuinely thought the fresh air would be good for her, but Sara was so incredibly winded by the time we'd hit the first crosswalk that I suddenly realized this might have been more of an undertaking than I'd planned for.

"You want a piggyback ride?" I asked, starting to wonder if we should just go back upstairs.

"I'm not that pathetic, am I?" She winced, already out of breath.

"I'm just saying it's your birthday weekend and piggyback rides are free. Limited time only."

She scoffed at that, but it didn't meet her eyes. "I'm fine." *Only she wasn't.* We didn't make it to the puppies because Sara collapsed before we got there.

"What the hell did you do?" Liam yelled before I was even all the way through the door.

"She fainted." I shouted frantically, heading towards the couch with Sara limp in my arms. "Call a doctor."

"I'm fine." Sara muttered weakly, eyes fluttering.

"Like hell you are," Liam basically snarled.

"*Call the damn doctor.*" I demanded, my voice cracking.

"I'm fine." She insisted, except she definitely wasn't.

Several hours later, Sara was sitting upright on the couch, scowling like her life depended on it. An IV tube was in her arm, hydrating her, and a prescription protein shake was sitting on the table in front of her, *untouched*. Supposedly, it would help her gain back some of her weight—it was like liquid rations, and I expected it tasted about the same, because after one sip, she didn't touch it again.

I'd never known blinking could look so furious, but as Sara stared at me, blinking furiously, it was the scariest thing I'd ever seen.

"Drink the shake." Liam demanded sternly.

"This is the most disgusting thing I've ever tasted." She argued vehemently.

"You're being dramatic."

A furious narrowing of her eyes. "Why don't you try it, then?"

"Fine. I will." He sipped and failed miserably.

"Come on." I groaned when Liam's eye twitched, and he struggled to keep a straight face. "It can't be that bad. Pass it over." I'd eaten all kinds of nasty food on long assignments. When push came to shove, you'd eat whatever you needed in order to stay fueled. This chocolaty-looking shake couldn't possibly—I took a sip and had to *force* myself to swallow as I held back a grimace. "It's just a little bitter." I conceded as neutrally as I could muster.

False. It was possibly the worst thing I'd ever put in my mouth. I bit back a cough as the sludgy, gritty texture coated the back of my throat.

Gina waved her hand, looking determined. "Give it here." But her eyes went wide, and she immediately gagged, chasing it down with whatever highly caffeinated drink was probably in her pink tumbler cup. "That's *awful*." She covered her mouth with a grimace. "Oh, Liam, she can't possibly drink that, it's inedible."

"If you would just try to eat some solid food." Liam started, but the look Sara gave him was crushing.

"You know I try, I just can't." Her voice was so small, and Liam looked utterly crushed as she continued. "*Now*, will you cancel the surprise party? I don't want everyone fussing over me, especially while I'm all hooked up." She looked like she was considering ripping the IV straight out of her arm, and I was grateful she was clearly too exhausted to actually do it.

His shoulders sagged. "Is that what you really want?"

"Yes." She closed her eyes, leaning back against the couch. "I appreciate all the work you put in, but I'm just not up for it."

Shit, I think I just single-handedly ruined her party.

Gina left to deal with a work emergency, and between Liam and me, saying we waited on Sara hand and foot would have been an understatement.

We were just about to cue up another girly movie, that *we* had to pick because Sara kept saying she didn't care, when Liam muttered under his breath. "Fucking hell." He stood up, texting furiously, and disappeared into the kitchen. When he reappeared, he had his jacket on, and he dragged a hand through his dark hair. "I have to take care of something at the restaurant."

"Now?" I asked incredulously.

"I'm sorry." Liam apologized profusely to Sara. "I wouldn't go if I had any other choice, but this is—I just have to take care of this. I'll be back as soon as I can, I promise."

"Go." Sara lamented, limply waving him away. "I'm fine, stop your worrying, you can leave me with my babysitter."

I walked with Liam down the hallway. "What could you possibly have to do at the restaurant that's so important?" Something passed across his expression that made my chest tighten. "Liam?" He only shook his head, begging me not to push. "Liam, what's going on?" I demanded quietly.

"Keep an eye on her." He gathered his keys and phone, heading for the door. "And do me a favor," he sighed over his shoulder, locking eyes with me. "Keep your hands to yourself and no midnight walks, please."

I put my hands up in surrender. "No fresh air, got it."

Something was definitely off with him, and it wasn't just tonight. He'd been more distant than usual lately, but I supposed he was dealing with his grief in his own way. Doing the best he could. We all were.

I wandered back into the living room, not totally heartbroken by the situation.

"Can I get you anything?" I asked.

Sara sighed. "My sanity?"

"Darn, I'm fresh out of that." I snapped my fingers.

The corner of her mouth pulled. "Thought so."

"Seriously, anything at all?" I swallowed hard, listing things while she shook her head *no.* "Ice cream? I could have someone come do your nails? I know, I'll go get you one of those puppies." I offered, not joking in the slightest.

"Thank you, but really, I'm fine." She gave me a weak smile.

"Do you want to open your gift?" I asked nervously.

Her eyes shifted. "You got me a gift?"

"Don't get too excited." I shrugged and gripped the back of my neck. "It's small."

Her whole face lit up, making my heart stutter as she nodded. "Of course I want to open my gift."

CHAPTER 16

Nightmares & Googly Eyes

CARTER

I retrieved the large gift bag from my room, suddenly regretting getting her something so stupid. Her real gift wasn't ready yet, and I could have literally bought her anything under the sun as a placeholder, and I'd basically gotten her a jar of dirt. I started panicking as I stood there in front of her, hesitating with that stupid bag.

"What is it?" She asked, eyes bright as she sat forward, reaching for the gift. "*Oh, it's heavy.*"

Together we set the bag on the coffee table, and I reluctantly let go, watching while she quickly pulled the tissue paper out with something that could almost be called excitement. *Frick.*

"They uh, they were doing a carnival next to the base for the kids, and I don't know, I saw these and it made me think of you. It's probably a dumb gift, it's not really—" I swallowed hard not sure what to say as I suddenly realized I was standing an awkward distance away that I couldn't close without it being obvious, so I just stood there on the carpet like an awkward schmuck.

Sara shot me a puzzled look from under her lashes as she unrolled the first tube of sand, trying to figure it out. One after another, she lined up the colorful vials across the coffee table. I'd gotten one of everything, just to be sure, and now, it seemed incredibly silly.

Sara finally pulled the glass figurine vase out, quickly piecing together what it was. "Oh, Carter! I've always wanted to do one of these." She reached into the bag again, finding a second glass bottle. "And would you look at that." She shot me a shy little smile. "There's *two* of them—should we make them now?"

I shrugged, suddenly feeling incredibly pleased with myself as *she grinned.* "Only if you want to."

Twenty minutes later, we were sitting on the floor in front of the coffee table with two very colorful sand art vases. I'd picked the sand people shaped ones for us because they kind of reminded me of the Sour Patch Kids she loved so much. Both had googly eyes, and were plugged with a colorful sprout of bouncy hair coming out the top—Sara's was yellow, and mine was blue. *Very fitting.*

"I'm glad these made you think of me." Sara chuckled, and sitting a little too far away, she leaned forward to give me a hug. My breath stalled out as her arms slid around my neck, and my arm instinctively found its way around her middle—an awkward angle for a hug, but she lingered all the same, making my every breath come faster and faster, the longer she held on. I could hardly breathe at all by the time she finally pulled back and smiled at me, *a real smile.* "Thank you, Carter."

"I'm glad you like it." I cleared my throat before looking down to play with a piece of fuzz on my jeans—to check *things.*

While Sara was washing her hands, I did a quick vacuum of the rug, and it wasn't until she returned that I realized my mistake. *My seat choice.*

I internally kicked myself while I sat so incredibly still, watching her hover in front of the couch. The whole debate flashed through her big brown eyes as she eyed the middle cushion before she nervously dropped her gaze and took the opposite corner. My eyes shuttered, realizing a few seconds of foresight would have made all the difference. *Fuckity fuck dammit.*

Liam was gone, and I had just blown my one chance to be close to her this weekend. The googly-eyed sand people judged my poor decision making from the coffee table, and I didn't blame them.

~

I never knew five feet could simultaneously feel so close and yet so damn far away as we sat on the same couch, feeling miles apart.

By the time the world's longest movie was over, Sara was fast asleep, curled up on her corner with me quietly scrolling my phone on my corner just letting her sleep—until it finally dawned on me that she hadn't moved in quite a while.

Not even an inch.

"Hey." I crouched in front of her, gently brushing a hand over her knee, but she didn't stir. "Movie's over." I murmured, but she didn't respond at all.

My pulse spiked.

"Sara?" I wasn't whispering anymore as I came to the sickening realization that something was wrong.

I'd been sitting here while she was fucking unconscious—for God knows how long.

"Come on, sweet girl." My voice cracked as I reached for her face, just waiting for her to stir.

Any second now.

But she didn't.

"Wake the fuck up." I demanded, terror slicing through me.

Was she even fucking breathing?

"No, not like this, please not like this." I begged, frantically shoving her hair out of the way as I jammed two fingers against her throat, desperately searching for a pulse. *"Please stay with me, baby."* My voice broke, knowing I'd done this. I'd pushed her to go on that walk when she was so incredibly weak. She'd told me she was too exhausted, and if she—because of me—

The corner of her mouth pulled, and for a split second, I

thought she was having a stroke, but her eyes flicked open. "Gotcha." She laughed sleepily.

I gaped at her, feeling dizzy as I struggled to register that she was totally fine. "Are you shitting me right now?" I might actually have been in shock.

Sara grinned deviously, pillow creases lining her face as she slowly pushed herself up. "Now we're even."

"Even?!" I demanded, head dropping between my knees with a disbelieving laugh.

"Aww, come on, Kensington. Don't tell me you're not up for a little harmless prank."

I blew out a shaky breath before collapsing back onto the floor in a heap of frayed nerves. "Yeah, harmless prank. Right." *Holy fucking shit.*

She tapped my foot with hers, and I pushed up to my elbows. "Too much?"

"You're never too much for me." I joked, but I couldn't find it in me to laugh. Not when I'd thought I'd fucking lost her for the longest second of my life. I felt like I wanted to puke, wondered if I actually would.

My payback was carrying Sara to bed. "Come here, you little troublemaker." I leaned forward to scoop her up. "Let's get you to bed."

"What are you doing?" Her brows shot up as my arms slid around her. "I'm perfectly capable—"

"It's cute that you think this is optional." I scoffed, and she sucked in a sharp breath as I lifted her all too easily, pulling her against my chest. "Because it's definitely not." I had to touch her, feel the breath rising and falling out of her from under my own palms, because that moment had flipped a switch for me that I didn't know if I could ever turn off.

Despite her every protest, I smiled to myself because even as she argued with me, her head was tilted against my shoulder, pressing closer while her fingers clutched my shirt like maybe she didn't want to let go.

Best feeling ever.

I couldn't help but linger at the edge of the bed as I gently set her down and found her gazing up at me. "Carter?"

"Yeah?" I responded all too eagerly.

Her lips parted for a long moment, forming and un-forming a question until she finally murmured, "Thank you for the gift."

"Of course." I nodded breathlessly.

Whatever she'd intended to ask me, she never did.

I was lying in bed, wearing nothing but sweats, while I scrolled through my phone looking at vintage watches, just waiting for Liam to get home so I could have a word with him—*when the sound of Sara's scream made my blood curl.*

I scrambled out of bed and tore down the hall, but when I shoved against her door, I was horrified to find it was locked. A muffled whimper filtered through, and panic-saturated instinct took over—I shouldered it open, ready to kill someone.

Inside, I found Sara thrashing in the bed, fighting *no one* as she cried a strangled noise for help, and I realized with heartbreak and relief that she was dreaming. My chest caved in as I raced for her, loosening the sheets that were tightly tangled around her body before pulling her into my arms.

"Sara, sweetheart, wake up." She gasped a breath and shoved against me the minute her eyes flew open. "It's me, it's Carter." I pushed her hair out of her face, cupping her cheek as her eyes darted around wildly. "It was just a nightmare. I've got you. You're okay now."

It took her a moment to get her bearings, her gasping breaths coming more and more steady by the second as she finally slumped forward, face hidden by her hair as she dropped her head into her hands.

"It was just a dream." I hummed, my panic morphing into

heartbreak as her gasps slowly turned into quiet, broken sobs. "Not real."

The sound she made was the most heartbreaking noise I'd ever witnessed. I'd heard it only once before. *That night.* The night I'd watched her break right in front of my very eyes.

"It's me." She cried, slumping against me.

"What's you?" I asked, gently stroking her hair.

"In my dream, I'm the one who's dead." She sobbed. "I'm the one who's trapped in the coffin, and I can't get out."

"Oh, Sara." I sighed, completely understanding the guilt, the nightmares, the ache of it all. "I'm so sorry I missed the funeral."

"I know you would have been there if you could have." She said, and I hummed in agreement. "You'll never guess who showed up."

"Who?" I tensed.

"Taggart fucking Caldwell." She practically hissed.

"That fucker." My jaw flexed.

"He's in every single one of my nightmares—right before Liam accuses me of not doing enough and before my mother disappears and I appear in her place."

"After my parents died," I started slowly because I'd never really talked about this. "I couldn't sleep for months." I admitted, leaving out that I'd always felt like someone was going to come for me next. "It gets better, it takes a while, but it does get better." I promised, not bothering to admit that eventually she'd be able to sleep soundly again, but that during the waking hours, the ache would never fully go away.

I hated this for her so much, wished I could bring her mother back, for both her and Liam. They were clearly dealing with the loss in different ways, but it was taking its toll on both of them, and from personal experience, I knew it would for a long while.

"I'm so exhausted." Sara sighed. "All the time I'm so exhausted."

"You have to try to eat." I gently coaxed.

"I really do try." She admitted. "I don't know why I can't keep anything down. Every time I force myself to eat—it just makes me sick."

I loosed a heavy breath. "I know."

We sat quietly for a little while, basking in each other's warmth, me selfishly stealing this tiny moment of closeness before my mouth curved in amusement.

"That protein shake... is nasty as shit." I confessed, playing with the end of one of her curls.

She huffed a laugh. "I knew it."

"Like, really bad." My chest shook with laughter.

"And why is it so freaking gritty?" She exclaimed. "It's like drinking sand."

"I don't know, but you have to try and get it down, or some real food. Just try to eat something, even if it's only a little bit."

"I'll try." She promised.

I was still holding her because she hadn't pulled away yet. "Padawan no try. Just do." I said, in a terrible Yoda accent.

"Fine. Drink the nasty shake, we will." Sara retorted in her own much better Yoda accent, and we both chuckled.

"Yeah, that's my girl." I huffed a laugh, tried to compartmentalize, even while her skin was warm under my palm as I rubbed her back.

A ghost of a smile pulled at the corners of her lips, and she peered up at me through her lashes before she quickly dropped her gaze, but still, she didn't pull away.

My heart started pounding faster as the air in the room suddenly shifted.

In the darkness, Sara traced the pattern on the sheets before she slowly trailed her delicate fingers up to the palm of my hand, making my breath catch. "I was sad you weren't at the funeral, but I honestly expected it with your work." She admitted.

"I'm really sorry I couldn't be there." There was so much more I wanted to say, but I couldn't—I could hardly speak with her touching me.

"Don't be. You're here *now*." She shrugged, adding sarcastically, "Remember that time we stopped talking for three years?"

"Yeah, that was really stupid of us, wasn't it?" I chuckled quietly.

"Yeah. Let's never do that again."

"Deal."

Sara hesitated as she slowly trailed her fingers up my arm, making me shiver. "Does that tickle?" She tilted her head, exposing the long column of her neck as she slowly, lightly, traced the lines of ink up my forearm—the floral sleeve I'd gotten tattooed in honor of my mother.

"Yeah." I huffed a laugh that was quickly cut off when her fingers floated over a small addition hidden amidst the foliage. I tensed, wondering if she realized what it was, or if it was too dark. Her fingers resumed their tracing until she ran out of ink, and then her hands were floating over my bare chest—*just because.* I wondered if she could feel how fast my heart was beating as she rested her palms against me.

Breath ragged, I stilled when her eyes dropped to my lips. "Carter?" She murmured.

The sound of my name in her mouth.

"Yes?" I rasped.

"Can I ask you something?"

"Always." I nearly panted. "Anything." As if I wasn't dying to know what was bouncing around in that pretty little head of hers, every hour of every day.

But just then, the front door opened, and it cleaved my chest in half when her grip tightened as I quickly slipped out of it, like she didn't want to let go—*I know I didn't.*

"I should go before he finds us." I explained, gripping the back of my neck regretfully.

"Nothing to find." She breathily reminded me, but it couldn't have been further from the truth.

Her wearing whatever silky excuse that was for a nightgown, with her hair flowing all around her like a goddess—me, shirtless, angling my body away from her in the darkness to hide what Liam would castrate me for if he found me in her room like this, at this hour.

"Sweet dreams, pretty girl." I cast her a long look, feeling hollow inside, before I slipped out of her room, desperately wishing everything was so much different.

I intercepted Liam before he could see which room I had come out of. "You get everything all sorted?" I asked, noting the sort of wild look that was in Liam's eye.

"Yup." He threw his jacket over an armchair.

I crossed my arms over my chest. "You want to tell me what kind of restaurant emergency requires you to leave for five hours when your sister is sitting in your living room with an IV bag in her arm?" I questioned, not because I was reprimanding him but because I knew if he'd left there had been a damn good reason for it.

He responded with a simple, "Nope."

I searched his expression. "Liam?" I called after him as he walked around me to head down the hall. When he turned, he looked so exhausted, so defeated. "I'm here for you. Whatever you need, I'm here for you."

The corner of his mouth tugged, but the smile didn't meet his eyes. "I know, Kensington." He disappeared down the hall and into his room.

In that moment, I realized I didn't know my best friend quite as well as I thought I did, and my chest tightened, wondering what the hell he was up to.

CHAPTER 17

The Bucket

A full semester behind, I finally returned to school, but I was just going through the motions. My grades were passing, *barely,* but I had zero inspiration to paint. I just couldn't seem to start, couldn't seem to even pick up a brush.

If I didn't figure something out soon, I was going to flunk out of my classes, and there would be no way for me to graduate on time.

I just felt so behind, like I was already supposed to be bouncing back, but I wasn't. I wasn't even remotely close. The world was moving on, but I was impossibly stuck.

After Carter's parents had died, he'd handled it so well, kept it together. Even as a teenager. Only, it had slowly been dawning on me that he'd been in *so* much more pain all those years than he'd ever really let on. Carter had been all alone in that big house of his for all those years. I wondered how many nights he'd woken up screaming... with no one there to hear him.

Over these last few months, I'd experienced a depth of grief that I didn't even know was possible, and I couldn't possibly fathom doubling it.

My phone buzzed, and I reluctantly opened my texts.

LIAM

Did you eat today?

> Yes

A lie. I lied most days. To my credit, I really was trying. There had been a few days where I'd forced myself to eat something substantial, but I'd immediately thrown up. I literally could not stomach anything. My body had an appetite for one thing. Grief. Heaps and heaps of it. My phone buzzed again.

What did you eat?

Have you been drinking your shakes?

I silenced my phone, not bothering to answer it. I knew he meant well, but he was pestering me day in and day out, and I just didn't have the energy. He wasn't the only one either. Everyone had come out of the woodwork to badger me. I supposed I should be grateful that I had anyone at all to check in on me, but truthfully, it was really just wearing me out even more. Everyone had these expectations of where I was supposed to be in the process of all of this, and letting everyone down—it was just too much to deal with. Everything and everyone was practically moving at the speed of light, and I doubted I'd ever catch up.

So I sat in my art studio in the dark and just waited. For what? I had no idea. My eyes flitted to the canvas I'd at least wrapped for Carter. It was leaning against the wall by the door, but I still hadn't gotten around to actually mailing it. He'd already paid me, despite my best efforts, so I knew I *really* should mail it, but I just couldn't muster the willpower to actually get it done.

Day in and day out, anger pulsed through me as I stared at the bright, colorful canvases around the studio. I hated them. Resented that I'd ever been so happy when that emotion felt so far away now. I'd been so oblivious to how good my life had been, taking it all for granted.

I was *barely* making it through my classes, the numerous extensions, and my professor's patience was running thin. I'd permanently stepped down as a teacher's assistant, unable to juggle all my responsibilities. I still could hardly eat, and I still hadn't mailed Carter's painting. I just needed to get the damn thing out of my sight for my own sanity, at least, but I couldn't, for reasons I couldn't exactly explain. It was just too damn hard.

Carter had texted me dozens of times, even sent me an exorbitant amount of money to cover the shipping. We'd sent the balance back and forth several times, with him increasing it every time he sent it back, before I finally gave up and just stopped responding altogether. I didn't have the energy to fight him. So the balance just sat in my account, looming over me like an anvil ready to crush me. Part of me wished it would.

Over the last several weeks, Carter had tried a dozen different tactics to get me to respond to his texts, but I just didn't have the energy to care. What would I even say? There was nothing to say. It was taking everything I had just to get out of bed in the morning, and many mornings I didn't even accomplish that.

I was stuck. I knew it, but what I didn't know was what to do about it.

I'd lay in the studio for hours, wearing my painting clothes, waiting for inspiration to strike, but it just wouldn't. What I really wanted to do was *destroy* everything.

Last week, I'd finally picked up a paintbrush for the first time and found myself just wanting to stab it straight through the canvas—punch a gaping hole to match the one in my heart.

I checked the time and groaned. I was going to be late. *Again.* Apparently, this is who I was now, and I couldn't find it in me to care.

I dragged myself up, wondering if I should just drop out of class, because what was even the point? I didn't want to be here anyway, but I didn't want to be at home either.

So I went to class. For some reason, I went. I didn't bother taking notes, didn't even bother bringing a notebook with me, and when the lecture was over, my professor pulled me aside before I could escape.

"Sara, can I talk to you?" She asked, concern lighting her expression, and I could tell whatever she was going to say was gonna suck.

I could take it. I would be the master of things that sucked.

At least that was one thing I could be good at.

And then I realized even that wasn't true.

My professor motioned me over, and dread filled me. "Sara?" She crossed her arms, leaning against the front of her long, worn desk.

"Professor Alden?" I pulled my sweater tighter around me, because I was always cold these days, even in the dead of summer. Today I was freezing.

"I received a phone call this week." Her eyes searched my face, and I waited as she buried the lead.

It used to make me so anxious knowing someone was about to drop a bomb on me, *waiting for the worst-case scenario—* waiting for the proverbial other shoe to drop. But the thing was, I'd already experienced the worst-case scenario because nothing could be worse than the long pause the doctor had taken before he told us my mother hadn't made it. It was one of those moments where I knew, before the words had ever left his mouth. Maybe there was some sort of energetic bond that had been severed the moment my mother had taken her last breath. I didn't know.

What could Professor Alden say that was worse than that? Nothing. Literally nothing.

So, in a way, I felt invincible now. Nothing could hurt me because there was no room for any more of anything. Pain, happiness, grief—I was full to the brim. No get-out-of-jail card for me.

"I believe you sold your first painting over the holidays?" Professor Alden asked, concern still lacing her expression, as if all my thoughts were on broadcast. I swallowed hard. How did she even know that? "I'd like to help you get that shipped to the buyer."

I took a deep breath, knowing I couldn't really say no. "Okay."

She reached out and touched my arm. "You doing okay?" I only nodded, leaning a hip against her desk. I felt *so* fatigued today, needed to sit. Desperately. "Have you picked up a brush yet?" I'd picked up the brush many times, but I knew what she meant, and I shook my head *no*. "Why not?" She asked curiously.

I knew she meant well, but I was so over this conversation. I picked at my nails, trying to figure out how to explain it—my nails, I realized, had never been this clean, this paint-free. "Nothing interesting enough to paint." I shrugged indifferently, rather than explaining that I was all dark and twisty, all fucked up inside. Ruined. Probably for good.

She nodded, and I knew she was about to lower the axe. "Sara, I'm going to give you an assignment, and it will account for your entire grade this semester."

I was slightly surprised by the panic rising in my throat. So much for not caring.

She pointed to a big bucket next to her desk. "Your semester assignment is to use this entire bucket of paint. No exceptions." I stared at the bucket, totally confused. It was just cheap wall paint from the hardware store. It wasn't even a good color... I *never* used black in my pieces.

"I'm not going to be grading you on your technique." She watched me closely. "You'll be graded based on the amount of paint left in the bucket."

"Professor?"

"If you use fifty percent of the paint, you'll get a fifty percent, if you use seventy-five percent, you'll get a seventy-five percent. My only stipulation is that you must use the paint on a canvas." She added with a narrowing of her eyes. "Or many canvases, I don't care. You just can't pour it out somewhere. Understood?"

Dread filled my stomach. It was *so* much fucking paint. I hadn't even been able to go through a tiny little tube the past several months, and this, this was impossible—no, that didn't even cover it. This was *insurmountable.*

I couldn't do it. I was going to fail my class.

"Sara?" A lump lodged itself so deep in my throat, I couldn't even swallow, so I just nodded. "Meet me here an hour before class tomorrow, and I'll bring a moving truck to transport your painting."

I gasped as I hefted the bucket up with two hands, realizing how heavy it really was. How the hell was I going to get this down to my studio?

"And Sara—I want you to carry that bucket around until it's empty. Everywhere you go."

"*What?*" My mouth dropped open. "It's *really* heavy, Professor Alden." Did she know how weak I was? That I was on the verge of passing out, like, all the time?

"I know." She smiled. "That's the point. You can do this, Sara. Just get the paint onto a canvas. That's it." She went back to the papers she was grading as if she hadn't just handed me a death sentence.

Now, the neck of my artistic career was stretched across the executioner's block, and she seemed indifferent to the fact that I was incapable of moving my head—not before the axe dropped anyway.

The next morning, with my painting loaded up, Professor Alden drove us to the post office, and when we got there, it dawned on me I didn't even have Carter's address.

Shit.

"Is something wrong?" Professor Alden asked.

"I don't have the buyer's address." I admitted, hoping she'd let me off the hook, knowing she wouldn't.

"Isn't he a family friend of yours?" She opened the back of the truck.

Not getting off the hook.

"Yes, but he's moved a few times in the last few years."

She turned and smiled knowingly. "Why don't you give him a call, and I'll go find someone to help me carry this inside?"

I nodded and blew out a frustrated breath, because I'd returned Carter's texts here and there, but we hadn't *spoken*. In fact, I'd kind of been hiding from him since my birthday. The way he'd looked at me was just too damn hopeful. When I knew I was just going to let him down. Just like everybody else.

Maybe I could just flee the scene and never return? I could quit and just be done with it already. The thought sounded appealing until I realized I'd already reached my limit of lying around in my childhood bedroom, and I'll admit, even I was surprised at that realization.

My hand trembled as my thumb hovered over his contact card, and I suddenly realized I needed privacy for this. So I wandered further away from the truck and leaned against a tree across the parking lot, sliding down to sit.

I closed my eyes. This was Carter. Of all people, he'd understand.

So I dialed, and as I lifted the phone to my ear, my insides immediately knotted up, and I wondered if I was going to puke.

He answered on the second ring, a little out of breath. "Sara?" I immediately couldn't speak, a lump lodged itself in my throat, and silent tears streamed down my face instead. *Fuckerson.*

"Sara, are you there? Is something wrong?" There was noise in the background. He was probably busy, and I didn't want to waste his time, but God, I just couldn't get a word to form.

In my best effort to make my vocal cords do their job, I choked out an embarrassing, strangled sob.

"I'm here, sweetheart." His calming voice filtered through the phone with immediate understanding.

I must have sounded like a serial killer, just breathing heavily into the phone, but Carter just started talking to me, slowly filling the silence. "I'm glad you called." The sound of his voice was *so* comforting. "I know this is hard, but you're strong, Sara. So fucking strong, and I know things will never be the same without her—"

He was right. They wouldn't. I shook violently, crumpled over my knees and sobbed, hard and ugly, practically feral, not caring who saw.

I don't know exactly what he said, or how long I stayed like that, but eventually my insides started unknotting and I let the soothing sound of his voice bring me back to reality.

"Where are you?" He finally asked.

I glanced across the parking lot and found my professor sitting on the bench outside the post office, patiently waiting for me. I hiccuped sharply, remembering why I'd called to begin with. "I-I'm in a parking lot." I finally got out.

"What do you see?"

"What?"

Gently, "What do you see, sweet girl?"

"My uh, my professor." I hiccuped again, wiping the snot running down my face with the back of my hand.

"Good." I could hear his smile through the phone. "What can you feel?"

"Feel? Uh, gravel? I'm sitting on sharp-ass gravel." I laughed and pulled in another deep breath.

He chuckled. "Sounds about right. I wish I was sitting on that sharp-ass gravel right next to you." *I really wished he was too.* I took another deep breath. "Sara, tell me, what do you smell?"

I closed my eyes and inhaled deeply. "Some kind of fried food and—car exhaust." Each deep breath seemed to make the sun shine a little brighter and the world seem a little calmer.

"Attagirl." He hummed. "I'm really proud of you."

"I wish you were here." My voice cracked, and I nearly started crying again.

"I wish I was there too." He sighed. "More than you know—are you alright? Are you in a safe place?"

I cleared my throat, cramming all my emotions way deep down. Enough already. "Yeah, I'm alright."

"Safe?" he asked again.

"Safe." I confirmed with a roll of my eyes.

"Good." He murmured and then, "Hey listen, I'm at work right now, but you know you can call me anytime, day or night, right?"

"I promise I won't bug you again." I tipped a pile of rocks out of the palm of my hand.

"Sarafina, sweetheart." He huffed a laugh. "I really hope you do." There was a gap of empty space before we said goodbye, and when the phone went dead, I forced myself to uncoil and brush myself off.

I patted my cheeks dry with the back of a sleeve and headed towards my professor. "How'd it go?" She asked, looking up from her phone. "Did you get the address?" *The address.* Shit. I'd completely forgotten.

Carter picked up on the first ring this time, sounding frantic. "Sara?"

I cleared my throat. "I'm so sorry to bug you again—I need your address."

"You're mailing my piece." He exhaled, pure delight in his voice. "I'll text you, okay?"

"Thanks, Carter."

"Anytime, pretty girl. Let me know if you need anything else, okay?"

"Okay." I shook my head, embarrassed at myself.

"Gotta go. Bye." He hung up the phone quickly, but I got a text from him with an address a mere minute later.

I nodded to my professor, and we went inside and did the impossible thing.

We mailed it.

~

Professor Alden patted my back as we stood outside the post office soaking in the sun, basking in its warmth for a moment. "You realize this makes you a professional."

I scoffed. "It doesn't count if a friend bought it."

"Was money exchanged?" She asked.

"A wad of hundred-dollar bills." I rolled my eyes and muttered, "And an obscene amount of money for shipping, that I have to send back." I added, "Again."

"Well, if the amount you keep is enough to profit, that means you're liable for taxes, Sara." She smiled knowingly. "Do you know what that means?"

"I need to hire an accountant?" I asked, puzzled.

She chuckled. "That means *you're in business.* Family friend or not." She shrugged. "Besides, that's what being an artist is. Selling art to your friends. Because in this industry, it's all about *networking.* Everybody is a friend of a friend, and everybody want's to buy their friends' art because they want to brag about how well they know the artist." I chewed my lip. I hadn't thought of it like that.

I supposed there was no going back now. She was right. The ball was rolling whether I liked it or not.

"Now, you just need to use that bucket of paint." She reminded me. "Or don't." She looked me up and down. "You might put some muscle back on, which it looks like you could use."

I realized maybe I wasn't fooling everyone as well as I thought I'd been. "Is that what this assignment is?" I asked as we got back into the truck to drive back to campus. "A workout regimen?"

"Is that what you think it is?" She looked at me as she turned on the ignition.

"Honestly? I have no idea. A punishment for falling behind?" I winced, trying again.

She looked me square in the eye. "No, Sara, it's just a physical manifestation of the process. We all carry emotional baggage around with us all the time. Some things are heavier than others, and unless we go through the process of letting go, we have to keep carrying our shit around with us. Whether we like it or not. And right now you're carrying the weight of the world on your shoulders." She eased out of the parking space. "The more we let go, the lighter we feel. It's going to be painful as hell, but your mother would want you to keep moving forward. Even if it's just a tiny bit every day." She smiled sadly, keeping her eyes on the road. "Don't get stuck. It's harder than you think to get unstuck." And then she added more sternly. "And don't you dare send that money for the painting back."

"Why?"

"When the universe gives you resources, *receive it*, don't reject it. Life is about flow. Motion. If you reject that money, you're putting a stopper in your flow. Give it away, donate it if you want, but don't reject it. Stay in the flow, even if it's just a tiny little trickle, because that, Sara, is the secret to getting unstuck." Damn. I hadn't thought of it that way either.

Just get the paint on the canvas, I told myself. That's it. I could do that. Right?

Wrong.

CHAPTER 18

Casanova and The Dirty Blonde

CARTER

All around us, patrons hooted and hollered, rowdy and inebriated inside The FlatHatter, the dive bar everyone from the base liked to frequent.

I tipped my beer bottle to my lips before quickly shielding my face as Tatum threw a spray of peanut shells at me. "You just couldn't help yourself, could you, Casanova?"

"Aww Blaze, I can't help it if I'm just better than you." I chuckled with a condescending shrug, but I was more than glad to have a flight training week to be back at home with my OG flight squad. Most of my covert tactical missions were spent with people that I never really got the chance to know. Mostly because the team was rotating, but sometimes, and it was becoming all too frequent—I was bringing my team members back in a long box. One of these days, I wondered if it would be me.

"You wish." Tatum popped another peanut into his mouth with a roll of his eyes.

"Can I get you boys anything else?" The smiley, red-headed waitress asked, folding her now empty serving tray under her arm.

"How about your number?" Ezra Williams asked with a flirtatious wink.

The waitress smiled. "I'll do you one better. I'm off in five."

"It's a date." Ezra crooned.

"Or you could go out with *me*." Mike Rochester grinned with his oh so charming smile. "I promise to show you a better time than this loser." He hooked a thumb at Ezra.

"You don't want him, Gorgeous—you know what they call him up there," Ezra grinned, ready to drop his next insult, "*Grandma.*"

"At least I'm not hot off the block." Mike countered, adding with a smirk, addressing the waitress again. "This guy wants to get to the end as fast as possible, and me, well, I'm incredibly patient. *In fact, I prefer taking my time.*"

"Don't you two make an interesting pair," the waitress laughed and walked away, tossing her hair over her shoulder casually. "Why choose? You're both invited." Ezra and Mike looked at each other, a silent question passing between them.

"Fuck." I muttered. "You two have fun with that." They both stood up at the same time and grabbed their jackets in agreement.

"Have fun in Paris." Tatum called after them with a shake of his head. "Shit, that's either going to make things really funny or really fucking awkward tomorrow."

I chuckled, feeling fingers walking around my shoulder, before a hand slid into the base of my hair. "Hey soldier." A sultry voice purred into my ear, and then a bleach-blonde woman came around my side, fiddling with her necklace, not so subtly drawing attention to her cleavage. "Looking for a good time tonight?"

"I'm good, thanks." I smiled politely.

She scrunched up her nose. "Come on, it could be fun." She made a pouty face.

"You might try that table over there." I nodded toward another crew that I knew would definitely take her up on the offer.

She hopped up on her tiptoes and pulled herself into my lap, nearly knocking over my beer bottle. I grabbed it before it spilled, tensing as she threaded her arms around my neck and leaned into my ear. "What if I'm not interested in them? What if *you*'re the one I had my eye on?" Tatum shot me a look, like *come on, she's hot.*

I threw Tatum a roll of my eyes before addressing the woman. "Sorry, ma'am, I gotta wife back home." I said, putting a little twang in my voice for Tatum's benefit.

"I don't see a ring." She scrunched her nose in annoyance. "Don't break my heart. I don't think I could take it. I promise I'll make it worth your while." She wiggled in my lap, and I flinched, grabbing her wrist as she slid her hand down, down, down.

Tatum stifled a laugh.

"Sorry, I'm really not interested." I gently pushed her out of my lap to stand, and I flinched when one of her nails pricked the back of my neck in protest.

She scowled. "Whatever. Your loss." She left, putting extra sway in her hips as she stomped off.

"What the hell?" I rubbed my neck. "She scratched me." I pulled my hand away, half expecting blood.

Tatum burst into laughter. "I gotta wife back home." He mimicked me in a feminine, twangy accent, clutching his hands together. Which looked utterly ridiculous, given his size and stature.

"I don't know, okay." I chuckled. "She wasn't getting the memo."

Tatum shrugged. "Looked like it could have been a good time."

"Maybe." I murmured, knocking back the last of my beer.

"Listen, I know you've got a thing for your sweetheart back home or whatever, but my man, you've gotta get *laid* from time to time."

"Sara is not my sweetheart." My jaw flexed as I begrudgingly admitted it.

"Semantics." He countered, "And if she's really not, then there's nothing stopping you from selecting something off the menu." He turned and motioned around the bar at the countless women, many of them specifically on the hunt to pick up a guy from the base. "How long has it been anyway?"

"I don't keep track." I gritted.

"Better get back on the horse before your dick falls off."

"I don't think that's how that works." I noticed the blonde was still watching me from across the bar with a scowl.

"Dude, you got it bad." Tatum shook his head. "You gotta lock that shit down, otherwise you're gonna be miserable."

"It's not like that." I shrugged.

"What's it like then?"

"She's just a family friend." *That I possibly love.* "Besides, her brother would kill me."

"You sure about that?" He sipped his beer.

"Yeah." I nodded emphatically. I really was. Losing Liam as a friend was not an option. I couldn't afford to gamble our friendship on something like this, especially when Sara hadn't really responded to any of my advances.

We flirted, sure, but over her birthday it'd just been a game. Something to cheer her up. When it came down to it, I didn't want to make her uncomfortable. Didn't want to push her away again. Besides, I was here, and she was there. It wasn't even remotely practical. I shook my head, wondering why I was even considering it. Friends. That's what Sara was, *my friend*.

"Whatever, man, your blue balls, not mine."

I sighed, trying not to think about it at all. "And how is long distance treating you?" I asked pointedly.

"It fucking sucks." He rolled his eyes. "But what are you gonna do? She's the love of my life and all."

"Didn't know you were so sappy." I picked at the paper label on my beer bottle, feeling sorry for myself.

"Neither did I." He scoffed, standing to stretch his arms over his head. "Next rounds on me."

I wondered how Sara was doing after earlier. Wondered if she'd pick up the phone if I called. It was definitely worth a shot.

"Actually, I'm gonna head out." I stood and grabbed my jacket off the back of my chair, hoping for the best.

"Suit yourself."

I swung my jacket around my head, slipping it on. "See you tomorrow."

"Drive safe." Tatum called, pushing through the crowd towards the bar.

The drive home was relatively short, and I blinked my eyes, trying to keep them open. It was only eight, and I was surprisingly tired. I was always a *little* worn out after combat training, but tonight I felt totally out of it.

I parked my Tesla outside my apartment. Surprised when I got out to see, I'd parked on the line, like a total schmuck.

I shook my head, feeling a little dizzy, and decided to leave it for the night as I climbed the stairs, heading for my second-floor apartment.

I definitely wasn't drunk. I'd only had one beer, but maybe I was dehydrated? Flying at mock speeds was pretty strenuous on the body. I'd drink some electrolytes before I went to bed, maybe use some of that magnesium lotion Charlotte had talked me into getting last summer. Staying in peak physical performance was a top priority for me, and I wasn't against supplementing where I needed to.

I fumbled with my keys, cursing as I dropped them on the ground. It took me three tries to get the door open, and when I finally did, my skin pricked, finally realizing there was actually something wrong. *This wasn't exhaustion at all.*

I blinked, staring at my hand as I gripped the door handle, watching it blur in front of me. What the hell was wrong with me?

Before I had time to consider, or even step inside, I suddenly became aware of a large presence looming behind me, and a millisecond later a bag went over my head. I whirled to throw a punch, but I realized I was about to be in deep shit—because *I was already moving in slow motion.*

CHAPTER 19

Speed Dating Psychos

CARTER

Bag tied around my neck, I stumbled around and couldn't quite get the damn thing off. Without my sight, my other senses heightened, and my head snapped up as I heard the slide of metal and then felt the barrel of a gun press into my chest.

Instinct took over as I twisted the gun out of my assailant's hands using a maneuver I'd done countless times and launched a hard kick that landed square in his thick chest, trying to figure out what the hell was going on.

I didn't use the firearm for several reasons, the main one being the young family that lived across the hall. Instead, in several swift movements, I ejected the clip of bullets and emptied the one in the chamber before I frantically grappled with the bag on my head.

I finally yanked it loose, and my eyes blew wide the instant I ripped the bag off, because a second later I was tackled to the ground.

As we fell through my now open door, I took the impact of both of our bodies, and my shoulder hit the ground first. There was a sickening, nerve-numbing crunch as he came down on top of me, and I growled out a gasp, instantly realizing my shoulder had *dislocated*.

Shoulder barking with pain, I dragged myself up, eyes narrowing in on my attacker. Good shoulder down, I rammed into the man's stomach, and we slammed into the TV stand, breaking it clean in half.

I shook my head, blinking as I scrambled up, realizing I was getting dizzier by the second. "What do you want?" I demanded, circling with the man around my living room, with one arm dangling totally useless by my side.

I inched towards the kitchen where my gun was when a figure appeared in the doorway.

"It's over. Sit your ass down." I realized it was the blonde from the bar, and she was aiming a gun at me.

What the fuck?

I put my good hand up in surrender, and just as I was about to launch myself at her, another man filled the doorway behind her.

"You've got to be shitting me." I muttered. "What the fuck do you want?" I demanded.

"What I wanted was a good time." The blonde rolled her eyes. "Guess we have to do this the hard way." She pulled out a kitchen chair and motioned with the gun. "Sit."

I stumbled, grabbing the arm of the couch as my legs started to give out.

Oh shit, I had minutes. Maybe.

"Get him." She snapped, waving the gun around wildly enough that I knew she was dangerous, simply for the reason that it was clear that she had no idea how to handle that thing.

As I backed away, my knees betrayed me and gave out beneath me—a moment later, the men grabbed me by each arm, and dragged me into the kitchen, making me scream in pain as my dislocated shoulder wrenched the wrong way.

I was immediately in a cold sweat as the two men slammed me down into the chair, and my head erupted with a dull headache. My hands were zip-tied behind my back, further wrenching my arm, feet zip-tied to each leg of the chair, and a nylon rope tied ghastly tight around my chest.

Still, the front door was open. "FIRE!" I shouted as loud and long as I could.

"Shut up." Pain bloomed behind my eye as I took a hard punch to the face.

I groaned, desperately trying to bring the room into focus, as it steadily became more and more fuzzy.

I blinked as they closed the door and then stood in front of me in the kitchen. "If you're planning to have a threesome on my kitchen table." I panted. "I must warn you, it's only rated up to two hundred pounds." My heart was racing far too fast now, and I hoped that whatever drugs were in my system didn't kill me.

"Ha ha, very funny." The woman snapped and pointed between us with the gun. "No, we're gonna have a little chat, you and I."

I blinked, trying to shake the black spots speckling my vision. "Excuse me if I'm not inclined to cooperate with your method of speed dating." The rope was the only thing keeping me upright now, and my head felt heavier than lead.

"The Society is tired of waiting for your cooperation." She said, and my wheels immediately started turning, shocked, as I tried to sort this out, figure a way out of this before I lost consciousness.

"I don't know what the hell they're waiting for." My left ear started to ring, my eardrum fluttering painfully, and I felt like I was going to puke any second now. "I gave you all my answer years ago." I pulled against my restraints, but it only made the excruciating pain in my shoulder shoot down my arm and up my neck. I bit back a whimper and tried again with no luck.

"Yes, well, you were young and dumb then." I lifted my head to see the woman shrug as she spun the gun around her finger carelessly. "The director has been wildly patient, and now he's ready to put some pressure on you. He *will* get what he wants.

Eventually. And right now, you have two options, join or turn over the estate."

I closed my eyes, trying to ground myself, trying to breathe through the pain, trying to draw in a full breath to steady myself. "You can tell him that's never going to happen." My head snapped to the side from the punch I didn't see coming. I laughed as blood dripped out of my mouth with a metal tang and black edged around my vision, all while I fought to stay conscious.

"You gave him too much." A male voice said.

"How was I supposed to know? I'm not a fucking pharmacist."

My heart was pounding way too fast. Could a heart explode? It felt like it was going to. "What did you give me?" I demanded weakly.

God, I didn't want to die from a fucking overdose. I had things I needed to do, things I needed to *say*.

"You'll be fine." The woman responded. "If you cooperate."

My response was jumbled and nonsensical, my tongue a dead weight in my mouth.

"Your membership is not a request; it is a requirement, and I suggest you concede in a timely manner. Otherwise, our little party here will be the least of your problems."

That was the last thing I heard before I blacked out.

<u>Sarafina</u>

I laid in bed that night and stared at the giant bucket of paint in the corner of my room, debating if I should text Carter about the whole ridiculous thing. Debated even calling him instead, but ultimately decided I didn't want to seem like a sad, needy nuisance after my embarrassing breakdown earlier today.

I scrolled through his latest messages anyway.

CARTER

Hey, just wanted to check on you today. It's
supposed to be a beautiful day. Get outside
and get some fresh air. Hope you have a great
day, pretty girl.

You're going to get through this. I know it
doesn't seem like it, but you WILL have good
days again. I'm here for you anytime. Day or
night. I mean it.

Also, I'm really excited to get my painting btw

Fucking excited!!!!! But you get the point

I smiled and thumbed over to my banking app and sent the
balance for the painting back to him, and waited. I understood
why Professor Alden had said to keep it, but right now, this was a
bit of a ritual between Carter and me—somehow easier than
texting actual words. Besides, Carter always sent the money right
back within a matter of minutes. It was our weird little game
of tag.

I laid in bed scrolling social media and periodically thumbing
over to my banking app, checking, but still no response from
Carter.

Hours went by as I laid there just waiting, feeling worse and
worse. I wasn't sure how long I waited, but eventually I realized he
wasn't going to send the balance back this time. I shook my head,
feeling silly that I had expected him to be available on demand. He
had his own life, and it's not like he was waiting in great anticipation for my texts. Maybe he'd decided the painting wasn't worth
that much anyway, because it definitely wasn't.

The sad truth was, he was just probably being nice when we'd
spoken on the phone earlier because that's who Carter was. He
would have stayed on the phone with me while I cried like a
lunatic, simply because that's what he would have done for any
one of his friends. I wasn't special.

I laid in bed and went back and forth, tormenting myself before finally composing another text to him.

> Sorry it took so long to send the painting.

I hesitated before typing out another message.

> Don't sue me if I put too much bubble wrap on it. It's going to take you a WHILE to get it all off. Hah. I just wanted to make sure it got to you in one piece.

I stared at the thread, but the three little dots never popped up. The longer I waited, the more I wished I would have just played it cool and thanked him for earlier. I groaned. Was it too needy to send *another* text thanking him? Should I wait for him to respond first? Maybe he was annoyed with me. *I* would be annoyed with me.

I composed another text just in case. I didn't want to seem like an ungrateful ass. Thanking him was the least I could do.

> Thanks again for earlier and sorry I've been so lame.

I sent the message, forcing myself to plug in my phone and hide it inside my nightstand. Out of sight. Out of mind.

Tossing and turning, sleep completely eluding me, I finally caved in the wee hours of the morning and checked my texts, *but still no response*. I threw the phone back into my drawer, hating the tears that streamed down my face as I stared at the ceiling. I'd definitely pushed him away with my psychotic emotions.

Why was I so needy? Why couldn't I just get a grip and move on like everyone else seemed to be able to? Why did everything feel so damn hard?

I just wanted to go back to those perfect moments at Thanksgiving, when my mother was alive, when Carter and I had mended things and were talking again, when I had an appetite for life and for food. When things were *normal*.

I was desperate to grab onto something that I just couldn't seem to wrap my fingers around, because it didn't exist. Not anymore.

Carter had his own life, and I just needed to let it go. Needed to let *him* go.

CHAPTER 20

Palms Down Ass Up

SARAFINA

I stood, hands on my hips, staring at the paint bucket in the corner of my room, deciding whether or not I was going to participate in this delusional assignment Professor Alden had given me.

I had nothing to lose and nothing better to do anyway, so against my better judgement, I hauled the damn thing outside. The minute I hit the threshold, I knew I'd made a mistake.

By late afternoon, I thought I might faint. I hadn't so much as lifted anything heavier than a cheese stick since December. Saying I was out of shape would have been the understatement of the century.

As I struggled across campus in the heat of summer, I was really beginning to resent Professor Alden. Dragging that heavy bucket across the concrete, I decided if I didn't wear a hole in the bottom by the end of the week, I'd just pour the damn thing out. She'd never know.

In a burst of delusional motivation, I hefted that fucking bucket up, and its very scratched rim snagged on the cement—I tripped, falling over the top of it before I could recover. I went down hard, palms first, ass up.

I cursed, wincing at my raw, stinging palms before I gave up completely. Silent tears streamed from the corners of my closed eyes as I laid in the middle of the sidewalk, wishing someone would just end my fucking misery already.

I hated this.

Hated this stupid assignment.

Hated dragging myself out of bed for class.

Hated dragging this damn bucket across campus.

Hated that my mother was dead.

Hated that my father had turned into a ghost, and that Liam seemed to be going on with life, while I was just stuck.

Hated that Carter didn't text me back.

Hated that *I* didn't text any of my friends back.

And most of fucking all, I hated *myself* for being so fucking weak.

My lower lip trembled as I suppressed a guttural scream that I didn't even have the energy to utter.

An unfamiliar voice from above asked, "You okay?"

"No." I snapped bitterly, not bothering to open my eyes. "You can't tell from my pathetic form that I'm clearly trying to lay here and wallow?"

"Should I just leave you here, or?"

"Yes," I grumbled. Who in God's name was—

"You sure you're okay? Because you don't look okay."

"I literally just said I wasn't okay." I muttered, opening my eyes to find a random guy silhouetted against the sun. I couldn't make out his face. A new paparazzi? I sighed, realizing I'd have to cut him a check, just like all the others I'd bribed to back the fuck off.

"What are you doing?" He asked, standing too close for comfort.

"What does it look like I'm doing? I'm taking a nap." I threw an arm over my eyes and sighed because I had no fucks left to give. "If you're here for a photo, that's old news."

"Really? Because it looks like you fell, your shit is everywhere." He cleared his throat. "And no, I'm not here for a photo, whatever the hell that means."

"Sure you aren't." I glanced at the scattered contents of my purse before throwing an arm over my eyes again.

"Do you want help with that?"

I assumed he meant the bucket. "Can't. It's an assignment."

"Carrying around the bucket?" He asked, and I could feel him still hovering.

"Go away." I demanded, relieved when he didn't respond. I wasn't sure how much longer I laid there, but the sun was scorching, and I finally forced myself to sit up, because if I didn't move, I was actually going to faint from heatstroke. I groaned when I realized he was sitting on a nearby bench. "I thought you'd left."

"Nope." He shrugged. "Just wanted to make sure you didn't pass out down there." He crossed back over to me, and I tensed. "So, are you going to tell me what the deal with that bucket is?"

"Nope." I pushed a strand of hair out of my face and stood feeling more than a little lightheaded as I ignored his outstretched hand.

"Fair enough." He smiled and grabbed the bucket anyway.

"Put it down; you can't carry that." I argued, frantically grabbing for it—I nearly fell over when he let go of it and the weight swung back to me.

"Why?"

"Because *I* have to." I snapped. God, what was his problem? Just go away, guy.

"You have to?"

I groaned, waving towards the bucket. "I have a dead mother." I practically shouted. "Okay? Is that a good enough reason for you?"

He grimaced. "Are those her ashes?"

"No," I said defensively. "I'm not a complete weirdo, despite what it may look like." Maybe I was, but I certainly wasn't going to admit it to this asshat. I stared at him while he watched me closely. Maybe he was a journalist. If he was, he was a really bad one.

"So if it's not your dead mother's ashes, what's in the bucket, then?"

I groaned, shielding my eyes from the sun. "Seriously? Why do you care?"

He shrugged. "I don't."

"Good, I'm glad we got that settled." I hefted the bucket up, dying to get away from him.

He walked backward in front of me. "So, you gonna tell me or what?" He blocked my path, and my shoulders slumped as I dropped the bucket. I did *not* have the energy for this.

"It's paint. Okay? Black fucking paint." This entire ordeal was probably going to end up on some shitty website tomorrow. Whatever.

"Well then, that wasn't so hard." He smiled. "I'll just walk with you then, while you carry your big bucket of black paint."

"I don't even know you." I glowered.

"I'm Isaac." He stuck his hand out, and I didn't shake it. "I'm in some of your classes." Maybe he was, he did look vaguely familiar.

I took off again, and he paced alongside me, which wasn't hard given my speed. "You know, this is typically the part where you tell me your name."

"You don't want to know me." I grumbled, wondering if this was a new angle.

"I think I might."

"I'm a mess."

"I don't mind messy."

I stopped and looked at him. "You are very persistent, you know that?"

"Yeah, well." He shrugged. "You're really pretty." I squinted against the sun, looking at him for a long while. What the hell did he want? "You thinking about letting me carry that bucket for you? It's okay to ask for help, you know."

"I didn't ask." I reminded him.

"Right." He laughed. "I think that's the point."

"I have to do this, okay?" I put my hands on my hips, staring at him. "It's important. I don't know exactly why it's important, but it is. I'm—I'm doing a process." I explained.

"Okay." He nodded, still not sold on the idea. "You're doing a process."

I was, and I wasn't about to cheat, because I think I knew deep down there really was no cheating any of this.

Carter

I blinked my eyes open as something soft brushed against my mouth.

Meow. A cat was rubbing against my face. I didn't own a cat.

A smattering of blood drops came into focus in front of me. I groaned, realizing my face was smashed against my kitchen floor, because I was still tied to a kitchen chair, but I was alive, so that was something.

Sharp pain dotted through my fingers as I tried to wiggle them. My hands were zip-tied so fucking tight I could hardly feel them at all.

The cat rubbed against me, and I groaned in disgust when it turned, nearly putting its butthole in my face. Despite my protests, he started purring and flopped over in front of me, blinking his giant bug eyes from upside down.

Then I realized how it'd gotten inside in the first place, my door was busted, hanging off the hinges. I opened my mouth to call for help, but my throat was dry as sandpaper and my voice came out barely louder than a whisper.

I attempted to push myself up, but my head slammed back against the floor, making my head pound even harder.

Straining my neck to look around, I realized the apartment was utterly trashed. Couch filling all over the place, broken glass all over the kitchen floor, every drawer, and cupboard was open. I shuffled towards the kitchen as best as I could, every heave making my shoulder scream with pain, but if I was lucky, maybe there was a steak knife on the floor. I hoped I didn't pass out from the pain before I could get there.

I tensed when my front door groaned open. "Carter?" Tatum filled the doorway.

I swallowed, my voice coming out hoarse. "Get me out of this, would you?"

Tatum hurried through the living room towards me, taking in the mess with complete shock. "What the actual fuck." Tatum hauled the chair upright, and I winced as the blood rushed from my head all too quickly. He quickly pulled out a pocketknife and bent to cut the zip ties at my ankles.

"How did you know to come find me?" I rasped, head pulsing.

"You didn't show up for work." He said, chest rising and falling rapidly. "You weren't answering your phone. Now I see why." His voice was full of question.

I stared at the ceiling as Tatum cut the rope around my chest and the zip ties on my hands. How was I going to explain this?

"Oh fuck. Your shoulder." He came around the front of me.

I grimaced. "Pop it back in." He didn't hesitate. He grabbed my arm and did it fast, before I had the chance to tense.

I cried out, cursing every word under the sun as I gasped for breath. "Fuuuuck." I couldn't pull a breath in.

"It's in." He frowned, and I rotated my arm gingerly, nodding in agreement as I forced slow steady breaths through the nose. "So, what the fuck happened last night?"

I rubbed my wrists, pins and needles shooting through my hands. "Would you believe me if I said it was the cat?" I shot him a small smile before my face contorted in pain.

The orange stray was now sitting on my kitchen counter, licking its paw and dragging it over its ear—with total disregard for the situation.

"Was this some fucked-up sex shit?" Tatum asked, glancing around the room.

What the hell was I even supposed to say? Tatum just waited, totally dumbfounded.

"The blonde from the bar last night..." I started.

"What about her?" He asked, his expression perplexed.

"Apparently, she likes it rough." I joked.

"Seriously?"

I shook my head in disbelief. "No. She, uh, she drugged me."

Tatum blinked. "Drugged you?!"

I nodded, rubbing the back of my neck where I'd felt the prick. "Is there a mark?" I asked, leaning against the kitchen table as I turned.

He came around and looked. "I don't know, I can't tell." Feeling weak, I slumped back in the chair. "What the hell happened? She robbed you, or?"

"I guess she must have seen my car and figured I had money." I shrugged indifferently. "She had two guys with her."

"This is so fucked up, man. They didn't have to trash the place. Just grab the valuables and leave, you know." Then Tatum groaned. "I'm guessing you haven't even seen your car." I winced, waiting. "It's beat to shit. Like some real Carrie Underwood shit."

I stared at him.

"You know?" He asked, and I shook my head no. He reluctantly sang a bar for me. "Dug my key into his car..." He waited, and then rolled his eyes and sang another line. "Carved my name..."

"Carrie Underwood fan, huh?" I teased.

"Jillian likes that crap, okay? It's not my fault, and besides, her range is—*it's like really good*." I wondered if he was impersonating Jillian as he said it. Tatum shook his head, disbelieving he'd even admitted that. "But yeah, your car is definitely in bad shape." My head popped up in realization. Finally, something was going my way. "Why the hell do you look so happy about it?"

"The Tesla has cameras around the whole thing."

"Fuck yeah." Tatum threw a fist into the air in triumph. "But seriously, let's get you to the hospital first. You look like absolute shit." He grinned. "I'll even give you door-to-door service, like a gentleman." His grin dropped when I faltered as I stood. Tatum lunged and grabbed my good arm, looping it around his neck to support me. "You gonna be okay?" He asked, worry crinkling his brow.

"Yeah, I think so." I panted.

He nodded. "Note to self, don't piss off a dirty blonde."

"I thought Jillian was blonde." I mused.

"Exactly." He muttered.

CHAPTER 21

But I'm a Nice Guy

I sent one more follow-up text, but I never did get a text back from Carter that following week, so I finally decided to let it go. Let him go.

I didn't know why he was suddenly ignoring me after being so sweet on the phone, but I didn't have the energy to overthink it, because I was busy using every ounce of energy, I did have to drag that damn paint bucket around campus.

The task was utterly exhausting and left me feeling like I was going to faint at any given moment. It also garnered a cacophony of confused looks from other students, though I found myself surprised at how easy it was now not to care about things like that anymore. A few assholes recorded me, but it wasn't anything I hadn't dealt with before.

"Morning." Isaac's far too chipper voice sounded from behind me.

I grunted at him in response, and he went on filling the air with whatever it was he talked about while he strolled alongside me to class everyday now.

I really needed to use some of the paint because I was going to wither up and die if I didn't get rid of some of the weight. That or Isaac was going to talk my ear off first.

How hard could it be? I was overcomplicating this, I knew that.

I'd just dump the bucket out on a canvas and be done with the damn thing—I'd just do it.

Easy.

Open the lid, and pour it out, bada bing, bada boom, didn't even have to pick up a paintbrush.

Only when I got there that afternoon... I couldn't do it.

Instead, I sat on top of the bucket and just stared at my paintings from last year.

The more I stared at them, the more I hated them. They made me feel like an impostor. I knew I could never recreate a series like the one in front of me again, and it made me feel panicked. I was breathing, but it felt like I was suffocating. Everything was so different now. *I* was different now. I had no idea how to move through the world anymore. Maybe I wasn't even a painter at all. Maybe I never had been.

And yet, knowing there was literally no point, I pushed the paint bucket out into the hall, and went through the effort to haul the damn thing home with me.

By the end of the following week, I was, of course, exhausted, because that stupid bucket was *still* full to the brim. I hadn't been able to use a single drop. Which meant I'd been hauling around a full paint bucket for nearly two weeks now.

This morning to keep my strength up, I'd eaten *two* cheese sticks for breakfast, which I supposed was Professor Alden's plan all along—trick me into eating more, out of sheer survival, but even with the extra cheese stick for breakfast, I was still running on fumes.

Professor Alden periodically checked in on me throughout the week, but she never pushed for an explanation as I hauled that paint bucket in and out of her class. I think she appreciated that I was taking her assignment seriously. Though, for the life of me, I didn't know why I even bothered.

Oddly, I found myself growing attached to that stupid bucket. The weight was... comforting in a strange way.

Every day was the same. Cheese sticks, paint bucket, collapse into bed without dinner because I was so exhausted. The bucket was becoming so ingrained in my daily routine, I almost forgot I had an assignment to complete. *Almost.*

Isaac was a thorn in my side, since he'd figured out my schedule, and while I'd grown less and less suspicious of him, he was still talking my ear off every day—all while I nodded and grunted at him. Clearly, he wasn't smart enough to be a journalist, and the paparazzi would have taken their damn photo already. What he wanted exactly, I wasn't sure, but everyday he asked if he could carry the bucket for me, and every day, I told him the same thing. *No.* And then he'd respond back, "Right, because you're doing a process." Only today, that's *not* what he said.

"Aren't you supposed to be *using* that paint or something?" He scratched his head as we passed under the rustling trees.

I sighed. "Don't judge me. I'm not in the mood."

"I'm not judging. I'm just curious."

I looked over at him and decided it was too much work to keep being aloof. "I give up."

He laughed. "On what, exactly?"

"On trying to avoid you." I set the bucket down. "You can carry it."

"Really?"

I gave him a small smile. "No."

He made a face at me. "Are you serious?"

"That was called a joke." I flexed my hand to get the circulation going. The thin handle was a nightmare. My hands had blistered last week, and now they were peeling.

He grinned. "You're telling jokes now?"

"I suppose I am."

"That means you're warming up to me." He nudged my shoulder and reached for the bucket.

"No, seriously, you can't carry it."

"You're dedicated, I'll give you that."

I smiled to myself at the realization. I hadn't accomplished anything of substance this year, but he was right, I *was* dedicated. I had *committed* to this assignment. Even if it was dumb.

"So, are you going to give me your number now?" Isaac crossed his arms over his chest, shaking me out of my thoughts.

"Nice try." I scoffed. "Just because I've decided not to ignore you doesn't make us friends."

"Come on, how am I supposed to even try to be your friend if I can't invite you to anything?" He pulled out his phone, and I realized the loneliness of the last few months *had* felt like a suffocating blanket. "We're ten digits away from having a good time." He said, a flirtatious little smirk on his face.

Heart thundering in my ears, in a moment of pure insanity, I blurted out my number.

Isaac's thumbs tapped away on the screen. "Check your phone."

Oh shit. What did I just do? I swallowed hard. "Now?"

"I want to make sure you didn't give me a fake number." He smirked as I groaned and set the bucket down, checking my phone. I waited, but no message came through. "That's what I thought." Isaac laughed and plucked my phone out of my hand, tapping away.

"Not my fault you typed it in wrong." I muttered immediately wishing I *had* given him the wrong number.

"Yeah, right." When he handed my phone back, a new text thread at the top of my messages was addressed to:

MY BEST FRIEND ISAAC

Hey

I shook my head and stuffed my phone into my back pocket. "You're very presumptuous." I muttered, and then curiously, "What did you save *my* contact as?"

Isaac smiled, and his thumbs flew over his phone screen. "Check your messages." He wiggled his brows and peeled off in the direction of his class. "Bye, baby."

I saved your contact as Bucket Baby

Very cute.

Not as cute as you

Now go to class you slacker

I hauled the bucket up, and a small smile threatened to tug the corners of my mouth up. I shook it off and headed towards my studio. He was *not* my friend.

The next week, after following me around like a sad puppy as usual, Isaac made his move. He invited me over for pizza and a movie that Friday, and to my surprise, I said yes.

I showed up at his apartment after my evening class, sans paint bucket.

He opened his front door dressed in a t-shirt and jeans, looking shocked. "Woah, no paint bucket." He motioned for me to come in.

"It's my weekend." I shrugged.

He smiled and shut the door behind me, tipping his head for me to follow him into the kitchen, where he handed me a plastic plate. I looked around his space, taking it in. Typical college guy apartment. It was clean at least, pretty empty though.

"Take your pick," he said, opening all three boxes of pizza, each a different type.

"You got this all for us?" I asked, wondering how much he planned on eating.

He dropped his hand down onto my shoulder and squeezed. "I think you need to eat, young lady, so I came prepared. I wasn't sure what you'd be in the mood for." His thoughtfulness caught me off guard.

Truth be told, the smell of the pizza was making me queasy though, so I grabbed a single slice of cheese pizza and headed for the table just off the kitchen.

Isaac sat across from me, several slices piled onto his plate. "You want a beer?" He asked, setting an open one down for me. I shook my head no. "Suit yourself." He used his t-shirt to twist off the cap of his own beer.

In the time it took him to finish his plate and go back for seconds, I'd barely gotten half a piece down. He looked at my plate with slight concern.

"I ate before I came. Sorry." I tried to lie convincingly. "It's hard to get through that evening class without dinner."

Isaac nodded, clearly trying to decide if he believed me. "No worries. My roommate and I will probably finish all that off by tomorrow anyway." Finishing his seconds in record time, Isaac wiped his hands on his jeans and asked, "You want to watch a movie?"

"Sure." I nodded in agreement. That was what he'd invited me over to do in the first place, so might as well.

We picked a new release, and he sat at one end of the couch and I sat at the other. "You avoiding me?" He asked flirtatiously, and I didn't know what to say. Kinda yes. His arm was draped over the back of the couch, and he waved me over. "Get in here."

"I don't know." I said uneasily. Maybe I hadn't fully thought it through, coming here, evaluating what his intentions were. I mean, I didn't *really* know the guy.

"You look so damn sad all the time, a little cuddling isn't going to kill you," he argued and patted the couch next to him. "Might even be good for you." Maybe he was right though, maybe a little human contact wouldn't be so bad. I moved to the other side of the couch to sit next to him, leaving an inch of room between us so we weren't touching. He chuckled, and he spread his legs wider, so we were *just* touching, and I supposed I was okay with that. "I'm here when you're ready." He winked, arm wide open, waiting for me.

As the movie progressed, I let him move a little closer, and I eventually did snuggle into Isaac's side. I was a little tense, but man, it felt good when he dropped that arm around my waist and pulled me in a little closer.

I couldn't remember the last time I'd been hugged, let alone held. Except that I did know. It had been months, but Carter had been the last person I'd snuggled up with. Kinda. Clearly, Carter was over whatever weird thing we'd rekindled—since he'd completely ghosted me.

As Isaac pulled me closer, I tried not to think about Carter at all. I didn't realize how badly I'd needed it. Human contact. So in a moment of self-preservation, I decided to stop being so hard on myself for once and just enjoy this for what it was. Comforting.

Halfway through the movie, I glanced over at Isaac and realized he'd been looking at me, probably for a while. I quickly looked back at the TV.

Shit. Every girl knew what that meant.

"You ignoring me?" His voice was low.

"Huh?" I played dumb, trying my hardest to look super focused on the movie.

His thumb stroked my side. "I'm really attracted to you, you know." I blew out a shaky breath, hating how good his touch felt.

Time to pump the brakes. "Isaac, we're friends, right?" I asked as he shifted closer.

"Yeah, of course we're friends." He licked his lips. "We could be friends with *benefits* if you want." Damn. At least he was direct.

"I don't really do that." I explained.

"Why not?" He asked, no judgment in his voice, only a simple question, but I couldn't come up with an answer. Maybe there had never been anyone who fit the criteria I'd need to make that type of situation work. I honestly had no idea.

Isaac's voice dropped a bit lower, his thumb moving up to the sensitive place on my ribcage as he continued stroking, waking me up in all kinds of ways. Damn, being wanted, being touched. It felt good. "I could make you feel better, you know." He sounded sincere as I searched his face.

Maybe I *should* change it up. Maybe I *should* do something different. Maybe this was *exactly* what I needed. Maybe this was a version of letting go. Of more things than one, for that matter.

Slowly, he leaned forward, and I didn't pull away, letting my eyes fall shut when his lips met mine.

It was nice. He was a decent kisser, he smelled really good, he was an attractive guy—this could be good for me, I decided.

Slowly, he pushed me back onto the couch, not breaking the kiss. With his body hovering over mine, his kissing turned more urgent, more dominant.

"Isaac." I murmured, turning my head towards the TV to break away.

"I've been dying to kiss you since the first time I saw you." He rasped, and with my lips out of reach, he moved down my jaw to my throat.

"Isaac." I said again, and his mouth crushed against mine, silencing me, the kissing deeper, too intense.

He was moving so fucking fast. I lifted my chin, forcing his lips off mine. "Slower. I need to go slower." I put my hand on his chest, pushing him back.

He nodded intently. "Of course. Yeah, no problem." He kissed me more slowly, and I relaxed slightly, threading my arms around his neck. "We'll go as slow as you want."

Not ten seconds later, his hands slid up underneath my shirt and I pushed them back down mid kiss, but a moment later he tried yet again, and with his body pressed against mine, pinning me against the couch, tongue sliding aggressively down my throat. All take and no give—*panic seized me.*

"This is too much." I gasped into his mouth, pushing against him. "I need to sit up."

"I know, right." He murmured, hands everywhere, ignoring my request.

I pushed him back, but he was much bigger than me, and he didn't budge. Not even a little. In that moment, everything flipped in an instant. "Isaac, stop." My voice came out so incredibly paper-thin.

"What's the matter? You shy?" He was on the second button of my sweater already.

"Stop!" I shoved against him as hard as I could. "Stop it. I can't do this." I quickly shimmied out from under him *while I still could.*

He sat back on the couch, irritated. "What's the matter? I thought we were having a good time."

"Yeah, well, you thought wrong." I held back the tears as my body quivered with adrenaline.

He shrugged. "I'd settle for a blowjob at least."

"What the fuck is wrong with you?" I cried.

"Geez." He stood up, walking towards me as I backed away. "Sara, at least finish the movie." He motioned to the couch. "Come on, you're acting like I'm not a nice guy."

"You aren't a nice guy!" I screeched incredulously. "*Nice* guys don't pull *that* kind of shit." God, I could have slapped him for that statement alone, but I buttoned my sweater back up, tears finally falling, and as I sprinted for the door, that's when I noticed *a camera* in the corner of the room.

I looked back at Isaac in horror as he pulled something out of his pocket and took another step in my direction with a look in his eyes that made my blood run cold. I sprinted out the door, making a panicked mad dash for my car.

Peeling out of the parking lot with a screech, I watched Isaac's silhouette disappear in my rearview mirror as my stomach churned.

I drove several blocks away and finally parked somewhere random before completely breaking down. I'd been so fucking stupid to trust him—I had spent the last few weeks letting this asshole in, letting him work my emotional walls down, when he only had one fucking goal in mind. Fuck the sad girl and make a quick buck.

I'd spent what little energy I had left on him, and it was such a waste. I felt used, defeated, tricked, stupid, and most of all, I felt so fucking sad.

In that moment, I knew it was time to return the calls and texts I'd been ignoring. Paying attention to what had been right in front of me had been the weaker, easier move.

There was one person I was desperate to hear from, but he clearly didn't feel the same, so I would let that one go.

Picking up the phone, I did what I should have done weeks ago. I turned to someone I knew I could always count on.

I called Sloane. "I need you."

"I'm there." She said without raising a single question. "Packing a bag right now."

CHAPTER 22
That's Where I Draw the Line

SARAFINA

Sloane grunted, attempting to pry the lid off my stubborn bucket of paint, muttering to herself when she broke a nail. As she cracked the paint bucket open, I realized this was the farthest I'd ever gotten. In all these weeks, I'd never even opened the damn lid.

She grunted victoriously and then we both stood over the bucket, peering into its inky darkness, as if it held some kind of magical dark power. An ominous black hole ready to consume the entirety of my art studio. I wanted to climb right in and sink to the bottom.

"You could just dump it onto the canvas." Sloane offered indifferently, still staring into the depths of my uncompromising assignment.

"That feels like cheating." I countered. I had to do something of meaning with it. Otherwise, what was the point?

She sighed. "You're making things harder on yourself than you need to."

"I'm not making anything hard, it just *is* hard." I snapped and then immediately covered my face with my hands and groaned. "I'm sorry." This wasn't like me, but I was so edgy all the time, and I didn't know how to make it stop.

"Don't be sorry. You have absolutely nothing to be sorry

about. You need to yell, shout, break shit—do it. I'm not going anywhere, Sara." She raised a perfectly waxed brow, promising, "I can take it. You can't get rid of me that easily."

I think a part of me knew I needed Sloane's thick skin, and I realized that out of everyone, that's why I'd called *her*. She could handle me being an asshole, and we'd still be fine.

When I pulled my hands down from my face, Sloane was staring at me, and my skin prickled as I saw her make a decision in her eyes. What exactly she'd decided in that moment, I didn't know, but I immediately went on defense. I suddenly wished I would have called Jules, because not only could Sloane take shit, she could give it too, and I could tell she was just about to fling some right at me. I was about to get a love filled, ass kicking. *Fuck.*

"Do it, Sara. Dip the brush in and make a stroke on the canvas." She instructed me firmly.

I scratched my neck. It wasn't even remotely that simple. "I have to plan, I need to sketch, back paint, prep the canvas."

"That is not the point of this, and you know it." She said. "Just put the paintbrush on the canvas. Just one tiny little stroke."

"I can't."

"You can." She implored, and I couldn't breathe as *I shook my head no, suddenly regretting calling her.* "You're a brilliant artist, Sara. Fucking brilliant. Your mother would want you to keep going." She pushed harder, and the walls started closing in, and I knew what was coming. I was going to have another panic attack. "Your mother would want—"

"Well, she's not here, is she?" I shouted desperately, fighting the cascade of bodily responses that were taking over. *Fuckerson, it was happening again.*

"How much weight have you lost?" Sloane's voice was calm, and there was love in her tone but also brutal, stark accountability.

I dropped my gaze, heart racing so fast I felt like I could puke. "I don't know."

"How much weight, Sara?"

"I don't have a scale." I knew the number.

Sloane's expression turned both compassionate and terrifying. "You are skin and bones. You are literally starving yourself, and if you keep it up, you're going to kill yourself. Like actually." Tears welled up in my eyes as she asked more softly. "Is that what you want? To die?" I honestly didn't know the answer to that question. I was just so fucking tired, wanted it all to stop. Wished I could tap out for just a minute, just to catch my breath. She didn't move, and I didn't move. An invisible string held us exactly where we were. "You have so many people who love you so desperately; all you have to do is *let* them love you."

"I'm alone." My lower lip quivered.

"You're not."

"I am." I trembled. "You don't understand. How could you?"

"You're right. I don't understand what you're going through, but I'm here for you anyway. You have Liam, Jules, Ariana." Sloane laughed. "You have *Cade* and Theo, you have your father, your cousins." And then she added knowingly. "You have *Carter.*"

"Carter hasn't texted me in over a month." I snapped before I could think better.

"Yes, he has." She argued, brow arching with skepticism.

"What?"

"Sara, he texts you every day. Texts me, asking if *I've* heard from you. He's worried, and he cares about you so freaking much. Why are you ignoring his calls again? I thought you two made up?"

"I never got a single call." I countered quietly, feeling dizzy.

She thought for a moment. "I don't know. He got a new phone, but he's been calling and texting you. Every single day, Sara."

I stared into the paint.

"Choose to live, Sara. Not this shell of a human being, not this strange commitment you have to your own suffering. Choose to live."

"I am," I said defensively. "Every day, I drag myself out of my bed when I just want to lay there and rot."

"And I'm so damn proud of you for that, but it's not enough. You *have* to do this. You *have* to put this paint on the canvas." She hesitated. "Not for your mother. For *you*. This is *your* big, beautiful life, Sara, and it's the only one you get."

My lower lip trembled, but everything else was frozen.

"Fine, if you won't do it, I will." Sloane grabbed a random paintbrush and headed for the bucket of paint.

"No!" I screamed, lunging to rip the brush out of her hands. "I can't do it, okay? I can't fucking do it! I can't live in a world where my mother doesn't exist—I can't try to make beautiful things when she's dead. She's fucking dead, and there's nothing I can do about it." I sobbed.

Sloane crushed me in a hug, refusing to let go of me when I struggled. Her voice was softer and more gentle in my ear. "Then don't make beautiful things. Make ugly things, make sad things, make compelling things, but make something, anything at all, because *anything* is better than *this*." She squeezed me tighter. "Don't die with her, Sara. You lost your mother, and I feel like I'm losing my best friend." She cleared her throat. "I know this is selfish, but *I* need you. If you won't do it for yourself or for your mother—maybe you could do it for me? I'm begging you to try." We sank to the floor, and she held me while I sobbed. Ugly, dirty, raw vulnerability, the kind that would push most people away. But she hugged me through it all and didn't let go.

When my crying had slowed, I felt the long handle of a paintbrush as she pushed it into my hand. "I can't." I cried.

"You can." She was crying too. "I know you can."

"I don't know how to do this. I'll *never* be able to make anything beautiful again."

"Then make grief art, make hate art, make something, anything, just to remind yourself that you're fucking alive." She gripped my hand and gently pushed the brush into the bucket, even as my hand trembled. "You're alive, Sara, whether you like it or not, you're still here. So let go of the past and choose to live. Otherwise, you might as well have died with her." Sloane let go of my hand with a tremor in her own voice. "But I'm so glad you didn't."

I sobbed as I moved the brush over the canvas, letting big imperfect globs drop onto it, and then I lowered my hand and made a line. One single line. The feel of the brush against the canvas, scratching an itch I'd long forgotten about.

I stared at that black line for what felt like an eternity, and then I screamed. I kept screaming as I threw the paintbrush across the room and plunged my hands into the paint, scooping, and dumping, and heaving it onto the canvas with my bare hands. Smearing the paint *violently,* until the canvas was completely black, until I was covered up to my elbows, my clothes ruined, my hair matted.

Breathless, I narrowed in on the colorful paintings stacked against the wall. *I fucking hated them.* Had fantasized about destroying them for months now.

I hadn't known shit when I'd created those joyful, happy, colorful paintings. I'd been an ignorant rainbows and butterflies child that didn't know a damn thing about the world. About real pain. About grief. I'd been naïve, and stupid, and ignorant, and those paintings deserved to burn, right alongside my old life. I wanted my old art to disappear into the ether, never to exist again, and I decided maybe that was okay, maybe that was what I *had* to do. The thing I'd been guiltily considering this whole time. I had to burn something to the ground before the despair inside me consumed me first.

Throat raw from screaming, I didn't say a word as I grabbed that first canvas and dragged it across the studio, already my black handprint ruining the corner.

I threw it onto the floor and lifted that heavy-ass paint bucket, because even if I was struggling, I *was* stronger after carrying it around all these weeks. I poured the entirety of it out onto that massive canvas and ruined it, one palmful of cheap black paint at a time.

When I was done with that one, I grabbed another, and another—sliding the pool of paint from one canvas to the next, scooping it off the floor, making it stretch as far as it would, until nearly all the pieces were ruined. Some were completely covered, some just a single angry slash when I'd lost interest and moved on to the next one.

So entranced in the task at hand, I'd almost forgotten Sloane was in the room with me. When I finally looked up, transported back from wherever it was I'd gone, she gently called my name, saying, "It's empty. You did it."

A strange sort of quiet settled over me as I put the lid back on the bucket and picked it up. I don't know why I was surprised when it was light in my hands, but I was.

So fucking light, like—*a weight had been lifted.*

I swung the bucket in a wide circle over my head and then threw my head back and laughed. Actually laughed. Sloane chuckled quietly, and then we looked at each other and broke into hysterical, maniacal laughter.

I placed a hand on my belly, gathering myself, and still, she didn't say anything. She just waited. Let me have my moment.

"Let's go turn in my assignment." I panted, and Sloane walked with me, a quiet reassuring presence, while we crossed through the buildings with me covered head to toe in paint.

Isaac looked surprised from across the walkway, and I didn't say a word to him, nor did I say a word to anyone else that stopped and stared.

Sloane opened the door for me as we stepped into Professor Alden's office, and my professor looked up, a split second of surprise on her face, before she smiled wide and proud. "You did it."

"I did it." I breathed as she simply pointed to her trash can. "Throw it away?" I asked in disbelief, half wanting to keep the bucket for some strange reason I couldn't quite explain.

"You don't need it anymore." She sat back in her chair and crossed her arms. "It served its purpose."

"What if I'm not ready to be done with it?" I gaped. I couldn't just get rid of it, not after everything. It just felt wrong.

"Then I'd say it sounds like you have a new series in mind." She went back to grading the papers on her desk. "Best get to it if you're going to submit in time for the exhibition at Basecoat Gallery." I stood there not knowing what to say, but Professor Alden didn't look up once after that.

I walked back to my studio dumbfounded. Professor Alden was right. I think I did have an idea. The need to create, to translate everything I'd been feeling all these months onto a canvas, had exploded out of me, and now there was no putting the dark, twisted thing back in the box.

The next morning, Sloane and I cried and said our goodbyes, and then I went to work gathering supplies. As I stared at the gallons upon gallons of clear wax and stacks of multicolored embroidery thread, I knew full well that I was going to regret my bright idea by the time I was finished.

But I'd done it. I'd used the paint, and it had all started with a simple line. *And a damn good friend.*

The grief was still there, but Professor Alden was right about another thing. I felt the tiniest bit lighter.

But I still had one more thing to do.

Sloane had already shared Carter's new contact card with me, and with trembling fingers, I opened up a new text thread and composed a message.

> Hey, heard you got a new number

A mere minute passed before I got a response.

> CARTER
>
> Hey sweet girl, where you been?!

Sloane and I figured out that I had a random setting turned on, blocking unknown numbers

Ahh that makes much sense

After the funeral, I was getting too many messages from random people

I forgot I had that setting turned on

Totally get that

People mean well, but it gets to be a lot

Glad I made the cut

I hesitated before admitting the next bit.

I thought after that phone call... that I had pushed you away.

I'm really sorry about that btw I didn't mean to call you in the middle of a workday and dump all my problems on you

The phone rang immediately, and I reluctantly answered it.

"Sara," Carter said, scolding and gentle all at once.

"Yes?" I bit back a wince.

"Please tell me you don't really think that."

"I don't know." I shrugged nervously. "I just—I know it was a lot. I was too emotional, and when I didn't hear from you—I just thought maybe it was too much for you." *That I was too much for you.*

"You're never too much for me."

I felt like I could burst into tears from the relief, but I shoved it down rather than repeat our last phone call as I cleared my throat. "So why'd you get a new number, anyway?"

He sighed. "That... is a long story."

"I have time." I waited with bated breath, unsure how he would respond.

He hesitated for a long beat. "Someone actually stole my phone."

"You're going to have to give me more details than that, *Mr. It's a long story.*"

"Yeah, uh." I could hear the hesitation in his voice. "My place was robbed."

My pulse spiked. "Carter! What happened? Are you okay?"

"Yeah, no, I'm fine now. I'm just sorry about the timing." He chuckled, but I wished I could see his face. The feeling that there was something between his words that he wasn't saying made me anxious. "I wanted to call you that night after work and see if you were okay." He admitted with a long sigh. "But alas, no phone."

"I'm just glad you're okay." I murmured. "What happened?"

"Oh, it's not a big deal." He said casually. "There have been some thefts at the apartments around the base."

"That's surprising."

"Just some smash and grabs." He assured me. "I accidentally left my phone in my car."

"Oh, it was your car?" I asked, feeling slightly relieved. "I thought you meant your house."

"Really, I'm fine." He chuckled. "It's *you* I'm worried about."

"Sloane came by this weekend." I started slowly.

"I heard." He admitted, and I groaned. "All good things." He assured me. "You painted again."

"Yeah," I murmured, wondering what exactly she'd told him.

I could hear the smile in his voice. "I'm so proud of you."

"Thanks." I smiled into the phone, far too wide, feeling grateful he couldn't see my expression now.

There was an awkward silence as I wandered into the bathroom and turned the phone on speaker. "Are you brushing your teeth?" Carter laughed.

"Yeah, I'm getting ready for bed." I mumbled through a mouthful of toothpaste.

"Getting ready for bed, huh?" His voice lowered, but I could hear the mischievous smile that was definitely on his face. "*What are you wearing?*"

"Carter!" I pulled my toothbrush out of my mouth, scolding him with a grin of my own.

His laughter was deep, warm, and comforting as it leaked through the phone. I could almost feel it wrapping around me like a warm embrace. "Can't blame a guy for trying."

I spit into the sink and threw my toothbrush into the drawer. "Shouldn't you be doing the same?" I accused.

"I'm already in bed." He teased. "You going to think of me tonight?"

"Maybe I will." I teased back, feeling lighter than I had in months.

He was quiet for a moment, and my pulse spiked at the pregnant pause, waiting to see what he would say next. "Maybe I'll think of you too." He said, his voice low, gravelly.

"Yeah?" I breathed as a tendril of desire wandered over my skin like a caress.

"Yeah," he admitted, and then I could sense the playful jab coming before he even said it. "I'm going to think about how you looked on your birthday, after you got your protein shakes." I groaned at the memory. "And wonder why you're so damn cute, even when you're more pissed off than a rabid badger."

"Hey!" I said with mock offense, even though I was now grinning from ear to ear. "You admitted it yourself. Those shakes were disgusting."

"Speaking of, have you been drinking your very nutritious, very delicious shakes?"

"Yes," I answered before even realizing it was a lie.

"Sarafina, you pretty girl, are you telling me the truth?" He asked flirtatiously, but I realized he *knew* I was lying.

Whoopsie! "Who wants to know?"

"Someone who cares about you very much." He was teasing, but it was still nice to hear.

I snuggled into the sheets, and suddenly it was hours later, and I'd been asleep. The call was still connected and quiet on Carter's end, so I left it running and drifted off into a peaceful sleep for the first time in months.

CHAPTER 23

Who Left a Dildo in My Bed

CARTER

Inside the Rosewood Athletic Club, I dribbled the basketball across the court and passed it to Liam before gingerly rolling my shoulder to test my mobility. I was still a little sore, but thankfully I'd avoided surgery after my shoulder dislocation, and the doctors seemed pleased with my overall recovery. I'd taken brutal beatings before, but with the dangerous cocktail of drugs I'd been given, I'd spent several days in and out of consciousness while the doctors worked to clear my system. When I finally left the hospital several days later, it was with terrible tinnitus due to a ruptured eardrum and a sore, somewhat useless arm.

Now, I was almost finished with my medical grounding, and while I didn't mind the break from the tactical missions, it absolutely sucked not being able to fly. The last few months had been frustrating, to say the least, but there was, however, one thing I looked forward to these days.

My long phone calls with Sara.

Some nights, we talked about absolutely nothing, and other nights, I could feel Sara's walls slowly coming down as she trusted me with more and more. The crazy thing was, I found myself doing the same. Our late night talks had become a lifeline during my recovery, because when we weren't falling asleep on either end of the phone, my mind was swirling with theories that made my stomach churn, wondering what kind of organization would hunt me—with no fear of retribution.

The problem was *I already knew the answer.*

The kind of organization that my father had been in business with. The kind of organization that could possibly influence and infiltrate even the most prestigious government organizations. The kind of organization that could very likely be behind—

"Damon, pass the ball." Rowan Belacourte shouted from across the court, shaking me out of my thoughts. Liam stole the ball out from under Damon Kingsley before he could pass it.

"Nice try." Rowan intercepted the ball from Liam and took his shot. The net swished a moment later. Rowan, was the oldest Belacourte, and was about as ruthless on the court as he was in the boardroom.

I grabbed the ball and headed back down the court. I was trying to take it easy on my healing shoulder, and I was. Mostly. Which meant Liam and I were currently losing by a mile.

"Let's go, Kensington." Liam shouted at me in frustration.

"Dude, he's injured." Rowan rolled his eyes at Liam as he attempted to steal the ball from me anyway, but I quickly dodged around him and passed it back to Liam, not wanting to strain my shoulder any more than this game already was. I had to get back to work ASAP, and I wasn't going to fuck that up over a pickup game, no matter how important Liam was currently convinced it was.

Liam took the ball the rest of the way down the court, and the net swished as the ball went in.

"That's game." Damon panted, half folded over, hands on his knees while sweat poured off him.

I shook my hair out, a spray of sweat flying off me. It felt good to get some exercise. Slowing down had absolutely wrecked me these last few months.

The gym doors opened a moment later and Eva, Rowan's

other half, came into the gym looking like she was about to pop as she neared the last weeks of her pregnancy.

"How's she doing?" Damon asked Rowan, watching Eva slowly waddle over—she stopped to talk to someone in the bleachers.

Rowan shook his head, a wary look passing over his face. "She's hanging in there, baby's healthy, Eva's healthy. That's all I can ask for."

I raised a brow, and Liam shook his head and shrugged. "No idea."

Rowan jogged over to Eva, giving her a sweaty peck on the lips that made her turn her nose up while he grinned.

Damon pulled his shirt over his head and wrung it out. "How long you home for?"

"Just this weekend." I crushed an entire bottle of water, wishing it were still cold.

"Damn, I was hoping to connect you with one of my contacts."

"You know I'm not coming back." I countered.

"Don't bullshit me." Damon panted, "I know you've got one foot in, one foot out."

"Dame." I groaned. "Seriously? Not you too."

He shrugged, "You've gotta stop running sometime."

"I'm not running." I headed towards my bag on the bleachers.

"Sure you're not." Damon said, walking backwards towards the gym doors. "I'll see you later. I've got an investor meeting, but it's really good to have you home. Let's do this again."

Damon Kingsley, Theo's older cousin, had been a family friend for years, and he'd been another one of those key people to come through for me after my parents had died. I considered his words. The only problem was, Damon had no idea what I was dealing with because the Kingsleys were *new money*. He wasn't from my world, where things were run more quiet and powerful, where there were decade-old agreements practically drawn up in blood. He didn't know how deep the old-money conflicts ran. It was a fucking nightmare. One I intended to avoid at all costs.

"I'm going to head back and shower." I told Liam. "Meet you for lunch?"

"Yeah... see you there." He grumbled and didn't look up.

I paused. "What's up?" He looked up at the ceiling in exasperation, phone in hand, and I caught Gina's name on his text screen. "Everything going okay with the Mrs?" I asked.

"Not exactly."

"Want to talk about it?" I stretched my shoulder, rotating it in a slow, wide circle.

"I don't know if there's going to be anything to talk about soon." A wary look passed over his expression.

"What's going on?" I asked genuinely concerned. They'd been on the road to marriage for sometime now, though I supposed if he hadn't popped the question, maybe there was a good reason for it.

His phone rang, and Gina's contact card popped up. "I've gotta take this," Liam shot me an apologetic look.

"Do your thing. See you at lunch."

At the lounge inside the Vandenbergh Hotel, I dug into my usual Cobb salad with extra steak and extra shrimp, all while my heart broke for my best friend—because Liam looked so defeated, so hopeless, as he explained that him and Gina were on the verge of breaking up. He was already on his third drink, words growing less articulated by the minute, as he desperately struggled not to fall apart.

"I don't know, I feel like I'm slowly losing her. *She's* busy with work, *I'm* busy with work, and the long distance is taking its toll —it was just supposed to be temporary, but it's not. We started down two separate paths without even realizing it, and I have no idea how the hell to find my way back."

"Maybe you've both grown into different people." I said quietly. "A lot has changed for you both since college."

"Maybe, *but we're great together.*" Liam pushed the food around on his plate, voice nearly breaking. "It wasn't supposed to be like this—we were supposed to—I was gonna—" He shook his head and threw his fork down in disgust. "I was waiting until she moved back, because that's what we'd discussed, but now she's not moving back, and I've had *this* fucking thing sitting in my sock drawer for *three years*." He reached into the pocket of his suit jacket, and my shoulders sagged as he softly set *a ring box* on the table.

I stared at that little velvet box, knowing whatever laid inside was a sparkly representation of Liam's hopes and dreams.

Liam pinched the bridge of his nose as his voice caught. "It doesn't even matter. I can't give her what she wants—what she *needs*, and at the end of the day, I just want her to be happy. Even if that doesn't include me anymore." He sighed heavily, eyes shuttered. "*But I waited because she asked me to.*"

"I'm so sorry, Liam." I murmured.

He loosed a heavy breath, jaw flexing for a long moment before he finally murmured, "I'm sorry, we don't have to talk about this anymore."

I desperately wished there was something I could do for him, but there wasn't. "Don't be sorry, I wish you would have talked to me about this sooner, especially after the year you've had. How are you doing with all that?" I asked cautiously, knowing there was never a good time to bring these things up.

"It fucking sucks. I can hardly sleep. My father is God knows where these days. Work is a fucking nightmare. I've hardly had time to slow down and process everything." He huffed a heavy sigh. "It's just been one thing after another, but I'm hanging in there, really I am. It's Sara I'm worried about. She's back at school, and I hardly ever hear from her—after what happened in the spring, I'm just worried about her all the damn time."

I shook my head knowing he was right, Sara was an expert at

keeping everyone at arm's length, and she'd only *barely* started opening up to me again—even in the midst of his heartbreak, Liam was still taking care of everyone else, but I sensed he was changing the subject, so I let him.

"Have you seen her lately?" I asked casually, trying my best to keep my tone even. "Sara?"

"No, but she'll be in town on Sunday."

"Any reason in particular?" I quickly realized he had no idea about her art show tomorrow, and in light of everything, that fucking sucked. "It's not winter break yet."

He shrugged. "Same as you and me, I guess. Sometimes you just need to be home."

Shit, why hadn't Sara told him about her exhibition? The only reason *I* knew was because Sloane had texted me, and thank God she had. It was Sara's first completed series since losing her mother, and her first ever gallery showing. It was a huge accomplishment, and I was extremely proud of her for it.

I stabbed at a piece of steak, wondering if I should say something to Liam, because *I knew* he'd want to be there for her, but the last thing I wanted was to betray Sara's trust. Not to mention Liam would be hurt if it came from me anyway. *What a mess.*

I hoped maybe she was planning to tell him when she got here, but I honestly doubted it. So I bit my tongue and said nothing, knowing *I* was already showing up uninvited. There was a good chance that was going to blow up in my face anyway.

After lunch, I drove home, dropping Liam off at his family manor, and we ended up playing video games until the early hours of the morning. The more we talked, I could tell Liam was still holding on for dear life, even though his relationship was clearly at an end. I knew the timing of this impending breakup couldn't have come at a worse time for him. Losing his mom, working on his restaurant on top of his other responsibilities, attempting to maintain a long distance relationship, it was a lot by anyone's standards.

"I'm just gonna sleep down here." Liam said, half asleep on the couch already, and I realized that was his way of saying goodnight. It'd taken all night, but he'd basically polished off the entire fifth of whisky by himself. Now the empty bottle was shoved between the couch cushions next to him, as he slung an arm over his eyes, hiding the damp on his cheeks.

"You know where to find me if you need anything." I sighed, getting my stuff together. As I headed towards the entry, I realized the house looked a little empty. "Hey, where is all the furniture? All the paintings?" I asked, poking my head back into the living room.

"That is a great fucking question." Liam scoffed, but didn't open his eyes. "You should see upstairs." *Odd.*

I hummed a nod, chewing on that for a minute. "Alright, well, I'll see you later."

Liam waved a hand, eyes still closed, and I wandered through the corridor and let myself out the front door, locking it behind me.

On the short walk over to my estate, I mulled over how empty the Devereux manor had felt, hollow, like the life itself had been sucked right out of it. Kinda felt like my family manor. Devoid of life.

It was drizzling outside when the sound of a car engine coming up the wide street made me look over my shoulder. I watched as Brad Devereux slowly crept into the courtyard and then parked diagonally, halfway across the lawn of the estate. He didn't even bother pulling around to the garage—just parked right on top of the landscaping, and then I realized why. He stumbled out of the car, clothes rumpled and wandered back to the garage entrance on foot.

He was drunk. Plastered, by the looks of it. *Damn it.*

No wonder Sara and Liam were having such a hard time.

They'd lost their mother, and their father was pulling this shit. Lost in his own grief, no doubt.

My shoes crunched over the crushed stone as I crossed through the moonlit courtyard. Liam and Sara had lost their mom, and I'd lost... I didn't even know what I'd lost. Charlotte had been the only motherly figure I'd had left after my own mother had died. If Charlotte hadn't stepped up, I honestly didn't know where I'd be. There were lots of people I was grateful for but she'd kept my freezer stocked with lasagna for four years straight, and in the early years she'd even taught me how to drive —refused to let my hired driver be the one to help me get my practice hours. The memory made me smile, she was the reason the three of us had a lead foot. Her words echoed in my mind, *if you're going to drive fast, then you'd better know what the hell you're doing.*

That night at Thanksgiving, I felt like Charlotte had known how I felt about Sara—but now, I'd never know for sure, and wondering about it was pointless. She was gone, and there was no bringing her back.

For me, this was par for the course though. Just when it felt like I was getting my feet back underneath me, figuring out how to do life, everything would always shift. Again. Maybe that's what life was, always adapting. I didn't know. I craved the mundane while simultaneously craving anything but.

I let myself inside the manor, and my footsteps echoed on the marble as I crossed through the formal entryway to climb the sweeping staircase towards the living quarters. I didn't take a second look as I passed my parents' wing of the house. It'd been closed off for years now, and I knew what I'd see, canvas covered furniture and depressing, empty space. Trudging down my wing of the house, it felt awfully dark, and I did a double take as I passed a narrow table in the hallway, swearing there used to be a lamp on it. But maybe not. I shook my head, lost in my thoughts, but when I finally stepped into my bedroom, I went on high alert, realizing immediately that something felt off.

I'd showered after I'd gotten home from the Rosewood Athletic Club, but I'd been in a rush. Now, standing at the threshold of my bedroom, I was starkly aware that someone had been in here.

My pulse spiked, senses sharpened, wondering if this was some sort of trap. The Society had been the one to lure me home after all.

My eyes fell to my bed across the room, noticing it was slightly mussed, as if someone had slept there. I cautiously approached, and as I pulled back the rumpled sheets, I half expected to find a poisonous snake, but that's not what I found at all.

I stood there dumbfounded.

There was a fucking dildo in my bed. I looked around the room, utterly perplexed as I found everything else perfectly in place. The fuck? I shook my head, realizing it had to be a prank. Liam probably, though when he'd had the time, I had no idea. I snapped a picture of it and texted it to him.

> Haha very funny.

LIAM

> Listen, I'm all for sexting, but I typically prefer it to be with the person I'm fucking.

> This wasn't you????

> Not a chance in hell.

> Let me know when you figure it out

> Fucking hilarious.

> I wouldn't touch if I were you. Might have been used.

I scratched my head as I stared at the massive rubber dick in my bed, wondering who the fuck had put it there. It was pink, sparkly, and veiny. I shook my head, and fished the thing out of my sheets with a tissue before heading to the ensuite for a shower. I'd solve this mystery tomorrow, when I wasn't deliriously exhausted.

Soon, the bathroom was filled with steam, and my hands were braced against the stone wall as I stood under the rainfall shower, letting the scalding droplets pelt over my back. I was basically sleeping standing up, but as I stood under the hot water, I could have sworn I heard something downstairs. I brushed it off, wondering if I was imagining things in my exhaustion.

A minute later, there was a much closer *thump*.

I quickly shut the water off and listened—there was no doubt in my mind now. Someone was in the house, and they were already upstairs by the sound of it.

My heart thundered in my chest, knowing my gun was in the safe.

Another *thump. In the bedroom.*

Shit.

They'd put me in the hospital, and this time, I was sending someone to the morgue. With nothing but my bare fists and determination, I charged into the bedroom, adrenaline pumping through me like a freight train.

I stopped dead in my tracks when I saw my attacker—to my utter shock and confusion, the small intruder swaying in my bedroom doorway was none other than my darling Sara.

Her dripping wet hair clung to her rosy cheeks, and nestled in all that gorgeous thick hair was a pair of little black cat ears that sparkled as they caught the light.

My eyes flared as I took in the rest of her, soaked to the bone, wearing nothing but a sheer slip dress that clung to every forbidden curve that I knew—would lead me straight to salvation and then to hell.

Temptation didn't even begin to cover it. I was so completely and utterly *fucked*.

CHAPTER 24
The Unicorn Horn

SARAFINA

Three minutes earlier...

I punched in the door code a second time, and it beeped at me in warning. "Come on." I muttered, knowing full well it was user error as I squinted at the keypad in the darkness. "Please, please, please open." I tried again, my shoulders sagging in relief as the locking mechanism finally whirred and the keypad flashed green. *Thank God.*

I looked over my shoulder where my creepy Uber driver was still waiting, parked in the courtyard, and bolted inside the grand entry. The ornate door thundered as I slammed it shut, plunging me into eerie darkness as I promptly locked it, triple-checking that it was *definitely* locked, before I stumbled under the Kensington coat of arms and into the massive manor.

Fucking creep.

My footsteps echoed as I blindly made my way down the dimly lit corridor. I thought I was doing pretty well, until I crashed straight into a table, nearly knocking an antique vase off its surface in the process. Wide-eyed, I gripped the intricate ceramic piece, settling it back down on the tabletop. I didn't even want to know how much that thing was worth—probably a one-of-a-kind, gifted to some royal, somewhere at sometime. I peered into the darkness behind me with an uneasy shiver, feeling the shadows move as I quickly darted towards the stairs in the back.

I practically crawled up each slippery step. The deep green marble staircase blended with the shadows, making it next to impossible to see where one step ended and another began— where the carpet runner had suddenly gone, I had no idea. I made it to the top in what felt like three business days and then promptly ate it, realizing I was on the *second to last* step.

Still cursing at my throbbing shins, I braced a hand against the wall to steady myself. The carved wood was smooth and cool under my palm until I rounded the corner into the last narrow hallway, and my fingertips rippled over the embossed wallpaper— I gasped as I inadvertently knocked a priceless painting clean off the wall. Narrowly missing it falling on *me*, it fell to the unforgiving marble floor with a sickening crash. *Ahh!*

Hardly able to keep myself upright, I propped the painting up as carefully as I could, desperately hoping it wasn't damaged before I headed past the first five, widely spaced bedrooms to the only one that was made up.

I gripped the brass doorknob, wondering if I was going to vomit as the thick door swung open with my weight, but there was no time to figure out how I was going to cross the long distance to the bed, because just then, the door to the ensuite bathroom ripped open.

Murderer!

A growling blur came barreling through the sitting room, directly towards me.

No! Murdering bear!

I clutched my chest and screamed, waiting to be mauled to death. This was it. I'd escaped the creepy Uber driver only to become bear jerky. "Sara?" I was still screaming as a deep velvety voice sounded from across the room, coming closer. "What are you doing here?"

I cracked one eye open and then the other. "Carter?" I blinked slowly, registering the miles and miles of wet, sculpted chest in front of me. *Oh my.* The tanned muscles were coming closer by the second, and if I wasn't dizzy before, I certainly was now.

Carter was completely and utterly *naked.* Except for one thing. *A thin pink hair tie around his wrist.* Had he been wearing it since last Thanksgiving? That couldn't be right. I clearly wasn't thinking straight, but how could I—in front of me was the most astonishing thing I'd ever seen.

I grinned, wide-eyed, as I tracked a bead of water all the way down those sinfully sloped obliques, *straight to heaven's door,* watched that lucky little droplet dance over his muscular legs like an absolute tease before finally disappearing into the lush carpet.

Now *that* was a rare piece of art, a sculpture fit to display for one very lucky queen. *Might as well call me Your Highness, because giddy up, this knight had a horse all of his own, and I was ready to skip the carriage and ride him.*

"You're naked." I whispered, staring at *it* in all of its proud, hard glory. I blinked, wondering if I was seeing things, but no, it was *definitely* getting bigger by the second.

I swallowed hard and forced myself to avert my eyes from the incredible specimen in front of me, craning my neck up to meet Carter's gaze as he came even closer. My mouth formed and unformed words with no success, because there *were* no words. Nope. None. I'd seen him naked before, but not like this.

No, no, no. Not. Like. *This.*

"What are you doing here?" Carter looked as shocked as I felt. "I mean, I'm glad to see you and all, I just uh, what are you doing here?" He raked a hand through his wet hair, and I realized he'd grown it out again. Even wet, it had that effortless, old-money, *sexy can I,* look that made me want to rake *my* fingers through it. "It's the middle of the night. Are you okay? Are you hurt?" he asked, with nothing but pure concern in his voice.

I swayed in the doorway. "I was, uh, I just came over because..." How the hell was I going to explain this? I had no idea he'd even be home this weekend. I motioned towards the bed. "I was just sleeping here until—" I gasped!

My pink dildo was sitting *erect* on his nightstand, sparkling translucently under the lamplight in all its veiny glory, *an absolute atrocity* amidst the elegant decor of his bedroom.

When I looked back, Carter's gaze locked with mine, and we both realized the same thing at the same time. His eyes glimmered with wicked realization, and that was all I saw before I took a flying leap to apprehend—what would undoubtedly be—the source of my eternal shame.

"No!" I screamed, diving for the contraband.

Carter got there first, grabbing it out from under me with a wicked chuckle. He full-fisted it; his eyes darkening to a color I'd never seen before.

He grinned, looking back and forth between it and me. "What is sweet, little Sarafina Amara Devereux doing in *my* bedroom with *this*?" he asked, a cocky grin plastered across his face while the thing wobbled around in his massive hand, with total disregard for the situation.

I practically clawed my way up his sculpted chest, frantic to get that thing back, but it was no use. He yanked it higher, higher, higher, out of my reach. I was never going to live this down. I *had* to get it. I lunged, and the back of his legs hit the bed, sending us flying backwards onto his luxurious sheets. When we finally stopped moving, I gasped for an entirely different reason, realizing every inch of me was draped over the top of every inch of *him*.

Oh God.

Now, there was only one dick in this room I could think about because it was snugly nestled between my thighs, my short dress now conveniently bunched up around my waist.

Carter's eyes flared darkly, and heat surged through me as my stomach did *the* flippy thing. *Shit! Say something! Anything!* "I'm sorry." I whispered at the same moment his cock flexed against me and everything emptied out of my brain. "*Ohhh God.*"

Carter's hands flew to my hips, gripping them as he swore, grinding out, "You shouldn't make those kinds of sounds while you're sitting on my cock, sweetheart."

Palms on his chest, the heat of his body was deliciously warm against my damp skin. I wasn't wearing any underwear, and I knew if he so much as *flexed*, he'd slide right in. "Why is that?" I whispered with a hard swallow.

His Adam's apple bobbed, chest rising and falling rapidly as he gritted, "Because, if I had any less self-control, you'd be on your back right now, taking my cock like a good girl." Carter's voice dropped even lower, practically vibrating out of him and into me. "Keep making sounds like that and everything you were imagining while you were using your cute little unicorn horn in *my* bed," he trembled with restraint, his voice dark and raw. "Well, it wouldn't hold a candle to all the things *I'd* do to you, sweetheart. Is that enough of a reason?"

Oh God, was I even breathing? I sucked in a deep breath, remembering I needed air, and that was enough to shift us, forcing the tip of his head to graze across my *oh so very* slick clit. *Bah-zing-gah!*

Carter groaned gutturally, as if he were in pain, and I whimpered as heat flooded my whole body with throbbing, desperate need, all while I fought the dangerous urge to slip low enough to let it happen again. Carter's eyes flared as he gripped my hips with more strength than I'd ever felt in my life, *keeping me lifted*, and his every muscle rippled beneath me with the exertion. I realized I was digging my red lacquered nails into his chest, but I didn't dare move a fraction of an inch.

What I said next was the alcohol speaking, surely, because I was never this bold. "Tell me why I shouldn't *let* you do all those dirty things to me." I whispered, *desperate* for him to brush against me just once more. At least. Ten times ten would do nicely too. With a nice hard—

"Don't ask questions I know you already know the answer to." He rasped, every vein in his arms flexing as he gripped me, *determined* to keep me from sinking down onto the one thing that I *desperately* wanted him to skewer me with.

I searched his eyes, feeling confused—he was hard as a rock

underneath me, there was no denying it, but I swallowed thickly, suddenly realizing that maybe this was *just* a physical response for him. I mean, I didn't blame him, I too was having a *very* physical response.

"I should put some clothes on." He said tightly.

Yes, I nodded, *only* a physical response. I was literally sitting on his hard cock, offering myself to him, and he was trying to politely tell me what he always had. That this was never going to happen. I tried not to let the sting of rejection wash over me, but it did anyway. "Yeah, you should put some clothes on." I nodded emphatically, heart still racing a mile a minute. "Good thinking." I stared down at his body, realizing he really *was* like one of those ancient sculptures of a Roman warrior, and I couldn't help wondering if he fucked like o—

"You mind, uh, dismounting?" Carter was physically trembling, a pained look on his face.

Oh God, why was I still on top of him? "Of course." I breathed, my gaze snapping back up to his, and the look in his eyes made my heart pound even faster.

The room was a little topsy-turvy as I slid one leg over the throbbing stallion and rolled onto the bed in a breathless heap.

Carter quickly pulled on some thin gray sweatpants, *as if that was going to help the situation at all.* Even drunk as a skunk, I could see everything outlined, clear as day. And dear God, there was *a lot* to outline. Last time I'd seen it, it hadn't been *inflated.*

Carter sat at the edge of the bed, keeping a little distance between us, and we both stared at that damn dildo in the sheets and then back at each other. I was sure my cheeks were as red as they'd ever been.

Carter's smirk quickly disappeared as his eyes dragged over me with a look I couldn't decipher. "Can we talk about what the hell you're wearing?" He scrubbed a hand over his face. "Please tell me you didn't go out like that."

"What the hell is that supposed to mean?" I frowned, lying back on the bed.

His jaw flexed. "That's barely a scrap of fabric. I'd hardly even call that a dress."

"What would you call it, then?" I raised a brow and tried to ignore the pounding in my clit. I'd deal with that traitorous bitch later. As soon as I got my toy back, I'd schedule her in for a ruthless beating.

"Fair enough." He said roughly, "And these?" He reached out, making my breath catch, but he only tapped my sparkly cat ears. I'd forgotten I was even wearing them.

"Just something I picked up along the way." I said, eyes glued to his chest again. *Those abs*, you could probably climax just rocking over those abs, there were that many grooves.

He sat there for a long moment, broad chest rising and falling rapidly before he asked, "Who did you go out with, anyway? Are the girls home too?"

"Nobody."

"Seriously, who?" His tone was protective, and my vagina clamped around nothing. Sheesh, I was struggling out here.

"No, I literally went out alone." I shrugged, cataloging this moment away to use for later. Did that make me a bad person?

"You went out by yourself, looking like that?"

"Mhmm?"

"Christ, Sara." Carter muttered with a shake of his head. "It's a wonder you even made it here in one piece. You're plastered, you know that, right?" He turned serious. "You didn't drive, did you?"

Rude. I would *never* drive drunk, and he knew that. "Of course not. I had a creepy Uber driver take me home." I snapped, realizing my last jello shot was coming back for me with a vengeance.

Carter's warm brown eyes darkened to something lethal and sharp. "What?"

"Yeah, he was asking me all these questions. Do I have a boyfriend? Was this my house? Was I alone tonight?" I waved my arm around and quickly regretted it as a wave of nausea hit me hard. "He might even still be down there, because I couldn't get the door code to work at first, and he just sat there and watched me." I pressed my hand against my lips. I knew I should have skipped that last jello shot. Maybe the last three.

Don't puke, don't puke, don't puke.

Carters stood up abruptly, jostling the bed.

Oh God.

DO NOT PUKE IN HIS BED, SARAFINA.

"Don't move, I'll be right back." Carter stormed down the hall, the vein in his neck ready to pop.

I watched the gilded ceiling move in waves, wondering if I was going to pass out, as hours worth of drinking suddenly caught up with me all at once.

A few minutes later, Carter came back into the room, startling my eyes open. "Fucker was skulking around down there, looking into the windows." Carter fumed, shutting the door firmly.

"What did you do?" I asked halfheartedly. Carter was here, and I was safe now, so who the fuck cared what happened to the string bean with a mustache.

"I sent him packing." Carter paced the room, a strand of his hair falling over his face as he shook his head. When he finally stopped, he put his hands on his hips and just stared at me for a long minute, and the intense weight of his gaze was almost too much to bear. "I'll contact the company and deal with it tomorrow." He finally sighed, expression softening, as he raked a hand through his hair, pushing it back.

"What do you mean?" I asked, closing my eyes to slow the spin of the room. No, that was worse, definitely worse. That made it feel like I was careening down the Alice in Wonderland hole, towards hell itself. I opened my eyes again and tried to focus on Carter's face instead. Such a nice face.

"It means I'm going to take care of it." He said matter-of-factly.

His utterly pissed off, protective streak was kind of cute. I wondered if I'd ever seen him this upset, and damn if that didn't stir something in me. I squeezed my thighs together, wishing I could do something, anything, just to ease the throbbing between them. The ache was painful at this point.

Carter's gaze drifted down as if he could read my mind, as if he could tell I was slick as a horny little otter. Smooth too, I'd waxed.

"Do you have any clothes here?" He asked rather sharply.

I nodded to his dresser, covering my mouth as I burped quietly and prayed nothing else came up.

Carter chuckled, shaking his head. "Of course you unpacked." He opened the drawers one by one until he found the drawer I'd stashed all my stuff in. He dug around, jaw flexing for a moment before he silently continued looking. "How many days have you been here?" He asked quietly.

I sighed, twirling a strand of hair around my finger, relieved that the drunken feeling had finally peaked. The room was still spinning, but at least it didn't seem to be getting any worse now. "I don't know, maybe three."

"Sara." Carter looked over his shoulder.

"I don't need a lecture, okay." I snapped. "Nobody will just let me be sad. It's exhausting."

He shot me a long look, brows crunched with concern, and then went back to digging through my clothes. "I don't see any pajamas in here?"

"That's because I didn't bring any." I closed my eyes and admitted shyly. He wasn't supposed to be home! I was *obviously* going to change the sheets when I left.

Carter's gaze snapped up to mine, sharp and assessing. "*Fuck, Sara.*" He muttered. "Here, you can wear something of mine."

He opened a different drawer, grabbed a few things and approached the bed. "Come here, drunkie." He crooked his finger with an amused smile.

I sleepily crawled over to him on all fours, and he swallowed hard, taking a nearly imperceptible step back. Or maybe I imagined it. The room was still moving in waves.

"Here." He handed me the clothes and stared at me for a beat before finally turning around.

I struggled to peel off my wet dress, grunting as the clingy fabric rolled, catching around my shoulders.

"Sara, please." His tone was sharp.

"Huh?" I mumbled from inside my wet dress prison, my arms stuck above my head.

"Stop making those noises." He begged. "You're killing me."

"I'm not making *noises*." I gritted, finally wrenching the dress free and flinging it across the room. It landed on the floor with a wet plop.

I pulled on his old football t-shirt and the blue striped boxers he'd set out for me. It was kind of crazy, actually. I'd imagined wearing his number more than once in high school, and here I was about to sleep in it. Hehe!

When I was done changing, I couldn't help but stare at his back. He was fidgeting, and every smooth line of muscle was rippling with his impatience. There were several scars I'd never noticed before, and I felt compelled to run my fingers over their raised edges, but I didn't.

"Done." I sighed, climbing into the silken sheets.

He turned, gripping the back of his neck as his eyes darted around. "Do you need anything else before I head downstairs?"

"Are you getting a snack?" I perked up, actually feeling hungry for once.

"I was going to sleep on the couch." His lips quirked. "Are you hungry? I can get you something."

"Why wouldn't you sleep here?" I frowned, patting the bed next to me. "This is *your* bed, after all."

"Sar," His lips parted and then he didn't say anything for a good minute as he dragged a hand over his face. "I don't think this is a good idea."

"What about the other bedrooms?" I asked, not wanting him

to be downstairs while I was upstairs. I'd honestly been a little spooked in this enormous mansion all by myself the last few days.

"They're not made up." He said so quietly his breath was just a push of air.

I hated that he'd always had the power between the two of us. It sucked. "Carter?"

His eyes were soft, nervous almost. "Yeah?"

"Don't leave." I asked, giving him my very best sad eyes. His jaw flexed as he looked towards the door and then back at me, his chest rising and falling rapidly for a long while. "Please."

"Okay." He finally conceded with a nod. "I'll stay." Slowly, *carefully*, he slid into the sheets next to me, and turned off the lamp. He left ample space between our bodies, threading his hands behind his head while he stared at the ceiling, wide awake.

I smiled to myself and stared at *him* in the darkness until I couldn't keep my eyes open. Such a nice profile, perfect for drawing—sharp jaw, strong nose, full lips, long lashes. Why did guys always have such long, beautiful lashes? What a waste.

I was almost asleep when Carter let out a heavy sigh. "Tomorrow we are going to have a serious conversation about the fact that you went out alone and got drunk." He paused in frustration. "Not to mention literally *nobody* knew you were home." His voice caught. "Sara, if something had happened."

I inched a little closer to the heat radiating from his side of the bed. "Carter?"

He answered softly, turning onto his side to face me. "Yeah?"

"I'm really glad you're home." I tentatively reached a hand out, resting it on his chest. I was surprised to feel his heart racing under my palm. "I missed you so much." Oopsie, my filter had clearly been dissolved via alcohol into a net with gaping holes. What was I even saying? Inside thoughts. Had to keep the inside thoughts *inside* my head.

He placed his hand on top of mine with an involuntary shiver. "Geez, you're freezing, Sar, your skin feels like ice."

I breathed a laugh. "I'm *always* cold." I couldn't remember the last time I'd actually felt warm.

He sighed and threaded an arm around my waist. "Come here." I yelped as he easily hauled me across the bed.

"Hi." I giggled, tucking my hands under my chin while I buried my face into the solid warmth of him.

"Hi." He breathed, and I was enveloped by the scent of the minty soap, still clinging to his skin. He pulled the covers up over us and rubbed my back, trying to warm me up.

"Carter?"

He chuckled. "Yeah?"

"Why are you still wearing my hair tie?" He tensed, and then it suddenly dawned on me that maybe it wasn't mine at all.

"Your hair tie?" He started slowly. *Shit. It was someone else's.* Carter drew a long breath before speaking. "Do you want it back?" *Back.* Relief flooded me. Carter moved to slip the hair tie off. "It's probably all stretched out now."

"You keep it." I smiled. "You've been wearing it for almost a year."

He blew out a small breath in response. "Yeah, a year."

"Mmm." I hummed, feeling sleep quickly closing in as his fingers trailed over my back, tracing a mystery pattern over and over again. I shivered, not sure if it tickled, soothed, or aroused, but I didn't care. He was touching me, and it felt incredible.

Actually, I didn't know if anything had *ever* felt so good as being pressed against him, as being wrapped in his arms. He felt... like home. Like the thing I'd so desperately been trying to find all these months. Like I was finally safe again and finally had somewhere to land.

As I drifted in and out, there was another question I'd been mulling over that I couldn't quite make sense of since the last time I'd seen him. I searched my drunk and tired mind trying to find it. He'd mentioned it back at Thanksgiving.

I sleepily relished the soothing rise and fall of his chest against my body as the question finally came to me. "So tell me about this yellow Gatorade thing." I sleepily demanded, while his body heat seeped into my very bones, staving off the cold I'd been enduring this whole year.

He was quiet, and I wondered if he was asleep already, but then I realized he was still tracing. "You really want to know?"

"Mhmm." I hummed, barely a grunt.

"You falling asleep on me?" He asked, a smile clearly evident in his voice.

"Mmm." I was drifting in and out and having a hard time telling what was real and what was dream now. This was probably just a really good dream. That was okay. It was better than having another nightmare.

"Let's save that story for another night." He pulled me a little tighter, and I let him.

"Carter?" I tilted my head up, my nose scraping against the underside of his stubbled chin.

He shivered, but his chest shook with laughter. "Yes, Sarafina?"

"Thank you for not leaving." Definitely a dream.

He stilled and then whispered back, "I'll never leave you." And then his nose dropped down to graze against mine.

"This is so much better than a phone call." I mumbled.

"Yeah. It definitely is."

CHAPTER 25
Counting Sheep and Panties
CARTER

I must have woken up fifteen times during the night, my raging hard on, aching with want and need. Sara wasn't sober, so nothing was going to happen, of course, but it didn't change the fact that I'd imagined her in my bed at least a thousand times, and now, here she was, curled up in my arms. Her curly hair was tangled around my arm, shoved into my face and mouth, and it was even better than I'd ever imagined.

Knowing she'd slept in my bed naked—shit, I couldn't think about that right now. Not to mention the lacy fucking underwear I'd found stuffed into my dresser between all her clothes.

Knowing what her underwear looked like...

Fucking hell. One imagined. Wondered. But now I *knew.* They were all kinds of colors and styles, but they all had one thing in common, they were soft, lacy and skimpy as fuck.

I needed a cold shower.

And that dildo. Damn that fucking dildo, it was still somewhere in the bed with us. I swallowed hard and tried not to picture what she looked like, using it on these very sheets.

Her sliding that sparkly thing in and out of herself, making more of those little noises that I could easily swallow down my own throat—all while her skin was damp on *my* sheets, head thrown back on *my* pillows.

It was all like a fucking wet dream come to life.

And what had *she* been thinking about, using that sparkly thing in *my* bed? Had she been thinking about me?

Just then Sara murmured and threaded her leg over mine, leaving my knee now snugly jammed against the place I was desperately trying not to think about. Only the thin cotton of my borrowed boxers stood between me and the warm damp spot I could feel.

Fuck. Fuck. FUCK.

I forced a slow, steady breath in through my nose and out through my mouth, over and over until I wasn't a live wire ready to explode. It didn't do much good, though. She smelled too damn good, and it wasn't just her shampoo this time. It was everything, her skin, her arousal, all of it was mixing into a delirious cocktail that forced all my blood in one direction, *no matter how hard I tried.*

I started counting backwards from a thousand before I got distracted.

Why had she decided to sleep here, anyway?

Then it hit me... Brad stumbling up his driveway, drunk. We'd talked about a lot of things over these last few months, but we hadn't talked about that.

Death was a clusterfuck of pain and misery that continued to unravel, no matter how hard you tried to stop pulling the thread. I understood at a certain point, there was only so much you could say about it.

What had happened was devastating, but what the actual fuck?

Seeing Brad like that was wildly disappointing. In fact, that didn't even begin to cover it, and yet, to a degree, I understood it. The falling apart because of the loss. I couldn't help feeling like even though it was only Sara's mother who was gone, that it didn't matter. In her own way, she'd lost both of her parents.

Just like me.

I hated that for her, and for Liam.

Liam. Fuck, what would Liam do if he found out about this? Us? I started counting backwards from a thousand again.

Before I knew it, the sun was coming up, and it didn't matter that I'd hardly gotten any sleep. I was as wound up as the energizer bunny.

I pushed the covers down, trying to cool off. It had taken all night, but Sara had finally warmed up. Now that her skin was warm against mine, she seemed to radiate heat like her own personal furnace.

I wasn't complaining about the situation by any means, but I never slept in sweats, and between every inch of her body pressed against mine, and my heart pounding arousal. I was ready to combust. I needed an ice-cold shower, and fast.

I just couldn't stop staring at her, hardly believing this moment was even real. Sara's mouth hung open, snoring softly— her tongue was stained blue from whatever God-awful sugary drinks she'd no doubt slammed down, one after another, last night.

I smiled to myself as I gently shifted, trying my best to untangle our limbs without waking her, but Sara grumbled, reaching for me as I slid to the edge of the bed. I quietly pulled the covers back over her, tucking her in, and then propped an arm over the other side of her body, utterly mesmerized by this little slice of heaven.

She looked so peaceful that I couldn't resist stroking a thumb over her cheek. She swallowed, closing her mouth, and I pushed a curl behind her ear, gently enough not to wake her.

I could hardly peel myself away, wanting to brand this moment into my memory forever, because I doubted it would ever happen again.

When I finally made it into the shower, I locked the door and immediately fisted my hard, aching cock under the hot water. I bit down on any moans, as I remembered how wet she'd been, splayed over me last night. I wondered what it'd feel like to actually slide into that tight warmth, and I imagined the whimpering little sounds she'd make when I did it.

Stuff I shouldn't be thinking about at all, but it wasn't two seconds before I was pumping into my hand hard and fast, and thick hot ropes were spraying onto the shower walls. When I was done, I braced both hands against the stone, letting the steaming hot water wash away my guilt.

Fuck me. I was never going to get last night out of my mind.

The image of her body in that soaked, see-through dress, the way I could see the outline of everything important. The heat of her wet, pulsing pussy, gliding over me, just that once.

That one would follow me like a ghost, day and night, until the day I died. I pushed the thought away, because I couldn't spend all day jacking off in here like a horny teenager.

When I got out of the shower, I grabbed my phone and checked the security cameras, making sure the Uber driver hadn't come back last night. I'd promised to do something horrific to his eyes if I ever caught him trying to peep a look again, and I'd meant it.

A strange sort of possessiveness washed over me as I watched the footage. Sara frantically trying the door, multiple times, glancing over her shoulder nervously when the code failed. What killed me is that even though I was right here—I would've had no idea if that piece of shit had gotten out of the car and tried something.

The thought enraged me, and I couldn't shake the feeling that was building in my chest.

Something that softly whispered, *mine, mine, mine,* like a drum that ruled the beat of my heart.

Nobody was going to touch what was mine.

Towel wrapped around my waist, I came out of the bathroom

desperately trying to silence that ridiculous voice. The sheets rustled, and I realized Sara was propped up on her elbows, a shy little smile on her face, looking sexy as fuck, in *my* bed, wearing *my* clothes.

The drumbeat pulsed on, and I quickly shoved it down. "Hey." I said, putting my phone down on the dresser.

"Hey." She was all swirly and nervous like she'd been the day of her art class. I freaking loved it.

"Did I wake you?" I asked, hoping she'd gotten enough sleep. At least that would make one of us. She shook her head no, and I noticed a sparkle still glinting in her hair. "I see the cat ears lasted all night." I chuckled as her eyes flicked away from my bare chest. Last night she'd done *a lot* of staring, but then again, so had I.

She reached up, her voice still raw from sleep. "I don't even remember where I got these." She struggled to untangle the sequined headband from her hair.

"Here." I crossed the room. "Let me."

Her eyes flared as I walked closer. "Thanks." She murmured, wrapping her arms around her legs, dipping her head while I carefully detangled the headband from her frizzy curls. When I finally got it loose and handed it to her, she tossed it on the bed—before slyly tugging the covers over the dildo that had reappeared amidst the sheets.

Damn it, I was already hard again. Imagining her using that damn thing had me tenting my towel. I used the opportunity to turn my back to her and head towards the walk-in closet. "So you went out drinking alone?" I asked, keeping my voice light as I changed around the corner.

Sara cleared her throat. "It's really not a big deal."

"Yeah, Sar, it kind of is."

"I didn't mean to scare you last night. I didn't even know you'd be home, otherwise, I wouldn't have come."

With the important parts clothed, I leaned in the closet doorway and crossed my arms. "*You*, scare *me*?" I raised a brow. "How about *you* nearly peeing your pants you were so scared?"

"I thought you were a bear." She admitted.

"A bear?"

"You were practically growling when you came out of the bathroom."

"Was I growling, or were you just totally wasted?"

She scrunched her nose in the admittance of guilt. "Both?"

I chuckled. "Sure." I opened my mouth to tell her why I'd come tearing out of the bathroom, but quickly caught myself. "Don't think I don't see what you're doing." I scolded.

She tilted her head innocently. "What?" *God damned angel.*

"Changing the subject." I said, as if it weren't obvious.

"Is it working?" She batted her long dark lashes at me, the smudges of makeup around her eyes making her that much more endearing.

"No." I shook my head with a chuckle. "Why'd you stay here instead of your place? The walk too far?" I teased.

She winced. "I'm sorry. I should have asked you first. It's totally weird, right?" She nervously looked at her nails, adding quietly, "Probably should have stayed in a guest bedroom too."

"The beds weren't made up." I reminded her.

"That's not why I picked your room." She said so softly I wasn't sure I'd heard her right.

She'd *meant* to sleep in my bed—*pink dildo and all?!* My mind started whirring with possibilities. I swallowed hard. "You didn't answer my question."

"No." She laughed, "I guess I didn't."

"Why are you hiding from Liam? From your dad?" I asked gently.

She was a terrible liar. "I just, uh, I wanted some alone time before I went over there." Was her father coming home drunk a regular occurrence?

"You could've had alone time at your apartment." I countered. She looked at me for a long moment, like she wanted to tell me the real reason, but she closed her mouth again. I moved to the dresser and put my watch on, knowing that was all the answer I was going to get for now. "I know about your art exhibition."

"What?" Her voice turned slightly panicked.

"Sloane told me." I said over my shoulder, meeting her wide brown eyes.

Sara flopped back onto the bed with a groan. "Why would she do that?"

"Because you need people there to support you." I sat on the edge of the bed.

She threw an arm over her eyes, hiding. "You don't want to see it."

"Sure I do." I pulled her arm down so I could see her face. Even now, I could tell she was still hurting so damn much. I wished there was something I could do to ease her grief, to help her find her spark again.

She exhaled. "No, really, you don't."

"Care to tell me why?" I tugged on her shirt, and she finally looked at me.

"It's just, it's *different* than the piece I sent you." She looked down.

"That's okay. Different is good, different is moving forward." I wanted to touch her, and even though we'd been pressed together all night, for some reason, I didn't know if I should. "Every collection is bound to be different, besides it shows your versatility as an artist." I encouraged.

"Maybe." I could hear the sadness in her voice. It had snaked its way into her heart and stolen everything from her, sapped the joy right out of her, and I hated it, seeing her so sad.

"Well, I guess I'll just have to see what it's all about tonight." I teased gently, and her gaze snapped up. "Oh yeah, I'm coming, and there is nothing you can do to stop me, sweetheart." I leaned back on my forearms, snapping my teeth at her bare feet.

She yanked her feet back with a gasp, and something lusty passed through her eyes. She chewed on her lip, considering whatever it was playing through her pretty little head, and then smiled to herself.

God, I wanted to dive into the bed and crush her, wanted to kiss her, wanted to give her something good, anything good. She deserved it so damn much.

I didn't do any of that. "Do you want to grab a shower? I was going to pick up some breakfast for us."

She nodded emphatically. "Yeah, a shower would be good. *Really, really* good."

Just for a minute, I didn't stop myself from staring. She was so beautiful even after just waking up, actually, *especially* after just waking up. "You want your usual?" I finally asked, and she smiled softly at me and nodded.

Damn, she looked way too good in my bed.

CHAPTER 26

Knock Twice or Snap Once

CARTER

"Ham for you, sausage for me." I pulled our loot out of the Breakfast Bar bag.

I almost never ate like this, except with Sara. In high school, me, Liam and Sara had been in sports all year round, and had to eat and train accordingly. Liam and I would trade off, picking Sara up after soccer or track practice. When it was my turn, she got really good at begging me into sneaking her fast food with those impossibly big, brown puppy eyes, and I got really bad at saying no.

Over time, it had just turned into our thing. If there was something to celebrate or even something shitty going on, we'd hit the drugstore, grab our Gatorades and Sour Patch candy, and then get Burrito Bell, unless it was a Saturday morning, in which case, The Breakfast Bar was our go to.

This was throwing me back, only now, everything was just so much different.

I pushed her orange juice across the table, another more domestic fantasy coming to life as she sat there, flushed cheeks, wild morning hair, looking freaking adorable.

The drumbeat inside me banged on, pulsing through my very

blood like a war song. I ignored what it said, or tried to at least, while Sara sat there looking like ancient royalty, looking like she belonged on the throne of all this grandeur. She suddenly seemed to give purpose to this dusty old excuse for a home, because if she asked me to, I'd certainly be hers to command, would swear myself to worship at the foot of her altar, *day and night.*

"Since you already know about my exhibition, would you mind if I stayed here through the weekend, just until it's over?" She asked, stabbing the straw through the plastic lid of her orange juice.

My heart raced as I considered several more nights of sleeping under the same roof with her, but I didn't miss a beat. "Of course not. You're always welcome here, you know that." I was going to have to buck up some serious self-control and keep my goddamn hands to myself.

It would have been one thing if Sara wasn't... Sara.

But no, she'd been sitting on my dick like a goddamn temptress, not wearing any fucking underwear. Asking what if she *wanted* me to do all those dirty things I'd threatened, all while she batted her lashes innocently.

Innocent my ass, she'd sealed her request by teasing her gloriously drenched pussy right over my throbbing dick. I was freaking Houdini for getting myself out of that one.

I noticed Sara fiddling with the sandwich paper rather than eating. "Why are you home anyway?"

I cleared my throat, hedging. "I had some meetings in town." It was partially true.

She looked utterly confused. "With who?"

"Investors," I said quickly, taking another bite.

"That doesn't make any sense, I thought you wanted to stay in the Air Force?"

"I do."

She narrowed her eyes, head tilting as she assessed me. "What aren't you telling me, Kensington?"

"I may have had some extra time off." That was *kind of* a lie.

She astutely poked me again. "I wasn't aware the Air Force just dolled out extra time off."

"I may currently have some schedule flexibility, due to a medical leave. Thought I'd make the most of it." I shrugged, jamming another bite in.

"Medical leave?" Her face went pale, and it suddenly occurred to me that was a terrible choice of words on my part, considering her mother's unknown health condition before she'd passed.

"It's nothing bad. I just dislocated my shoulder." I quickly reassured her through my mouthful. She nodded slowly, wheels turning, and I swallowed without chewing, adding, "I'm fine, Sara, truly I'm fine."

"Okay." She sort of played with her sandwich, but still didn't take a bite.

By the time I'd finished my two breakfast sandwiches, she'd barely eaten half of hers, if that.

Oh fuck. I'd just assumed that when she'd started painting again that she'd started eating too. It was dumb logic, I knew, but in that moment, I realized it was clearly still a big problem. Thankfully, she didn't look as gaunt as she had on her birthday, but she was still much thinner than usual.

Sara noticed me looking, and she pushed the paper over to me, waiting for me to finish her food like I always did when she was full. "You're finished?" I asked, worry filling my chest.

"Yeah, I'm not really a breakfast person anymore." Bullshit.

"You don't want to save it?" I offered. "You might be hungry a little bit later."

"I doubt it." She leaned back in her chair and stared out the window. *Damn it.*

In an attempt not to make a big deal about it, I dragged the half-eaten sandwich towards me—I finished the rest of it, feeling like it was ash in my mouth. I tried to convince myself I was over-reacting, but deep down, I knew I wasn't.

Dusting my hands off, I leaned back in my chair and rested my arm on the back of the neighboring one. "I really think you should tell Liam and your dad about your exhibition. I know they'd love to come." She groaned. "What? I'm just saying." Why was she hiding this from everyone? We all should be celebrating her. She deserved it so damn much.

"Please don't tell them." Her shoulders sagged in defeat. "I know you don't get it, but I really can't handle that right now."

"Alright." I nodded. It wasn't my place, but part of me wondered if maybe I should make it my place.

"It's bad enough that Sloane told *you*." She grumbled and then, getting an idea, she perked up. "Is there anyway I could bribe you not to come?"

As if I'd ever let that happen, *although*, there were *quite a few* things I could probably be bribed with right now. Not the point. "Not a chance in hell." I grinned. "You're stuck with me, sweetheart."

She made a fake disgusted noise, but her eyes sparkled just a tiny bit. "I guess I can live with that." She sipped her orange juice absentmindedly.

At least she was getting her blood sugar up. I'd have to find a way to get something of substance into her though, some protein or carbs at least. She needed something solid to sustain her, so she didn't faint again. And the drinking had clearly not gotten better either. I blew out a slow breath. One thing at a time. Baby steps. Healing was not linear. I knew that firsthand.

She glanced up at the clock. "I should probably get ready. I have a few things I need to check on before the showing tonight."

I looked at the time and groaned, not sure how so much time had passed so quickly. "Shit, I gotta get going too." I pushed my chair back. "You need a ride tonight?"

"I'll just bring a change of clothes with me and stay until the showing."

"A ride home then." I said, punctuating my plan with a nod.

"Don't make plans afterwards. I'm taking you to dinner to celebrate."

"Burrito Bell?" She laughed.

"No, something nice."

She bit her lip and nodded tentatively. "Yeah?"

"Yeah." I grinned, and for some reason, I wanted to kiss her goodbye, like it was something I'd already done a thousand times, but I caught myself just in time. I sucked in a tight breath and tapped the back of her chair instead. "See ya tonight." I called, wondering how the hell I was going to get through the day with this aching feeling in my chest. I didn't want to leave her.

I stood outside the exclusive gentleman's bar across town and gave the password before I was permitted entrance. Even though it was ten in the morning, it was surprisingly busy as I entered the lounge.

Cigar smoke curled through the air as I passed rows of emerald-green tufted couches that were curved in half moons for close intimate conversations, under low chandeliers.

I nodded politely as I passed several groups of men who continued their conversations quietly, but watched me, as if they'd all been expecting me. If I hadn't already been on high alert, I certainly was now.

The only woman in the entire establishment had been the hostess, and she'd clearly been dressed to appease the club members. I grimaced, heading towards the table number she'd given me. I wondered how my father had endured things like this, or maybe he was exactly the kind of man who enjoyed these kinds of establishments. I'd been a teenager when he died—what did I even know about him? Truly, when it came down to it. The thought was sobering.

"Carter." A man with graying hair and a cigar hanging out of his mouth stood to greet me.

Richard. I gritted my teeth and looked around the table, noticing there were four other men seated, two I didn't recognize. "I supposed I should have expected that you'd be here."

"Have a seat." Richard didn't bother with introductions as he nodded to the only open place at the table.

"Where's the Director?" I asked, very quickly realizing this was just another game of smoke and mirrors, and a waste of my time.

"Couldn't make it." Richard motioned to the booth, and I reluctantly stepped into the velvet-tufted section that made up one of five separate seats that curved all the way around the circular booth.

One of the men I didn't know but recognized, motioned to the bartender and a moment later, I was served a drink. Unease prickled over me, and while the chatter across the bar didn't change, I got the odd feeling that I was being watched by everyone in the room.

"I prefer to pour my own drinks these days." I smiled thinly. "From an unopened bottle, if you don't mind."

A moment later, a fresh glass appeared in front of me, and I poured myself a modest serving of scotch from a new bottle. It was ten in the morning, but when in Rome, I supposed. Getting a whiff of smoke, I sipped the amber drink, and it went down smooth as I surveyed my surroundings, quickly understanding that the men who drank here had the kind of influence and power that even money itself couldn't buy. I knew right then and there that my father and his friends dealt in currencies much more sinister than money. If my attack hadn't been evidence enough, and it was, the undercurrent in this room left me feeling more than a little agitated and uneasy.

I kept my face bored and uninterested, all while I catalogued *everything* around me. People, exits, armed guards near those exits.

Richard lifted the original glass that had been placed in front of me and poured it into his own drink, giving me a smile that didn't meet his eyes.

"You look more like your father every time I see you," Samuel Mortarulo mused from across the table while he casually shuffled a deck of cards in his hands over and over.

"I have things to do today, so why don't we just cut to the chase, since you're already wasting my time. I'm a very busy man, and I don't appreciate accepting a meeting with someone who can't even bother to show his face." I rested my arm on the back of the booth and looked around the table. "I guess I'm stuck with you all. I'm sure you've no doubt summoned me here in an attempt to persuade me to join the organization or turn over the estate." I swirled the scotch in my glass, adding mildly, "And I can assure you, just like I've said since the very beginning, neither of those things is ever going to happen."

Looks were exchanged across the table, and one of the men who hadn't introduced himself started a bit nervously. "I think we've gotten off on the wrong foot."

I couldn't help but scoff at that, whoever in this organization had orchestrated that attack on me—starting off on a bad foot didn't even begin to cover it. The retribution that was in store for them if they attempted that little trick a second time would cost them dearly. I'd already begun to identify key financial pillars across the members of this organization, and I wouldn't hesitate to start bringing those pillars down if I needed to.

The man continued, "Your father built a great many businesses that were beneficial to him and his business partners, and since you've decided not to follow in his footsteps, we are merely suggesting that if you were to turn over the estate, we'd make certain you were fairly compensated."

"Oh, I don't doubt that one bit." I scoffed, filled with ire.

Richard laughed, the sound crawling over my skin like a dying insect. "Carter, you are a man of great potential. That is very clear, but so was your father. A great man, who *died* far too young for very avoidable reasons." He gave me a look that made my skin prickle as he continued. "Don't make the same mistakes your father did, or you might end up like your mother." Richard mused, and my heart might have stopped beating as he finished by saying, "Collateral damage."

"Excuse me?" I uttered, my blood running cold.

"A tragedy. Truly a tragedy." Richard said, leaning back with enough smugness that I couldn't help but let the question blossom in my mind. Was he admitting to involvement in my parent's deaths? Or was he just toying with me? What would the motive have been, if this entire table was so obsessed with the money my father made them? Why kill him, *kill my mother?* Another look was subtly shared between several of them.

"What exactly are you implying?" I asked, gripping my glass of scotch, while something inside me finally started to unravel after years of keeping it at bay.

Samuel spoke, "With *your* recent accident, we figured it would be a good time to reconsider your membership with The Society. You've been so diligent in ignoring the invitations for the last several years. Perhaps your altercation has persuaded you?"

My heart was pounding as the pieces started slowly falling into place, as I started to read between the lines, wondering if it could really be true.

"*Accidents* have been known to happen when the rules aren't adhered to." Richard shrugged.

I knew better than to let my emotions get the best of me, because the moment I did, I'd only be playing into their hand, so I kept my face stoic, neutral, wondering what rules he was referring to, wondering *what exactly* my father had done in this organization.

"It wasn't an *accident* that I was drugged and attacked." I offered with a thin smile, feigning stupidity. "Don't deceive yourself into thinking that it will work a second time."

Richard smiled and didn't even bother denying it. "We would never."

Out of the corner of my eye, I noticed several muscular men hovering a bit closer than they had been before. "You want the estate. Why?" I demanded.

"Start by accepting your invitation, and then we'll talk."

My temper flared as I noted all the exits, all the bodies, and all the weapons in the room. I knew with a broken bottle of scotch, and all my pent-up anger, it wouldn't be too hard to fight my way out, with little to show for it.

"We're done here." I stood abruptly enough that the nameless man's drink sloshed over the rim of his glass and onto the table.

"For now." Samuel said, casting a glance at Richard.

I was already two steps away when Samuel's words stopped me in my tracks. "You may not have any family left, but we know you have people you care about."

I clenched my fists at my sides and turned slowly, thinking of the girl who'd slept in my arms all night.

"It'd be a shame to lose another Devereux, don't you think? Especially a particularly beautiful one who seems to have caught your eye."

My eyes flicked between his, and narrowed. "*Is that a threat?*" I asked quietly, a thousand possibilities spinning through my mind all at once.

"It's merely an observation." He said, nodding behind me. "You've already lost so much, and it'd be a shame to keep going at this rate."

Something inside me snapped, and I hummed darkly, "Maybe I haven't been clear up until now, but let me take this opportunity to enlighten you. If this organization and it's members don't back off, not only will I bankrupt every single one of you just for the hell of it—if you *ever* threaten the Devereuxs ever again, I will flay every single inch of skin off your body." I practically growled. "And if you even think about breathing in *her* direction, I will make your death so slow and painful you'll be begging for me to end it." I didn't dare speak Sara's name, but I wanted to throw every single one of them through the wall. "Stay the hell away from me and stay the fuck away from the Devereuxs." I seethed, quietly forcing a shaky breath out through my nose, and that's when I noticed Richard's glass.

It was untouched. He'd bluffed, hadn't touched it, not even a sip.

Richard followed my gaze and offered me a slippery smile of a man whose power was wholly unchecked. "Don't bother with juvenile threats when you don't even understand the stakes of the game you're playing, son." He swirled the liquid in his glass contemplatively, practically daring me to accuse him directly. "Next time, you leave when we say, Carter. Or there *will* be consequences."

"You are absolutely right, there *will* be consequences." I threatened darkly, towering over him. "If you attempt to touch *anything* that is mine, *the debt will be paid in blood.*" I was trembling with fury, but I kept my voice low and even as I promised, "I swear on my mother's grave, if you ever threaten her again, you will regret it until your dying breath, and it will be my hands that decide when that is."

"We'll see about that."

Two burly armed guards appeared at my sides, reaching for me.

"Did you know you can peel all the skin off a man's hands with only two cuts?" I threatened quietly, my voice laced with more venom than I knew I was capable of.

With a nod from Samuel, they escorted me to the door, hovering closely behind.

Every single eye in the room was on me, and I doubted it was from the scene I'd just made. They'd *all* been waiting for me. But why exactly, I still couldn't say.

I left the club as calmly as humanly possible, but inside, I was dying to smash something, and as they shoved me out the door, I locked eyes with Taggart fucking Caldwell, who smirked at me just before the door slammed in my face.

I hit the door. Hard. That fucking prick was lucky I didn't see him before they locked me out—I was half tempted to break the door down and give him exactly what he deserved. Whatever the hell had happened between him and Sara was her story to tell, but even if she never confided the details—he was at the very top of my shit list, right next to Richard Sinclair.

I was seething, physically trembling as I climbed into my McLaren, and floored it.

These men were dangerous, and now, the only question was, would they kill to get what they wanted? Because it was entirely possible that *they already had.*

CHAPTER 27

Casanova Takes No Prisoners

SARAFINA

"Who is *that*?" Lila, the owner of Basecoat Gallery, asked, as she ogled whoever was coming inside next.

A sleek sports car had pulled up outside, and I stood on my tiptoes trying to see out the front windows. My breath caught when I realized it was *Carter,* and he'd driven the yellow Lotus Evija tonight, which meant he was in *a mood* to show off.

My stomach flipped as I watched Carter hand his keys to the valet, looking angsty and sexy as shit, and then he strolled into the gallery smooth as sin. "*That* is Casa-fucking-Nova." I breathed suddenly aware of every part of my body.

"*Who?*" Lila didn't take her eyes off him, and neither did I.

Carter slipped his hands into his pockets and strolled into the crowded gallery with a smoldering expression painted across his face. Standing an easy head above everyone, the sea of bodies began to part around him as he cut through the crowd with a devil may care attitude.

Quiet wealth rolled off him—the suit he was wearing was no doubt custom, cut to fit every perfect line of muscle on his incredible body. The top two buttons of his crisp dress shirt were undone, and between the clothes and the tousled hair, it was difficult to tell if he'd rolled out of bed looking that good, or if he'd just come from an actual romp between the sheets.

A pang of jealousy washed over me, as I hoped it wasn't the latter.

Carter's whisky-brown eyes were dark and assessing as he scanned the bustling gallery and then his eyes locked onto one thing. *Me.*

Every nerve in my body jittered with the realization that *I* was the target that *this* man had locked on to.

Carter's lips hooked up on one side into a devilishly charming grin that would have any woman dropping her panties, *including me*, and I steadied myself, heart pounding, as all that sexy, powerful energy finally reached me.

He made no apologies as he dragged his gaze over me, taking his sweet time. My skin seemed to scrape against the silk of my plunging red gown while he took in every single inch of me with lusty adoration.

I was grateful when he stepped into my space and steadied me —surprised when he kept on coming.

Carter leaned in intimately close, his lips brushing the shell of my ear as he murmured. "You look absolutely fucking beautiful, Sarafina, but I'm not going to lie." My dangly earrings tinkled against my throat as he leaned in even closer. "I might be partial to that little number you were wearing last night." His fingers tightened around my waist, his breath an igniting caress on my skin as his voice dropped even lower, vibrating against me. "Tell me, did you skip the underwear again tonight?" Carter pulled back and winked at me, but there was no boyish charm in it. It was all raw, confident, powerful man.

Heat rushed to my cheeks and neck, and my plunging gown wasn't going to do a damn thing to hide it. "You came." Breathless, it was all I could utter.

He took my chin between his fingers, his eyes dropping to my lips. "Of course I came." The way he looked into my eyes in that moment, into the deepest parts of my very being, as if he could read every word written on my soul—I didn't know if I wanted to jump him or sob with relief. Time seemed to stop completely and then start again when he gave me the most earth-shattering smile.

"Sara?" a voice asked nearby, and just like that, every warm feeling I'd had was vacuumed out of me. Like a jello shot being slurped down by an already drunk frat boy, and speaking of frat boys.

I apparently had a terrible poker face because Carter immediately slid a possessive arm around my waist, *like I belonged to him*. In fact, it was so effortless, it felt like something he'd done a thousand times.

"And you are?" Carter asked, his gaze sharp, his tone low and assessing.

I shook myself out of my stupor. "Carter, this is Isaac." I cleared my throat as it closed up involuntarily.

Isaac just stared at me, an entire unspoken conversation passing between us that made me want to puke.

Carter's gaze was unforgiving as he stared Isaac down, and when Isaac finally looked up at Carter, his eyes flared with the realization that I was here with someone. Isaac immediately postured. Great, we were going to have a dick-swinging contest. Yippie.

"Um, what are you doing here?" I asked, attempting to keep my voice steady while I ignored how good Carter's fingers felt, curled around my hip, how sensual his thumb stroking the small of my back felt.

God, I could hardly stand up straight with him touching me like that. Did he have any idea what he was doing to me?

"I have a couple of pieces showing." Isaac explained, "And you?"

I nodded breathlessly as Carter continued his caress.

"Which ones are yours?" Isaac asked, and I hated every second of his gaze on me—the judgment as he dragged his eyes over me.

When Carter had just done the same, his gaze was steeped with adoration and longing—and it felt so wildly different from the way Isaac was currently looking at me. In that moment, I knew—I had been wrong to second guess what had happened at Isaac's apartment that night. I wasn't just being sensitive about what had happened *before* I'd even discovered that camera. He'd crossed a line. I knew it, because Carter had never ever made me feel the way Isaac had that night—like my voice didn't matter. And the fact that he'd tried to record it, well, that was just the icing on the cake.

With Carter like a guard dog, ready to attack at any second, I cleared my throat, finding my voice again. "I'm the main one." Why was I downplaying it?

"You're the feature?" Isaac asked, shocked. Ouch, if that didn't hurt.

I nodded, my voice getting caught in my throat as a lump formed. I hated that he was here. I hated it so much. Just when I was finally starting to enjoy myself for once.

"How the hell did you manage that?" Isaac asked, and then he looked at Carter suspiciously. "Never mind. It looks like you had a hookup. I see you found another *friend*." *With benefits* is what he didn't say, but I could practically feel the words sitting on the tip of his tongue.

That fucking prick assumed Carter was my benefactor. I didn't know why it bothered me so much. Lots of incredible artists had them, but I had earned my place tonight, all on my own. I had gotten here with literal blood, sweat, and tears. It was the only thing of note that I'd achieved this year, and him reducing it down to—well, it didn't matter. He was an ass. An ass disguised as a *nice guy*. Ugh! My heart thundered as his words looped in my mind over and over.

I tried to find that kernel of accomplishment, that pride for what I'd created, but it felt so far out of reach now.

Carter's grip released as he stepped into Isaac's personal space, a full head above him. "Let's see if your pieces are worth their salt." Carter said, pretending he was, in fact, an interested investor. I mean, in reality, he could have been. He could support the entire gallery if he wanted, let alone a single artist.

"What?" Isaac asked, taking a step back.

"Unless you're not pursuing a benefactor." Carter mused, becoming mildly disinterested. Something was different about him tonight. Whatever it was, it was hot as fuck. "Perhaps it *would* be a waste of my time." Carter droned, and casually checked his watch as if he had other more important things to do —I smiled to myself, catching a flash of pink.

Carter was basically ripping Isaac to shreds with his eyes, and I jabbed him in the side as subtly as I could, but Carter was having none of that. He stepped forward and gripped Isaac's shoulder. "What do you say?" Carter practically growled, and my stomach flipped at the sound. *Damn.*

I suppressed a smirk, kind of loving how protective he was being. I'd never seen him so—commanding, so intense. I tried to ignore what it was doing to my body. I failed. It was doing wild things to my insides. Feral things. Ungodly things.

Isaac winced under the grip. "Uh, sure, that'd be great."

That's when a whole new set of nerves hit me. I realized Carter was better educated about fine art than most people I knew. He wouldn't even be pretending as he evaluated Isaac's work... as he evaluated *my* work afterwards.

Oh God, I was going to puke.

Growing up, I'd seen the priceless pieces that had filtered through the Kensington Estate, one after another. Pieces that most people wouldn't even dream of seeing in their lifetime, Carter had casually hung on the walls of his house.

Panic hit me like a freight train. This wasn't just my friend looking at my art, this was someone whose eyes were trained to evaluate art for investment purposes. Someone who was trained to spot shit from a mile away.

Oh God. I should have tried harder to keep him away tonight. The worst part was I knew he'd be nice about it, even if he thought my collection was utter trash. How pitiful that would be. This was going to be humiliating.

"I'll only be a moment, sweetheart." Carter turned to me again, fingers trailing down my arm, leaving a trail of goosebumps as he took my hand. He pressed a supple kiss to my knuckles, giving me a smoldering look that could only be interpreted one way.

I wasn't wearing any underwear tonight because panty lines, and now I had an entire situation happening between my legs. I was panicked, I was turned on, I was a fucking mess. "Of course, *sweetie.*" I bit out in warning, shooting Carter my own determined look, but Carter was having none of that as his eyes flashed with something lethal. As if he fucking knew everything that had happened that night, without me ever saying a word. I swallowed hard as his gaze turned venomous and he slid his hands into his pockets, trailing Isaac like a shark who smelled blood in the water.

"You didn't tell me you had a boyfriend." Lila, perky as ever, materialized next to me, shooting me a wide-eyed jealous look.

No point in explaining. Not when Carter was practically acting like he *wanted* people to think he was my boyfriend. What the hell was up with him tonight? "It's new." I said, grabbing a champagne flute off a passing tray and knocking it back in one go.

"I'd knock back a few more of those if I were you." She scoffed. "I think you're in for a *long* night." Lila left, grumbling to herself. "I need to get back on the apps."

Just then, a buyer came up, inquiring about purchasing the collection in its entirety. As they gushed over how fabulous it was, I thanked them profusely and kindly directed them to the gallery desk to place a bid request. Lila had been right. I was going to be able to sell the collection in its entirety, and there were so many interested parties that it was going to auction.

In fact, there were several bidders who were *adamant* they get their hands on it, and a few had offered absolutely *outrageous* prices to ensure they would be the ones to take the pieces home. The whole thing was surreal, and I wondered if it was a dream, or maybe this was another one of my nightmares, and everyone here was just a monster in disguise. Totally possible.

Across the gallery, I could basically figure out what Carter was saying to Isaac. His face was laced with mild disgust, and though he pointed out different elements of the piece giving an analysis, Carter was no doubt shredding him apart. One subtle but calculated comment after another.

When Carter finally left, Isaac's shoulders slumped. In disappointment or relief, I wasn't entirely sure.

I breathlessly realized Carter was coming straight for me, and I whirled around, darting across the gallery. Before I could hide, I found myself stuck in a conversation with a very sweet Swedish couple while they so kindly gushed over the collection.

It wasn't that I didn't want to talk to them. The woman was very generous in sharing how she'd lost her own mother, and that my exploration of grief had impacted her deeply. In fact, I was thrilled to hear that my collection was resonating with so many people. It was just that, the longer I stood here, the closer Carter got, and if he reached me, it was totally possible a tear might actually start running down my leg.

Right on cue, I felt Carter's presence looming behind me, and then his hand slid over my stomach possessively, and he pulled me flush against him. I might have been on the verge of fainting as that hand *stayed* splayed wide over my belly, and I couldn't help but notice the solid wall behind me growing even harder. It was an effort to keep on conversing as if I couldn't smell his cologne, as if I couldn't feel what had been nestled between my legs last night, now that it was pressing firmly into my back.

"Would you excuse us?" Carter interjected politely, adjusting his moonstone cufflinks in front of me. "I've yet to view the collection, and I'd like to do so with the artist."

The woman's eyes sparkled, and she shot me a smile. "Yes, of course."

"Thank you so much." I said, "You can connect with the gallery owner, Lila. I believe she's already taking bids."

"Fantastic," the man said, and they quickly headed to the back of the gallery.

Carter spun me around, his hands gripping my hips as he pulled me to him. "My turn." His voice was low. "No more hiding. Let's see this fantastic collection everyone is absolutely obsessed with."

I bit my lip and nodded, suddenly feeling even more nervous than I had. Carter took my hand and guided me through the crowd to the center of the gallery. "Here it is." I waved my arm in front of the start of the piece nervously.

Carter didn't let go of my hand as he clasped his own behind his back, observing it, taking it in. I pointed to the plaque. "Read this, and then I'll explain how it works."

"How it works?" His eyes were twinkling, but he focused intently on the plaque, reading the poem about mothers and daughters that I'd written.

His eyes moved to the next plaque, a brief explanation of my mother, the woman she had been, and then finally the last plaque. A short explanation of my grieving process this year, and how the collection had come into formation.

"A single thread." Carter read the title of the piece aloud, and his eyes were already glassy.

I smiled to myself, relishing in the warmth of his hand around mine, and we started at the beginning.

The very first painting was actually one of the few paintings I hadn't totally destroyed from my previous collection. I explained how it represented nurtured girlhood. It was colorful, complex, innocent, naïve, joyful, and unrestrained.

As we moved down the display, the pieces became progressively more covered in black paint, and less of the original collection was visible underneath. A representation of how female innocence gets stripped away over time. Girlhood, adulthood, relationships, experiences, and how they all begin to overtake that original purity of essence.

In the center was the all-black piece, the one I'd literally scooped black paint onto with my bare hands that day in the studio. It was the death of girlhood, the separation of mother and daughter, the ultimate darkness that choked out everything it touched.

Carter leaned in, squinting at the black paint, and his eyes flared as he found it. "Is this your mother's handwriting?" He asked.

I nodded. "Everywhere there is black paint, her words are overlayed because even in the lowest, darkest parts of my grief, she's still with me. We are two threads braided into a strand that can't be separated. Not really."

It had been a painstaking process to transfer her words, one by one, onto the canvas. Emotionally devastating too, but also healing. I'd come across so many special discoveries.

"I love you to the moon and back. Don't forget your art project." He cleared his throat. "We may have a maid, but this builds character. Take this upstairs and fold it, please." He chuckled. "I've made the most beautiful thing I ever could have," Carter looked at me, misty-eyed before he finished reading the passage aloud, "My daughter. Nothing I do, no matter how grand, will ever compare." Now *I* was nearly crying. When I'd come across it in her journal for the first time, I *had* cried. So hard my eyes had nearly swollen shut, and there were dozens more, just as poetic, just as devastating, just as precious to me.

"What are these?" He asked, gripping my hand tighter in his.

"Birthday cards, sticky notes with chores." I shrugged as nonchalantly as I could. "Entries from her journals."

"You kept all this stuff?" He asked in wonder.

"I've always been a bit of a hoarder, I guess." It was a relief realizing that he didn't totally hate the collection. "There's more." I gently tugged him down the display, and he let me, even as his eyes lingered.

Beyond that darkest piece, the paintings began to get less and less black again, and they shimmered as if liquid were running over them, representing the process of moving forward, the darkness being washed away.

"This is beautiful." Carter murmured. "It's symbolic, raw, profoundly moving, visually captivating."

"What's this?" he asked, pointing to the plaque that said, *start peeling*.

I smiled, nodding. "Go ahead."

He reached out and found one of the thousands and thousands of colorful threads that I'd painstakingly embedded in black wax over several new pieces I'd painted. "It's interactive?" He asked, waiting for my permission to start pulling the thread. "I saw one of these at your school."

"It's on trend." I teased, shrugging with a shy smile. "Go ahead."

Carter slowly pulled one of the threads, and it peeled up in a wild swirling pattern, revealing a new colorful painting underneath, exposed only by the thinnest line of color exploding out where the thread had once been.

He looked at me curiously, and I tipped my head towards the bucket. He dropped the thread into the all-black bucket and suddenly, the clear tube that fed out the side exploded with color, swirling around to the other side of the display.

It was a bit of an illusion I'd rigged up with the help of someone from the engineering department, but it looked like the threads were swallowed up into the darkness and then transformed into liquid color.

"This represents the process that you have to go into the darkness, into the grief, to find the light." I said. "You pull one thread at a time and then you let them go. It seems insignificant in the moment, but in reality, this is what you're creating."

I tugged Carter to the other side of the display, where the explosion of color swirled through a complex network of tiny clear tubes that weaved around the new collection I'd created. It was colorful and joyful, but in an entirely different way than my old work had been. It was chaotic, nuanced, and a bit dark in some places, too.

"The joy was always there under the surface." I explained. "Turns out grief and joy can coexist. You just have to know where to look."

This side of the piece was a living, breathing visual that represented the ever-changing dance of grief and joy. A push-pull that would probably never stop being part of my life.

Carter was quiet, and I nervously filled in the space. "The piece will continue to change over time, because that's how grief works."

"And this blank canvas?" He asked, adorably intrigued by the small white canvas at the center of the colorful display.

"It's not blank." I grinned nervously.

He leaned in, finding *my* handwriting all over the canvas in white.

"This is the final journey of the mother-daughter relationship." I explained as he puzzled over it. "When the daughter becomes a mother." A slow smile crept onto his face. "It's not filled with color yet, because I haven't gotten that far—I don't know what the color of motherhood is yet." I didn't bother adding that I wasn't even sure if I wanted to be a mother anymore. "And it's the third strand in the braid." I explained. "The triple goddess. Mother, maiden, crone— *queen.*" I amended because I'd always liked that version better.

He shook his head in awe. "I love it." He wrapped his arms around me, picking me up as he spun me around, and for a moment, I didn't care who was watching. I laughed freely for the first time in a long while, and Carter moved us to a quiet corner, setting me down behind a pillar.

His hands hit the wall behind me. "I'm so proud of you, Sara."

I shyly looked away. "You're just saying that. Everyone is just saying that."

He tipped my chin up. "You want to bet? I'm telling you, I'm incredibly impressed. This is real inspired art, Sara. It makes you think, and feel, and the more you look, the more you find," he said passionately. "You have a real gift, don't doubt that, not even for a second." He stared at me in awe, and I blushed at the praise. "What you did, the concept, the lived-in practicality of it all, the vulnerability you showed. It's commendable."

I swallowed hard. "You think?"

"I know. In fact, I already bid on the piece."

"You bid?" I gasped. "You hadn't even seen it yet."

"This is going to be worth a fortune." He mused, sounding like a pleased investor. "This will continue to gain value as you develop as an artist. I mean, the fact that this is your debut collection is wild. Not to mention, there is so much potential for subsequent connected collections."

His wheels were turning, and I could see his work-brain turning on. That's how I knew he really liked it because now he wasn't busy spinning up flowery compliments. No, he had gone full-out investor mode. It made me feel the slightest bit better to realize he genuinely believed that the piece had value—he of all people would know.

I shifted nervously. "What if I don't want you to own it?"

"Why not?" He asked gently, reading my anxiety, already locked in, right there with me.

"Because I think I need to let this one go. My professor's assignment, this piece, it was about going through the process. The process of *letting go,* and I don't think I could look at it every day because I *need* to let it go."

He nodded, concealing a small smile.

"What?" I asked, feeling embarrassment flush my cheeks as my confession seemed to miss the mark.

"You just said every day."

"What? No, I didn't." I swallowed involuntarily, realizing I in-fact had. I wished I could melt into the wall behind me, but there was nowhere to hide from my mistake.

He grinned, "*Yes,* you did."

"Well, I just meant—"

Carter leaned in even closer, his lips nearly grazing mine, breath dusting across my mouth as he uttered, "*My, my, my, pretty girl, aren't you just full of bright ide*—"

Suddenly, there was an *explosion*—Carter's eyes blew wide, and before I could even gasp, he grabbed me.

Screams erupted across the gallery as the strength of his arms wrapped around me so tightly, it knocked the breath from my lungs.

It was all happening in slow motion, as more strange and horrifying sounds rang out—I was falling, and he was with me, but my arms were pinned against his body as the room went sideways, and I braced as the ground closed in.

Carter's arm shot out and took the brunt of the impact as we hit the floor, and the weight of his body over mine was unyielding as I disappeared beneath him, disoriented and panicked.

My scream was muffled against his chest as the floor vibrated with every continuing explosion.

"I've got you." He frantically promised, wrapping himself even more tightly around me, cocooning me beneath his broad frame.

Panic and confusion slashed through me, but his body stayed against mine, solid, steady, and sure.

When the explosions finally stopped, I was shaking like a leaf, and my stomach churned at the eerie crackling and tinkling noise that now filled the air.

"Stay down." Carter commanded, and I'd never heard him sound like that before as his wide hand tucked my head back down the second I'd lifted it.

People started quietly murmuring all around us, and trembling, I slowly came to the realization that we were okay.

I shakily peered around his arm, discovering there was colorful broken glass *everywhere*—I covered my mouth in horror, suddenly realizing what had happened. One of the artists had an elaborate collection of glass sculptures, and the *entire thing* had fallen from the ceiling.

"*No,*" I breathed, nausea flooding me for an entirely new reason. I gaped at the mess, feeling *devastated* for the artist. It had been a *massive,* incredibly intricate collection of pieces that they'd spent over a year on. The fact that it had fallen, that the display mount had failed—*was utterly sickening.*

I dizzily tried to sit up, but I was surprised when Carter's weight stayed against me, feeling oddly firm, as he scanned the gallery a final time, and lying beneath him—my breath quickened for an entirely different reason.

"Carter?" I murmured, and his gaze finally dropped to mine, his face looming just above me, as my pulse spiked again.

"Are you okay?" he panted, eyes wild and worried as his chest pulsed against mine with every heavy breath.

"Yeah," I murmured breathily. "You?"

"Yeah." He nodded and slid his arm beneath me.

As he hauled us up in a quick motion, his fingers slid around my waist, and I swallowed hard as he scanned around us one last time. When he finally looked down at me, he had a strange look in his eyes that made my chest tighten.

His gaze suddenly softened, returning to that warm brown color, and he *almost reverently* grazed the backs of his knuckles down my cheek. My eyes might have shuttered as he followed the line of my throat, *rather intimately,* and then gently pushed my hair over my shoulder, before his hand slid all the way down to the small of my back, pulling me into an embrace.

My breath caught at that hug for some reason. "Are you okay?" I asked.

"How long do you want to stay?" he murmured, and I could feel him looking around *again.*

"Why?" I whispered, wondering why he was so on edge. Why he'd dropped me to the ground like that, clearly expecting the worst—though I supposed in his line of work, those kinds of sounds *were* typically life-threatening, and something about that made my heart ache for him.

"I made us dinner reservations." He reminded me cooly, a little smirk finally tugging at his mouth as he finally gazed down at me again.

I nodded. "Let me talk to the gallery owner, and then I'm ready." It was finally time to let the piece go. It had served its purpose.

"I'm so proud of you, Sarafina." Carter said, his eyes soft and shimmering all at once. Carter reluctantly let go of me as I headed towards the gallery desk.

"I'll be right back." I said over my shoulder.

"Take your time, just know I'm waiting in *great anticipation*."

I caught his eyes traveling down the back of me as I walked away, and I smiled to myself.

CHAPTER 28
Michelin Star Rednecks
SARAFINA

In the car, Carter rested his hand on the middle console, palm up, and wiggled his fingers in request. "You waiting three whole business days, or are you gonna get in here, pretty girl?" Carter crooned, while the dim glow of the console illuminated his devastatingly beautiful face.

"What does this mean?" I asked nervously, sliding my hand into his. We'd held hands lots of times, but not just because, not like this.

"I just want to be close to you tonight, that's all." He shrugged casually. "Is that okay?"

"Yeah." I smiled to myself. "I guess that's okay." I tried to steady my breathing as his callused thumb stroked over the back of my hand, making me feel all kinds of things that I tried to shove down and forget about.

Entirely distracted by the feel of his hand around mine, we drove along the scenic waterfront for some time before I suddenly realized where we were going.

Carter pulled up at The Pearl, a seafood restaurant that I'd been dying to eat at for years, but for one reason or another, I'd never booked the reservation. How he'd remembered that, I had no idea.

Carter rounded the car and opened my door, extending his hand to me. "How did you get a reservation at the last second?" I asked as he guided me inside with his hand on the small of my back.

Carter shrugged and raked his free hand through his hair. "I know a guy."

Inside, a very pretty woman greeted us, and she gave me a warm, polite smile before she gave Carter an extra-long look. My stomach clenched as I waited for him to reciprocate, and to my relief, he didn't seem to notice her at all.

Carter and I were shown to a candle-lit table in a quiet corner of the solarium that jutted out over the river, and the view was incredible. Boats drifted by with twinkling lights, while the moon reflected off the rippling surface of the water, and just beyond the solarium was an art déco inspired bar. There was a live band serenading us with sultry music, the entire space was beautiful, and utterly *romantic.*

Was I reading into things? What did all this mean, exactly?

Carter stepped in front of the server and pulled out the tufted, high-back chair for me and then settled into his own, a mischievous look in his eye as the candlelight flickered between us.

"I've always wanted to eat here." I said suddenly, wondering if this was a date. It couldn't be though—right?

"Oh, I know." Carter smirked.

I fidgeted nervously while the server placed our napkins on our laps and took our drink order.

After our glasses of white wine were sampled and then poured, Carter grinned, unable to contain himself as we started on an appetizer of chilled oysters and caviar. "I have a surprise for you, and if you're not into it, you can totally veto it."

"Okay?" I placed my empty oyster shell back on the pebbled ice with peaked curiosity. "What is it?"

"I know you've wanted to eat here for a while, and if you want something off the menu tonight, we can totally do that." He leaned forward on his forearms. "But, I also know you well enough to know that you typically prefer Burrito Bell over caviar, and since this is a special occasion," a small smile tugged at the corner of my mouth as I listened intently. "Remember that one summer at the beach house?"

Of course I did. That had been one of the best summers of my life. The boating during the hot summer days, the big family meals in the evenings, the campfires and s'mores on the beach, long after our parents had gone to bed. The flirting. Even back then. Well, *I'd* been flirting, or trying to at least. "What about it?" I asked, turning the memory over in my mind fondly.

"I thought maybe we could share a seafood boil tonight instead of whatever stuffy menu they have planned."

"Like where they dump it on the table?" I quirked a brow, looking around. Carter nodded, a grin spreading even wider across his face. "How did you even remember that I liked that?"

"It's not hard to remember the important things." He watched me intently.

I blushed, unable to hold his gaze. "I don't think they do that here, Carter." In fact, I knew there was no way they were dumping a giant pot of seafood directly onto the pressed table-cloth in front of us.

Carter smirked, all too proud of himself. "They don't, but if you want it, they'll do it for us."

"You never cease to amaze me with your thoughtfulness." I admitted, shoving my emotions back down before I slowly grinned. "Let's ruin the tablecloth."

"That's my girl." He grinned back, and something exciting and electric hummed between us as we gazed at each other, leaving me feeling more hopeful than I'd felt in a long time.

This time, I didn't push the feeling away. He was soothing something inside of me, even if I wasn't sure exactly what that was. I decided I could let myself have this moment, could let myself feel... *happy*. Just for one dinner at least. Surely that was allowed.

Carter's gaze shifted over my head, and he pushed his chair back as a deep voice sounded behind me.

"Would you look at this riff-raff." A tall, muscular man in a chef's apron shook Carter's hand and pulled him in for one of those bro-hugs where they clap each other on the back, way too hard.

"Riff-raff?" Carter grinned. "You're one to talk." He motioned to me a moment later. "Ethan, I'd like to introduce you to Sarafina Devereux."

"No shit." Ethan shot Carter a look as he reached for my hand. "It is *very* nice to meet you, Sarafina." Ethan bent, bringing my knuckles to his lips with a wink, and I blushed when his lips lingered a little longer than I'd expected.

"Okay, okay. That's enough of that." Carter said stiffly and gripped Ethan's shoulder *hard*.

Ethan chuckled deviously and crossed his very buff arms, pleased he'd confirmed what I'd been trying to figure out all night. Carter and I *were* on a date.

Heat bloomed across my chest at the realization, and I suddenly realized Ethan had been talking to me. "It sounds like you two are going to throw off my whole service tonight." Ethan said, and I looked at him blankly as he pointed a thumb over his shoulder. "I owe this guy a favor, and he wants me to horrify my regulars and set up a redneck, backyard boil in here." Ethan rolled his eyes at Carter. "Because that's totally what I earned the Michelin Star for."

I could feel my cheeks heating even more. "If it's too much, we don't have to—"

"Hey now." Ethan waved his hand, cutting me off with a sympathetic look. "Gorgeous, I'm totally joking."

"Oh," I breathed, my head still in the clouds. "Okay." I took a heavy sip of my wine and glanced at Carter, who was *already* looking at me.

A date.

We were on a date?

Oh my.

"I'm happy to do it, truly." Ethan looked at Carter. "I'd do anything for this guy, *and* for Liam's kid sister, for that matter." I nearly choked on my wine.

Shit-what?

"I'm going to whip up the best damn boil you've ever had. We're going backyard, but elevated as fuck." Ethan nodded to himself, his mind clearly occupied with the options already.

"Appreciate it, man." Carter clapped him on the back.

"Anytime." Ethan nodded. "Holler if you guys need anything at all."

We watched as Ethan strutted over to the bar and threw back a shot of something clear, before disappearing around the corner, presumably towards the kitchen.

"Pays to know someone." Carter said as he settled back into his chair.

"How exactly do you know him?"

"Through Liam," Carter said, watching my reaction too close for comfort.

"Right." I chewed on the inside of my cheek and adjusted the silverware nervously.

"Does that worry you?" Carter asked, tracing his finger over the rim of his glass.

"Uh, yeah."

"Why?" His voice was low, thoughtful, as he cocked his head, still watching me carefully.

"What if he says something? What if Liam finds out about—" I shifted, unable to find just the right words.

"He won't." Carter purred, and the timbre of his voice caressed my very bones. "But I'm glad to know you're worried."

I swallowed hard, realizing I'd outed myself. This *was* a *date-date*, and Carter wanted to see if I knew it. How I felt about it.

Sneaky bastard.

My heart fluttered, and I suppressed a smile. I was on a date with my best friend. With the guy I'd been crushing on since forever. Was this real life?

I tried to keep my cool, and more importantly, not make it mean anything more than it was. Just a simple dinner between friends... *that was romantic.*

Shit. There was no way I was going to keep my cool. I was freaking the fuck out.

CHAPTER 29
Strawberry Taste Test
SARAFINA

Twenty minutes later, Carter and I were either the cutest or most annoying dinner guests they'd ever served.

Carter had his crisp white sleeves rolled up to his elbows. *I know.* I was in my plunging red silk gown, and we both wore matching plastic bibs to protect our evening wear.

We shared longing glances over our pile of seafood dumped on newspaper, and while the candlelight flickered between us, we giggled and hammered the shit out of our crab legs, fighting for every last bite. It might have been the most romantic thing I'd ever done.

"Everybody's looking." I laughed, dipping another piece of crab into the ramekin of herby melted butter.

"They're just admiring how beautiful you look," Carter said, eyes pouring over every facet of my face.

I quickly looked away and laughed again. I couldn't help it. "They're looking at the mess we're making."

"Let 'em. Ethan wouldn't serve this shit if he didn't want us making a mess."

Just then, a scrap of something flew into the air, emphasizing my point. We shared a guilty look, and our shoulders shook silently as we stifled our laughs, trying not to disturb the live performers, whose music still tinkled softly in the background.

"They *don't* serve this shit." I reminded him with a chuckle while I worked on freeing another piece of meat from one of the smaller crab claws. If I was being honest, I was actually surprised at how few of the massive pieces there had been. Not that I minded the extra time it took to crack open the smaller pieces, *it prolonged our date.*

When I looked up, Carter was still watching me, a devious smirk on his face that made me blush. *Again.*

I wondered what exactly he was thinking, wondered if it was similar to what I had been thinking all night. "Are you going to eat, or just watch me eat?" I finally teased.

Carter leaned forward on his forearms, voice lowering. "Oh, don't you worry, I'll get my fill tonight." His eyes dragged over me. "One way or another."

I sucked in a quiet breath while Carter started back in on his meal so casually, I wondered if I just had an abnormally dirty mind. We'd been shamelessly flirting all night, but I wondered if Carter understood that it was so much more for me. It always had been. I'd never admit it, of course, because I'd nearly done that once, and we'd almost lost our friendship over it.

If I lost him again, I didn't know if I could survive it. Not after the year I'd had. I realized as I stared down at my plate how badly I needed him. His friendship.

I'd rather settle for friendship than nothing at all, I decided. That's probably what this was to him—a friend date.

Carter was thoughtful and kind, and this was my debut as an artist. The more I thought about it, *of course, he'd take me out to celebrate.* This wasn't anything special, this was just Carter being who he was. Thoughtful and generous.

As if he could read my mind, Carter asked, "What's going on in that pretty little head of yours?"

"I'm just thinking."

"About what?"

"About how Sloane sold me out." I rolled my eyes, trying to ignore the empty pit that had formed in my stomach over the last thirty seconds.

"Ah, well, if she hadn't, you wouldn't be eating this delicious meal." Carter drawled.

"So I guess I have Sloane to thank for this?"

"I guess we both do." Carter pulled off his gloves and bib before setting his napkin on the table. "It's a good thing, too. Otherwise, I wouldn't have been able to give you your real birthday gift."

Carter reached into his jacket pocket and pulled out a flat, square box. "I'm sorry it's late. It's bespoke, and it wasn't ready in time." He cleared his throat. "I know I could have mailed it, but I wanted to give it to you in person."

With trembling hands, I slowly pulled off my plastic gloves as he slid the beautifully wrapped box across the table. "What is this?" I asked quietly, admiring the beautiful hand-painted gift wrapping.

"Open it, and you'll find out." He mused.

Starting at the tape seams, I carefully peeled the paper off because it was far too pretty to rip.

"Live a little." He chuckled, egging me on. "Rip the paper."

"I want to keep it." I said, fluttering my lashes to keep the water in my eyes from escaping down my cheeks.

"Not to worry, that's the second part of your gift—a whole box of this wrapping paper, because I knew you wouldn't want to ruin it."

"Really?" I asked, as he went blurry through my watery eyes.

"Obviously."

"You know me so well." I didn't dare blink.

"I'd like to think so." He crossed his arms and ran a thumb over his lower lip, concealing his smile.

I swallowed down the lump in my throat and ripped the wrapping off, reveling at how freeing it felt. It was a flat, square box, navy blue leather with gold detailing around the edges, and my fingers trembled as I hesitated to open it. My heart thundered realizing *he'd bought me jewelry.*

Carter smiled to himself, just waiting for me to discover what was inside. When I tipped the lid up, I was speechless. I knew what it was right away.

Inside, was a delicate filigree chain that shimmered as it caught the candlelight, and in the center was a small gemstone pendant. It was bespoke, understated, elegant, *and the pendant...*

"Carter." My lower lip wobbled. "This is beautiful."

"It's opal." He said softly. "Your mom's birthstone." I fluttered my eyes rapidly. "It's kind of fitting that your piece is releasing the same month as her birthday, isn't it?"

I tried, I really tried to hold it in, but warm tears streamed down my face as I looked between him and the necklace. "Will you put it on me?" I whispered.

"Of course." He rounded the table, and I laughed, wiping away my tears as I ripped my plastic bib off, exposing my neck.

Carter's hands were warm and steady on my skin as he swept my hair to the side, and a moment later, he'd deftly clasped the delicate chain. I leaned in breathlessly when his thumb swept up the column of my neck, just once, and heat cascaded all the way down to the tips of my toes. "This means so much." I breathed.

"I'm glad you like it." He hummed, returning to his seat.

"Thank you, Carter." I touched the pendant as it warmed to my skin. "I'm never going to take this off."

He looked pleased as he nodded, eyes warm and soft, and then asked, "Got room for dessert?"

I sniffled with a laugh. "I honestly don't think I could take another bite." This was more than I'd eaten in one sitting in— well, I wasn't sure how long.

"Maybe not a bite, then." Carter mused slowly. "Maybe just a lick or two." He smirked, letting that sit for a beat while everything in me sparked awake. "How about some ice cream?"

I bit my lip as I met his gaze, it was laced with something wild. "Ice cream?"

"I dare you." He said with a glimmer in his eyes. "To make room for dessert."

My heart started racing. Oh, we were back to this. *Our dares.*

Ice cream in hand, we strolled along the moonlit waterfront, hand in hand. I was now draped in Carter's suit jacket, shyly licking my strawberry ice cream cone, brazenly aware that he watched my tongue sweep across it every single time.

"Truth or dare." I uttered, casting him a glance out of the corner of my eye.

Under the moonlight, he glanced back at me, something unspoken humming between us. "Truth."

My heart started pounding. "Why are you wearing my hair tie every time I see you?"

"I like it." He said rather cryptically, looking down at the hair tie in question.

"Why?" I breathed, as his thumb grazed over the back of my hand.

"I just do." His eyes settled on my mouth and then away, his hand warm and steady around mine as we walked side-by-side. "Your turn. Truth or dare."

"Truth."

"Why didn't you tell your dad or Liam about your exhibition?"

"Carter." I sighed, not wanting to get into the long list of reasons that I wasn't sure I could even vocalize if I tried.

"Why?" He pressed gently, and I threw the rest of my ice cream cone in the trash can as we walked past it.

I shrugged. "I was scared, I guess." I licked my hand where the ice cream had dripped. He nodded, eyes tracking the movement. "Truth or dare?" I quickly asked him before he pressed for more details I didn't have.

"*Truth.*" He said with a low chuckle as the tension built

between us, and I wondered how many truths we'd divulge before one of us caved and picked *a dare.*

I shook myself out of the lusty haze I was in. "Was the salted buttercream actually better than strawberry?" I asked smugly, referring to our vehement debate back at the ice cream shop.

He stopped again, facing me. "I'd say we should do a taste test, but somebody just threw away their cone." He teased. "So I guess I can't taste the strawberry now." His eyes dropped to my lips again, and he swallowed hard as if he were considering getting a taste straight from the source.

"Too bad." I breathed.

"I guess you'll have to be the judge for the both of us." He rasped and lifted his ice cream cone to my lips. "Though I think you're probably a little biased, if we're being honest here."

"I promise to be as unbiased as humanly possible." I looked up at him through my lashes and slowly licked his ice cream cone. As my tongue dragged across it, I watched his eyes turn feral.

I licked my lips, aware of every cell in my body. "Strawberry was definitely better." And then I added, against my better judgment, "It's too bad you didn't get to try it."

Carter swallowed hard, and we stared at each other for the longest minute of my life.

"Ask me, it's my turn." I said, heart pounding in my ears.

Carter's breath was coming in ragged sweeps as we stood hand in hand, silent except for the soft sound of water lapping against the pier. "Truth or dare?" He uttered.

"Dare." My heart thundered. "I dare you to try the strawberry."

"I'm supposed to dare you." He rasped.

"I know." I breathed exhilaration and panic simultaneously surging through me.

This was a mistake.

What the hell was I doing?

And then something in his gaze shifted, like a tether deep

inside him had suddenly snapped. "I suppose I can make an exception." Carter said, closing in. "Just this once."

"You will?" I squeaked as he slowly backed me underneath a shadowy tree, gasping when my back hit the smooth bark behind me quicker than I'd anticipated.

Carter licked his lips, and I gasped again when he slipped his hand under the jacket I was wearing and slid that hand over my stomach and around my waist. His thumb dragged over my silken hip, slow enough to make me combust.

Date! Romantic date! This was a date-date!

Screaming inside.

Was he going to kiss me?

Please say yes.

Oh my God, it was happening. I couldn't breathe, couldn't catch my breath, as his other hand threaded around the back of my neck, as he tilted my face up towards him—where his ice cream cone had gone, I had no idea.

"I've been thinking about doing this all night." He murmured, his breath a caress across my fluttering eyelids.

"Yeah?" I hummed, unable to get more than a single word out.

"Yeah." His thumb stroked down the column of my throat, and I nearly whimpered. "I've been trying to convince myself why this is a terrible idea." His chest brushed against mine with every panting breath he took. "And I just can't find it in me to care anymore, but I do need to be clear about one thing."

"What's that?" I trembled as his fingers curled tightly around my hip with promise.

"While I can think of one way, I'd *love* to taste that strawberry ice cream. I'm going to need you to be crystal clear with me." His voice lowered. "Can you be a good girl and answer one question for me?"

Holy mother of God. "Yes," I rasped, on the precipice of melting into a puddle of goo.

"Yeah, that's what I thought—you are going to be a good girl for me, aren't you?" He chuckled deeply, his voice filled with approval and amusement, while I proceeded to melt into that aforementioned puddle. "Sarafina, my darling, since you threw away your ice cream cone—tell me, where could I possibly go to get a taste of this delicious strawberry ice cream you keep going on about?" He practically purred, all raw male arrogance as the backs of his knuckles grazed over the bare skin between each plunging panel of my dress, so feather light. Down his knuckles grazed between my breasts, leaving a wake of fire in their path.

"*Ohhh.*" I arched into his touch as his knuckles skimmed over my stomach and then disappeared before they drifted lower.

"Hmm?" His hand returned to my hip, anchoring me firmly between him and the tree. The silk of my dress against my skin was nearly unbearable as I shifted, desperate for more. "Tell me where I should go, Sarafina." Carter hummed, reminding me of his question, eyes crinkling with amusement, lust, longing, and everything I'd ever wanted.

I lifted a shaky finger up to my lips and tapped them, my words coming out breathy and uneven, despite my best efforts. "One taste and you'll know the strawberry is definitely better." Carter groaned. "I dare you." I whispered. "To prove me otherwise."

As I pulled in each ragged breath, he shifted closer, and the clean, intoxicating scent of him seeped into my very skin. "I might burn in hell for this," he murmured, leaning down.

"Then I'll burn with you." I breathed.

"Never." His lips dusted over my cheek as he vibrated with restraint. "Angels don't get a hall pass to hell."

"Then let's hope you're my salvation." I breathed, "Because I'm already burning." I'd been burning for him for as long as I could remember. My hands rose and fell on his chest with each panting breath he pulled in as he hovered in front of me, hesitating, while my entire world threatened to fall out from beneath me.

I was a big dumb idiot for risking everything I'd grown to rely on these past few months, a reckless, desperate idiot, but with nothing left to lose, I begged. I'd been broken before, and I could survive it again, if I had to.

"Please." I whimpered, hoping it was enough to break his resolve.

It was.

CHAPTER 30
An Angel with Wicked Intentions

CARTER

One minute earlier...

Sara loomed in front of me breathless, her dare hanging in the air like a crime waiting to be committed. I wanted to kiss her so fucking bad, but I knew there was no going back, no undoing it once it was done.

This was a big night for her, a weird fucking day for me. Maybe we were caught up in a moment, maybe this would pass.

God, she looked so beautiful right now, her wide brown eyes gazing up at me through those dark lashes. You'd almost think she was innocent until you saw the rest of her—the God-damned red dress she was wearing.

Fingers trembling with restraint, I closed my eyes and willed myself to keep my hands where they were, despite every silken curve resting under my fingertips, just begging to be touched, explored, *tasted*.

This was madness.

I should stop before I ruined everything, before someone got hurt. Probably me. *She was my best friend. I needed her. Couldn't afford to lose her.*

Her voice was heartbreakingly soft as she uttered that one little word, "Please."

And I was the weakest man alive as I let that one-syllable word break my resolve. "Fuck it." I rasped, reckless and greedy—dying to finally taste my little strawberry temptation.

Sara was utterly pliant as I took her face in both hands, as I tilted her lips up to mine, and the sound she made was nearly enough to undo me right then and there.

Suddenly, it didn't matter that this was a terrible idea. I didn't care anymore. Now, here, this—there was nothing but the smell of her, the feel of her, the sound of her.

"Carter." She whimpered, clutching my shirt as my lips brushed against hers gently, the first stroke of contact enough to make us both combust.

God, the sound of my name in her mouth.

I wanted everything.

I traced her lips with mine, relishing in the soft feel of her skin, wondering if I was dreaming. My zipper was painfully tight as I scented the trace of strawberry and buttercream lingering on her supple mouth.

More, I needed more.

I slotted my mouth against hers, tongue sweeping across that delicious lower lip as I tasted her for the first time. Fuck if I could remember my own name, but I didn't have to as she uttered it again. I swallowed her whimpers down my throat while she slid her arms around my neck and I pulled her even closer, desperate for so much more.

I kissed her slowly at first, discovering the feel of her lips on mine, of her body pressed against every inch of me. Her needy little sounds, desperate and wanting, as I discovered how perfectly she fit against me. Just like I knew she would.

She tasted better than I could have imagined. She was all sweetness, ice cream yes, but her very essence, the smell of her, it was almost too much.

Sara's tongue met mine as I swept it into her mouth, and every little sound she made, the feel of her perfect tits pressed against my chest as she pulled me closer, was all too much, and simultaneously not enough.

I could feel myself becoming ravenous for her, and I didn't want to go too far, too fast. Didn't want to be another guy who took more than she was ready to give.

It took everything in me to break the kiss, but I did, and I was already aching for more as I gazed down at her, breathless and a little undone. *Perfect.*

Sara broke into a shy smile and giggled nervously, but she didn't look away. Instead, she gripped me by the lapels and inched up on tiptoe. "Why'd you stop?" She rasped, giving me a look through her lashes that made me want to throw her over my shoulder like an uncivilized brute.

I was so fucked.

A lopsided grin spread over my own face as I gazed into my best friend's eyes and knew nothing would ever be the same again. "Oh, you want more?" I practically purred, letting her pull me back down to her mouth. "Aren't you a greedy little thing."

"So what if I am?" She laughed breathily, and I couldn't help myself as I went back for seconds.

The next slow-burning kiss was like water running over river rocks. Smooth and fluid, and quickly turning more rapid.

Sara's fingers threaded through my hair, tugging, as her supple body writhed against my own, and I groaned at the contact, at the incinerating need for her.

I slid my hand up her neck and tilted her face, angling her the way I wanted, relishing that she let me. Her back arched as I pulled her closer, deepening the kiss, being careful to keep her arms around my neck and away from the heavy weight at my back.

Our kissing quickly turned more frantic, more desperate, as we pulled at each other, panting, and tasting, and claiming. The comfort of our friendship a seamless bridge into this new territory.

My hands wandered over one silken curve after another, stopping just below the tempting swell of her breasts, where my fingers rose and fell on her ribs with her every rapid breath. Under the cover of darkness, I knew I could easily push the plunging panel of her dress to the side. Release one of those pert nipples I'd been struggling not to look at all night. Instead, I pulled myself back again, breathless and instantly desperate for another taste.

"So, was the strawberry better?" She whispered between panting breaths. "Since you went back for seconds?"

I rested my forehead against hers. "Careful, pretty girl, or that arrogance might get you into trouble." I hummed, brazenly letting my thumb dust over the bottom curve of her breast.

Her eyes fluttered as she arched into my hand. "Trouble is my middle name, didn't you know?" I chuckled roughly and did it again, loving how she pretended to be unaffected by it.

But in that moment of pure ecstasy, in that moment of her surrendering to me, softening for me—something more sinister crept in.

Fear.

I pulled her against my chest, hiding my face in her hair as the panic began to sink in.

All night, *that voice* had been banging around in my head.

It was relentless.

Chanting at me like some primal, barbaric brute.

My eyes shuttered as I replayed the sound of those explosions in the gallery. The sickening panic I'd felt for that split second. I'd tried to brush it off, tried to convince myself I was just being jumpy. Yet, after this morning and the threats those men had made, threats against Sara that absolutely terrified me—I'd nearly reached for the gun that had been a solid weight at my back all night.

Those men, whatever it was they wanted from me, were willing to do whatever it took to get it. Including hurting the ones I loved.

Suddenly, I wanted to puke.

Sara rested her chin on my chest and gazed up at me with a

soft smile I struggled to return. She looked so vulnerable, so inno-cent, her eyes finally bright and alive again.

In that moment, I realized what everyone else seemed to know already. Realized the truth of that chanting voice I'd tried *so dili-gently* to silence.

Sara's body seemed to know the truth of it too as she swayed in my arms, completely trusting, depending on *me* to take care of her, to keep her safe.

So I let that single word in. Let that war drum beat inside me. Let it fill me, primal and protective, lusting and wanting.

Mine. Mine. Mine.

Sara was mine, and maybe she always had been.

I surrendered to the realization that no matter how steep the cost, I would do whatever it took to keep her safe and out of harm's way.

The guilt that washed over me was near unbearable as I scanned the waterfront, scanned the shadows all around us, looking for anything out of the ordinary. Water lapped softly against the pier, and the stars twinkled softly in the sky, as if nothing was amiss. All the while my skin prickled because I could feel it—*we were being watched.*

When I pulled into the garage and turned the off the car, there were a million and one things I wanted to say, but Sara beat me to it as she cleared her throat, "If you want to pretend like it never happened I completely understand. I got caught up in the moment, and I'm sorry if I—"

"*No,*" I rasped, seeing the doubt in her eyes as she tried to undo our entire night.

She continued on nervously. "It's really okay. We can just go back—" she yelped as I hauled her over the console, into my lap before she could finish whatever ridiculous thing she was about to decide. Before I lost her again.

"I don't want to pretend," I started and simultaneously heard a soft rip as she settled into my lap. *Her dress.* I quickly shifted her and made it even worse. "Shit, I'm sorry."

Sara's lips crashed against mine, silencing my apology. "Don't be." She briefly pulled back and reached down. "I don't mind if you rip my clothes off." She breathlessly admitted as I suddenly began to recline.

So fucked.

Sara gave me a devious look as the soft whir of my seat going back filled the air. I would have laughed, would have teased her, but there was nothing humorous about her sitting in my lap looking like that.

Nothing at all.

I swallowed hard as Aphrodite herself slid down, heavy lidded on top of me, and I gripped her thighs as she straddled me, settling in on either side of my waist. "You're perfect, you know that?" I rasped.

"Carter," Sara demanded achingly. "Kiss me."

So I did. I kissed her until she was writhing and swollen lipped, until the car was fogging up, and I was basically dry fucking her over her dress—the damp heat between her legs a tempting invitation as she rode my tented zipper, leaving me wanting so much more.

However, I was not about to fuck my best friend in the car, like a horny teenager. Though it took all my strength once again, I finally broke the kiss, because Sara was not just a quickie car fuck, and definitely not for our first time.

First time. What was I even saying?

We were already so far past a line we should have never crossed.

"We stay in here any longer and we're going to get ourselves in trouble." I panted.

"I don't mind."

It was a strain to keep my hands still, to keep them from roaming, exploring, ripping more fabric. "I don't want any of our firsts to be impulsive, or quick, or in the car."

"What would be so bad about that?" She batted her lashes.

"My sweet, sweet girl." I breathed. "You are an irresistible temptress hiding behind innocent wide eyes, you know that?"

"Took you long enough to figure it out." She said with a breathy laugh.

"Just the same." I swallowed hard as she loomed over me, tempting as fuck. "I can hardly move in here, and while having you on top of me is the stuff of wet dreams, this just won't do, not with what I have in mind." I gripped her hips, wondering if I'd gone too far.

"Then take me upstairs." Sara said through her lashes, and my cock jumped. How could I say no?

Sara screamed with delight as I hauled her over my shoulder and did just that.

When I opened the garage door and closed it behind us, we were all shrieking laughter, but the house was quiet, and Sara's laughter suddenly turned quiet and breathy.

As she swayed over my shoulder with each step towards my bedroom, I could tell she was incredibly nervous, and, fuck if I wasn't a little nervous, too.

It took the entire walk down the hall for me to get my head on straight. I was going to kiss her goodnight and then go sleep downstairs.

I was going to fucking behave.

I was an idiot for implying otherwise.

As I approached my bedroom, I set her down against the wall in the hallway and caged her in. Only the faint outline of her lips parting was visible in the dim light.

I leaned in as her eyes fluttered shut, knowing I'd never get enough of this, *of her*. Should have never started because I didn't know if I could stop now.

"Carter," Sara moaned breathily as I kissed a path down her jaw to her neck, finding the hollow beneath her ear, and then traveling back up to her perfect lips. She was like putty in my hands, open, inviting me in for more.

A goodnight kiss, I reminded myself, pulling back to give her a chaste kiss on the forehead before I pushed off the wall, creating much needed space between us.

"Thank you for dinner." She whispered.

"Let's do it again sometime." I teased, leaning on the wall across from her, practically sitting on my hands as I nodded towards the bedroom—time to bid my girl goodnight.

She looked at me for a long moment and swallowed hard before she headed into my bedroom, the soft lamplight illuminating her divine silhouette.

I stayed in the hallway and tried to steady my breath as I gazed at her walking away from me. I wanted her so fucking bad. I had for a long while now.

Having tasted her, kissed her, felt her writhing against me making all those fucking little sounds, it was difficult not to imagine what she'd look like, riding my hand desperately.

Taste like. Head thrown back and squirming on my tongue.

Feel like. Taking my cock underneath me.

She was intoxicating, and she was *everything* to me.

Which was why I should just go downstairs before I could change my mind.

But I didn't. Whatever was going to happen or not happen, she'd be the one to decide. I'd let *her* set the pace. I'd walked away once before and regretted it ever since. I wouldn't do it again.

I blew out a steady breath, trying to ignore the fact that I was nearly dizzy as all the blood in my body rushed in one direction.

She was watching me with a sleepy expression, only, that's when I noticed she was trembling. *Was she afraid?* Or was it something else entirely? I didn't know what exactly was running through that pretty little head of hers as she fidgeted in front of my bed.

So I stayed in the hallway, unsure if I should come in. I didn't want to push her too far, too fast, and most of all—I needed to know that I wasn't going to lose my best friend. I couldn't afford it. I needed her. So fucking badly, and she had no idea.

I knew she'd had bad experiences with other guys. I didn't know the specifics, but I knew enough to be worried. She'd been with people who'd taken when she didn't want to give.

I knew Isaac from the gallery was one of them. He'd crossed some line with her, and it was completely evident by the way Sara had shrunk into herself the moment she'd heard his voice. The thought made my blood boil.

There was a reason she'd never been in a long-term relationship all these years, a pattern that seemed to be repeating itself in her love life. That night of the charity auction flashed through my mind, and I still didn't know what exactly had happened in that car before Taggart had dumped her on the side of the road, covered in blood. She'd never confided the details of that night, even amongst all the secrets we'd shared over the last few months, but I did know one thing. In one way or another, he'd hurt her too, and after the way she'd responded at Thanksgiving, I didn't dare ask her about it again. I knew she'd come to me when she was ready, but right now, I had no fucking idea what she was thinking. One minute she was mounting me with enough boldness that you'd think it was something she'd done a thousand times, and the next, she was visibly trembling as if she were trapped—I wondered if I was to blame for making her feel that way.

She had so much confidence one minute, and the next, it was like she'd forgotten all about it. Forgotten the strength, of who she was. That was what healing looked like, I supposed, but still, part of me was terrified that I was about to walk over a landmine that Sara didn't even remember she'd buried.

I wanted to help her move forward, hopefully with me. I just didn't know how to do it without getting us both blown up. It was a terrifying prospect to consider.

Not to mention, Liam would lose his shit if he knew his little sister was standing here, like a merciless seductress in front of my bed—he was probably in his own bed, just across the street at this very moment, and he had the door code. In fact, if he saw me pull into the garage, he could come over at anytime.

"Are you coming in?" Sara asked nervously, her eyes lusty and skittish all at once.

I'd worry about Liam later. "Do you want me to?" I cautiously asked, wondering if I *should* just turn around and go downstairs.

"Maybe I dare you to," Sara breathed, licking her lips.

Fuck me. This woman.

My eyes darted between hers as I processed that she *did* want me to come in, and everything shifted.

Fuck yeah. Internal fist pump.

"You dare me to, huh?" Something about the inviting way she retreated begged me to advance, and like a hypnotized man, *I did.*

"Mhmm." She backed up a step, reeling me in with every one of hers.

I could practically see her pulse fluttering wildly in her neck, nipples peaked, hard against her gown, practically begging to be touched.

I gripped the top of the doorframe, staying at the threshold, not coming an inch closer until I got this wild feeling inside me contained. "Are we playing truth or dare now, pretty girl?"

"Yes, and Carter," she batted her lashes. "I dare you to come in here." In a flirtatious invitation to play, she pointed to the floor in front of her several times.

I realized my beautiful angel had intentions wicked as sin.

And who was I to deny her?

CHAPTER 31

The Dare

SARAFINA

Carter loomed in the wide doorway, looking sexier than any human should as the soft lamplight glittered against his dark, watchful eyes.

I was doing my very best not to disintegrate under his intense gaze, while he was busy looking at me, like I was the only thing that existed in the entire universe.

My heart was racing, my hands were trembling, I was fluttering with anticipation, dying to see what might follow the kiss of all kisses.

In a matter of hours, *everything* had changed.

Carter hesitated in the doorway. "Will he or won't he accept the dare?" I mused as nonchalantly as I could muster, though I could hardly steady my voice. This was all such new territory for us.

Carter pushed off the doorframe and sauntered into the room without a word. My entire body vibrated with awareness as he gave me a simple look that had me on the precipice of begging. I retreated a step towards the bed as he softly closed the ornate door behind him, *before he fucking locked it.*

The tension between us was a band ready to snap as Carter

strolled over the lush Savonnerie rugs, and shrugged off his suit jacket, casually laying it over the arm of the closest chair.

I retreated another step, *towards his luxurious bed.*

The feel of his lips on mine was still a burn, branded on my skin as he unbuttoned one sleeve and then the other, before slowly rolling them up.

I suddenly bumped into the bedpost and fumbled, gripping it for stability while he leisurely unclasped his belt, pulling it out loop by fucking loop. My mouth went dry as he rhythmically wound it around his hand and then set it on the dresser, watching me very carefully as he did so.

Finally, Carter spoke, his voice exceptionally low and smooth. "I won the last dare. Now what?" He crossed his arms with a smirk and leaned against the dresser, keeping ample distance between us.

I could tell he was letting me guide the pace of things, letting me control how far tonight would go. That's why it was so easy to trust him, why I'd always felt so safe with him—I knew he would never push me past my limits.

That tiny voice in the back of my head immediately went to work, reminding me that he was capable of rejecting me, that he'd done it before and he could do it again. But that didn't stop me from imagining that muscular body looming over me, doing very dirty things.

"I guess that would make it my turn." I whispered, still clutching the bedpost for dear life.

"Truth or dare then?" He murmured.

"Truth." I breathed like a chicken.

He nodded, all too amused, and considered, finally, in a voice as soft as the starlight at the pier, "Tell me what the fuck Isaac did to make you react like that."

Oh fuckerson.

I thought I'd been so clever by averting a dare, and *this* is what he wanted to talk about? Talk about a cold bucket of water.

"Pass." I said, as Carter settled in against the ornate dresser, like he'd be there a long while. Just great.

Carter chuckled darkly. "You know, pretty girl, part of my job is getting people to talk." His eyes glimmered, something determined lurking just beneath the surface, and I felt myself bristling. I could dig in my metaphorical heels too. Watch me. See if I tell you a damn thing. Arrogant jerk. What was he going to do, muscle the answer out of me?

Carter continued, "You could save me some time and tell me yourself or alternatively," His voice dropped low and menacing, and I suddenly realized he hadn't been talking about *me* at all. "I could just pay him a little visit. The options are really endless, but I doubt he'd hold out very long." Carter continued on as my lips started to form a question. "Since the moment he laid eyes on you, I've been considering all sorts of *interesting* things."

"What the hell does that mean?" I demanded.

"It means," His lips twitched, cocky confidence rippling off him like smoke off a signal fire. "Well, I don't need to fill that pretty little head of yours with violent things, now do I?"

He was going to what? Beat him up? "You wouldn't." I set my jaw, wondering if in fact he would. All bets seemed to be off now.

"Try me, sweetheart." Carter smirked. "Besides, if you don't say your truth, then you lose, and that would bring our little game to an end tonight." He tilted his head, a predator assessing its prey.

And how damn badly I wanted to be caught.

"Do you want our game to be over?" He asked too quietly.

Abso-fucking-lutely-not.

"How do you even know there is a story to tell?" I countered, inching towards the bed. Wondering when I'd grown so bold. I'd only had one glass of wine with dinner, and now I could hardly feel it—I suddenly wished I'd slogged down a second or third before we'd left, but Carter hadn't ordered the wine by the bottle like he usually did. I knew a little liquid confidence would be *so very* nice right about now, but simple bravery would have to do.

Carter's eyes flared as he watched me sit on the edge of his bed. "You think I didn't notice how your entire body recoiled the moment you heard his voice?" He spoke softly, though his voice bordered on outrage. "Or how you belittled yourself in front of him."

I shimmied back on the bed until only my heeled feet were dangling off the edge, arguing, "I did not."

Carter's jaw fanned. "I seriously beg to differ."

"I did no such thing." Heat flushed my cheeks because I couldn't reasonably admit what he was saying was true. Not to him, not to myself. I didn't want to acknowledge that I'd felt so horribly weak in that moment. Helpless.

Not like I felt now though, right now, I felt pretty damn powerful. Carter had always been so freaking restrained with me, and right now, it felt like he was wrapped around my finger, and I *loved* it.

"Did you sleep with him?" Carter asked, a wave of dark jealousy passing over his expression.

"With Isaac?" I raised a brow, tossing out casually. "Maybe I did."

The look. On his. Face.

Jealous Carter wasn't on my bingo card, but damn if I wasn't happy to check off that box anyway.

I grabbed the cat ears off the nightstand and fiddled with them, trying to decide if I should tell Carter what actually happened or if that would ruin the mood. "Why do you want to know?" I mused, watching him carefully. "Would you care if I had?"

"*He* was looking at you like he'd slept with you." Carter glowered. "And *you,* on the other hand, did not seem to share that same enthusiasm." *Always so perceptive.*

"I didn't sleep with him." I said smugly, shoving what I was really feeling down even harder.

Carter's eyes narrowed, not buying it for a second. "So tell me your truth." He drummed his fingers on his arm patiently. "What happened between the two of you?"

I stared at him for a long while before I finally dropped my gaze to the floor. "He befriended me when I was at my lowest this summer, and let's just say he only had one thing in mind."

"And what exactly was that?"

"I think you can guess." I slid the headband into my hair and cocked my head against my shoulder flirtatiously before I leaned back on my elbows, trying not to think about it.

"I can guess a lot of things, but this isn't a guessing game." Carter hummed with a subtle smirk, clearly amused with the cat ears. "*You* picked truth, so let's hear it."

"He wanted to be friends with benefits, and I—" Friends with *financial benefits*, is what I didn't say because I couldn't bear to admit that humiliating little detail. How to put the whole thing delicately? "I didn't know I didn't want it—until I knew, I didn't want it."

"Care to elaborate?" Carter asked darkly.

"Not particularly." I avoided his gaze, suddenly feeling less into my game than I had a moment ago.

"Well, there's only one thing I need to know." His tone eased up because he noticed me withdraw, because of course he did.

"What's that?" I asked, fiddling with my new necklace. His eyes tracked the movement.

"Do I need to bury him in a dark hole where no one will ever find him?"

I scoffed, wondering if he actually would. "I'll let you know when I decide." There was so much context I could add. About how I thought Carter was ignoring me, so I had tried to move on, albeit very unsuccessfully, but I didn't say any of that, because it would have been humiliating to admit. "It's really not that big of a deal." I tried to shrug it off, tried to convince myself of that fact just as much as him.

"It's a big deal to *me*," Carter said quietly. "I don't want to hurt you, and if I don't know where your wounds are, I might."

"Carter." I sucked in a small breath at the devastation in his voice, the fear there. "You have nothing to worry about." He nodded once, but didn't say anything.

So I offered him a tiny piece of the truth. "I was lonely, and we kissed. He was moving faster than I was comfortable with, so I left, and then things were really fucking awkward after that." I left out the most horrifying bits because it was humiliating—the fact that I hadn't seen straight through it. I should have known better.

"And are things moving too fast for you now?" Carter asked gently, and I could tell he had this messed up idea in his head that he was the bad guy in all this, but that couldn't have been further from the truth—he seemed to completely miss the fact that I was desperate for him, and that I always had been.

I swallowed hard, not sure what I was so afraid of as I looked Carter square in his kind, patient, brown eyes, and decided maybe I could admit this to him, and everything would be alright. That *I* would be alright if I unburied one of my dirty little secrets.

I didn't give myself time to second-guess as I threw myself off the ledge and hoped he'd catch me. "You don't get it. It wasn't just that he was moving too fast, Carter." My voice wavered, but I kept going. "I told him to stop multiple times, and he didn't. Nothing happened exactly, but I had to shove him off me, and it fucking sucked." Carter's eyes shuttered, his knuckles going white as he gripped the dresser so hard it groaned, but I kept going. "The worst part is, I wasn't even into him. I was just lonely and confused. The day he met me, I was literally lying in the middle of a sidewalk on campus, crying." I admitted against my better judgment and immediately hated how heartbroken Carter looked at that. "Sad, lonely, vulnerable girls are apparently his type." I added quietly while I anxiously fiddled with a single sequin on the cat ears, wondering if I had it in me to admit the rest.

"Is that what *I'm* doing?" Carter asked warily. "Are you sad and lonely, and I'm taking advantage of you when you just need a good friend?"

I looked at Carter for a good long while and then huffed out a frustrated noise. "Why do you always think you're the bad guy?"

"Maybe I am."

"You're not."

His eyes dragged over me, making my skin heat. "I'm no better than—"

"You're better than everyone." I quietly cut him off. "You're my best friend, and no, a friend is not the only thing I need. What I need—" I huffed, knowing I should keep my mouth shut, but he had me all worked up and I couldn't think straight, so I hid behind my eyelids.

"Tell me. Whatever it is, I'll give it to you." He said earnestly.

"What I *need is* a good, God damn fucking." I snapped, and Carter's eyes flared with surprise. "My thighs are literally a slip-and-slide right now because—to answer your question from earlier, *no*, I'm not wearing any underwear! It would have given me panty lines, and because of *you*." I motioned up and down his body, and Carter could hardly suppress his laughter as he hid a wildly amused smile behind his fist. "Well, you know why." I stuttered out ineloquently. "I know you do. You gave me the kiss of all kisses, and you showed up for me tonight, and you always show up for me when it matters most, and this," I touched the necklace breathlessly. "You're so incredibly thoughtful, and you're worried about hurting me? Sometimes you're too damn protective. You know that? Maybe I don't want to be protected. Maybe I want to be fucked." I said incredulously, and his eyes heated at that. "You're worried you're going to break me, but sometimes it feels like you're the only thing putting me back together—*truth*." I quickly stopped myself before I confessed the most brutal thing of all.

"Don't stop." Amber-flecked eyes begged. "Please don't stop."

"Truth." I admitted, eyes shuttering because I couldn't bear to look at him when I said it. "*I'm terrified.*"

"What are you so afraid of, pretty girl?" Carter's eyes darted between mine, trying to decipher.

"Of *getting* what I want." I shrugged. "Of *not* getting what I want." I let my gaze drag over his tall, imposing figure *very* slowly.

Carter licked his lips, his mouth parting as each breath came a little faster. "What exactly is it that you want?"

I smiled deviously, trying to hide my nerves. "I think it's your turn, Casanova. I've had enough truth-telling for now." I leaned back on my forearms, dangling my feet off the edge of his bed.

He gave me a long look and shook his head. "I see how it is."

"Truth or dare." I asked sweetly, my heart still thrumming a mile a minute from my word vomit.

"Truth." He smirked, shaking his head.

"Why did you take my hair tie that day?" I was desperate for the answer.

His brown eyes shimmered like molten caramel, and he considered for a long while before he finally answered. "To replace the one I took—*the night before I left for basic.*"

I sat straight up. "What?"

"I wanted something to keep you close while I was gone." He admitted. "That flimsy little thing survived through some of the shittiest days I've had, and you know when it finally broke?" He shook his head. "I had it on that morning, Thanksgiving, and I was so nervous to come up to your room and talk to you, *that's* when it finally broke." He looked away. "I was trying to figure out what I was going to say because I was terrified that you never wanted to speak to me again." His voice was hardly above a whisper. "This one was a replacement. Just in case you decided you were done with me for good."

My pulse thrummed, realizing what he'd just admitted.

He looked devastated as he gazed at me, eyes so full of yearning. "You're my best friend too, Sara, and I'm terrified of losing you. I don't want to screw up what we have because I need you more than you even realize, and fuck." He gripped the back of his neck, looking distraught. "I've tried not to cross the line with you,

I really have, but then you show up here, looking like *that*, and you're sleeping in *my* bed with *that* fucking thing." He motioned to the dildo, still buried in the sheets. "And I can't help but hope that maybe you feel the same—*truth*." He added, desperation drenching his beautiful eyes.

I could hardly breathe. "Carter."

"Not to mention, seducing me with strawberry everything." He added wildly, with a dramatic roll of his eyes and then more quietly, "Why do you smell so fucking good. *All the fucking time.*" His eyes shuttered. "And taste so fucking good." I smiled quietly as a fluttering swell filled my chest. "Feel so good." His shoulders caved slightly at the admittance.

"Carter." I whispered.

He swallowed hard, and kept going, eyes glued to the dildo in the sheets. "Truth or dare. Are you going to use that thing when I leave?" He rasped.

"That's not how truth or dare works. I have to pick first." I whispered.

He took a step towards me. "Then pick truth."

"You're going to leave?" I asked, teetering between the thrill of him coming closer and the confusion that he was going to leave. Why? After everything we'd each just said.

"Answer. The. Question."

"Yes," I answered breathily even as heat flushed my cheeks at the admittance. "I'm definitely going to need to do *something* after that kiss." I'd been hoping it would be with him though.

He smirked.

Oh. My. God.

What was I even saying?

Shut your goddamn mouth, Sara!

I didn't know if I'd ever been this honest in my life, and what a terrible time to start.

"Your turn." A wicked look stirred in his eyes.

"Truth." I buried my face in my hands. "I'm *horrified* that I just said that—that you know I used that thing in your bed."

"Truth," he hummed, "why exactly were you using that thing in *my* bed? Hmm?" Then brazenly, "Don't you have a boyfriend to take care of your needs, pretty girl?"

I shook my head no. Obviously not. He just wanted to hear me say it. Again.

"No?" he asked, feigning surprise, his voice low and pleased.

"Truth." I breathed, my entire body trembling.

"Yes?" he rasped and took a step closer.

"I've had real shit luck with guys." I whispered, admitting another little secret, and he stilled halfway across the room. "I don't think I know how to trust anyone anymore."

"I know." He said *so* gently, and waited there, glued to the floor. I knew he wouldn't move, not until I asked him to. As if everything about him wasn't already turning me on, his patience was too.

"Truth. You should probably know before we go any further that I think there might be something wrong with me." I admitted, my voice shaky as I spoke the inner fear out loud for the first time. "Truth. I haven't been with anyone in a while because I'm honestly not sure I'm any good at *it*." Oh boy, I should shut my mouth now, before I said something I couldn't take back. "Truth. It took me an entire month to muster up the courage to buy that thing, because I needed to take things into my own hands— because nobody's ever made me finish before, and I-I-wanted to see if I even could."

His eyes gleamed at that. "*Nobody?*"

"There's something wrong with me." My voice wavered, because a small part of me was terrified I wouldn't be enough for him, for anyone. "I don't think I can." Shit. The cat was out of the bag now. That's right folks, I willingly outed myself as the broken thing I was. What the hell was wrong with me? I had zero game.

"How many people have tried?" Carter asked, a confident sparkle in his eye at the unspoken challenge in the air.

"A few?"

He raised his brows.

"Three." I whispered, wondering if he thought that was a lot or a little.

"Truth," Carter said carefully. "Can you make *yourself* feel good with that?"

"Carter." I pleaded, heat flushing my cheeks. I was never going to live this down.

"Sarafina." He waited, *so patiently waited*, even as I begged him with my eyes.

"I don't know." I admitted under my breath. "Kinda?"

"Hmm." He mused. "That's *very* interesting."

"*Carter.*" It was practically a whine.

"And you still think there's something wrong with you?"

"Maybe?" I whispered. "Probably."

His smile was feline. "I can prove to you in fifteen minutes there's not a damn thing wrong with you, pretty girl." He smirked adding, "But just because I *can* prove my theory quickly doesn't mean I will. In fact, when I do finally get my hands on you, sweetheart, I can promise, *I'll be taking my sweet, sweet time.*"

Oh God. I swallowed hard, the ache of desire blooming within me was growing more excruciating by the second, tempered only by my anxiety. "I think you're underestimating my problem—not to mention that sounds more like a *dare* to me."

"*Fact,*" Carter emphasized cockily, but still didn't move from where he stood. "I could make you come ten ways to Sunday." He motioned to the dildo. "Using *only* that." He lifted his hand and wiggled his fingers lazily. "Or these. *Dealer's choice.*" He sucked his teeth with a smirk, waiting.

"Fact." I swallowed hard. "Maybe I would let you try."

"Fact." He suppressed a smile, and it was the longest pause of my life before he finished his thought. "I wouldn't have to *try.*"

My heart was about to take flight in my chest. "I think you're overly confident." The words were thin as mist on my tongue.

He shrugged incredibly arrogantly. "*Truth,* I'd be more than happy to test my theory." His smirk was wicked. "All *you* have to do is ask."

My kryptonite. Speaking up for myself. And he knew it. I fidgeted, not quite able to voice what it was I wanted—*why was it so damn hard to ask for what I wanted?*

"*I dare you.*" He whispered encouragement. "Tell me what you want, pretty girl."

I wanted *him!* Obviously! I wanted him so fucking bad, and he wasn't going to make a move until I explicitly asked him to. Why did he have to be so damn chivalrous?

Everything ached with pounding desire as his gaze dragged over me, just waiting for me to say the word, but what if he couldn't do it? What if *I* couldn't do it? By myself, sure, kinda, I could make it feel good, but I wasn't entirely sure if I was *really* finishing. With someone else—*I'd never even gotten close.* It'd always been way too fast, over before it ever really started feeling good.

Then again, I'd never been with anyone like Carter before. Never with someone I wanted this badly. Who turned me on this much.

Who felt this right. This *safe*.

What I wanted was dangling right in front of me, just waiting for me to reach out and grab it. *Him.*

I couldn't quite do it though. So instead, I grabbed the next best thing. The sparkling pink thing.

Carter's chest rose and fell with every heavy breath he took just a few feet away, still glued to that same spot.

Fisting the heavy rubber sparkler, I pulled it into my lap, completely embarrassed by the monstrosity of the thing. "I dare you." I rasped. "To prove you can make me come ten ways to Sunday—with this."

That was all it took.

His eyes gleamed, as he crooked his finger. "Stand up."

CHAPTER 32

Noodles for Legs

SARAFINA

Heart racing, I slid off the bed and stood as Carter closed the space between us in two powerful strides. "Turn around." Carter's jaw flexed as the air filled with thrilling anticipation. I looked up at him nervously as the intoxicating scent of him enveloped me and heat surged through me. "Do you trust me?" he asked, his voice filled with quiet calm. I looked at him for a long moment and knew I did, I trusted him more than anybody in the world, so I nodded yes. "Good. Turn around for me, sweetheart."

I turned slowly, fingertips tingling, knowing I was handing over my power, giving him the ability to crush me if he wanted to, but I did it anyway. Reckless, stupid, and greedy, I did it anyway.

I stood there, waiting for him, feeling like I was about to combust just at the *idea* of him touching me. Behind me, I heard a drawer open and close and then, a moment later, the warmth of him was hovering behind me, the heat of his breath on my neck, making me shudder.

Carter slid his wide hand over my stomach and pulled me flush against his strong, solid body from behind. I clamped down on a moan as he gently fisted my hair and tilted my neck to the side, the caress of his breath at my ear, as he said, "I've been dying to get my hands on you all night, pretty girl." His voice was gravelly. "Should we lay down some ground rules, seeing as this is technically a dare?"

"Sure." I instinctively arched back as his lips grazed my neck, leaving me breathless and desperate.

Carter chuckled, and the sound vibrated against me. "To prove my theory, that you aren't broken—I'm going to use your cute, sparkly little unicorn horn to make you come ten ways to Sunday." He rumbled. "Agreed?"

"Agreed." I nodded dizzily. He wasn't even doing anything yet, and I was already disintegrating under his touch. The power he held over me was thrilling and terrifying. I'd always been susceptible to his charm, his kindness, always been a weakling in that regard.

"And tonight, just so we're both on the same page, I'm only going to penetrate you with this." Carter took the dildo from me and tossed it onto the bed. I. Was. Dripping. He stroked my neck, and my eyes fluttered. "Are we agreed? Dildo penetration only?"

Was I dreaming? I must be dreaming. There was no way I was really this bold, this daring, this willing to leap off a cliff, knowing I might splatter at the bottom. "Agreed." The word came out strangled as I tried to catch my breath.

"Good." Carter hummed, bringing me back into my body with the simple caress of his fingers over my skin. "Now for the rules." I whimpered as he nipped at my ear, and his voice was calm and commanding as he began. "You are going to tell me if you want me to *stop* at any point."

"Okay," I breathed, doubting that would happen.

"You are going to tell me if you're *uncomfortable* at any point."

"Carter." I fidgeted nervously.

His hands came around my body to grip both my wrists and still me. "I want you to feel safe with me, sweetheart. *Always.*"

"That's good." I practically panted in agreement, though my

brain was short-circuiting as his thumb stroked the tender inside of one of my wrists.

"You are going to tell me if there is anything you know you don't like." He smelled so damn good, and I dropped my head back against his chest, wondering if my knees might give out beneath me. "Sara, is there anything that's off limits tonight?" He asked.

I nodded breathily.

"Good." His nose traced the shell of my ear. "Tell me."

"I—I don't want." I was suddenly afraid of sounding stupid. I'd honestly let this man do anything he wanted to me.

"I'm going to take such good care of you." Carter's grip tightened around me, and he kissed the hollow beneath my ear as I swayed. "But in order to do that, I need you to tell me what you're comfortable with. Can you do that for me, Sara?"

I could hardly think straight, let alone string a sentence together. "I—I don't want it in my mouth."

"Good girl." He murmured against my skin. "Thank you for telling me, and you have my word, I won't put it in your mouth."

"Thank you." I rasped, surprised at the relief that brought me in saying it, the relief I had knowing for certain he'd keep his word.

"You're welcome." And then he added, with an arrogant low chuckle, "*But what I will do,* is put that rainbow sparkler so deep into your tight, wet pussy—play with you for so long, that you won't even remember your own name."

I gasped, fluttering around absolutely nothing at all, realizing Carter was so much dirtier than I'd ever anticipated, and *fuck it was hot.*

"Are you ready for your first real orgasm?" He chuckled far too confidently.

"I've had an orgasm before." I tried to respond smartly, but my voice came out paper thin, giving me away.

"Not like this, you haven't." He murmured, his voice a caress against my throat, and my breasts tightened as he gripped the zipper at the back of my dress. "The last rule is the most important one."

I hummed in acknowledgement because I could hardly speak. My insides felt like a lava lamp—gooey, crumbling and liquefying all at once. Everything in me was molten, for one thing. *Him.*

"Most importantly, sweet girl, I want you to tell me exactly what you want and where you want it. Understood?" Carter rasped into my ear. "Communication is key to a mind-blowing orgasm."

"Okay," I whispered as arousal literally slid down my thighs. I had no dignity left. None. I was desperate for this man, and I wondered if he knew how badly he could hurt me.

"Are you going to be a good girl and follow the rules?"

"Yes," I breathed, knowing I would do literally anything he asked of me.

"*Yeah, I know you are.*" Carter rumbled into my ear, and the slow sound of my zipper sliding down was the only sound in the room besides both our heavy breathing.

I shuddered as his fingers trailed over the bare skin of my back, but instead of undressing me immediately, his hand slid around the nape of my neck and everything else disappeared as he claimed my mouth with his. His body was hard and unyielding behind me, but his mouth was soft and gentle against my own, like his lips were offering me a sensuous, lazy hello. The kiss was completely unhurried, despite the fact that his grip on me was tighter than it'd ever been—like he was worried I would slip away in the wind if he didn't hold on tight enough. Or maybe he just needed somewhere to put all the intensity he was feeling while he kissed me *so very* gently.

Slowly, he coaxed my lips open and swept his tongue into my mouth, tasting of something familiar and yet not, something I needed more of and something that felt so damn right.

His broad body pressed against mine. Strong, steady, in control, but always listening, each stroke, each touch, a call and response, a sensuous building melody. He groaned when I pushed back against him, and I found that enthralling, the way *he* responded to *my* touch.

"You." He kissed me again. "Are." He pulled back only for a moment. "Trouble."

I laughed breathily, but it quickly turned into a moan as he tipped my chin up, igniting a desperate charge between us as he deepened the kiss, almost trembling with restraint as he claimed me, cautiously, carefully—each kiss, each caress coming in waves, giving me time and space to communicate if I needed anything before the next claiming of his mouth on mine. Carter kissed me so *thoroughly*, it was literally difficult to stand.

Panting, filled with anticipation and need, I finally ground back on him more freely, feeling his considerable length pressing hard into my lower back like a promise. I moaned his name, a desperate plea for some sort of release to the tension that had been steadily building between us for months now. *Years actually.* And over the last few days, the ache had become excruciating, near unbearable—all of this was either going to lead to the best or worst day of my life. *I was going to be left with everything or nothing at all.*

"Still want to do this?" he asked, breath ragged as he reached around me to drag the toy out of the bed.

My heart had never beat faster, skin never flushed hotter, as I took a flying leap off the edge of my cliff, knowing that jump would either save or destroy me. "Make me feel good, Carter." I rasped and then added with a devious smirk, because I just couldn't help myself. "If you can."

He groaned, but it was me who ceased to exist as I became nothing more than desire itself when his fingers slid over my bare skin and then lower. "Don't you know, you really shouldn't say things like that to a man like me? *Tempt me like that.*" His eyes shuttered as he promised darkly, "Keep running your mouth like that and I'll *make sure* you don't remember your name when I'm done with you."

And I believed him, but maybe that's exactly why I breathlessly egged him on—just for the thrill of it. "That's quite a promise. Will there be a pop quiz? Do we need a control for this hypothesis?" I smirked and started spelling it. "That's S-a-r-a-f-i—"

"Pretty girl, you are going to be the death of me." Carter turned me around to face him, chest rising and falling as he fingered the thin straps of my gown for a beat too long—his expression reverent, and terribly focused.

Lips swollen, I reached up and slid one strap down my arm before he could change his mind. Carter slowly pushed the other strap down, murmuring as my dress slipped down over my body and pooled on the floor around my feet.

His eyes flared, and his voice was rough as he murmured, "So fucking beautiful, Sarafina." It came out like a simple fact, not even a compliment, and there was nothing but pure adoration in his voice, as he worshipped me with his eyes.

My response got caught in my throat as I stood in only my heels and jewelry, otherwise, on complete display for him. The soft lamplight was my only savior as my nipples peaked and he made a meal out of me with his eyes, took his time too.

Carter licked his lips before he reached out to grip my ribcage as if he needed to make sure I was actually real. Breath ragged, he ran a thumb over the bottom swell of one breast and watched me very carefully as he dragged that calloused thumb over my nipple, causing me to take a sharp, sudden inhale. I wondered if I might collapse as the sensation cascaded through me, making every part of me throb for more.

Carter didn't bother taking my stilettos off as he gripped my waist with two hands and guided me backwards towards the bed, gently laid me back onto the silken sheets. My feet were still on the floor, but the cool swath of fabric beneath me was a welcome reprieve against my burning skin as he planted a hand next to my head and leaned over me. The way he was looking at me—I'd never felt more desired in my life. Never felt so *beautiful*. The hopeful but nervous expression in his eyes was an illuminating look into the fact that maybe he was jumping off a cliff of his own. That maybe we were in this together. Maybe things weren't as one-sided as I had led myself to believe.

He was almost in a trance as he dragged a thumb roughly over my bottom lip and then trailed the backs of his fingers down the plane of my chest and over my stomach. I arched as his knuckles grazed below my belly button and whimpered when he pulled his hand away—a cautious explorer.

"Remember the rules?" Carter rasped, swollen-lipped, while he adjusted himself. "Do you want me to keep going?" He asked, and I nodded breathlessly. "You have to use your voice. Can you do that for me?" The look in his eyes told me I could pull the plug right now, if that's what I wanted.

The feeling of safety with him—felt like pure freedom.

"Yes," I whispered. "I want to keep going." Would curl up and die if we didn't keep going.

"Good girl." Eyes dropping to my breasts, he licked his lips before pushing a knee between both of mine, and I clutched the sheets, nodding for him to continue.

His breath was ragged as he pushed my knees open, baring me to him for the first time—he swore, eyes dilated so much they looked wholly black.

Corded arms flexing, he reached over me and grabbed the toy, turning it over in his hand. "Oh, the things I'm going to do to you, sweet girl." I trembled beneath him with anticipation.

In all the years I'd known Carter, he'd never allowed our harmless flirting to escalate, never turned the full force of his charm on me, and thank God for that because *this* version of Carter was utterly panty-melting and completely commanding. He could have anyone he wanted, and for the life of me, I couldn't figure out why that seemed to be me at the moment, but I wasn't about to start asking more questions.

Carter briefly looked at the toy in his fist, not saying whatever it was he was thinking, before he looked back at me with an expression I couldn't even begin to describe.

When he slowly lowered the toy, finally dragging the pink dildo across my collarbone, his eyes turned glazed and animalistic —he dragged it so slowly, over the swell of one breast and finally over that nipple, making me arch with a sharp intake of breath.

"You like that?" He murmured, and my eyes were squeezed shut as I nodded. "*Say it.* I want to hear that beautiful voice of yours, Sara."

"Yes," I whimpered as he repeated the motion and everything in me grew deliciously tight and loose at the same time.

"What about this?" He dragged the toy over the plane of my stomach and then down my inner thigh, making me tremble as he teased me. "I never thought I was a greedy man, but right now I'm feeling *very* greedy." He started up the other thigh, deliciously slow, as he trailed up to the other nipple, slowly circling it while he asked, "Tell me, sweet girl, where should I go next?"

He knew exactly where I wanted it. "Lower." I squeaked out.

"Here?" He asked, circling my belly button with a cocky tilt of his head.

"Lower." I whimpered.

"Oh, here?" He slid the length between my legs.

"Yes." I gasped at the contact, wishing I could snap my legs shut for more friction, but he kept his feet firmly planted, anchoring me open while he watched what he was doing to me.

I should have felt embarrassed or exposed maybe, he was still fully dressed—but the sight of him slightly undone in his dress shirt, hair mussed, looming over me with that look on his face, it told me everything I needed to know about how he felt.

I whimpered involuntarily as he dragged the toy over me again. "Look at you." His free hand was planted next to my head and he was awed as he dragged the toy back up my stomach, leaving a slick trail across my body. "So wet. So ready for me already, and we've barely even started."

He circled that one nipple until I was panting and writhing. "Please, I need more." I nervously begged, and he licked his lips, heeling off his shoes before he hauled me into the center of the sheets, murmuring his approval. I felt precious as he carefully laid me back, but I knew I looked anything but—I was wearing stilettos, sparkly cat ears, adorned in my new jewelry and nothing else.

Who was I right now? I didn't know, but I liked her. A lot. The thought of doing this with someone else, never in a million, but with Carter, something about it felt so damn right.

He lowered his bodyweight onto me, gazing at me with worshipful adoration and hungry lust, before he captured my mouth with his, and I suddenly relaxed, realizing he wasn't even remotely in a hurry at all. I don't know how long we kissed like that, with me writhing underneath him, naked and desperate, but I gasped when the toy finally slid between my legs again.

Carter chuckled darkly before he swallowed up my sounds and went to work.

"Ohh, Carter." I moaned into his mouth. "That feels good."

"Yeah?" he crooned, kissing down my jaw and throat as he teased me over and over. "You look so pretty when you need me— I bet you'll look even prettier when I make you start begging." He added cockily, but I didn't have it in me to argue with him. He was right, I did need him, desperately. "Do you know why you're on your back?" he asked between kisses.

"Why?" I cried as he flicked the toy over my clit again, his biceps flexing under my white-knuckle grip on him.

"Because I want to see how beautiful you look when I wreck you for the very first time."

A long moan was my only response as he set a delicious pace.

In another one of his fuck-boy moves, Carter knelt on either side of my legs, pinning them snugly together, while he fucked me mercilessly with that toy.

I felt that coil of warmth starting to build, and I began to move, meeting his hand thrust for thrust. "There's a vibrating setting." I gasped, not sure why I felt like I needed to share that random fact. Why was I trying to make awkward conversation?

"Don't need it." He chuckled arrogantly, making me cry out

in the next instant—like my pleasure was my punishment for even suggesting it.

He teased me until I didn't know if I could take it any longer, because I'd never spent this long having sex in general, let alone sex *just for me.*

I was just about to start freaking out that I couldn't do it, that I was taking too long to get there, worried that I was going to frustrate him, lose his attention—when something unfamiliar started to unravel within me.

"C-Carter." I whimpered, realizing it was going to happen.

"Yeah, there it is." he purred, his mouth at my ear as I started to lose a sense of time and space.

"I think I'm going to—I think it's—" I gasped, unable to string a full sentence together.

"I know." He dragged the toy over my clit for emphasis. "I know." He was giving me everything I needed and more. "You're so beautiful." He murmured. "I want you to come for me, sweetheart. Let go and come for me."

The magic-O was definitely going to make an appearance. Holy. Shit. Yes.

This had never happened before. Truth be told, nobody had ever spent this much time trying to get me there, and it showed.

"Look at you squirm, baby." He crooned as I rasped in each breath, and light started to speckle my vision. "You're mine right now. All *mine.*"

God, I was almost there. *So fucking close.* I clutched the sheets, thighs fighting against his while he kept me pinned, unable to escape the building tension in my core. I was thrusting up onto his hand with abandon, and I didn't care if it made me look like a desperate, needy slut. Maybe I was. Maybe for Carter I was. I was chasing the high, and all the while I wished it were his hands, or better yet his cock, instead of the toy, but still, he was right there with me every step of the way.

"Oh, God." I panted, ripping at his hair, pulling it, blubbering about I don't even know what, as I teetered on the edge of coming completely undone.

Carter was patient, relentless, and diligent, and I was so freaking close, but I just couldn't quite—I didn't want to let him down, I wanted to be enough for him, but maybe I really *was* broken, maybe this wouldn't work. I wondered if the other women he'd been with had taken this long or if I was the outlier.

"Sweetheart, stay in your body. I want you to focus on how this *feels*. It's going to happen, you'll see." He captured my mouth with his, and kept the pace—didn't deviate until everything started to coil tighter and tighter, as if it were inevitable.

"Carter." I gasped, throwing my head back into the sheets as my back arched with pleasure.

"My name sounds so good in your mouth when you're so wet and needy for me. *Look at you*," Carter groaned. "My fingers aren't even inside you yet, and they're a fucking mess."

Oh, I was so screwed.

"I love the way you look, taking your pleasure, Sara. You're so fucking pretty, you know that? I've honestly never seen you look more beautiful than you do right now." He murmured, adding, "You look free."

And then it was happening all at once.

"That's it, let it all go." He crooned. "Give me everything you've got, pretty girl. I want it all. *All of you*." I couldn't think, couldn't speak, didn't even exist at all as my climax finally tore through me, like an explosion of fucking fairy dust, leaving a limp wreckage in its shimmering wake.

I rode each shuddering wave, realizing I was crying Carter's name as I came back down from my high. I also realized I had a death grip on his hair, and I roughly released him, all while he grinned down at me triumphantly.

That was all I saw before I collapsed back and closed my eyes, still practically convulsing, aching with pleasure.

The months of tension that had been building between us were relieved in one mind-blowing orgasm, confirming that no, I really hadn't experienced a *real* orgasm before, just little mini, almost ones, if that was even a thing.

I felt invincible. Someone else making me come—made me feel free, powerful even. I couldn't quite explain it. I thought I'd be giving up my power, but honestly it felt a lot like I just took it back.

I shuddered as wave after wave rippled out of me, finally slowing down, and Carter finally removed the toy from between my legs, with one last shuddering stroke over my clit.

I was so relaxed-exhausted-delirious that I nearly fell asleep, but skin still sticky, I forced myself to find my brains so I could shove them back into my cranium in a desperate attempt to function again. *So much for remembering my name.*

Still panting, I found Carter lying beside me, gazing at me with such admiration in his eyes, I wondered if he was hallucinating, or maybe I was the one hallucinating. Totally possible.

After what felt like an hour but was probably only a few minutes, I could finally form words. "You have magical powers." I breathed. "I guess that means I'm not broken."

"Told you." He hummed, fingers trailing absentmindedly over my stomach as he added softly. "Perfect as always."

"That was," there were honestly no words. "Incredible."

His mouth crooked up, adorably proud of himself. "That good, huh?"

I shook my head sleepily. "Better. I don't think I'll ever have an orgasm that good again."

Carter's fingers flattened over my stomach, stilling, and he got a devilish grin. "That's an interesting theory."

My eyes went wide. "What is that look—Carter?"

"Oh sweetheart," he purred wickedly. "You are a naïve little thing, aren't you—*that was just the warmup.*"

"The warm-up?" I practically gaped.

"Always such a Rookie." He chuckled, "Now that we got a quick win and we know you're not broken, it's time to have some real fun." Carter popped up with all the energy in the world. "You ready to play, pretty girl?" I yelped as I was suddenly being flipped over onto my stomach.

I wanted to be dramatic and tell him I didn't know if I'd survive another one, but I knew what he was doing, he was checking in, asking for my consent again. So I nodded breathlessly. "Yes."

"That's my girl." Carter's muscular arm was a band around my waist as he lifted me up onto a stack of pillows and then settled in behind me. "I hope you're ready." He murmured possessively. "Because tonight, you're all *mine.*"

I knew right then and there, it was over for me.

There was no escaping the gravitational pull of Carter.

Not tonight, maybe not ever.

Finally.

CHAPTER 33

Palms Down Ass Up 2.0

SARAFINA

I gasped when Carter suddenly gripped my ankles and pushed my knees forward, forcing my ass up into the air as he dragged my legs wide open, baring me to him completely.

"Fuck." Carter muttered to himself as cool air hit my already swollen clit and whatever else was now exposed to him. *I tried not to think about it.*

Before I could close my legs even a little, or protest that he couldn't possibly want my ass in his face, Carter's knees slid between mine, anchoring me wide open, as he settled in behind me.

"I could take a fucking bite out of you." He groaned, but added quickly. "But I won't, not tonight anyway." This position had me exposed in every way possible, and I tried to steady my breathing. Thank God I'd waxed. "Doing okay?" Carter checked in, his hand skating up my back, to the nape of my neck, like a solid, reassuring weight, before he brushed my hair out of my face.

"Mhmm." I swallowed hard.

"Sara?"

"I trust you." I said, remembering he wanted full words.

"Good." He hummed. "You're safe with me." I knew he could

see as my core tightened, fluttering in response to his words. "We can stop at any time."

"Please don't." I lilted, already desperate and needy for another release, as his breath dusted over my skin like a promise.

He chuckled, toying with me a bit. "Pretty girl, do you know why you're on your stomach now?"

I gasped when I felt the toy dragging up my inner thigh. "Why?" I choked out.

"So you can scream into the sheets without waking up *the neighbors.*" He murmured in my ear with a wicked chuckle. "I love how vocal you were about twenty minutes ago, but we wouldn't want to get caught now, would we?"

I rolled my eyes, knowing he was right. "Carter?"

"Yes, sweetheart?" His hands skated over my skin.

"Fuck you."

He chuckled. "Oh, I plan to." Heat rushed through me as he dragged the toy over my ass, and then down, just barely avoiding the place where the sun doesn't shine. Which confirmed that he did in fact have a bird's-eye view of *everything.* I wasn't sure exactly how I felt about that, but I didn't have time to think about it as he slid the toy against my already drenched vulva and I cried out, burying my face in the sheets.

I whimpered as he traced *around* everything for long enough that I was desperately pushing my ass into the air, trying to get that contact on my clit again. Anytime he got even remotely close —it was enough to make me beg.

He'd almost let me have it and then he'd pull back slightly, humming when I pushed my hips higher, higher, higher, chasing the contact I desperately needed. "Look at you." He rasped. "So fucking greedy."

I gave in and begged *desperately,* as if I had any control over it at all.

Carter chuckled and obliged, sliding the toy against me several times as I moaned into the sheets. And then he went back to teasing until I was rocking back, desperate for penetration, desperate for release, desperate for anything he'd give me.

I pushed my hips back in unabashed request. "Carter." I begged. "Please." The unravelled sound of my voice shocked me.

"Are you going to take it like the good girl I know you are?"

Fuck me. "Yes," I whimpered into the sheets as he circled my clit, making me physically tremble.

"I know you are," he purred and slid the tip of the toy into me just barely.

I gasped, the sound muffled as it turned into a needy moan. "More." I demanded, and he slowly slipped it in a little further, stretching me carefully as I moaned into the mattress.

"You should see yourself." He murmured, "The way you're taking this fucking sparkler, the way your perfect pussy is wrapping around it, sliding over it." He groaned, muttering a curse, while he continued to work me excruciatingly slowly.

"More, I need more, Carter." I begged.

"Whatever you need, baby." His free hand gripped the crease of my hips, guiding me with that hand while he speared me with the other. He thrust the toy a little further each time, until he began to brush against that place, deep inside me.

"Oh, God." I cried out as he thrust harder. "Yesss." I rocked my hips back to meet each thrust, my ass tilted up in the air as I begged for more, more, more.

"I need you to tell me if this gets too intense." Carter instructed. "I'm not inside you, and I can't feel if this is too deep."

"More." I blubbered into the sheets as the toy swept over that spot again.

Carter's chuckle was a dark rumble. "As you wish."

His knuckles slapped against my clit with every thrust of the toy, and the ache inside me was growing near unbearable. "Faster." I begged, growing more exhausted by the second.

"That's my girl." Carter said, picking up the pace. "All you have to do is ask." Suddenly, I flinched as pain mixed with my pleasure. "Too far?" He quickly paused.

"A little." I panted. "Don't stop though. *Please,* for the love of God, don't stop." I could feel his body shake with laughter behind me, but I didn't care as he started up again.

He shifted my hips, and the next thrust just barely bottomed out, full and rough, still stealing my breath as he swept over that spot, but it was no longer painful. "Better?" Carter attentively asked.

I nodded, breathless and unable to get the words out, as he brushed against that spot again and again. I was sweaty, and growing exhausted by the second as that coil built. My throat was raw from the sounds I didn't even realize I was making, didn't recognize at all.

"Seeing you like this, I wish I could taste you." Carter rumbled, his other hand slipping between my thighs. "Maybe next time I will." He threatened, and I nearly screamed when his thumb *almost* swept over my clit. *He* still hadn't touched *me* with anything but the toy.

I was crying, practically sobbing as I let go, letting him take everything I'd been holding onto and turn it into exactly what I needed.

His voice was rough and low, the timber like I'd never heard before as his lips brushed the shell of my ear, as his teeth tugged on my earlobe. "Part of me wants to draw this out as long as possible so I can stare at your perfect pussy for another hour." He panted and drew the toy out so fucking slowly. "So I can watch you pink, and wet and desperate." He circled my entrance, stretching me, and I whimpered into the sheets.

"C-Carter." I begged.

"Do you have any idea how beautiful you are?"

I spasmed as the tip filled my entrance, and desperate to be full again, I pushed my hips back.

He asked again, "Do you have any idea?" *Thrust.*

I screamed into the sheets as he drove the toy against my G-spot.

"Answer me, pretty girl," Carter rasped into my ear, but a strangled cry was all I got out. "I know." He murmured and drew the toy out. "I know." *Thrust.*

I screamed as those spots began to speckle my vision again. My ass was in the sky, my face buried in the sheets, every part of me was sticky, or sweaty, and every part of me was on fire. The smell of him, the feel of him, how erotic what we were doing was. And I was so fucking close to a wildly different kind of orgasm than I'd ever had before. I was desperate to find that release, desperate to fly down the mountain he'd so diligently carried me up.

"You're doing such a good job." *Thrust.*

"You should see how well you're taking this." *Thrust.*

"I can't help but wonder what you'd look like taking my cock instead of this toy." *Thrust.*

I might have screamed. "Carter," I begged, voice raw. "I want *you*." I wanted his skin on mine, wanted *him* inside me, needed to feel *him* claiming me, fucking me, worshipping me. Wanted the weight of him to bring me back down to earth.

"I know." He panted, and it was almost a whimper. "But this is why we made the rules, so we didn't get caught up in the heat of the moment and do something you'd regret."

Why, oh why, had I dared him to fuck me with the dildo and not just slept with him like a sane person? *"Please."* I cried, desperate to undo my stupid mistake. *"Please, I need you."*

He was breathless as he asked, "Can I touch you with my hands, Sara?" *Thrust.*

The way my back arched, desperate for just that—whatever I said was merely a strangled sound.

"Use your words." Carter chuckled, but the sound was practically predatory.

"Y-yes." I panted.

"What do you say?" *Thrust.*

I screamed. "C-Carter." I whimpered desperately. *Thrust.*

"Where are your manners, sweet girl?" He hummed a melodic caress wrapping around me. "I've never known you to be so demanding."

I cried into the sheets as his fingers trailed up my inner thighs. "P-P-Please." I begged.

"There it is." He murmured, rough and soft all at once, his voice like dark velvet, the sheets hardly muffling my screams when his fingers finally brushed over my clit. *Thrust.*

"That's my girl." He rasped, low and controlled, but there was something dark and wild underneath—his voice was a command that I had no other choice but to obey as I started to black out. "Now be a good girl for me and wash my hands with your holy water, make a mess all over my fingers and come for me, baby." *Thrust.*

Stars speckled the darkness behind my eyelids.

I was putty in his hands.

I was nothing and everything all at once.

I had no idea if I screamed or cried, or made a fool of myself as the orgasm of all orgasms began to descend down on me. Warmth like I'd never felt before began to unravel in my core, and everything in me went tight and desperate. In that moment, I would have sold my soul for the release that was on the precipice of descending down on me. The feeling of his body hovering over mine, the feeling of his breath on my skin, the smell of his sheets, his cologne in my nose. The feeling of that spot deep inside me, waking up from a long slumber I hadn't known it was taking.

And then everything in me went limp and taut at once as my orgasm exploded around me like a supernova, pulling me into a delicious black hole as nothing but pure ache and pleasure filled every cell of my body—and it just kept on coming as Carter rocked wave after wave of pleasure from me, holding me hostage up in the heavens until the sensation was so intense, I actually blacked out.

Trembling and twitching, I felt myself finally float back down to earth.

I shuddered as Carter slowly pulled the toy out of me, the sound wet as fuck. I felt like a broken rag doll, my throat raw as if I'd been screaming, like time and space didn't exist as pure exhaustion and satisfaction ebbed and flowed in unison with my every breath.

Carter's hands were warm and steady as he hooked an arm under my hips and slid the pillows out, laying me flat on the bed. It was only then that I realized my heels were still on, when his steady fingers unclasped the straps and he slid them off my feet.

A moment later, he was pushing my hair away from my face, pulling the cat ear headband off, and then his hand was broad and strong as he rubbed long soothing strokes down my back while the aftershocks continued to twitch through me.

With the greatest effort I'd ever exerted, I blinked my eyes open and found him lying next to me, elbow propping his head up as he just gazed at me, with a look I couldn't decipher.

I suddenly felt wildly shy and looked down with a quiet puff of air that wasn't quite a nervous laugh.

Carter only hummed, the sound all too cocky and amused as he lifted just the sheet over my naked body. As if he knew I was suddenly self-conscious, even though I had just bared it all.

I tucked my arms under myself, folding my hands under my chin, and we just laid there staring into each other's eyes for a long while.

Carter's expression broke into a small smile and he whispered. "*I win.* The dare—just so that's on record."

I weakly huffed a soft laugh in response.

"Aww, look at you, all tuckered out." He teased and then all too cockily, "I wonder if you can remember your name now? *Hmm?*" All I could do was grunt a little noise that made him grin and whisper, "*Told you.*"

I shook my head. "You didn't even use the vibration."

"Didn't need to." He breathed a laugh. "Something to look forward to next time."

"Can't wait." I murmured, and his gaze fell to my mouth

before he dragged me on top of him and tenderly took my face, giving me a soft, slow kiss that was quiet and intimate, and in complete contrast to the way he had just destroyed me.

His hand slid around the nape of my neck, his other at my hip, pulling me closer as I threaded a leg over his, no doubt ruining his suit pants with what was dripping between my legs. "I don't think I'll ever get over this," he murmured, "but I want us to slow things down a bit."

"No," I grumbled between kisses, and he chuckled. I was not about to give up the best orgasms I'd ever had in my life. I was hungry for *more.*

"Consider this a prequel for what's to come." He nibbled on my lower lip with a playful snarl. "It would've been practically criminal for you to go another day, thinking there was something wrong with you, and I can't wait to show you again and again how right my theory is, but I want to slow things down a bit. Take some time to figure this out."

"You sure about that?" I slid my hand down his stomach, finding a hard, gratifying length that I palmed over his pants.

His face looked pained. "Sara, I—We—" The words were an ache, and I loved that he responded to my touch like that, but as I went for the button at the top of his slacks, his fingers circled around my wrists, stopping me.

"I want to do something for you." I whispered earnestly. I was exhausted and knew I wouldn't be able to match his skill, but I was certainly willing to try.

"There's no way in hell I'm letting you put your hands or your mouth on me before I've even had a chance to taste you." He said, eyes wild. "And besides, we agreed. Dildo only, tonight."

I swallowed hard. "I want you to feel good too."

"That was just as good for me as it was for you." He brought my hands up to his chest. "Honestly, probably better." I raised a skeptical brow, but he doubled down, clearing his throat. "I'm serious, I may or may not have *already* blown a load—watching you slide over that fucking thing, hearing you beg like that, for *me*." He confessed, eyes growing glazed.

I bit my lip, absolutely loving that he came just from looking at me. "How is that even possible?" I puzzled, not totally sure if I believed him.

"I think you're seriously underestimating how goddamn sexy you are." He murmured, "You have no idea how attracted to you I am. None." And then he clarified, "And about last night, I wanted to, trust me, I wanted to *so* bad, but just so we're clear—I will *never* put you in a position where you can't give your full consent. *Ever.*"

I swallowed hard, knowing I'd needed to hear that. *For so many reasons.*

"Carter," I pleaded, feeling even more desperate to get my hands on him as I realized he was already hard again. I was dying to make sure he knew this wasn't a one-way street.

He wrapped his arms around me, crushing me to him so I couldn't reach him. "I don't want to move too fast. I've—"

"What?" I murmured, cheeks squished against his broad chest.

"You matter so much to me, and honestly, this is probably way too fucking fast—I should've had more self-control. Don't get me wrong, I loved every fucking second of it, and I'll remember this until the day I die, but I don't want to scare you away before we've even started."

"Do you not want *me* to touch *you*?" I tried to quell the tears that immediately pooled in my eyes. "Because if you don't, it's really okay. I just want to know." I started rambling. "Just so we're on the same page—so there's no confusion." I was wrong about what I'd said earlier... this was going to break me clean in half.

"Stop it." Carter rolled on top of me and kissed me breathless. "I've wanted this, *wanted you* for so fucking long, and we don't need to do everything all at once. Please don't push me away because you're afraid." He pleaded, his expression turning boyish, filled with so much concern that I couldn't help but believe him.

"I need you, sweet girl. So damn much. Just let me take my time with you. Can you do that for me?" He asked. "I know we joke, and tease, and flirt, but I'm not going anywhere, I promise. We just need time to figure this out, time to sort this out for ourselves, especially before we tell anyone."

"Right, Liam." I nodded, wondering how the hell we were going to tell him. He'd be furious.

Carter groaned. "*Please* don't say your brother's name while you're lying underneath me naked."

I laughed softly. "Fair."

He cupped my face, eyes narrowing. "I'm half tempted to punish you for bringing your brother into *our* bed." I rolled my eyes at him. "Don't think I won't do it." He threatened, walking his fingers up my stomach.

"Carter." I tensed.

"Yes, sweet girl?" He cocked his head innocently, all while digging his fingers into my rib cage.

"I'm not even ticklish." I tried to keep a straight face, even as I was squirming.

"I'll take that under advisement." He said, a gleam in his eye. "But here's the thing, if that were true." He lowered his mouth to mine. "Then this wouldn't bother you a single bit."

"It's the truth." I squealed as he started tickling me.

"Little liar." He pinned me, kissing and tickling until I was howling for mercy. "Promise you won't bring Liam into the bedroom and I'll stop." He demanded, grazing his teeth over my jaw more sensuously.

"I promise." I gasped out, panting for breath.

"Good." He finally conceded, and I giggled, threading my arms around his neck as he lowered his lips to mine, kissing me slow and deep, holding me like he just couldn't get enough.

Every plane of sculpted muscle under my fingertips was like a drug to me, the solid, reassuring weight of his body on top of me like a balm to all the pain still buried inside of me, and I wanted *more*. Begged for it—for him to start all over.

"Slow." He pulled back, panting. "We need to slow *way* the fuck down." His shirt was completely untucked, his hair a mess. I didn't even want to know what *I* looked like.

"Fine." I huffed a laugh, teasing, "Just so it's on the record, this is also a win for me—you may have created an addict." I warned.

"Lucky me," he rumbled. "And good thing for you, I'm more than happy to be your dealer."

"Carter." I gazed into his molten brown eyes. "I'm scared." I admitted. *Fucking terrified, actually.*

"Don't be. We're going to figure this out together." He promised, but what if this didn't work out? What if we'd just crossed a line that we never should have?

"I don't want to lose you." I admitted with a hard swallow.

His expression softened. "Pretty girl, don't you know, I've *always* been yours."

When I woke up the next morning, I had a pleasant ache between my legs, and I blushed as the night before came rushing back in heart-pounding snippets too good to be real, *but they were.*

And maybe even better, Carter had held me all night long, his heavy arms a warm, comforting band around my stomach. So much so that I could hardly roll over, as if he couldn't bear the risk that he might lose me.

And maybe even sweeter, I smiled to myself, I'd learned that Carter was a bit of a sleep talker. Every time I'd adjusted, his hands had found my boobs, and he'd hung onto them like a freaking security blanket while he sleepily grumbled at me, complaining I'd taken *his* boobs away.

I chuckled to myself, but finally blinking my eyes open, I sat up, heart catching when I realized the bed was *empty*.

My heart sank, and then I checked the time and immediately realized why. It was nearly *noon*—my eyes lit up when I noticed the note waiting for me. I rolled over and plucked it off the night-stand so fast I nearly flew off the bed.

You looked too peaceful to wake. Had to run out for a few business meetings. Breakfast is keeping warm in the oven. I already miss you.

Sweet. He was always *so* sweet.

I bit my lip as I set the note down next to my crusty-dusty dildo discarded on the nightstand. Gross. I'd have to wash that thing before Carter got a second look at it in the daylight.

On the floor, our clothes from the night before were strewn about, and I grabbed Carter's dress shirt, grinning as I slipped it on. It hung to my knees as I buttoned it up halfway, and after a tiny moment of second-guessing myself; I tugged the shirt open a bit and snapped a cute, sleepy selfie, sending it to Carter before I could change my mind.

I wanted this to be easy, didn't want to overthink things with him. So I wouldn't, I decided. Fun and easy. That's what I'd be.

I wandered downstairs while I scrolled through my texts, catching up on everything I'd missed in the chaos of yesterday. Sloane and Jules would be in town in an hour, and everyone was going to a Halloween party at the club tonight.

I smiled to myself, realizing, for once, I was going to have a date. Except, no, I wasn't, because nobody could know anything yet. *UGH!*

On my way downstairs, as I passed one of the backdoors, a shadow flitted across the floor. I startled, looking up from my phone, but when I peered out the window, no one was there. Nothing but the vast expanse of gardens that opened up behind the estate, and nothing seemed out of the ordinary.

Still, the hair on my neck raised, and for some reason, I couldn't bring myself to open the door and step outside. I tried to shrug it off, but that's when I noticed the crumbled leaves just inside the door. I swallowed hard. Carter *never* used the backdoor. He always came through the garage, not to mention he hated going into the massive botanical gardens behind the estate at all, because that had been his mother's favorite place.

My eyes darted to the lock on the door, and the metal was cool under my fingertips as I triple-checked it was in fact locked, because of course it was locked. The striated marble was toasty warm under my bare feet as I headed towards the kitchen, trying to convince myself that it was probably just one of the gardeners coming in for a glass of water. Carter was hardly ever home, and even after all these years, he'd kept the estate in pristine condition. There were always staff members coming and going for routine maintenance and cleaning.

Still, as I rounded the corner to the kitchen, I couldn't help but glance over my shoulder one last time as prickling unease settled in my gut.

Three ovens later, I finally found my breakfast, feeling a pang of sadness for Carter as I padded through the industrial-sized kitchen that probably hadn't been used in ages. It was such a massive house for just one person. Kinda depressing.

I plopped down at the breakfast nook and opened the paper bag. Inside was an enormous breakfast sandwich and a tall cup of hot seasoned broth from the health food store up the street. The note inside read:

OJ is in the fridge. Be a good girl for me and finish your breakfast. All of it. You'll need your strength for tonight.

Oh my. I would *not* be the first one to tap out tonight. So I ate everything, finishing my entire breakfast in record time.

I opened my text thread with Carter, giggling to myself as three little dots popped up and disappeared once, and then twice, in response to my sexy morning selfie. I grinned, feeling pretty damn pleased with myself, and deviously decided I was going shopping this afternoon because tonight definitely called for a new dress.

If Carter and I had to keep our hands off each other tonight, and keep this a secret, then it wouldn't hurt to make sure at least his eyes stayed on me.

CHAPTER 34
Little Secrets
CARTER

The view of the city skyline from the floor to ceiling windows in the Vandenbergh building was incredible, but as I waited for my appointment, I hardly noticed it.

I couldn't think, couldn't breathe, couldn't hardly remember why I was even here.

I jiggled my leg as the images from last night replayed through my mind over and over. Sara's hair fanned out underneath her as she writhed on the sheets beneath me, begging, moaning my name. Her head thrown back, cheeks flushed while she let me do things to her that a man could only dream about.

The sight of her, face down, swollen and wet, taking that fucking unicorn horn, the mattress useless to muffle the beautiful sounds she was making—my leg bounced faster, all while I wished it were *my* cock buried in her, all while she had *begged* me, for exactly that.

I was the energizer bunny, and I was practically drunk off her. Desperate for more. Fucking obsessed with waking up and remembering she was still in my bed.

I'd wanted to wake her up *so badly* this morning, laid there holding her for as long as humanly possible, until I was actually running late, and when I'd finally dragged myself away, I'd been dying to wake her up and kiss her goodbye, but how could I? Not when she looked so peaceful and perfect.

I wanted that feeling every morning.

Forever.

Minus the slightly panicked feeling that she'd unlocked inside me. Minus the realization that I should have jacked off one more time before I left the house this morning because I was already aching for her again.

I hadn't though, because my dumb shoulder was acting up after last night. Nothing could have been more worthwhile, though.

A buzz vibrated in my pocket, and my heart skipped a beat when I saw it was a text from her. My breath turned more thin than it already was as I clicked on the selfie she'd just sent me—stared at it, zoomed in on it, quickly looked around to make sure no one else could see, and zoomed in on it some more.

I dragged a hand over my face and stifled a groan. She was the sun in my world, and *everything* revolved around her.

Fucked.

She was in *my* shirt from last night, with far too many buttons undone for me to think straight. So I started in on a response that was something to the effect of *You won't be able to walk straight when I'm done with you tonight* and then I immediately decided that was way too intense, since I was determined to slow things down with her. So, I erased that and started over. *You look beautiful.* True, but what a stupid, completely inadequate response. I immediately erased that too. Beautiful didn't even begin to cover it.

Fuck it. I started in again.

> You look sexy enough to take a bite out of and I had to jack off multiple times this morning wishing it was you I was pumping into because I couldn't stop picturing the way your pussy swallowed up that goddamned unicorn horn. I wish you could have seen it. It was hot as fuck. YOU were hot as fuck. And I know I said I wanted to take things slow, but honestly, I'm a simple man. All I want to do is bend you into a million and one shapes, and fuck you in every single one of them... until you can't speak, or walk, or do anything at all, and baby, I'll do it all for you. I'll be every damn thing you need. Forever.

It was way too much, but just for kicks, I kept going.

> I want to give you the world on a string. I want to worship you, devour you, explore you, Sarafina. And it's not just your body, it's your laugh, your spirit, your kindness, your softness. You make everything better. You make me want to be better, and right now, like the single brain cell man that I am, all I can think about is how desperate I am to fuck those gorgeous tits of yours. Respectfully, of course.

And then I erased the entire message.

Fuuuuuuuuck me.

I stared at the photo again and zoomed in on that sliver of soft, perfect cleavage, all while my cock jumped like an untrained dog.

Someone cleared their throat, and I looked up, breathless. The receptionist had clearly been talking to me. "Theodore will see you now." She repeated.

"Thanks." I stood and stuffed my phone into my pocket, using the opportunity to discreetly adjust myself after she went back to her computer. I needed to get a grip. I was in public, for Christ's sake.

I headed through the massive doors into the large, dimly lit office and found Theo inside, looking broody as usual, sitting behind several glowing screens. Behind him were even more screens with live video feeds.

"Kensington," he said, and didn't bother standing. "To what do I owe the honor of this impromptu visit?"

I grimaced and gripped the back of the chair across from his desk. "I need a favor."

His brows raised, and he motioned, inviting me to sit. "I owe you." He settled back into his chair and cocked his head. "But you already knew that, so what exactly can I do for you?"

I settled into the high-back chair, wondering how long it'd been since I bailed him out of prison and hired a damn good lawyer to get the charges dropped.

That was one thing I had learned from my mother, to always reach a hand out to help because eventually, you'd be the one needing that hand to reach back. She, of course, was right.

And right now, I desperately needed Theo to protect the one thing that mattered most to me. "I need a security detail." I started, "Best team you have."

"I see." Theo nodded thoughtfully. "For whom?"

"Sara."

His whole face shifted, his grin feline, and I didn't know if I'd ever actually seen him smile. "I should have known." He mused, more to himself than me. "How'd Liam take it?"

"We're not together." I swallowed hard, hating the words even as I said them. "Which is why she can't know she's being watched, and neither can he."

Theo outright laughed at that, and it nearly knocked me out of the chair with surprise.

"Sure." He chuckled and brushed a thumb thoughtfully over his lower lip. "Whatever you say, Kensington."

He was always such a fucker. "Can you do it?" I asked, growing more irritated by the second.

"Of course I can do it." He folded his arms across his chest. "It's going to cost you, though."

I rolled my eyes, so much for owing me. "You know price doesn't matter." I'd spend every dollar I had and more to keep her safe.

Theo nodded thoughtfully, his mind wandering elsewhere. "Yes, I do."

He was still quiet when I finally asked, "How's Ariana?"

His jaw clenched. "We're not on speaking terms at the moment."

"You haven't spoken to her since—"

"No," Theo snapped, his eyes simmering with disdain. "She's as stubborn as ever."

I wandered over to the coffeepot. Sloane had invited Ariana to the club tonight, but I wondered if Theo already knew that.

Theo scrubbed a hand over his face. "She's a massive pain in my ass, is what she is."

I stirred my coffee, even though I'd added nothing to it. "Sure." I parroted his words from earlier. "Whatever you say, *Theodore*."

Theo scowled at me. "Fuck you."

"Likewise." I took a satisfied sip of the steaming black brew and returned to my chair. "You could always assign someone else to her."

"No, I can't," Theo said matter-of-factly.

I knew Theo would never forgive himself if something happened to Ariana. The irony was, I'd feel the same about Sara. I wondered when we'd become so similar. The only difference was Ariana wanted *nothing* to do with Theo—for reasons that weren't entirely clear, because I knew exactly what had sent him to prison, and it was what he'd done for her. In the same position, I couldn't say I would have done differently either, but clearly there was more to the story, and now, they were like two magnets, doomed to have opposite polarity —never quite able to touch again, and I honestly felt bad for the guy.

"Well, it's a good thing she has you to keep an eye on her." I offered.

"Why do you think I got into this line of work?" Theo grumbled.

I chuckled softly, moving on. "When can you have the detail ready?"

If The Society's threats were real, and I knew they were, then it was wise that the security team was placed as soon as possible, and even wiser that Sara and I kept things quiet between us, at least until this was all smoothed over.

"For you. I can have the team placed in less than twenty-four hours." Theo said.

Perfect, she'd have someone watching over her the moment I left, with no gaps.

I pursed my lips, wondering when my life had gotten so complicated. "I'll need a detail for Liam as well." I grimaced as I reluctantly added, "and for Brad." It was the right thing to do.

"Interesting." Theo nodded. "Very interesting."

"Don't ask." I warned, setting my coffee down on the side table.

"Wouldn't dare." He mused as a quiet alarm started beeping in the background. Theo spun around in his chair and clicked through several video feeds before picking up his phone. "You sure you want to involve Brad in this?" he asked, but didn't look at me as his thumbs flew over the keyboard, composing a text.

"What do you know?" I searched his stoic face.

He continued typing. "I know enough."

Bastard had his hand in everything, which was why he really was the best. "Theo, this is important." I implored him.

"Yes, it is, so I would choose wisely if you're going to get involved in Brad's affairs." He gave nothing away as he set the phone down and looked at me warily.

"I'm not going to leave him out to dry." I blew out a breath. "Even if I wanted to, Sara would never forgive me." I gripped my temples, supposing I owed him this, even if I was disappointed in him. For so many reasons.

Theo was quiet for a moment as he watched me, but finally he spoke. "Brad's accumulating gambling debts at a rather alarming rate."

My eyes snapped to his. "How much?"

"Too much."

I grimaced. That would explain the missing furniture and antiques around the house. "Who is he gambling with?" I asked.

Theo sat back in his chair. "I believe you're already well acquainted with the organization, actually." Before I could comment on how he knew anything about The Society, Theo turned to his computer, clearly done revealing his intel. "Is there anything else you need?" he asked, and I shook my head no, pondering Brad's situation. "Then I'll set up a detail for each of the Devereux's. Is this protection only, or surveillance as well?" He asked.

I hesitated. Part of me wanted to know what Sara was up to, who was in her life on campus, but it wasn't my place, and I wouldn't betray her trust like that. On the other hand, she wouldn't even have to know... I could eliminate problems like Isaac before they ever crossed her path.

Tempting as it was, protection was one thing; surveillance was another. Besides, while I trusted Theo to place a team that would keep her safe, I knew he would gather as much intel as he could for his own benefit anyway.

"Protection only." I sighed.

"Your loss." Theo said with a smirk. "Just so we're clear, I *always* surveil. It'd be irresponsible not to. It's just a matter of whether or not you want to know about it."

"I won't betray her trust like that." I grimaced, hating that I had to keep this from her, but she was still so fragile, and she didn't deserve to walk around in fear. She needed normalcy in her life as much as possible. She'd already had so much taken away, I wouldn't take away her sense of safety too.

"Very well. I'll only inform you if anything seems out of the ordinary." He turned to his computer. "Precautionary courtesy."

I nodded, that would be fine, I supposed. "What do you need from me?"

Theo pursed his lips. "Nothing. I've already got a file on all of you, so this should be pretty seamless."

I rolled my eyes. "Of course you do."

"I'm the best for a reason." He shrugged. "You need a detail for yourself?"

"I'm good." I stood up and headed for the door.

"Is that why you're carrying?" He was looking at the computer when I turned.

"I'm not." I lied.

"Right." Theo rolled his eyes, reaching into his drawer, and he thumbed through a file before plopping a stack of photos down on his desk.

Even from across the room, I could see the blood in the photos, and my heart started to race as I walked towards his desk. I picked up the stack, realizing they were photos of me, one after another, of me unconscious, the night of the attack.

"Where the fuck did you get these?" I demanded.

"I know a guy," Theo said, not even mildly concerned as he typed away on his multi-screen surveillance setup.

"*What guy*?" I demanded.

"Hacker guy." He shrugged uncouthly. "You know the type, and you also know I protect my sources."

"Did you know they were coming for me?" I growled.

"Of course not. You know I would have warned you." He shrugged. "A contact offered me the information after the fact, and I'm never one to pass up intel. You, of all people, should know that." I was fuming. "I waited for you to reach out after the whole thing, but you never did." Theo shrugged. "And I'm not one to stick my nose where it's not invited."

"Oh, you're not, huh?" I growled.

He steepled his fingers together, expression totally unbothered. "*You know*, I have other services." Theo mused. "Off book. Untraceable."

"You're going to land yourself right back where you started." I snapped, tempting as that offer was.

"Perhaps." Theo shrugged. "Perhaps not." He leaned forward on the desk. "The only question is Kensington, when it comes to her safety, how far are you willing to go?" His eyes darkened.

There wasn't a question in my mind. All the fucking way. Which is why it could never come to that. "If anything happens to her, it's your neck I'm coming after." I threatened as I stormed towards the door.

"Easy, Carter." Theo warned. "Let's not get ahead of ourselves."

"If so much as a hair on her head is touched, I will buy this whole goddamn building, just so I can burn it down with you inside." I said from the doorway. "You have my word."

"And you have mine." Theo nodded, completely unbothered. "As long as my team is watching, nothing will happen to her, or to Liam, for that matter." He stared at me as I hesitated in the doorway. "Carter, I've got her. I'll keep her safe." He offered more gently.

"Thank you." I said, my eyes shuttering at the dark reality of the situation.

"Anytime, old friend," Theo said, already picking up the phone as I closed the door behind me.

Fucking prick.

Jules shot me a look as we waited outside The Inferno. The security team was running my ID because—

"Why the fuck do you have a gun?" Jules hissed under her breath.

"No reason." I avoided her outraged expression.

The bouncer checked my gun, informing me I could pick it up afterwards.

I rolled my neck as Jules and I headed through the dark velvet tunnel towards the club entrance. "Jesus fucking Christ, Carter." Jules groaned as we walked through the darkness.

"Jules, it's really no biggie." It wasn't and after yesterday, I wasn't taking any chances.

"Do you always carry?" She asked, bumping into me in the dim light—it was next to impossible to see in here. "When the hell did that start?" She demanded, "I thought you were a freaking pilot."

I wondered what exactly she thought I did when I went up in the air, because I certainly wasn't doing loopty-loops just for fun. Okay, fine. Sometimes yes, I did do loopty-loops for fun, but that wasn't all I did up there. "Just do me a favor and don't mention it to anyone, would you?" I asked, hauling the heavy curtain open.

"Fine." She rolled her eyes as we stepped into the club. "But you owe me."

"Consider me indebted." I shouted over the thundering music as it hit us, the bass pulsating through my entire body.

"I really, really hate guns." She muttered just loud enough for me to hear as she trailed along behind me.

I cut through the tightly packed crowd and took in the scene, realizing The Inferno was insane. I'd heard about it, but I'd never been. Tonight, it was decked out in Halloween decor that was as outrageous as you'd expect for the city's most notoriously sexy nightclub.

We neared one of the four columns that were planted at each corner of the massive dance floor—each pillar had a different fanged animal carved into the marble. I eyed the cages hanging above the stage where the DJ was and peered over the sea of dancing bodies, wondering how the hell we were going to find the group in here because tonight, it was jam-packed.

"This way, Kensington," Jules chimed, her dark auburn hair

glinting under the orange and red strobe lights as she ducked around me.

We broke through the crowd on the other side of the dance floor, and I spotted our crew at a table in the reserved section. Liam stood at the edge of the table, drink in hand, and next to him, I was surprised to see Cade. Jules squealed and slid into the booth, throwing her arms around Ariana and Riley.

Meanwhile, tucked away in the back of the booth, looking happier than I'd seen her look in a damn long time, was Sara.

The moment our eyes locked, my heart stopped beating. Sara offered me a shy little smile, and then quickly made herself busy talking to Riley Kingsley, Theo's younger cousin.

She'd only looked for a split second, but the way Sara's eyes lit up when she saw me had me doing internal somersaults. It was the best feeling in the world. God, she was so fucking gorgeous.

Sara looked back at me, and suddenly her eyes went wide, and I realized Liam had been talking to me while I'd been busy drooling over her. I quickly recovered and cleared my throat, clapping Liam on the back. "So loud, I can hardly hear." I joked. "Surprised you got a spot, it's packed tonight."

"Yeah, they go all out for Halloween." Liam motioned to the table, explaining over the music. "I'm doing the menus for the club."

"Gotta love a hookup." Cade drawled, hanging one arm over the tall booth.

Liam shrugged and sipped his beer.

"Cade fucking Blackthorn." I clapped him on the back. "Who let you in here? Long time no see."

"That's your own damn fault." Cade shook his head. "What's the body count up to these days?"

"It's high enough." I shrugged. "I don't keep count." Except I did. Every single one. I did.

"Sure you don't." He looked me over and was smart enough to read between the lines. "You headed overseas anytime soon?"

"Probably." I nodded, adding, "I rarely know until the last

second, though." I looked at Sara, who quickly looked away when I caught her eye. We had so many things we needed to talk about, to plan for. "It's not so bad, usually a few months at a time, and then it's back stateside for a while."

"If you wanted to fly, you should have gone commercial." Cade drawled. "We could have gone into business together."

I shook my head. "I don't even want to know what shit you're smuggling around."

Cade pursed his lips. "No, you probably don't."

"Besides, flying an F-16 isn't even remotely the same as flying a jumbo." I chuckled. "Being up there, flying that fast—there's nothing like it." Although, as of last night, there was one thing that might even be better than flying at mock speeds.

"Adrenaline junkie." Cade muttered.

I scoffed. "You're one to talk." Cade had grown up fighting, drawing blood just for the hell of it, and honestly wrestling around with him was probably the reason I was still alive. Cade was nearly as thick as Theo, but he had an inch of height on all of us, including me, making him lean enough to be fast and bulky enough to be dangerous. I'd seen him in the ring, and whatever was driving him was way more than adrenaline and disciplined training—he had something to prove, no doubt a result of his hard upbringing. Cade hid it well though, all behind that lazy grin of his.

Cade chuckled and took a sip of his amber drink. "How long you in town for?"

"Tonight's my last night." I said. "Had to make it out for the birthday redo." Since I was the one who had ruined Sara's birthday in the first place. I still felt terrible about that.

Liam chimed in over the music to Cade. "We got a cake for later. If you've got time, you should stick around."

"Wouldn't miss it for the world." Cade said, giving Sara a long look that made me grit my teeth.

Ohhh fuck no. When had that started?

I curled and uncurled my fist, trying to look unbothered as

Liam leaned in. "By the way, I know your time is limited when you're in town, and I know it really means a lot to her that you showed up." Liam clapped me on the back, looking genuinely appreciative. "You're a great friend. To both of us. This has been a hard year, and I've been dealing with a lot of bullshit lately. It's just—it's nice to know I can always count on you." He added, "Especially with her."

I finally looked at Liam, and my hands went instantly clammy. "Of course." I swallowed hard, doing a piss-poor job of pretending like I hadn't just fucked his sister sideways with her own dildo, less than twelve hours ago. "I had to make up for ruining her birthday in the spring." I shrugged, panic rising in my chest.

Right on cue, the girls started sliding out of the booth one by one, with temptation itself headed straight my way.

"It's all good." Liam nodded, looking relieved. "She just needed a little time, I think. She seems like she's finally bouncing back. Actually, she's been really happy all day."

I bet she has.

"Yeah, she looks good." I agreed casually, wondering how the hell I was going to keep what I'd done from Liam. "Healthier." I quickly added, tamping down a dangerous smirk. I felt guilty, I really did. I hated lying to my best friend and betraying his trust, but selfishly, keeping it a secret... made it that much hotter. *Fuck. I was definitely going to hell.*

I wasn't an idiot though. There were so many ways I could get screwed over. If Sara decided she didn't want this, I knew exactly who Liam would side with. And even if she decided she did want me, Liam might never accept it. I could end up with everything I'd ever dreamed, or absolutely nothing at all. The realization was sobering.

Over the years, Liam had always been incredibly protective of her, and he'd been very clear about the rules—nobody touched his sister unless they wanted to lose their teeth. And seeing the way Cade was currently looking at Sara—I was fucking glad for the rules. Rules were great. *Cade especially* should remember those rules. We all should. *Except for me, of course.*

Jules nudged Liam's arm, checking in. "Hey, how's everything with Gina?" Liam grimaced and shook his head.

Meanwhile, I tried to act casual and uninterested, but I could literally smell Sara hovering nearby, and when I finally stole a glance, my vision went red.

Fucking Cade. Now he had his arm slung around Sara's shoulders!

I clenched my fist, knowing I couldn't say a damn thing with Liam standing right there.

"I thought your birthday was in June?" A strand of Cade's jet black hair fell over his face as he leaned down and rumbled into Sara's ear. "If I would have known we were celebrating you tonight, I would have gotten you a gift, gorgeous."

Sara rolled her eyes. "My birthday *is* in June." She adjusted her short, shimmery green dress. Fuck, she looked good tonight. "I wasn't feeling so hot on my actual birthday, and if I don't let them pretend that this is my party tonight. They'll just keep doing this, planning more fake parties, until I cooperate."

"Maybe you're just worth celebrating twice." Cade crooned, and I wondered if I was going to be sick.

Tonight, Sara had her hair up in a high ponytail with curly strands hanging out around her face, and I couldn't help wondering if I'd get to wrap it around my fist later tonight. "I'm going to get a drink." I extended my hand to Sara, more than ready to steal her away. "You want one?"

Before Sara could answer. "I just topped her off." Cade said, not moving his eyes from her face, keeping her locked snugly into his side.

"*Great.*" I bit out tightly, wanting to peel the skin off Cade's hand as it gripped the bare shoulder I'd had in my mouth last night.

Jules was still talking to Liam when Ariana and Riley came up. "You want to come to the bar and get a drink with us?"

"Duh," Jules chimed, and they linked arms and headed into the packed crowd.

"Coming, Carter?" Ariana asked over her shoulder.

"I'm going to say hey to Sloane first." I forced a smile, knowing I had to keep my fucking eyes on Cade.

Sloane just looked at me sweetly as I slid into the booth. "Hey Carter."

"Sloane," I said tightly before taking a sip of a random drink at the table. I stared Cade down as he leaned in and whispered something into Sara's ear, and she laughed, *actually laughed.* What the hell was he saying to make her laugh like that? *Goddamn it.*

"They look good together." Sloane said, snatching what was apparently her drink back. "They'd have the most gorgeous dark-haired babies. Don't you think?" Sloane threw her head back and laughed, clearly enjoying my misery.

Actually, *we'd* have the most gorgeous dark-haired babies is what I wanted to snap, but I didn't. "No, I don't." I bit out, stealing Sloane's drink again, knocking it down in one go.

"Hey," she complained. "Don't take your girl problems out on me."

"I don't know what you're talking about." I bit out as Cade proceeded to rub a strand of Sara's hair between his fingers. *Now he was touching her fucking hair!?* Why the fuck wasn't Liam saying something!? Fuck! Liam was on his goddamn phone, didn't even see Cade coming on to Sara! I whipped my gaze between Liam and Cade, just waiting for Liam to notice, but he didn't. *Come on, Liam. Look up! Any second now would be really fucking great. Knock his teeth out, it's what we all wanna see.*

"That's not what Sara tells me." Sloane chimed.

My gaze snapped to Sloane. "What'd she say?"

Sloane just shrugged and zipped her lips before throwing away the imaginary key. "Girl code."

"Right." I muttered, slamming my glass down too hard on the

table to get Liam's attention, but the music was too loud and it didn't make a world of difference.

"We're burning daylight. Why isn't everyone dancing?" Ariana asked cheerfully, returning with a drink in hand.

"*I'm* ready to dance." Sara chimed, and Cade immediately extended his hand to her.

My mouth dropped open with hope as Sara shot me a look, but before I could scramble out of the booth, Cade headed out to the dance floor, pulling Sara along behind him—she threw me a little grin over her shoulder right before she disappeared between the packed bodies.

Fucking bastard!

Touching what wasn't his to touch, and there wasn't a damn thing I could do about it.

My brain was short-circuiting as I hauled myself out of the booth and stormed across the dance floor.

She was mine.

CHAPTER 35

Jealous Wittle Wabbit

Cade was all over Sara on the dance floor, and I stormed right past them, towards the bar, wishing I could rip his arms out of the sockets.

It took me several minutes to get my order in, and I spent that time leaning over the counter, pouting and feeling sorry for myself, but a moment later a familiar smell hit me, strawberry and amber. *There you are.*

"Hi." Sara breathed, her cheeks flushed as she leaned back against the bar.

"Hi." I rumbled, and I couldn't help myself as I placed a hand on the other side of her, and scooped her into the space in front of me. *Fucking mine.* "I thought you were busy dancing?"

"I was." She had the audacity to bite her lip as she shyly looked up at me through her lashes. "And now I'm not."

"Don't give me that innocent little coquette act." I teased and leaned in, almost close enough to kiss her. "I know you're all wicked, lusty thoughts in there."

"Maybe I am."

The bartender set my drink down, and never leaving Sara's gaze, I pulled out my card and slid it across the bar. "I'll start a tab." The bartender took the card as I asked Sara, "What are you drinking?"

"Are *you* an option?" She hummed, eyes dropping to my mouth.

I dragged my knuckles down her arm, leaning in even closer. "What happened to taking things slow?"

"You're the one who wanted to do that, not me." She tilted her head onto her shoulder and crinkled her nose adorably.

"Oh, you are so very mistaken, pretty girl. That is the exact opposite of what I *want* to do, but it is what I think we *should* do."

"Good luck with that." She said sweetly and grabbed my drink off the bar, throwing it back with a long sip that made her sputter endearingly. "*Yelck.*"

"Yeah, that was whiskey. Your favorite." I chuckled and leaned in, deciding I could steal a quick kiss.

Sara pushed off the bar top just before my lips hit hers, and I got a mouthful of ponytail as it swished, smacking me in the face.

Jules and Douglass broke through the crowd a moment later. Fucking hell. Thankfully, neither of them saw.

"Hey you made it," Sara said tensely, giving Douglass an awkward side hug.

"Of course." He nodded at me. "What's up, Kensington?"

"Nothing much." I watched Sara run her finger around the inside of the necklace I'd given her last night, eyes still honed in on my mouth. This was pure torture.

Just then, the music changed. "This is my song!" Jules squealed, dragging Sara out onto the dance floor, and Sara threw her head back and laughed, shooting me one last wide smile before she disappeared into the crowd.

I shook my head with a grin and turned back to the bar to order another whiskey. Goddamn, she was an angel. I couldn't wait to get my hands on her again, couldn't wait to just talk to her even. I missed her. She was in the same room as me, and I missed her.

So so fucked.

Douglass was dressed in a full suit, like he usually was, and he leaned on the bar top next to me, neither of us saying anything to break the awkward silence between us. Instead, he made conversation with the girl on the other side of him, chatting her up as if Jules hadn't been standing here a mere second ago. I shook my head, waiting for my drink to be made, watching him smile a little too big, and lean in a little too close, flashing a little too much of his cash when he went to pay.

When my drink was ready, I didn't bother sticking around to watch. I'd never really cared for Douglass. We were cordial, but what Jules saw in him, I had no idea. Frankly, I thought she deserved better, she was a sweet girl, and how he had bagged her, I honestly had *no idea*. Truthfully, he was a bit of a jackass, even when he wasn't flirting with random women that weren't his girlfriend. It was an odd match, to say the least.

I took my double whiskey and headed back towards the booth, but I caught Liam's gaze over the sea of heads and headed across the club towards him.

When I came out on the other side of the crowd, I immediately surveilled the men standing next to Liam. They were just as tall as us, and each of them was covered in tattoos, necks, hands, everything.

"Carter, this is Dante and Luca Leone." Liam nodded between the two men. They looked nearly identical. They had to be brothers, or at the very least, closely related. "Dante owns the club." Liam explained rather tensely.

"And I'm along for the ride." Luca said, smiling like a Cheshire Cat.

I felt like I was being sized up as prey when I shook Dante's hand. "Hey, what's up, man? Nice to meet you."

"You all having a good time tonight?" Dante asked, and something in me immediately went on defense. This guy was dangerous. They both were, but so was I—we shared a glance that established exactly that.

"Yeah, this is a great place you've got." I nodded. "Liam tells me he's doing the menu for you."

Dante smiled wide. "He's a visionary when it comes to flavors."

"He's in high demand these days. You're lucky to have him." I agreed, watching this strange interaction unfold.

"Indeed, I am," Dante said, while Luca stood, toothpick hanging out of his mouth, looking bored and uninterested—I knew he was anything but. "Even luckier that we have an ongoing agreement." Dante mused, and I looked at Liam. What an odd thing that was to say, but Liam shot me a look like, don't ask.

I felt Luca quietly watching me, and when I finally met his gaze, there was something behind his eyes that I couldn't quite figure out, *like he knew something I didn't.*

"If you'll excuse us, gentlemen, we have matters to attend to." Dante said. "Enjoy the evening."

"Happy Halloween." Luca winked as he trailed off in the opposite direction. "Stay safe out there, kids, and be sure to watch out for the monsters under the floorboards."

When each of them strolled off through the crowd, it parted around them like butter on a hot knife. I watched as Dante disappeared into a backroom, and that's when I noticed Cade inside, just before the door closed.

"What's their deal?" I asked, watching Liam closely.

Liam shook his head warily. "It doesn't matter." Bullshit.

"How'd you guys meet?"

"Here." Liam said, already cutting back through the crowd towards the group while an odd feeling settled in my chest. What the fuck was he up to, running with guys like that? Cade too— another reason he was going to keep his filthy paws off Sara. I didn't want her anywhere near The Society, and anywhere near whoever the hell *that* had been.

~

Throughout the night, the group took turns rotating from the dance floor to the booth, taking breaks to refill their drinks and catch their breath.

Of course, there was only one person I cared to dance with, and all night my eyes were on her, just waiting for the right moment to steal her away.

I found myself alone for several songs when Riley stumbled back to the table by herself. "Doing okay?" I asked, wondering if she was even old enough to be in the club at all.

"Great." She beamed.

I chuckled. "Just take it easy, would you? You've got your whole life to party."

She rolled her eyes, and then asked, "Do you want to dance with me?"

"Why don't you have some water? You look like you could use it." I offered, pushing a glass towards her. "How did you get in here, anyway?"

After she'd chugged half the glass, she explained, "Gemma is one of my best friends. I can come anytime I want. I just have to come through the back." She rolled her eyes, and I chuckled. "Her brother Dante owns the club." Riley explained. *Interesting.* She rattled the ice in her empty water glass, looking bummed. "I was dancing with Cade, but I don't know where he went. Have you seen him?"

"He's a little old for you, don't you think?" I mused.

"Not you too." Riley rolled her eyes. "For your information, I'll be twenty-one next month. If you see him, will you tell him I was looking for him?"

"Actually, I saw Cade in a meeting with Dante earlier."

"You did?" Riley said, her demeanor shifting. "Oh."

I sat forward. "What's the matter?"

She looked around. "You don't know?" Her eyes widened a little as she leaned in and lowered her voice. "Dante Leone?" She raised her brows as if I should know what that meant. The name did sound familiar, but I couldn't quite place it.

"Is that supposed to mean something to me?" I asked warily, turning the name over in my head.

"The Leones run the mob. Or they are the mob, I guess. I don't know. Gemma doesn't tell me, and I don't ask. She just told me to stay away from her brothers—I heard Dante murdered his fiancée." Riley said nervously. "But don't tell anyone I told you that, though."

I nodded, but I didn't hear anything else Riley said after that, because I kept turning Dante's words over in my mind. *Liam and I have an agreement.*

What the fuck kind of agreement did Liam have with the mob? And even weirder, why had Liam introduced us when he seemed anything but happy about it.

"There you are, Riley. We've been looking for you." Jules lilted a worried mother hen. "Come on, guys, we're all going to dance to the next song." Riley popped up immediately, but I was still lost in thought as Jules motioned. "You too, Carter. You're not getting out of this one."

Drink in hand, I let the girls drag me out to the dance floor, and even though she wasn't anywhere near me, my eyes were glued to Sara as she *moved* to the music. Her short green dress shimmered, catching the light as it hugged her every gyrating curve. Except for a few shimmery, silvery straps across her bare skin, the dress was open-backed, and I was all lusty thoughts, utterly mesmerized by her—I couldn't help it.

A little while later, Sara dragged a finger over my chest before she disappeared with Jules and Riley towards the bathroom, strutting away from me with a wink. I was getting incredibly desperate to steal her away for a dance when no one was looking, which, as the night ticked on, seemed to be getting harder and harder.

However, at that moment, I noticed Douglass had already found someone else to dance with. Someone who was *not* Jules. I wondered what he was like when Jules wasn't around at all. Fucking dipshit.

When the song changed and Douglass put his hand some-where it definitely shouldn't have been, *I'd had it.*

I finally gripped his shoulder and said loudly, "Your girlfriend has been gone a while, maybe you should go check on her?" *Aka, what the fuck are you doing?*

Douglass gave me an irritated look and lowered his voice to hiss, "What the fuck?"

"Yeah," I mouthed back, shooting him a look. "What the fuck?"

He glared at me, wiping his nose. "I'm just having a little fun."

I squared up to him. "Why don't you go find *Jules*, and have a little fun?"

"You know, Carter here is right. I *should* go check on my girl-friend, make sure she's not getting herself into any trouble." He practically snarled through his slightly slurred words. "But he'll dance with you. Won't you, Carter?" He shoved the girl into my arms roughly before storming off like a petulant child.

I righted the girl, making sure she wasn't going to fall over before I let go. "Sorry about that. He's involved." I added quickly. "And so am I."

A tart little voice sounded from behind me. "You're involved, huh?" Sloane came around my side.

Just great. "Maybe I am," I muttered, heading for the bar.

Sloane cocked her head and promptly blocked my path. "With whom?" She asked sweetly.

"I don't know what you're talking about." I dodged around her.

Sloane followed after me, not letting up. "Hmm, for some reason, I'm not finding that particularly convincing."

"Did she say something?" I finally stopped and asked, shouting over the music.

"I don't know. Do you want her to have said something?" Sloane grinned, ineffectively hiding her smirk behind her drink. "Oh, this is too much fun! You've both got it *bad*. You finally kissed her, didn't you?" Sloane sang, and I pursed my lips and said nothing, realizing Sara hadn't said a damn thing to Sloane.

Good. I wanted Sara all to myself for a little bit. "Don't you guys talk about these things?" I asked, starting for the bar again.

"She'll tell me when she's ready, and I'm not going to push her. Not when she looks happier than she's looked all year." Sloane nodded to Sara, who was already coming back from the bathroom.

Sara did look happy. She really did, *she had a glow*. I smirked, knowing *I* did that—me and my little pink pony friend.

"You kissed." Sloane decided rather matter-of-factly.

I rolled my eyes, as if kissing even covered what I'd done to Sara last night. "Maybe we did." I shrugged.

Sloane narrowed her eyes. "Just do me a favor, Kensington." She lowered her voice to a menacing whisper. "Don't fuck it up this time."

"I don't plan on it." I gritted, kind of loving how protective Sara's friends were.

"Do you have a plan at all?" Sloane asked pointedly. "You know what they say about a man without a plan."

"I'm working on it." I gave her a sarcastic smile. "Okay?"

"I guess we'll see, won't we?" Sloane shot me a menacing look.

"What are you two talking about?" Sara came up, rosy-cheeked, her ponytail swishing behind her.

Sloane tilted her head at me and said sweetly, "We're talking about what a good planner Carter is."

"Huh?" Sara grabbed Sloane's pink drink out of her hand, taking a big sip.

Cade appeared and slung his arm around Sloane's shoulders. "Wanna dance, blondie?"

Sloane rolled her eyes. "No."

"You owe me." Cade grinned.

"May I remind you that your DD-ing, is because *you* owe *me*." Sloane said, staring down her nose at Cade, even though he was so much taller than her, even with her height and her heels.

Cade put his hands up. "Fine, if you don't think you can handle all this."

"Please." Sloane grabbed Cade by the tie and dragged him behind her. "Let's see if you can keep up, Blackthorn." Cade raised his brows in surprised victory while he trailed behind Sloane's lion's mane of blonde hair.

Good. Let one *feral* animal chase the other *rabid* animal and leave *my sweet wittle-wabbit alone*! I was finally all alone with the girl I couldn't seem to track down all night, and it was about damn time!

"I wonder if something is going on between the two of them." Sara pursed her lips, watching them disappear between the packed bodies.

I could give two shits about whatever was going on between the two of them. The only thing I cared about was the fact that they were both finally gone. "Think I'm going to get a dance with *you* before the night is up?" I cocked my head, drinking Sara in.

She bit her lip, looking around. "Should we?"

"I don't see why not." I said, loving the way her breath picked up when I closed the space between us. "You've danced with everyone else tonight."

"True," she breathed.

"Your brother didn't seem to mind Cade putting his filthy, fucking hands all over you." I said lowly.

"Oh my," Sara bit her lip with a flirty smile. "Jealousy looks good on you, Kensington, you should try that look on more often."

"You know what looks good on *you*?" I leaned in with a rumbling chuckle. "Nothing at all."

Her eyes twinkled. "I would say the same, but I wouldn't know, because *someone's* a prude."

"Please, you've gotten an eyeful several times now." I nearly lost it when she palmed me unexpectedly. "Fuck, Sara."

"Maybe an eyeful just isn't enough for me." She pouted innocently as I grabbed her wrist with a groan. "Maybe I'm not wearing any underwear again, and maybe I'm desperate for you to find out for sure."

I snaked my arm around her and hauled her against me, hardly able to pull in a full breath. "Dance with me, pretty girl."

She gazed into my eyes, sliding her arms around my neck. "I thought you'd never ask."

CHAPTER 36

Poker Face

The bass was low and sensual as it thundered around us, and Sara *moved* on me. She turned, pushing her ass against me, and dragged her hand down through my hair, while I buried my face in her neck, and I couldn't help biting her. She gasped and rubbed herself against me even harder as we gyrated to the music, letting our hands wander, grasp, and explore. "We're being reckless." I panted.

"Who cares?"

"Liam might."

Sara turned towards me again, looking around as she gripped my neck. "Actually, where is Liam? I haven't seen him in a while."

"Uh, I don't know." I wondered if Liam had somehow ended up in that shady backroom with Cade and Dante. My gut told me he had, but I didn't want to think about him. Not right now.

I was so tempted to steal a kiss, but after nearly getting caught once, I didn't dare. Dancing I could explain. If we got caught kissing, Liam might actually kill me.

After a couple of dances, Sloane appeared all too soon. "Come on, lovebirds, it's cake time."

"Sloane." Sara groaned, shooting her a look, but Sloane was already headed back.

Sara pushed up on her tiptoes and pecked me on the lips with a sweet smile before she grabbed my hand with a sigh. "Let's go, Lover Boy."

I grinned like a schoolboy and tugged her ponytail as she dragged me back to the table, putting a little extra sway in her hips with every step.

~

At the booth, there was hardly room for us to fit. Everyone was crammed in, Jules in Douglass's lap, Sloane, Riley, and Ariana crammed together at the back of the booth. Cade smashed in on the far end, nearly falling over the edge, but Liam was nowhere to be found.

I motioned for Sara to take the only free spot on the edge of the booth next to Douglass. "Actually, you sit for a second." Sara said, pulling out her phone. "You guys are too cute. I have to get a picture."

Jules, who was in Douglass's lap, shifted over for me, and Sara snapped the picture with an adorable grin.

"Right here, birthday girl." Cade patted his lap as Sara put her phone away.

I pushed up to stand because there was *no way in hell* I was letting her sit in Cade's lap. She could have my spot.

Sara shoved me back down with surprising force, all while smiling sweetly at Cade. "There's room over here. Thanks though." Sara planted herself square in my lap, and my fingers instinctively slid around her waist as she wiggled back.

Cade nodded at me with an understanding smirk, and I just shrugged, struggling to conceal my pleased smile.

It was hard to hear everyone over the music, and the girls were practically shouting, trying to carry on a conversation at the back of the booth when Sara whispered over her shoulder to me. "I dare you to see how long you can go without touching me." She pushed herself back, grinding against me, ruthlessly.

I was already hard, and this wasn't helping in the slightest. "Careful." I warned softly. "Or I might have to teach you a lesson for teasing me all night." I murmured, fingers grazing against her bare leg. "See how good your poker face is."

"I think you're the one who's bluffing." She challenged quietly.

"Oh, yeah?" I dragged a lazy caress up the inside of her thigh, and she flinched. "You sure this is a game you wanna play right now, pretty girl?"

Sara's legs parted beneath the table, inviting me in. "Deal me in, Kensington, *I dare you.*"

"Oh, you are trouble, aren't you?" I chuckled, cautiously glancing around the table as I continued lazily, just barely inching higher. "You can fold anytime—show me your cards." I offered, giving her an easy out as the rise and fall of her breaths against me became more shallow by the second.

"Call. I raise you double or nothing." She dared, and my own heart was thrumming a mile a minute as I inched beneath the edge of her dress, feeling wicked as ever. "You shouldn't raise when you have no idea what's in my hand, pretty girl." I gave her one last warning, as my self-restraint snapped down to the last wavering thread.

"If this was a dare, and it totally is," she leaned forward onto the table, resting her chin on one hand casually, while the other slipped beneath the table, sliding up *my* leg. "You'd be losing right now." Naughty girl, egging me on like that—she gasped when I slid my feet between hers, snapping her legs wide open under the table, anchoring them there.

"If you want to fold, now would be the time." I hummed a final warning as she tried to wiggle free.

"Hit me." She rasped, begging me to keep going.

Breath ragged, I slid my fingers higher, making her jolt. "Then while we're at it, why don't we up the ante?" I purred against the shell of her ear, "You always were a rookie when it came to poker. *Let's see if you've gotten any better at bluffing.*"

I felt Sara choke back a sound as my fingers grazed higher, discovering she *was* wearing underwear and there was a warm damp spot, already waiting, just for me. Fucking hell. She chased my hand as I lazily moved elsewhere, testing her limits one last time because I was about to have some fun with my little daredevil.

"Are you going to actually do something, or not?" Sara challenged breathlessly. "Because I'm starting to get bored."

I chuckled. "Oh, sweet girl, you are about to be in *big trouble*." I threatened quietly and then cleared my throat, finding my voice rough, as I called across the table, "Sloane, Sara wanted to ask you something." I tugged those thin panties to the side and dragged my fingers across the very edge of her, and Sara practically convulsed.

Sloane turned, shouting across the table. "What's up?"

Sara was fucking soaked, desperately squirming as I locked my forearm over her thighs, halting her escape. "I—was just wondering," She struggled as I slid the tip of a finger through her wet heat, counting on her to keep it together. "Water!" Sara gasped out, slamming her hand on the table, reaching towards the pitcher a millisecond too late. "Could you pass the water over here?" She begged, fluttering against my fingertips as I began a slow, wide circle around—

"What the hell is this?" Liam barked, coming up to the table.

I might have actually been having a heart attack as I frantically unpinned Sara's legs, grateful it was so dark in here.

"Tables full." Sara quickly interjected, saving us, albeit far too breathily, while I tried to pull her dress back down as discreetly as possible, hoping my own poker face was holding.

"Here they come, here they come." Jules announced, our saving grace, as everyone started singing happy birthday.

Liam shot me a look, but I knew he hadn't seen, because if he had, I would have already swallowed my teeth.

Someone set down an epic cake on the table that Liam had no doubt made, or at least ordered with detailed instructions—it was covered in flowers and glitter with six-inch sparkler candles shooting off the top.

The entire table was singing, staring at that epic cake, and I couldn't have given two shits about that cake, because the dessert I desperately wanted a taste of—was already glazed across the tips of my fingers like sweet, sweet icing.

I rubbed my slippery fingers together under the table and tried to shake myself out of the lusty haze I was in, as I finally joined in the singing. Sara threw her head back and laughed, so carefree, and then she took a deep breath to blow out the colorful sparkler candles.

"Make a wish." I said quietly into her ear as the chorus ended.

Sara leaned forward and blew out the candles, only they didn't blow out. She squealed adorably in her frustration as she tried again.

"Blow harder." The girls cackled hysterically as Sara tried again. "Put your back into it!"

"Help me!" Sara finally pleaded, and before anyone else could lean in and spit all over the cake, Douglass licked his fingers and snuffed out the candles, one after another, sort of killing the vibe.

"Doug," Jules complained in shock. "Now her wish isn't going to come true."

"It wasn't going to come true anyway." He shrugged indifferently.

Jules made a frustrated noise, but pulled the cake towards herself and started cutting slices for everyone, muttering quietly.

The first plate was, of course, passed down to Sara, who continued to wiggle in my lap as she leaned forward and started eating. "Look who finally has an appetite." I murmured, suppressing a smile.

"I got your note," Sara said, even quieter, as I popped one of the birthday hats onto her head with a chuckle.

Sloane announced to the table, "I got us all tickets to Rattlesnake Ranch. They have an epic corn maze, and the most insane haunted house, it's so fucked up." She grinned. "So finish your cake and have another drink if you need a liquid jacket because it's going to be chilly out there."

"I'm so sorry, but I'm going to have to head out after this," Ariana called across the table to Sara. "I have an early morning at the embassy tomorrow."

"Oh my gosh, don't even worry about it. I'm just so glad I got to see you at all." Sara grabbed Ariana's hand across the table, and they did a girly, whatever kind of thing that made me chuckle. It was cute. *Sara was cute.* "You're here for the cake. That's the most important part anyway." Sara winked, and I was so glad to see the old Sara back, and happier than ever. Everything felt right. Better than right, actually.

The table broke into chatter, and while Liam was waiting for his piece of cake, he leaned in. "Hey, did you ever figure out who left the dildo in your bed?"

Sara immediately choked, and Cade looked between us and sucked his teeth. "I could take a wild guess." Asshole.

"Sorry." Liam chuckled to Sara. "Guy talk." If only Liam knew.

Sara shoved a massive piece of cake into her mouth, chewing furiously, and I pushed her water cup towards her, doing my best to keep a straight face while I talked to Liam.

Suddenly, Theo appeared out of thin air, looking like a bull ready to charge. "What in the ever-living fuck are you doing here, Riley?" Theo thundered, and the table froze.

"Oh, shit." Riley hissed and quickly knocked back her drink, quickly shoving the last bite of cake into her mouth.

"And *you.*" Theo pointed a finger at Ariana. "You are in deep shit, princess."

"Don't you dare speak that way to me," Ariana bit out harshly.

"We had an agreement." Theo snarled.

"*You* had an agreement." Ariana crossed her arms in defiance.

Everyone's eyes ping-ponged between Theo and Ariana as they argued.

"I should have known I couldn't trust you with anyone else."

"I. Don't. Need. A grumpy beefcake, following me around everywhere I go!" Ariana gritted out angrily.

"Tell that to your fucking father."

"I did." Ariana practically screamed.

Meanwhile, Riley was quietly sliding over everyone, trying to avoid the crossfire. "Sorry." She grimaced, literally climbing over Jules and Douglass. "So sorry."

"If your brothers find out about this," Theo grumbled, grabbing Riley and hauling her over the table entirely.

"You're not going to say a damn word." Ariana threatened Theo from the back of the booth. "Otherwise, I'll tell my father what *you* did!"

Theo barked a sardonic laugh. "You go right ahead and do that, cupcake!" Everyone gasped as Theo ripped the table out from the booth, sending cake and drinks flying everywhere.

Ariana's eyes went wide. "What are you doing?" She tried to scramble away as he closed in, but there was nowhere to go, we were packed in like sardines, and he was blocking the only path out. "Theo—Theodore! Don't you fucking dare." Ariana cried, scrambling up.

Theo grabbed an arm, bent low, and in one motion he hauled Ariana over his shoulder, as if she'd even had a chance.

"You bastard." Ariana screamed, beating against his muscled back, her strawberry blonde hair swinging with his every step. "I'm going to have you arrested for kidnapping."

"In case you forgot, princess, making sure you don't get abducted *again* is exactly why I'm here." Theo scoffed, a satisfied smirk on his face. "Better me than someone else."

Riley's shoulders sagged as she trailed along behind Theo and an outraged Ariana.

"Bye, cutie." Cade called with a wave of his fingers to Riley.

Without even turning around, Riley threw her hand up behind her and flipped off Cade.

Sara clapped a hand over her mouth as the girls erupted in

shocked giggles. "Why was that kind of hot?" Jules gaped at Sara, who headily murmured her agreement. *Noted.*

"Okaaaaay." Sloane chimed as we all gawked at each other. "I guess we're done with cake. Who's ready for the haunted house?"

My grip on Sara tightened. Why did I have a bad feeling about this?

CHAPTER 37

Monsters in The Dark

SARAFINA

A shrill scream erupted in the distance, and I sucked in a sharp breath, jerking toward the sound. Relief flooded me when muted laughter quickly followed, but my skin still prickled with unease.

You're fine.

The soft hum and chirp of bugs filled the air around me. Minutes stretched long, and dead ends grew even more frustrating as I tried to push down the panic that had sunk its teeth deeper into me with every wrong turn.

With mud squelching under my caked tennis shoes, I started down the next tall row of corn, hating the darkness that suffocated me from all sides as I very unsuccessfully tried to navigate my way out of the maze.

I told myself my mind was playing tricks on me, but ominous shadows seemed to move within the dense walls of corn, seemed to keep pace with me.

When I reached the end of the row, my stomach dropped, realizing the path split in three different directions. *Again.*

There was a strong chance I'd been going in circles for quite a while now, and I'd had just about enough of that. I quickly tied several corn husks together and placed the large, recognizable knot at the entrance of one path before starting down it.

I pulled out my phone and turned on the flashlight, not caring about the rules as I hurried down the row to see if I made a loop back to my marker.

Cold mud splattered up the back of my bare legs, and I desperately wished I'd changed into leggings, but of course, the outfit had been my priority.

Well, actually, the look on Carter's face when he saw me in my leggy little dress had been the priority. A twist of heat bloomed in my chest, making me smile as I recalled Carter's quiet simmering outrage when Cade had taken me to the dance floor. Jealous Carter was *hot*. Got *me* hot just thinking about it. As fun as dancing with Cade had been, he'd only been a part of my cover. There was, of course, only one person I had really wanted to dance with.

It was the guy who had fucked me into next week like it was a casual Tuesday night. The guy who had practically turned me inside out, using in his own words *a cute little unicorn horn*.

To put it delicately.

I rubbed my collarbone breathily as I turned his words over in my mind. He wanted to take it slow. I rolled my eyes. Please. I wanted to do anything but. I wanted to make up for lost time. I wanted—

God, I was desperate for him. Whatever. It was what it was, and what it was—*was all freaking consuming*. But I'd always been like that about Carter, always been drawn to him. I couldn't help it.

I shook my head, knowing Liam was going to be *so* upset when he found out; it'd feel like a betrayal to him. We'd have to figure out a way to tell him eventually, but Carter was right. We deserved a little time to figure this all out, just the two of us.

Plus, the sneaking around was kind of hot too.

Replaying last night's shenanigans in my mind, I clung to that little kernel of warmth as I turned down another tall row of corn, lost in my dirty little thoughts.

The way Carter's eyes had tracked my every movement all

night, what we'd almost gotten caught doing underneath the table.

Whew.

It wasn't just the physical side though, the feeling of being wanted, desired, looked at in that way. It was ecstasy. I'd never felt anything like that in my life. Didn't even realize the way other guys had looked at me had been so devoid of the devotion that was already so apparent with Carter.

Even the way Cade had looked at me, it was all lust and desire. When Carter looked at me, there was hunger and desire there for sure, and thank God for that, but there was something soft, and protective too. Like he wasn't sure if he wanted to handle me like a precious, fragile artifact, or ruin me entirely. The juxtaposition of it was utterly thrilling if I was being honest.

A quiet laugh bubbled up as the warmth of being *wanted* filled me, making me feel woozy and lightheaded. It was like floating away into thin air and being crushed with the most powerful force all at once. Sure, it had taken us a lifetime to finally get over the hump, but now, everything just felt so—being with Carter just felt *different*. In every way. Exciting yes, but also calm, steady, *right—*

I screamed as something smashed into my face at mock speeds, followed by the disgusting sound of buzzing. I sputtered and spit, frantically trying to get the feeling off my mouth as I exploded into a windmill of flailing arms. The thing skittered over my face before finally flying away.

Grumbling, I smoothed out my hair, a little paranoid that the bug was still on me, and adjusted myself. Stupid, fucking confusing corn maze. Why Sloane had been dying to do this, I had no idea. The only thing worse than being alone in the dark was being alone and half-naked in the dark with gross bugs. The worst cherry on top you could possibly ask for.

I turned the next corner, feeling more and more anxious by the minute. Was I anywhere close to getting out of here? I had to be. How many turns could there possibly be... in the city's most notoriously complicated corn maze?

Shit.

I'd started this whole damned thing with Jules and Douglass, and when they'd started bickering, I'd tried to give them some privacy. Which led to me making a turn too quickly, and before I'd even realized it, they were long gone. I grimaced, knowing something had been going on between the two of them for a while now, and I honestly just wished that she'd cut him loo—

Suddenly, I realized everything had gone eerily quiet... that it had *been* unnaturally quiet for some time.

My hair raised as I turned in all directions, shining my phone flashlight into the dense corn, as if I'd find something or *someone* lurking between the stalks.

I knew I was being ridiculous because—*something rustled behind me.* I whirled, the light revealing nothing as I twisted in all directions, breath shaking, heart pounding wildly in my ears. "Carter, is that you?" I swallowed hard as my voice came out alarmingly timid and quiet.

No response.

The corn rustled. "This isn't funny." I complained, unnerved by the panic lacing my voice as I tried to steady it. "Liam?"

No response.

I started to feel dizzy as adrenaline crashed through me, and I abandoned my plan, taking the first turn away from the noise.

I turned my phone light off and hurried down the long muddy path, looking over my shoulder before I rounded the next corner, slightly out of breath.

Forcing silent breaths in and out, I listened quietly, but every-thing was still eerily silent.

Quietly as I could, I continued onward, all the while feeling like the shadows in the corn were following me. Which was delu-sional. I knew that.

Finally, with bile rising in my throat, I stopped and stared into the dark row of corn, wondering if I was imagining things as a dark shadow seemed to stare right back. I lost my nerve, frantically fumbling for my flashlight again, but when I finally got it on— there was nothing there.

And then I heard the footsteps *behind me.*

My throat closed up as I turned in wild panic, horrified to find a terrifying face looming over me—I wished I were one of those girls who threw a punch, or did something to defend myself, but the only thing I could do was scream. Even that took the longest second of my life to produce. The mud gave way beneath me, and I was already falling backwards as the scream seemed to stick in my throat before finally cracking out of me with a thin screech.

"Boo." Someone grabbed me by the waist, catching me before I fell into the mud.

"*Carter.*" I gasped after another long second, relief washing over me. "That's not funny." I complained shakily.

"Did I scare you?" He chuckled.

"No." I gritted, all the while relishing in the protective warmth of his touch as he steadied me.

He blinked against the bright light in his eyes. "You mind aiming that thing somewhere else, scaredy cat?"

"I'm not sure I'm done blinding you yet," I huffed before shakily tapping the light off, my stomach swirling with adrenaline and nausea. Stupid fucking corn maze.

It was hard to see as my eyes adjusted back to the dim light of the moon, but the darkness didn't seem to matter as much anymore.

"Geez, you're freezing, sweetheart." Carter pulled me tighter against his hard body and rubbed my arms, trying to warm me up.

"Oh, you have no idea." I wormed my arms up his chest with a sly grin and slid my icy hands against his bare neck.

He yelped. "Hey now."

"You deserve it for scaring me like that." I grumbled with a small smile while the buzz in my body morphed into something totally different.

A glimmering look flashed through his eyes and I think I felt it more than saw it in the darkness, "And you deserve all kinds of things that I can't wait to give to you, pretty girl." Carter cupped my hands between his and blew hot air on them before kissing each of my palms, sending a strike of heat through my entire body. *That was certainly one way to warm up.*

"Was scaring me worth it?" I asked skeptically, already missing his warmth as he stepped away from me. "I would have wandered all night before I cut through all those creepy-crawlies to get out of here." I involuntarily shivered with the heebie-jeebies.

Carter pulled his hoodie up over his head, and I shivered for an entirely different reason as I watched his shirt slide up, revealing his toned stomach. "What?" He asked, shaking out his hair in that adorable way he used to before he bunched up the collar of his hoodie.

"So help me, this better not have a single spider on it." I complained, my voice muffled as he pulled the warm fleece over me.

"Why would it have spiders on it?" Carter said, while he adjusted the oversized hood around my face, looking amused.

"Didn't you cut through the middle?" I shoved my arms into the sleeves, relishing in the intoxicating smell of him now wrapped all around me.

"No, I followed the light you were waving around like a madman." He huffed a laugh.

"Oh." I looked up at him for a long minute, a weird feeling settling in my chest.

His jaw flexed, and an equally strange look settled over his expression. "Sara, why are you asking me that?"

I shook my head and cinched the hood tightly around my face, not caring if I looked dumb. I was freezing my tits off, and besides, Carter had already seen more of me last night than my short little dress was currently revealing. So much for being mysterious. "I may or may not have gotten spooked—I thought someone was following me." I admitted, shoving my nose into the fleece, eyes practically rolling back as I inhaled deeply.

"Hmm." Carter looked around, a mildly concerned look flooding his expression. "Come on, let's get you out of here."

"Yeah," I quietly agreed. "This place is giving me the creeps." But I was completely startled by Carter's *very quick* pace as he deftly moved us through the maze.

"You know you've been going in circles for the last ten minutes?" He seemed distracted as he pulled me along.

My breath curled in the air as I huffed a laugh. "I was just getting my steps in."

"Sure you were, pretty girl." He chuckled, but it sounded hollow, and my stomach dropped when he looked over his shoulder—his jaw tense as his eyes swept each row in an almost tactical sort of way.

Did he really believe that someone had been following me? That would be ridiculous, right? "You're in a hurry." I said as casually as I could.

Without missing a beat. "Just trying to get you out of the cold." *Hmm.*

With Carter's powerful hand wrapped tightly around mine, I followed him through the maze as he made one confident turn after another.

"How do you even know where you're going?" I still couldn't make heads or tails of where we were.

He shrugged. "I'm directionally blessed. What can I say?"

"Thank God for that." I wondered how Sloane, Cade, and Liam were faring. "By the way." I lowered my voice to an outraged whisper. "I *cannot believe* you told Liam about the dildo!"

Carter chuckled, shooting me a long look. "I may have texted him, thinking it was a prank when I initially found it."

"For the love." I groaned. "He can *never* find out it was mine."

Carter's thumb brushed over the back of my hand. "Yeah, we're definitely in agreement on that."

Several turns later, my shoulders sagged in relief when the exit sign illuminated the end of the path. *We were going to sleep in our own beds tonight! Yippy-ki-yay-motherfucker!*

Carter squeezed my hand three times before letting go of it and then he gripped my shoulders, steering me out of the exit in front of him. "Found her." He announced proudly, and I gasped when he immediately yanked me back against him—just before a hulking man in a cowboy hat stalked by. The man nearly ran me over with a wheelbarrow full of zombie bodies, looking grumpy as shit. "Watch it." Carter hissed and then muttered, "Fucking cowboys."

"You made it!" Sloane laughed, shoving a steaming paper cup into my hand.

"Thanks, I'm freezing." I groaned, blowing on the sweetly fragrant hot apple cider before I gingerly tried a sip. It was the most delicious thing I'd ever tasted in my life.

"Same." Sloane groaned. "I don't know why I didn't think to bring a change of clothes." She smirked and jutted her hip into mine. "At least we look good."

I eyed her wearing Cade's leather jacket, and she eyed me wearing Carter's hoodie. We exchanged a silent look of a thousand words. "Later." I quietly mouthed with a smirk, and she nodded in agreement.

Soft folk music played from the snack bar speakers, and the cackling sound of the city's scariest and most debauched haunted house echoed in the distance.

Everything was fine. I had just gotten a little spooked in the dark, that was all.

And yet, I could tell Carter was still tense, anxious almost. It was making me feel anxious, but I didn't know exactly why.

"Where's everybody else?" I asked, letting the curling steam from my paper cup bathe my face in wet warmth.

"You guys were taking forever. So, Liam and Carter went back in to look for you." Sloane pulled Cade's jacket tighter around her shoulders. "Jules and Doug must have gotten really turned around."

I shoved my nose under the collar of Carter's hoodie and blew into it. Next to me in a tight, black t-shirt that he looked far too good in, Carter's skin pebbled in the brisk air. "Do you want your hoodie back?" I asked, feeling a little guilty.

I could feel Sloane's gaze shift to us as Carter wrapped his arms around me and pulled me into his chest, murmuring softly. "Naw, I'll be fine. I've got a cute little hot pocket to keep me warm." I rolled my lips over my teeth, hiding a grin, and Sloane wiggled her brows at me before she made herself busy talking with Cade.

A few freezing cold minutes later, Liam appeared, prompting Carter and I to quickly step away from each other. Liam looked pissed, and I panicked for a split second thinking he'd seen us, but when Jules came into view a second later, I realized something was wrong. Liam ushered Jules towards us, with a protective hand on her back, while Douglass stalked off towards the bathrooms, mud splattered up the back of his suit. When Jules got closer, I could see her eyes were puffy and swollen, like she'd been crying *hard*.

"Here, Jules." I handed her a fresh cup of hot cider, and then Sloane and I crowded around her, rubbing her arms to warm her up. "What's the matter?" I asked gently as Jules tried to hide her sniffling.

She stared down at the hot drink, blinking rapidly. Her lips parted, but then she just shook her head, unable to get the words out.

"Jules." I asked softly. "Are you okay?"

Her lower lip trembled, and the word was a push of air. "No."

"What happened?" Sloane asked as we shared a look.

"We just got in a fight, that's all." Jules voice broke. "I really don't want to talk about it right now."

"Are you up for the haunted house?" I asked. "We can totally skip it if you want."

"Uh, yeah, sure." Jules said, clearing her throat. "No, yeah, let's do it."

I looked at Carter, and he nodded icily towards Douglass, who was walking straight past the bathrooms and towards the parking lot. Doug didn't so much as look back as he disappeared between the cars. *Still wearing his jacket.*

Jules caught our glances and followed our gaze, her lower lip trembling fiercely as she tried with all her might to keep it together. "I'm going to need a ride home." She whispered emptily.

"I can take you home. You're on the way." Liam offered sympathetically, even though she wasn't even remotely on the way home.

Jules just stared blankly towards the parking lot, and a tear slipped down her cheek. My heart caved in, and I handed Carter her drink before I wrapped my arms tightly around my friend and just held her. I felt Sloane's arms pile in over the top of mine as we sandwiched Jules. Her shoulders shook, and the smallest noise squeaked out of her as she held back a sob. *Damn it.*

We all shot each other silent looks while Sloane and I held her like that for several minutes, until Jules finally pulled back, wiping her eyes.

Liam cleared his throat. "Jules, I can really take you home now, if you want." When she didn't respond, Liam reached out and touched her arm gently. "I was actually getting kind of tired anyway. You'd just be giving me an excuse to ditch." He tried lightly. "You ready to go home? Call it a night?"

There was a long pause, and she wiped her nose with the back of her hand before straightening. "I don't want to go home and be all alone." She said quietly but firmly.

Liam nodded, his lips parting as he searched for the right words. But what could any of us say that would truly help? Nothing. We could just be there for her, like she'd been there for all of us when we needed it.

"You should sleep at the house tonight." I casually offered. "I was actually thinking we could do a girls night. I know I should have planned better, but I was thinking we could do breakfast in the morning?" I looked at Liam, who nodded in agreement.

"Oh, please say yes," Sloane chimed in. "I miss you guys so much."

Jules nodded and then shook her head in a circle as we watched her silently change her mind multiple times over. "Yeah." She sniffled, her mind clearly somewhere else. "Okay."

Without another word, as if knowing we'd try to talk her out of it, Jules turned and slowly started towards the haunted house line.

"Should we try to convince her to call it a night?" Sloane asked cautiously. "I don't know that the haunted house is the best idea right now. It's pretty intense in there."

When none of us responded right away, "I think she needs the distraction." Cade said, his piercing blue eyes swirling with some memory of his own. "She probably wants to feel some sort of normalcy." I stared up at Cade for a long moment, wondering what exactly he meant by that.

In line for the haunted house, Sloane promptly paired us all off. "Carter, you can go with Sara." She pushed us together with a smirk. "Liam, you go with Jules?" She asked, but it wasn't really a question as she dragged them to the front of the line, pushing them together.

I knew Liam would have Jules laughing and distracted in no time. He was always good at that—lightening the mood, smoothing things over, taking care of people. Over the years he'd been a big brother to *all* my friends in one way or another. Finding too much entertainment in making our lives miserable of course, but he was *always* there if any of us needed him. Protectively stepping in when a boyfriend needed an ass-kicking, picking someone up if they were too drunk to drive, offering sage advice, it didn't matter—if anyone in his life ever needed help, he was there. I knew she'd be in good hands with Liam, and so did Sloane.

Liam nodded, understanding his task—he was on Jules duty for the rest of the night. "Don't you worry, kiddo," Liam said, throwing an arm around Jules shoulder. "No zombies will be getting by me tonight."

Jules laughed softly, her nose still stuffy. "Thanks."

"And what about me?" Cade practically purred at Sloane.

"*I* can hold my own in there." Sloane tossed her hair over her shoulder flippantly.

"I don't think it's the monsters inside we have to worry about." Cade hummed, and slid his hand over Sloane's shoulder and around her throat, growling playfully. Her eyes flared. Only for a split second, but both Cade and I caught it, and Cade smoothed his smirk as quickly as it formed.

"You are insufferable." Sloane rolled her eyes and smacked him. "I'm not scared of monsters inside or outside."

"We'll see about that." Cade tugged her closer, and I watched as Sloane *let* him. *Fascinating.*

At the front of the line, Jules and Liam signed a waiver before their tickets were collected. And then they disappeared through the gauzy curtains, into the city's most fucked-up haunted house, as Sloane had put it earlier.

As soon as Liam and Jules were out of earshot, Sloane turned on heel. "What the actual hell?"

"What do you think happened?" I asked before Cade added with a shake of his head. "What an ass." Carter's jaw flexed, but he said nothing as he listened with crossed arms, buffering against the chill. "Carter yanked Douglass off a random girl at the club." Sloane announced.

"What?" I whirled to Carter. "Why didn't you tell me?" Before Carter could answer, Cade added, "And Doug-ass was definitely doing snow in the bathroom earlier."

"What?!" Sloane and I both yipped in unison, whirling to look up at Cade with our mouths agape.

Cade grimaced. "I don't think it was his first hit, either."

Sloane narrowed her eyes. "And you would know that how exactly?"

"Don't you start with me, Blondie," Cade said lowly, his eyes flashing with something surprisingly sharp.

Carter's jaw fanned, and he shook his head, not paying attention to whatever sparks were igniting right in front of us. "I don't know what she sees in him."

"Do you think it was just tonight?" I asked, and we all looked at each other, nobody answering, because how could any of us really know? Carter gave me a sympathetic look, and I knew *exactly* what he thought.

"Well, nobody say anything until we know for sure." Sloane pursed her lips contemplatively. "There's no use making things worse, not until we know, and definitely not until she's gotten a good night's sleep." Except Sloane sounded anything but sure about that decision.

"Maybe," Carter said, a protective tone lacing his voice, and a tingle ran through me, watching him. "I'm interested to know what Liam overheard in there. There might be more going on that we don't know about."

"What do you mean?" I asked, trying to stay focused, but damn, he was sexy when he was being protective, and it was really sweet that he cared about my friends that much.

"If she's getting steamrolled like that all the time, she might not even realize the relationship is dysfunctional."

Was she getting steamrolled all the time?

A pang of guilt hit me, realizing I'd been off in my own little world this year. Everyone had been so focused on me while I was busy falling apart, and I hadn't even bothered to notice if my friends were okay. Hadn't even considered that they might not be.

Douglass wasn't my favorite, but Jules loved Douglass *unconditionally.* Why, I couldn't say exactly, but I knew one thing for sure, she deserved someone as kind and caring as she was, and there was only one way she was going to find it. She probably had to let go of a man that nobody could understand why she was with in the first place. She'd *always* been a giver, and Douglass had always been a *taker*. Someone could only do that for so long when things weren't being reciprocated. But the more I stewed on it, I wondered if maybe Carter was right.

"Sloane and I will talk to her in the morning. We could all use a good night's sleep first." I sighed tightly, and everyone nodded in agreement.

I cast a long look at Carter and hoped *we* had a fighting chance. I'd heard what he'd said to Cade earlier at the club. He was going to have to deploy soon. The thought made me want to puke. Not just because he would be gone for months on end again, but because there was a very real possibility he might never come back.

I blinked the thought away, hardly able to even consider it as my eyes stung with tears. If something happened to him, I didn't know if I'd survive it.

CHAPTER 38
Catch Me if You Can
SARAFINA

We were the last couple to enter the haunted house. "Don't get scared." Carter hummed into my ear. God, even the sound of his voice was sexy.

I tightly clutched Carter's arm as our eyes adjusted. I *hated* being scared, but with a date, maybe it was the *tiniest* bit fun being chased with chainsaws and bloody knives. Besides, if this was the price I had to pay to hold on to Carter's bulging biceps, I supposed it was a steal of a deal.

As we navigated our way through the haunted house, I hardly paid attention to all the creepy stuff. Closing my eyes as Carter chuckled at me and guided us through each room, completely unfazed.

Suddenly, something cold and wet splattered on us, and I screamed as a gurgling zombie jumped out, dragging a bloody hand over my cheek before he tried to drag me away.

Carter straight-armed the guy and hauled me into the next room, slamming the door shut behind us.

"Disgusting." I muttered, using the back of my hand to wipe my face. "I definitely could have done without that." Carter grimaced, looking stressed. "What's the matter, big guy?" I asked,

390 · CHARLIE LENNON

pushing up on tiptoe, threading my arms around his neck as I batted my lashes at him innocently. "Are you scared?"

"Says the girl who's had her eyes shut this whole time." He chuckled.

"What's wrong?" I asked, wondering why he was so incredibly tense.

He looked around warily. "I don't love this kind of thing."

"Me neither, but I love doing it with you." I poked his stomach. It didn't give, not even a little. The corner of his mouth quirked up, and he grabbed my hand, pulling me down a new hallway quickly enough that no monsters pounced on us.

He locked onto a dark corner, and I yelped with delight as he hauled me into the alcove. Wide hands slid under my sweatshirt, circling my waist as he gazed down at me, a little breathless. His thumb brushed over my cheek, wiping away the residual fake blood, but it sent a zing of awareness through me. The corner of my mouth pulled up in a sheepish grin, and I bit my lip as he cupped my face in both his hands.

"Hi." I breathed.

His eyes softened like he was looking at a helpless baby deer, and I wondered if I could melt into a puddle from just a look.

"Hi." He whispered, a sweet boyish grin enveloping his whole face.

Suddenly, he cocked his head. "What?" I hissed nervously.

He put his index finger over his lips, signaling me to stay quiet. "Liam and Jules." He mouthed, blocking my body with his in the alcove.

I listened as the voices came closer. "...you ever wonder what would have happened if you and Gina hadn't stayed together after high school? Like who you would have met instead? How your life would have been different?" Jules asked.

"Do you wonder that about you and Doug?" Liam asked, avoiding her question altogether.

"Maybe? I don't know." Jules sighed, coming closer, and I couldn't help but dig my fingers into Carter's side. Payback for last night. He flinched, but he was grinning at me like a fool from behind his hand while he shushed me.

Suddenly, there was a scuffle and a roar before an eerie howl rang out and then disappeared just as quickly.

"Yuuuck!" Jules yelped, sounding like she was right next to me now. "I didn't know it was going to be so goddamn *sticky* in here." I stifled a laugh, realizing they were right on the other side of the wall.

Liam chuckled. "Honestly, Jules, I've really been trying not to think about it."

"Oh, eww." she said. "You just made it even worse, and now *it's* all over my hands." She complained.

"Here," Liam laughed gruffly. "Let me."

"Thanks." She groaned as their voices slowly disappeared. "But I've probably already contracted some filthy disease. It's too late for me." She sighed dramatically. "I'm a goner."

Liam's laugh was muffled in the distance, and I didn't hear his retort over the thundering music and screams.

Before I could comment, Carter's fingers tightened around my waist, and he pulled me into him with a swift, needy tug that pushed a gust of air from my lungs. "I wish you could come home with me tonight." He had a sad, yearning look painted across his expression.

My heart swelled as I sheltered in his embrace. "Yeah, me too."

"I keep telling myself all the reasons this is a bad idea." He rasped, wide hands sliding up my ribcage. "And for some reason, I just can't bring myself to care." His lips hovered over mine, his breath caressing my skin with all kinds of sinful promises. "All I can think about is those fucking sounds you were making last night." He rasped. "I think it's my new addiction. *You* are my addiction." He added, but someone ran by screaming, and I startled. "Don't worry, I'll keep you safe." He murmured, lips dusting across my lashes.

"You sure about that?" I teased, hearing a gurgling noise

approaching in the distance. Despite my better judgment, I inched away from Carter with a sly little grin.

"Are you toying with me, you little troublemaker?" His fingers tightened, unsure if he should let go of me or not.

"Maybe I am." I stepped out of his grip.

"Oh, you are wicked." He crooned, watching me with a dark gaze, letting me creep away, inch by inch, with curious hunger etched on his face.

"If you want to hear any more of those little sounds you love so much, I guess you'll have to catch me first."

He smirked, looking like he was ready to pounce on me. "You sure you wanna go exploring in here by yourself? Seems like quite the rookie move to me."

I tilted my head innocently as I backed fully into the hallway. "Better hurry, or some monster might steal me away."

"You are going to be the death of me," Carter chuckled, his hands flexing at his sides, eyes filling with something that made my blood thrum. His voice dropped a bit lower. "Take one more step, pretty girl, and I won't be responsible for what happens when I catch you." He threatened, all while the corner of his mouth curled, telling me he was having just as much fun with our little game as I was.

I giggled. "Can't wait." I took another step back, a thrill filling me as he took a step forward and something electric sparked to life between us.

And then I backed up—one more step.

Into the intersection of the hallways.

Into the danger zone.

I hardly had time to brace as something slammed into me so hard it knocked the wind out of me. I flew through the air before crashing into the wall. *Hard.*

I couldn't breathe, couldn't get my lungs to work, and there was no time to process what was happening as I was being dragged backwards, being choked by the hood of Carter's sweatshirt.

Carter was a blur above me as he tackled the zombie to the ground in the next instant. "Shit. Are you okay?" Carter hissed, kneeling over me as I finally sucked in a breath, all while the zombie hobbled away groaning.

"Ow." I grimaced with a broken laugh. "Yeah, I'm fine."

"Are you sure?" I nodded, coughing as he helped me up. "This place is a fucking hellhole." He muttered, adjusting the hoodie around me, and then his face morphed into a smirk. "Got ya."

"That's not fair." I complained, rubbing my chest.

"What's not fair is how fucking sexy you are," he hummed, leaning in for a kiss.

I shoved a finger against his lips, grinning while he groaned. "Not so fast, Kensington." I slipped out of his grip. "If you want to kiss me tonight, you have to earn it. I chased you for *years*— now *you* can chase *me* for once."

"Wow." He threw his head back and laughed, deep and throaty. "That is not at all how that went, and I'm going to give you a head start, because I promise you're going to need it." He held up his hand, giving me a lazy, wicked smirk. "If you really want me to chase you, then I just have one last thing to say, pretty girl." My stomach flipped as his eyes narrowed, growing dark and predatory. "*Run.*"

My eyes blew wide as five fingers went to four, then to three, and that was all I saw—I gasped and hauled myself down the hallway before launching myself up a set of rickety stairs, narrowly avoiding a guy with a chainsaw as he chased a screaming woman down the steps.

As I hit the top step, I realized how incredibly out of shape I was, but I was even more stunned to see Carter, *already* upstairs, at the other end of the hallway. "How the hell—" *The look in his eyes.* No time for questions! I shrieked and took off in the other direction, his footsteps thundering right behind me as I grabbed a corner to swing down the next hallway.

Heart pounding with very real adrenaline, I kept sprinting and breathlessly launched myself around another corner, and then another, before I finally looked over my shoulder and realized he was gone—and when I looked back, I screamed, finding Carter standing right there in the middle of the hallway in front of me. *Waiting for me.* Arms flailing, I gasped, skidding to a frantic stop.

"Somebody's going in circles again." He smirked, the towering, intimidating mass of him only a few short paces away. "Come here, pretty girl." He taunted, and my throat went dry as he dipped his chin with a monstrous expression and crooked a finger at me. "Do as your told." His expression was full-out predatory as he chuckled darkly, "Or I'm gonna take a bite out of you when I catch you."

I screamed and hauled myself back in the other direction, hearing him right behind me again—he was taunting me, letting me stay just barely ahead of him, and I panicked and sprinted through a door, something primal taking over as I frantically looked around, only to realize I'd backed myself into a corner.

I whirled as the hulking mass of him came straight at me— and for a split second, I got scared, suddenly realizing how formidable he really was.

I froze, as Carter stepped out of my way, motioning for me to escape. "Run for me, pretty girl." He demanded, and grinned wickedly, gaze dragging over me like he was about to make a meal out of me. "Go on."

Wide-eyed, I slowly inched around him, slowly backed towards the door—*and then he pounced.* I screamed as he grabbed me clean out of the air and hauled me over his shoulder like a sack of potatoes.

"Now I shall take you back to my lair and drink your blood, my fair maiden." He laughed an evil Dracula laugh, and we were moving before the world spun and suddenly I was pinned between him and a wall, right side up again. His lips crashed against my own, desperate and hungry, and I screamed with adrenaline-filled laughter when he bit my neck with a dark chuckle, making good on his promise—only, we were suddenly falling.

The wall gave out, and we fell through it, getting tangled in a mess of fake cobwebs right as a fake spider came crashing down on our heads. "Fucking hell." Carter hissed, ripping the thing clean out of the ceiling while I howled with laughter, wondering if I'd ever seen him so worked up. "This mother-fucking shit-hole!" He muttered a string of grumpy, pissed-off curses under his breath, each more riled than the last.

I was crying, I was laughing so hard, nearly peeing my pants, still shaking with adrenaline as he hauled me through several more rooms, finally banging open a swinging metal door that said *operating room*.

"Out." He actually growled at the sexy nurse, covered in blood.

She was on her phone, and she looked up with a sigh. "You've entered the operating room, and now I'm going to cut you up."

"Get out!" Carter snapped, holding out a folded bill. "Now!"

She perked up slightly. "Come on, Trevor, let's take a break." A guy who was dressed like a rotting corpse banged open a metal medicine cabinet door and hopped out. "Unless you're shooting blanks, I suggest the top drawer on the left."

Heart still pounding, I opened the drawer and giggled— *hundreds* of Halloween-themed condoms. Carter slid a heavy metal table in front of the door, and when he turned, *the look he gave me* had a tear rolling down my thigh. *Alone. Finally.*

Carter strode across the room and took my face in his hands and kissed me. Hard. Desperate. Wanting. I whimpered as he pushed me against the wall, hauling my legs up around his waist before he snapped his hips against mine, pinning me in place with his strong, unyielding body. With the barrier between us finally broken after all these years, one night of teasing and we couldn't get enough of each other fast enough at all.

I moaned a desperate plea into his mouth as our tongues tangled ravenously—his desire growing more powerful and unleashed, as he devoured me like he was actually starving. New and exciting, comforting and familiar all wrapped into one deliri-ous, passionate, perfect kiss. There was no doubt in my mind anymore, he wanted me just as badly as I wanted him.

The second I tried to wriggle down from his grip, he released me, and I turned, shoving *him* up against the wall, *hard*. I slid down as he watched me from above, breath ragged while my fingers frantically grappled with his belt.

"Wait." He rasped, fingers circling my wrists as he pulled me up. He backed me up against a table, where I yanked him down to my mouth again, giddy he couldn't resist as I hauled him against me and hiked my leg over his hip. His fingers slid higher as he groaned and lifted me onto the table—then with great effort he finally peeled himself back.

I grinned when he gave me a warning look that said, *stay there or else.*

Carter dragged both hands down his face, looking absolutely tormented as he backed across the room and planted himself against another metal table. "We need to lay some ground rules." He panted.

"Perfect. I love breaking the rules." I shrugged with a grin.

He groaned. "Don't I know it."

I chuckled, relishing the bite of cold metal against my legs, because my skin was on fire, everywhere his fingers had been, everywhere I hoped his mouth would go.

"We are going way too fucking fast."

"Are we?" I asked innocently.

"This has been a hard year."

Oh great. This again. "And this might be the only thing making it better."

"That's exactly what I'm saying—I don't want to be your rebound, or just a fling, or whatever."

"Carter," I groaned. "You're not."

"You said Isaac took advantage of you, that you were sad, that he only wanted one thing."

"This," I pointed between us, growing frustrated with him. "Is not that at all."

He barked out a frantic laugh. "I'm really glad to hear you say that, Sara, but I know you've had shit luck with guys, you said so yourself, and I know something fucked up happened with Tag that night—so how can I possibly let you get on your knees for me when you specifically didn't want the dildo in your mouth last night? I need to know how to take care of you." He panted. "I need to understand your boundaries better, because I have no fucking idea where the lines are."

I froze. Why was he bringing this up *now*? "I don't want to talk about that." I murmured, not quite ready to let go of that little secret just yet.

"And I'm not asking you to—not until you're ready, at least," Carter said. "But I, we—are moving way too fast. We need to slow this down."

My lower lip wobbled against my will as the sting of rejection washed over me.

"Sara." I couldn't meet his eyes. "Sara, look at me."

What he was saying made sense, so why the fuck did it hurt so badly? Why did it feel exactly like rejection? What was wrong with me?

"Sarafina," he said, his tone softer and more lusty. "Be a good girl and look at me." His tone was gentle but still commanding enough that I couldn't help but look. "Please don't cry." He gripped the metal table while I batted my lashes, trying to keep the water in them from spilling out. "I need you to know something," he lamented. "It's taking everything in my power not to rip across this room and grab one of those party favors so I can fuck you against the wall until you're screaming my name again." My skin tingled, wishing he would do exactly that. "But I'm not going to do that because you're the kind of girl, I could—" He swallowed hard and stopped himself. "I'm not going to fuck it up because we moved too fast before you were ready." My heart stalled out as his words hung in the air like dynamite, ready to blow up. *Marry?* Is that what he was going to say? I was the kind of girl he could marry? "I want to do this right." He panted frantically, adding, *"Have to do this right."*

"What about what I want?" I asked, emotion getting the better of me.

"We need time to figure this out."

"I know what I want—I want you." I declared, knowing I should try harder to play it cool, but I was so damn tired of pretending.

"Sara, I don't want to screw this up."

"This." I pointed between us. "Is kinda screwing things up." I headed for the door feeling—I didn't even know. Everything. Nothing. Not enough.

"Sara, please don't walk away." He begged.

I crossed my arms, jiggling my leg, trying not to cry. "Move the table." I just needed a breather, a second of space to think.

"Can we talk about this?" he pleaded.

"I can't do this right now." I admitted quietly as I stared towards the door, "Please, I just—I need a minute to think." I added, unable to look at him. "I hear what you're saying, I just—" Something panicked started clawing its way up my throat, the feeling of being trapped, out of control, I didn't know. "Carter. I need to get out of this room. Right the fuck now." I snapped, the music feeling too loud, my skin feeling too sticky, the air feeling too hot.

He reluctantly moved the table, and I headed down the hallway, feeling his presence a few paces behind me. Only I wasn't watching where I was going, and suddenly, the floor dropped out from under me.

I was falling, flailing, screaming, and then my body barked with pain as I landed on a filmy, stained mattress. Something cold and wet splashed all over me as gargling and screeching creatures grabbed at me.

"Carter!" A dirty hand clamped over my mouth, and my

hands were tied before I even realized what was happening, and suddenly, I was being hauled away with alarming speed.

Carter had already dropped through the ceiling when we locked eyes. The look in his expression was terrifying—it made me feel like something was actually wrong. Something more than just haunted house theatrics.

"Carter!" My voice cracked as I thrashed against the goblin, but Carter was already in motion, already closing the space between us, and nearly to me already. He was going to get to me, just like he had minutes earlier.

And then I saw it, as if in slow motion, a thick metal door started to roll shut, and Carter's panicked expression disappeared as the hallway grew darker and darker, until finally, the door seemed to thunder as it slid into place, sealing off the hallway.

It was all happening so fast, hands all over me, body slamming into one wall after another as we rounded so many corners, and I was screaming, but suddenly I was being dropped into some sort of container.

A sickening feeling lurched through me as I scrambled up, but there was a heavy click as everything went dark and quiet. *Trapped.* And as I frantically pounded on the lid, I realized something awful.

I was not the only thing in this container.

Carter

There are moments in your life when you can think, plan, strategize. Moments when there is time for rational thought, and then there are moments when the reptilian brain takes over, when there is nothing but instinct, muscle memory, and survival.

Unlike the adrenaline that I'm so used to at work, the adrenaline that flooded me at the sound of Sara's terrified scream was wholly different.

My body reacted before my brain did. I was already moving, launching into a sprint. How she'd gotten so far, so quickly, was horrifying, but there was no room for guilt, and no room for second guesses. There was only instinct and action.

I saw that fucking door as it started to roll across the hallway, and I pushed harder, ran faster. I was nearly to her, almost there, when it slammed shut. Separating us. I slammed straight into the door, yanking on it, but it didn't open.

"Let me go!" Sara screamed from the other side, making my stomach bottom out.

"Sara!" I heaved against the door, over and over again, but it wouldn't budge.

Frantically I fumbled at the seams, when Sara screamed in the distance, "Get off me!" My gaze snapped up and a new sort of fear drenched me.

Muscle memory took over as I pulled my gun out and unloaded the entire clip along the seam of the door before the locking mechanism released. I heaved the door open and slammed a new clip in as I followed the sound of Sara's screams, shoving monsters into walls as I sprinted through the haunted house after her.

And then, what was worse than her screaming was when I couldn't hear her at all. Loud music blared, and there was cackling and howling from every corner of this hellscape, but no sound of her.

I sprinted from room to room, screaming for her without a response.

A zombie sprinted past me, cackling, and I grabbed it clean out of the air, shoving it against the nearest wall. "Where the fuck is she?" The zombie screamed as I ripped its mask off. "I will make you hurt in ways you didn't know you could." I growled, adrenaline and panic pounding through me as precious seconds slipped away. "Where is she?" I shook him.

"I don't know." He gasped, wide-eyed. "It's not real, it's just part of the performance."

With a broken laugh, I lowered my voice to a lethal growl.

"You have exactly two seconds to give me an answer before I start making things hurt."

"There's a room." He sputtered. "Please don't shoot me. I just work here."

"Where?" I dropped him to the ground, holding him by the scruff of his neck.

As he led me through several rooms, I hoped this was all just part of the haunted house theatrics, but what if it wasn't, what if someone more dangerous had abducted her—say someone who had just threatened that, a mere twenty-four hours ago.

One thing at a time.

The zombie quickly led me down into a basement, and when I saw one goblin guarding a locked door, I dropped the zombie.

"Is she in there?" I demanded.

The goblin launched into a script, and I shoved him out of the way, trying the door. It was locked.

A hand landed on my arm. "You can't just go in, you have to break the code, and then sacrifice—"

I pinned him with a lethal look, because I was not fucking around. "The only thing I'll be breaking is your fucking arms if you don't get out of my way." He immediately backed up.

I shouldered the door open and inside, I found a woman tied to a chair, looking mildly alarmed. Not Sara. My stomach rolled. If she wasn't here...

"Who are *you*?" The woman asked as I stared at her, recalculating.

A man, who I assume was her date, hurried in. "What the hell took you so long?" She complained as I stormed out of the room and grabbed one of the goblins.

"The brunette in the Air Force hoodie." I demanded. "Did you take her?"

One of the goblins in the corner chimed in, "Yeah, I think that hot piece of ass in the green dress is upstairs in the cooler." My eyes snapped to him. "I got quite a handful, if you know what I mean." He shook his head with a laugh, not looking up from his phone. "It's always easier to cop a feel when they're flailing around." Then he added more quietly, "God, I love this job."

Everything went red. "What did you just say?" I stalked towards him.

He turned to look at me. "Oh, shit!"

I kicked his chair out from underneath him and sent him crashing to the floor. "You're the one who fucking touched her."

He scrambled back, but I stepped on his chest, slamming him back into the floor. "I was just joking around." He pleaded.

"Was it a joke when she was screaming at you to get your fucking hands off her?" I leveraged more of my weight onto him as he wheezed. Good, let this piece of shit suffocate in that mask. "It's not so fun when you're the one who can't fight back, is it?" I growled, bearing down harder.

He started begging, and this was wasting time. I hauled him up and twisted his arm behind his back, right before the point of breaking, muttering. "Take me to her right now, or I promise you, I will break every bone in your useless body."

CHAPTER 39

So Incredibly Generous

It was muffled, but I could hear it from down the hall. *Her screaming.* I'd never heard a more sickening sound, and my body took over as I dropped the goblin and launched myself towards that scream.

I burst into the room and rushed to the long, body-sized cooler that was shaking violently. Sara was sobbing inside it, screaming, all while two goblins leaned against a nearby table, laughing hysterically—only one thing mattered right now. *Her.*

I dropped to my knees in front of the cooler. "Sara, I'm here." I frantically shoved at the lid, but it didn't open.

To my horror, I realized the cooler was locked.

They'd fucking *locked* her in.

I had to get this thing open. *Right-fucking-now.*

"Help me!" She *screamed.* "Please, somebody help me!"

Using the butt of my gun, I smashed the first latch. "I'm here! I'm gonna get you out!" I shouted as the cooler shifted across the floor. Something was wrong, so incredibly wrong. Whatever they'd done to her—I smashed the second latch and shoved the lid open.

Sara exploded out of the cooler faster than I could grab her, and as I looked inside, I suddenly realized why. *Ohhh shit.*

She was hysterical. "Get it off me!" She ripped my hoodie off, crashing into a wall as she wrenched the fleece off her body, rope still dangling from one of her wrists.

I grabbed her, skin damp under my fingertips, ducking to her eye level. "Sara, baby, it's in the cooler." I gripped her tightly as her thrashing turned into breathless sobs. "It's not on you." I forced her to look down. "I got you." I chanted, crushing her against me. "You're safe now."

"It—b-bit me." Her voice broke, and the sound cleaved me in half.

Fuuuuuck.

"I know it's painful—but it's not poisonous." Red hot anger pulsed through me as I gently stroked her hair. "You're going to be okay." I assured her, but Sara's sobbing quickly morphed into hyperventilating—she was having a full-on panic attack, and for good fucking reason.

I gripped her face in both hands, and her skin was so incredibly hot to the touch, as she gripped my shirt in her curled fists, a wild, panicked look in her eyes.

"Let's take some slow breaths." I tried coaching her through it, but we were so far past that—she was spiraling and I couldn't get through. "Sara. You're going to be okay, you're just having a panic attack, and we're going to take some nice, slow—"

Her hands flew to her throat as her lips parted in panic, because no matter how many breaths she pulled in, she couldn't speak, and she couldn't breathe.

"Look at me. We're just going to ride the wave—don't fight it. This *will* pass." I said calmly as the red tint of her face started to fade, her lips turning a pale color as she hyperventilated. "Sara. Eyes on me." I commanded, and her gaze jolted to mine. "I've got you. Whatever is happening right now, you're gonna be okay— even if you pass out, *I have you.*" A moment later, her hand slid from her throat, eyes fluttering before she went limp in my arms.

I gently lowered her to the floor, brushing the hair out of her face as I pushed two fingers against the pulse point on her neck.

"Shit, it was just supposed to be a prank." One of the goblins started quietly.

My gun was a tempting, heavy weight at my back, but bare hands were good too. Slower. I ignored them altogether and forced a slow breath out as Sara stirred awake.

Sara whimpered softly as her eyes flickered open, her breathing weak but steady.

"I know, baby." I brushed her damp hair off her neck and pulled her dress down, covering her. "I've got you now, you're gonna be okay."

"Sara?" Jules gaped from the doorway.

"What the fuck is going on in here?" Liam barked, thundering into the room. "What happened?" Liam dropped into a squat, taking Sara from my arms, his tone lethal. "Sara, who did this to you?" Sara didn't even attempt to answer him, and Liam's gaze narrowed in on the goblins across the room.

His expression went icy as he stood, leaving Sara in Jules arms. "What did you do to her?" He demanded.

"They touched her, Liam." I curled and uncurled my fists. "And then they locked her in there—with *that*." I dipped my chin to the cooler, towards *the eight-legged fuzzy thing that was bigger than Sara's hand.*

Liam leaned over to look in the cooler. "*Oh, fuuuck no.*"

"So, who wants to go first?" I asked, hands now free, aching to do some damage.

"Listen, this is all just a big misunderstanding." One of them started. "It was just a prank."

"You think I give a shit what your reasons were?" I bit out lethally soft. "She was *screaming for help* while you stood there and laughed at her—you are so incredibly lucky she doesn't have a goddamn medical condition."

"We aren't liable, you know." Another one argued. "You signed the waiver."

"You're right." I agreed quietly. "They did say *everyone* who entered this building risked bodily injury."

"Listen, the monsters are allowed to do whatever they want in here, so—"

"*Lucky me.*" Liam murmured, cracking his neck like a twitch, as he stood next to me, breathing heavily.

"Masks off." I demanded calmly, and the goblins all looked at each other and then back at me, while I chuckled darkly, explaining, "That wasn't optional."

They shifted nervously.

"*NOW!*" I barked, and they startled, quickly pulling them off.

"It was just a—"

"Shut. The fuck. Up." I bit out cooly. "Here's how this is going to go, two of you are going in that cooler, and one of you gets whatever the fuck I decide, and I can promise you—it'll be a hell of a lot worse than the cooler." Their eyes went wide. "Decide amongst yourselves."

One made a run for the door, and Jules stuck her leg out, tripping him. Atta girl.

"Bitch." The guy spat, and Liam decked him square in the nose before shoving him in my direction.

I shrugged. "I guess that decides that, then." I hauled the first goblin over to the cooler.

"Wait, it was just a joke. Please." The goblin begged, nose pouring blood as I dropped him in.

"Then I'm sure you'll find this fucking hilarious, won't you?" I shoved him into the cooler, and there was a hard crack and groan behind me, and then Liam was stuffing the other guy in, right on top.

I forcefully shoved the lid down, and Liam and I dug in, shoving the cooler under a table so it wouldn't open.

They were already screaming. *Good.* I hoped that thing bit the shit out of them.

Meanwhile, the other guy was headed for the door, but Jules had already shut it and was standing, wide eyed, blocking his way out with a determined look on her face.

The guy grabbed her, and she yelled as he threw her to the ground and ripped the door open, but not fast enough—Liam had him by the scruff in the next instant, shoving him against the wall. "Don't you fucking touch her."

"You're the one who touched something that wasn't yours to touch." I tilted my head, and my blood thrummed as white-hot protective rage blinded out everything else—because after everything she'd been through, this shit was going to end here. Now. With me.

"It was nothing."

"It was everything." I seethed, quietly demanding, "Now, for starters, you can apologize—to both of them."

"You're fucking insane."

I seized him by the throat and shoved him into the wall, coming nose to nose with him. "I am *not* going to ask you again." I reached behind me and grabbed my gun, jamming the barrel into his neck.

"Shit." Jules hissed somewhere behind me.

"Apologize." Liam growled right next to me. "Or you *will* regret it."

"I'm sorry." The guy ground out in a childish tone.

I actually laughed as I cocked the gun. "I swear to you on my mother's grave, I will pull this goddamned trigger if you don't make it sound like you mean it."

"Carter?" Jules said softly, coming around my side, tentatively placing her hand on my arm. "Let's just go. She's going to be okay."

"Jules." I said calmly, glancing back at Sara, who was currently lying on the floor like a fucking starfish, just staring at the ceiling.

"Yes?"

"Take Sara and go wait in the hallway." I instructed.

"Liam, you have to do something." Jules turned to him, alarm rising in her voice.

"Do as you're told, Julia." Liam murmured softly, but she didn't move. "*Please.*" He asked, eyes shuttering.

"Liam?" Confusion and worry washed over her face as she looked up at him.

Liam loosed a heavy breath and quickly gathered the girls, moving them towards the door as Jules argued at him.

"Carter? Carter! You aren't thinking clearly." Jules yelled over Liam's arm as he pushed them out into the hallway. "*Liam, you can't let him do this!*"

"Do *not* open this door." Liam demanded firmly, and Jules just gaped at him as he simply flicked the door shut in her face, without another word. Meanwhile, I watched the perverts eyes linger on the girls a little too long, as if he wasn't in life-threatening danger. Fucking moron.

"Since you don't seem to understand choice. Let me give you a little lesson." I said, my fingers twitching because I wanted to pull the trigger so fucking bad. "You didn't give her a choice." The cooler behind us rattled violently, and I smiled at him, and clarified, "But I'm a generous guy, so I'm going to give *you* one—*a choice.*"

"Fuck. I'm *so* sorry." He begged. "Please don't kill me."

"I'm not going to kill you." I shook my head with a dark chuckle. "I'm going to make you suffer so much you'll wish you were dead though."

"Please."

"Option A. I shoot you in both kneecaps." I continued calmly. "Option B. I break every-single-one of the fingers that touched her."

He gaped at me, understanding washing over his face.

"Take your pick, but I promise each will be equally as horrifying."

He started begging, but there was nothing he could say, because he'd made her scream and now I was going to make him do the same.

"Pick one." I finally roared, trembling with restraint, as my patience wore thinner and thinner.

Liam gently reached out and lowered my gun to the floor. "I

think we both know there's only one choice here." He stepped around me and grabbed an arm. "Let's not make the mistake of leaving any evidence behind." *Option B was a superb choice.*

Sarafina

Liam carried me to the car on his back. "Are you okay?" He turned his head to mine and asked quietly.

"No." I sighed. "But I will be. I just need to sleep it off, I think." My leg hurt like hell, though, and I didn't know if I'd ever felt so exhausted, or so sticky.

I slid into the back seat of Liam's Range Rover and rolled the window down as Sloane rushed up. "Sleepover still on?" She asked, and I nodded. "Okay, I'm going to grab a few things and then I'll head over." She headed for Cade's motorcycle. I could hear her talking to Cade more quietly. "I guess you aren't the only psychopath around here."

He shrugged, totally indifferent. "If the punishment fits the crime." He pushed the helmet onto her head and tightened the straps before he put his own helmet on and did the same.

"Sara?" Carter ducked his head into the open window. "Put an ice pack on the bite. It'll help with the swelling." I nodded as he added, "Text me if you need anything at all."

"I lost my phone, remember?" And then I offered hopefully, "You should join us for breakfast?"

"I have to leave pretty early." His face fell. "I'm sorry." He tapped the door as Liam called goodnight and started to pull away.

Next to me in the back seat, Jules sighed heavily. "Stupid, stupid men." She muttered, shaking her head.

I leaned on her shoulder, letting my eyes fall shut. "I'm sorry about you and Douglass." *She deserved to know, I'd want to know.*

"We'll work it out." She murmured quietly. "We always do."

"I don't know this for sure, but Cade thinks he saw Douglass using drugs in the bathroom at the club."

Liam's gaze snapped to us in the rearview mirror as Jules took a sharp intake of breath. I hugged her tightly, supporting her in every way I physically could while we waited for her response. "He said he'd stopped." She breathed.

"Jules," Liam muttered from the driver's seat. "How long has this been going on?"

"No." She bit out more sharply than I think I'd ever heard her speak. "I can't right now. I just—can't."

"Well, there's one thing I know for sure." I offered.

"What?" they both asked.

"Fuck. Spiders."

Liam and Jules chimed in agreement. "Yeah, fuck spiders."

Carter was leaving in the morning, and we still had so much to talk about, to plan for. Our argument seemed so stupid now. He was deploying soon, and I *had* to see him before he left.

CHAPTER 40
I'm No Gentleman
CARTER

My cock was in my hand when I heard a soft knock on my bathroom door. I tensed, and then the melodic sound of Sara's voice called through it. "Can I come in?"

I released my grip, cock aching just at the sound of her voice. "I'm in the shower?"

"I know." It went quiet.

I should say no. I should definitely say no. Besides, it was early. What was she doing up at this hour? Especially after last night. She should be sleeping, recovering. Was something wrong? "Uh, yeah, come on in."

Sara slid through the door, looking devious as ever, as she closed it behind her and leaned against it.

Uh oh.

The steam on the shower glass wasn't any sort of real visibility barrier as she took a good long look at me, still hard.

I immediately started counting backwards.

Thinking of gross stuff. Thinking of my mom.

Sara heeled off her running shoes.

Never mind, definitely not thinking of my mom right now.

The sound of her zipper dragging down made my mouth go

dry, and her tight little running jacket slipped to the floor a moment later.

Uh oh.

Her shirt was up over her arms next, leaving her in a sports bra that made her tits look *incredible.*

She was angelic, divine—except for the bruises she had forming all over her body, the red lump on her leg, and I hated that.

I could hardly breathe as she walked towards the shower. She looked me dead in the eyes and slowly shimmied her running shorts down over her hips.

Pink. Lacy-fucking-pink underwear.

Nope. *Thong.*

Never mind. *Never-fucking-mind.*

She wasn't angelic—she was diabolical. A wicked little temptress who knew exactly what she was doing. Doing—

What was I doing?

I was about to lose it on the shower wall, my hand right back where I'd started.

I should stop. I should look away at least.

But I wasn't a gentleman—not when she was in here, looking like *that.*

Apparently, I was a man with no morals at all, devouring every inch of skin she revealed like a parched man who'd just found holy water in the desert.

She reached for the bottom of her sports bra, and my chest seized up, knowing what was coming next. She peeled the tight thing off, getting comically tangled before she freed herself, but I didn't have it in me to laugh. Not when I was staring at the world's most perfect tits.

How lucky was I about to be?

Fuck.

No.

I was a disciplined person.

Friday night had been a one time thing, and from here on out, we were going to slow this all down. Take our time. We deserved that. *She* deserved that. I dragged both hands down my face in agony.

Discipline was my middle name, *yeah*, I could stay in control. She approached the open section of glass and pushed that sorry excuse for underwear down her legs, and my eyes shuddered as I bit my knuckles with a groan.

She moved to pull her hair out of the ponytail. "Leave it." I demanded hoarsely before I even realized what I was saying. Apparently, I was no better than a simple-minded brute. Sara dropped her hand, eyes glimmering while she left her hair in that *oh so tempting* high pony.

My fingers tingled, dick ached. I couldn't remember what I was supposed to be doing, or rather, *not* doing. I wanted to wrap that ponytail around my fist. Wanted to haul her up against the wall and—

No!

But she's in here looking like *that*.

Stick to the plan.

No fucking way. It's not a want, it's a *NEED*.

She's forever.

Would it really be so bad if forever started today?

Stick to the plan.

—what was the plan again? My brain short-circuited.

Sara sauntered across the walk-in shower and casually grabbed a washcloth off the teak towel stand. I clenched and unclenched my fists as she stepped under the stream of hot water, just barely brushing against me as she reached past me for the soap.

Fucking hell. I squeezed my eyes shut—maybe if I didn't look. If I couldn't see her, she couldn't see me. Right? Like an ostrich. I'd just jam my head in the proverbial sand. Only now, very dirty things were playing on my very own personal movie screen, torturing me from inside my head.

It didn't matter that I couldn't see her, I could smell her. She'd just come from a run and had that slightly sweaty smell, the one that reminded me of other cardio-type workouts—of the horizontal variety. *Fucking hell!*

"I've been doing some thinking." She started innocently enough, and I peeked as she lathered up the washcloth and began to scrub her arms.

I swallowed hard, immediately realizing I should have kept my eyes closed. "Yeah?"

"Mhmm." She hummed, all too amused with herself.

I wanted to reach out and touch her so badly. Wanted to slip my fingers between her legs, *no*, wanted to drop to my knees and worship at the altar of her body, get a taste of heaven itself.

"You said we shouldn't do more *things* until we figure this all out."

I swallowed hard. Did I say that? *Me?* There was no way. Why would I do such a stupid, stupid thing? "Yeah, I did." I regretfully agreed, practically panting as Sara slowly trailed the washcloth over her breasts. Such perfect tits. I wanted to reach out and grab one, wanted to mark that silky skin with my teeth.

"*Caaaarter.*" She sang softly, moving to the other one.

"Yeah?" I whispered, in a trance.

"My eyes are up here." She smiled deviously as I dragged my eyes up and swallowed. Looking into her eyes was actually worse.

That thread pulled tighter and tighter inside me—

She should have known better.

I was just a simple man.

She'd underestimated herself, and she'd underestimated *me*.

She should have known how powerful she was when she came in here looking like that. Everything I'd ever wanted was just dangling in front of me, waiting for me to reach out and grab it.

—that thread of control snapped.

I took a step forward, and her eyes flared. It was such a stupid rule. I was leaving today, wouldn't see her for months, possibly. The ache in my chest was too much to stay away. *The ache in other parts of me was too much too.*

"So I was thinking." Sara continued quickly, alarm lacing her voice as her eyes went wide, realization slowly washing over her, discovering that maybe I didn't have the strength to restrain.

Not when she was teasing me like this. Not when she was in my goddamn shower, naked and perfect, begging to be devoured. Not when I'd literally been ready to kill a man for her last night. Not when she was—*mine*.

I took another step forward, and she retreated.

"*Carter.*" She warned and then her back hit the stone wall, nipples peaking from the cold.

My hand hit the wall above her head, the other sliding up her soapy ribcage as the water cascaded over us, quickly rinsing the bubbles away.

"*Carter,*" she whispered.

"Yeah?" I rasped, dragging a thumb over a nipple, watching it immediately tighten for me.

She whimpered, eyes fluttering as her head dropped back against the wall. "I was," She swallowed hard. "I was just thinking —that we need to even the score."

"How so?" I slid my fingers up her stomach, up the slippery center of her chest and around her throat, tilting her face to me.

"Well," she panted breathily, the water saturating her hair. "I —I—was just. We," she rasped, as I dragged a thumb roughly over her lower lip.

"Open for me." I begged before sliding my finger inside.

She wrapped her perfect lips around my thumb and sucked, and my eyes might have actually rolled back in my head.

I fisted my cock, pumping it a few times before stepping close enough that her perfect, *perfect* tits were now smashed against my stomach.

"Tell me, pretty girl." I demanded roughly. "Tell me what you were planning on doing when you came in here, and forgot how mouthwateringly tempting you are?" I replaced my finger with my lips, tracing her mouth, not quite stealing a kiss just yet, just feeling, exploring, discovering as the hot water poured over us.

Closing the remainder of space between us, I anchored her

hips to the wall with mine, eliciting a sharp gasp that melted into a needy moan. *Good.*

"I want you to come for me." She got out with great strain, as I slid my hands up her sides, guiding her hands above her head where I pinned them against the wall.

"Is that so?" I kissed the corner of her mouth before slowly moving to the other corner.

"Since you said we couldn't touch each other yet." She was trembling, arching into my every touch, but she tugged her hands down and I released my grip on her immediately. Too much. This was exactly why we needed to slow down.

I cursed when her slippery little fingers slid between us and she fisted my cock for the first time.

Shit-mother-fucker. *Not too much.* She just had plans all of her own.

She brushed her thumb over my already leaking head. "I want to watch while you come." It was taking everything in me not to blow as it was.

"*Fuuuuuuck.*" I groaned. Her hands on me felt too good, better than I ever could have imagined.

She giggled breathily and did it again, eyes sparkling with amusement, while I watched her discover she had me wrapped around her finger—that she always had. I was in big fucking trouble now.

"You are a greedy, wicked little troublemaker, aren't you?" I chuckled lowly, but my laugh was cut off as she stroked me again, making me jerk.

"Do I make you feel as good as you make me feel, Carter?" She hummed.

"Yeah," I panted. "But I meant what I said."

"I thought you might say that." She admitted, but her smirk didn't falter. "And I think it's only fair that you come for me before you leave." She pushed my hand towards my erection, her small hand over mine, as we stroked my cock in unison. "I want to watch you come for me, Carter, and if you won't let *me* do it, then I want to watch while *you* do it." She demanded.

The thing she didn't realize was that at this point, I would have let her keep going. Desperately wanted her to. "You're going to pay for this later." I narrowed my eyes, coming up with all kinds of sinful retribution.

"That's the plan."

Evil little kitten.

I thrust involuntarily, head tipping to hers as I surrendered when she swept her fingers over my head before she let go.

"Fuck me." I rasped, pumping my cock in my hands as she watched, excited and breathless underneath me.

"Yes, exactly." Her lips quirked adorably. "Let's fuck you."

I captured her mouth with mine and wished it were her hands on me, but I shouldn't have been complaining at all. I mean, she was right technically, this was keeping to the rules. Sort of. And I would take anything she'd give me.

I started to go tense as her hands roamed over me, grasping at my hair, teeth yanking on my lips as I got closer, fucking my own hand, imagining it was her I was sinking into instead.

"Are you going to come all over my stomach?" She murmured, and fuck if that wasn't hot.

"Do you want me to?" I whimpered against her lips, hardly able to get the words out as she pulled me closer.

"Yeah, give me something for the road, flyboy." She demanded, nails raking over my scalp, over my shoulders, over my chest as she dragged her teeth over my bottom lip.

Oh, this woman, I could give her something for the road.

"Fuck the rules." I panted, and I couldn't help myself as I let go and grabbed that ponytail, wrapping it around my fist several times.

I claimed her mouth with mine, desperate, sloppy and needy, as I slid my hand up her smooth inner thigh.

Her sharp intake of breath was her only response as she shifted and gave me open access, inviting me in.

"Fuck, I should stop." I rasped, pleading with her, knowing I wasn't strong enough to do it on my own. "You have no idea the things I'm thinking about doing to you." My fingers inched closer to heaven. "Tell me to stop." I begged, feeling myself starting to come apart at the seams.

"Nope, can't do that." She gasped when my fingers slid higher. "Do you feel that, Kensington? That's all for you." She moaned as the pads of my fingers brushed against the slick heat between her legs. "I wanted to touch myself yesterday, but I didn't. I saved myself, all for you."

Fuck me.

"If you wanted a gentleman—you're out of luck." I warned, my control unravelling, un-spooling faster and faster by the second. "You undressed in front of the wrong man."

"Why would I tell you to stop when I finally have you right where I want you, hmm?" She huffed out a strained laugh. "When you're finally doing what I've fantasized about a million and one times."

Yeah, fuck the rules. They were made up anyway.

Only one thing mattered. This. Us. Her.

The sound she made as I dragged a knuckle from her center to clit was a chorus of angels singing. "Again." I demanded and repeated the motion in reverse, earning a sharp gasp in and a breathy whimper out.

Slick heat fluttered against my hand. "Carter." She cried and hiked her leg over my hip as I teased her clit and claimed her mouth. I was tempted to sink to my knees and claim her the way I really wanted to. Hike those beautiful thighs up over my shoulders and quench the thirst that had been driving me mad for months now.

"Wait, no." She groaned against my lips. "*You're* supposed to be coming for *me.*"

I let out a low chuckle with nothing but pure amusement. "I love that you think you can come in here, looking like *that,* and boss me around." I tugged her ponytail, forcing her eyes to mine.

"You silly girl." I reprimanded, nipping at her lower lip. "Don't you know I'd turn you inside out a thousand times over before I let you get your hands on me?" I watched her closely as I slipped a finger into her for the first time and swore at the tight, wet heat that enveloped my finger. "Fuck, you feel incredible." I murmured, heart pounding when she made a sound that was most definitely the hottest thing I'd ever heard.

"*Ahh Carter.*" She gasped and threw her head back against the wall, desperately begging for more.

"Yeah, this is exactly what I wanted." I rasped, "You're gonna look so pretty riding my hand, I can already tell." I slipped a second finger in, eating up the fact that she was already soaked for me, *that fast.* "You're going to ride my face next." I practically purred into her ear, "And then, when your legs finally give out, you're going to take every fucking inch of me like a good girl, aren't you?" I was going to be late, but it was worth it.

Her nails dug into my skin as she loosed a strangled noise. Good, let her carve me up while I made a meal out of her.

She was so beautiful like this. *For me.* "Look at you." I murmured, curling my fingers, watching her go taut and loose all at once. She trembled, whimpering another one of those glorious sounds when I did it again, tweaking a nipple with my free hand. "Yeah, you like that? Tell me, pretty girl, tell me how much you like that."

"Y-yes." She moaned loudly, sinking deeper onto my fingers— and then I heard a voice that made me clamp my hand over Sara's strangled moan in absolute terror.

"Carter?" *It was Liam. Knocking on the bathroom door.*

"Oh, shit motherfucker!" I hissed, and Sara whimpered into my hand as I pulled my fingers out of her fluttering pussy as innocently as possible.

Everything was happening all at once. I was a tornado as I frantically grabbed a fresh towel and threw it around Sara, hurrying her into the sauna. From behind the glass door, she mouthed one panicked protest after another. I waved her back away from the glass.

"Carter, you in there?" Liam asked as I shuffled around.

"Uh, yeah, a little busy at the moment." I threw my hands up in a silent scream.

"Oh shit, are you with somebody?"

"Nope! Just me!" Panic didn't even begin to describe what I was feeling.

What the hell was he doing over here? It's not like we'd snuck up on each other and doused each other with ice water in years. Not since high school.

No, something had to be wrong—

He knew.

Fuck. HE KNEW.

"What's up? Is everything okay?" I called through the door, trying and failing at steadying my breath.

"Not really." Liam said, his voice tight. "But I'll wait for you in the kitchen."

"Uh, sure, I'll be down in a couple of minutes." I said.

Liam didn't respond, and Sara cracked the sauna door open, still slightly sudsy, and I waved her back. She motioned to herself in silent outrage as soap dried to her skin in the heat of the sauna.

I threw out a frantic hand, silently demanding she stay put. My eyes bulged when I realized the bathroom door wasn't even locked, and I quickly locked it, listening until I was sure Liam wasn't upstairs anymore.

"*Fuuuuuck.*" I whisper-hissed, racing back under the stream of water and quickly rinsing, while Sara sauntered over. "He knows." I cursed to myself, spiraling.

"He doesn't know." I scrubbed furiously, and Sara reached up and grabbed my face in both of her hands. "Carter, he doesn't know. Why would he?" Fuck, I hoped she was right.

"Do not. Under any circumstances. Come downstairs until he's gone." She grinned. "Sara." I switched to begging, clasped my hands together, pleading desperately. Now was *not* the time to play daredevil.

"Kiss me and I'll think about it."

"Now?" I gaped in full-out panic.

She tapped her lips.

"Woman." I grabbed her face and kissed her hard, kissed her for what it was.

A goodbye.

CHAPTER 41
The Note
SARAFINA

Liam, uncharacteristically, pretended not to notice as we stole fruit from the tray he was neatly arranging with little bits of pretty foliage and edible flowers. But I knew the truth. He didn't even have the energy to snap back with some clever response because of what he'd shared with Carter this morning—the heartbreaking news of him and Gina. *They'd broken up.*

At the kitchen counter, Jules leaned back in her chair and raised a knowing brow. "So, Sloane, tell me about you and Cade."

"I have no idea what you mean." Sloane shrugged with a grin.

I laughed and threw a grape at her. "Sure you don't."

"Oh, we're going to get to *you* next." Jules chuckled, shaking her head. "You and Carter were awfully cozy last night. *All* over each other, in fact."

"Jules!" I hissed, shooting a nervous glance in Liam's direction. He thankfully didn't notice because he was zoned out on his phone—in fact, something smelled like it was burning on the stovetop.

"Liam," I called gently. Nothing.

"He's out of it today." Jules said absentmindedly, playing with the necklace she *always* wore. "I think what happened last night really upset him."

I shook my head *no* and lowered my voice. "Him and Gina broke up yesterday morning." I grimaced and my heart broke, realizing he'd put on a brave face *all day* yesterday, probably because he didn't want to ruin my birthday redo.

"Oh, shit." Sloane sat up. "Do you think they'll work it out? They're so great together."

"No, I think it's been a long time coming." I admitted. "Gina's career is really taking off, and so is Liam's, and neither of them can really move in the foreseeable future."

I grimaced as Jules shoulders sagged and wondered if she was thinking the same thing I was. Long-distance relationships seemed next to impossible to maintain. It made me wonder how Carter and I would fare. We hadn't even made plans for his upcoming deployment. I hadn't even hugged him goodbye. Not really.

The stove was *really* smoking now. "Liam!"

"Oh, shit." He startled, shoving his phone in his pocket.

He yanked the smoking pan off the burner, grumbling under his breath as he carried it across the kitchen and chucked the entire thing into the sink. It hissed with steam as he gripped the edge of the counter, and his head hung between his shoulders in defeat.

Oh Liam.

"Don't say anything." I murmured, hating that he hadn't told me himself. I only knew because I'd eavesdropped from the stairs at Carter's. "He'll say something when he's ready."

Jules nodded sympathetically, and Sloane zipped her lips.

I changed the subject with a grin. "So Sloane, how was your motorcycle ride with Cade?"

"Fast." She chuckled, shaking her head, and I didn't doubt it.

"You two have been hanging out a lot lately." Jules prodded with a smirk.

"It's been quiet around Briar Rose." Sloane shrugged. "We bump into each other a lot."

"I'll bet you do." I grinned, but Sloane quickly changed the subject, looking at Jules. "So, are we going to talk about what happened with you and Douglass last night?"

"What can I do?" Jules sighed, twirling a long silky strand of auburn-brown hair around her finger. "I love him." She looked so conflicted.

"Love can only go so far." I countered carefully, but Jules eyes heated in defense. Why was telling your friends the truth so damn hard sometimes? "You deserve *so* much more than you're getting." Sloane nodded in agreement, shooting me an encouraging look.

"I'm not entirely sure that's true." Jules admitted, staring down at her plate.

Sloane reached out to touch her arm. "It's true." She hesitated. "Can I say something brutally honest?" Jules nodded, clearly holding back tears. "Watching you with him this last year —I'm worried you're like a frog in boiling water." Sloane said *so* gently. "I know you love him, but he's hurting you. Just because it's not with his fists doesn't make it okay."

"Sometimes he's actually really, really sweet." Jules whispered. "It's not always bad."

"Of course not, that's what makes this all so difficult." I said quietly. "If it were *just* the bad, you would have left him a long time ago."

"It's complicated." Jules admitted tearfully. "And I'm just so fucking tired."

"I think that means something." Sloane said. "You should feel clear. *He* should make you *feel* clear. Not confused."

"I don't know." Jules pushed her food around on her plate. "Maybe this is as good as it gets."

"Oh Jules, it gets so much better than this. I just know it." I slid off my chair and wrapped my arms around her. "I'm here for you. Always."

"Thanks." She sniffled, and I found Liam giving us a long look.

I didn't envy either of them.

Heartbreak was the fucking worst.

I hoped I wasn't next.

~

I was retrieving my suitcase from the side porch when Liam came out of nowhere, startling me.

"Everything alright?" I asked, hoping he didn't ask why I was bringing my suitcase in from outside. Carter had dropped it off before he left.

Liam didn't, he was far too distracted. Poor thing. "Yeah, everything's great. Why?" He forced a smile, and my heart crumpled a little, realizing he wasn't going to tell me about Gina.

Fine, I wouldn't push. Not today, at least, but I hated how he shouldered the weight of the world, worried about burdening anyone else. Especially me. Though I supposed I was busy keeping my own secrets.

"Sara," He hesitated. "I need to show you something."

My skin immediately prickled with anxiety. "What is it?"

"It's better if I show you." The anxiety I thought I'd conquered rolled over me in a massive wave. Something was *very* wrong.

I followed Liam down the corridor, into our father's office, feeling like my stomach was going to fall out of my nether regions.

Liam went straight for the desk and opened a drawer. The air became so charged I wondered if I was going to puke as he pulled a folded note out.

"Liam?" I demanded, panic clawing at my throat. "What's this about?"

His jaw fanned, eyes darting between mine. "I'm not even sure I should be showing you this. I don't want to give you more than you can handle, but I'm assigning you a bodyguard, and the only reason I'm telling you is because I know you won't let this go unless I explain." He didn't extend the note.

"Liam, you're scaring me." My voice wobbled, wondering what the hell was going on.

"Just," He gripped my arm, and my mouth went dry. "I need—"

"For Christ's sake." I grabbed the note out of his hand, unable to wait a second longer.

I mean, how bad could it possibly be? Our mother was already gone. There was no undoing that. I'd been photographed nude. What could possibly be worse than any of that? My hands trembled, and the room might have been spinning as I tried and failed to read that damn note.

I stared at the words written on the page, but no matter how hard I tried, I couldn't make my eyes focus on the words. I couldn't think. Couldn't breathe. "Who wrote this?" I asked, willing my eyes to bring the letters into focus, that little smear of red at the bottom, but they just wouldn't.

You know those moments where you're trying to read a restaurant menu—but the server is approaching the table and the very fact that you're running out of time is making it damn near impossible to read the words on the page? This was like that, only so much worse. I could have been trying to read hieroglyphs as I stared at that one line note, and it wouldn't have made a difference.

Liam jerked as heavy footsteps sounded down the hall, and he grabbed the note out of my hands as I whirled towards the door.

A wary figure appeared. "Dad?" I wasn't actually sure when I'd seen him last.

My father eyed both of us in his office, and the air felt oddly thick as Liam shifted forward towards my father. "What are you two doing in here?"

"What are you doing home?" Liam asked, with an unprovoked bite in his voice.

I glared at Liam over my shoulder as I rushed across the room. "I missed you." I threw my arms around my father, and he returned the hug with an awkward pat on the back.

"I heard about your exhibition." My dad pulled back.

I swallowed hard as guilt hit me like a freight train. "Who told you?" The words nearly got stuck in my throat.

"A colleague." My father said, "They told me it's going to auction." I nodded, feeling smaller than small. "That's good." His words were filled with something I couldn't quite decipher. He looked at me for a long minute, his expression unreadable. "I'm disappointed I didn't get to be there."

Shit. I'd messed up big time. Carter had been right, I should have told him. I hadn't meant to hurt his feelings. Hadn't meant to push him away when I already felt like he was impossible to reach. "I'm sorry." I started stumbling over my words. "It's just, I didn't mean to—"

"You had a gallery showing?" Liam looked utterly gutted, and my stomach bottomed out with immediate regret. "Why didn't you tell me?"

It was one of those moments that I suddenly wished I could take back. I'd been overwhelmed and didn't know how to let them in. "I'm sorry I didn't tell you." I said quietly.

"You should have." Liam said emptily. "I wanted to be there for you."

"I'm not the only one keeping secrets." I near whispered under my breath.

"I won't apologize for protecting you—" He gritted and cut himself off.

A wave of emotion overcame me as I raised my voice. "You don't have to do all this on your own, you know."

"Except that I do." Liam bit out.

"Pretty necklace." My dad commented tightly, trying to diffuse the building tension, "Opal was your mother's birthstone."

My heart thundered. "Since her birthday is coming up, I thought maybe we should all do something..." I trailed off, not knowing where I was going as my father tensed, withdrawing slightly. I opened and closed my mouth with no idea what else to say.

My father ignored my invitation entirely. "If you two could excuse me, I have some work to do."

I nodded, heart breaking that *this* was all he could give me. I hadn't really seen him in months, and he didn't even seem to care.

My mother had clearly been the glue in our family. Did he even want a relationship with me when my mother wasn't encouraging him to participate in my life?

Liam waited for me to leave the office first and then followed closely behind me, the note safely tucked into his bag.

I opened my mouth.

"In the car." Liam said under his breath as we headed for the foyer.

Down the street, we sat in Liam's Bugatti, and he handed me the note. I forced out a slow, steady breath and read the simple but damning note.

> **I KNOW WHAT YOU DID. I HAVE EVIDENCE, AND IF YOU DON'T GIVE ME WHAT I WANT, I'LL TAKE IT ANYWAY.**

It was signed with a thumbprint.

In blood.

I looked at Liam and swallowed hard, my lip trembling. "Liam, what does this mean?" His jaw flexed while the questions poured out of me like water, my mind spinning a million miles a minute. "Who wrote this? Who did they write it to?" It had been in my father's office. Did he have something to do with this? But why? "Did Dad do something? Does he know?" I caught myself realizing Liam was carefully monitoring my reaction. I had to keep it together, had to make sure he didn't cut me out of this, thinking I couldn't handle it.

"I don't know anything for sure." Liam grimaced. "But I promise you, I'm going to get to the bottom of this."

"Thank you for sharing this with me." I carefully steadied my breath. "I'm surprised you told me, but I'm glad." What the hell was going on? I could feel myself starting to shut down again, but I wouldn't let him see that. I couldn't burden him with my emotions any longer, especially not now.

"There's a reason I told you." He said, his voice was low and tense, and I realized Liam's eyes were locked on the rearview mirror.

I froze. "What is it?"

"Don't look." He said, pulling out onto the road. "Someone's been following us."

"Liam, what the hell is going on?" I breathed shakily.

"Everything's going to be fine." He said, "I'm going to make sure you're safe. I promise."

CHAPTER 42

The Rookie

CARTER

Tatum dropped his loaded barbell to the ground with a thud. "Someone's in a good mood today."

"Fuck yeah, I am," I grunted, watching the sweat trickle down my brow in the gym mirror as I dropped into another repetition. "I nearly cleared my PR." The feel of a good workout had always been meditative for me, but I was especially grateful my body was mostly back to normal and I was feeling stronger than ever. "It's just a matter of time." I added more to myself, forcing that sliver of doubt out of my mind.

"Obviously." Tatum agreed, chugging from his water bottle.

"Oh," I added nonchalantly, though I was anything but, "And the love of my life is flying in this weekend." *On the private jet I'd bought just for her,* but I didn't mention that little detail to Tatum.

"Ah, there it is." He shot me a mischievous look. "I'm actually surprised you're going so hard today."

I could sense an incoming jab, but I humored him anyway. "Why's that?" I huffed, dipping into my next repetition.

Tatum grinned wide and made a vulgar gesture, lifting his spread fingers to his tongue. "You're going to wear yourself out before she does."

I choked on my laughter, nearly throwing my back out as I quickly racked the bar, bracing against my shaky legs to catch my breath. Dirty motherfucker. But it was true. Sara wanted to go at mock speeds—I smiled, having never considered it quite like that before.

"Good luck with that, Casanova." Tatum snickered, "Don't go too hard, or next week is going to be a bitch." He considered for a moment, his expression turning more sobering. "Or maybe in that case... do. Last hurrahs and all."

I grimaced. This would be the last time I'd see Sara before I deployed. While it was good to be back to work as usual, the thought of being away from her for so long made my chest ache in a way I didn't know it could.

"I can't help it. I have zero willpower when it comes to her." I panted, lifting the bar again, fingers flexing over the grooved metal grips.

"That's how I knew Jillian was *the one*." Tatum said, heading for the locker rooms.

The one.

I didn't even bother shooting back a clever remark because I think a part of me knew the truth of that statement. A part of me had always *known* I felt that way about Sara. I just hadn't allowed myself to *admit it*. As hard as I'd tried to stay away from her, I just couldn't do it anymore.

I dipped low and dug into my heels as I forced myself to rise and then do it all over again. Sara was consuming me, dragging me into her orbit like gravity itself.

Selfishly, I didn't want to fight it anymore.

She occupied my mind, day and night. The sound of her laugh, the dimple on her left cheek when she was being snarky. The feeling of her curls tangled around my fist while I kissed her. The whiny, frustrated sounds she made when I whispered very, very dirty things into her ear, even over the phone.

I wanted to give her the moon on a string. Wanted to give her everything money could buy, and anything it couldn't. I tried not to get ahead of myself, but she was going to be here this weekend, and when I got my hands on her.

I was so whipped.

"I'm happy for you, Casanova. You deserve it." Tatum chuckled over his shoulder. "You finally grew a pair."

"You should try it sometime." I shot back, hating that he might be the tiniest bit right.

"Don't need to." He turned in the doorway and over his athletic shorts, gripped his sack proudly. "Robert and Bobert locked Jillian down a long time ago."

"You named your balls?" I quirked a brow and teased. "Poor Jillian."

"You mean *lucky* Jillian." He motioned palms up and disappeared down the hallway with a grin.

I huffed out a laugh and dropped into another repetition. Anything to take the edge off. I needed to wear myself out— needed to try and keep some ounce of control when it came to my darling, Sarafina Amara Devereux. Which was next to impossible.

Sara simultaneously made me feel like the weakest man alive for not being able to resist her, while also making me feel invincible, like if she believed in me, I could literally do anything. Be anything. Have anything.

Including having a family again.

I shook my head, almost not daring to admit it, even to myself.

It was something I'd decided a long time ago that I was never going to have again. A family.

When my parents had left me alone in this world, it'd taken everything in me to keep going. To survive, I'd had to wall myself off completely.

I'd been pretty successful too, not letting anyone get too close. Sure, I'd been with plenty of other women over the years, but it had been about the sex. Strictly a physical moment of release and never anything deeper.

Which was one of the many reasons I was so adamant about

taking things so slowly with Sara. I *wanted* to build that emotional foundation with her. Because whether she realized it or not, she'd found all the dark, ominous cracks in my heart and easily slipped through every wall I'd ever built. It was terrifying.

The thought of building a family with Sara, *not to mention picturing Sara pregnant with my dark-haired babies, which was sexy as fuck to fantasize about,* filled me with a strange and unfamiliar hope. I, of course, was getting way ahead of myself.

All of it was unnerving, because feelings and shit, but for the first time in my life, I felt like I belonged to someone. *Her.*

And she sure as hell belonged to me. That girl was *all mine.*

My muscles were shaking as I forced out another repetition, forced the jittery feelings in my chest to settle because I had to ask her something important this weekend. Because *girlfriend* had to come before the four-letter word I couldn't shake out of my brain. The word that made me hard just thinking about it. *Wife.*

Sarafina

"Are you ready, Miss Deveruex?" Vaughn, my new security guard, asked, coming into my class to collect me.

"I thought we discussed that you would wait *outside* my classes." I practically hissed, and I stuck my hand up, cutting off his gruff voice. "I know. I know." I grumbled. "Where you go, I go." I mimicked his useless explanation for everything.

The moment Liam had dropped me back off at school, there had already been private security set up for me. As much as I hated it, that note in my father's office had been wildly unsettling. If I could admit it to myself, I hadn't been able to shake the feeling that someone *had* been following me. I knew I was probably just being paranoid, but it was hard not to be.

I murmured my goodbyes to Carmen, and her cheeks flushed as she gobbled Vaughn up from head to toe with a glazed stare. I was shocked to see him give her a smirk before he practically dragged me out into the hallway. He looked halfway human when he wasn't scowling like his life depended on it.

Outside, I asked venomously sweetly, "So how was your day?" I was pissed as hell that he'd already broken the rules we'd agreed upon. Vaughn ignored me altogether as he all but shoved me into the bulletproof SUV and then abruptly closed the door on me. *Jerk.* I rolled my eyes as we headed for the airport, and a swell of excited nerves suddenly hit me.

I was dying to see Carter this weekend, especially with his upcoming deployment closing in, but honestly, there was a terrified part of me that wasn't exactly sure what we were doing. We hadn't discussed being exclusive, and I'd been too afraid to ask. I sure as hell wasn't seeing other people, but it didn't escape me that Carter had options. He always had.

The minute he'd turned eighteen, the tabloids had named him the city's most eligible bachelor—they still ran stories about him, even now, grabbing photos whenever he came home, starting the whole news cycle all over again. Women literally threw themselves at him, and I was just little ol' me, hoping he wouldn't forget about me if I wasn't smack dab in front of his face.

Truth be told, I was *pretty sure* we were exclusive, but that doubt still lingered, because Carter was either totally on the same page as me and I'd look stupid for asking. Or he totally *wasn't*, and I'd look even more stupid. Because officially—we weren't anything official.

I groaned at the utter nonsense of it all, but I didn't want to seem too needy. Didn't want to scare him away by asking for too much too soon. Not when I *finally* had his attention after all these years. And I really, really, *really* wanted to play it cool.

The only problem, I knew I'd be gutted if he couldn't give me what I needed from him. *Real vulnerability,* and a little commitment would definitely be nice too.

I wasn't stupid, the jokes, the teasing, the humor. It was all a carefully crafted facade to hide behind. His defense mechanisms were intentional. He wanted to keep everyone at arm's length.

My heart thundered as I refused to admit to myself what I already knew. I was falling for him. Hard and fast, and the realization that he could easily break my heart was sobering.

I'd barely made it through the last year in one piece, and if I lost Carter, I didn't know if I had the strength to put myself back together *again*.

~

When we rolled onto the tarmac, I sucked in a small breath, staring at the private jet sitting in front of us.

The Rookie was painted across the side of the plane in bubble gum pink letters and painted on the tail of the plane was a goddamn unicorn.

I couldn't help but grin, and even from behind his sunglasses, I could practically smell Vaughn's eye roll as he opened my door. I ignored him altogether until I realized he was heading towards the plane with me.

And Vaughn was definitely not part of my dirty little fantasy of how this weekend would go—Carmen's maybe, but not mine.

"Not to be rude, but you weren't exactly invited on this trip." I walked in front of him, blocking his path, trying to feel out if he was going to board the plane with me.

"You don't want me here?" Vaughn asked with a surprising amount of emotion as he hefted up my heavy bags. I opened my mouth and tried to find a polite way of saying *hell-to-the-fucking no way* but he shirked back before I could form an answer, looking very offended, "You know, I can see when I'm not wanted."

My mouth parted in surprise as he headed back to the car... *with* my bags? I hadn't expected that to be so easy. In fact, now I almost felt—

He smirked as he looped around the car, faking me out, before heading for the plane again.

"Ha ha, very funny." My shoulders slumped, wondering what Carter was going to think of our plus one.

"Thank you." Vaughn said dry as ever, "I do comedy on the weekends."

"Careful, some might consider that an invitation." I threatened. "Watch out, I might crash *your* party next time."

"Oh, I'd love to see you try, Devereux." He muttered, adding my luggage to the cargo area while I climbed the steps onto the plane.

When I ducked inside, I bit my lip with a grin—the aisle, the plush seats, everything was littered with rose petals. It was outrageous and romantic as hell.

My heart fluttered as I spotted a note in Carter's handwriting, and I sank into the plush, oversized seat to read it, discovering that the Rookie was a gift. For me. So I could come see Carter whenever I wanted to. A lump formed in my throat as I let it sink in that Carter had bought me a freaking plane. That had to mean something serious... right? Even for someone as filthy rich as him. Plus, he *never* spent money, but he'd bought me a freaking plane! I was giddy.

I was even more giddy when Vaughn stuck his head through the plane door and told me to have a safe trip before the door slammed shut. *He wasn't coming after all.*

Score.

As the plane took off, I settled into my seat and pulled out a fresh magazine, immediately skipping the article about Liam—reading about my friends and family in print usually made me nauseous. Best to avoid it altogether, because most of it was usually staged, completely made up, or photoshopped. My stomach rolled, hoping they were saying good things about Liam and his restaurant, but I didn't have the stomach to look for sure.

I was busy reading an enthralling article about the best waterproof mascara when a deep, smooth voice crackled through the intercom, wrapping around me like a caress. "Good afternoon, this is your captain speaking." My head whipped around so fast, I practically morphed into an owl. "We're currently cruising at an altitude of thirty-thousand-feet, and an airspeed of four-hundred-knots." I rolled my lips over my teeth, realizing *Carter* was my pilot, and hearing Carter talk shop was hot as hell. "With clear skies as far as the eye can see, the only turbulence you can expect this afternoon will be right here *inside the plane*." I grinned, shaking my head. "I'd now like to invite Miss Devereux up to my *cock*, excuse me—up to *the* cockpit. I repeat, the captain requires your immediate attention in the cockpit, Miss Devereux. Please proceed to the front of the plane at your earliest convenience. Thank you for your cooperation, and thank you for choosing Mile High Airlines."

I hurried up the aisle and found the door to the cockpit already cracked. "Hi, sweetheart." Carter whispered, eyes so filled with longing it stole my breath.

"You're here." I breathed, eating up the cute little hat, the headset, how sexy he generally looked, flying the plane.

"Couldn't wait." He admitted, patting his lap, which I immediately slid on to.

"You bought me a plane." I murmured with a devious smirk as he reached around me, flipping switches. "That's a tough move, you know."

His chest shook with amusement, but his words were soft as he finally gripped my waist and met my gaze again. "Oh? And why's that?"

"Because it's going to be hard to top a gift like that." I said tartly, sliding my arms around his neck, becoming enveloped in his smell—fresh, clean, and intoxicating as fuck. I smiled to myself, realizing if the sky had a scent, that's what it would be.

"Don't you worry your pretty little head about that." His grip on me tightened as he pulled me to his lips. "I have all kinds of plans for you, Miss Devereux."

I smiled against his mouth. *Plans* were an excellent step in the right direction.

CHAPTER 43
Mile High Club
CARTER

"You know the hat is pretty damn cute." Sara teased as I put it onto her head, "But you know what would be even more fun?"

"What's that?" I asked, kneading her hips as she settled into my lap.

She bit her lip. "Your jet helmet."

I chuckled darkly. "Oh, you are going to get yourself into all kinds of trouble up here, aren't you?"

"Yes, sir." She saluted me with an adorable scrunch of her nose while my cock jumped with excitement. "I have to ask—did you buy me this plane just so you could join the mile-high club?" Her head tipped back, exposing the elegant curve of her neck as I ran my nose down it.

"Maybe I did." I ran my tongue over the column of her throat before sucking on it. "Because I have all kinds of things planned for you way up here in the sky, pretty girl." I was going to send her to heaven as many times as she'd let me.

Her eyes heated with understanding as she teased, "What about what I want?" She palmed me, and I rested my forehead against hers with a breathy chuckle. "I'll let you have a turn once I've had mine."

A smirk flashed across her face. "I dare you to prove it."

"Careful, Sarafina, you sure you want to start that game all the way up here?" I threatened, "There's nowhere to hide today, nowhere to run." I rumbled greedily, triple-checking I'd set the plane on autopilot.

Sara bit her lip, and I wasted no time sucking that pillowy thing into my mouth, loving every minute of my two favorite things. Claiming her and being in the sky.

As I kissed her, the feel of her in my arms, so small and delicate, reminded me how vulnerable she was. And even if The Society's threats against her had proven to be empty so far, I was still on edge.

I didn't even care that Theo had accepted payment from Liam for additional private security on top of the team I'd hired. Liam couldn't have known—but Theo did. The bastard. It didn't matter, though. I was grateful she had an additional bodyguard glued to her hip. Closer was better. Safer. I wondered if Sara had confided in her brother about what had happened with Isaac. Socialite or not, Sara was breathtakingly gorgeous by anyone's standards, and that was reason enough to draw attention. Either way, Isaac and every other asshole she'd been with was a piece of shit. She was mine. And she was never going to be pushed past her physical or emotional limits again. I'd make sure of it.

"Carter." Sara moaned into my mouth, swollen-lipped, looking perfect as ever.

"Fuck." I blew out a breath, knowing I'd never wanted someone this bad in my life and any illusion of control I had—she decimated with a simple bat of her lashes.

Sara gave me an innocent smirk and sunk her teeth into her bottom lip, her mass of chocolate brown curls completely disheveled thanks to my handiwork.

An odd wave of nerves washed over me, anxiety that bringing her deeper into my life would somehow endanger her lingered at the edge of my mind. Then again, never letting her out of my sight was an equally appealing alternative.

"Hey," I whispered, "I uh, I have to ask you something." She tensed. "It's good, I promise." I quickly amended, realizing she was expecting the worst. My sweet, sweet girl, I hated it so much that she ran so anxious—that she was always waiting for something bad to happen. I brushed a strand of hair out of her face and leaned in for a slow but chaste kiss on the lips to reassure her. God, she smelled so incredible, all the time. It made it hard to think—sweet but sexy, warm and tempting, like strawberries and honey, like something that I desperately wanted to take a bite of. *I wanted to taste every inch of her, actually.*

I also loved how much she trusted me, as she instantly relaxed, raking her nails over my scalp with an adorable giggle. "I *like* good."

God, I loved this girl. Fuck! Too early to say it? Yeah. Way too soon.

I booped her nose with mine. "I like *you*." I murmured instead, feeling like my chest was about to explode. "Like really like." I knew I must be in love, because I couldn't even string an intelligent sentence together.

"That's good." Her eyes were soft as she teased me affectionately. "I like, really like you, too." Her hands slid lower, making my brain stutter. "*Like really.*" Cheeky girl.

I cleared my throat a bit dramatically, loving how she was already giggling, hanging on my every word with expectant wide eyes. "Sarafina Amara Devereux." She straightened slightly. "Will you do me the great honor of being my girlfriend?" I added, "Officially."

Oomph. Sara slammed into me with surprising strength, basically choking me as she squeezed her arms around my neck. "You want me to be your girlfriend?" She squealed with delight. "Carter Ambrose Kensington, I thought you'd never ask."

I chuckled nervously from within the curtain of hair draped over my face as she loomed over me. "What do you say, pretty girl? Should we make this thing official?"

"I think the plane sort of solidified our relationship." She teased, pretending to be put out, "But okay, *I guess* I can be your girlfriend."

"Wow." I sunk my teeth into my bottom lip. "I like *that*." I murmured, gripping her ribcage, loving that she was even more filled in and healthy than the last time I'd seen her.

Her eyes sparkled. "Do you like *this*?" She deviously trailed her fingers down my chest, and her hands were a little chilly as she slipped each of them under my shirt, making each breath come a little tighter.

"I know you're not trying to get your hands on me before I've even touched you—tasted you." Her eyes flared, but she quickly pushed my shirt up, peppering my neck and chest with soft kisses that led lower.

"But what about this?" She looked up deviously. "Doesn't this feel good?"

Fuck. I couldn't breathe, couldn't think with her hands on me, so I just nodded with a hard swallow.

It was taking everything in me to keep control. If I moved a muscle, I was going to flip her underneath me and sink into her. The way she'd looked, and sounded taking that damn unicorn horn back home, the way her tight heat had felt wrapped around my fingers in the shower—tonight I wondered what she'd look like when *I* sank into her, what kinds of sounds she'd make, taking *me*.

It was a moment of wet dreams, knowing I was going to claim her for the first time, way up here in the sky. I *did* want to take my time with her, but I was also deploying, and after years of pretending, I honestly didn't have the strength to stay away anymore, not when so much of my time with her was already out of my control.

Before I could think better, Sara's long, slender fingers wrapped around my aching cock. "Fuuuuck." I rasped, nearly losing it at the sight of her looming over it with such an eager and determined look on her face.

Fuck me.

My girlfriend.

Sara was my fucking girlfriend.

Who had decided to let me win the lottery?

Control snapped.

In one deft move, I hoisted her up on the dash—the dash I'd had custom made just for this, because right now, I fucking loved being rich. "It's cute that you think you get to call the shots." I murmured as she wrestled me for the upper hand.

"Hey, I was in the middle of something." She giggled with a grunt.

"So was I." Something primal in me sparked to life as I tipped her back, laid her out under the big blue beautiful sky and pinned both her hands above her head.

She looked up at me, eyes flared with need. "No fair." She whimpered breathlessly.

"You're just going to have to wait your turn, sweetheart." I hummed, feeling very greedy. It was a tight fit, but I stood between her legs as I leaned over and kissed the exposed curve of her soft breasts with a lusty grin. "How much do you like this shirt?"

She was breathless and swishy as she started to ramble shyly. "A regular amount? I don't know? It's just one of my lounge shirts—"

"Great answer. Perfect Answer." I breathlessly slid my fingers into the collar, and her eyes blew wide with understanding.

I couldn't help but give her a panty-melting wink just before I ripped the soft material straight down the middle. "Carter." Sara protested with a needy gasp, sounding anything but mad, as her hips bucked up, and I anchored her against the dash with a thrust of my own.

"That was in the way." I explained, eyes nearly rolling back in my head as I drank in the delicate red lace that was encasing both her perfect tits. I wondered if she always wore lingerie like this, or if it was just for me. Using my index finger, I tugged the soft material down, letting one breast spill over the top. "So was that." I rasped, dusting my thumb over her nipple, watching it tighten for me.

In broad daylight, I could see every mouthwatering inch of her, and I honestly couldn't get enough. "God, Sara, you're so beautiful." I admitted, hearing how my voice had turned rough as I leaned down to drag my tongue across a pebbled peak.

She arched into my mouth with satisfying need as I flicked my tongue over her slowly, and then I moved to the other side. She was like a gourmet meal, and I was just getting started.

"I missed you." She murmured, hands tangled in my hair, no doubt staring into the endless sky above her—I loved sharing this with her, this slice of freedom, this slice of *me*.

All of it felt so right. "I know, sweet girl. I missed you too." And as much as I loved the sky, I was entirely mesmerized by the two soft peaks in front of me.

"Carter, I want you." My eyes dragged up to her pleading ones. "I *need* you."

I read the urgency in her voice. I was leaving. All we had was this weekend, and then—I couldn't think like that. Wouldn't. "Not going to lie. Those words sound pretty damn good coming out of your mouth." I mused lazily, despite the anxiety lodged in my chest, "I wonder what else would sound good coming out of your mouth?" I trailed a finger across her waistband, watching her reaction as she sucked in a hard breath. Fuck, I loved the way she went so soft and needy for me.

I lowered my mouth to her stomach, swearing she actually tasted like strawberries as I tasted every available inch of skin between her waistband and belly button.

Mine to taste, mine to worship, mine to devour.

She whimpered as I moved lower, chest heaving with every panting breath. "Yeah, that's exactly what I imagined it'd sound like when I kissed you here." I purred, eating up all her little sounds.

Using my teeth, I dragged her waistband lower, leaving another kiss on her too soft skin as her fingers tightened in my hair. "Carter?" Her breathy voice was slightly uncertain, the look in her eyes reminding me exactly why we needed to take things slow. Not just for me, but for her.

I leaned my forearm on the dash next to her, while I traced her stomach with the pads of my fingers, just gazing at her, mesmerized, waiting. "Yes, pretty girl?"

"Never mind." She quickly rasped.

I stopped tracing. "Sara." I slid my hand up the center of her and gently gripped her throat, tilting her face towards me. "Talk to me." I pleaded with a puppy-dog pout that earned me a soft laugh. "You can tell me anything."

She sighed. "Why do I believe you when you look like that?"

"Because it's true." I waited quietly all the while, admiring how beautiful she was. Rosy-cheeked, encased in a halo of long goddess-like curls. I didn't deserve her.

She absentmindedly played with my hair. "I don't think I'm as experienced as you are, and I..." She trailed off, and I could practically smell her overthinking things in her head.

I stroked her cheek. "There is nothing you can say that will make me feel differently about you. I'm all in, sweetheart." I promised, wondering if she understood what I was really saying. "I'm not a mind reader, though, and it would be helpful to know what's going through that pretty little head of yours."

An exasperated breath out. "Truth. I'm not sure I know what to do." She said shyly and then added even quieter. "Truth. What if you don't like how I taste?" She threw an arm over her eyes, covering her face.

Ohhhhhh.

"Trust me, you don't have to worry about that." I chuckled, knowing what was between those long, lean legs was a buffet ready to be devoured, and I. Was. Hungry. Starving actually.

Her cheeks were quickly turning a deep shade of crimson, and it was adorable. There was something electric about the pull between us that she responded to me like that—like she couldn't help it. I fucking loved it.

"It's—I don't know—you know?" She groaned, wide-eyed, and too damn adorable for her own good.

"Trust me, I'd *love* to know." I huffed a quiet laugh, my cock thickening. "And you don't have to *do* anything." I brushed the pad of my thumb over the soft spot below her hip bone, watching her reaction. "You just have to lie back and let me feast." I could see her pulse flutter—she was nervous, but she was definitely into the idea.

"It just didn't go well last time." She blushed a bit, clarifying, "The only time."

God, my girl had been through so much. I nodded, grateful she trusted me enough to share that, heartbroken that she'd ever gone through it in the first place. "We don't have to do anything you're uncomfortable with." I leaned down and kissed her forehead.

"I'm comfortable with *you*." She offered breathily, fingers clutching my shirt like her life depended on it.

I chuckled. "Oh, I know."

"Carter." She smacked me with a grin, going swishy again. "I just don't want to disappoint you." She admitted, and my jaw flexed.

Part of me loved that she was a little shy about all this stuff, a little naïve, and being the first one to make her feel good, in this way, was *hot*, but I hated that someone had made her feel this way to begin with. "Sar, the thought of tasting you drives me *wild, and you will never, ever be a disappointment to me. Ever.*"

"It does?" Her eyes heated, and I smiled, loving that's what she'd locked in on.

I offered her a playful shrug. "I think my tongue would drive *you* pretty fucking wild too." I teased. "But I don't really care what we do tonight, as long as we do it together—I'm just glad I get to spend the weekend with my girl." I rested a cheek on my propped-up fist, offering her a mischievous smirk. Fuck yeah, I loved saying that. So. Fucking. Much. Mine. Mine. Mine. Wanted to climb up on a roof somewhere and sing about it, and I didn't even sing.

Sara rolled her lips over her teeth. "I guess... you don't have to stop what you were doing earlier." She quickly flopped back, embarrassed by her request, but this was already a huge improvement—she was using her voice and asking for what she wanted.

"What's the matter?" I grinned and peeled her hands away, *again*. "Do I make you nervous, pretty girl?"

"Of course not." She breathed as I settled my hips between her legs, twirling a strand of her hair around my finger.

"Liar." I chuckled deeply and hummed, "Do you like the thought of my mouth on you?" My cock twitched as I slowly dragged a finger over the swell of her breast and then over a nipple. "What about the thought of my tongue on you? Tasting you." I nudged her head to the side to access that tender little place below her ear.

"Ohhh." She sighed, wrapping her legs around my waist.

"Tell me." I hummed against her skin.

"Yes."

"Yes, what?" I nipped and quickly soothed the place where my teeth had been with my tongue.

"Yes, the thought of you ... tasting me." She said the words slowly, as if it was making her nervous to admit it. "Turns me on. A lot."

Fuck yeah. Challenge accepted.

CHAPTER 44

Eye Contact

"Good." I rumbled. "It turns me on too." I lowered and kissed every available inch of bare skin from Sara's lips to her waistband until she was trembling. In the process—exposed in the broad daylight, I discovered a jagged scar on her lower stomach, and I brushed my thumb over it gently, eyes narrowing. "What's this from?"

Eyes squeezed shut, she squirmed beneath me breathlessly before she finally got the words out. "I had an ovarian cyst removed."

"Laparoscopic?" I asked, and she nodded quickly, as I left a soft kiss there. "I didn't know." I hummed, holding her a little tighter.

"Outpatient, one-day thing at Montclair." She panted as I swept my tongue over the scar and then lower, making her practically whine, "*Carter.*"

I hooked my fingers into her stretchy yoga pants. "Do I have your enthusiastic permission to remove these?" I murmured with a smug grin, even while I watched her closely.

"Yeah." She nodded breathlessly. "Always."

"You know the rules. You want to stop at any point. We do." I slowly dragged the soft fabric down her legs, trying to steady my own breath as I gave a tug at each of her feet, releasing her. I threw the stretchy thing across the cockpit. "We won't be needing those for quite some time." I grinned, knowing the pilot was just making long loops in the air, killing time—

It was me! I was the pilot! And I'd never loved it so much as I did right now.

"Carter?" She suddenly propped herself up on her elbows, and I immediately halted. "If you think I taste gross, just—" She couldn't find the words, and I tried to give her a minute, to let her speak, but I honestly couldn't bear to let her finish the thought. "Nothing about you is gross, and I want you to stop saying that about yourself." I rasped, heartbroken, as I gripped the base of her skull and kissed her hard, hoping she'd finally believe me. "Baby, I can promise you, this is a feast I've been thinking about consuming for a very long while now."

A breathless, "Really?"

"Uh yeah." I nodded, eyeing the matching red lace underwear and the damp spot currently waiting for me.

"Please don't be weird if you think I taste bad." She pleaded as I descended.

"It's not going to be a problem, but if it makes you feel better —I promise, *I won't be weird.*" I shook my head, we were definitely going to have to work on that one.

"Thanks." she said hilariously formally as she stared up into the sky.

"You may want to save your thanks for later." I panted as I dragged the soft lace down her legs, flinging it against the window like a slingshot, earning me a nervous little laugh. "You're not getting those back, by the way." I warned, sinking into the captain's chair.

She swallowed hard as I lowered my shoulders between her legs and pushed her thighs apart. "I wouldn't dream of it." Her voice was wafer-thin.

"Good, because I'm keeping those as a souvenir." My breath caught in my throat as I took her in, *fucking gorgeous,* utterly soaked, and fluttering desperately for me. "Baby," I groaned, "Is this all for me?" The smell of her alone was nearly enough to make me lose it.

"Mhmm." She squirmed as I lifted a knee over my shoulder and pressed a kiss to the inside of it.

"You're safe with me." I murmured, inching my way up her leg. "Always."

"I know." She rasped as I kissed a path up to her inner thighs, loving the show as she quivered beneath me, glistening.

"Look at you, already squirming." I hummed with a chuckle, moving closer and closer to the main attraction. I watched her when I finally brushed my lips over her shiny, swollen clit, and it earned me a sharp gasp before she immediately clapped a hand over her mouth, covering a strangled cry.

"No, sweetheart, I want to hear you." I hummed possessively as I immediately pulled her arm down. "I want to hear how good I make *my girl* feel. Let me have this." I begged.

"Oh, fuck, Carter." She whimpered, writhing under me when I licked a wide path up her center. "That feels incredible."

"Atta girl. Keep using your voice." I rasped, relishing in the flutter of her against my tongue as I went to work, worshipping her body with my mouth. "You know how fucking sexy you are, laid out like my own personal buffet, with the sky as your tablecloth?"

"Holy shit." She gasped, hands flying to the glass above her as I devoured her ruthlessly.

"Yeah?" I crooned, lips glistening. "What about this?" I slid two fingers inside of her, cock twitching at how easily they slid in, at how tight and warm she was.

Her hands speared into my hair, pulling hard. "Oh God, oh God, oh God."

"God's not coming to save you now, Sarafina." I warned, licking my lips. "You're all mine, but I promise I'll take you straight to heaven."

"Y-yes." She moaned as I razed my teeth over her clit and then soothed it with my tongue.

"You like that?" I threaded one hand around her leg and pressed on her stomach, meeting my fingers inside her.

She was so fucking beautiful. My undoing.

I never wanted the moment, the taste of her on my tongue to end, because as much as I wanted to be inside of her—I loved learning her body like this, loved taking my time with her.

I paused, feeling quite greedy. Like gollum. We wants it, we needs it, so why shouldn't we haves it? I pressed my tongue to my cheek while my fingers continued, "Eyes on me." I rasped the command.

"What? Carter, please." She gasped, frustrated, teetering just at the edge of release and looking too damn breathtaking and innocent while I held her there, begging—with a beautiful striated cloud in the background, framing her like a priceless painting. She *was* priceless, and *I* certainly loved painting my face with everything between her legs.

"I'm feeling pretty damn greedy right now, and I want to watch while you surrender to me, pretty girl." This beautiful, strong girl, who had walls of her own, had dropped them for me, and I didn't want to blink, didn't want to miss a single minute of it. "Come on, brown-eyed girl, let's see em."

"Carter." She slammed her eyes shut as I dragged a languid stroke of my fingers against her fluttering inner walls.

"Open your eyes, pretty girl, or I'll stop." I hummed, dragging again, grinning as she shuddered and then complained a moment later when I paused. "Can't help myself with you." I shrugged greedily, her legs rising over my shoulders with the motion.

Desperate for me to keep going, her heavy-lidded eyes met mine, lusty, nervous, and surrendered. When I resumed the slow drag of my fingers inside her, her lips parted in ecstasy, eyes filled with everything I needed as I watched her. Heart to heart, soul to soul.

For long minutes, I alternated between sucking and stroking, just watching her body respond. Paying attention to what exactly made her eyes slam shut and arch her back with desperate need. Just exploring her, never wanting the moment to end.

But when she was breathless and begging, with a sheen glittering across her skin, I let my girl have it. Legs shaking on either side of my ears, she went soft and wild, surrendered, and powerful all at once as she began to unravel.

For me.

Her lips parted in a silent cry, and her eyes squeezed shut as she spasmed around my fingers, letting me know my cock would be a tight, perfect fit.

I pulsed against that inner wall, leaving long, firm strokes that met the flat palm of the hand on her stomach. I sucked her sweet clit into my mouth, tasting, as she gave me everything—as she arched with an exhausted, broken scream.

Beautiful. Undone. Mine.

She was trembling, still whimpering those fucking little sounds when I finally withdrew my fingers. And I just couldn't help myself as I slid my glistening fingers into my mouth one by one and sucked all of my hard work clean. "Fucking delicious, sweetheart." I leaned forward and slid a finger into her mouth, pressing down on the pad of her tongue. "Taste that?" I asked. "I can't get enough of it."

Her eyes flared as she wrapped her pert lips around my fingers and sucked like the good girl she was, and damn if I didn't imagine that pretty little mouth wrapped around my cock. *All in good time.*

"You did so good." I crooned, moving a few strands of hair that were sweat-slicked to her neck—just then a quiet alarm started beeping. "Hold on." I kept my hand planted against her stomach, keeping her in place.

Sara's mouth tugged up. "It's okay. I could use a minute to recover."

"Don't move." I instructed, listening to the radio.

"Wouldn't dream of it." She grinned, lying spread open, swollen, used, and every bit angelic.

As I listened to the radio, I felt like my heart was being shredded into little pieces. "Sweetheart, I've got some bad news." I swallowed hard. "My assignment got moved up, I have to take you home tonight." The whole special weekend I had planned, went straight out the window. No parachute.

Her face fell. "Now?"

"Yeah," I murmured, "I'm so sorry." I had wanted to take her to The FlatHatter, and introduce her to some of my buddies. The only people who could really know we were together. I wanted to show her off a bit. Was dying to, actually.

"Don't be." She said as I carefully pulled her off the dash. She sank into the copilot chair. "It's not your fault, and I'm really glad I got to see you one more time before you left, even if it's only for a few hours." She tried to sound cheerful.

"Yeah, me too." I nodded emptily. "Hey, while I'm thinking about it, grab my bag over there." I nodded to the corner as I shifted my attention back to flying the plane, turning it around. "Can you grab my wallet in the front pocket?" She quickly handed it to me, and I dug out a thick black credit card. "Here, this is for you."

"Why are you giving me your credit card?" She puzzled.

"It's not my credit card." I smirked. "It's yours."

She cocked her head, flipping the card over. "But why?"

I shrugged, grinning at her sitting in her red bra, ripped shirt, otherwise naked in my copilot chair. "Just in case you need it."

Her lips parted, taking a small breath in that didn't lead to any word being spoken. I could feel her gaze drilling into me, asking a question that I preferred not to answer—because her father was gambling, because the house had been stripped of precious antiques—telling me, he was no doubt, quickly running out of money.

I shrugged. "Use it for whatever you want, but just keep it, just in case you need it."

She nodded contemplatively and then, "Captain, how well can you fly this plane?"

I huffed a laugh. "Uh, fine? Why do you ask?"

"Good. Then it's finally my turn, Casanova."

"Ohhhh fuck me." I groaned, white-knuckling the yoke as I realized what she meant. She slid down in front of me, hands sliding up my thighs. "Sara." I choked out, pleading, as she quickly pulled out my cock—it immediately thickened in her hand.

"Keep your eyes on the road." She murmured, but I'd already turned the autopilot back on. There was no way in hell I could focus on flying this plane with her on her knees, looking at me like that.

She stared at my hard cock with slightly wide eyes, and when she glanced up at me through those dark lashes, with that innocent little look; I knew it was game over for me.

I felt like a horny teenager, ready to blow at the first suggestion of contact. I stilled as she gave me the most devious look I'd ever seen, and her tongue darted out, swirling tentatively around my head while she watched my reaction.

Mother-of-fucking-pearl-holy-fucking-shit.

I whimpered, knowing I'd been wrong—I wasn't Gollum at all, I was the volcano in Mordor and I was about to erupt.

"I'm sorry I'm not very good at this," she admitted, gripping me with both hands.

"Sweetheart, I think you're doing just fi—" I groaned as hot, wet heat enveloped me.

I gripped the yoke rather than the back of her head, just to be safe, given her comment the other night—but she was so impossibly sexy, and it took all my energy not to thrust into her mouth hard and rough. Not to sink myself down the back of her throat like I wanted to.

"You look fucking incredible with my cock between your lips." I panted, and the eager look on her face didn't help as she bobbed up and down, eyes starting to water. "Yeah, baby, just like that, suck me like a good girl." I groaned, realizing it was hotter than I'd imagined. The look she gave me from underneath her dark lashes while her plump lips slid up and down my length. Her cheeks hollowed out, and I swore as I hit the back of her throat and she gagged.

"You don't have to go that deep." I rasped in warning, not wanting her to push herself too far. "Anything you do feels amazing." But she did *not* like that comment one bit, and I white-knuckled the yoke as she swallowed me down with even more determination—a ruthless punishment for even suggesting she slow down.

I wasn't going to last long at all. "Fuck, baby, I'm close." I whimpered, head falling back on the brink of ecstasy. "If you don't want me to come in your mouth—"

Her words were muffled, and I caught a flash of a brief mischievous smile before her cheeks hollowed out ruthlessly, making me cry out. Loose coils of hair tangled around my hand as she swallowed me deeper, as I fucked her gorgeous mouth. Her eyes watered and she gagged as I climaxed, jerking hard as I came, straight down the back of her throat. But like the devious thing she was, she swallowed everything I gave her, and then proceeded to release me, flicking her tongue over my head to get every last drop—she had the audacity to lick her lips like she just couldn't get enough.

"Fuck, you're incredible." I panted, shuddering as I collapsed back into the captain's chair, realizing that had really just happened, that she'd just sucked me off while I was flying a damn plane—I couldn't think straight, couldn't hardly catch my breath.

"You turned the autopilot back on, didn't you?" She grinned, clearly feeling very proud of herself, before she crawled up my chest and gave me a peck on the lips. I didn't bother answering as I grabbed her before she could pull away and hauled her into my lap, tasting myself on her, because I just couldn't get enough of her. *Of us.*

~

On the short flight back, we chatted about everything under the sun, each of us shooting each other small smiles, just enjoying each other's company. We'd spent the last few months laying those important foundational pieces, the ones that made me feel even more confident that I was falling head over heels for my best friend, despite all the alarm bells going off.

And when we landed, I did something that shook me to my core. I told her my feelings.

As she turned to get into the car, I grabbed her wrist, relishing in the way her breath hitched as I brushed my thumb across her delicate skin. I doubted it would ever get old. "Sara."

"I have to go." She groaned, thinking I was pulling her back for one more kiss. For the umpteenth time. "*You* have to go."

"I know." I took her face in both hands, panting as I gazed into those big brown eyes that held everything I'd ever needed. "I know this is way too soon." I admitted nervously. "But it's also way too fucking late." She searched my eyes trying to figure out what I was about to say. "I'm deploying, and I can't leave without telling you how I feel."

"Carter." She breathed, her eyes blowing wide with sudden understanding.

I was trembling, literally shaking like a leaf, I was so terrified. "I love you." Saying it out loud was scarier than flying at mock speeds, scarier than facing down any enemy, any threat. "I think I've always loved you, Sara. I think there has always been a part of me that has known it, too. Even if this means risking the only family I have left, you're worth it. Whatever happens, I'll always love you, Sara."

"Kensington." Rage flashed through her eyes. "How dare you throw that out there like you're not coming back from this assignment in one piece!"

Oh shit, oh shit, *oh fucking SHIT!*

I'd leapt, and the parachute hadn't opened.

I should have kept my mouth shut. Too soon. Way too fucking soon. What the hell was wrong with me?

Sara hauled herself up on tiptoe and yanked my face down to kiss me. I kissed her back, but I couldn't help feeling like the world was falling out from underneath me.

Except she pulled back breathless, eyes shiny. "Don't say I love you like it's a goodbye, Carter, because *I love you too,* and if you don't come back." Her voice cracked. "I *need* you, so you *have* to come back to me. *Promise me.*" She demanded.

Did she just say she loved me? She did, right? She freaking loved me!? I picked her up and spun while the world painted itself in a rainbow of rose-colored hues. Life had never felt so full. I'd never felt so alive. Sara was all the way at the very center of my heart, and she could gut me from the inside out if she wanted to. It was simultaneously the most exhilarating and terrifying thing I'd ever felt.

"It's not a goodbye, sweetheart. It's the most exciting hello of my life because I'm just getting started with you." I promised.

"It better be, because if you die over there, Kensington, I promise I'll kill you myself." A tear streamed down her cheek.

Oh God, I was never going to let her get in this car and leave me now.

She loved me too.

CHAPTER 45
Banana Dick
SARAFINA

My knee bounced as I anxiously sat on the stool in my art studio and reread the last text messages from Carter. I knew I should be painting. I needed to make some serious progress on this piece, but I was dying for a message to come through—one teensy-tiny little message that would give me proof of life and remind me that I was overreacting.

Actually, I was really proud of myself for keeping it together. The first couple of times Carter had gone radio silent had been absolute hell, and while I hated it, I was slowly learning to deal with the anxiety.

Honestly, it'd only been a couple of weeks since I'd heard from him, and this wasn't even the longest stint. But for some reason, this time, it just felt harder.

I knew he loved flying, loved his job, but this fucking sucked —and even when I knew he was safe and sound, I hated the long distance. As much as I loved Briar Rose, *I loved him more*. Since I could really paint from anywhere, I'd already hinted at the fact that maybe after graduation I'd be willing to move, because when we did talk, in between all the flirting and sexting...we were talking about the future, and making plans—*he was making plans,* and I wanted them to hurry up and start already.

So I did what I always did when I missed him so bad my chest felt like it was going to cave in. I set my phone down and recorded him a funny little video.

A musical was blasting as I pranced around like a loon. "Hi baby! I hope you're having a good day. I'm in my studio, painting, and managing my anxiety like a champ. Look what I painted—it's your massive dick." I giggled and picked up the camera, showing him the vulgar little doodle I'd made and then aimed the camera at the trash can. "And I even ate Thai food for lunch. Aren't you proud of me?!" I turned the camera back around, telling him how much I loved and missed him, before I kissed the camera goodbye.

My smile faded as I quickly ended the video, knowing if it was too long it wouldn't go through at all. But staring at the wall of messages I'd already sent him, my shoulders sagged.

> I miss you so much

> Good morning, thinking of you.

> *Image*

I had a really bad nightmare last night. Womp womp

I wish I could talk to you right now, something real shitty happened today.

Also Vaughn is an ass, and I give you full permission to kick his butt when you get back. He deserves it. Grumpy rude asshole!

> *Image*

Think of me the next time you jack off, because I'm thinking of you right now.

Remember that thing you did with your tongue. Let's do it again sometime. Same place? Same Time?

> *Image*

Carter?

Carter!

Flyboy

Hey big boi

Biggie dick boi

Bing bong

Bing bing ring a ding ding

Did you get any of those? I thought maybe if I sent enough messages, maybe one would get through.

IDK maybe some of them are.

Image

This is the biggest banana I've ever seen in my life. Look at the girth.... and speaking of girth.

Image

Hey look, I have a banana dick. What do you think? I think I look quite dashing.

It's not as big as yours but I think I could do some real damage.

When you get back, I'm going to bounce on yours until it falls off.

Your banana dick that is.

Just warning you.

JK. No but really

Yours is so much prettier than my banana dick

I mean more manly. You have the biggest, most manly dick of all the dicks.

I shall name him your obi-wand. And I would like to politely request that you split me in half like Darth Maul. Only make it hot dog style instead of hamburger. Please and thank you.

Hold the mustard but I'll take the ketchup

I don't even know what that means, but I can't wait to hear what you come up with.

Okay... I don't know. I miss you

SIGH. I miss you so bad

Ten four. Casanova please report for duty

Roger. We need proof of life. Stat.

Any day now.

Fuck.

This is really hard.

I wish I at least knew where you were.

The gremlin is being really bad today, and I feel like something is really wrong.

I know I promised you that I would keep my anxiety in check, but I'm really starting to freak out. I hope you're okay.

I love you.

So much.

...

I decided I would rather be Princess Leia instead of Darth Maul. But you can still split me in half hot-dog style when you get back.

CHAPTER 46

If Martin Baker has no fans, I'm dead

CARTER

Months deployed, and I missed her so badly my chest felt like it was going to split in half. I was out of cell service again, and I couldn't wait for the flood of texts and pictures that would come in the moment I was back in range. Those daily texts she sent me were a lifeline, but it wasn't enough.

I was head over heels for this girl, and I couldn't help the sinking feeling that maybe all my priorities were suddenly changing. What I wanted for my life was changing. She filled me with so much hope for the future, and I was slowly realizing that I'd do anything in the world to make her happy, and keep her safe. *Anything.* Maybe even consider coming back to Briar Rose, because as much as I loved flying—*I loved her more.*

Being away from Sara was going to be difficult—I knew that, and before I'd gone out of service, I'd spoken with Theo. Sara was doing amazing—Vaughn reported that she was painting, and eating, and that she was *safe and happy.* All good news, and yet, I couldn't stop the sinking feeling from settling into my chest that something was off.

That evening, just as the sun dipped below the horizon, I couldn't help but feel like something terrible was about to happen. Tonight my mission was simple enough. We'd done the simulation dozens of times, and we were more than ready. We'd fly into the mountains, into the compound that was only accessible by horseback trail, or aerially, extract the hostages if there were any still alive, and kill the targets.

With hostages to bring back, it was a little odd that most of us were in our individual jets, but we did sometimes split up to hedge for casualties, and if things went sour tonight, there was always plan B.

The flight in, however, had gone beautifully. Actually, we'd slipped into the airspace *completely unnoticed*, and it was almost too smooth for my liking—eerily quiet, almost like a jinx.

I tried to talk myself out of the quiet panic that had settled into the pit of my stomach as we landed and then proceeded to hike the last mile towards the compound in the pitch black. But honestly, this was exactly why I'd made myself unattached all these years. I wouldn't trade Sara for the world, but this feeling, this fear—it made me slow, made my mind fuzzy, made me a danger to myself and to my team.

So I forced myself to push the fear away and box it up while I silently rappelled down the side of our target building and then swung into the open window.

Inside, I silently unclipped, and next to me, several members of my team were doing the same.

With a silent motion, the team slipped down a dark hallway, fanning out, as we looked for our targets.

With another silent motion, I kicked a door down, and with calm adrenaline pumping through my veins, keeping me sharp, I realized that my night vision revealed absolutely nothing.

The room was empty.

As we moved down the hallway, we cleared room after room, finding more of the same, and my skin prickled with unease—because something wasn't right here.

"This was bad intel." Someone muttered through the comms. "We need to get out of here."

On high alert, the team quickly slipped back out into the night, and we started the steep hike back to our aircrafts.

Sweating and anxious, I breathlessly slid into the seat of my jet and mentally locked in, forcing all my worries to fall away as we headed for the midnight skies.

The drag of the jet as I sliced through the air was a comforting feeling as I finally crested over the top of the mountains, feeling my heart rate start to settle.

The familiarity and control of the aircraft was a soothing balm to my nerves. A midnight lullaby of familiarity, and I shook my head—being in love made me a heartsick fool. I was going to have to get a grip on this, and soon.

Only a moment later, I realized that my gut feeling had been right.

I started losing altitude for no reason at all, and the next dial I touched didn't respond. Everything in my chest went tight as I went through the sequence with no response.

I frantically switched dials and levers, but I was rapidly losing altitude, and there was nothing I could do about it. My equipment was malfunctioning, and it took me about two seconds flat to realize that my jet had been tampered with. My stomach churned quickly piecing it together—*the bad intel.*

"Mayday! Mayday!" I called through the comms as black edged at my vision.

I plummeted down the side of the craggy mountains with nothing but dark earth in my field of vision, suddenly realizing something horrific.

"Eject! Eject! Eject!" someone screamed through the comms, not realizing what I'd figured out a mere second earlier—*the release was jammed.*

"Bailout!" they screamed, but I couldn't.

The ground was closing in with alarming speed, and I was frantic, but no matter how hard I pulled, I was stuck.

I knew I only had seconds, and the only thing I could think in that moment was *this was going to break her—but at least she knew I loved her.*

Everything went quiet, and I knew this was it—with tears streaming down my cheeks, I shakily let go of the release.

And then I braced for impact.

CHAPTER 47

Intuition

SARAFINA

I stood in my art studio, hands on my hips as I stared at the massive canvas in front of me, desperately struggling to paint. I tried to tell myself that the churning feeling in my gut, the fact that I hadn't heard from Carter in several weeks, was just an over-reaction.

But every day that I didn't hear from him, it became harder and harder to convince myself that I *was* overreacting.

I'd made a promise to Carter before he'd left that I'd try to keep my anxiety in check. We'd shared many long, frustrating conversations about scenarios just like this. Where he'd be unable to contact me for weeks or possibly months on end—only he was supposed to eventually call me, tease me about being so worried and tell me everything was okay. That he was coming home.

I knew the rules—anytime I felt anxious about not hearing from him, I had to text him. So I did. All the freaking time I did, and every day that passed without getting a response, was absolute hell.

Today, even with the pit in my stomach that I couldn't seem to shake, I had somehow managed to get into that elusive flow state while I painted.

Dip, dab, stroke. The smell of the paint, the feel of the brush dragging across the canvas. Those messages would come through. Any day now.

I was humming along to the music when my studio door creaked open unexpectedly, and I spun around ready to rip Vaughn a new one—but I was startled to see Liam standing in the doorway, with Vaughn just behind him.

I read the expression in both their eyes, the tight posture, the worry, and I could suddenly hear my heartbeat in my ears as everything went quiet—numb. I didn't even have to hear the words, because I already knew.

It was all bullshit. I'd known deep down in my gut that something was wrong. And I'd fucking ignored it. Ignored *him*. I'd gotten so used to writing off that gut feeling, and now my worst nightmare was about to be a waking reality.

I dizzily sank into a chair, eyes shuttering as I waited for the words.

"There's no easy way to say this, so I'm just going to come right out and say it." Liam murmured, "*Carter's missing.*"

CHAPTER 48

Pudding Cups

SARAFINA

Inside the Montclair Medical Center, Briar Rose's private hospital, the smell of disinfectant stung my nose as I rushed down the hallways, refusing to cry.

Liam's grounding presence followed closely behind, and if he wasn't clearly on the verge of tears himself, I could have just reamed him. They'd found Carter, and Liam had spent the last week getting him home. He'd known for over a week where Carter was, and he hadn't said a word—because *he didn't want to get my hopes up;* which was a horrifying truth all on its own. But precious days he'd known, while I puked my guts up, and now Carter might not even—

No, I wasn't going to lose it until I saw him, until I got to his room. Worrying wouldn't help him, I knew that—but it didn't matter, the guilt was thick as mud to wade through anyway. I'd known something was wrong for weeks because I'd felt it. *Felt him.*

My lunch threatened to make a reappearance as the numbers crawled higher on the doors and then, *there he was.*

Even from the hallway, my throat seized up. Even from here, I could see how black and blue his face was. A strangled noise clawed its way out of my throat as I lingered on the threshold.

Liam's hand was a solid, comforting weight at my back as I hovered in the hallway on the verge of collapsing, because when I stepped through the door, it'd finally be real, but out here, it was just a bad dream.

A few people were already in the room, and they cleared out as I drifted closer, watching the nurse change his IV bag—he was just laying there, so incredibly still.

"Carter?" I approached the hospital bed, already sobbing. "Can he hear me?" I choked out.

"He might be able to. We can't say for sure." The nurse shot me a sympathetic look as she finished up. "There certainly isn't any harm in trying." She nodded reassuringly as she closed us into the private hospital suite.

I covered my mouth, failing to silence another sob.

We loved each other. That had to mean something. To someone, somewhere. *It had to.*

Liam and the others fell into quiet conversation with the nurse in the hallway, and I pulled up the padded armchair. It slid easily across the smooth floor as I brought it right to the edge of Carter's hospital bed.

I so very gently took Carter's hand in mine, not caring about Liam seeing, and folded over onto the bed and wept. Even his hands and arms were bruised. He'd always held me like I was something delicate and fragile, *precious*, and now it was *him* I was worried about breaking.

In the car, on the way to the hospital, Liam had warned me, told me that Carter was in rough shape. It wasn't exactly clear to me what had happened in the days he'd been missing, but the fact that he was breathing on his own—that there was no major organ damage, was a good sign. The only problem, we wouldn't know until he woke up if he had *brain damage*.

With every sniffle, I got another smell of his skin, and it smelled awful. Wrong. Like chemicals and sickness, and that made me cry even harder.

A tissue was pressed into my hand, and when I finally lifted my head to blow my nose, I realized several more people had arrived. Jules dabbed her eyes with her own tissue and squeezed my shoulder. Next to her, Sloane's lip trembled while she tried her very best to give me a reassuring look, but I could see it in everyone's expressions. No one expected him to pull through.

Liam was stoic, leaning against a shelf at the back of the room, staring into space with glassy eyes. Several of Carter's guy friends had settled in at a card table in the corner and were talking softly. I recognized a few of them, Ethan from the restaurant, several of the Kingsley brothers, Cade and his cousins, someone I was pretty sure Carter had worked with on base—I'd seen a picture. There were flowers, and cards, and balloons in every corner of the room—and while I hated it so much that I'd been one of the last people to know, it was proof that *so* many people cared about him. *That had to mean something.*

I forced myself to look at Carter's face again. Forced myself to keep it together. Crying wasn't going to help him any, but maybe feeling all the love from everybody in this room would.

I gently squeezed his hand. "Carter?" My voice came out disgustingly clogged from all the crying, and I didn't expect him to respond, but a part of me hoped he would.

He didn't. He only breathed in-and-out in slow, steady beats. Otherwise completely unresponsive, but I watched the heart monitor, grateful for each and every one of those heartbeats.

"I missed you." I cleared my throat, offering him a reassuring smile he couldn't see. "So much." The palms of his hands were calloused and familiar against my skin as I promised. "You're going to get through this. You take all the time you need, because I'll be right here with you every step of the way." I was crying again. "Well, actually, it'd be great if you decided to wake up *sooner* rather than *later*." I gripped his hand tighter, swearing I could sense him squeezing back, but I knew I was just imagining it.

"You have to wake up for me." I lowered my voice to a soft,

inaudible whisper to beg. *"Please don't leave me, Carter, because I don't know if I can go on without you."*

~

I wasn't sure how long I sat like that, but eventually I heard Liam murmur that he was going to pick up our dinner. I cast him a long look and found him exhausted and puffy-eyed as he left the room.

Not caring if anyone else saw, I finally climbed into the hospital bed and curled myself around Carter's too-still body, feeling like I was on the verge of passing out from emotional exhaustion.

"Just remember you love me." I whispered, leaving him a soft kiss on the corner of his bruised mouth, hardly able to continue, "And I love you."

In that moment, I knew if he ever woke up—I wasn't going to hold anything back anymore. I was going to let him all the way in. I had to, because the fear, the nerves, it all seemed inconsequential now. Silly. I should have tried harder, been more honest, more open with him so much sooner.

I drifted off to the sound of quiet voices murmuring as more of Carter's friends showed up, but I didn't bother greeting any of them. I couldn't.

I awoke to the crumpling sound of food bags, and a moment later I felt my brother's steady arms slide beneath me before he settled me onto the couch, planting himself right next to me as he crushed me against him and I sobbed.

I don't know how I even got the words out because I just couldn't stop crying. "They said they don't even know if he'll wake up, we just have to wait." I'd heard the question asked again and again, as more people filtered in and out, and a little piece of me had died every time the nurses answered.

"I know." Liam murmured, his own voice raw, like he'd been

crying in the car. "We should go home, get some rest. We can come back in the morning."

I didn't want to leave. I wanted to climb right back into the bed and sleep next to Carter. Next to the man I loved. Chemical smell and all. I wanted to talk to him, just in case he was in there somewhere. Just in case I could convince him to try his hardest to come back to me.

Panic threatened to take me out at the knees, and in a split decision, I decided I couldn't let it. Carter needed me to be strong for him, so I would be. This wasn't like what had happened with my mother. He would pull through *because he had to*.

"He's going to be okay." I announced with a nod as I stood up and straightened myself, adding simply. "He's strong, and he has a lot to live for."

"I certainly hope so," Liam offered emptily.

"Go fish." I admired Carter's face as he laid there, unaware of our riveting game. Even swollen and bruised to high heaven, he was still so handsome.

I finally sighed and threw my cards down, tired of playing by myself.

Footsteps sounded behind me—Sloane was here for her shift. "I was thinking for lunch we could get some Thai food today." I started, but when I turned, it wasn't Sloane at all. It was a man I didn't recognize. I sucked in a surprised breath and stood, an uneasiness I couldn't explain, washing over me.

He was extremely tall, maybe even taller than Carter, wearing an expensive-looking suit that perfectly fit his broad muscular frame beneath. Gold rings flashed on his tattooed fingers.

"I'm sorry, I thought you were—" The way he was looking at Carter made my pulse spike. "Who are you exactly?" I asked, coming to the foot of the bed between the stranger and Carter.

"An old friend, and you must be?"

His smile made me swallow hard. I wanted to shrink as he stepped closer, but I forced myself to hold my ground. Some part of me knew I couldn't let him get anywhere near Carter.

"Sarafina Devereux, I believe?" he said, slowly coming to his own conclusion as he removed the toothpick that had been hanging out of his mouth.

In the silence between us, his eyes dragged down. Whether he was checking me out or assessing me, looking for something, I couldn't tell. Either way, I didn't like it one bit.

With the hair on my arms raised, I didn't bother sticking my hand out. "I don't believe we've met." I didn't like being in the same room with the man, let alone voluntarily touching him.

His features were sharp, eyes dark, and everything about him felt dangerous as he huffed a deep laugh. "I suppose not, though from what I know, that one has a real soft spot for you." He nodded to Carter.

The man still didn't bother introducing himself, and that's when I noticed he wasn't wearing a visitor badge. I inched towards the nurse's call button as my heart started to race with fear.

The button was on the other side of Carter's body; there was no way for me to reach it discreetly, and I got the sense that if I dove for it, I wouldn't get there first. "How do you know Carter exactly?" My voice came out too strained, giving away my nerves.

"We have an understanding." The man said with a predatory tilt of his head, and I wondered what the hell that was supposed to mean. "At least we will." He gave me a smile like the Cheshire Cat, and I realized he knew exactly what I was doing.

His gaze suddenly flicked to the monitor as Carter's heartbeat spiked, and I whirled, shocked to see Carter's fingers twitch. I slid my hand into his. "Carter?" I breathed, hope exploding in my chest.

Eyes still closed, he weakly murmured something inaudible.

I leaned over the bed, careful of his IV. "I'm here, baby. I'm right here." I took his face gently in both hands. "Carter, it's Sara.

Can you say that again?" His eyes remained closed, and he murmured again. "I can't understand you, but I'm here." I tried again, my excitement growing. He was waking up!

"My strawberry's." He mumbled out so quietly, I wasn't sure if I'd heard him right.

"You want strawberries?" I asked excitedly, knowing I'd bring him an entire truckload of them, but he didn't respond again.

I suddenly remembered to hit the nurse's call button, and that's when I realized the stranger was long gone. Thank God.

"He's awake, he woke up." I was buzzing with excitement and hope as Andie, the nurse I'd gotten to know a little bit, came in. "I mean, kind of." I wrung my hands. "What do we do?"

Andie smiled warmly and started checking his vitals. "Now, we wait."

Hours later, when Carter had finally come to, I was ready to put him right back under.

His first coherent words to me were utter delusion. "We need to break up." And my first thought was, *oh fuck, he has brain damage.*

We were going to be like that movie, 30 First Dates or whatever. Only he was Drew Barrymore... which I supposed made me Adam Sandler. Which was honestly sort of fitting, but he was alive and I loved him, so I'd do whatever it took, for as long as it took.

Concerned, I reached for him, but Carter withdrew, a hard, cold look in his expression that made my stomach sink. "You've been through a lot." I started quietly, "And you don't know what you're saying."

"I do know what I'm saying." He stared at the wall behind me, refusing to look at me with those purple-ringed eyes. "More than you know."

"Carter, look at me." I tried gently.

His gaze dropped to his hands. "I've made up my mind. It's over. We're done."

Something in me erupted, overriding the panic. I was sleep deprived, I'd missed lunch, my emotions were so strung out I didn't even know how I'd kept it together, and now this?

Fury didn't even begin to describe it. I'd been at his bedside day and night, worried sick. This stupid idiot had nearly gotten himself killed, and now he was pulling this shit?!

"If you wanted to get rid of me, you should have stayed comatose." I snapped angrily as Carter blinked, his greasy hair sticking in every direction. "We love each other, remember?! So you're not getting rid of me when I don't even know if it's you or the brain damage talking."

His jaw flexed for the longest second of my life as I gaped at him. "That was before. This is now." He said firmly.

"Are you kidding me?" I demanded. "Are you seriously trying to break up with me right now?"

"I'm not *trying* anything. I *did* break up with you, and you're just going to have to accept that." Carter bit out so cooly that I wanted to strangle him with his own IV tube. We were in a hospital. They'd already brought him back once. They could do it again.

Ultimately, I decided not to strangle the love of my life with my bare hands, purely on the principle of the matter. "Un-fuck-ing-believable." I stormed out of the room, past Liam, who was mouth agape in the doorway next to Cade.

"The fuck did you just say?" Liam demanded.

I shot Carter a look over my shoulder. "*That* is your fault." I ignored Liam's stream of outraged questions as I added sourly, "Have fun with that, Kensington. I'll go ahead and order the dentures for you too because you're gonna fucking need them! Because if Liam doesn't do it, I swear to God, I'll knock out your perfectly straight teeth myself!" Carter looked stunned as I shouted at him, and the peanut gallery stifled shocked, wide-eyed, disbelieving laughs from the corner of the room. "I've been sitting at your bedside day and night, worried sick, and I warned you what would happen if you got yourself killed, so don't look so surprised—and will somebody get the damn doctor up here to look at his stupid brain already!?" I demanded, holding back a sob.

I practically stomped down to the cafeteria like King-Kong and angrily ate a chocolate pudding cup, unable to finish it as I finally burst into tears.

A little while later, I smelled Sloane's signature perfume behind me, and she rounded the cafeteria table and slid into the chair across from me.

"How mad is Liam?" I asked, staring into the abyss of my pudding cup, feeling nauseous.

"If Carter wasn't already in a hospital bed, I'm pretty sure Liam would have put him in one." What a mess. "It'll all work out." She gripped my hand across the table and grimaced. "He's probably disoriented, and he's obviously been through hell—I'm sure he's not thinking clearly yet, even if he thinks he is."

I nodded, hoping she was right, but a small part of me knew she wasn't. "You think I should go up there and check on him—on Liam?" I sighed halfway, wishing Liam *would* knock his teeth out. Maybe knock the sense right back into him, I certainly wanted to.

"Cade is trying to talk Liam down right now," Sloane said. "Plus, Theo and his cousins are up there. They won't let Liam hurt him. At least not while he's still in a hospital bed." Sloane nodded confidently. "Let's give it a few minutes."

Only I knew a few minutes wasn't going to change his mind. I'd seen the look in his eyes. Seen the determination to push me away.

Why? I couldn't say exactly. But he'd done it before, and I knew exactly what it looked like, and even worse, what it felt like.

CHAPTER 49

I Know You

CARTER

Standing in my kitchen, I knocked back a second pill from my prescription bottle as a pounding headache stabbed through my head, threatening to turn into another nasty migraine.

Liam yelling at me from across my new penthouse in the city wasn't helping.

But this was progress, at least. The yelling.

"How. Long. Has this been going on?" Liam demanded, and I realized he'd stopped yelling long enough to actually ask a question.

I stared at the ceiling, *since the moment I laid eyes on her.* "Halloween." I admitted.

Back at the hospital, he'd ripped me a new one, but this was essentially the first time he'd spoken to me since—he'd made a special visit just to ream me. Again.

Liam stared at me, jaw rippling. "Did you sleep with her?"

"I—" My lips formed and then unformed the words. What the hell was I supposed to say? I didn't want to lie to him, but any version of the truth was only going to make things worse. "We—"

His eyes narrowed. "I knew it was fucking weird that she was in your lap on Halloween." I could see his wheels turning, and I closed my eyes, just waiting for it. "Was that my sister's dildo in your bed?" Liam demanded. "Fuck!" He shoved both hands through his hair, still pacing furiously. "I don't even know if I want you to answer that." He stopped and stared at me, wheels turning, a shred of hope still there. "Kensington, I need you to be straight with me. Did you sleep with my sister?"

I was about to lose my best friend, but if it meant protecting the woman I loved, it was a painful cost I was willing to pay. "Technically, no," I muttered, hating how awful that sounded.

"Technically?" He growled darkly, fists curling and uncurling.

I dragged two hands over my face in exasperation. "What the hell do you want me to say, Liam?"

"The truth!" He demanded.

I didn't say anything more, and that was damning enough.

Liam shook his head in outraged disbelief. "I thought I knew you." Then, "Actually, fuck that. I *do* know you. Which is exactly why I told you to stay the hell away from her."

"Liam—"

He pointed a trembling finger at me, every word seething. "I warned you."

I put my hands up, muttering quietly, "I know."

"There was a reason I told you to stay the hell away from her." He was barely contained as his voice cracked. "Because even at twelve, I saw the way she looked at you—*the way she always looks at you*. Damn it, Carter! I *knew* you'd break her fucking heart."

There it was—the truth of how my best friend saw me.

And just like that, I was alone in the world again—I'd just lost the one friend I could always count on.

I'd known it was coming, but I prickled all the same because Sara hadn't just been a friend with benefits, or a fuck buddy, or whatever he thought. She'd been my *everything,* and it'd been the best few months of my life, finally acting on what I'd been feeling for years.

"It's not what you think." I started, knowing I should just

keep my mouth shut, but the truth gnawed at me and I couldn't stop myself from trying to right the pain of his words. "Liam, I lo—"

"No! You do not get to speak right now." He growled. "Because I swear to God if you weren't still recovering, I'd knock your fucking teeth out."

I'd deserve it too. The look on her face. The shock—the quick recalibration as she put a brave smile on, instead of crumbling, while I broke both our hearts, telling myself it was for her own good. But the truth was, in those flashes of consciousness between the excruciating pain, I'd come to a single realization—my crash was a perfectly timed attempted murder, and I only had myself to blame because The Society had warned me, clear as day. They threatened *my* life, and they'd threatened *hers*, because of what she meant to me—I'd been naïve, not realizing their connections went all the way to the top, even in the military.

I'd survived that crash by mere luck. A miracle if I dared to believe in such things, and when I didn't kick the can like they'd planned, they'd done the next best thing. Ended my career. Issued an honorable discharge without medical evaluation or opportunity for reinstatement. Continuing to toy with me, brazenly flaunting their power—making it clear that even if they couldn't kill me, they could still control me. *Take away the things I loved.*

In the passing weeks since leaving the hospital, I'd launched a private investigation. Only the jet in question had mysteriously disappeared. To cover foul play, no doubt.

The only question was, what did The Society want from me that was worth killing for? I wasn't naïve enough to believe it was a square of dirt anymore.

The first time they'd approached me, I'd been a heartbroken teenager. I'd been badgered by them so many times over the years. It'd almost become mundane, and I'd never slowed long enough to look at the absurdity of the whole thing, and after the initial attack, I fucking should have. They'd tried to kill me, and they'd threatened to kill Sara—I could kick myself for being so damn careless with the only thing that really mattered to me. Which was precisely why I had to let Sara go.

For years, I'd tried to avoid the mess that my father had left behind, not really understanding the magnitude of it, but there was no hiding it, no sweeping it under the rug. No, the problem was going to knit itself a goddamn sweater and try to strangle me with all the loose threads.

I was more than ready to burn it all down, and I didn't want Sara going up in the flames too. The simple fact was that with me she'd always be a target. They had known what she meant to me, had threatened her by name, and I'd let my emotions get the better of me. I'd shown them the cards in my hand, and I couldn't regret it more.

The Society had taken just about everything from me. My family. My health. My career. Sara was the *only* thing I had left, and I wasn't about to let them take her, too. I loved her with everything I was, which is exactly why I had to let her go, because if something happened to her because of me—

"Are you even listening to me?" Liam shouted angrily. "She's just barely putting herself back together again. You have no idea what she's been through." He swallowed hard, his voice nearly cracking. "What she's dealing with, *even now.*" I wondered what he was even talking about, what other secrets Sara had kept tucked away. Though I supposed I couldn't be upset when I was keeping secrets of my own. "Just—stay the fuck away from her." He pleaded. "If you ever cared about her at all, just leave her the hell alone."

I was spiraling into the depths now, and I wouldn't take her into the darkness with me. Not with my chunky knit sweater, not with anything. "That's exactly what I'm doing." I muttered.

"Really? Do you know what you're doing?" He narrowed his eyes as he laid into me. "Because it seems like you're just fucking around, with total disregard for a girl who has been through hell and back." He shouted, "I would think you of all people would understand how difficult this has been for her."

"You don't think I know that." I shouted back, head pulsating. I felt like I was going to puke, but I wasn't entirely sure it was the headache.

He looked at me point-blank. "Stay the hell away from her. Or I'll fucking kill you." He headed for the door without a second glance. "I mean it, Kensington."

I groaned, wincing as I sagged onto the couch. Everything hurt.

Halfway through the door, Liam added, "And take a goddamn shower, would you. It smells like a frat house in here." The walls shook as he slammed the door.

I had bet everything, and I'd lost even more. I felt like an empty shell.

The TV burned the backs of my retinas as I stared into the blue pixels, not really watching it at all.

Only one thing mattered now.

Revenge.

Suddenly, my penthouse door exploded in a burst of thunderous knocks.

"Let me in, you stupid boy," Sara shouted from the hallway.

My shoulders sagged, and I reprimanded myself for the relief I felt hearing her voice. I was supposed to be strong enough to let her go, but I wasn't even close.

If I got off this couch and opened that door, I was going to let her inside. So despite her shouting from the hallway, I walked into my home office and ignored her altogether.

It was easy to ignore her too because I could hardly hear. That was another thing they'd taken from me. My hearing. I was fucking deaf in my left ear. Permanent.

I stewed on that fact and quirked my head, wondering why it

sounded like Sara's shouting was coming from inside. "Don't you dare ignore me."

My stomach dropped when she waltzed into the room looking like a bright star, a smile painted across her face, eyes alive. For me. Even while she was yelling at me. "How did you even get in here?" I rocked back in my office chair, feeling simultaneously devastated and relieved to see her.

Her eyes flicked over my bare chest, the dirty sweats I'd been in for days. "I thought you'd try to ignore me again today." She announced, "So I took the liberty of making friends with the front desk. But you apparently don't lock your door, so I guess that was unnecessary on my part."

I groaned and dragged a hand over my stubbled face. "Why are you here?"

"In case you forgot, we love each other." She bristled. "And whatever brain damage you've sustained is not going to change that." She waved around me irreverently.

"I don't have brain damage." I sighed. "I just—"

"I know, I know. You can't hear." She cut me off. "But guess what? You actually *can* hear, because you just heard what I said. Good thing you have two of those things on your head, isn't it?" She looked at me for a moment, taking in my disheveled state. "I'm not going to lie, I don't mind the scruff." She scrunched her nose. "But when was the last time you showered?" I could only groan.

She turned and hauled the heavy grocery bags in her hands into the kitchen, and I followed her, hating how good she looked from behind. Hating how good her skin felt when I brushed my hand against hers, reaching for the grocery bags.

"Don't." She snapped, yanking back sharply. "You shouldn't be lifting heavy things." I reluctantly let go as she went right back to her cheery tone. "I'm not saying it doesn't suck, but I am saying you're alive and you still have one good ear. So we should try to be grateful for that."

I really didn't deserve her. Even after what I'd said... she was still here, still showing up for me. Why was this so fucking diffi-cult? For both of us.

"Sara—you really shouldn't be here." I rubbed my thumb against my palm. I didn't doubt *they* were watching the building, tracking who came and went. If I was going to keep her safe, I needed to keep her *far away* from me; otherwise, this whole charade was pointless. "It's—it's over between us." The words felt like ash in my mouth.

She crossed her arms and glared at me. "You said you wouldn't let anybody hurt me ever again." She quoted me, and I grimaced. "Not even yourself."

"That's what I'm doing."

"Is it? Or are you pushing me away because you're scared?" She raised a brow. "I know that I can't understand what you've been through." She started slowly. "And I know you're upset about your hearing and your career, but I love you, Carter, and you love me." Her eyes softened. "You were there for me when I couldn't reach back out and take the hand you were giving me, and now, that's exactly what I'm doing for you. Whatever you need, I'm here for you. We'll get through this." Her mouth pulled into a sad smile. "Together."

My heart sank—I was going to have to hurt her to make her leave. Fuck! Why couldn't she just listen to me and walk away. Why couldn't she just do what was best for her. Why'd she have to be such a goddamn angel. And why, for fuck's sake why, couldn't I just let her go.

I had to. For her safety. I had to. I'd *never* forgive myself if something happened to her because of me. I'd never been good enough for her, anyway. She deserved someone good and now I was all fucked up inside. Broken.

"What I need is for you to leave." I steadied myself, reminding myself that she had to believe what I was saying, otherwise, this was pointless. "Thing is, Sara, I don't want this anymore. Us." I practically choked on the words as I watched them chip away at her resolve. Just barely.

I forced myself to keep going. "Every thing was different when this was long distance. It was just a nice idea." I fucking deserved to go to hell. "Now—you just don't fit into my life anymore." I said cooly. There went another chip of her confidence and another shard of my heart. "My career is over, and the only thing left for me to do is to pick up where my father left off, and that requires a certain lifestyle."

She scoffed. "A certain lifestyle? What the hell is that even supposed to mean?"

"I can't be tied down." I hardened my face while I watched myself break her heart. "I need to keep my options open." I didn't even know what the hell kind of excuse that was.

"You're trying to break up with me so you can fuck around?" She demanded. "Because what? It's good for business?"

I was going to puke. "Yeah, I guess I am." My head was pounding even harder, and I'd never hated myself more.

She waved down her body, and I swallowed hard. "Go ahead —fuck around." She demanded. "You've been *so* careful around me, wanting to take things slow." She seethed dramatically. "So, which is it? Do you love me so much you have to stay away, or do you not care at all and you can just fuck me?" She unzipped her jacket and threw it on the ground, revealing the most innocent amount of skin, and it was still far too much. "Which is it, Carter? Hmm?"

"Stop." I breathed, gripping the marble countertop.

"Here's an idea for you—if you're going to throw me away, you might as well actually *use* me first." She laughed humorlessly while my heart cleaved in half. "Come on, *fuck-boy*, let's go!" She started to yank her hair out of her ponytail, but aggressively halted. "Oh wait, I forgot. You *like* my hair up." Her shirt was up over her head next, leaving her in a white, lacy, everyday bra that pushed her perfect tits up just right. "Because I know things about you, Carter. Like when you're bullshitting me, for instance." My heart thundered in my chest as she reached behind her back for her bra clasp.

I wasn't strong enough for this. To deny her. Panic seized me. "Stop." I demanded, slamming my fist down on the counter, freezing her in her tracks. "You're not listening to me. I don't want you here." I bit out. "Why don't you get that?"

She crossed the room, and my eyes shuddered as she rested her hands on my bare chest so gently and gazed up at me, pleading. "Why are you doing this, Carter?" Her voice was so small, hurt. "What changed?"

She was too damn close, smelled so sweet and soft—like home, but she was never going to be my home. That had been a pipe dream, and I was ignorant for ever pretending otherwise.

I gripped her wrists to keep from taking her face and kissing her. "You ever think there was a reason Liam told me to stay away from you?" I whispered. "*I'm no good for you.*"

"I can see through this." She breathed all too knowingly. "What you're doing." She moved to pull away, but I couldn't let go, and she stilled. "I just don't know why you're doing it." She pleaded. "Just tell me why. Please."

"I can't commit." I admitted, grasping at straws. "I've never been able to. You know that about me." The truth was, nobody had been her—because I was terrified to lose anyone else I loved—that I wasn't strong enough, that I refused to endanger her in whatever mess I was now smack dab in the middle of.

"Whatever twisted punishment you think this is—that you deserve. You don't." She pleaded. "Carter, you're good. You're so good. Please don't throw everything we have into the dumpster fire that is my life right now."

I cupped her face because I just couldn't help myself. I hated how selfish I was, that even when I was breaking her heart, I was still taking from her. That I needed her touch to ground me while I worked up the courage to break her heart. I was a fucking asshole. "You're a great girl, Sara. You're just not great for me." I braced myself for the final blow. "I just need someone less needy."

She jerked back as if I'd burned her.

Good. I'd done it. I'd taken her biggest fear and used it against her.

I was lower than low. *I was nothing.*

I felt faint as her lip wobbled, and she straightened. "I would say I would try to be less needy for you, but I'm not going to bother. You stood by me at my worst, at my ugliest." She said with surprising strength, though her voice trembled. "And as someone who's been living at rock bottom for a while now, I know what you're doing. You're pushing me away. For reasons I don't understand, and you're being damn cruel while you're doing it." She added as tears started rolling down her cheeks. "But *I love you, Carter.* I know you, and I know when you're bullshitting me." I swallowed hard as she grabbed her shirt, quickly throwing it on, her voice quickly losing more and more bite. "So, I'm sorry, you big jerk. You're not getting rid of me just because you're hurting." She stormed towards the door, wiping her cheeks. "I'll see you tomorrow. Same place. Same time." She sobbed a broken laugh as she stopped in the threshold, something quiet and confident shining in her eyes even as they shimmered with hurt. "I *know* you love me too, and I'll give you all the time you need to remember it." She refused to blink, but a tear rolled down her cheek anyway.

This was torture. I wanted to apologize, to tell her I didn't mean any of it, but I didn't. If I loved her, then I would keep my goddamn mouth shut. So that's what I did, tasting blood as I literally bit my tongue because my insides were screaming for her. This was how it had to be in order to keep her safe, to keep her *alive*—I wouldn't become my father and let Sara end up like my mother. *Collateral damage.*

The door slammed, leaving me all alone, and once again it was because of the mess my father had left behind. I knew I should be used to it by now, but I wasn't.

I staggered to the counter, hating myself. My medication was kicking in and my heart raced faster, each breath coming a little more shallow than the last.

Fuck, when I got emotional. When was the last time I'd eaten something? My blood sugar was way too low. I gripped the counter weakly, feeling the edges of my vision closing in as I tried to stagger into the kitchen.

The door banged open. "You made me so mad I forgot my purse." I slid down the counter. "Carter!" My head hit the ground, erupting in another sickening migraine. Sara's panicked scream was the last thing I heard before I blacked out.

It was dark out when I woke up in my bed. Sara's chest was rising and falling peacefully as she slept fully clothed, curled up beside me.

How she'd gotten me into the bed in the first place, I had no idea, and then I realized I had an IV in my arm—she called the doctor over, because of course she had.

I rolled onto my side and felt a tear slip down my cheek as I stared at her face, illuminated in the moonlight. The soft slope of her nose, her dark lashes against her full cheeks. I wanted to reach out and touch her, but I didn't. She was too good for me, and I didn't deserve her, even when I wasn't being the world's biggest ass.

Which is why I had to make her let me go before it was too late. I quietly slipped out of the bed, angrily ripped the IV out, focusing on the sting of pain and wandered into my office, sitting in front of my too-bright computer screen.

That's when I noticed the stack of mail on the desk because, of course, she'd brought the mail in. I shook my head, and then a small black envelope caught my attention, and my heart stopped beating altogether.

I cracked the wax seal and slid the heavy envelope open.

An address and a date. *Let's put this behind us once and for all.*

I knew the letter for what it was, not an invitation at all, but a threat. And the only thing they could use against me was currently lying in my bed, looking like an angel.

For her own safety, I needed her far, far away from me, because when I started tipping the dominoes I'd been setting up these last few weeks, I wasn't entirely sure that I wouldn't be the last one to fall.

I quickly responded to my PR team's most recent email, wondering if it was a huge mistake, but as soon as Sara let me go —I could burn it all down and maybe I'd let the flames consume me too.

CHAPTER 50

A Spiral of Chaos

SARAFINA

"Did you see?" Jules worried voice asked through the speakerphone from the kitchen counter.

"See what?" I asked, mulling through Liam's fridge absent-mindedly.

"I texted you." Sloane explained. "Let's not jump to conclusions, it was probably staged."

I had a cheese stick hanging out of my mouth. "Hold on, I'm pulling it up." I leaned over the counter and opened the message, looking at the picture she'd sent me. The cheese stick dropped to the floor as I gasped.

"Oh, shit." Jules breathed. "I knew she hadn't seen it—do you want us to come over?"

A lump formed in my throat, and I couldn't find the words to respond.

I'd given Carter the space he'd asked for and had waited several weeks before driving back to the city. Big mistake.

～

"Didn't know those short little legs could go so fast." Vaughn

muttered under his breath when I shoved through the Vandenbergh building doors faster than he could open them for me.

"Try to keep up, would you?" I stomped through the massive
lobby towards the elevators.

"I would not want to be him." He muttered, following closely
behind.

"No, you would not." I smashed the elevator buttons,
grinding my teeth as the doors slid shut. Up, up, up we rode, the
elevator music comically perky despite the fact that I was
seeing *red*.

Vaughn cleared his throat, breaking the silence. "You think
you're going to be a while?" He asked warily.

I quirked a brow sassily. "Why? Do you have somewhere you
need to be?"

He put his hands up in surrender. "I was just going to check
in with the boss upstairs."

"Sure." I shrugged dramatically. "And why don't you get yourself a little ice cream cone while you're at it." I didn't know if I'd
ever been so brazen, but Vaughn was a dick. He could take it.

"Just call me when you're done." He sighed as I marched off
the elevator.

I banged through the ten-foot wooden doors into Cade's
office. "Sup, small fry?" Cade rumbled from behind his desk as I
stormed in. "*Damn, girl.*" He hooked a thumb at me. "Check out
the drip on this one." I'd gone shopping, gotten a blowout,
bought a new dress. I looked incredible because I was out for
fucking blood.

"Get out." I screeched at Cade, kicking him out of his own
office.

"I can see you two need a minute." Cade dipped his head and
wisely pushed out of his chair, heading for the door.

"Sorry, Cade." Carter sighed, shoulders sagging.

"Feel free to Picasso it up in here, and paint me a pretty
picture with all the blood." Cade whirled, smirking at me as he
grabbed a decanter of amber liquid, and then he had the idiotic

audacity to proposition me, while steam was practically blowing out of my ears. "And when you're done with this idiot, I'd be more than happy to sponsor your next shopping spree." He winked. "I could show you a real good time in the dressing rooms too. You, me, and some three-sixty mirrors—"

"In your dreams, Blackthorn." I snapped at the same moment Carter barked, "Get out!"

Cade just shrugged as he lingered in the doorway with a smirk. "All I'm saying is—if someone is going to have hate sex on my desk, I think it should be me." Carter was halfway to the door when Cade finally shut it, grinning like the shit-stirrer he was.

I stopped Carter in his tracks, redirecting my own vitriol. "Carter Ambrose Kensington, what do you have to say for yourself? Because I don't think you have any right to be pissed at Cade. Not after what I saw in the tabloids this morning." Carter quickly turned, heading towards the tall windows that overlooked the city in a futile attempt to escape my wrath. "Don't you dare walk away from me." I snapped. Cade's office was big, but not that big.

Carter was *supposed* to be recovering, but I guess he was busy. Busy working with Cade, doing God knows what, and apparently —busy *kissing other people*. Tall, beautiful blonde people with impossibly perky tits, because *blondes had always been his type*. In fact, I didn't know if I'd ever seen him with a brunette growing up. Never. I wondered if I should have plopped down in Cade's lap and laid a big, wet, sloppy one on him to kick this whole thing off. See how Carter liked that.

"What are you doing here?" Carter asked, eyes flashing with pain, but I didn't feel a damned bit sorry for him.

"I'm checking on you, like I do every day." Even as I yelled, I hated how badly I wanted him to wrap me up in his arms and tell me everything was going to be okay. How badly I wanted him to tell me it was all just for show. A bit. A game. Not fucking real. I of all people, knew how easily the media could use a photo to paint a story that wasn't even remotely true. I would probably have been named Briar Rose's sluttiest socialite if I hadn't bought out the images straight from the photographers, *or worse.*

So it was entirely possible the blonde in the photo had literally thrown herself at him, because women *actually* did that when it came to Carter.

Please, please, please let it be a PR stunt.

"Yeah, well, you're not my girlfriend anymore, so don't." Carter bit out sharply, shoving his hands into his pockets.

I smarted back, pretending to be shocked. "Wow, I haven't heard that ten times in the last month."

"Maybe you should start listening."

"You know how I know you still care?"

"How's that?" He didn't bother looking down at me.

"Because I still have my plane." It had to be a sign.

A muscle ticked in his jaw. "It was a gift."

"And because you authorized all the charges, I made this morning." I shook my arms, showing him what I'd bought on his dime—a new set of diamond everything, and shoes. Really freaking cute shoes, too. Something, anything, to get his attention.

"I gave you that card to use if you needed it." He shrugged indifferently, but I had spent *a lot.* Maybe too much. Like maybe I should return the jewelry at least.

"Because you care about me." I practically screamed. "And by the way, I hope all this sparkly stuff puts a dent in things." I crossed my arms, feeling ridiculous as the chunky diamond bracelets clinked against each other. It wasn't my style at all, but that wasn't the point. The point was, I'd spent upwards of forty million dollars on diamonds and he hadn't even so much as flinched—on a Tuesday!

"It didn't." He almost smirked but quickly dropped the corner of his mouth when I shot him a murderous look.

What. A. Prick. Filthy rich *asshole.*

The tiny pendant he'd given me for my birthday burned against my sternum, practically mocking me from beneath the gaudy diamond-cluster-necklace currently attempting to strangle me.

I could feel myself getting flustered, pissed off that I couldn't get a rise out of him. I'd hoped a shopping spree on Mr. Frugal's card would elicit some sort of reaction, and this was rather disappointing if I was being honest.

"Fine, then I'll make a really, really *big* charitable donation on your behalf—how about fifty million to the Montclair Medical Center! How about that!" I threatened rather petulantly, wondering if that'd be enough to make him flinch.

This time he did smirk. "You go right ahead and do that, and while you're at it, why don't you go ahead and double it. Make it a nice round hundred—and then you can double *that*, pretty girl." He winced, catching himself using his favorite term of endearment while I erupted.

"Fine!" I shouted, with a stomp of my foot. "I will." Asshole!

A tense silence hung between us for a long while, as the question I really wanted to ask tightened around my throat like a noose. I didn't voice it as I motioned to the paperwork that had been between him and Cade, my voice feeling thin. "What's all this?"

He shifted uncomfortably. "Just business."

"Carter, I'm worried about you." I apparently could only keep up the raging bull act for two seconds. I collapsed against the edge of the couch and groaned. "Why the hell are you even working with Cade?" Whatever they were doing couldn't be good. I didn't know exactly what Cade did, but whatever it was, I knew it was shady as shit.

"We have mutual interests now." Carter wandered back to the desk and shuffled through the paperwork, and I could swear I caught a flash of pink, hiding under his Patek.

Maybe I was hallucinating.

Give me something, anything, Carter.

I was actually beginning to believe he really *was* done with me.

I watched him out of the corner of my eye while I pretended to look at my newly manicured fingernails. "Someone has been following me."

His eyes snapped up to mine, sharp and assessing.

Ah hah! That's fucking right. Pretending he doesn't care. Please.

"Someone's been following you?" He demanded protectively, finally turning his body towards me.

"Yup." I shrugged indifferently as I eyed his suit, hunting for any signs of that stupid, beautiful blonde. No stray hairs glimmered anywhere on the dark material. Thank God.

Carter closed the space between us. "Fuck Sara. How long has this been going on?"

"Thought you didn't care." I flopped back into the deep couch, running my fingers over the leather tufting.

"This is different." His jaw fanned, as if I'd caught him actually caring—what a fucking mistake. "Actually, Sara, where *is* your bodyguard?"

I smiled sweetly. "Waiting upstairs for me, like a good boy."

"This is serious."

"I know." I shot back. Saying it out loud made it feel real. Like it wasn't just in my head. "To be fair, I've never seen anyone, but I can feel it—feel a presence watching me." And it *had* felt different from the paparazzi because eventually the paparazzi always showed themselves. This presence was ever-present and *never* showed itself.

Carter dragged both hands down his face in exasperation before admitting quietly, "It might be your security team."

I could just strangle him for writing me off. "I'm not talking about Vaughn." I muttered harshly.

"Neither am I." He quickly fled for the door.

That got my attention. "What do you mean?" I shot up, and he walked faster. "Carter?" My voice went up an octave as I teetered on too-high heels, shoving my body against the door, blocking his exit. "What the hell are you talking about?" I asked breathlessly.

He stalked into the adjacent conference room and cracked open a bottle of water. "I hired a security team for you last fall." The words tumbled out of his mouth like he knew he was about to be in deep shit—and he'd be right.

My mouth dropped open as he white-knuckled the heavy glass bottle and nervously guzzled, "And you didn't think to tell me?" I demanded. "I've been feeling paranoid and anxious for months— because of you?!" I put my hands on my hips and stared at the ceiling. I'd been losing my marbles over nothing, thinking it had been related to that damn note. "Unbelievable." I muttered, knowing he couldn't possibly understand what it was like to be a woman walking through the world, already a little on edge as it was. "I know why Liam assigned me security." I started slowly, realization dawning on me.

"Yeah, you want to tell me the real reason he did?" Carter asked warily. "That was a bullshit explanation he gave me."

I tapped my lips, ignoring his question as I continued my line of thinking. "You know, I'm really curious, *Kensington*." His name was like a curse word in my mouth. "Why the hell did *you* hire security for me?" My heart rate increased as a different kind of sickening feeling settled into my stomach.

"Just being safe." He quickly took another long swig of water, draining the bottle.

What the actual hell? Liam had been keeping secrets for months, and now Carter? Both of them, making decisions about my life without bothering to consult me first. This was getting *really* old.

"If you won't tell me, then you don't get to keep tabs on me." Totally reasonable.

"You *will* keep your security team." He demanded, and the authority in his tone made my core tighten like a horny fucking traitor.

Moody, broody Carter, was apparently doing it for me. Fan-fucking-tastic timing. "Who the hell do you think you are?" I demanded, feeling myself starting to unravel as he closed the space between us. "Trying to keep tabs on me while simultaneously pushing me away?"

"I'm trying to keep you safe." He snapped, closing in.

"You have a real funny way of showing it." I breathed, my eyes going wide as he entered my space with several more long steps. My tongue darted out, wetting my bottom lip, and his eyes were dark and angsty as he tracked the movement.

"It's not. Up. For discussion."

I'd never seen this side of him aimed at *me* before.

Something protective and simultaneously predatory, dangerous.

Fuck, it was hot.

He smelled good too, familiar, minty, masculine, alluring. *Focus, Sara!* "You're right, it's *not* up for discussion because you've made it very clear you don't want to be in my life anymore." I bit out, already dialing a number on my cell phone. "And it's well within my rights to fire your little minions."

His hand hit the wall above my head, and I swallowed hard, tingling as the energy crackled between us like a strike of lightning about to ignite. "Good luck with that, because they're on *my* payroll."

"If I can't fire them, I'll have Gina help me get a restraining order." I threatened as Theo answered the phone, sounding irritated as usual.

"Why are you calling me, Sara? I know you're in the building."

"Hi Theo." I started sweetly, but Carter yanked the phone out of my hand and hung it up, making me want to scream as he stuffed it in his pocket and pushed off the wall.

"I was attacked." Carter practically choked out. "Last summer."

That stopped me in my tracks. "What?" I breathed, looking him over as if his body were currently injured—and it was, from his accident. He should be in bed, recovering. Why was he pushing himself so hard, so soon?

He started pacing. Nervously. "Some people my father worked with made some threats." He turned towards me, almost pleading as he explained, "They're dangerous and they mean fucking business, Sara."

"I don't know what the hell that has to do with me."

"Everything!" he shouted.

"Then why the hell didn't you just say something?"

"I didn't want to scare you." He softened breathlessly. "You'd had such a fucking hard year." His chest rose and fell wildly. "I didn't want you to be looking over your shoulder, constantly worrying. I know how important having a normal college experience was for you. So I made sure they'd stay out of your way." He swallowed hard. "But I had to be sure you weren't in any danger."

"I wasn't." I reached for him, almost surprised when he let me take his hand. "I wish you had just told me." I breathed, eyes darting between his. Searching. Hoping. Waiting.

Whatever I was waiting for didn't come.

My chest tightened as that cold exterior settled back over his face.

Shit.

The question was out before I could stuff it back down. "Did you kiss her back?" I asked breathlessly, feeling his big hand calloused against mine.

He didn't hesitate as he pulled away. "Don't ask me questions that I can't answer without hurting you more than I already have."

Oh. The photo was real?

I felt dizzy as the fog cleared all too quickly. He'd been telling me over and over again that he didn't want me, but I had just done a shit job of actually listening to him. Why did I actually believe I knew him better than he knew himself? How mother fucking delusional. I'd been a plaything when it was fun and convenient and when it mattered most. He didn't want to commit.

The reality check *stung*.

But I shouldn't have been surprised. In fact, I should have expected it from him. I was still so naïve—after *all* those years of pining. I was still trying to force a freaking happily ever after with someone who clearly didn't want me. Who does that?! Apparently me.

I wasn't supposed to chase *him*, and yet that's all I'd done, *my entire life*. I realized in that moment exactly what I wanted. *I* wanted to be pursued for once. I was *done* doing the chasing.

He was telling me loud and clear what he wanted, and it wasn't me—it was another one of those fucking blondes he loved so much.

I fumbled with the clasp of the tiny pendant around my neck. "I always want the best for you, but I can't pretend this isn't exactly what I expected from the moment you kissed me on the pier." I hesitated, the heartbreak quickly catching up with my ambition and fury. "I thought—this was all moving so fast, but I thought you were my person, Carter. I guess... I was wrong." I swallowed hard, the word sticking in my throat. "Goodbye." It came out a whisper as I trickled the necklace down onto the desk, not waiting to see if he picked it up.

"Sara, I—"

"Don't." I cut him off with a sound that was more a sob than a word. "I'm finally finding the strength to do exactly what you asked me to. Please don't follow me. This is hard enough as it is." I practically sprinted to the elevator, violently punching the close door button to escape. Hot tears burned an acidic path down my cheeks—I was ready to tear somebody's throat out... even if it was my own.

I stormed through the lobby, eyes blurry. I didn't give a shit what Carter or Liam wanted for me. What about what *I* wanted for me? For fucking once. Everybody treating me like glass—and, yes, maybe last year I'd needed it. But I was strong too. I could be a lot of things, in fact. I could be soft, and I could be strong, and I could be complex and difficult and fuck—I couldn't even think.

On the street, my new red-bottomed heels clicked with every thunderous step I took. I wasn't watching where I was going, could hardly see through my tears as I slammed so hard into someone it nearly knocked the breath from my lungs.

I felt myself starting to fall, and the man grabbed my arms as we spun behind a tree, planted in the sidewalk. "I'm so sorry." I huffed, trying to right myself, but he wasn't letting go.

Why wasn't he letting go?

As I peered up, I didn't catch his face because he shoved me backward. *Hard.*

I gasped as I fell to the ground, but before I hit—hands grabbed me, yanking me into an SUV with tinted windows.

Everything was happening so fast and simultaneously so slow. I gagged as rough, salty fabric hit my tongue, something painfully tight around my wrists before I could pull it away, a sharp pinch in my neck and then a flood of nausea as the panic set in.

The edges of my vision started blurring before I could even scream.

None of it had been in my head, my bodyguard was upstairs, and I'd just told the one person who knew where I was... not to follow me. *Oh God.*

CHAPTER 51

I'm the Bad Guy

Traffic was a bitch as I drove to my last and most important meeting of the day. Pissed as hell, I started weaving around cars like a speed demon, because I *needed* to go fast—*needed* to enter that narrow, peaceful space between life and death to stop the pain.

It didn't matter though. Arriving at my destination far too early, I was still agitated enough to strangle someone. I couldn't help but wonder if this had all been a colossal mistake. Sara had finally done what I'd asked her to. She'd let me go. So why the hell didn't I feel better about it?

I slammed my hands against the steering wheel of my Aston Martin, hating myself. For hurting her. For being so fucking weak. For letting myself fall for her in the first place. I loved her more than air itself, and that's exactly what letting her go felt like. Suffocating.

Then there was the rage quietly growing within me, smothering out everything else, leaving my insides shredded up between all the dark and ugly pieces left behind.

I groaned, resting my eye sockets against my palms in a futile attempt to soothe the pounding in my head. Reality was slowly setting in. Eventually, she'd fall for someone else. Get married. Start a family. Would she end up with some cardboard cutout like Eric? Someone who didn't really *see* her, or even hear her voice—someone with no passion who would just kiss her on the forehead and believe the happy smile she painted on, not bother to read between the lines, not bother to *know* those deepest parts of her—the pain she buried, the secrets she kept, the joy she had. God forbid she ended up with someone like Doug, someone who steamrolled her, who kept her without caring for her—someone who plucked her instead of watering her and letting her bloom.

Someone else was going to take that gift, that privilege of knowing her, protecting her, loving her. All the while, *I'd* be the bad guy in her happily ever after—a reality I was okay with if it meant keeping her out of harm's way, and keeping her alive. I would *not* become my father. Loving Sara from afar would *have* to be enough for me.

But it wouldn't be. The thought of someone else taking, touching, claiming what was *mine*. Mine to *cherish*, mine to *protect*, mine to *love*—I wanted to break something.

I laughed, a strangled sound in the silence of the car. In one swift move, I'd joined this world of chaos and deceit. Manipulated Sara into choosing the outcome I was trying to achieve. Let her believe all kinds of things that weren't even remotely true. I was bending, twisting reality—I wasn't just *playing* the bad guy, I was actually turning into one.

It hadn't been quite a lie exactly, but it certainly wasn't the truth. The paparazzi photos *had* been a PR stunt to make it clear to her and everyone else that I had moved on. That she was inconsequential to me. *Not worth targeting.*

The fact that the woman I'd been photographed with had yanked me down for an unplanned kiss the moment the paparazzi started clicking away—well, it solidified what I'd always known. People only wanted what they could take from me. Access to my status, wealth, power.

Everyone was desperate for a taste of me, and if they all wanted it so bad—I'd fucking give it to them, spoon it down their fucking throats like poison. If they wanted me in their world, playing their games, wanted to take away the things that were *mine*—then they would have to deal with the goddamn consequences.

I hardly recognized myself anymore. The rage was turning me inside out. Turning me into something empty and tortured. *Pathetic.* I slammed the car door and opened the trunk, staring at the tactical bag I'd packed. I took what I needed, and headed into the building, knowing I had nothing else to lose. A person could only take so much loss before nothing mattered anymore.

Inside, I followed an attendant through a series of concrete corridors that felt more like a prison than an office building. I wasn't sure what I had expected, but I was beginning to understand that once you went in, you might not come out.

My gun was secured underneath my suit jacket as we stepped into the elevator, and the attendant tapped a key card to begin our descent. Below the basement level, the elevator numbers stopped counting, but I estimated we were about ten floors below ground level when we finally came to a stop.

The elevator doors finally slid open, revealing an ominous black marble hallway lined with armed guards. Halfway down the hallway, I was left in a dimly lit room without a word of explanation.

I approached the long panel of glass on the far side of the room, peering into the darkness beyond, when a shadowy figure appeared from the corner.

"Carter Kensington." I was surprised to hear a sultry voice. "I'm so glad you could make it tonight. I've been looking forward to speaking with you in person for quite some time." She stepped closer but kept her face out of the dim light, her voice soft but sharp. "May I offer you a drink?"

"Why don't we just cut to the chase?" I studied her as best I could in the shadows. "I'm here for one singular reason." I tossed the envelope onto the low table, quoting its contents. "To end this once and for all."

She didn't bat an eye as the envelope sliced across the glass table, knocking a single ember from the flickering candle that lit the entire room. The black paper immediately burst into flame, the orange embers shimmering against the woman's dark eyes.

"So why don't you summon the Director out of his slimy little hole and let's get this over with."

The room darkened as the envelope extinguished into a pile of ash. "Who's to say you're not already speaking to her?" The soft voice mused, just a silhouette gliding through the shadows.

"Careful." I warned, "Don't get caught in a crossfire that was never meant for you." An amused laugh was her only response, and I checked my watch, a strange feeling washing over me. "I'm convinced half the reason it takes so long to get in touch with this damn organization is because of the elaborate games you all play."

She stepped forward, the flicker of candlelight illuminating her dark, striking features. "I'll admit, you are not quite what I expected." Her eyes narrowed as she calculated, "And I unfortunately for you, am not who you're looking for."

"Then you're wasting my time." I slipped my hands into my pockets, and the delicate metal of Sara's necklace was warm as I ran my fingers over it like a prayer charm.

"Perhaps." She tilted her head, exposing a flash of something on her cheek before she pivoted into the shadows again. "Perhaps not."

I turned back to the void beyond the glass, oddly drawn to what it might be hiding. "Is the Director going to grace me with his presence at all? Because if not, I have pressing matters I need to attend to." I was done playing games. He wanted my attention, and now he had it.

The woman laughed, offering an apology I doubted she meant. "No, he unfortunately won't be able to meet with you tonight."

I blew out a slow breath, that restless feeling inside me beginning to unravel. "Then you can tell him he's left me no choice." I headed for the door. *Time to start tipping dominoes.*

"Not so fast." She lilted. "I've been given *one* assignment for this evening, and I haven't completed it yet."

"I wish you luck with that."

"I suspect I'll need a little luck." She hummed, "Seeing as I've been given the delightful responsibility of obtaining *your membership* tonight."

My eyes narrowed as I paused. "Hate to break it to you, but they set you up for failure with that one. My answer still hasn't changed in the last ten years. So, in case you didn't get the memo—"

"I *always* complete my assignments—tonight will be no different." There was an odd bite of danger in her tone, as if she were trying to scare me.

But we were alone in this room, and I could snap her like the delicate twig she was. Maybe that would get me an audience with someone who mattered, but I could see it in her eyes, she knew I wouldn't. "Who are you?" I closed the space between us, hating the feeling of being toyed with.

"You're asking the wrong questions, Carter." She taunted me as she slipped back into the shadows. "Who I am is of no concern to you."

"Enlighten me then. What questions should I be asking?" Was this woman a pawn or a player? I honestly couldn't tell.

"Do you know what your father did for us?" She mused, answering her own question. "I suspect not." She began a wide circle around me, and I was beginning to feel like she was coiling me up in her tail, ready to start squeezing at any moment so she could swallow me whole. "Do you really know what made your father tick? Do you even know what makes *you* tick, when it comes down to it?" She continued her loop until she was in front of me again, keeping herself half in the shadows. "Do you know what motivates you? Hmm? How about what *terrifies* you?

Because *I* know." Her jewelry tinkled as she pushed her dark hair over her shoulder and continued, "In fact, I know *everything* there is to know about you." She spoke softly, but there was nothing meager about it. "I know all your dark, dirty little secrets, and I know you'll help me complete my assignment before the night is over." A saccharine-sweet smile that was nothing but venom underneath.

Except despite her best efforts, I could tell there *was* something underneath all her swagger...*fear.*

"What will *you* gain?" I asked, trying to make sense of her. "Or maybe I should ask, what will you *lose* if you fail your assignment?"

"Everything." She bit out. "Which is why I *will* succeed. No matter the cost."

"I'm afraid you have no idea who you're dealing with." I studied her as a chill settled over me while she countered, heat rising in her voice, "Don't fight what's inevitable." I crossed my arms continuing, "Keep pushing me and maybe you'll be lucky enough to find out."

She scoffed, the tension breaking. "Aren't you naïve, tossing around idle threats when you have *no idea* what's really at stake." The woman checked the watch on her slender wrist as she headed for the door. "Enough of this. Follow me." She turned, "Now. Or you'll miss the event, and then we'll both be screwed." She droned, a bored expression painted across her face.

Her heels clicked over the striated marble as she sauntered smooth as a panther down the dimly lit hallway while I reluctantly followed. I knew she could be leading me to my demise, but what other choice did I have, but to let them show me the pieces in play so I could finally tip the board—once and for all. We passed several more armed security guards before she swiped a key card and opened a set of tall, heavy doors and motioned me through.

Several dozen shadows moved within the dark room. Soft

conversation held in careful whispers filled the space, just barely audible above the quiet music playing from the speakers.

My pocket began to vibrate, and I pulled out my phone, realizing it wasn't *my* phone, *it was Sara's.* Shit, I'd been so upset, I'd forgotten I'd taken it from her. The phone continued to buzz—it was Theo.

Stepping away from the woman, I quietly answered the call, but before I could even speak, Theo was barking through the phone, "You are in some deep shit, Sara."

Oh, hell no.

"I know you're *never* going to speak to her like that again." I murmured, keeping my voice low. "Or I promise you, Theo, I'll cut your goddamn tongue out myself."

"Perfect, you two kissed and made up," Theo admonished, irritation lacing his voice. "You mind telling me the next time you two feel like sneaking off to fuck in secret?"

"We didn't sneak—" My chest tightened with realization. "Why the hell are you calling her phone, like you don't know where she is?" My blood pressure went through the roof, senses sharpened. "Tell me, you know where she is, Theo."

"Fuck!" Theo hissed. "Call you in five."

"I swear to God if you hang up—" I stared at the phone as the line went dead. He'd lost her. She'd been in the building with us, and he'd fucking lost her. I was going to kill him.

Richard Sinclair approached me. "You should know your attendance tonight is purely a courtesy to your late father."

"Excuse me?" I pocketed the phone, ruthlessly running my fingers over the necklace in my pocket. Where the hell was she? She'd been *so* upset when she'd left earlier. Where had she gone? Damnit, she was so impossibly stubborn, ditching her security detail purely to piss me off. *Fuck.*

"Despite the fact that you refuse to be formally inducted, we here at The Society understand you have a special interest in tonight's merchandise, and as such, we've voted in favor of your attendance." I could hardly think. I had to leave, had to get out of here, get eyes on her. Richard smiled. "Sometimes all the pieces align without you even trying. Isn't that right, Bradford?" I turned, surprised to see Sara's father.

I gripped his shoulder, confused at the panic drenching his expression. "Do this for me, Carter." He begged, pressing something into my hand just before two armed guards closed in. "No matter the cost."

"Brad? What's going on?" I demanded an explanation, but an armed guard stepped between us, and several more promptly dragged him away. The sound of his begging disappeared into a back room, while my fingers tingled against the cool, curved metal beneath my suit jacket. "What the hell is going on here?" I demanded, but no one seemed the slightest bit alarmed. Except for me.

Richard watched me, all too amused. "Why don't you ask Seven? Tonight will go a whole lot smoother if you decide to cooperate." He nodded to the woman with the dark features, who was glaring at Richard with a death wish in her eyes.

Had Brad's gambling debts finally caught up with him? "Is this a ransom?" I grabbed Seven's arm, murmuring into her ear, "Whatever the cost, I'll pay it." For Sara, I would.

"I know." She said simply. "But you'll find I prefer to operate in favors rather than dollars."

I gripped her arm tighter. "*What* do you want?" I couldn't deal with two crises at once. Not when one was so much higher priority to me. Sara would never forgive me if something happened to her father, but I'd never forgive myself if something happened to her.

Seven shot me a warning look even as she traced my lapel with a sharp burgundy fingernail, murmuring, "Tonight *will* cost you. The only question is—how much?" She turned her head, and I sucked in a sharp breath as she revealed a brutal scar down one side of her face. "Don't worry." She patted my lapel condescendingly. "I think you'll find our selection to be worth every penny." Underneath all her swagger was a flash of something else. It was gone almost quicker than I could detect. Pity? Resentment?

I released her as an armed guard approached us. "Who are you?" I demanded softly, unable to determine if this woman was here against her will—she had a damn number for a name, add that to the growing list of crises to deal with. "I can help you. What is your *name*?"

"I am the seventh." She murmured, her voice a push of breath as she ignored my question altogether and tapped the object in my hand, drawing my attention back to it. It was a remote, with a two-digit number inscribed on the top and a single button on the bottom. "As an honored guest, the elite members of the organization have voted, and you'll be allowed to take part in tonight's event." She added. "You're quite lucky, you know—they've never voted to include an outsider."

"What is the event?" I demanded.

"All will be revealed in due time." She lifted a folder, holding out a pen. "Now sign your intention to join the organization or you *will* regret it."

I shook my head. "I'm sorry, I can't." What would they do to her when she failed, I wondered.

"Your funds will be limited as a guest." She warned.

"Seven," Richard warned sharply, and as small as it was, her flinch was unmistakable. She shot him a glare from beneath her dark lashes and stalked away, disappearing into the darkness without another word. I stared at the slender metal object in my hand, its shiny gold surface reflecting the dim candlelight.

"Sad really, what a man will do to pay for his debts." Richard shrugged, sipping his cocktail. "However, one man's loss is usually another man's gain."

"How much does he owe?" I asked.

"Enough to hurt."

I bristled, shoving my personal feelings down. "I'll buy out the loans. Tell me who to talk to." Why hadn't Brad just come to me? He must've known I'd help him. If not for the guidance he'd offered me over the years, however skewed, then for Sara, and for Liam.

"They've already been bought out." Richard said blandly, and an odd feeling washed over me as I looked back in the direction they'd dragged Brad off to. "He made a donation to cover his debts in full." Richard explained.

Donation? What did that even mean?

"Almost time." Richard checked his watch, looking pleased. "You really should grab Seven and sign the membership addendum before it's too late." He added, "Although this is undoubtedly more entertaining. I wonder if you'll fight as hard as your father did?"

"Excuse me?" I demanded, all while feeling a pull towards the glass that I couldn't explain as I peered into the darkness, took stock of the guards blocking the room they'd dragged Brad into.

"You could have been a great asset to this organization and not the liability you've turned into." He said. "You know, I heard a rumor that several people pooled assets to bid against you. Makes it a fair fight, I suppose."

So this was an auction. "Who did?" And what was the merchandise they all thought I was so interested in? They were going to be sorely disappointed. I'd never been hypnotized by all the glamour like everyone else.

"We owned your father." Richard ignored my question. "And don't you forget for a minute that now *we own her too*." I stared at him, panic rising in my throat. "You didn't think that messy little PR stunt was really going to deter us, did you?" A slimy smile. "This is just the beginning, boy. You can use your father as an example of what happens when you deviate from the organization's wishes. Your membership was just a formality. Always has been." He scoffed. "We owned you the minute you took over the estate. Your childhood entanglement only makes all this that much easier." He added menacingly, "Let me make one thing clear. From here on out, you will offer the utmost loyalty and *respect* to this organization. Otherwise." He gripped my shoulder, amusement painting his ugly expression. "*She dies*, unavoidable collateral damage, *just like your mother*. Though, even I can admit how wasteful that was." He shrugged irreverently, as if he hadn't just admitted what I'd always suspected—*he'd murdered my parents.*

Everything went red hot as I shoved him against the glass, and even reaching for my gun, I felt powerless. "You bastard—"

The void beyond the glass blasted us with a burst of too-bright light. I couldn't see, and I couldn't look away—my eyes stung as my vision adjusted all too slowly. Sara's phone started vibrating in my pocket over and over again as a vague outline on the other side of the glass took shape, all while Richard chuckled.

I shoved him out of the way, blinking to bring the horrifying reality into focus. The long dark hair, the plunging dress plastered over her every curve, how she wobbled on too high heels—*my throat went dry.*

She was the merchandise. The only thing I had left. *Sarafina.*

The sounds in the room ceased to exist. Only my heartbeat in my ears as time slowed. She'd always be mine, and I'd been a reckless fool to pretend otherwise. Seconds turned long and deadly as my training took over.

One. Hands cuffed to the podium.

Two. Eyes glassy, *terrified—drugged.*

Three. My fingers against the cool glass wall between us—*bulletproof.*

Four. Armed guards at all the exits.

Five. Approximately thirty disposable suits spread evenly across the room.

Six. Taggart-fucking-Caldwell was here, eye-fucking, what was *mine to protect.*

Seven. Fingers sliding over the familiar curve of metal. *My gun.*

Eight. A voice crackled through the speakers, clear, crisp, and perfectly grating. "The bidding will begin at five hundred million." I finally slipped into that narrow space, that quiet, lethal calm settling over me. The cost was child's play, and *my woman* was fucking priceless. Not. For. Sale.

Nine. I spoke. "Now it's *my* turn to make one thing clear, if she doesn't walk out of this room with me—*no one does.*" I slid the barrel of my gun against the throat of the man responsible for my mother's death. "You're not the first man I've killed, and tonight—*you certainly won't be the last.*"

Ten. Time to burn it all down. *I pulled the trigger.*

CHAPTER 52

Highest Bidder

SARAFINA

I was upside down as I screamed, hearing gunfire explode from somewhere in the building, sounding all too close. The guard who had me over his shoulder dropped me the second his radio crackled to life, and I cried out as I hit the unforgiving marble floor, *hard*.

I had to get up, had to move—this might be my only chance to get away, because the words *sold to Taggart Caldwell* still rang in my ears like a nightmare, and I wasn't entirely sure this wasn't another one of them.

The gunfire and screaming continued, but my heels refused to find purchase on the shiny marble floors spanning the wide corridor. With trembling hands, I quickly wrenched each too-tall stiletto off, not wasting a second, to enjoy the relief as I reached for a nearby door handle. I dragged myself upright, horrible things appearing and disappearing in front of my eyes every single time I blinked. I rattled the door, panic clawing at me when I realized it was locked.

The dark, ominous hallway seemed to get bigger and smaller as I stared down the long row of doors, and I could hardly make myself move. This was exactly like my nightmares—*I was trapped*.

My eyes blew wide as one of those doors burst open, the

gunfire inside growing louder as people fled, screaming, covered in splatters of blood. Whatever this place was, I had to get out. *Right now.*

I frantically stumbled to the next door, covering my head when more shots rang out and glass exploded somewhere nearby. *Locked.* Each door was spread apart by far too much distance, *each of them locked.*

There was nobody around me, and I screamed in surprise when someone appeared, seemingly out of thin air and grabbed me. I dizzily looked down, finding a delicate hand, adorned with sharp, red-tipped nails. "Come with me." Her sultry voice demanded.

I gasped, "Who are you?" She was the most beautiful human I'd ever seen in my life, and she was perfectly terrifying.

"I'm the one who is going to get you out of here." She yanked me along irreverently.

"WHERE IS SHE?" A voice bellowed, and I froze, but my heart sank, realizing I must be dreaming, probably another hallucination. Carter had no idea where I was, and he wouldn't come for me anyway. He said he was done with me. For good.

An explosion of gunfire rang out, and then everything stopped all at once. The woman holding me quickened her pace as she all but dragged me down the hallway while I tripped over my long, tight gown, only staying upright because of her grip.

"Seven." Someone growled. "Get back here with my merchandise."

"Run." She let go of me and produced two glimmering gold knives out of thin air—she cast a glance at me from over her shoulder. "Right now!"

But I froze—there he was, at the end of the hallway, *Taggart Caldwell.*

The room was spinning, and armed guards were closing in from all directions—there was nowhere *to* go, but she was already moving through the hallway like a shadow. I blinked, realizing one guard was already keeled over, another went down a second later, and long dark hair slid over the smooth marble behind her as she slid between the next one's legs, slashing as she went. She headed straight for Taggart, who was backing away with wide eyes, when several shots rang out and she went down. The sound of her scream echoed off the walls as she clutched her thigh, a pool of red leaking from her hand.

A beefy guard lumbered over, and whatever he was saying didn't register to me as I watched him lift his gun to her face with a smile. *Oh my God, he was going to kill her point-blank.* Whoever she was.

Time seemed to slow, a gift, as I stumbled towards a fallen guard, pulled the gun away wide-eyed as he groaned. I slid my finger over the trigger, lifting the heavy thing into the air, just staring at it for more time than the beautiful shadow could afford, wondering, could I even do it?

Her dark eyes slid to mine, and she nodded just once, in permission, no, *pleading.* There was no time to think. I couldn't let her die for me, so I pulled the trigger, and then I pulled it again.

Nothing happened.

I gasped. Where the hell was the safety? I frantically fumbled, feeling the man's brutal eyes slide to me as I stumbled back, but that was all the window she needed. The woman spun, slicing the man's Achilles, sending him to the floor with a cry before she climbed on top of him with her knife already dripping his own blood.

I looked away, nearly vomiting as wet, awful sounds filled the hallway like echoes from another one of my nightmares.

And speaking of nightmares, "Hello Sarafina." Fingers gripped my cheeks roughly, forcing my face up to his. "Long time no see."

"Tag." I breathed, taking him in—he seemed so much bigger than the last time I'd seen him. Looming over me, he was incredibly intimidating, maybe not as muscular as Carter but nearly as tall, and certainly *much* bigger than me.

"I've been looking forward to today for quite some time." His charming smile was like a Venus flytrap, hiding what he really was. "Years, actually."

"Why are you doing this?" I pleaded. "This is insane."

"Because I can." Taggart hauled me away roughly, and when I looked over my shoulder, the woman he'd called Seven was already gone. The dark marble shimmered with reflective pools of blood everywhere I looked, but she'd disappeared into thin air. "Don't pretend you haven't had this coming for a long while now." Taggart added, sliding his arm around my waist.

I struggled to keep up with his long legs as he hauled me through a door, basically dragging me behind him.

"Get your fucking hands off her!" A man bellowed—it *was* Carter. He was on his knees, hands cuffed behind his back. "I'm going to take you apart, piece by fucking piece." Carter raged darkly, violently thrashing against his restraints—his voice didn't even sound like his at all. *Was I hallucinating?* There was a circle of bodies all around him. "I'm going to kill you so slowly you're going to beg for me to end it."

"Not if you're dead." Taggart nodded, and a guard irreverently pressed a gun to Carter's temple.

"No, please!" I screamed, jerking to a halt as Taggart yanked me back, shoving something hard and unforgiving into *my* ribs— Carter's eyes flared and he went *deathly still*.

"Don't kill him yet," Taggart droned. "I want to make sure my new wife has incentive to be compliant." *Wife?* A hot tear streaked down my face, and I refused to let any others escape.

Wake up. Wake up. Wake up.

I had to be dreaming. Taggart was always in my nightmares, along with my dead mother. *Just another dream.*

"Let me go, or else!" I screamed, and the room was rippling as I desperately tried to break free from Taggart's grip, but I couldn't.

"Or else, huh?" Taggart chuckled, but something flashed in his eyes, because we both knew what I had done in that car all those years ago. "Naw, I've waited long enough. I think I'll keep you, it's about damn time anyway."

"I fucking dare you to try." I cried. "I will never marry you."

There were some snickers in the room. "Maybe you bit off more than you could chew. Are you going to let her get away again?" Someone teased. "Maybe we need to get someone else to handle her this time." Another voice chimed in, and people laughed as Taggart grew more agitated by the second.

I braced as Taggart's hand lifted—

"Don't you lay a fucking finger on her." Carter growled. "Why don't you come over here and see what happens when you pick on someone your own size—or can't you count in inches—I bet you can't, can you?" Taggart paused as Carter fought the only way he could, *verbally*.

"What's the matter? Mommy never teach you math, cause you could only count to one? Can't solve problems with your skinny little pencil dick?" *Carter definitely had Tag's attention now*. "I bet fun-sized isn't so fun, you single-inch-worm piece of shit." Carter mused cockily while Tag's outraged breaths came faster by the second.

"Come over here, you coward—yeah, that's right, come over here and hit *me*. I fucking dare you." Taggart swung, and I screamed as Carter's head snapped to the side with a sickening crunch, but Carter spat blood on the ground, laughing as he grew more condescending by the second.

"Wow, I've had bee stings that stung worse than that. You hit like a wet noodle, but I bet you're too busy sucking your own little cocktail-weenie to learn how to throw a proper punch, huh? Or can you even find that pathetic little tic-tac? I bet you can't, can you? Yeah, look at him—*you can always tell*." Tag hit him *hard*, and I stifled a sob, suddenly realizing what Carter was doing —and Carter didn't look at me once as I silently backed away, tears streaming down my face.

"What's the matter, you cocksucker, overcompensating for your little cornichon down there?" Carter gave Tag a shit-eating grin, and I could hardly see as Tag hit him again and I silently sobbed—heart breaking with every single step I took, wondering why he was sacrificing himself for me if he didn't even love me anymore.

Tag had Carter by the collar. "We'll see how fun-sized she thinks I am when I'm halfway down her throat." Taggart hissed and hit Carter *again and again and again.*

Carter's insults were coming slower by the second as he spat a mouthful of blood and panted, "You sure about that? It seems like you might have a sweet-tooth of your own—did you gobble down your own Rollos, or did you get jipped and the sleeve only came with one nugget to start with?"

Tag roared, and Carter rocked back, only upright because of the men holding him, as he sagged between their grip.

Taggart finally paused, panting to catch his own breath as he turned—*looking for me.*

I stumbled back, desperately trying to disappear into the shadows, as Carter erupted, blood streaming down his beautiful face while he frantically tried to keep Taggart's attention. "Come on, you limp-dick, is that all you got?" Carter screamed, knocking a guard off balance as he thrashed. "Hit me, because this is your one goddamn chance, you brainless piece of shit. Get over here and hit me."

I was still *so* far away from the door, and the room was spinning like crazy as I reached towards a nearby table to steady myself —but my hand plunged through the air as I grabbed at *absolutely nothing at all*—I gasped as the ground came rushing towards me.

"You're gonna be wearing a fucking bib when I'm done with you, you spineless roach. *GET BACK HERE!*" A pair of shoes appeared by my hands as I tried and failed to push myself up. *"DON'T YOU FUCKING TOUCH HER!"*

Taggart yanked me up so hard I could hardly get my feet underneath me. He was practically twitching as he thumped the gun against my temple, over and over again, making my head pound harder than it already was.

I dizzily watched the firearm split into two and mash back together as he waved it around in front of me, lips moving as he violently shook me—behind him a red blur was hurtling towards us. Taggart's eyes blew wide, and he whirled, lifting the gun, and I all too slowly realized that red blur was *Carter*.

The sound was deafening as Tag pulled the trigger, over and over again, emptying *bullet after bullet* into Carter's blood-soaked chest, until there was only the empty click of the trigger.

The ground seemed to thunder louder than my screams as Carter staggered back, gasping for breath, before he crumpled with a strangled cry.

My throat burned with a scream as I clawed my way towards him, desperately trying to reach him, as red seeped onto the ground beneath him, but no matter how hard I fought, I couldn't seem to get any closer.

I begged, offered *everything*, powerless as Taggart loomed over the man I still loved, threatening to end it for good.

"Now, now, let's not be hasty, Taggart. No use in starting off on a bad foot." Samuel Mortarulo murmured. One of my father's friends... why wasn't he helping us? I begged him, but he wouldn't even look at me.

"You're right." Taggart twitched as he checked his watch. "We have a flight to catch."

"Sara—baby, it's going to be okay." Carter frantically rasped. "I'm going to come for you. There's nowhere they can take you that I won't find you—*look at me, baby*." Carter pleaded, panic saturating his gentle voice as he crawled towards me, a streak of red dragging behind him. "I'm going to find you."

Taggart had shot him so many times, and Carter was *still* crawling, reaching for me as I fought to get to him, *was I hallucinating this too?* Carter was saying all the things I wanted to hear, but *that* wasn't real. I'd given him—*us*, my all, and it still wasn't enough. He'd thrown me away like it was easy. Moved on in two seconds flat, because blondes had *always* been his type. *That* was real. If the sight of him dying in front of me wasn't so horrifying,

I might have smiled, relieved I'd caught the nightmare red-handed. I was going to wake up *any minute now*, and what a relief— because if this *was* real, if Carter *was* bleeding out in front of me... *I'd never survive it.*

Taggart lingered because his ego was wounded, and this was just another one of my nightmares, so of course he did. "Can you picture it?" He motioned, waving the gun between us. "Little mini me's with *our* genetics running around. You could have had that, Kensington, and you almost did, but you ran away instead." Tag panted wiping his face with the back of his hand, "Which is lucky for me, because after all these years, she's finally *mine*, and I don't want you to forget for a single second what that means." Carter's eyes shuddered as he panted and dragged himself another inch, and Taggart leaned in with a menacingly soft whisper. "She's *my* prized mare, and I'm going to bend her over and fuck her like one too."

Carter's screams were in my ears as I dizzily looked at Taggart. "Don't worry, I'm not a savage." He threatened psychotically. "I won't breed you until after I've ma—"

"You're not going to *breed me* at all!" I cried, throwing an elbow at his groin that barely landed because he yanked me back, laughing sardonically. "Oh, you bitch, you and I are going to have fun. I'm gonna take real good care of you, Sarafina *Caldwell*." My head snapped to the side, and the room went sideways as I hit the ground in a crumpled heap, light dancing behind my eyes.

Carter might have been screaming for me as I sank further into that cold marble floor while Taggart loomed over me.

"Just think, if you play nice, your father gets off the hook. Scotch free. Debts paid." Taggart threatened. "But if you don't play nice, Sarafina." He gripped my cheeks, forcing me to look up at him as he went in and out of focus. "Don't forget I own you now. If you break the agreements of his contract. You're both dead."

"I'm begging you!" Carter's voice was growing quieter in the distance. "I'll do anything!"

"My father?" I murmured, confusion washing over me as it hit me like a freight train, all at once. *The note.* Had my father done this to me? I blinked as darkness started to close in.

"Sara, I love you!"

Why wasn't I waking up?

CHAPTER 53
Good Little Wife
SARAFINA

"You will do what is required of you when the time comes, or there will be consequences." Taggart threatened as he leaned against the wall next to the door, arms crossed over his wide chest.

"You think you can threaten *me* into submission?" I barked. "You tried that once before, and it didn't go so well."

"You *will* marry me." He said simply, tilting his head as if he could still feel it, what I'd done to him. "Despite your little stunt, you don't have a choice, and you never did."

"I won't, and there's not a damn thing you can do about it." I practically spat.

He hummed, cruel amusement twisting his handsome face like cyanide poison. "I don't think you have any idea what I'm capable of."

"What's the matter? You couldn't get yourself a real wife, so you had to buy one?" I demanded. "What the hell do you want with me?"

He murmured arrogantly, "All will be revealed in good time, wife."

"I'm not your fucking wife."

"You will be."

"You always did have a big ego." I laughed humorlessly, the

sound coming out too thin as I tried my best to hold my ground. "You know what they say about men with big egos."

I screamed as he launched across the room, shoving me into a wall, his fingers digging into my cheeks as he roughly grabbed my face. "You are a crude little thing, aren't you?" Taggart bristled with a smirk, reading the fear in my eyes as he threatened quietly. "We'll see how small you think I am when I finally shut that bratty mouth of yours up."

"It's only a matter of time before he comes for me." I whispered, hoping maybe that was true, choosing to believe that it was —even if a sliver of doubt lingered at the back of my mind. Carter might not love me anymore, but I knew he'd never let me suffer this awful fate, he'd said so himself. *I think.*

"Kensington?" Taggart's smile was cruel as he cocked his head like a predator, and my heart bottomed out, feeling like helpless prey. "You really don't remember, do you?"

I stared up at him, my mind swirling. The events of that night were still so fuzzy around the edges, so many gaps in between, so many horrible things I wanted to believe I'd dreamed up. "He said he'd come for me." I desperately tried to remember Carter's face, the exact words. The promise was more of a feeling than an actual memory.

Taggart let go of me and wandered over to the vanity, ducking down to adjust his suit collar. "Hate to break it to ya, but Kensington isn't coming for you—he isn't going anywhere at all, actually." Taggart laughed, looking at me through the mirror. "Goddamn, they must have given you a heavy hit of the good stuff. How were the hallucinations, by the way—I've heard they're quite the ride." I stared at Tag, heart pounding as sickening fear churned in my stomach. "Let me fill you in on the important details. *You* were crying—so much fucking crying." Tag rolled his eyes. "And *I* pumped Kensington full of so much lead it took multiple people to drag him away. And *he* is probably already in the dirt." Tag mused, clarifying. "*He's dead.* Finally, the immortal bastard." Tag fussed with his hair in the mirror. "I tenderized him up real good, so I'm sure the worms are already busy making a meal out of him." I closed my eyes and clamped down on a sob. Tag strolled back over to hook a finger under my chin with a glazed look. "Don't look so sad, it's just you and me now, baby, and I promise we're going to have all kinds of fun."

"Don't call me that." I whispered, lower lip trembling. "I'll never be your baby, and definitely not your goddamn wife."

Taggart leaned in, his breath rushing across my face as a tear slipped down my cheek. "I'll call you whatever the hell I please, you little cunt, and you'd damn well better get used to answering to me, because *nobody's* coming for you." He dragged his finger out from under my chin roughly and walked backwards with a shrug. "Play nice, and it won't be so bad for you." He finally turned, not bothering to look at me as he explained rather indifferently. "Or don't, but I'll make you regret it, I can promise you that." He locked me in the opulent room, leaving me to crumble.

The next night, a dress box was sent up to my room with a request to join Taggart and his father for dinner. As I lifted the skimpy thing out of the tissue paper, eyed the lingerie underneath, I knew I'd never survive as Tag's plaything, and I also knew my one small act of rebellion would cost me.

It did.

When Tag discovered I wasn't coming down for dinner, he came upstairs to scream at me and left me with another bruised cheek and without dinner, but I'd gone hungry before, and I could do it again.

He was emotional, and if that was the only thing I could use against him, I would. *It had worked once before.*

Weak from days of not eating, days of grieving, and all the residual sedatives still lingering in my system—I knew the truth of what Taggart had told me. Over the last few days, I'd had plenty of time to lay here and piece all the scraps together—Carter taking a chest full of bullets that was meant for me, him crawling, bleeding out in front of my very eyes. Even if he'd been rushed to the hospital, which I knew he hadn't been—it would've been a miracle for him to survive. And even if he hadn't loved me at the end, *I had still loved him, never stopped loving him.*

Now he was gone, and the only way I could be with him was in my nightmares, where his broken and battered body, his screams, echoed through my mind, whether I wanted them to or not.

My tears had long run dry as I laid in a puddle of too-soft bedding and cried, staring at the broken glass all over the floor when Taggart let himself into my room several nights later.

His brow raised as he took in the mess I'd made, and I shakily pushed myself up as he approached, shoes crunching over the glass. "Clearly, withholding food isn't an ample motivator for you." Taggart sucked on his teeth, and I couldn't help the small smile that formed at the tiny win.

"You think this is funny?" Tag scoffed. "We'll see how funny you think it is when I carve my name into your skin to remind you who you belong to. As you know, if you don't do what's required, I have all kinds of ways of making you comply. You can scream and cry, and break every damn vase in this house, but just remember that you were purchased for one reason and one reason alone." He snapped. "So when the time comes, you *will* comply and provide me with an heir, wedding vows or not." He threatened, "Or I'll throw you into one of the cells downstairs, with someone a hell of a lot bigger and meaner than me." I swallowed hard, trying to keep my features neutral as he approached the edge of the bed, his voice dropping to a low, contemplative tone. "Or maybe you like it rough? Hmm? That wouldn't surprise me one bit." I flinched as he reached for me, dragging a finger down my cheek with violent softness. "Don't forget, Sarafina, there are lots of ways I can make you suffer, make *your father* suffer. And you'd deserve it too—wouldn't you? So why don't you just accept the fact that you belong to me now. You were always going to be a Caldwell, one way or another."

~

Tag didn't feed or check on me the next day and it finally occurred to me that maybe he was waiting for something. For what, I didn't know, but after the threats he'd made, and what had happened in that car all those years ago—I was going to fight for myself, even if I was the only one doing it. I was growing weaker by the day, so if I was going to try to escape, I needed to do it now.

I'd given up on the windows after the first night, which meant the only way out was through the house. Ear pressed to the bedroom door, I stared absentmindedly into the lavish room that was my prison cell. There hadn't been any movement in the hallway for a long while now, so I was hopeful, if not pretty confident, it was empty.

Thankful for my foresight, I jammed the butter knife I'd stashed that very first day into the first hinge on the old door, hoping the pin would slide free. *It did.*

The second one slid right out too, and I started to get hopeful, but as I stood on a chair and pried and pried at that third pin, begging and cursing at it, it didn't budge. I was growing more frustrated by the minute. I was so close and yet so damn far away —it was an old door, probably hadn't been greased up in ages—I suddenly had a thought.

A few minutes later I was giving that old door hinge the best hand job I'd ever given. I lubed it up with one of the old lady scented bath oils that'd been left next to the claw-foot tub—sweet talking it so filthy I could rival Carter's dirty mouth, and that realization gutted me. I tipped my head against the door and silently sobbed, realizing I was never going to hear another one of his witty little remarks again. I knew I had to get out of here, but part of me didn't have the strength to keep going. Not when the reality outside this room seemed just as grim.

When the pin finally wiggled loose, I was exhausted. Emotionally and physically. Spots laced my vision with the exertion as I relied solely on adrenaline to get that door off the hinges —this was clearly an ancient estate given the decor in this room, and the thick wooden door was obscenely heavy. The door groaned, and I barely got my fingers out before it thumped to the ground, the hardwoods groaning in protest. I winced, waiting, but no one came running.

Quietly slinking through the massive manor, I found most of the bedroom doors were locked. Blowing out a frustrated breath, I headed down a new corridor, muscles locking when voices in one of the rooms became apparent.

I could hear my heartbeat in my ears as I slowly crept across the old floors, hoping they wouldn't creak as I pressed myself against the wall, and moved closer. I listened for a long minute before I lowered, daring a peek inside. Tag was having an argument with his father—I'd only met him a handful of times, but I recognized him.

There was no other way out except to cross in front of this open door—which meant I'd have to make a run for it and hope for the best. I was terribly weak as I waited for my window.

"I'm trying." Taggart yelled, pacing the room.

"You have one job." His father seethed, "Find those goddamn files."

"They don't exist." Taggart exploded. "There isn't a single painting of roses or flowers anywhere in that damn house with—"

His father was seething as he cut him off. "It cannot be that difficult to find a flower mural, your incompetence is testing my patience, boy."

"We've checked every painting in the entire fucking neighborhood and then some."

His father was glowering as he opened a box of cigars and

pulled one out. "Then use the damn girl to make him concede."
Him who?

"She's too stubborn, and scaring her isn't going to be enough.
I guarantee she's not going to cooperate until they send the de—"

"We're out of money." His father snapped, and my eyes blew
wide with understanding. "And it's not going to take them very
long to figure out the rest of that damn payment is never
coming."

"I've done my part." Tag shouted. "In fact, I've done everything you asked me to and more, for nearly a decade now!"

I jolted when Tag's father grabbed him by the neck and
slammed his face down onto the desk suddenly. "I will not be
blackmailed by this organization any longer." He growled,
twisting Tag's arm behind him as he continued. "I've lost everything I own, so you can waste time toying with your little mail-
order bride." Taggart grunted as his father released him. "I will
give you one more chance to get that information, *by any means
necessary*. If you can't manage that, then I don't see the need for
either of you. Useless, just like your brother."

I had to get the hell out of here. *Now.* Before I couldn't.

My muscles were locked with fear, but I must have shifted,
because the floor creaked mercilessly—both their eyes snapped
up, and I launched myself down the wide hallway like my life
depended on it, because horrifyingly *it did*.

I suddenly wished I hadn't let myself get so out of shape, but
weak as I was, adrenaline kicked in and took over. My panic
propelled me down one hallway after another, and hope filled me,
realizing this might actually work.

Except as I came flying down a set of stairs, a bulky armed
guard appeared at the bottom, aiming a gun at me, and he didn't
hesitate to pull the trigger.

I went down with a scream, and footsteps thundered down
the stairs behind me. "I tried to warn you, Sarafina, this could
have gone so differently, and now, you've given me no other
choice."

CHAPTER 54
The Three Stooges
CARTER

The smell of something musty was in my nose as I blinked to consciousness and pushed up to sit. I stared down at the stained cot, and then out the metal bars, into the concrete prison cell I was in. Everything came rushing back in a flood of horror as I registered the trail of crusted blood dried down my chest, the bullet wounds festering in my shoulder—I'd been stripped down to my underwear—bulletproof vest, clothes, the love of my life, *all gone.*

My eyes shuttered as the sound of her helpless cries filled my memories—the image of her so small and defenseless while Taggart threatened her at gunpoint—as he struck her soft precious body and then dragged her away unconscious, promising to do things that terrified me.

I had to get out of here, had to find her. There wasn't a second to waste. Every minute she was with him—no, I couldn't let my mind wander. My sweet, sweet girl, she was strong and clever, and she would fight to stay alive—I had to believe that.

Pain barked through my bruised and beaten body as I stumbled barefoot to the prison bars, feet stinging against the cold concrete floor while panic threatened to take me out at the knees —but that was a luxury I couldn't afford.

I frantically and systematically started checking every seam of my prison cell, every nook and cranny, wondering how long I'd even been out. Hours? Days?

A buzzer rang as a heavy metal lock snapped open—the woman Richard had called Seven sauntered into the room, and I swallowed hard, realizing she was in different clothes. *Not good.* She carried a plastic lunch tray, looking mildly disgusted as she slid it through the food slot.

"Where is she?" I croaked, finding my throat dry, the taste of metal still coating my tongue.

"I wouldn't touch the food if I were you, but I'd drink the water." She nodded at the cup. "It'll help with the headache— flush the sedatives out of your system."

"Where?" I demanded hoarsely, hanging on the bars. "Is she?"

"Drink the water and then we'll talk." Seven droned, and I reluctantly stared into the clear liquid, wondering if it was poisoned. She raised a brow as I studied the thin plastic cup, wondering how far I could get with a shiv and no shoes.

Seven paced lazily across the long room while I took the first tentative sip—I knocked back the entire cup a moment later, realizing I was parched. *Days.* I'd been out for days. *No.*

"Your father took something that belongs to us. Bring it back and we'll discuss Sarafina's contract."

I wiped my mouth with the back of my hand, knowing I had no other choice but to play these stupid, nonsensical games with them. "What is it?"

"Sensitive information." She fussed over her nails.

"How very cryptic of you." I countered, flexing the plastic cup in my palm, testing its give.

"Bring the information to *me*, and my employer will consider releasing Sarafina." She shrugged. "Simple really."

I narrowed my eyes. "The Director?" I cracked the cup.

"*My employer.*" She corrected, eyes dropping to my hands. *Interesting.*

"Great." I stuck my hands through the food slot and

presented her with my handcuffs, shoulder barking with pain. "Let me out of here, and I'll gladly bring you anything you want —which toy do you want with your Happy Meal?"

She laughed melodically. "Don't try to play checkers with me while I'm busy clearing the chessboard." She winced as she turned.

"You're injured?" *I could definitely work with that.*

She straightened, all signs of pain vanishing. "Just a scratch." Who the hell was she? Who was her *employer*—was she helping me or playing me to help herself?

It honestly didn't matter; I'd do whatever it took to get Sara back, and that started with cooperating so I could get the hell out of here. "Just tell me exactly what you need and I'll get it."

"We believe your father hid the information at the estate." She looked at her nails as they shimmered in the light, and I tensed in realization—they were painted a glittering gold to match her dress. She hadn't just changed her clothes; she'd had time to do her nails since the last time I'd seen her. *Oh fuck.* Is that why my head hurt so bad? Had they kept me sedated?

"How long have I been out? How many days?" I swallowed hard, terrified of the answer.

"Long enough that I'd stop interrupting me, if I were you." She snapped.

"Before your father died, he said—"

My eyes flared. "What the hell do you know about my parents' deaths?"

She paused contemplatively. "You know, you and I are more alike than you realize." She mused, "Orphaned far too young—"

"What exactly is it that you do here, *Seven*?" I emphasized her not-name with a bite that she rolled her eyes at.

"Whatever is necessary." She shrugged.

"What do you know about my parents—about my mother?" I demanded, eyes shuttering as a new, unfamiliar sort of hatred built within me. My father had made his choices, whatever they were, and my mother? *Collateral damage?* Murdered because of his selfish choices? Had there been no one there to save my mother when she needed that help? Charlotte and our shared secret flooded my mind—*her arranged marriage*—maybe it hadn't been an arrangement at all. Maybe Brad had bought her, in this very building, turned around and sold his daughter to the same fate—had my father done the same? The question made me nauseous—I couldn't let Sara end up like her mother had, tied to someone dangerous who thought she was their property—or worse, like *my* mother, her life sacrificed because of someone even more dangerous. I would burn the earth to ash before I let my darling Sarafina suffer either of those fates. Sarafina was mine to protect, and mine to cherish. I'd been a fool to pretend otherwise. "Did she suffer?" I loosed a defeated breath, not knowing if I could even handle the answer.

"Bring me what I need, and someday I'll tell you all about it." Seven said sweetly.

I scowled, knowing that wasn't even remotely true. "Tell me where to look and I'll—"

"Did your father keep any of his paintings in storage?" She asked rather suddenly. I nodded, shocked as she began listing places she definitely should *not* know about. But apparently she did. "Anywhere else, I might check?" She asked, one arm banded across her stomach, while she propped the other arm up, snapping her nails in the air with irritation.

I shook my head. "Not that I know of."

"There must be." She mused to herself, deep in thought as she paced. "Because it's not in *any* of the paintings I checked, or anywhere else for that matter."

"It's been you." I said, realization washing over me. "Breaking into the house, leaving the letters—how'd you get in and out without the security system catching you?"

She smirked, "Wouldn't you like to know." Then she turned more thoughtful. "I know for a fact it's not in any of the paintings in the house." She turned up her nose with disdain. "Because I've checked them all—*thrice*."

Most of the paintings around the house were just investment commodities, many of them I just hung up to enjoy purely for the hell of it until I sold them again—I couldn't count how many pieces had filtered through the house the last ten years, not to mention the portfolio—if what she wanted was hidden in a painting—it was most likely *long gone* by now. If the information was that important, a painting would be the last place my father would hide it.

"Why do you think the information is behind a painting?" I mused. "Why not tucked away in a safe, or a deposit box?" I continued sharpening my plastic shiv.

"Because I checked those too." She scoffed.

"What did he say?" I asked. "Specifically." Plastic dust rained down on my feet.

I found her eyes cold and calculating when she met my gaze again. "When I took little bits of flesh from his body, he said I'd never find it, because it was behind your mother's favorite painting." Seven said, and I started sharpening faster. Had she been the one to actually do it then? Had she drawn the last breath from my helpless mother? Maybe I'd give *her* seven perfect breaths before I—

The buzzer sounded again, and a towering figure filled the glass window in the door—Seven groaned, but I was grinning.

"Oh goody, the Three Stooges and their lapdog," Seven spat, slipping out the back just as Theo kicked the door open, looking pissed off at the door itself. "Damn door locks."

Theo, Liam, and Cade filled the room, and Cade wasted no time attaching a small device to the prison bars. "Step back." He instructed. "Explosion in three, two." The device detonated, and a small wisp of smoke curled in the air.

"I'm surprised to see you here." I said to Liam.

"Daddy's here to save the day." Liam grimaced with a small smile, pulling the cell door open. "I heard what you did for her— saw it too." He shook his head. "It's a goddamn massacre out there."

"I did what I had to." I grimaced, *would do it again* is what I didn't add as I quickly pulled on the clothes he handed me, wondering what the body count was up to now. "Temporary truce?" I asked.

"For now. Let's just get her back safe and sound and then I'll decide if I'm going to beat the shit out of you." The corner of his mouth pulled into a stressed almost-smile. "Though it looks like someone already got a head start, you look like shit."

I turned to Theo. "Taggart Caldwell has her. Said they were getting on a plane, we're going to need to hack into—"

Theo shook his head. "We've been poring over the flight logs for days, but they never arrived at their destination." He hesitated, and my chest tightened as I searched his face. "We traced them back to the Caldwell Estate, and then they just *disappeared*."

I stared at him, panicking because if Theo couldn't find them —*this was not good. Not good at all.*

"We're going to find her; it's only a matter of time." He assured me. "There's a solid chance they're hiding out somewhere in Briar Rose. They have to be close by. We would have found them already if they had left—which means they probably didn't."

"Probably?" I snapped. "We're wasting time." I stormed out the door, wondering how much time they'd wasted rescuing me, when they should have been looking for her.

As we headed through the compound, I didn't bother looking at the mess I'd made. Only one thing mattered now, *getting her back*, and I'd gladly leave another pile of bodies, if that's what it took. Taggart had threatened Sara at *gunpoint*, and now they'd just disappeared? If anything happened to her, I'd never be able to forgive myself.

∾

Bouncing around in the back of the tactical van, I bit back a scream while Liam and Cade pinned me down—the medic was busy digging bullets out of my shoulder like I was a fucking sandbox to play in.

"Hold the damn flashlight still. I can't get the right angle if I can't even see." They muttered to someone else on the tactical team while I chuffed heavy breaths out through the nose, really wishing I wasn't playing Cavity Sam in this shitty game of Operation.

My scream finally ripped free as we hit a bump, and the medic just went for it, making me thrash—they pulled the last bullet out a moment later. "Got it." They announced proudly, and I collapsed back in a sweaty heap, trembling as they added insult to injury, wiping my shoulder down with a disinfectant that stung. "Alright, *this* is the one you're gonna wanna brace for." They warned, grabbing another bottle. "This is just a temporary patch, and it's gonna burn, *like hell.*"

I was still gasping for breath, eyes fluttering as Cade loomed over me, giving me a shit-eating grin. "Hey princess, don't focus on that—focus on how this feels." He purred like I was one of his sexual conquests and then proceeded to slap my face—right as something that burned like the devil's asshole hit my open wound.

"*Fuuuck.*" I cried, tipping my head back with a whimper while black spots laced my vision.

"Aww, look at him, taking it like such a good boy," Cade teased, as the medic started bandaging me up.

"*You're an asshole.*" I panted, body shaking, dripping with sweat.

"You're welcome." Cade chuckled, patting me as he and Liam finally let go when they were sure I wasn't about to punch the medic in the face.

"That should do it for now." The medic announced.

My eyes were closed as I lifted my good arm with a sarcastic thumbs up for the sandcastle builder before throwing a middle finger in Cade and Liam's direction.

"Look alive." Liam chuckled, and I groaned when a sandwich bag hit me in the face a moment later.

I held the plastic baggie up. "Is this shitty little sandwich your way of telling me you're still pissed at me?" I sighed, realizing it was PB&J.

"I hope it's the worst damn sandwich you've ever eaten." Liam grinned, looking all too pleased at my misery. "I used grape jelly."

I hated grape jelly.

CHAPTER 55

Where Is She

CARTER

The sun dipped low in the sky, setting blazing red streaks across the horizon as we quietly waited, hidden in the foliage of the Bishop's apple orchard. It was almost eerie, considering the carnage that was about to unfold in a matter of minutes.

Next to me, Liam shifted impatiently, muttering, "What the hell is taking them so long?"

The comms in my ear were a quiet flurry of commands and updates as we waited the torturously long minutes for each unit to clear its respective section.

Theo's team was sweeping the outside of the manor, while his cybersecurity team hacked into the security system from the comfort of the tactical vehicles.

"Almost there." Someone murmured an update, and I could hear their fingers flying over the keyboard. "Likewise." One of Theo's men responded.

We had confirmation that Sara was inside the manor, but we didn't have confirmation that she was unharmed or even alive. It was only my tactical training that kept my feet in place, knowing that every precious minute that passed was a minute Sara could be injured, in mortal danger, or worse.

"Any day now," Liam muttered.

"She's strong; she'll pull through this." I shifted, fingers pressing into the soft earth beneath me, willing my words to prove true.

"You don't know that," Liam murmured. "People do terrible things when they're desperate."

"Well, let's hope she's the one doing them." I countered, my chest feeling tighter than ever. "We both know she's capable of raising hell when she wants to." Liam huffed a heavy breath that might have been amusement.

Sara was resourceful, yes, but Tag—I worried about the lengths he would go to prove himself, in whatever larger picture was playing out. He'd threatened her at gunpoint and then proceeded to empty an entire clip into me—that reality left every cell in my body drenched in fear, and it was a luxury I couldn't afford. So, I returned to my box-breathing in an effort to steady my panic as I watched the sun melt beyond the horizon in blood red hues.

"I don't know how I didn't see this coming." Liam admitted quietly. "I should have known the lengths my father would go to save his own skin—should have seen the signs, the way he was pillaging the estate, I should have known something was up."

I exhaled a long breath, thinking the same. "I don't think anyone could have predicted this." I added, "It's not your fault."

"Is it yours?" Liam asked, no vitriol in his voice, as he finally turned to look at me.

I looked down, jaw fanning. "Honestly, it might be."

He hung his head, giving it an exhausted shake. "It's not." After a moment, he added with such disgust, "What a fucking cocksucker—trying to buy a wife."

"Liam, I need you to know she wasn't just a fling." I admitted quietly, and he shot me a glowering look. "I love her."

"Why the fuck did you break her heart, then?" He demanded softly, keeping his eyes on the manor rather than looking at me.

"Back then?" I swallowed hard. "You made it very clear that I'd be dead to you if I ever made a pass at her. And when my parents died, you, your family, her, it was the only thing that kept me alive." I felt his gaze on me, but I couldn't bring myself to look at him as I admitted something I was incredibly ashamed of. "You think I was going to jeopardize the only family I had left by making a move? You're practically my brother, Liam. You can be pissed at me all you want, but back then, no matter how I felt, I stayed away because of *you*. I couldn't admit it to myself that I loved her, because I was terrified of alienating you. Terrified of losing your parents' support." I studied the dirt beneath me. "You don't know what it's like to be all alone—to have no one."

"You've never had no one." Liam huffed.

"Because I played by the rules, you set up for me. Read between the lines when your father warned me."

"You ever think that was for a good reason?" Liam's eyes were dark, unforgiving. "You went behind my back with her and then decided to break her heart anyway. Just like I knew you would, from the very beginning."

"Liam, they drugged and beat the shit out of me and then turned around and threatened to do the same for her—worse, actually. What the hell was I supposed to do?" He stared at me for a long minute. "I stepped back for her own goddamn safety." I huffed, lowering my voice further. "Because no matter how much I love her, keeping her safe is always going to be my top priority— no matter the cost."

"So I'm supposed to believe you broke her heart for the better good." He asked quietly, as if that's what he wanted to believe, but couldn't. "How can you love her if you've never been able to hold down a serious relationship?" He muttered. "Do you even know what love is? What commitment really means?"

"Are you even hearing me?" I demanded, "They kidnapped her, sold her like it was nothing—Liam, they threatened to kill her, and I believe them, because they *murdered my parents*." I barreled on even as his eyes snapped to mine in realization. "This organization, this Society your father is so proud to be a part of, they're not playing fucking games, and they will stop at *nothing* to get what they want. I get that you're angry, and you have every right to be, but tell me you wouldn't have done the same damn thing for Gina—if you thought it's what would keep her safe— keep her *alive*."

"This is *not* about me and Gina." He grumbled, "Sara's just too fragile for this. Everyone just hurts her, over and over again. She carries the weight of the world on her shoulders all the goddamn time, and I just want to see her happy, *safe*."

"I think she'd say the same about you—and she's not fragile, Liam. She feels deeply, yes, but give her credit where it's due, for Christ's sake. She's strong, and determined, and resilient—not to mention, she's a grown-ass woman who's perfectly capable of deciding who she's *allowed* to love." He glared, but I kept on going. "And if you really do care about her happiness, when I ask her to marry me, don't be the one that stands in the way." He opened his mouth to object, but I didn't stop. "I've always loved her, and that's why there wasn't anybody else, because it was *always* her. She's my forever, Liam, and if she'll take me back, I can't step aside for you or anyone else. Not ever again. Don't draw a line in the sand when it doesn't have to be that way."

"And when you're done playing house?" Liam demanded softly. "Marriage means something to her."

"The day I'm done with her is the day they put me in the dirt." I looked back towards the manor cooly. "And even then, I'll never stop loving her."

Liam stiffened as he returned his gaze to the manor. "She'll be the one to decide, then."

"And Liam?"

"What?" he snapped roughly.

"When we get in there, I need you to get her out because when I get my hands on him," My blood went red hot as the sound of Tag's hand meeting Sara's cheek rang through my memory, the feeling of metal biting into my wrists, the helplessness I felt as she crumpled to the ground. "*I'm gonna kill him.*"

Liam opened his mouth to argue, but just then Theo

murmured, "Alright kids, put your seatbelts on, we're in, and it's time to raise hell."

Liam and I pulled our masks down over our faces, and the next several minutes were quick and precise as we took the mansion room by room. The house staff was quarantined in the kitchen, the security staff subdued by whatever means necessary, and still no sign of Sara or her captors.

As we moved to the next wing of the house, Liam handled his firearm with far more skill than I would have expected, but I didn't waste a precious second to demand an explanation.

I combed the upstairs bedrooms, feeling more and more panicked as each yielded no sign of Sara.

At the end of one wing, my pulse spiked as I approached the only room with an open door—a bent butter knife was discarded at the threshold, and just inside was a puddle of oil leaking from a tipped bottle. I lifted the bottle to my nose, realizing it was a fragranced bath oil, and I smiled grimly, piecing together what she'd done. *That's my girl.* Resourceful. In the ensuite bathroom I found a few telltale strands of dark curly hair, and a quick smell of the pillows in the bedroom confirmed my suspicions. She *had* been in here at one point, but how long she'd been gone, I couldn't say.

Over the comms, "I'm upstairs. It looks like she greased up the door and pulled it off the hinges to get out." I eyed the old door, knowing how difficult that must have been for her—it was solid wood.

"Clever girl." Cade muttered in the comms.

"Are you a hundred percent sure she didn't leave the estate? Are there *any* blind spots she could have slipped through?" I asked, dangerous hope filling me, as I wondered if she'd actually gotten away, and then the anxiety that she might be somewhere in the woods all by herself swept over me in the next instant. I felt like I was going to puke, hoping she wasn't injured.

"There's no sign of that." Theo commented before murmuring instructions through the comms to sweep the grounds again. "But that doesn't mean there aren't alternate routes out."

Liam's voice echoed across the hall and in my comms, frustration drenching his voice as he asked, "*Underground?*"

"It's not on the schematics." Theo grunted. "But that's certainly possible."

"*Fuck!*" I muttered, biting back my panic as I continued my sweep of the upstairs bedrooms. "Does anybody have eyes on *Deadwell?*"

"Nothing here."

We finished the sweep of the upstairs bedrooms, and there was still no sign of her. I gripped a doorframe and tried to steady my breathing, feeling my chest tighten, wondering if I was about to have a panic attack.

I felt Liam hovering by my side. "Breathe." Head hung, I nodded, forcing another slow breath out. "We're gonna find her." Liam said, but when I finally met his gaze, his dark eyes looked as frantic as I felt.

I took three slow breaths and forced myself to move. I had no doubt we'd find her, *but what if we were too late.*

Suddenly, "Anybody looking for a rat?" Vaughn asked all too cheerily through the comms. "Because I just cornered one in the study."

Liam and I locked eyes, and I jammed a fresh clip into my gun as we hurried downstairs, chaos erupting in my earpiece. *Must go faster.*

I burst into the study, finding Tag on his knees, blood already pouring from his face.

"*WHERE IS SHE?*" I demanded, hauling him up and slamming him against the wall. God, it was so incredibly tempting to lighten my clip a few rounds, but I knew wherever Sara was—we'd find her a hell of a lot faster with his cooperation, and her safety was far more important than my revenge.

"Fucking hell, how are you still walking?" Taggart muttered, his cuffed hands rattling. "Can't you stay dead for once."

My finger twitched on the trigger. "Tell me where she is," I started, lethally soft. "And I'll *think* about letting you live."

"It's nothing personal." Taggart tried negotiating, lifting his cuffed hands. "I'm sure we can work something out. I'm very willing to sell you my contract for the right price."

"You really are a moron." I shoved him back against the wall with a disbelieving laugh. "Here's how this is gonna go. Every time you make me ask where she is, I'm going to make it hurt." I promised calmly. "Do you understand?"

"I'll make you a deal. I'll sell you the contract for the bid price plus ten percent interest." Tag offered.

I dropped my head, my finger flexing over the trigger as I lifted the gun. "I must not have made myself clear." I emptied half the clip into the wall next to his head and then jammed the hot barrel into his throat. "*WHERE THE FUCK IS SHE?*" I growled, crushing his windpipe as I burned him.

"If you kill me, my fingerprints won't work." He gasped a strangled cry with just enough amusement to push me right to the edge of my restraint.

Seeing red, I never moved my eyes from his face as I holstered my gun and pulled out my knife. "I don't need your goddamn fingerprints to get behind a door." I grabbed his hand, and he screamed as I took the first fingerprint before he even had time to realize what was happening. "Let's see how many you have left by the time you finally decide to talk." I went for the next finger.

"Basement! She's in the basement." Taggart screamed as I took the next fingerprint just for the hell of it.

I threw him towards the doorway, wiping my knife on my pants. "Lead the way, and you'd better start praying to whoever it is you pray to because that's just a taste of what I'm going to do to you if you laid hands on her again." *He'd already laid hands on her, and that was already enough for me to kill him. Now, I was going to do it slowly.*

Taggart was cradling his bloody hand, staring at it, when Liam shot the floor around Taggart's feet several times. "Let's make haste Taggart, I don't have all day, and neither do you."

"Yeah, giddy up, motherfucker." Cade clapped Taggart on the back. "And don't look so surprised. You took one of the most beloved people in Briar Rose and thought nobody was going to come looking for her? You're a fucking idiot."

Vaughn just grinned, and my gaze fell to the brass knuckles he'd slipped onto his fingers.

Theo pushed past Vaughn, grumbling, "I doubt you'll get your turn while the body's still warm; *don't forget we haven't even discussed your disciplinary action yet.*" Vaughn's jaw flexed as guilt flickered through his eyes, and I didn't pity him a damn bit. It *was* his fault. He'd dropped his guard, and it was his neck I was coming for next.

The sound of footsteps was heavy behind me as the team followed us down into the basement. Taggart led us into a dusty storage room and hesitated in front of a closet door, seeming to know he was already damned.

I yanked the door open, half expecting to find Sara tied up inside, but I blinked as row after row of bright lights clicked on, illuminating a long white hallway.

"What the hell?" I murmured, realizing it was clearly an addition. The shiny floors, the massive vault door at the opposite end —it all felt incredibly out of place in the historic estate.

"Why the fuck do you look so nervous?" Liam demanded. "If you laid a *finger* on her."

"Of course not." Taggart swallowed hard, and for the first time, fear flashed through his eyes, and I got the sickening feeling he was lying through his teeth.

Liam wasted no time jamming Tag's fingers onto the vault door scanner.

I'd rescued dozens of hostages on covert missions over the last several years, but this wasn't anything like that. This was my whole world, this was my future, this was *the love of my life*.

The heavy metal door groaned open, and a terror like I'd never known hit me at the same moment a gust of musty, dank air did. The light from the hallway poured onto a set of ancient stairs that led down into a pit of darkness.

I stared at the crumbling stone masonry for a beat too long as pure shock washed over me. Several variations of *what the actual fuck* were murmured behind me.

My gaze slowly slid to Theo and then Liam, finding equal shock and worry in their eyes.

Suddenly, I didn't care about retribution anymore. My body was shaking with fear as I plunged into the darkness. If I was too late... I'd never forgive myself.

CHAPTER 56

For Fucks Sake

"Please. Please. Please." I murmured, hurrying into what was effectively a medieval dungeon. Just when I thought my heart might beat right out of my chest, the sound of Sara's voice trickled up to me.

"Is that—am I hearing that right?" Cade asked over the comms from farther up in the dark stairwell. "Is she singing— *Popular*? From Wicked?" He chuckled grimly. "*Of course she is.*"

I ripped the comm out of my good ear, straining to hear.

"At least we know she's alive." Theo muttered, and I couldn't have been more grateful for that realization.

The singing got louder, and when I finally rounded the last corner, several bullets went whizzing past me as gunshots rang out —I was shocked to find it was *Sara* with the gun.

"Don't shoot." I begged, hands up, as I quickly strode down the dimly lit corridor. "I'm here, baby." I dropped to my knees in front of her, frantically looking her over. "Are you hurt?"

Her lips parted, and she stared at me as if she were looking at a ghost.

My breath stalled in my lungs as I shakily took her face in my hands, illuminated by the headlamps behind me. "Oh my God, look at your face." The sound of my voice was strangled as rage and relief simultaneously pumped through me—noting every mark, every bruise, every tear. *I was gonna kill him. Slowly.*

"You came." She breathed. "*You're alive.*"

"Of course I came." I knelt before her, eyes shining. "I told you, there's nowhere on this earth you could go that I wouldn't find you."

My eyes shuttered as she tentatively reached for my face, gaze roaming my chest in disbelief, and then her eyes slid past me, and out of nowhere she started laughing uncontrollably—I suddenly realized she was *in shock.*

"You *all* came for me." She threw her head back, giggling deliriously, and that's when I finally processed what she was *wearing*—a hideous wedding dress, so puffy she was practically drowning in it.

In fact, I realized she was basically lounging in a metal folding chair with her bare feet kicked up, as if she didn't have a care in the world—and then I realized why at the same moment Theo did.

"*For fuck's sake.*" Theo muttered as I took the flask from Sara, smelling whiskey in it.

The corner of my mouth slowly pulled. "Are you drunk, pretty girl?"

She got suddenly serious and snatched the flask right back. "Oh, didn't you hear? I'm getting married." She snapped. "So yeah, I think I deserve it after this whoooooole fiasco." She waved the flask around, sloshing amber liquid onto both of us in the process.

My gaze swept the corridor, finding a cell door open, and even though one of Theo's men had secured the guard in the corner, Sara was still aiming the gun at him. That's when I noticed the *many* holes in the stone wall around his body, and I looked back at Sara with quiet surprise, a million and one questions sprouting in my mind.

Sara's fingers were in the air, her words a bit slurred as she declared to no one in particular, "Just so we're all on the same page, it is important that you know that I am *not* a lightweight." With determined focus, she counted on her fingers, the gun suddenly waving in every which direction.

"*Watch it!*" Theo growled, ducking alongside everyone else.

"Easy there, Rambo." I carefully took the gun from her and passed it back to Liam, who was eerily quiet as Sara stared at her fingers far too hard, and then announced, "I haven't eaten anything in four days? Five days? A week?" She barked a laugh. "I'm not really sure, cause there aren't any windows down here." She sang, and any relief I'd momentarily felt evaporated in an instant.

"You didn't fucking feed her?" Liam whirled and slammed Tag into the wall, and I suddenly decided Liam could have Tag all to himself because the only thing I really cared about was getting Sara out of this pit of despair. She'd been in the fucking dark for God knows how many days.

I reached into the pillowing layers of fabric around Sara's waist to pick her up—only *she winced* when I grabbed her, and I pulled my hand away, realizing it was *wet*.

Pure shock washed over me as I discovered the warmth against my palm *was blood*. "Oh my God, are you shot?" I gasped in horror—how much blood had she already lost? Fuck! I jammed my palm against the injury, applying pressure, only—

"Don't you dare touch me, Carter." Sara snapped, jerking away as hurt filled her eyes, as if the pain of her injury had suddenly reminded her exactly where *we'd* left off—fighting tooth and nail in Cade's office, me pushing her away, *breaking her heart.*

Panic clawed up my throat, and I tried as gently as I could muster, "Sara, you're shot. We need to get you medical attention. Right now." I reached again, but she jerked away, making me hesitate.

"I am not going *anywhere* with *you*." Her eyes were teary. "Get away from me." She snapped, and when I didn't move, *she screamed*, her voice breaking, "I said get the fuck away from me!"

My ears rang, heart ripped clean in half as I took a dizzying step back, while the dense walls consumed her pain and wrath. She'd been through a lot, she was in shock, she'd been fucking shot, and she was acting like I was the one who'd hurt her, *because I had.*

Liam materialized, squatting down in front of her, his voice incredibly gentle. "Sara, please go with Carter. I'm begging you."

Her lower lip trembled. "I can't." Tears rolled down her cheeks, one after another, as she lifted her gaze to Taggart, who looked like he was about to shit himself. "If I don't marry him, they're going to *kill* Dad."

Liam took Sara's shoulders. "Don't worry about Dad, we're going to find him, but first we need to get you somewhere safe, and you desperately need a doctor. So please, I'm begging you, just go with Carter." Liam looked over his shoulder at me, glaring, before he returned his gaze to Sara's. "Whatever is happening between the two of you, he's the only one I can trust to keep you safe. I know, you know that."

"Not him." Sara covered her face, shoulders starting to shake. "Liam, please. Why can't I just go with you?"

"You know why. I have to stay here and make sure—" Liam's voice lowered further, and my eyes slowly slid to Taggart.

One of Theo's men was holding him. "I warned you." I slid my gun into my holster. "You touch a fucking hair on her head and I told you what the consequences would be."

"I bought her, and she's still mine to do whatev—"

I swung, and the sound of bone crunched as he reeled back, and then I was on top of him, still swinging. "You never should have laid a fucking finger on her." I bellowed, and something warm and wet was dripping from my fingers as my hands found their way around his throat.

He'd starved her. Hurt her. Broken her.

I watched the life slowly drain out of him as I bore down harder. "I should have done this a long time ago—the very first time you made her bleed." My hands stung where he was desperately clawing for breath. "I should carve you up, because that's exactly what you did. Didn't you?!" I roared at him, not giving him an inch to answer. "I *know* what you did." He jerked underneath me, eyes wide with understanding, and I knew I should stop, knew I should carve him up slowly, just like he deserved, but I couldn't seem to let go.

Someone squeezed my good shoulder as I realized Sara had bought into every lie I'd told the last few weeks and then some. "Get your girl and get her out of here." Theo murmured. "Let us take care of the rest."

Taggart jerked as everything in my head went quiet.

"Carter, take Sara, now!" Liam's voice felt so far away, and I couldn't seem to let go. "Do you really want her to see this? After everything she's been through."

No, I wouldn't be the one who subjected my sweet, sweet girl to another horrific thing. *I had to let go.*

Taggart clawed for breath as everything inside me quieted— just me and him in that narrow space between life and death. Just another line of ink to add to my arm. I knew he deserved to die *slowly*, but I didn't have the strength to pull away.

"Carter!" Someone was shaking me.

I had to stop.

For her. I had to stop.

But it'd be so easy to hold on for just a little longer. We were almost there—*just a little longer, and then it'd all be over. For good.*

I was panting as Cade appeared in front of me, his hands carefully sliding against mine, pushing me out of the way. "He's not going anywhere," Cade murmured softly. "Carter, I have him. *Let go.*" I met Cade's gaze and gasped as his hands took over, falling backwards.

"We've got this, he's not walking out of this room." Theo promised and pushed something into my hands. "You know where to go, a doctor is already on his way."

I was panting wildly as I wiped my wet hands against my pants and shakily pushed up, as my gaze finally drifted to Sara—who was just staring, stunned at what I'd done. Almost done.

"Don't look at that, sweetheart, look at me." I commanded softly.

Her eyes slowly lifted, and the look she gave me hollowed me out three times over. Now she'd seen me for what I really was, and her reaction was exactly what I'd expected. Horrified.

I extended a shaky hand. "We need to go." But she stumbled back, something devastating flashing through her eyes, and I knew what I had to do. "I'm sorry." I croaked, dropping a shoulder low to push into the mass of white fabric as I softly took her arm.

"Carter, please." Sara protested tearfully as I tipped her over my shoulder in a gentle motion, doing my best to avoid her injury. "Why?" She demanded.

"I'm so, so sorry, Sara." I muttered, feeling her go limp in submission and defeat—feeling shockingly grateful as I felt her shake against me, crying, because that meant she was still conscious and I had no idea how much blood she'd lost, how much time we had.

Theo closed in on Taggart, checking his watch. "Lucky for you, Taggart, my schedule just opened up." Theo cracked his knuckles. "You should know, walk-ins are my favorite."

"I—can pay you." Taggart countered, wheezing hoarsely—hardly able to speak.

"We know you never had the funds to complete the transaction." Liam hummed calmly as I hurried up the steps—and I suddenly recognized the lethal cold rage in his voice, knowing that I had mere seconds to get Sara out. *If that.* "They were going to come for you one way or another, and you didn't honestly think you could get away with this, did you?" Liam mused calmly, far too calmly. *Oh God.* "This is the second time you've laid hands on my sister, and you don't have any idea how much you're about to regret that." He laughed humorlessly. "There's something you should know about me, Taggart—*I'm a professional butcher.* I carve up all kinds of flesh all day long, and now, you waste of a human carcass, *I'm going to carve you up.*" Liam promised darkly, his voice fading in the distance. "Don't worry though, I'll be right here with you every step of the way. You can count on that."

We were only halfway up the stairs when Taggart started begging. "Cover your ears." I pleaded with Sara, sprinting hard, because a moment later, the screaming started.

Outside, the crunch of my footsteps against the crushed stone was practically deafening against the tense silence between Sara and I.

Gently setting her down on the steps of the circular stone fountain, I carefully cut open the side of her dress to inspect her wound, and she begrudgingly let me. I stared at the injury for a beat and then my head dropped in relief as I blew out a slow steady breath—furious that she'd been shot, grateful she'd only been grazed. The bullet had taken a chunk out of her side, and she'd definitely have a scar, but it didn't appear life-threatening, thank God. I didn't even want to consider what would have happened if the shot had been an inch to the right. Headlamps bobbed behind me as someone handed me fresh gauze, and I wiped down and then quickly packed Sara's wound.

I took Sara's face in my hands, feeling sick to my stomach as I gently examined the bruises, and a hard lump settled into my throat. "Did he hurt you anywhere else?" I asked hoarsely, "Touch you—" My voice cracked, hardly able to even ask the question.

She shook her head no, looking at her hands, and I released a breath I didn't realize I'd been holding. "Thank God." Brushing a strand of hair out of her face, my heart broke when she pulled away. "Let's get you a hot shower and something to eat." I offered her a hand that she ignored when she pushed up, but when she swayed, I scooped her up into my arms in the next instant, ignoring her scowl.

She was quiet as I loaded her into the car, shoving too much fabric in with her. "You know, no one would have guilted you for actually shooting the guard. It would have been self-defense."

"I tried to." She admitted quietly, "Turns out, I just have shit aim."

I realized the halo of shots around his body weren't mercy shots at all, she *had* gone for the kill shot. Maybe I shouldn't have been surprised, but I was. She'd fought for herself, and I was damn proud of her for it, but knowing she was alive, that she was going to be okay—I couldn't help but find her shit aim a tiny bit humorous.

"If you laugh, I'm getting out of this car." She muttered.

I looked down quickly, concealing an amused huff of air. "I'm not laughing."

"Sure you're not." She scoffed as I closed the door. At least her sense of humor was intact. It was a shred of proof that she was going to be okay. That maybe *we'd* be okay. I hoped.

I rounded the car, climbing into the driver's seat and stared at her, pure curiosity washing over me. "I have to ask, how *did* you manage to get the gun?" I was dying to know how she could have possibly outmaneuvered her guard, especially injured. I honestly couldn't figure it out.

She stared out the window. "I promised him a kiss if he shared his whiskey with me, the rest was only a distraction."

Now that—I did not like. Not a single bit. Not even if she was clever for playing to her strengths.

CHAPTER 57

Bread and Butter

CARTER

I thanked the doctor as he left the small countryside cottage, and Damon Kingsley pulled up the long manicured driveway and parked his Porsche.

"Change of clothes, his and hers." Damon handed me an overnight bag and then a thermal lunch bag. "And something hot to eat, compliments of the wife."

"Thanks, man." I said, already heading back to the cottage. "I really appreciate it."

"Not a problem. You guys are welcome to stay as long as you need." He jingled his car keys in his hand, looking concerned. "She gonna be okay?"

I walked backwards, desperate to check on her even though it'd only been a few minutes. "Too soon to tell." I said, wondering the same. "We'll get some food in her, get a good night's sleep and then we'll see what the real damage is."

"They're not going to let this go." He said quietly.

"Neither am I." I shrugged.

"Let me know if you guys need anything at all. I'm just a text away."

I watched as his headlights pulled off into the darkness, and a dull ache settled into my chest. Theo had sent us up into the hills to stay at Damon's summer cottage until they could secure Brad's safety. If I could just get my hands on the data Seven was looking for, that'd hopefully give me the leverage I needed to put this all to rest for good.

I'd lived through my worst nightmare, and yet, everything was still all wrong— part of me wondered if the worst was actually ahead of me.

Swallowing hard, I pushed through the front door and into the single-room cottage before dropping into the flower-upholstered chair in the corner of the room. Head hung in my hands, I waited for Sara to finish bathing.

I was so dehydrated my gums were dry, my shoulder hurt like hell, my head was pounding—I felt like total shit, but I didn't care. Not when the same fists that had left me battered and bruised had turned around and broken the thing that was most sacred to me in all the world.

I was slumped back in the chair, staring at the ceiling, deliriously fighting sleep when I suddenly realized the shower had been off for some time.

My hand curled and uncurled as I stood in front of the bathroom door, hesitating to knock—it was only the fear of that still silence that lived on the other side that propelled me to action. "You alive in there?" I asked, wishing that weren't a literal question, but it was.

A gust of hot steam poured into the room as Sara opened the door, bringing us face to face—she stood there quietly wrapped in a small pink towel, hair wet, clinging to her bare shoulders, while we just stared at each other for a beat too long.

I opened my mouth, but Sara beat me to it, looking away as she spoke softly, "I'm done—if you want to shower."

A tense silence hung between us, and I finally stepped out of the way, realizing she was waiting for me to move. "Do you need help with your bandages?" I asked, pivoting in the doorway as I gripped my neck.

"Nope, I'm good."

Fuck. "There's some fresh clothes in the bags, dinner too." I offered, but she kept her back to me and didn't say anything more as I stared at her, as I suddenly became uncomfortable staring, realizing that it might be unwelcome now. I blew out a shaky breath. "Uh, okay, I'm gonna shower—I won't be long, but I'll check to see if you're done changing... before I come out." I offered awkwardly.

"It's not like we haven't seen each other naked." Sara murmured, hands unmoving as they gripped the overnight bag.

I swallowed hard, any response becoming lodged in my throat. Where the hell did we go from here?

Maybe it was because I was too exhausted to take a long shower, or that I was terrified something would happen to her in the minutes the bathroom door was closed, or simply because I couldn't stand to be in a different room than her—I showered quickly. But when I cracked the door to ask if I could come back into the room, I didn't get a response.

Nearly ripping the door off the hinges, I rushed out of the bathroom, wrapped in a too-small towel, and found her already in bed, the lamp on her side turned off. My eyes shuttered as I sank against the doorway for a long moment, not sure exactly what I was feeling.

"Are you asleep?" I asked softly, but my shoulders sagged at the edgy silence that responded, because I could tell from her tight breathing—that she was still wide awake. My heart caved in, but I didn't push. Not tonight.

I sat at the small table just a few feet away, watching her chest rise and fall with more gratitude than words could ever describe, and by the time I looked down, soup gone, I realized how much bread and butter I'd eaten, *nearly all of it.* Reprimanding myself, I set the few pieces that were left to the side, and put Sara's half-eaten container of soup away in case she got hungry in the middle of the night.

When I finally slipped into the flower-printed sheets next to Sara, I discovered the pillow barrier she had shoved down the middle of the small bed, and my chest tightened. *I was in big, big trouble.*

But after the last few days, I would have gladly slept hanging from the ceiling if it meant being anywhere near her.

∼

I'd almost drifted off when I felt Sara reach for me in her sleep, and a tear slipped down my cheek as I laid there, totally uncertain if I should pull her closer—I didn't know how she'd feel about that in the morning. So I just put my hand over the top of hers, grateful for the warmth of her skin under my palm, grateful she was alive and grateful for this moment even if I was desperately terrified that this might be the last time we ever shared the same bed.

∼

When I finally woke, it was in sheer panic—I rolled over, finding the bed *empty*, my head whipped towards the bathroom, realizing it too, was *empty*. I realized she wasn't inside the cottage at all, as I simultaneously ripped the covers off—nearly falling to the ground as I flung myself out the front door screaming for her.

The sunrise drenching the garden foliage around the cottage with warm morning hues felt horrifying as I frantically turned in every which direction. If someone had forced entry, if they took her, I would have heard, I would have—I whirled, hearing her voice, barely audible above the sound of rushing water.

I sprinted around the back of the cottage and found her sitting in a garden that overlooked a shallow, bubbling stream. "Sara, you scared the shit out of me."

"Sorry." She murmured, just staring out over the water—I realized it might have actually been quite peaceful back here if I weren't about to shit myself. "Couldn't sleep." She said quietly.

I dragged a hand over my mouth, panting. "Have you been out here all night?"

"Just an hour or so." She was leaning against a mossy rock, wrapped in a tight ball with her chin on her knees.

Hands on my hips, I stared up into the gently swaying trees above me. "I didn't hear you get up."

"You looked so exhausted. I didn't want to wake you." She ran her finger over the tiny hearts adorning the pale pink pajamas she was wearing.

A tight silence hanging between us, I couldn't hold it in any longer. "Sara, listen, I have some—"

"Please don't." She murmured, cutting me off gently. "Whatever speech you have planned, it's fine. We really don't need to do this."

I rounded the front of her, blocking her view. "Yes, we do."

She didn't look at me, but her voice was firm. "I appreciate everything you did back there, and I'm really glad you're okay, that we both are, but it doesn't change anything for *us*."

"Actually, I think it changes *everything*." I tried to explain, but she didn't bother wasting a response as she played with a strand of grass. "I just need you to hear me out." I begged.

She still didn't look at me, but she was quietly determined all the same. "I'm sorry that's what *you* need, but when you ended this relationship, my priority stopped being your needs. Now I need to worry about myself."

"Yeah, but that's the thing—"

"You're not listening." Her voice sparked a little. "You don't get to say the things you said—to treat me the way you did—and then pretend that a few nice words will make everything all better."

"I'm not trying to do that at all. I'm trying to explain, if you'd let me."

"Is that what you're trying to do?" She laughed humorlessly.

"I get it, you've been through a lot."

"That is exactly what I said to you." Heat swirled in her eyes as she finally looked up at me.

"Sar," I begged. "*Please.*"

She pushed up and brushed herself off, bringing us chest to chest as she looked up at me, eyes suddenly filled with no emotion at all. "You decided you didn't want me, Carter. You did that. Not me. And that means you don't get unfettered access to me anymore." She started back down the narrow path into the cottage, and I watched her walk away, realizing she was taking our future with her.

I burst into the cottage a moment after she did. "Carter." She groaned. "Please, I'm exhausted, and I don't have the energy for this."

This time I demanded, because I clearly had nothing left to lose, "Just hear me out." I begged, because even if she still didn't take me back, she deserved to know the truth—that there was nothing wrong with her. God, the fact that I even had to set that straight—I didn't deserve her, but that wasn't going to stop me from trying to win her back anyway.

Sara straightened, but didn't say anything.

Fuck. This was do or die. Everything had to go on the table.

"I didn't mean any of it." I started totally ineloquently. She scoffed, and I could hardly fucking breathe. "I did it to protect you." A bigger eye roll from her and I clenched my teeth as my eyes watered against my will. "Sar, the people that took you—*they killed my parents.*" She stilled as my voice broke, her expression shifting in an instant, because that's just who she was. "They *murdered* my mother because of what my father did." Her eyes softened a bit more as I barreled on. "When my jet was going down, I thought it was over for me, and in those last moments, I wondered if it would break you—my death. After everything you went through with your mother, and how hard that was on you— I was terrified of what the news would do to you, but selfishly, in those final seconds—I kept thinking I was so glad I said *I love you,* because you said it back. I knew I was going to die, but it brought me so much peace to know you loved me back, that I'd been loved by someone who was better than I'd ever deserve."

She looked like she pitied me, but she shook her head. "If you really meant that, you wouldn't have pushed me away when it mattered most."

"*They threatened to kill you, Sara.* In hindsight, the way I handled everything was incredibly stupid, but you were right, my brain was all fucked up. I thought I was doing the right thing—I thought if I could pretend you didn't matter to me that they'd leave you alone, that you'd be *safe*. After what they did to me, what they *took* from me—part of me wanted to die, Sara." My confession hung in the air as I gasped for breath. "I just didn't see a way through, and I was so angry. I still am. I just didn't want to burn it all down and let you get caught in the crossfire."

"Carter," she scolded, with nothing but concern in her eyes.

"Do you know what it's like not being able to do the thing you love most? Being separated from the thing that defines you?" Even saying it out loud made me feel sick.

"Not like that." She admitted. "No."

"When I enlisted, I was so incredibly lost. Heartbroken. I didn't know who I was. Flying made me find myself again, and they took that away from me like it was fucking nothing. But you —" I was practically gasping now. "If they had taken *you* from me, I would have *never* forgiven myself."

Tears filled her eyes. "No, you just went and lost me all on your own."

"My mother was murdered because of who and what my father was, so I won't apologize to you for doing what I thought would keep you safe." I dared a step closer. "I did what I had to, to keep you alive and out of harm's way, and if I had to do it over— would I do it differently? Maybe. But I can't go back and change the past. The only thing I can do is apologize for what I did and said to push you away." I took a breath and continued more quietly. "I didn't mean a single one of those things I said, and it was lower than low of me to use what you had shared with me in confidence against you. I hated myself for saying those things, and I convinced myself that I had to, because I was terrified. I was trying to protect you." I looked at her unsure if she believed me. "I was scared that if I didn't let you go on my own, then I'd lose you forever, and if something happened to you because of me—I wouldn't have been able to live with myself."

She was quiet, but sorrow swirled in her eyes.

I kept going, so incredibly nervous. "All the cards on the table. I'm still terrified, Sara. They're asking me for information—for blackmail." I laughed, dragging a hand through my hair. "I don't even know if I can find what they're looking for, and I don't know how far this game goes if I can't give them what they want. I don't even know how to fight back, how to fight as dirty as they do—when I'm terrified of how my actions will impact *you*."

I felt like I could crumple, and she was quiet for another too-long moment. "Say something. Anything." I pleaded. "Because I'd rather fight with you about this than have nothing at all."

Her eyes were distant, and her voice was so quiet. "As hurtful as everything you did and said was, I just can't believe any of this happened at all. I can't believe it was my own father who—" She cleared her throat, eyes shining as her voice broke. "Who does that? He sold my hand in marriage—*my life*—to pay for his debts. Like I was just another asset in his portfolio. There aren't words to describe how devastating that reality is." Her lower lip wobbled, and my heart broke as she continued slowly. "Tag said you didn't even bid, and I honestly don't know if I believe him or not. It was easy to believe him, because of what you said to me. It was easy to believe you didn't want me anymore because that's what *you* told me." She looked at me, confusion washing over her expression. "He said a lot of things. Told me you were *dead*." Her voice caught, and she quickly recalibrated, eyes shuttering. "Everything was so horrifying and so incredibly hazy, whatever they gave me made me hallucinate such awful, awful things, Carter. I hardly know what was real, everything was happening so fast and simultaneously slow.

Standing here, I honestly can't figure out if I just made the whole thing up."

"I know." I breathed, wishing I could take all her pain away. "It was real, and you're here, and you're safe now, and I'm never going to let someone hurt you like that ever again." I promised, hesitating, "I'm only saying this since you asked, but of course I bid for you—I had the highest bid when the gavel came down." I promised, knowing it was silly of me to even mention, but I'd fought for her every step of the way, and she deserved to know it. Deserved to know I hadn't stood by, if that's what she was really questioning. "You're not something to be owned." I clarified, "But I was desperate to get you out of there anyway I could, and I would have paid any price to save you." I swallowed hard, meaning so much more than money. "Regardless, the whole thing was rigged from the very beginning, they were always going to let the Caldwells take you, though I still can't exactly figure out why. When he took you—I tried—I just—I couldn't get to you." My eyes shuttered, and I had to remind myself she was standing right in front of me safe and sound. "I'm so sorry, Sara. For everything."

Her mouth quirked in a sad smile, and she was quiet for a moment. "I'm sorry about your mother, Carter. I really, truly am."

"I know." I hesitated and then looked her dead in the eye. "Marry me."

She startled. "What?"

I swallowed hard, offering her a grim smile. "You know, technically, since I won the bridal auction, you don't have a say." I was taking a huge risk here, teasing her about that, but teasing had always been our shorthand, and I had nothing left to lose.

"Carter, you are walking on thin ice." She warned, eyes flaring. "I've been literally kidnapped, held prisoner in a dungeon, and *fucking shot*—I am not in the mood."

Which was exactly why I couldn't wait a second longer. Nothing was promised. I'd learned that twice now.

"Marry me." I advanced a step, hoping I wasn't being a total idiot. I mean I was, but I had nothing to lose, and everything to gain. "Marry me, Sarafina."

She crossed her arms. "Carter, you're being crazy."

"I *am* crazy." I advanced a step. "For you—always have been."

I could see her resolve wavering even as she fought it. "You can't just tell me a sob story and then expect everything to be alright."

"I don't." I admitted, "And I will spend every day for the rest of my life proving it to you."

"You haven't even asked for my forgiveness." Her eyes danced between mine as something shifted.

"I'm deeply sorry, Sara. For everything I said, for treating you so much less than you deserve." I said earnestly, hopefully, desperately. "Will you please forgive me?" I asked. "Will you please give me a second chance? I'll do anything you ask of me."

"If you really mean that," her eyes slowly warmed to a glimmer, and a ghost of a smile almost flashed across her mouth. "*I dare you to prove it.*"

CHAPTER 58

Beg Me Baby

"Beg." I pointed to the floor. "Down on your hands and knees, Kensington. Beg for my forgiveness."

Carter sank to his knees, his eyes turning molten, voice turning velvety. "Please, baby."

"Lower." I whispered, my heart starting to thrum. "Tell me how sorry you are for pushing me away at every turn."

"I'm so, so sorry, Sarafina." He dropped to his hands. "I never should have let you go, baby."

"No, you shouldn't have." I agreed, knowing I was letting the door of my heart open a teeny, tiny, little crack. Was that a mistake? I had no idea.

Earnest hunger painted his expression as he promised, "I'll do whatever it takes."

"Crawl." I demanded softly, and his eyes went hopeful and then wicked.

Slowly, deviously, he crawled across the room, and I suddenly realized he was coming straight towards me—there was no escape in this tiny cottage as he arrived, panting at my feet.

"Will you take me back, baby?" He begged. "Will you give a stupid, stupid man a second chance he definitely doesn't deserve?" He bracketed the wall on either side of my legs as he slowly rose to his knees, eyes pleading from beneath dark lashes.

My body was humming with the answer, but I was too prideful to say it. "I don't know." I bit out softly.

He slowly, carefully, rose to stand, hands sliding up the wall on either side of me until his face was looming over mine, just a breath away—too close to even think straight. "Just say the word and I'm yours forever." He murmured, "Just say the word and I'll burn the world down for you—or paint it in rainbows and unicorns. I don't care. I'll do whatever you need me to. My life is yours to command, and my heart is yours to love."

I wanted him *so* damn badly, but I couldn't—as easy as it would be to snap my fingers and pretend this all away, it wasn't even remotely that simple. "You hurt me, Carter." I ducked out from under his arms and made it a single step before I was halted, his hand threaded firmly around my wrist. "I honestly didn't know you were even capable of being so cold."

"I made a mistake." He panted, hands sliding over my waist, fingers tipping my chin to meet his desperate eyes. "I know I fucked up. Bad. But after everything that's happened, I also know you fully understand the severity of the danger that you were in—the reasons I did it." He challenged. "I thought keeping you at arm's length would keep you safe, but really, I never should have let you out of my sight." He admitted. "And I know that makes me sound like a single-brain-cell-caveman-brute, but that's what you do to me, Sara. You make my brain short-circuit. You fill my heart with all your goodness, and you push out all the bad." He swallowed hard. "I'd like to think I do the same for you—that you're better when you're with me."

"I thought I was perfect." I raised a brow, quoting the thousand times he'd chanted it at me.

"You are, which is why I want you by my side every day of my life. However long that may be." He gripped my neck, forehead tipping to mine in submission. "Anything you need of me, I'll do it. You have my word."

"I don't know how to trust what you're saying." I said, his fingers feeling like fire against my skin as my voice cracked with dangerous hope. "You broke me, Carter. Twice now."

"I'm not denying that, but you know why we couldn't be together back then." I swallowed hard, knowing the truth of it, even now. "Do you still love me?" He breathed.

Fuck. I couldn't answer. Of course I did. I never stopped loving him, and that was my problem. Those torturously long, empty days, believing he was dead, had been the worst of my life. Especially knowing what he'd done for me in that room, how he'd fought for me, but that didn't change how he'd treated me before all hell broke loose—it may have been fake for him, but it was *very real* for me. The hurt of his words still lingered in my heart like a festering wound, and I wondered if there was a small part of him that had truly meant what he'd said.

I stared at his bruised face, *feeling desperate.* Everything I'd ever wanted was hanging on a string right in front of me, but would that string move? Was it always going to be just out of my reach? That was no way to live.

His lips parted, and I knew he was so anxious, so scared, and it broke my heart. "I love you, Sara." He confessed, "Even when I was being an asshole, I loved you. Never stopped loving you." His voice broke. "I'll *always* love you."

"I don't know." I murmured, gazing into those eyes that felt like home, feeling so conflicted.

"You don't have to say the words if you're not ready, but if the answer isn't a hell no—then I'm begging you to let me back in. Let me earn the right to have you in my life."

"I'm not sure I know how." I admitted, "Even if I wanted to, I think I might be too scared, too broken."

"We can be scared together." He tipped my chin up, his mouth so temptingly close. "*Heal together.*"

"Don't break my heart again." I pleaded softly, "I don't think I'm strong enough to handle it."

"That's the thing." His thumb brushed over my lower lip

reverently. "You're the one with all the power here. You always have been."

"That's not true." I whispered, letting my eyes flutter closed.

"Oh, but it is, sweet girl." He murmured, "You've always had me wrapped around your finger, and I think you might know that." His breath was warm on my cheek, waiting.

"I can't make up my mind." I confessed. Was I supposed to be strong and kick him to the curb? Was I supposed to believe in second chances? All that stupid internet dating advice was so damn confusing. What about what I wanted?

It was him. I was terrified, but that's definitely what I wanted. To find a way to make this work, even if he was a stupid, single-brain-cell boy, and maybe, if I could admit it to myself, what he was saying made sense. I was still pissed off, sure, wished he would have handled it differently, yes, but nobody was perfect and it was an utterly bizarre and fucked up set of circumstances, one-in-a-million, actually. Literally life and death. How many second chances were we allowed in this lifetime? Because surely, we had to be coming up on our limit.

My eyes shuttered as the images from that dark room played in my mind like a horrific nightmare—my fingers roamed Carter's bare chest, his skin warm and real under my fingertips, even though I wasn't exactly sure how he was mostly in one piece. I felt a swell of emotion as I gently brushed my fingertips over the edge of the bandages on his shoulder, as that one horrifying image sat right in the middle of my mind, refusing to move. He'd been dying right in front of me, mopping the floor with his own blood while he literally crawled, *dragged himself across the ground to get to m*e, and somehow he was still alive. That had to mean something.

He'd shown up when it mattered most. He always had.

"Fuck it." I murmured as he tried to decipher what exactly that declaration meant. "I'm willing to let you *try* to remind me why we're so good together, emphasis on the *try*." He smiled as we crashed into the wall his hand protectively wrapped around the back of my head, shielding me from all the impact before it slid to my throat, fingers cradling me, claiming me, demanding me —his lips just a breath away from my mouth, just waiting for that permission, like he always did. "How do I know you're not lying?" I rasped. "Manipulating me like everyone else in my life. Taking what *you* need. Making decisions for me." Was he just saying nice words? Words were so easy to promise, and even easier to throw away.

His hands slid up my body, feeling so right, his body firm and unyielding as he pinned me to the wall as if he could shield out the world. "Blue Gatorade." He admitted, breathless and raspy. "I hate blue Gatorade."

"But you always—" His callused fingers pressed against my lips to silence me gently.

"I *hate* blue Gatorade." He rasped. "The day you twisted your ankle on the soccer field and your team lost the game—you looked like you had the weight of the world on your shoulders, and it was so small, but I knew you loved yellow, so I gave you mine."

"You practically begged me for my blue one." My eyes glassed over. "And you kept up that ruse for years? Why?"

"Because I never wanted you to feel like you were being a burden—you've always shouldered too much, felt too much, worried too much, and I wanted you to have what you needed without feeling guilty about it—without you having to ask for it first. I knew if I ever took a yellow in front of you again, my good deed would unravel, and I couldn't have that. Couldn't have you feeling bad, because I think, even then, I knew I loved you. Sarafina, I've *always* cared about what *you* need. Maybe I'm not the best at showing it, but it's always on my mind. Making you happy. Keeping you safe."

"When we were in that room." I started my throat nearly closing up, and Carter's gaze softened in immediate understanding. "I thought you were dead." He pressed closer, thumbs brushing the tears from my cheeks again and again. "For *days* I thought you were dead." My shoulders shook, voice cracked. "Carter—I watched him beat you within an inch of your life. Why did you do that?" I demanded angrily. "Why did you do that for *me?*"

"To keep you alive," he murmured gently. "I'd do it all over again too. I'll always do whatever it takes to keep you safe."

I rested my forehead against his chest, burying myself in his scent, his warmth, his familiarity. "He shot you *so* many times—how?" I cried against his heart, wondering how it wasn't filled with holes. "I watched you bleed out on the floor—you were *dying.*"

He cradled my head. "I had my vest on sweetheart."

"I didn't know. I thought—for days I thought you were—" My voice cracked as I sobbed against him.

"I know." He held me so gently. "I'm so sorry."

"That's twice now you've almost died on me." I finally looked up at him through blurry eyes. "That's twice now I've had to stand by, watching you teeter on the brink of death, your beautiful face all black and blue." I cupped his face gently. "Even when you pushed me away, I *never* stopped loving you, and then I had to watch them hurt you, Carter." *I was so angry at him for it too, at everything.*

A tear slipped down his cheek. "How do you think I felt? Watching him *hit* you, threaten to do those awful things to you, Sara—I've never felt more helpless or powerless in my life. He was hurting you, and I couldn't get to you." His eyes shuttered.

"I *can't* lose you, Carter. Not ever again." I cried desperately.

"You won't. You're the only one there has ever been for me, and the only one there will ever be."

His body was so comforting, so warm, so *alive* right in front of me, and as I gazed into those soft brown eyes, feeling like I was finally home again—I pushed forward that last little breath.

Maybe it was me, maybe it was him, but the moment our lips touched we were frantic. It wasn't one of those perfect kisses, it was desperate. Teeth clashing, moaning, hands everywhere. A question and answer over and over again. Confirmation that we were both alive, that this was real.

"Say you'll marry me." Carter groaned between kisses.

"No," I whimpered as his warm fingers slid up under my shirt, being careful of my injury.

"We're inevitable." He moaned into my mouth. Cocky bastard. He might be right, though.

I broke the kiss, pushing him back, and he let me. "This is crazy." I said, wide eyed. "You're crazy." Love was one thing—marriage another thing entirely.

"Why?" he demanded, scrubbing a hand over his stubble. "Because I know what I want?"

"Do you know what you want?" I demanded. "What about that fucking blonde you were kissing? Blondes have *always* been your type." Lest we all forget that damning little detail. Fuck. There went that damn string swinging away once again.

"Sarafina, sweetheart—why the hell do you think I always went for blondes?" He practically begged.

"Because you look picture-perfect with them." I gritted, hating how inferior that made me feel.

"No!" He rasped incredulously, as if I'd completely missed the point. "I've been so in love with you for so fucking long, and when I couldn't have you, I literally couldn't bear to be with anyone that looked even remotely like you—it was too damn painful." I swallowed hard at the confession, slowly realizing the truth of it. "And that stupid photo—I thought making it look like I'd moved on would keep you out of the crossfire. You were right. It *was* a PR stunt to throw off that goddamn organization, a fake date, and she yanked me down for an unplanned kiss the moment the cameras started flashing." He shook his head, eyes shuttering. "I would never have intentionally done that to you. I swear, I pushed her away the second it happened, but as you know, a picture is worth a thousand words." I realized he still didn't know how intimately I knew the truth of that statement, and my shoulders sagged with immediate understanding. "I already bought out the news outlets. That photo is long gone." He promised. "I'm so, so sorry I let you believe it was anything more than that." He begged, "You'd already seen it, and I was desperate to keep you safe, so I let you believe what you wanted to. Please say you believe me, if I lose you, I'm begging you, don't let it be over something I had no control over, *please*." He was gasping, begging, panicked.

I believed him, yes, but that still didn't change how insane this all was. "Well, that might be true, but you can't just ask me to marry you, Carter!" I threw my hands up. "This is ridiculous. I mean, we're like freaking trauma bonded now—or something." The urge to cry suddenly hit me again, and I felt like I couldn't breathe as I raced for the door, desperate for a breath of fresh air.

I felt so hopeful and simultaneously terrified as I felt him come up behind me. "I don't do divorce." I announced as I turned, not entirely sure why I was confessing that.

His eyes sparked alive and hopeful as they danced between mine. "Me neither."

"This is not how this is supposed to go." I waved my hand through the balmy morning air. "You're supposed to have a ring and get on your knees." I laughed, wiping my eyes. "Come on, Prince Charming, this is a mess. Right?"

"I just crawled for you, and I'll do it again with a diamond ring between my teeth if that's what you want." Victory gleamed in his eyes.

"That's not what I mean—not to mention we're in our pajamas."

His smile was feline. "I could get naked if you prefer."

I suppressed a smile.

He dropped to a knee in front of me, and my heart stalled out as the morning light painted his beautiful face in golden hues. "Sarafina Amara Devereux." He slid that thin pink hair tie off his wrist and looped it three times, making an elastic ring, and I started crying as he presented it to me with tears in his own eyes. "Fact. You took a piece of my heart the day I laid eyes on you, and you've stolen the rest every day since then.

Truth. I know how lucky I am to be one of the few people you've let in, and whether you realize it or not—you're the *only* one I've ever truly let in. From here on out, no matter the cost, I won't let anything or anyone stand in my way when it comes to my love for you—my devotion to you." He cleared his throat. "Sweetheart, love of my life, I dare you—to let me love you all the way to the altar and every day after." He grinned, albeit nervously. "Will you do me the great honor of marrying me?"

I wanted so desperately to say yes, *a thousand times over.*

I knew it was insane, but I also knew that maybe he was right, maybe we were inevitable. So I did what I'd been slowly learning to do this past year. I let myself have this moment, let myself choose the thing that made me happy, instead of forcing myself to suffer on some screwed up principle of the matter.

"Okay," I whispered with a slow nod. "Let's do it."

A tear slipped down his cheek as he smiled. "Yeah?"

"Yeah." I nodded, letting him slip the pink hair tie onto my ring finger as I yanked his mouth up to mine. "You better get me a rock so big you can see it from space! I want a freaking sparkle parade, mounted on my finger. Otherwise, no one will believe the city's wealthiest bachelor is tied down to a *brunette*!" I demanded on the verge of a sob or maybe laughter, I had no idea. I was never going to let someone else attempt to take what was *mine* again, because that's what Carter was. *All mine.*

We were already slamming into a tree when his lips crashed against mine, hands soft and shielding against all the impact. "I'm going to get you a ring so heavy you're not going to be able to lift your arm." He declared.

I laughed, and it quickly turned into a moan as his fingers worked the buttons down my pale pink pajamas and his lips followed the trail. He pushed me up against the rough bark of the tree as he sank to his knees in front of me, playfully begging. "Please, baby, let me have a taste of my *wife*."

Oh boy, *wife,* that was the biggest turn-on I'd ever heard.

"Yes." I moaned breathlessly, unable to find the strength to make him work for it as my fingers speared through his hair.

Fingers tugging at the strings, then hooking into the elastic of my pajama bottoms, he waited, like he always did, for that final word of permission.

I stared at him, heart thundering, and nodded in disbelief. "You're going to be my *husband*." That word might be an even bigger turn-on.

He grinned, yanking my pajamas down, "Hell yeah I am." I gasped as he hiked my legs over his shoulders, and I held on for dear life—my pajama bottoms still dangling from one leg as he pinned me against the tree.

"Carter, your shoulder." I warned with a gasp as his lips descended.

"I don't care about my shoulder." He practically spat, and there was no escape when his lips found my clit in two seconds flat. I cried out, back writhing against the tree as his stubble scraped against me in just the right way. He worked his tongue over and in me, bringing me right to the edge. This wasn't love-making; this was love declaring, and there was no time for teasing. We'd done more than enough of that our entire lives.

He came up to steal a glance, grinning, lips shining, and then, "Oh shit, there's ants in your hair."

I laughed deliriously as he scooped me up and laid me out in the soft grass, dusting my hair off before sliding an arm under my waist, other fingers slipping inside me while his tongue brought me to orgasm mere seconds later.

As I chanted his name, "Carter, Carter, Carter." The sound of my cries were swallowed by the rushing stream, the birds chirping in the air, the wind softly rustling through the trees as I trembled in the grass with pleasure.

His mouth was on mine as I shoved his pants down, reaching for his intimidating length. "Sweetheart," He rasped, frustration lacing his voice. "I don't have a condom."

"I have an IUD," I said, frantically kicking his sweats down.

"We don't have to do this right now." He swallowed thickly, pants stuck around his ankles because I couldn't reach that far. "We have the rest of our lives."

"Carter." I groaned. "Don't make me put you back on probation."

"Are you blackmailing me for sex?" his mouth curled as he teased. "Why is that kind of hot?"

"Time to put your money where your mouth is, flyboy." I rasped, sinking into the grass as the weight of his body finally descended over mine, as he laid me back like a precious, fragile artifact beneath him, all while looking devious as ever.

"Are you ready for the ride of your life, because I've been waiting *my* whole life to show you the ropes?" He smirked, leaning into my ear to murmur. "You always were a little Rookie, weren't you, pretty girl?"

"We'll see how funny your jokes are when your cock is buried inside this *perfect* pussy." I shot right back. "Because you're about to find out how ruthless she can be."

"Ahhh, there's that smart mouth I love so much." He chuckled, low and deep against me, but it was me who stopped laughing the moment his mouth claimed mine—the moment his muscular body rocked and he notched himself against me, already stretching me as the earth held me from below and his solid weight held me from above.

Watching me with a soft, wild expression, Carter pushed in. Leaving me writhing beneath him, breathless and gasping as I stretched wider than I ever had in order to accommodate him.

"*Fuck.*" He groaned as he pulled back and then pushed in a little further. "You're so damn tight, sweetheart."

"Is that all of it?" I managed to rasp out, feeling like I might actually split in half.

"Nearly." He gripped my hips, easing out.

"Nearly?! Oh, God, Carter, I don't know if it's going to fit." I cried as he swept his head over my swollen clit, making me jolt. "I don't know if I can—"

"You can take it, baby." He murmured, watching me totally entranced as he slowly pushed in again. "I know you can, because you were made for me." He rocked his hips, pushing that last bit in as my head tipped back, lips falling open in a silent cry. "Look at you." He murmured, "You look so pretty taking me like this." I was breathless as he settled there for a moment, peppering gentle kisses over my eyes, my nose, finally my lips. He rocked again, and I cried a strangled noise against his mouth, realizing *that* was all of it.

"There it is. See, *princess*, I knew you could do it, take my obi-wand—*hot dog style*, just like you wanted." He teased softly, and I whimpered but flexed around him in defiance, making him swear. "Careful, or I might be tempted to fulfill the other half of your request and split you in half, just like you asked me to." He threatened with a dark, amused chuckle, all while he cradled my face in his hands so gently.

"*Carter.*" I whimpered, unable to vocalize anything else as he slowly withdrew and then his muscles rippled against me as he rolled his hips, filling me again.

"Sar, you feel *so* incredible, just like I knew you would." The adoration in his eyes as he fucked me in broad daylight between a garden of roses was like nothing I'd ever seen. "I love you." He whispered into my ear and then proceeded to thrust so hard I couldn't speak.

"With everything I am." *Thrust.*

"Everything I'll ever be." *Thrust.*

"You're my everything, sweetheart." His tongue swept into my mouth as he kissed me breathlessly. "And I'm never going to let you go again." *Thrust.*

There was so much longing in his eyes, so much vulnerability there, and difficult as it was to speak, I had so much to say. "I love you too." I rasped, feeling him in me, and around me, shielding the world out as everything tightened. "The way you see me, the way you show up for me." He gazed down at me, eyes shining, just before my head tipped back, eyes slamming shut with pleasure when he thrust again. "I just want you to know that I see you too—all of your goodness, because you're *so deserving* of good things, Carter." I confessed breathlessly while a tear slipped down his face as he rocked against me again and again.

In that moment, I realized how much he needed to hear those words, realized that maybe he'd been waiting a lifetime for me to say them. "I want you to know that I'm your safe space too, that no matter what's happened, what you've done, *I will always love you, Carter. All of you.*"

His eyes were soft even as he wrecked me, even as another tear slipped down his cheek while he captured my mouth with his, and claimed me. "Thank you." He murmured against my lips, and in that moment, I knew my big strong man was as tender as they came. I knew I'd never take that for granted, his vulnerability with me, his gentleness.

The sun practically shimmered between the roses as it came up, and Carter was all muscles and sex looming over me as he stole my breath again and again. He was *so* beautiful, his body, his heart, his soul, and he was mine.

"Those damn ants!" Carter hissed, and in one motion he'd rolled me atop him, leaving him down in the grass with the ants as he shook my hair out.

I would have laughed at his determination to protect me, even from the ants, if it weren't for the sensation of him filling me even deeper. Breathless wasn't even accurate. I was so full, I wondered if I'd ever be whole again without him.

"You're the most beautiful thing I've ever seen." He dragged his palms down my breasts as I tipped my head to the sky, lips parted in a strangled noise of ecstasy. "Ride me, baby." He murmured, calloused fingers scraping over my nipples before returning to my hips, always being careful of the bandages on my side. "Use me for your pleasure."

He met me thrust for thrust, lifting and plunging me onto his cock until I finally fell forward, hands braced on his chest in exhaustion. And then it was all him, driving me down onto his cock until I finally shattered around him.

My fingers bit into the skin of his muscled chest as he worked the last waves of my orgasm and something raw and primal broke loose in *him*. His thrusts became rougher, more needy, soothing every insecurity at the edge of my mind. One hand was around my throat, the other broadly splayed over my hip as he used my body for himself.

I submitted to everything he was giving to me, taking from me, and demanding from me, let the intensity of being split in half, rip my soul wide open as I laid myself bare to him. My future husband. The man who'd fought for me, drawn blood for me, and even crawled at the threshold of death for me. His desperation was a balm to my heart as I let myself relish in the feeling of being used, wanted, desired, adored, and most of all *needed*.

"*C-Carter.*" I gasped as a coil built within me, brighter, deeper, more intense than anything I'd ever experienced.

"That's my girl, look at you." He rasped, thrusting faster and wilder, more frantic. "Taking me so well." I was still riding the crest of my last orgasm as something deeper and more intimate loomed. I was goddess divine, hair tumbling down my back, over my breasts, teeth grazing over flesh, sweat beaded on skin. It was simultaneously all too much and not enough. I ceased to exist altogether. I was eternal as light and darkness collapsed around me, leaving a pool of warmth in their wake. *I was loved.*

"Fuck, baby." Carter whimpered, driving into me so hard it stole the breath from my lungs as he climaxed. "Everything I've ever needed."

I collapsed onto his chest, breathless and satiated, shuddering with pleasure while he tenderly stroked my back and we each panted, totally breathless. "Perfect." He murmured. "Just like I knew you'd be."

"Inevitable." I hummed, knowing I'd never feel more safe, more nurtured, more cared for in anyone else's arms.

His chest suddenly shook with laughter against my cheek. "What's so funny?" I breathed.

"I just knew your pussy would be my kryptonite, and it definitely is. I can't wait for seconds—it's the only thing I ever want you to feed me." He declared, all too amused.

I pushed up on my elbows and lightly slapped his chest. "Carter."

"What can I say, *wife*?" He shrugged with a wicked grin from underneath me, and *I didn't know if I'd ever seen him look happier*. "You were made for me, and I am *never* going to get enough of you."

"Or maybe you were made for me." I poked him, and he captured the finger, bringing it to his lips. "And I can't get enough of you either, but I'm not your wife *yet*."

"Something I plan on amending very soon." He wiggled his brows proudly. "Is my dick your kryptonite?" He practically begged for the affirmation.

"He's certainly something." I murmured, and laid back down, at a loss for poetic words. "He's a hell of a lot better than the unicorn horn, that's for damn sure."

Carter barked a laugh. "I should hope so. And by the way, you can bounce on my *banana dick* as long as you want, because even if you ride him until the sun goes down—he's *never* falling off." Carter's chest shook with laughter, and I rolled my eyes, while he absentmindedly played with my hair.

Suddenly, I sucked in a sharp breath, and stilled.

"What's wrong?" He tensed, head lifting out of the grass, hand flying to my injury in worry. "Are you in pain? Was I too rough?"

"Never." I murmured and brushed my fingers over the inside of his arm, discovering a tattoo I'd never seen before—two tiny little Sour Patch candies hidden in his floral sleeve. *Our candy.* Holding hands. One yellow, one blue. "How long have you had this?" My gaze snapped to his.

His expression went sheepish. "Got it the day I left." The

corner of his mouth pulled as he admitted quietly. "I told you I'd think about you everyday I was gone, and I did. Every single day." I gazed into his eyes, those final questions inside me finally settling for good. "I wasn't lying when I said I've always loved you, Sara, and I always will."

I smiled, and laid my head back down on his chest, running my fingers over his skin where our tattoo was. *Ours.*

He played with my hair as I laid there and stared at his tattoo, at the *flowers* he'd gotten in honor of his mother, and I suddenly had a realization.

"Carter," my gaze lifted to the flowers all around us. "I overheard Tag and his father talking about finding a painting with roses."

Carter hummed, tucking a strand of hair behind my ear. "Yeah, there was a woman who's been checking all the paintings at the estate for some information."

"They said it was blackmail. Do you know anything about it?"

He was quiet for a moment. "Apparently, my father hid something behind my mother's favorite painting." He followed my gaze, realization slowly dawning on him.

"What if it's not an actual *painting* at all?" I breathed, "What if it's in your mother's—rose garden." We said in unison.

"You're incredible." He kissed me hard, being mindful of my bruised face. "You know that?"

"Oh, I know." I mused, smirking. "And I don't plan on letting you forget it."

CHAPTER 59
Shovels and Pennies
SARAFINA

I grimaced as Carter paused his digging and rested a hand atop the shovel. He panted, looking mildly distressed as he surveyed his mother's now torn-up rose garden. "We'll find it." I encouraged, passing him a cold bottle of water. We needed to find it soon or at least take a break. I was worried about his shoulder. He was trying to hide it, but I could tell he was in pain.

Carter guzzled the bottle down to the last drop. "What if I just destroyed all this for nothing?" He grimaced, wiping his brow. "I mean, it could be anywhere. We're probably just digging up another pile of decade-old pennies my mother buried. We could dig for months and still not find it."

He was right, the metal detector was lighting up all over the place, because there were literally pennies everywhere. I wondered if that was exactly what his father had intended. "Maybe if I go upstairs, I can get a better view?" I offered at my wit's end.

"When you come back will you bring me another bottle of water?" He asked, looking all too exhausted.

"Of course." I nodded, shoulders sagging as he started back in with the shovel.

Upstairs, I realized the best view of the garden was in the south wing, and it didn't take me long to realize his parent's bedroom was positioned with a perfect view. Because of course it was, his mother had probably planted the garden on that side of the house so she could look at it more often.

I hesitated before pushing the door open and finally slipping into the dark room. As I dragged the heavy brocaded drapes open, I coughed, a cascade of dust tumbling loose. The housekeepers had clearly left this room alone.

As I scanned the garden from the window, an odd pattern of flowers caught my attention, but before I headed back down to check it out, I couldn't help but take a lingering look at Carter, shirtless, sweaty, and sexy as hell, his muscles rippling with his every movement—then my heart froze, crossing the lawn, headed straight for the gardens was a tattooed man with a small army of men behind him.

I struggled to force the old heavy window open, only prying it up a mere inch—I screamed through the crack at Carter in warning.

His gaze snapped up to mine, and then across the garden. "Hide." He belted a panicked scream.

I sprinted into the hallway before skidding to a halt—the tattooed man from the hospital was blocking my exit out of the south wing.

"Hey curly whirly." He crooned, beckoning me towards him with heavily inked fingers. "Let's take a walk."

"Who the hell are you?" I demanded, slowly backing down the hallway, panic rising in my throat.

He lifted his hands innocently, revealing a gun at his side with the motion. "Now, now, let's not do anything impulsive." He murmured, following my gaze. "Just come with me. I'm not going to hurt you." Which is exactly what people said right before they did just that.

His footsteps were heavy and fast behind me as I bolted back into the bedroom—slamming the door shut behind me before I locked it.

"Open up." A smooth voice called in contrast with the

violently shaking door as I spun in every direction, feeling like a trapped animal. "Come on, cupcake, are you really going to make me break down this door?" He threatened all too cooly.

Bile rose in my throat as I tripped over myself, sprinting through the sitting room and into the bedroom. Terrified, I fumbled with the window, realizing it wouldn't open—the door to the suite burst open with a thunderous crack.

I whirled, eyes desperately sweeping the room, my gaze snagged on a heavy stone bust, and I hauled it off the dresser, launching it at the window. Glass shards went flying as I wasted precious seconds looking over my shoulder and found the tattooed man giving me a psychotic grin as he strode into the bedroom.

Oh my God, was he enjoying this? Chasing me like a cat playing with a mouse—I was not about to become a chew toy, I had a goddamn wedding to plan for Christ's sake.

I shoved the thick, heavy panel of curtains over the ledge of broken glass and out the window, hoping I wasn't about to break my neck as I slid over the edge. I gasped, feet dangling as the man lunged, but I slid lower before he could grab me.

"Take my hand." He barked, straining over the ledge. "*Now!*"

I laughed in disbelief, realizing I was hanging over a relatively sturdy-looking flower trellis. I scrambled over to it, ripping vines loose left and right as I hurried towards the ground, screaming when it gave way and I fell the last few feet. Crashing into a bush, I groaned when something hard bounced off my head, adding insult to injury.

I flailed, hauling myself out of the bush, and sitting on the manicured lawn, glinting in the sunlight, was a beautiful little metal box. I snatched it up, skin prickling as I fumbled with the latch, finding something small wrapped inside. This had to be it!

My gaze snapped up as the trellis cracked again, and I realized the man was almost to the ground. I shoved up and sprinted like my life depended on it, because once-fucking-again it did.

Crashing through the maze of gardens, I wove through the

hedges and finally dove into one, forcing silent breaths in and out as I quickly unwrapped the small object. Inside several layers of plastic, no-doubt to protect it from moisture, was a USB drive. I stared at it, realizing I had it—the blackmail. What else could it possibly be? Carter's father must have hidden it in the stone masonry outside the bedroom window, where Claire would stand and look at her favorite painting every day—her roses. We'd been halfway right about the garden.

The man's shoes suddenly appeared next to me, as he strode through the gardens. "Here, kitty, kitty, kitty." He crooned, and I clamped down on each panicked breath as a tear streaked down my cheek. "Don't you want to come out and play? I promise I don't bite."

The second he wandered into the next row, I shoved the USB drive into my pocket, leaving the box, and crawled towards the sound of Carter's voice—trying not to think about all the bugs that were probably all over me as I stayed hidden between the hedges. I was surprised to hear Carter talking in conversational tones as I got closer, but as I peered through the branches, I discovered a nearly identical, tattooed man was holding Carter at *gunpoint.*

Oh fuck no. Over my dead body were we doing this little number again.

I eyed the shovel lying on the ground behind the man who was about to shoot my damn husband to be. Heart pounding, I steeled myself and quietly crept across the lawn—whether or not Carter saw me, he didn't let on.

It was now or never. I inched up behind the man and grabbed the shovel, aiming for his head as I swung hard—his hand shot out, halting my swing with an iron grip that left me stunned and panicked.

I yanked, but his grip didn't budge and neither did the shovel. "*Let go.*" He demanded with such quiet, powerful menace that I did.

Just then, an arm slid around my shoulders from behind, and

I froze. "Damn, you run fast." The Cheshire Cat chuckled. "Not gonna lie, wasn't expecting that."

"She's a track all-star." Carter's head ticked to the side in a tense movement. "And Luca, if you don't get your hands off her in the next two point five seconds, you won't have any. I don't give a fuck who you are."

"What do you think, Dante?" Luca asked. "I'm thinking maybe I should keep this one for myself." My breath caught, and the muscles in Carter's arms rippled as his eyes went lethally dark.

"Didn't you hear what they did to the last guy that made that mistake?" Dante droned with a lazy roll of his eyes. "Your buddy likes to play with his food just as much as you do."

"Exactly, makes me think I want to see what all the buzz is about." Luca smirked, releasing his broad grip—I jolted when he patted my ass. "Alright, off you go, Legs, back to your keeper."

I glared, but quickly hurried over to Carter, who immediately pushed me behind him, and as he kept that one hand on me, I realized he was trembling—with fear or rage, I had no idea.

"You wound me." Dante touched his heart, still aiming the gun at Carter. "That you honestly feel the need to do that."

Carter was tense but didn't say anything, and as I looked at the two tall tattooed men in front of us, I suddenly understood why Tag had yelled and screamed and thrown his fists at me. Because looking at these men, truly dangerous men, there was a quiet, understated arrogance there, and I knew if they wanted, we'd already be dead. Taggart had been a powerless bluffer—his father's pawn. Just like Eric.

"So what do you say?" Dante asked. "Wouldn't it be easier if I just made this all go away?"

"As tempting as your offer is, I told you. I don't know where the information is."

"Oh, but I do." Luca ran a tongue over his teeth and grinned. I inhaled a sharp breath and frantically patted my pocket, realizing it was empty. "You may be fast, Legs, but I'm quicker." Luca held up the USB drive, giving me a wink.

"No," I breathed, realizing the ass slap had been a pick-pocket.

Carter squeezed me, murmuring, "It's alright."

"Well, I guess that's that." Dante put away his gun, and I tipped my head against Carter's back in frustration and relief. "We'll send you a copy." Then he turned his back and seemingly floated across the lawn, the group of men following after him like an army.

Did that mean my father was still in danger? I felt tears well up in my eyes because I was so incredibly frustrated. "I'm sorry." I finally murmured. "I had it, right here."

Carter watched the men load up and then finally turned, gripping me by the shoulders as he exhaled roughly, and I was startled by his sharp tone when he spoke. "You wanna tell me *what the hell* you think you were doing?"

"What?" My lower lip wobbled as I stared up at him.

"Don't you *ever* risk your life for me again." He scolded as I stood there dumbfounded. "Do you understand?" He brought his eyes down to mine, softening. "I am begging you, Sarafina." His eyes shuddered. "*Begging you.*"

My lower lip wobbled as emotion got the better of me. "You don't get to ask that of me! Not anymore." I said, tears filling my eyes. "You don't get to sacrifice yourself and not expect me to do the same—I couldn't just stand there and do nothing while someone pointed a gun at you *again*." I sobbed, and his expression softened. "When I tried to escape, I thought you were dead, and I honestly didn't even know if I had the will to go on." I confessed shakily.

"Don't say that." He rasped, looking devastated as he tipped his forehead against mine.

"*You don't understand.*" I sobbed, and he gripped me tighter. "I love you with every fiber of my being, with every breath that I take. You're a part of me, you're my safe haven, my landing place, *you're my home.* I may have made you crawl for me, but the truth is, I never stopped loving you. Even when you made me mad as hell." I laughed through my tears, and he did too. "You can't expect me to stand by while someone is threatening to harm you. Carter, I have the lines that crinkle around your eyes when you smile memorized, the sound of your laugh memorized—the curve of your mouth when your lips are pressed against mine is like a beautiful shadow, haunting me during every waking hour and every sleeping one too. Even if I wanted to, I could *never* escape you."

"Sara." His words were an ache of devastation, and understanding all at once.

"Promise me." I demanded adamantly, wiping my cheeks. "You said, anything that I needed, and what I need is *you*. Alive, and in one piece preferably."

"Okay." He promised gently and pulled me against him to give me a soft, reverent kiss.

Finally I pulled back, shaking my head. "I'm so sorry I lost it—it was right there, and I just let it slip through my fingers."

"Don't be sorry, sweetheart, your safety is far more important than a piece of plastic."

"Carter, it was way more than just a piece of plastic." I lamented.

"It's alright. It's done, and I made a deal with Dante, anyway—honestly, it might even be better this way."

"Who were those men? You knew them, one of them showed up at the hospital."

"You don't want to know." Carter muttered, slipping his fingers between mine and pulling me towards the manor, but I stopped him.

"Actually, I do. No more secrets, no more doing things you think I shouldn't know about, in the name of protecting me." His eyes danced between mine, hesitating. "You said anything I needed." I reminded him. *Again.*

Carter nodded slowly. "They run the mob, and whatever blackmail is in that file is damning enough to protect us."

"So they'll just leave us alone? What about my father?"

"If that USB contains what they think it does, it should be enough to clear his debts *and then some*."

"You don't think they'll come after you again?" I asked. "*Us?*"

"I don't see why they would." He admitted, watching me closely. "This whole time, it was never about you or me, or any of it. They were just desperate to retrieve the blackmail my father had collected. And now that it's out in the wild—now that Dante has it, it doesn't really have anything to do with us. I do have a whole host of security measures I'll be putting in place, but Sara, I promise I'm going to keep you safe." He shook his head with a heavy sigh. "Even if I have to dig a damn moat around this place."

"Like the Belacourte Estates?" I quirked a brow.

He rolled his eyes. "Okay, maybe not a mote, just a really tall fence."

"Yeah, okay." I chuckled as I led him to the house. "I don't know about you, but after all that, I could use another shower. How about a bubble bath for my fiancée?" I asked, raising a brow.

A grin slowly spread over his face. "If you can make it up there before I catch you, then I accept."

My heart started to race as I backed away. "And if I can't?"

"Then, as my future wife, I plan to give you a taste of what you can expect from your future husband." I bit my lip, backing away as he let me create some distance between us. "You should start running." He hummed, "Because I don't intend to be a gentleman for round two."

I only made it several paces before his strong arms wrapped around me, and I squealed as he hauled me up against his chest in a bridal carry. "That was cheating." I breathed. "You didn't even give me a chance."

"I'm never letting you get away from me again, that's a promise, Mrs. Kensington." He chuckled gleefully, "God, that sounds good." And I couldn't help but agree.

CHAPTER 60
Keep Painting
CARTER

"I can promise you, no one from the organization will be ignorant enough to disregard the agreements that have been made." Dante slid an envelope with several copies of the USB file across the desk with a wicked gleam in his eye. "Then again, people always surprise me." He shrugged. "You have my contact card should you need my services for any future *disposals*."

"Let's hope it doesn't come to that." I was anything but thrilled to be so intimately connected with the mob.

"Really, I should thank you for the intel." Dante looked all too pleased as he drummed tattooed fingers across his desk. "I must say, I had high hopes, but the contents of that drive have far exceeded my expectations."

I scoffed, "While I'm grateful for your assistance in putting all this to rest... I still can't figure out how you knew exactly where to find us." I watched him over the rim of my glass as I polished off my whiskey. He was not the kind of man you let out of your sights. Not for a minute.

"Right place, right time." He shrugged. "You know, I would certainly pay handsomely if you were to stumble across any other incriminating files. I imagine a man like yourself must have an orchard of blackmail, just ripe for the picking." He cocked his head. "Or perhaps you'd be more inclined to invest in the expansion of my business and maximize your profits." He said brazenly, offering to go into business together.

"I'm not interested in continuing the work my father started." I said, hoping there weren't any other dangerous skeletons hidden in my father's closet. "I have more important priorities."

"Ah yes, your little spitfire with the strong arm." Dante chuckled. "If it doesn't work out between the two of you, perhaps—"

My smile was flat as I leaned back, arm over the back of the couch. "You may have an army of men downstairs," I mused, while Dante's eyes twinkled, delighted I'd taken his bait. "But if you so much as blink in *my wife's* direction, I'll break your fucking neck."

"Duly noted." He chuckled with casual amusement as he rocked back in his chair. "But unfortunately for me, I doubt when I finally go, I'll be lucky enough to have such a quick death."

"I don't envy your outlook on life at all." I said, "Perhaps if you find someone of *your own*," the words were biting. "Maybe that outlook would change. Love has a funny way of coloring your perspective on everything." I admitted.

"Love." Dante muttered, and adjusted the rings on his fingers, drawing my attention to the mottled scars all over his hands, the letters inked over his knuckles—*Fate, and Lore.* "Love is good for one thing. Making you weak."

"Is that why you murdered your fiancé?" I watched him closely.

Something curious flashed across Dante's expression but was gone an instant later, leaving only lethal darkness. "That is what they say."

"Why do I get the sneaking suspicion that what they say isn't even remotely true?"

"Careful." He warned, "We wouldn't want you making me out to be one of the good guys."

"I think you've done that all by yourself." Whether I liked it or not, I was now indebted to him, and he to me. He could have killed us that day, taken the blackmail and been on his merry way, but he didn't. And in a curious unfolding of events, not only was The Society no longer my problem, now, a handful of very important politicians were about to bow to the whims of a very dangerous man. But Sara was safe, our future was safe, and the cascade of events that were about to unravel were no longer my problem. "In another life, I think I might have actually liked you, Dante."

He nodded. "Perhaps you and I are cut from the same cloth." I couldn't help but wonder if he was partially right. Each of us born into our own worlds, doomed to uphold the expectations that were placed upon us the moment we were born. "But then again, I'm on this side of the table, and you're on that side," he mused.

"And yet, we both have blood on our hands." I stood to leave.

"Ah, but you're an optimist." He murmured, looking like he felt sorry for himself. "I, on the other hand..."

I barked a laugh. "I'm curious why a man with as much power as you is playing a game he doesn't seem to enjoy very much."

"For the same reason you are." He flicked a knife up into the air, catching it before repeating the motion. "People see what they want to see, and we give them what they want." His hands slid behind his head, and the blade sunk into the wood of his desk, punctuating the end of our conversation.

"Thanks for everything." I headed to the door. "And please don't mistake my pleasantries for friendship." I warned, "I meant what I said. I don't care who the hell you are. If you so much as breathe in her direction, I'll give you exactly what you expect—a nice, slow death."

"It's been a pleasure doing business with you." He purred as I let myself out.

"I wish I could say the same."

The sound of his laugh faded as I headed out of Dante's office and into The Inferno.

The stairs in the nightclub were practically pulsating as I jogged down them towards the dance floor and the exit beyond.

But a familiar face coming up the stairs caught my attention. "Liam?" He looked terribly exhausted.

"Kensington." He was out of breath, as if he'd run here. "What are you doing here?"

"Just wrapping up with Dante. I think we've got the agreement all ironed out." I pulled out the envelope and handed him a USB. "We should all have one in case anyone double-crosses us."

"Good thinking." He nodded, wiping his mouth, eyes a little wild. "It's helpful—having friends in high places."

"Or low places." I murmured, noticing his shirt was incredibly rumpled. "What are you still doing lurking around here anyway?" I tried to lighten my tone even as worry filled my chest. "Didn't you finish the menus for the club months ago?"

"Oh, yeah." He shifted his suit jacket as if he were hiding something. "I'm just doing some consulting. The Leones have a lot of connections." He smiled, but it didn't meet his eyes. "Networking, you know?"

"Yeah." I swallowed hard, a pit settling into my stomach, knowing Liam already had lots of connections. "I know the breakup is still fresh, but if you ever need to talk... about anything." I fished.

"Yeah, I don't know, it's not a big deal." He gripped the back of his neck, his expression in contrast with his words. "I guess it wasn't meant to be." He checked his watch. "Hey Cart, I'm sorry, man, but I'm running a bit late." He hooked a thumb over his shoulder. "Catch you later? When I can beat your ass for getting in the sack with my sister?" He added with a grin. "Don't think I'm letting that one go this easy."

"You talk to her?" I asked, knowing Sara wanted to be the one to talk through everything with her brother, to explain our relationship.

"Yeah." He paused, already heading up the steps. "You already know what I'm going to say."

"If I hurt her—" I started.

"I'll kill ya," Liam finished for me, his head tilted with a smug grin.

I chuckled. "Beer this weekend? I miss you."

"I'd like that." He agreed, and relief flooded me, realizing he wasn't trying to push me out.

"Take care of yourself." I called as he excused himself and hurried up the steps. "And take a nap, you look like hell."

"You too, Kensington." He called over his shoulder with a laugh, but I couldn't help feeling like something was terribly wrong.

I started down the stairs again when my gaze snagged on the step he'd just been standing on. A faint red smudge where his shoe had just been.

Blood.

When I got home, I let *all* the housekeeping staff leave early so I could fully indulge in my favorite sweet treat, because the scent of brownie batter was in the air, and the only thing more tempting than the smell was how cute my *wife* was. I settled in against the doorframe of the kitchen, *our kitchen*, and dragged a hand over my mouth with a grin.

The soundtrack of some musical I didn't know was blasting through the speakers, and Sara belted the lyrics into a batter-covered spatula, completely oblivious to my presence. Her dark hair was thrown up into a messy ball on the top of her head, little wisps curling around the nape of her neck, highlighting the soft spot I intended to give my full attention to later.

She looked sexy as hell, practically swimming in one of my t-shirts, perfectly undone, soft lean legs flexing as she spun around, doing a piss-poor impression of her brother in the kitchen—there was brownie batter splattered in places I couldn't possibly explain.

My cock thickened as I watched—the song crescendoed, and she dramatically serenaded the little orange stray I'd kept after my attack, who was currently sitting on the countertop, enjoying the show just as much as I was. Something about the vulnerability of it, the fact that nobody else got to see her like this—except for me, *and Ranger*. Playful, uninhibited, joyful.

And the best part? She was all mine. *My wife.* Forever and always.

Sara startled, realizing I was watching her, and her face quickly morphed into a devastatingly beautiful smile as she leaned into her shoulder flirtatiously. "Hi husband."

"Hi wife." She was like gravity, drawing me in as I slid my arms around her, loving the way she immediately relaxed into me even as she kept stirring the batter.

"Want a taste?" She asked, dragging a finger across the batter-covered spatula before lifting it to me.

"Always." I sucked her finger into my mouth, loving how it made her eyes heat and then flutter. My lips innocently found their way exploring up the length of her arm, making a pit stop at her wrist, and then the inside of her elbow, and then her shoulder as her breathing turned ragged. I nudged her head to the side, relishing in the erotic little sound she made as I razed my teeth over that perfect soft spot at the base of her neck, and then my tongue was running over the skin, soothing the mark my teeth had left.

Her voice was raw with want. "I missed you all day."

"I missed you more." I greedily consumed her mouth as her lips met mine. "Mmm, how delicious."

She giggled breathily, "Me or the brownies."

I gave her ass a hard squeeze. "Both, of course."

Her smile broke the kiss. "Good answer."

"Come upstairs with me—I have a surprise for you." I dropped low, and she immediately sprang up onto my back—

wrapping her arms around my neck while I pulled her legs around my waist.

"Oh look, I'm like your little spider monkey." She giggled, referencing the girly movie we'd watched the night before.

I chuckled, "I am going to pretend like I don't know that reference."

She laughed. "I know you loved it, don't lie." I headed upstairs, not admitting that she might be a teensy tiny bit right. Honestly, I didn't really care what movie she wanted to watch, because what was even more fun than watching the movie with her was seeing how long she could focus on the screen, while I focused on her.

As I carried her upstairs, Sara peppered my neck with feather-light kisses that made me chuckle. "That tickles." I complained, not put out in the slightest as I set her down in the hallway. "Okay, no peeking." I slipped a hand over her eyes and shuffled her into the room—with her giggling and making dramatic noises like she was about to fall over, *she wasn't*, I had her every step of the way.

"What's it gonna be?" Sara chimed silly as ever while I pulled my hand away, but after a moment, she finally turned to me, wincing apologetically. "What exactly is the surprise?"

I grinned nervously, nodding to the clothes. "Give it a second. It'll come to you." Her face contorted while she mulled it over, and then her expression shifted as she sucked in a sharp breath, realization flooding her as she reached for a garment. I could tell she was trying not to get too excited before I confirmed it.

"Oh, my God." Tears immediately started rolling down her cheeks as she fingered the fabric, and my heart pounded, wondering if I'd fucked up. Maybe this would all be too painful. Maybe this was a mistake. "Carter, are these my mother's clothes?" She turned to me, a mixture of disbelief, heartbreak and relief simultaneously painting her expression. "Where did you get these? How?"

"Is it too much?" I asked, gripping my neck. "If it's too much, we can have them moved to storage."

"No." She quickly answered. "I'm just in shock. I can't even believe you were able to get these back?"

I shrugged. "It's not all of them, but I was able to track down a fair amount."

She buried her face in the clothes, her voice muffled as she inhaled deeply. "I can't tell you how much this means to me. Thank you doesn't even seem like a big enough word, but thank you, Carter." I rubbed her back as she turned and sheltered in my embrace to weep. "Thank you from the bottom of my heart. You're the sweetest, most thoughtful husband I could have ever asked for." She sniffled.

I rested my chin on the top of her head and smiled to myself. "I'm really glad you like it."

Her voice wobbled again as she lifted her head. "Are we in your mother's closet? Oh Carter, did you put our mother's clothes together?" She looked up at me, brows crunched, cheeks wet.

I cleared my throat and shrugged. "Our mothers were best friends, and I figured their clothes might enjoy each other's company."

"That might be the sweetest thing I've ever heard." Sara pulled me down for a soft, emotional kiss that made everything in my world right.

I brushed my thumb over her slightly swollen lower lip with a gentle smile. "There's one more surprise, this one is your wedding present."

"What?" Her mouth fell open? "Carter, you're all the wedding present I need."

I chuckled. "That may be so, but I have a sneaking suspicion you're really going to like this." I reached into the pocket of my suit and presented her with a blindfold. "No peeking." I murmured, and her eyes heated as she gave me a nervous but devious little look before she took the blindfold and slipped the silky thing over her eyes without an argument. *Noted.*

We had been slowly testing the waters in all kinds of ways these last few weeks, and that would be a fun one to explore *very* soon.

Blindfolded, I carried her caveman style to the opposite side of the manor, over to *our* wing of the house, and into the new addition I'd somehow managed to keep her out of for the last several weeks now.

"Surprise." I set her down in the sun-drenched room and nervously tugged the blindfold off.

"You built me an art studio." She breathed, turning in every direction to take it in—I'd spared no expense. The corner of her mouth hiked up in curiosity. "I know I don't have to tell you this, but there's a dozen other rooms in the house that could have been converted."

"None of them were perfect." I admitted, "So I had to start over." I'd made the studio to fit her *every* need, and I'd also built a beautiful outdoor area just beyond the long wall of floor to ceiling windows. Beyond the covered patio was all new landscaping to give her something pretty to paint, but if I was being honest, I knew she'd look just perfect sitting out there amidst all the flowers, framed like *my own* personal painting. "All the windows have blinds inside the glass." I explained, and grabbed the remote, showing her how to open and close them. "If you need to, you can actually get it pitch black in here." I pointed to the ceiling. "There's also a custom ventilation system—keep those pretty little lungs of yours in good shape." She rolled her eyes, and I grinned and slid a moving wall open to show her how the space could expand if she needed it.

She just stared at me for a long beat, eyes filled with something that made my heart swell. "I thought you didn't like spending money unnecessarily." She finally teased. "Especially making this *too big house,* even bigger." She mimicked me, a devious twinkle in her eyes.

"That was before I had someone to spend it on." I countered, already missing her touch from across the room.

"Hmm. If I had known that was the remedy, I could have started doing damage a lot sooner." She ran her fingers over the long work benches one after another, a pleased smile on her face.

I chuckled, watching her carefully as she took it all in. "What do you think?" I asked, wondering if I'd been overly presumptuous. "You can paint in the gardens if you want, or here in the studio. I just wanted to make sure you had the perfect space. If you don't like it, we can make any changes you want, or we can even get you a studio outside of the house. I just thought if you wanted to work from home, you know, in case that was easier with the baby—" I cleared my throat, realizing that didn't come out right.

"Not *the* baby, I mean *a* baby. Err *our* baby, obviously." I gripped the back of my neck, feeling like a total idiot. "Shit. I'm not saying—I mean, not anytime soon." She was grinning from ear to ear while I dug myself deeper. "I just—you know, whenever we're ready for that—if we're ever ready for that? I just wanted you to have a dedicated place for yourself."

Sara walked her fingers up my chest with a raised brow. "Are you trying to put a baby in me, flyboy?" I froze. "I don't think I'm quite ready to be a work from home mom yet, but I'm perfectly open to some baby-making practice." She winked.

I took her face in my hands. "I'm sorry that came out all wrong. You're just getting started in your career, and I'm not trying to put pressure on—"

She pressed her fingers to my lips, her expression softening. "I know."

"Fuck, I feel like I just put a shit ton of pressure on things." I admitted.

She threaded her arms around my neck. "Whenever we decide to start a family, I know you're going to make the best dad."

"You think?" I breathed.

"Yeah." She nodded. "And just so you know, Kensington, when the time is right, I can't wait to have your gigantic babies."

I grinned like the fool I was and fist-pumped. "Fuck yeah! I can't wait to make you my baby mama someday." We burst into a fit of giggles as I grabbed her hips and obnoxiously thrust my own against hers, both of us fully clothed.

She stared into the room for a moment, face slowly morphing into a devious grin. "Wanna make a sex painting?" She asked, and I barked a laugh. "Let's document those killer abs of yours so that when we're old and soft, we can remember the good ol' days."

The thought of growing old with the love of my life made my dick ache in the best possible way. "You don't have to ask me twice."

She dragged a canvas onto the floor. "What a perfect way to break in my new studio." She gleamed, already opening drawers, pulling body paint out, because *yes*, I *may* have already accounted for her bright idea. "Strip, Kensington, and let's see that eight-pack." She demanded, suddenly turning all business, and fuck if that wasn't hot.

"You know, the last figure modeling I did for you, I was trying desperately hard not to humiliate myself." I crooned as I loosened my tie slowly, watching her eyes heat. "You have no idea how hard I had to focus to stay flaccid." I undid my belt and stepped out of my pants before I quickly unbuttoned my shirt and eagerly shed that too.

"Is that why it took you so long to come out of the bathroom?" She chuckled as my cock bounced in front of her impatiently.

"Yeah, you have *no idea*." I reached for her.

"Ah, ah, ah. Wait your turn." She scolded, smiling to herself as she started smearing my body with different colors of paint using her fingers.

"What if I don't want to?" I threatened.

She clicked her tongue. "Too bad. I have a vision for this."

I swiped paint across her cheek quicker than she could get

away. "I'm sorry, sweetheart, but I've got a vision of my own, and as you know, I've *never* professed to be a gentleman."

"*WAAAAIIIIIIT.*" She screamed as I captured her in my arms, covering her clothes in paint—*my* clothes. Her shriek of laughter was music to my ears as I used about three percent of my strength to wrestle her onto the canvas before finally pinning her down.

Her giggles turned breathy when I claimed her mouth with mine. "We need a honeymoon." She moaned, "So we can stay in bed all day and have sex."

"Your back-to-back speed round this morning wasn't enough?" I chuckled, sliding her shirt up over her head.

"I'll never get enough of you." She moaned as I tweaked a nipple with blue and green fingers, making her back arch off the canvas. *Beautiful.*

"After the merger, we'll go anywhere you want, for as long as you want." I promised, getting even harder as I considered being able to keep her hostage in bed for days on end. I reached up to the workbench, knocking things over as I frantically grabbed for a brush. "Paint something for me, baby."

"Now?" she asked breathily, already writhing beneath me like a fucking goddess.

"Now." I flipped her over onto her hands and knees and slid her little shorts down her thighs, groaning when I realized she wasn't wearing any underwear. "Do as you're told and pick up the brush." I murmured, and she let out a breathy laugh and obeyed.

Her body trembled as I traced her with my cock, teasing and stretching while she doodled a shaky little pink thing—*a damn strawberry.*

"Make it a garden of them." I ran a paint-covered hand down her spine, leaving a handprint on her ass.

"Yes, husband." She breathed, and I ached for her. *For my wife.*

The little strawberry garden was almost finished by the time she was glistening and *begging* for me. So I notched myself against her, paint covered hands sliding into the crease of her hips as I sunk into the world's most perfect pussy with a groan of ecstasy and a quick thrust—she cried out and the paintbrush slid across the strawberries, ruining them, just like I was about to ruin her.

"Oh, God." She moaned when I pulled out and snapped back in. "*Yes.*"

"Come on, baby, can't you focus?" I set a languid pace. "Keep painting."

"Feels too good." She whimpered, palms flat on the canvas for stability, jolting forward every time I bottomed out.

"Then we'll do it together, yeah?" I wrapped her hair around my fist, panting as I lifted her mouth to mine for a searing kiss, as paint slid between our bodies. "Be a good girl and pick up the brush for me." She whimpered as I lowered her, trembling head to toe as she grasped the brush again. "Don't let go, *wife.*" I crooned and thrust hard—her hand slipped, streaking across the canvas as she cried out. "See, pretty girl." I thrust again, painting another streak, and another, and another. "Look what pretty art we make."

"C-Carter." She begged as we shifted across the canvas, thrust after thrust, painting our love story stroke by stroke. *Priceless and one of a kind. Just like her.*

"Yeah, that's right, beg me." I purred into her ear, executing a perfectly sinful method of retribution for the cottage.

"*Please.*" She whimpered, and I could tell she was getting close—I could feel her fluttering around me, tight and perfect, could see her stretching to accommodate me as I gave her everything she deserved and more.

"Fuck, you look so good taking me like this," I rasped, mesmerized as I watched the place where we were joined.

With paint getting too close to intimately important places anyway, our little game quickly gave way to frantic, demanding desire, and when her voice was raw and she was trembling around me with her climax, I finally spilled myself into her before collapsing onto the canvas.

I dragged her on top of me, painting my chest with her colorful tits. "Thank you, husband." She murmured, eyes heavy, completely satiated. "For everything"

"You are so very welcome, wife." I ran my fingers down the length of her back, I loved that word, loved calling her that, loved *being* her husband.

Meow. I turned my head and chuckled, realizing we'd had an audience this whole time.

"Ranger, no," Sara warned, "stay over there!" But it was too late. That darn cat was *obsessed* with Sara, followed her around the house, day and night.

Ranger wasted no time sauntering right across the painting, tracking little paw prints everywhere as he made a beeline for our favorite person. I chuckled when he climbed right on top of Sara's back and perched like a little bug, purring so loud, I could practically feel it vibrating through Sara's body.

Sara groaned with a laugh. "I guess it's fitting that everyone gets to make their mark on our family portrait." I smiled, obsessed with the start of our little family. "Why don't you take me up to the shower for round two?" Sara gave me a soft, satiated smile. "Because as good as you look naked, I need to get you cleaned up. I might have a little surprise for *you* too."

"Do you now?" I smirked, because the truth was, *I had one last secret of my own.* This right here was my family, my future, my everything, and it was time to let the world know she was *mine.* No more playing house in secret.

CHAPTER 61
His Last Secret
CARTER

Sara was beaming as she removed her hands from my face. "Surprise!" A chorus of voices shouted as several loud pops sounded, resulting in a flurry of colorful paper confetti.

I grinned, seeing the smiling faces of all our friends filling the roof of the Vandenbergh building, filling the elegant bar from corner to corner.

"Aren't you sneaky." I chuckled, keeping a secret of my own tucked away for later.

"You didn't think I was going to let you get away with your merger without celebrating, did you?" Sara grinned, making space as friends surrounded us. "I'll get us some drinks."

"Congrats, man." Cade stuck his hand out and winked. "I look forward to our future endeavors." His cousins crowded in. "Hey, I heard about the accident. Glad to see you're on the mend." Cash clapped me on the back.

Chase chimed in, "We're looking forward to flying Kensington Airlines."

I chuckled. "It's good to see you guys."

"You look a hell of a lot better than the last time we saw you. Besides, I couldn't pass up free booze and the chance to meet all these hot single women." Cash's gaze swept across the rooftop bar.

Damon Kingsley walked up and slung his arm around Cash. "You know what works best for picking up the ladies?"

"What's that?" Cash asked, absentmindedly adjusting his tie clip.

"Sympathy." Damon grinned and then shoved Cash straight into the pool, suit and all.

"Oh, my God." Sara groaned, returning with several glasses of champagne, looking bewitchingly beautiful. "You guys are relentless."

I caught Theo's eye from across the rooftop, and he dipped his chin to me before he returned to glaring at Ariana from several paces away.

"Congratulations!" Sloane waltzed up, slinging an arm around Sara. "You mind if I steal your girl away for a bit?"

"Don't keep her too long." I joked, but it wasn't all that much of a joke, not really. Sara shot me a little smile as Sloane hauled her off towards the girls.

I love you, I mouthed, and she beamed, mouthing it back.

"So you finally decided to join us in the real world." I turned finding one of Liam's cousins.

"Remi Devereux?" I shook my head. "Damn, everybody's coming out of the woodwork tonight."

"Oh, it's only going to get worse from here." He clinked his glass to mine. "That was some fucked-up shit that went down."

"I have no idea what you're talking about."

"That's fine, everybody else does." He smirked and then turned more solemn. "But seriously man, glad everyone's alright and glad that bastard got what he deserved.

"Again, I have no idea what you're talking about." I shrugged, taking another casual sip of my drink.

The evening was filled with raised glasses, claps on the back, and congratulations issued for my new business venture.

Now that I was officially back in the civilian world, I was juggling several businesses, one of them being my new commercial airline venture. Maybe I couldn't fly at mock speeds anymore, but with precious cargo, who would want to. I was more than ready to put the past to bed and focus on the promise of my future. My heart started to pound as I clutched a very special box in my pocket.

The sound of a beer bottle hissed next to me. "You been doing some home redecorating?" Liam asked. "Blue is a bold choice."

I shook my head with a chuckle, realizing I must still have paint in my hair. "Something like that." I wasn't about to correct him. I liked all my teeth right where they were.

Liam looked in Sara's direction. "It might take me a minute to warm up to all this, but you're right, she looks really damn happy." Liam admitted as he tipped the bottle to his lips.

"I'm glad you feel that way." I said, sipping my drink. "Because I already married her."

I smirked as my best friend sputtered. "Goddamn it." Liam groaned. "Please tell me you're joking."

I suppressed a smile. "There is nothing more serious than til death do us part."

He stared at me for a long beat and then clapped me on the shoulder. "Then I guess I should say welcome to the family. *Officially.*" He lowered his voice. "Don't forget, if you break her heart, make her cry, or knock her up—"

"I could make so many dirty jokes right now." I cut him off with a shake of my head. "Especially about those last two little details—"

"If you finish that sentence, you'll give me no choice but to break your neck," Liam grumbled. "Don't you ever say that shit to me again."

"Noted." I grinned, and his own mouth hooked up into a smile.

"In all seriousness, I'm really glad she has you, she's been through a lot." His expression turned glazed, and I hummed in agreement, knowing that fact all too well.

Sara may have been my wife, given me her vows, but I knew it would be a long while before she gave me the last of her secrets. I'd explored every inch of her body, but there were doors in her heart that were locked up so damn tight that the only key to opening them would be the passage of time.

But someday, when she was finally ready, I knew she'd come to me, explain the many lies she'd told to protect herself—the box of tampons she'd never opened that night, the surgery she'd never had—I'd pulled her medical records, heartbroken to confirm what I'd known the minute she'd said it, the scar on her stomach was very real, but the surgery to cover it up was not. When she was finally ready to explain, I would be ready and waiting. Until then, I could rest peacefully, knowing the man who'd carved up my wife was long gone, and I'd never let anyone hurt her like that ever again.

Liam looked at me sadly, and I couldn't tell if it was pity for Sara and whatever secrets he was keeping for her, or pity for himself. What he'd been through this past year. Or maybe it was simply the burden of whatever horrors had gone down in that dungeon after I'd left with Sara.

"Hey." I gripped my best friend's shoulder. "There's lots of fish in the sea. Give it some time, and you'll find that right person." He shook his head like he didn't believe it. "You could certainly join Cash on the hunt for hot singles." I teased, "Who knows, maybe your future wife is on this rooftop right now."

"Wouldn't that be nice." He shook his head. "Not likely though."

"Speech!" Cade shouted from the crowd, lifting his glass as the rooftop erupted into chants. "Speech, speech, speech."

I grinned, "Time to make things official." I handed my drink to Liam and clapped him on the back. "Wish me luck." I straightened my suit, feeling incredibly nervous.

"I would, but you won't need it." Liam gave me the first real smile I'd seen from him in a long time. "She's been obsessed with you since the first time she saw you, Kensington—I saw it in her eyes clear as day." Liam lifted his beer bottle with a shrug. "I suppose if I can admit it to myself, I think I saw that same look in your eyes too." I grinned at him, knowing it was true.

CHAPTER 62

Her Last Secret

SARA

"Speech! Speech! Speech!" The crowd egged Carter on as he cut across the roof and rounded the pool searching for me, and when his eyes locked on mine, it was as if his hands were already on me. Like the best kind of muscle memory.

Carter's hands slipped around my waist as if he didn't care who saw, and I couldn't help but giggle, like a silly girl, because that's how he made me feel, lighter than air.

He leaned down into my ear. "Mrs. Kensington?" he murmured, low, and intimate, *just for me.*

"Yes, husband." I whispered back, quietly enough that only he could hear.

"I have to ask you something." He planted me in place, motioning for me to stay put, and before I could ask what he was doing—people made space all around him as he backed up, several long paces, and slipped his hand into his pocket.

My hand flew to my mouth as he produced a ring box— plucked a massive diamond ring out of it and then swung his arm, chucking the empty box across the rooftop with a grin. Everyone was screaming and cheering as he slowly slid that ring right between his teeth and then dropped to his hands and knees in front of everyone we knew.

I was already crying, heart thundering as the love of my life crawled to me, grinning wickedly with a *massive* diamond ring between his teeth.

He was the only thing that existed as he finally reached me, looked up at me through his long lashes and took my hand while he presented the ring. "Hi, pretty girl."

"Hi." I whispered, eyes going blurry.

"You're the best thing to ever happen to me, and I want you to know, we were *never* just friends. I've loved you since the day I set eyes on you, and I'll love you until the day I die. Wherever my soul goes after that, I'll love you there too. I promise, there's nothing you can say or do that will ever change that. You're the air I breathe, the gravity that grounds me, the sun in my darkness. You're my everything, forever and always. Will you marry me, pretty girl?" He smirked, adding under his breath just for me. "Again?" I might have been crying as he crooned, "You said you wanted a ring so big you could see it from space, so I hope this fits the bill."

"Holy fuckballs." Sloane murmured from somewhere nearby.

"That's got to be at least twenty carats." Jules ogled.

Ariana chimed in, "Oh no, that's at least thirty, probably more, depending on the depth of the setting."

"Thirty-two, and I would have gone for double, but I knew she'd hate something that big," Carter murmured, never taking his eyes off mine. "So what do you say, sweetheart?"

I shrugged with a laugh, feeling several tears slip down my cheeks. "I'm not really the marrying type, but I guess I could make an exception."

"Is that a yes?" Jules asked excitedly.

"Yes," I whispered to Carter, both our eyes gleaming.

Carter grinned and slid the massive ring onto my finger. "She said yes!" Carter shouted gleefully, springing up to spin me around, and everyone cheered as he dipped me back and sealed his proposal with a long, sensuous kiss that garnered all kinds of comments from the peanut gallery, *kiss her real good, get a room, that's my sister you asshole!*

"I'm going to keep every promise I made." He murmured with a devastating smile. "No more secrets, just you, me, and our very bright future."

"No more secrets." I said, feeling a tear slip down the corner of my eye. "I love you."

"I love you more." He grinned, "Always will."

"I still can't believe you had to pee in a bucket." Ariana turned her nose up, and Theo rolled his eyes from nearby, always staying between Ariana and the pool, but she ignored him altogether. "That is seriously so deranged. I could never." She admitted.

"You guys are going to have the most beautiful wedding." Jules practically drooled. "And you'll be the most beautiful bride." She was basically crying as Sloane added with shining eyes, "I can't believe you're getting married to Carter! Finally!"

I only grinned, relishing the private little ceremony we'd had with just the two of us already—the rest would just be for show, but I didn't mind showing my husband off one bit. "It's going to be the party of the decade."

"You happy?" A shoulder bumped against mine—Liam.

"Yeah, I really am." I murmured, looking down at my *massive* ring for a long second. I'd asked for a sparkle parade, and that's exactly what I'd gotten—and then some. "I'm sorry this had to be so chaotic, and I'm sorry we didn't tell you sooner."

Liam scoffed as we wandered over to a quiet corner of the roof. "Well, I didn't exactly make it very easy for you, did I?"

"Can I ask why you were so opposed to it?" I studied him, noting the weariness in his eyes.

"Oh, it wasn't just Carter," Liam said. "Half the guys on this rooftop have tried to get closer to me in order to have a shot with you."

"Please." I rolled my eyes.

"It's true. It was never personal." He shrugged. "Okay, fine, I admit, maybe it was a little personal. I selfishly didn't want my best friend and my sister to have a falling out. That would have seriously sucked." Liam ticked his head and added, "I saw the way you looked at him, even back then, and I thought Carter wasn't capable of committing because of his history. I thought he wanted to fuck around just for the hell of it. In hindsight, I guess, it all makes a little more sense now."

I narrowed my eyes. "So what I'm hearing is, it's *your* fault my husband has a well-rounded sexual history?"

Liam grimaced. "Well, when you put it like that."

I stuck my tongue in my cheek with a devious grin, because I just couldn't help but tease him. "I suppose I can forgive you—since I'm reaping *the benefits* of all that experience." He nearly spit out his beer. "So I actually should be thanking you, because—"

"Nope. Nope. Nope." Liam clapped a hand over my mouth. "Both of you need to shut the fuck up. I do *not* want to hear a damn thing about any of it."

I chuckled and pried his hand away. "What about you? You've been awfully busy lately. You're not trying to avoid processing your breakup, are you?" I asked more gently.

"Are you kidding? I love processing hard feelings." He scoffed, adjusting the rolled-up sleeves of his button-down, *avoiding looking at me.*

"Liar." I laughed, and then placed a hand on his arm. "Do you think you guys will ever give it a second shot?"

"Naw." He admitted, "I held on for too long. Things were over, long before we called it, long distance was just the cherry on top."

"Liam, I just know you're going to find someone really, really great. Don't forget you're *a catch.* Seriously, do you even realize how powerful you are?" I asked innocently. "You've been out of the dating pool for a long while, so I don't know if you even know this or not, but girls *love* a guy who can cook, and *you* cook *real good*." I grinned.

He chuckled, "Says the girl who wouldn't touch anything I made for months."

"Hey, that's not fair." I narrowed my eyes and punched him in the shoulder, prompting his eyes to turn devious as he went in for the kill. "No! Don't mess up my gown." I gritted twisting his finger until he let go.

I gave him a warning look as he explained with a chuckle, "I think I'm just going to focus on work for a while."

"I just want you to be happy, you deserve that so damn much." He didn't say anything, and I lowered my voice. "You know, I really appreciate *everything* you've done for me, and I just wanted to let you know I'm always here for you."

"Thanks, Sar-Bear." My brother slung his arm around my neck before tipping his beer bottle back.

I admired my ring again, my thoughts wandering. "You know, the one thing I can't stop thinking about is that damn note—I'm worried someone knows something."

"Taggart's long gone." Liam murmured. "*They both are.*"

"But what if someone else knows something?" I said, staring out over the city, letting my quiet words slip away into the night air.

"*Then I'll take care of them, too.*"

I rolled my eyes. "I just wish I knew who wrote it at the very least, had that closure. You know?"

"We may never know." Liam muttered. "But at least we're protected and Dads off the hook. For now." He paused. "You talk to him lately?"

I shook my head. "I don't know. I think I just need some time."

"You don't owe him anything." Liam said solemnly. "Just make me one promise."

"Anything."

"Don't trust Dad. Ever again."

"I know what he did was terrible, but he's our dad." I countered. "He's the only parent we have left. Maybe if he gets the help he needs, I don't know. Maybe—"

"Sara, what he did was unforgivable." Liam's body went tight. "I'm glad you're okay, all things considered, but I'll never forgive him—you literally could have died. Both of you." He added, and my gaze found Carter across the rooftop, knowing Liam was right —Carter was already looking at me and he motioned me over with pleading eyes and a tilt of his head. "I'm not asking you to hold a grudge, but please don't let him back into your life, he doesn't deserve it."

I sighed and patted my brother's chest. "Maybe time will fix things, huh?"

"When did you become such an optimist?" The corner of his mouth pulled.

"Hey, I've always been an optimist." I argued, "And so have *you*. When did *you* become such a pessimist?" I challenged, seeing so much worry swirling in the depths of my brother's eyes as he shrugged. "At least we'll always have each other. You're the one person I know I can always trust." And thank God for that.

"Yeah, and that ass-hat." Liam nodded to the very dreamy man, who was putting on a little show for me, dancing, trying to lure me over to him with a suggestive curl of his fingers as he beckoned me over.

I shivered, this morning's shower escapades flashing through my mind, leaving me in a lusty haze. "You love him." I scolded with a breathy laugh.

Liam eyed me, lowering his voice. "Does he know?"

The pull of gravity itself was luring me away as I dropped my gaze. "No, of course not." I murmured, ignoring the guilt that punched through me at the admission.

"Honestly, that's probably for the best." Liam nudged me with a chuckle. "Go on, your fiancée is getting desperate, but just know, I'll always love ya, kid."

"I love you, too." I smiled and squeezed Liam in a big hug

before slipping through the crowd and into the waiting arms of my lover.

"You wanna?" Carter asked, tipping his head towards the pool. I looked down at my evening gown and grinned. "Oh sure, why the hell not?"

"God, I love you." Carter rasped, hauling me up into a bridal carry before he shouted for the whole rooftop to hear. "I have an announcement to make." I chuckled as everyone's heads turned and the music lowered.

Carter grinned wide and proud, looking mischievous as ever. "I just wanted to let you all know that I'm well aware of what a catch my darling wife is." I shook my head, just waiting for whatever was coming next. "And for all of you cocksuckers who thought you had a chance—*I win motherfuckers! She's mine!*" and then he jumped.

I screamed, howling with laughter, as we plunged into the sparkling water. Carter's mouth was on mine as we surged up, resurfacing, and everything else disappeared as my best friend, the love of my life, kissed me, *real good.*

Finally, no more hiding.

CHAPTER 63

The Butcher

LIAM

Seeing my little sister in my best friend's arms still wasn't something I was used to, but I was grateful she had him, because I knew Sara would be safe with him, *no matter what.*

Just like her little secret was safe with me, and it always would be, along with all the others I was keeping.

Which was exactly why nobody could know the real reason Gina and I had broken up—not even Gina, because it would be the unraveling of the carefully woven tapestry of deceit I'd been forced to weave. One lie, feeding right into the next, like a snake eating its tail.

Carter had been absolutely right. I *would* do whatever it took to protect Gina, *and I had.* I loved her too much to put her in such a compromising situation, because I'd become the very thing she despised—a criminal.

Someone who had sold out my best friend and my kid sister to the mob because that blackmail they'd found—was *payment called due* for the very first thread that had ever been woven. The knot that threatened to come back and strangle me at any moment—*the body I'd buried for my sister, the night of the charity auction.*

The night we'd both killed someone.

The golden boy, the optimist my sister once knew, he was long gone.

That note with the bloody thumbprint was just another thread with another steep cost, and that bill with the Leones, *wasn't even remotely close to paid.*

SARAFINA

Bad Boys

The lights were low, and a live jazz band was serenading us inside the lounge of the Vandenbergh wine bar. I was sipping a glass of merlot, catching up with Ariana, when Jules returned from the bathroom with a smug little smirk.

"Where's Sloane?" I puzzled.

"In the single-stall bathroom." Jules chuckled, and I suddenly realized what she meant as she tossed her bouncy auburn hair over her shoulder with an amused roll of her eyes.

"With who?!" we all demanded.

Jules raised a devious brow. "Who do you think?" She zipped the pendant of her necklace back and forth on the chain as she slid into the booth. "Her new best friend, Cade-fuck-boy-Blackthorn."

That would either be a match made in heaven or *hell*. Only time would tell, I supposed.

Cade

"Hello darling." I rumbled with an amused chuckle, seeing

my favorite hot, leggy blonde headed straight for me. Goddamn, she was a tall glass of water, which was perfect because I was thirsty—parched, actually.

"I need you." Sloane rasped, yanking me off the barstool by my tie. "Right now."

My cock twitched with delight, and I shot Theo a smirk. He just rolled his eyes and went back to pouting while he pretended to glare at Ariana from across the wine bar.

"After you, blondie." I grinned as Sloane dragged me into the bathroom like a dog on a leash—and if she'd asked me to bark for her, I sure as fuck would have. *Woof. Call me a good boy.*

Sloane shoved me inside, and I was all too happy to let her. I dragged a hand over my mouth, groaning as I ate up the view from behind while she frantically locked the door, a heavy click and then she whirled, slamming herself against the back of the door with a feral look in her eye.

I crashed against her in a single stride, hauling those long legs up around my waist, pinning her to the wall as I claimed that snappy mouth I'd grown to love so much. She tugged my hair, hard and desperate, as I grabbed her by the throat and tasted every fucking inch of her with a demanding kiss.

My hands slid around the bottom curve of her thighs, yanking her open, fingertips brushing against wet heat. A mere second later, she shoved me back, slamming me into a different wall, and my cock twitched as she frantically loosened my belt, going for the top button quickly after.

I chuckled. "You're in quite a hurry tonight. Did you miss me?" I crooned, not minding it a single bit.

"Yeah," she breathed, and I hauled her up onto the sink in a swift movement—just before she could get ahold of me, and she practically whined in frustration. "Fuck me, Cade. Right now. *I need you.*" And damn if that didn't make me feel amazing.

Her silky blonde hair rose and fell over the curve of her perfect tits as she panted, demanding for me to hurry up. I shook my head with a grin and reached into my wallet for a condom, but before I could rip it open—*she swatted it onto the floor.* "We don't need that."

I raised a brow. "You trying to get pregnant?" I chuckled, reaching for my backup, because I was always prepared for a good time.

"*Yes.*" She rasped, eyes wild. "Cade, I want you to put a baby in me."

I froze, realizing she was serious. "What?"

"No condom." She demanded, yanking the second one straight out of my hand, flinging it across the bathroom. Hard. I shouldn't have been surprised she had such an arm, she was a wild little thing, and I fucking loved it.

Still, I was stunned. "Darling, while I'd love to be your sperm donor—what the hell is going on?" I purred, mind internally whirring as I slid my hands up her too-soft thighs with a groan.

"I want to have your baby." She rasped, yanking my hips towards her desperately.

I chuckled with a shake of my head. "Great, let's do it." I was surprised, sure, but why the hell not?

"Really?" Her baby blues went wide and innocent. *Happy.*
Ohhh fuuuck.

That was an entirely different look than I'd ever seen from her, and that one was undoubtedly the most dangerous look of them all. Fucking hell. If she figured out what that look did to me—I'd be screwed before I could even bark.

"Cade, are you serious?" She searched my eyes so earnestly.

I grinned at her lazily. "Hell yeah, I am. Let's do it. Just take a little stroll down a short white aisle and I'll do anything you want me to, baby. I'm yours."

"Marry you?" She scoffed incredulously, like *I* was the one with the outrageous request.

"Why not?" I shrugged. "You like me, I like you." Maybe that was too simple a word for how I was very quickly beginning to feel, but what the hell did I know. I dragged a thumb against the crease between her hip and thigh, *very slowly*, and her head dropped back with a whimper. *Best sound ever.*

"I'm not marrying you." She huffed, trembling as I repeated the motion on the other side.

"Then I'm not putting a baby in you." I grinned, yanking her to the edge of the counter roughly. "And since you've disposed of both my condoms, you're going to be a good fucking girl and take *exactly* what I give you." I yanked her panties down and shoved her thighs wide open, sliding down to my knees for my new favorite snack.

Her hands speared into my hair as she tugged my head back roughly. "*Cade.*"

"Call me daddy." I purred with a savage grin. "And maybe I'll *think* about putting a baby in you."

"That is never going to happen."

I chuckled. "We'll see about that." I pressed a kiss to the inside of her thigh—all the while wondering what the hell my little wildling was really up to.

∼

Thank you so much for reading! Briar Rose is bursting at the seams with secrets, and trust me, all will be revealed in good time. So be sure to stay tuned as we follow this amazing cast of characters on their luxurious and treacherous journeys to find love!

If you're dying for more, right this second...

Download Carter & Sara's deleted chapter!

Poker Face 2.0 - A Vegas Wedding

www.CharlieLennonBooks.com/Bonus

Author Acknowledgments

Writing Dangerous Little Dares has been such an incredible experience. It's wild how so many unrelated things have fallen together to bring me to this exact point in my life. It's somewhere I never would have expected, but honestly couldn't be more perfect.

Inside this book are little bits of my heart and soul (did I just make a horcrux?) and as someone who has found great joy and comfort in fiction, I had to pay homage to some of my favorites. If you know where to look, you'll find a few Easter eggs sprinkled around here and there. It's also stuffed to the brim with some of the funny little colloquialisms from my personal life.

I'd like to mention the inspiration for Charlotte Devereux's love of holidays. My Nana, would *actually* turn on Christmas music in *July* because it was her favorite holiday. Decorations always went up early and stayed up late. Basically, we took a *summer break* from Christmas, and I'll never get that warbled, electronic version of Santa Baby out of my head either. My Nana introduced me to my love of gardening, and she taught me to read —which definitely makes her directly responsible for the way I devoured books like a little gremlin growing up.

Indirectly, my Nana is also responsible for my love of morally gray, fictional men, though I doubt she'd put it that way. A movie lover and a night owl, we would stay up into the wee hours of the morning watching old movies, just the two of us (accompanied by a bacon combo pizza, and giant bowl of chocolate chip cookie dough—made *exclusively* in the orange mixing bowl). Enter my obsession with Princess Bride and The Moon-Spinners with Hayley Mills. Well, really *anything* with Hayley Mills, among *many* other mystery movies and shows that sparked my resounding interest in comedy, adventure, and storytelling.

Putting a story of my own into the world is a truly surreal feeling—something about the permanence of ink on a page. I am certain I will have a vulnerability hangover after hitting publish, but storytelling has helped me find my voice, and while it's certainly a work in progress, I'm pretty damn proud of how far I've come.

Writing Carter and Sara's love story has been such a joy this past year. Being able to cozy up in the world of Briar Rose with all these characters has brought me *immense* hope in my life, and it is my profound hope that you found just as much comfort reading it as I did writing it.

I also *really* hope this book makes you cackle, because there was plenty of that too—me alone in my office, literally screaming at the walls, freaking out the fur babies. The flirting, the banter, the thrills. Many of these scenes had *me* blushing. That's how I know a scene is ready—when I'm giggling uncontrollably.

Sometimes, I'm not even totally sure where this thing came from, or how I managed to pull this off. This book is obviously massive, and while it breaks a lot of story structure rules—this was a story I *needed* to tell. I needed to go through this creative and emotional process as an artist. For whatever reason, this particular story chose to tell itself through me, and I'm so incredibly grateful, because just like my characters, *I* have grown and gone through a transformation in my own life.

While most of this book poured out of me like water, there were absolutely rough patches along the way. Doubt, imposter syndrome, writer's block and just straight up exhaustion from all the late nights. But I like to live my life by the mantra that you never judge yourself by your best day or your worst day. I try to let the highs and lows pass through me without judgment and know **it's the messy middle that matters the most.** That's what kept me going. On days when I was stuck, I let myself quit, knowing tomorrow would be a new day. I think, if you love something, you're allowed to quit it as many times as you need, because if it's meant for you, you can't escape it anyway. That's the beautiful thing about *your* dreams, they call to you because they're meant for *you*.

To anyone who knows they have magic buried deep inside themselves. That little voice, that little feeling—I know there's a million and one reasons to hide it, but just because someone else doesn't see the magic in you, doesn't mean it's not there. **No more hiding**. Take it from me. You *can* do it, and I think you might know it too.

I of course, have to thank the people who encouraged me throughout this process. I bootstrapped this thing, and as a recovering perfectionist, *that* was a painful process of letting go, accepting that my resources were limited, and letting this thing be perfectly imperfect.

Special thanks to my best friend, she was a *pillar* for me this past year, creatively and emotionally. It would actually take an entire book to write a proper thank you, but you know who you are, lady! I'm so incredibly grateful for you and the fact that we get to experience girlhood together—there actually aren't words. We will all anxiously await *your* debut novel! Going through the writing process side-by-side with you has been absolutely dreamy.

I'm always long-winded, as you've most definitely figured out by now, but dear reader, I hope you'll stick with me as we continue to explore the world of Briar Rose. Carter and Sara's story is just the tip of the iceberg, and you can't see it, but I'm smiling *oh so very* deviously because The Society of Secrets is about to get messy as hell. *Evil villain laugh* Can't wait to share more! ☺

Thank you from the bottom of my heart for picking up this book. Every page you read is a dream come true for me, which basically makes you my fairy godmother—a slow clap to YOU, dear reader.

As a reminder, reading for pleasure in this day and age is honestly an act of rebellion. And thank God I finally put down the self-help books, because fiction has improved my life far more than all those self-help guru books combined. Seriously. Fiction is deeply important. It's healing, cathartic, and educational; it teaches empathy and compassion; and it lifts up voices and stories that deserve to be told. And I for one, love being a little rebel.

Choosing to be kind is another little act of rebellion in our culture, and I think there's a lot more good out there than we get to see sometimes. Sometimes the loud voices are just that—they're just loud. I think so much of the good is *us*, connecting with each other, and supporting each other in all the small cumulative everyday ways. So let's stick together because life is so much better that way.

Today, this is my little contribution to making the world a brighter place. Tomorrow, it's your turn. The world is your oyster —so go ahead, *ruin the tablecloth.*

Wishing you all the light, love, and happiness.

♥ Charlie Lennon

P.S. I can't wait to share more of my creative projects with you. I promise this is only the beginning for me. **No more hiding.**

P.S.S. You can pry my em dash out of my cold dead hands—probably not even then.

Come join the amazing community of book lovers online, we'd love to see you there!

www.CharlieLennonBooks.com/Clubhouse

About the Author

 **Charlie Lennon** is an author of exciting, obsession inducing romances that will curl your toes one happily ever after at a time. Nestled between her page-turning plots where danger is always lurking around the corner, you'll find witty banter, heart-warming friendships, and morally gray men who will make you swoon. When she's not writing, you never know what she'll be up to! You might find her digging around in her vegetable garden, or starting yet another new hobby, knitting, boxing, rock climbing, paddle boarding, or even taking acting classes.

Don't forget to join the amazing community of online readers! We have tons of fun over there.

Tik Tok | IG | Pinterest | YouTube
@CharlieLennonAuthor

Reader Group|Charlie's Clubhouse
www.CharlieLennonBooks.com/Clubhouse

Also By Charlie

Shop books and t-shirts direct from Charlie's Bookstore:
www.CharlieLennonBooks.com

THE SOCIETY OF SECRETS

Book 1: Dangerous Little Dares

Book 2: Dangerous Little...

Reviews

If you enjoyed this book, would you do me a huge favor? Would you leave me a review? They help more than you'd think!

If you're shy or in a hurry, you can always just leave a star review. Written is best, but anything helps! ♥

You can find all the quick links here:

www.CharlieLennonBooks.com/Reviews

Amazon | Goodreads | Barnes & Nobels | Charlie's Bookstore